# WHEN FRANK OFFCUT
# WENT MISSING

Also by Tim Thompson:

When Doctor Manky Strolled In – *Book One of the Silver Button Saga*

# WHEN FRANK OFFCUT WENT MISSING

BOOK TWO
*of the*
Silver Button Saga

**TIM THOMPSON**

NATIONAL LIBRARY OF AUSTRALIA

A catalogue record for this work is available from the National Library of Australia

Title: When Frank Offcut Went Missing / Tim Thompson, author.

ISBN 978-0-6451994-2-0 (Paperback)
ISBN 978-0-6451994-3-7 (Ebook)

Graphic design and typesetting: Lead Based Ink
Map drawings: Tim Thompson

Typeset in 11.5/15pt Adobe Garamond Pro

# THE STORY SO FAR ...

We *pick up the Silver Button Saga on the morning of Monday, June 30. Sid Evily is recovering in Mary Brewer's bed after being bashed and robbed in the stables of her inn, The Harey Rabbit, on Saturday night. His bashers have left an incriminating silver button in his money pouch, tying him to the attack on the Duke.*

*Marmaduke Du Marma, Duke of Lower Icing, lies in a fevered delirium after being attacked and poisoned the night before Sid's bashing. Sir Richard Upson, the 'former' Seneschal of Lower Icing Castle, is leading the investigation into his poisoning, as well as the case involving the appearance and subsequent disappearance of Xavier, a young doctor (with a case of amazing curatives) who claims he is the son of the Duke.*

*In desperation to find Xavier, Sir Richard has enlisted the assistance of Frank Offcut. Frank is Lower Icing's only butcher and one of the wealthiest men in the Duchy. However, his youngest son, Billy, is in The Can for assaulting the niece of Will Plucker, the innkeeper of The Dead Duck. If charges are laid and Billy is found guilty, he will be sent to the dungeon, something Frank will do anything to prevent, including carrying out Sir Richard's dirty work.*

*Frank's search leads him to The Pits (after a tip-off from market vendor, Bert Muggins) where an encounter with The Slasher and the Moleson Twins leaves him battered, bruised and none the wiser. In fact, right now, Frank has just regained consciousness at the bottom of a valley... somewhere.*

# CONTENTS

**MAPS**

| | |
|---|---|
| Duchy of Lower Icing | 7 |
| The Five Duchies | 8 |
| The Township of Lower Icing | 11 |
| Mary's Neighbourhood | 16 |
| Sid's Neighbourhood | 92 |
| The Harey Rabbit Floorplan | 150 |
| Banquet Hall Floorplan | 194 |
| The Castle | 294 |
| Ophelia's Neighbourhood | 410 |
| Lower Icing and Stymouth | 554 |

**STORY**

| | |
|---|---|
| Part 1 - Ophelia, Mary and Olivia | 13 |
| *Monday, June 30* | 17 |
| *Tuesday, July 1* | 93 |
| *Wednesday, July 2* | 151 |
| *Thursday, July 3* | 195 |
| *Friday, July 4* | 295 |
| *Saturday, July 5* | 411 |
| *Sunday, July 6* | 547 |
| Part 2 - Marmaduke and Owen | 550 |
| *Tuesday, July 8* | 555 |
| Epilogue - Bethany and Juanita | 581 |

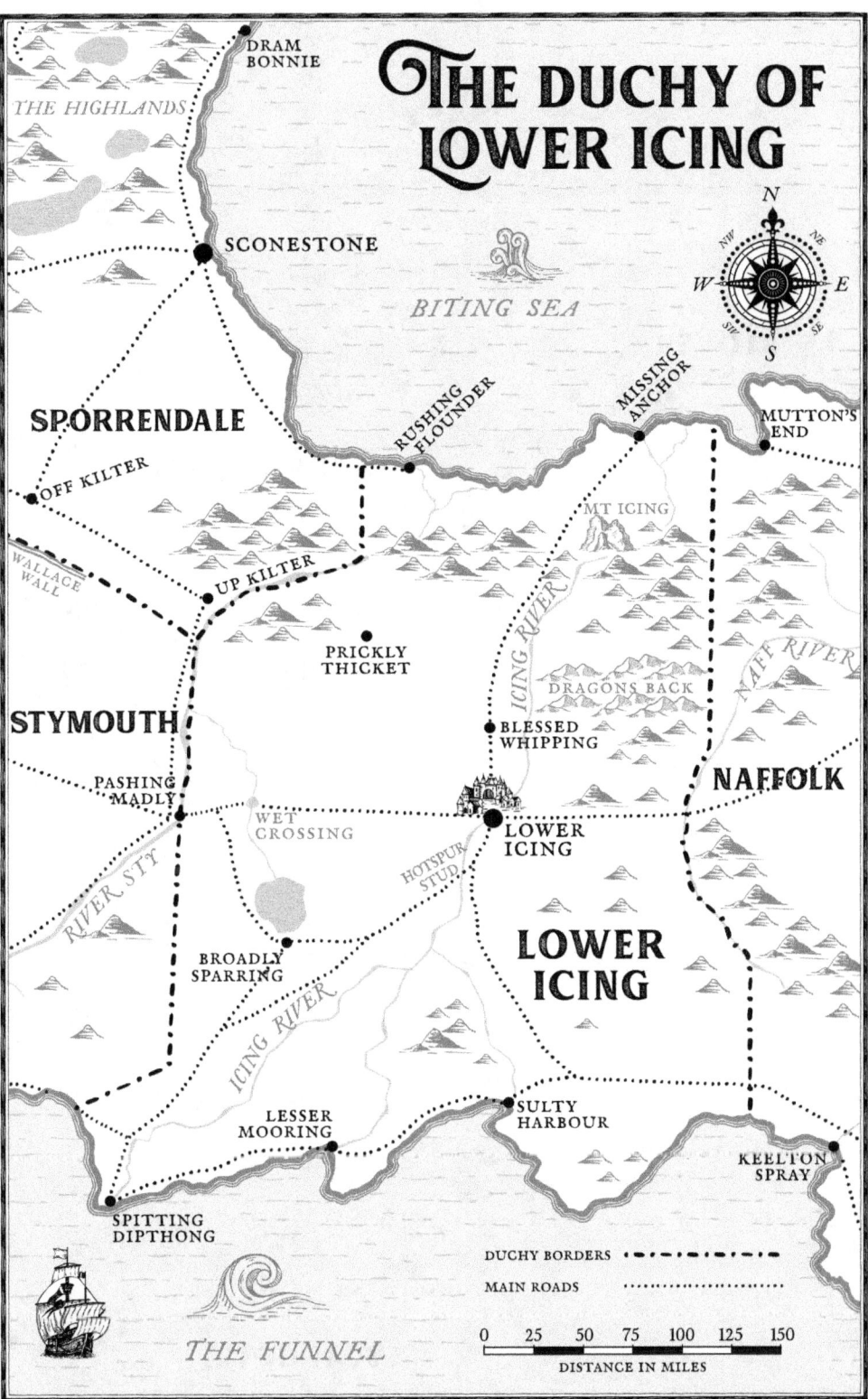

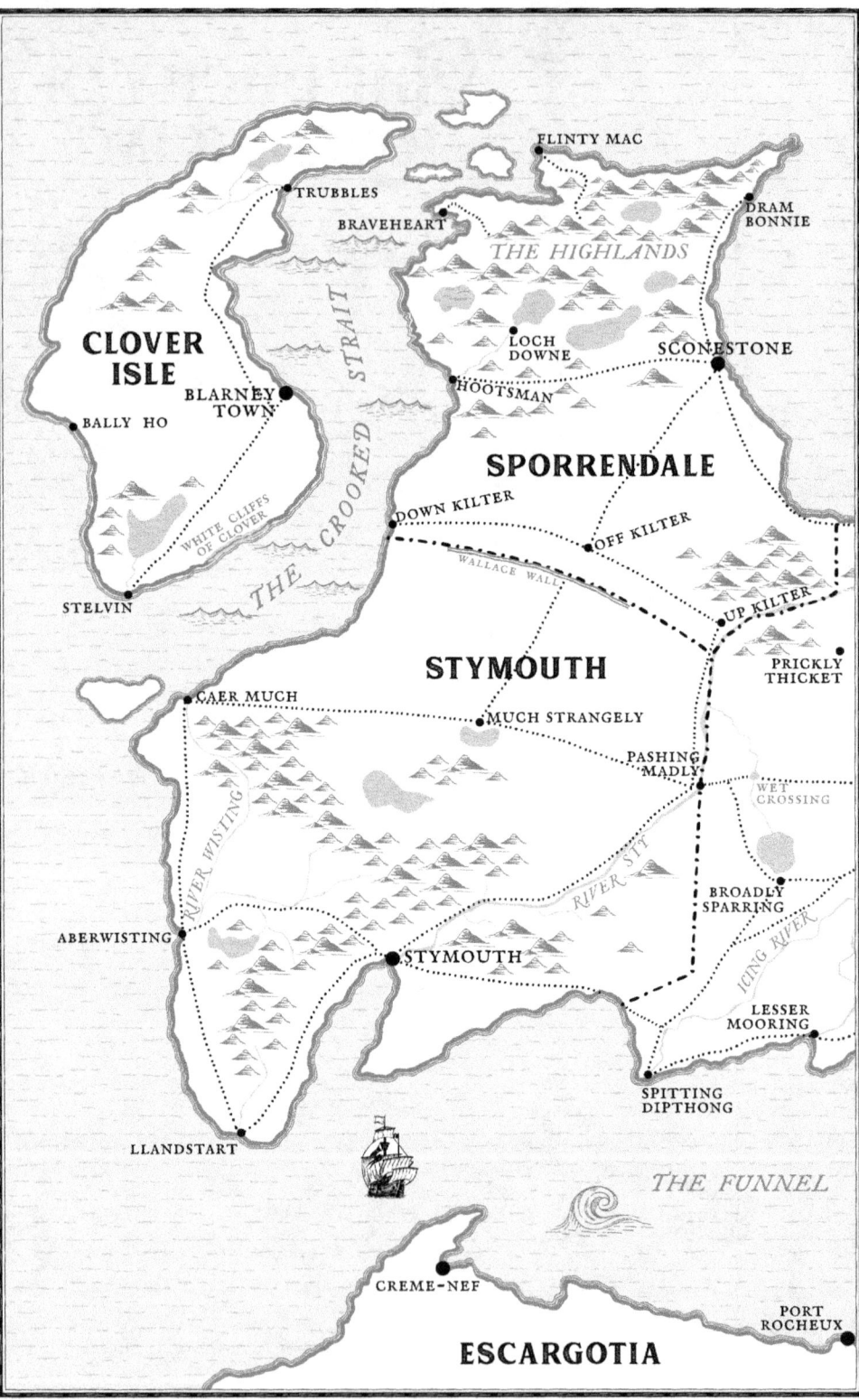

# THE FIVE DUCHIES

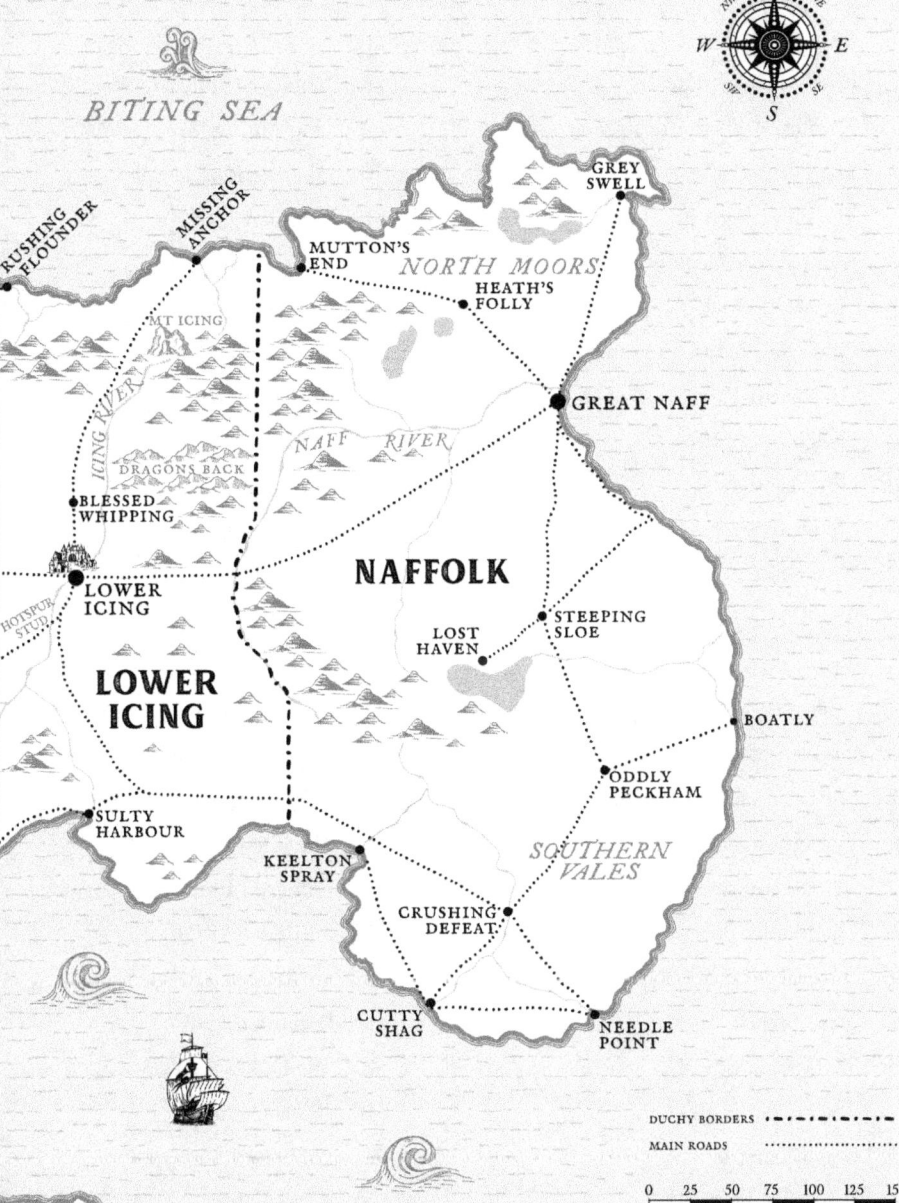

BITING SEA

N
NW · NE
W · E
SW · SE
S

RUSHING FLOUNDER

MISSING ANCHOR

MUTTON'S END

GREY SWELL

NORTH MOORS

HEATH'S FOLLY

MT ICING

ICING RIVER

DRAGONS BACK

NAFF RIVER

GREAT NAFF

BLESSED WHIPPING

HOTSPUR STUD

LOWER ICING

NAFFOLK

LOST HAVEN

STEEPING SLOE

LOWER ICING

BOATLY

ODDLY PECKHAM

SULTY HARBOUR

KEELTON SPRAY

SOUTHERN VALES

CRUSHING DEFEAT

CUTTY SHAG

NEEDLE POINT

DUCHY BORDERS ·—·—·—·—·—·
MAIN ROADS ···········

0  25  50  75  100  125  150

DISTANCE IN MILES

# Places of Interest

| | | | |
|---|---|---|---|
| 1. | Fraser Coin's Estate | 28. | Horace Dabbler Apothecary |
| 2. | Hamlet Macbeth Theatre | 29. | Hats on Big Wig |
| 3. | The Old Pit | 30. | Charles Bling Jeweller |
| 4. | The Pits Tavern | 31. | The Harey Rabbit |
| 5. | Munnymede (Jeremy Dupree's Residence) | 32. | West Gate |
| 6. | The Dead Duck | 33. | East Gate |
| 7. | Olivia and Sid's Old House | 34. | Stables |
| 8. | Du Marma Park | 35. | Castle Kitchen |
| 9. | Slaughter & Offcut | 36. | Office of Petitions |
| 10. | Sid's House | 37. | The Can |
| 11. | Ophelia's Secret Cove | 38. | Gerald's Office |
| 12. | Brown's Boarding House | 39. | Castle Laundry |
| 13. | The Burning Candle | 40. | Klob Hoofenhaus' Smithy |
| 14. | Trevor's Leather | 41. | Barracks |
| 15. | Tinker Taylor | 42. | Administrator Penman's Office |
| 16. | Crokery & Curios | 43. | Training Grounds |
| 17. | Oliver Lawson's Residence | 44. | Officers' Quarters |
| 18. | The Whysman's Residence | 45. | The Keep |
| 19. | Marcus Ironcase's Residence | 46. | Dungeon Entrance |
| 20. | The Bloody Bell | 47. | Sir Richard's Office |
| 21. | Rupert Smythe-Wheaton's Residence | 48. | Sir Richard's Residence |
| 22. | News Stand | 49. | Reception Hall |
| 23. | Town Square Well | 50. | The Duke's Residence |
| 24. | The Hiepants' Residence | 51. | Ducal Cemetery |
| 25. | Ma's Karaderie | 52. | Tom's Bathing Spot |
| 26. | Pierre Cardigan | 53. | Tom's Cabin |
| 27. | Humphry Tumbridge-Wills' Residence | | |

# THE TOWNSHIP OF LOWER ICING

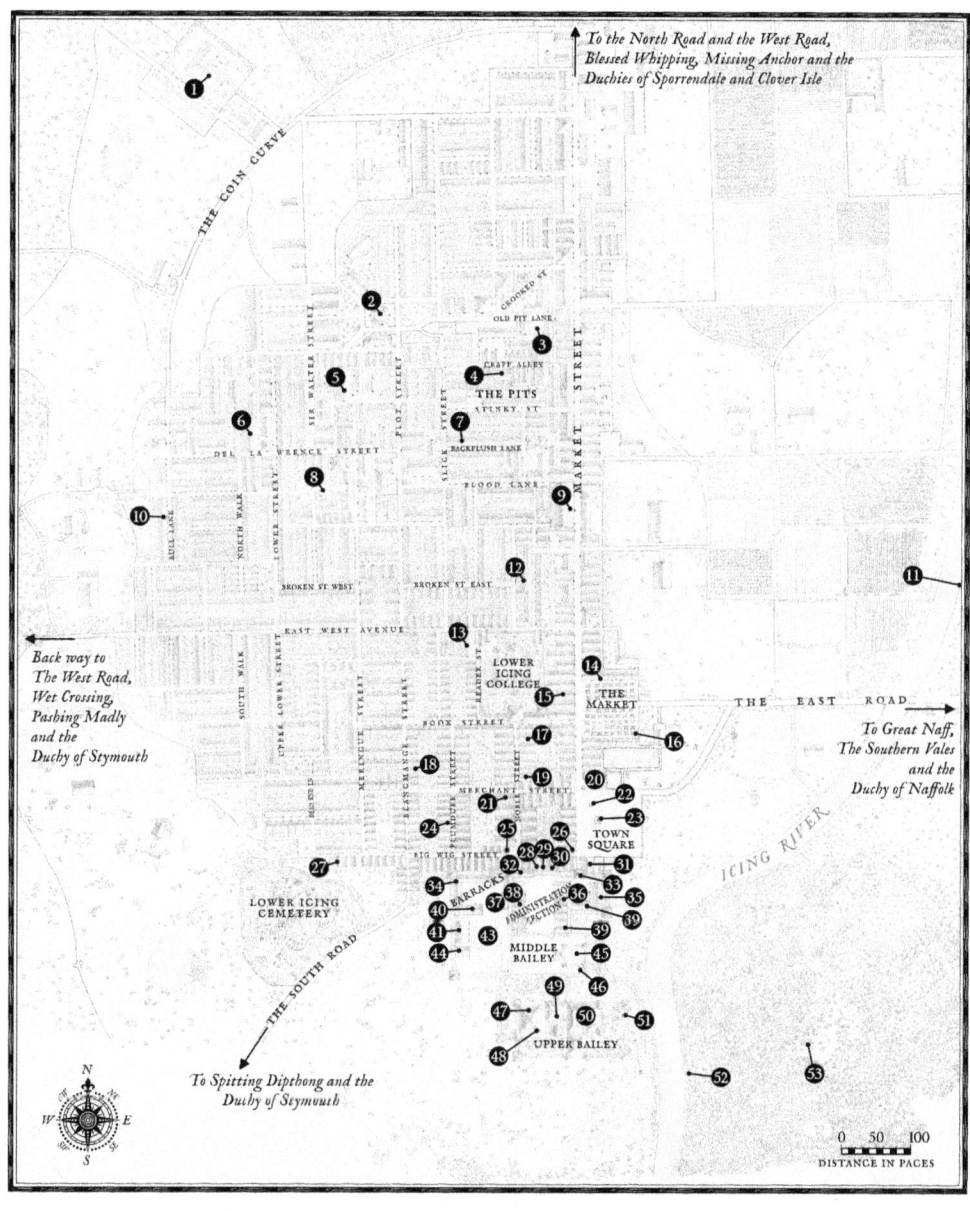

# PART 1

# OPHELIA, MARY

## AND OLIVIA

# INTRODUCTION

## *Damsels in distress*

OPHELIA OFFCUT, MARY BREWER and OLIVIA HIEPANTS certainly didn't know each other, at least not in any real way… only as names and reputations. Ophelia was Frank's promiscuous daughter; Mary was the engaging innkeeper of The Harey Rabbit; and Olivia was the snobby wife of the Town Crier. None of them had ever considered the people behind the reputations, nor had they ever felt a *need* to. They had their own lives to live.

And, at this point in time, they had far more pressing matters occupying their thoughts: Ophelia was worried that her father hadn't returned from a visit to The Pits; Mary was concerned by Sid's bashing and the silver button she'd found in his money pouch; and Olivia was consumed by the disappearance of Xavier, convinced he was the son of the Duke.

However, unbeknown to them all, their lives had just become entwined, the first strands woven together when Frank Offcut went missing…

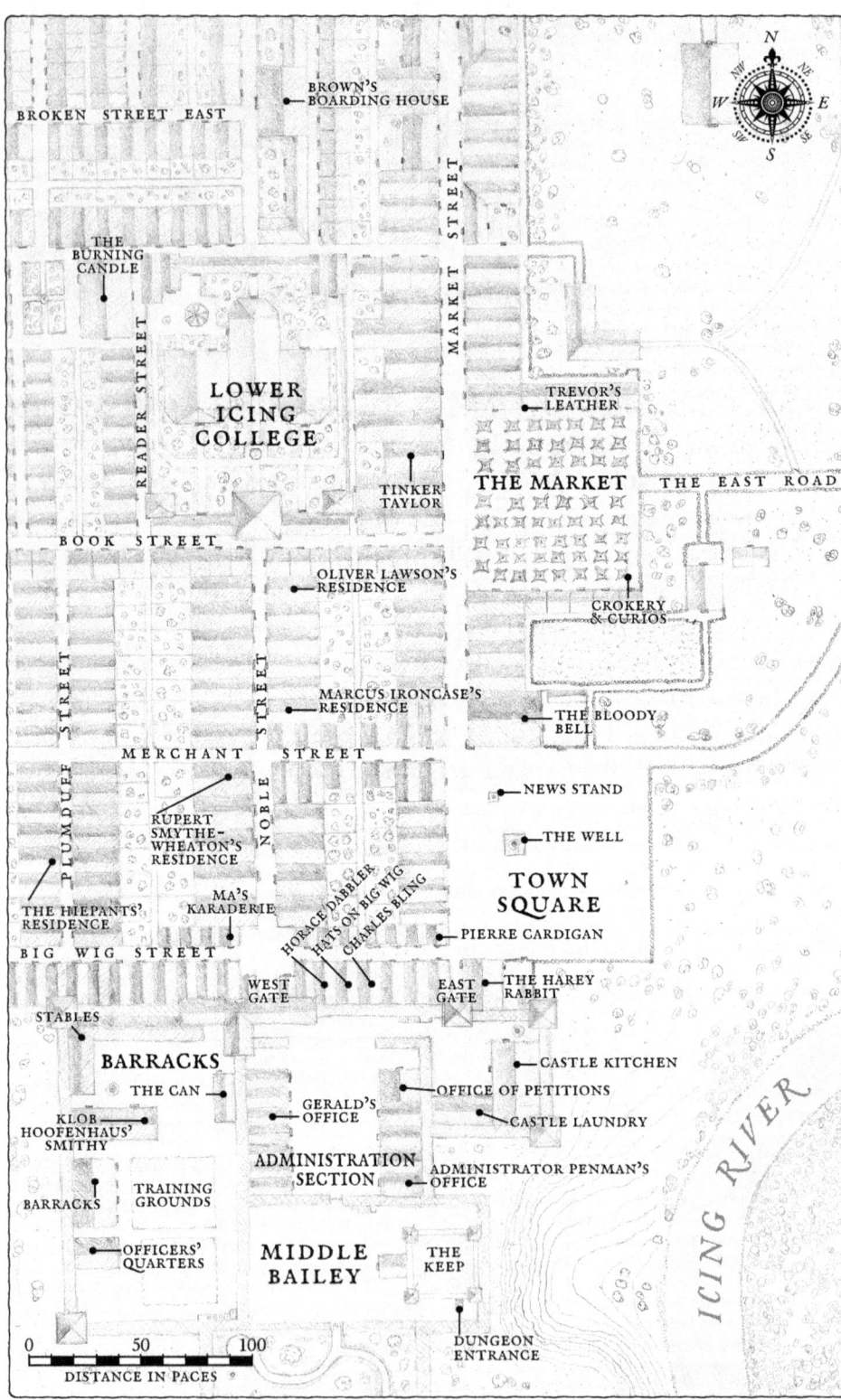

BROWN'S
BOARDING HOUSE

BROKEN STREET EAST

N
NW NE
W E
SW SE
S

THE
BURNING
CANDLE

MARKET STREET

LOWER
ICING
COLLEGE

READER STREET

TREVOR'S
LEATHER

TINKER
TAYLOR

THE MARKET

THE EAST ROAD

BOOK STREET

OLIVER LAWSON'S
RESIDENCE

CROKERY
& CURIOS

MARCUS IRONCASE'S
RESIDENCE

THE BLOODY
BELL

NOBLE STREET

MERCHANT STREET

NEWS STAND

PLUMDUFF STREET

RUPERT
SMYTHE-
WHEATON'S
RESIDENCE

THE WELL

TOWN
SQUARE

THE HIEPANTS'
RESIDENCE

MA'S
KARADERIE

HORACE DABBLER
HATS ON BIG WIG
CHARLES BLING

PIERRE CARDIGAN

BIG WIG STREET

WEST
GATE

EAST
GATE

THE HAREY
RABBIT

STABLES

BARRACKS

THE CAN

CASTLE KITCHEN

OFFICE OF PETITIONS

GERALD'S
OFFICE

CASTLE LAUNDRY

KLOB
HOOFENHAUS'
SMITHY

ADMINISTRATION
SECTION

ADMINISTRATOR PENMAN'S
OFFICE

BARRACKS

TRAINING
GROUNDS

OFFICERS'
QUARTERS

MIDDLE
BAILEY

THE
KEEP

ICING RIVER

DUNGEON
ENTRANCE

0        50        100

DISTANCE IN PACES

# MONDAY, JUNE 30

*The day after Frank Offcut's disappearance into The Pits, the second day of Sid's recovery in Mary's bed, and the third day after the attack on the Duke.*

## CHAPTER 1

### *Still waiting for Pa*

OPHELIA WOKE WITH a start. She hadn't meant to fall asleep. In fact, she hadn't gone to bed; she'd arrived home just after midnight.

Walking up the stairs, she saw candlelight coming from the lounge room. When she entered, her ma looked up expectantly from her petit point, her expression a mixture of worry and relief.

"Ophelia. Thank goodness." The embroidered material was shaking in her ma's trembling hands.

"Wha's wrong?" Ophelia said, stepping towards her. "Is it Pa?"

Her ma placed the petit point on the side table and drew Ophelia close. When the embrace ended, Ophelia was shocked by her ma's tear-streaked expression.

"Ma! Wha's 'appened?"

Her ma told her that her pa had returned home from seeing Billy and speaking to Will Plucker. Turned out it was Will's niece Billy had accosted. Then Bert Muggins had finally shown up, and, after a quick conversation with Pa, he'd left. Then her ma had heard her pa rummaging around downstairs and went to see what was going on. He'd told her he was going to The Pits to talk to the Moleson Twins, that it was the only chance he had to save Billy from the dungeon. Her ma had reluctantly acquiesced. Her pa had then disappeared into the night. Since then, her ma had been sick with worry; she'd spied a boning knife tucked under his belt.

Ophelia did her best to comfort her ma, but, in truth, she was just as concerned. As the night wore on and the minutes passed, her feeling of dread grew. She was attuned to every sound; waiting for footsteps on cobblestones, for the door to be unlocked and opened, for the creaking of stairs, for boots on floorboards, for breathing.

The last sound Ophelia remembered hearing was her ma working away at the petit point…

"Ma?" Ophelia asked of the empty gloom. The petit point lay on the divan where her ma had been sitting… moments ago? She sat up. There was no sign of life. Her neck hurt — she'd fallen asleep sitting in a chair and her head had obviously rested at an odd angle. She also felt groggy: a sure sign she had been sleeping for a while. She stood up and looked around the room, and her awareness suddenly awakened. *Pa!*

She rushed towards her parents' bedroom and opened the door. Her ma was staring out the window, motionless, framed in the light of breaking dawn. She didn't react to Ophelia's presence; she was gazing down Market Street… still waiting for Pa.

Ophelia's heart sank, and she quietly joined her ma at the window. Lower Icing was waking; vendors were setting up their stalls for another day of business. The jovial banter, the scraping and banging of wooden crates, the barking of orders, the rattling of carts and the neighing and spluttering of horses carried through the already-heated air. It was going to be another punishingly hot day.

A smattering of people made their way up Market Street. Some looked like they were market vendors, but most carried empty buckets: early birds trying to avoid a long wait at Lowing Icing's freshest well. None of them noticed two silent women standing, statue-like, at the window. They had their own burdens to bear.

Ophelia leant towards her ma and gently kissed her cheek. Her ma glanced at her and smiled weakly. She looked tired and haunted. It was a shock to see her this way; her ma had always been so strong and resilient.

"Ma," she whispered. "You need t'rest."

Her ma took her by the hand and squeezed it. "There'll be plenty of time for rest when your pa returns."

This was not a good sign. "I'll make a nice pot of tea then?"

Her ma nodded vaguely and returned her attention to Market Street. Ophelia silently left her side. Instead of making tea, she went to her brother's room. He was still asleep, as peacefully content in his dreams as he was in wakefulness. Of all her brothers, Ophelia felt most protective of, and closest to, Seth. There was not a bad bone in the butcher's number six son; all Seth wanted to do was please his family. He was two years older than Ophelia, but she felt more like the big sister.

She gently nudged his shoulder. He woke immediately, stared sleepily at her for a moment, then jerked into a sitting position. "Pheel," he croaked.

"Wha's wrong?"

Ophelia sat down on the bed. "I need you t'look after Ma."

He immediately looked worried. "Wha's 'appened?"

"She's worried 'bout Pa. 'E ain't come back 'ome."

He looked confused. Realisation followed shortly afterwards. "'E went t'The Pits!" Seth threw off his covers and leapt to his feet. "We 'ave t'go an' look for 'im, Pheel!"

Ophelia stood. This was exactly what she *didn't* want. Seth was barely capable of confronting a troublesome customer, let alone marching into The Pits and confronting the Moleson Twins. Even Ophelia wasn't *that* confrontational; she had a much less risky strategy in mind, one she could better handle without the good intentions of her brother.

"No, Seth. I need you t'stay 'ere with Ma."

Seth looked defiant. "Ain't no way I'm lettin' you go by y'self, Pheel."

"Don' need t'worry 'bout me. I ain't going t'the Pits."

He looked confused. "Where then?"

"Seth," she said, meaningfully. "Righ' now, y'best served 'ere. *You're* the man of the 'ouse 'til Pa returns."

He looked unconvinced.

"I promise I ain't gonna do nothin' silly."

He stared at her, torn between his instinct to protect his sister and his sense of duty to his ma. Eventually, he nodded his compliance.

## CHAPTER 2

# *Rattling of metal on wood*

**M**ARY WOKE AT dawn, as usual. She rarely felt tired (blessed, as she was, with bountiful reserves of energy) and, with the summer days being so warm, it seemed pointless lying in bed.

What *wasn't* usual was the fact that she'd woken up in one of the upstairs guest rooms. In fact, it was the second morning she'd done so. Her bedroom was occupied by a man, or, more precisely, a badly beaten-up man…

Sid was his name. He'd spent Saturday afternoon and most of the evening drinking with the Town Crier, who, as it turned out, was his brother-in-law. Mary had been surprised by this. She knew Gerald had been married for six years, but he'd never mentioned that his wife had a brother, and such a handsome one at that. Not only was Sid physically appealing, he had a roguish charm that Mary had instantly warmed to, and, unlike most of her 'refined' male clientele, he'd managed to refrain from slapping her bottom and ogling her cleavage.

It was strange that Gerald had never mentioned Sid. The Town Crier was not one for holding back information; words usually flowed out of him like ale from a keg. Still, any conversation she might have pursued about Sid's sudden existence was well and truly drowned out by the Saturday afternoon crowd at The Harey Rabbit. The intruder at the castle had been the loud topic of discussion, the silver button a point of conjecture. Gerald and Sid had kept to themselves for the most part and seemed to be in good spirits; Sid had even splashed out a gold coin on a fine Escargotian wine, while Gerald had stayed much later than usual, no doubt due to his brother-in-law's generosity.

Mary found herself drawn to their table — Sid was such a breath of fresh air compared to her stuffy regulars. Since she'd never seen (or heard of) him before, she'd assumed he was a visitor to Lower Icing and was more than surprised when he quipped, "Yes, I live north of Merchant Street, so I suppose you could say I'm from out of town." He accompanied the remark with a playful smile.

She returned his smile. "Well, I hope you enjoy your stay. If there is anything I can do to make it more enjoyable…" Flirting with customers went with the territory — it was second nature to her — and it helped fill The Harey Rabbit coffers. However, Mary felt strangely self-conscious talking to Sid, and she blushed furiously when he replied, "Meeting you has already done that."

So, when, hours later, Sid was discovered by John, lying unconscious by the stables, his face covered in blood, Mary had been more than just shocked, she'd been distressed.

Mary helped John carry Sid to the washroom. John was her errand-boy, a scrawny lad of fourteen, and Mary found herself bearing most of Sid's unconscious weight. She then sent John to fetch Doctor Whysman. In the meantime, she attended to Sid's battered head using a woollen cloth soaked in warm water infused with lavender. She wiped away the blood to isolate the wound — a nasty-looking gash above his left eye. It was still bleeding. She held the cloth in place, applying pressure to the wound until Doctor Whysman arrived.

Fortunately, it hadn't taken John long to fetch him, and Sid had been treated within twenty minutes of being found. Doctor Whysman acted quickly and decisively, stitching up the gash, dabbing it with a thick ointment (to further stem the bleeding) and bandaging it with thick gauze. During the process, Sid barely reacted — just a few groans during the stitching and, at times, laboured breathing, but he never regained consciousness.

Doctor Whysman put Mary's mind at rest, saying that nothing appeared to be broken and that Sid's heartbeat was strong. "His body has shut down to aid recovery, but I will see him first thing to make sure the wound has not festered."

Mary thanked him profusely and handed him a gold coin for his service, but he'd kindly refused, saying that a hearty Harey Rabbit breakfast would suffice.

She then went about the process of undressing Sid — his shirt was more blood-red than its original white, and the back of it was covered in stable grime. His black trousers and boots had escaped most of the blood splatter, but not the redolence of manure. After gently wiping him clean with another lavender-infused cloth, she and John carried him to her bedroom. Her bed was comfortable enough and, truth be known, she was exhausted. Lumbering

Sid upstairs to a guest room required too much energy.

Mary thanked John for his help and told him to get some well-earned rest. Before doing the same, she went over to Sid to make sure he was still breathing. He looked peaceful, like a little boy, and she gently stroked his dark hair away from his battered eye.

"Mmm… Lovely… lovely," he murmured.

Mary removed her hand, surprised by his voice. He opened his right eye, smiled feebly, and then fell back into unconsciousness.

Early the next morning, Sid woke as Doctor Whysman checked his wound; he was very groggy and the words he mumbled made little sense. Doctor Whysman was concerned by this. "His wound appears to be healing, but I expected him to be more alert."

Mary informed him that Sid had been drinking quite heavily, but the doctor offered another explanation. "The blow may have upset the balance of humours — yellow bile is particularly susceptible to hot weather, and this kind of injury could easily develop into a fever. The wound may actually benefit from exposure to air, so I think it would be best to leave the bandage off. Are you able to keep a regular check on him?"

Mary assigned the task to John. As much as Mary would have been willing to attend to Sid herself, Sundays were busy at The Harey Rabbit and her patrons had their *own* requirements — the main one being that Mary kept a regular check on *them*. In many ways, Mary *was* The Harey Rabbit.

John accepted the task without complaint; he'd been a real boon to Mary since he'd begun working for her three months ago. He'd been one of Reg Puffy's kitchen hands and had delivered eggs to The Harey Rabbit… up until Mary had poached him.

Still, even with the requirements of her patrons, Mary managed the odd visit to Sid, but each time there appeared to be no change.

"'E jus' mumbles ev'ry now an' then, Mistress," John informed her, "but 'e ain't got a fever, like."

Later in the day, after the lunchtime crowd had died down, Mary had retrieved Sid's pants and boots from the laundry. Juanita, her Icarumban cleaner and washerwoman, had done a wonderful job with them — she'd even made an attempt at getting the blood out of his shirt, but hadn't been happy with the result. "Too much blood, Meestress," she said, shaking her head. "You catch dee gringos who do thees?"

Mary shook her head. "Not as yet."

She left the laundry carrying his trousers and boots, and was walking towards her bedroom when Juanita called after her. The cleaner held something in her hand. It was a money pouch. "You forget dee signor's leetle bag for hees monies, Meestress."

Mary had her hands full — the boots clamped in her right hand, the trousers draped over her left forearm — but Juanita still handed her the pouch. "Thank you, Juanita," she said, taking it in her left hand.

"Poor Signor, ees no so reech no more — only one leetle coin left in dee leetle bag."

Mary had become used to the Icarumban's direct ways; for someone in her late teens, she'd experienced a lot of hardship growing up on the streets of Los Nachos, the Icarumban capital.

John was slumped on a chair, asleep, as she entered her bedroom. She couldn't really blame him. It was a tedious task, and the room was warm and stuffy. The unusual heat was good for business — her patrons had gone through ten barrels of ale this weekend, almost double what they'd normally drink — but it was not so good for sitting around watching a man sleep.

She quietly placed the boots down in the corner, next to her dressing table, and draped the trousers over the back of the chair. She nonchalantly tossed the money pouch on top of the table. It landed with a leathery slap, followed by the rattling of metal on wood.

The sound had jerked John awake and he was mortified by what he saw as a dereliction of duty. Mary assured him he'd done nothing wrong and that if anyone was to blame, it was her for leaving him cooped up in her stuffy room all day. She then sent him outside to get some air and stretch his legs.

Sid was still asleep. His breathing seemed strong and regular and there was no sign of fever — *she* was perspiring more than him. She then turned her attention back to the dressing table. The money pouch lay next to her hairbrushes and perfume bottles.

She glanced at herself in the mirror. She'd been serving for six hours straight in the stifling heat, and she looked like it. Then she noticed the silver coin that had spilled from the pouch... except, it wasn't a coin — there was a metal loop in its centre. It was a button. Turning it over, Mary saw a feather and a broken sword etched on to its smooth, silver surface.

She suddenly felt cold. This was the button everyone had been talking about, the one Gerald had heralded about, the one that had come loose from the clothing of the Duke's intruder. She looked at it again. There was no mistaking the markings — they were as clear as late afternoon sky.

Mary put the incriminating button back into the pouch and placed it in one of her dressing table drawers, as if doing so would undo her discovery. She thought about waking Sid, but she wasn't prepared to confront the possibilities the button presented. Instead, Mary went back to the bar and helped prepare for the teatime crowd. She needed time to think.

During dinner, she picked the brains of some her more connected regulars, but none of them were of any help. It seemed they were all in the dark. It was Mary who had a shiny secret.

Around eight o'clock, John informed her that Sid had woken up. Typical, she thought — just when The Harey Rabbit was full of blustering men and dainty women who expected everything to be 'just so'.

Mary sent John to the kitchen to fetch a bowl of vegetable broth for Sid. No doubt he'd be in need of nourishment, having been unconscious for some eighteen hours. On the way to her bedroom, she wondered what to say to Sid; she'd been so worried about him, felt responsible for him, and had even begun to invest in him emotionally. But since she'd found the button, she'd felt let down and… angry. However, her anger subsided as soon as she saw him. He looked so pathetic.

"Mary?" He looked confused.

Moving closer, she asked how he was feeling.

"I've had better ends to a night of drinking." It was obvious any movement, including speaking, was causing him pain.

"Doctor Whysman says you will recover," she said, sitting on the edge of the bed. "Nothing is broken." Then, leaning forward, she added, "And it looks like the swelling has gone down slightly."

A pained expression crossed his face. "So, how's the other fellow?"

Mary wasn't in the mood for trivial banter and her expression must have conveyed exactly that.

"Or was it *you* who took a dislike to my face, Mary?"

She smiled ruefully. *He* was questioning *her* integrity? "Faces don't bother me. It's the words that come out of them."

A period of silence followed: Sid seemed lost in the moment, his gaze turned inward, and then he looked past her. Mary was on verge of confronting him with the news of the silver button, but Sid commandeered the moment with a request for her hand-mirror. *Her* hand-mirror. So he knew where he was; he hadn't been beaten senseless then. She retrieved the mirror and also grabbed the pouch, holding it within the folds of her dress.

Sid took the mirror and stared at his reflection with distaste. "Glad you think the swelling's gone down."

His sarcasm caused her to snap. "Why did this happen to you?"

He was clearly taken aback by her tone. "I have no idea. The last—"

"Don't lie to me! I'm not a fool." She slapped the pouch into his right hand. "You've been robbed."

"Then I suppose the *robber* is why this happened to me," he retorted.

"Look inside the pouch," she said quietly.

"I can see it's empty; robbers don't often leave change."

"Robbers don't often leave pouches," Mary countered.

He acquiesced. Feeling inside the pouch, he pulled out the button and examined it. Then he gazed back at her, bewildered.

"Well?" she challenged.

He stared as if he couldn't understand why she was angry at him. "I have no idea how this got here."

Mary was unconvinced. "It's a warning, isn't it?" she said as she plucked the button from Sid's hand. "You know what happened at the castle, don't you?"

He looked deflated and in pain. Tears began to weep from his swollen eye. "I swear to you, I know nothing of what happened at the castle or why I was attacked."

There was a knock at the door. Quickly gathering her emotions, Mary stood and opened it. As expected, it was John with a tray of broth and bread. Mary directed him to the bedside table. He then asked Mary if she needed anything else.

"You've done enough, John. Thank you."

Mary turned her attention back to Sid. He was heaving himself into a sitting position. She helped him by rearranging the pillow and placing the tray in front of him. She almost picked up the spoon to feed him, but his hands and arms were in perfect working order. However, he struggled with the eating part. Manoeuvring the spoon into the right side of his mouth was difficult — the left side of his face was a swollen mass of black, purple and red. Mary found it hard not to grimace in sympathy.

"Please tell me the truth. If you're in some kind of trouble…"

He stared at her for a moment, his good eye appraising, looking for a reason to confide in her. Finally, he sighed. "Two days ago, Friday evening to be precise, a ghostly-skinned doctor with bacon-pink eyes walked into The Dead Duck and offered me money in return for information." Sid paused and gently dabbed at his dribbling mouth with the back of his hand.

Mary wondered whether the knock to his head had affected his mind. "Sid, I think you need more rest—"

"Hear me out," he said, grimacing in pain. "Please… you asked for the truth, and I'm giving it to you." Sucking back saliva, he added more calmly, "Though it may take me a little longer than usual."

Mary felt a sudden pang of guilt. "Sorry."

He twitched out a smile. Then he told her about the bizarre encounter he'd had with a person who called himself Doctor Manky, who'd asked Sid to use his relationship with Gerald to find out if anything unusual had occurred at the castle. He finished by voicing the same conclusion Mary had come to: This Doctor Manky must have either known that the Duke was in danger, or had some hand in the attack.

She shook her head in disbelief. "This is madness. What have you gotten yourself into?"

"Well, by the looks of things, your bed. So it can't be all bad." He smiled and grimaced; he seemed unable to grasp the fact that his face no longer did smiles.

Mary returned the smile despite herself. "Sid, this is serious."

He shrugged and inhaled another spoonful of broth.

"What are you going to do?"

Pausing mid-spoonful, his gaze turned inwards. "I haven't decided yet." Then his one good eye focused back on her. "I'll see what Manky has to say for himself."

He couldn't possibly mean that, surely. "And what if *he's* responsible for your beating? This Manky could have set you up."

"No, it doesn't make sense," he said, placing the spoon in the bowl. "I think it's more likely that I was marked out by someone in The Harey Rabbit. I'm not exactly one of the regulars."

Mary reacted defensively to his assertion; she couldn't imagine any of her regulars resorting to common thuggery — they'd employ far more sophisticated and damaging tactics. "How do you know it wasn't me?"

"I don't, but I'm not about to accuse the angel who's given me her bed and nursed me back to health."

Mary's indignation melted away. *How could he have this effect on her?*

She hardly knew him and he looked like a nightmare. "Well, it was cheaper than calling the undertaker."

She glanced out the window to hide her embarrassment. Outside, she noticed the stables were shrouded in evening shadow, highlighted in dusky pink. "It's getting dark," she said, standing, "I'll just light—"

Sid reached out and gently took her hand. "Mary…"

She looked at his battered face and, almost involuntarily, her hand tightened around his.

"Thank you."

She'd left Sid to finish his broth and spent the rest of the night working at being the perfect hostess, making each patron feel like they were her favourite. She'd checked in on him a few times, and so had John. Each time, he'd been asleep, and Mary had left him undisturbed…

Now, as the dawning Monday crept into the guestroom, realisation also dawned upon her, confronting her with a bigger picture — should she tell her brother about the silver button? He was, after all, the Seneschal of Lower Icing; it was her duty to inform him of anything that could be a threat to the Duchy. But Richard was such a… politician. And politicians needed to be in control (or, at least, be *seen* to be in control). Mary feared he would make Sid accountable regardless of his innocence… and she *did* believe he was innocent.

She pulled back the sheet and got out of bed. Her nightdress was crinkled and clung to her left thigh. It had been another hot and sticky night. She needed a bath.

Walking downstairs — there were currently no guests at The Harey Rabbit — she headed straight for the bathroom without checking on Sid. She needed time to think… and to soak.

## CHAPTER 3

# *My good wife, Olivia*

OLIVIA WAS AWAKE well before Monday's sun rose above the terraced houses of Plumduff Street. In fact, she'd spent most of the night staring into darkness *waiting* for it to rise. Her thoughts wouldn't let her sleep… and to think, just four nights ago she'd only *known* uninterrupted sleep. Last Thursday morning had put an end to that. The carefully maintained structure of her life had been washed away like the banks of the Icing River in flood.

Her husband, lying next to her, quietly snoring, had always been frustratingly predictable… until last Thursday morning, that is… when he'd brought a stranger home, a stranger who claimed he was the son of the Duke…

The existence of Xavier hadn't been a secret; Gerald had told her about 'the heir to the Duchy' the day he'd first met him in his 'prison cell of a room' at The Keep. He'd come home for lunch on Tuesday, bursting with excitement at the news. Olivia had never seen him so animated. "Imagine, my sweet, a *legitimate* heir." Then he'd kissed her fully on the lips. She couldn't remember the last time he'd done that. "It's certainly put the wind up Sir Richard!"

He'd gone on to tell her about the meeting he'd had with the Seneschal: how he'd *demanded* that Xavier be moved to quarters more befitting of a guest of his station; how Sir Richard had *acquiesced* and had made him responsible for Xavier's care and wellbeing. "Of course, my sweet, this is all very hush-hush until Xavier is officially recognised by the Duke, so no chirping to ladies, what."

Olivia had wanted to slap his face — a gossip was one thing she certainly was not! In fact, it was one of the reasons why she never joined her husband at The Harey Rabbit: she couldn't abide all the inane chatter.

She had then taken him to task on a few points. (Gerald was a born Town Crier; he couldn't help but embellish and exaggerate). For instance, she was able to establish that Xavier's identity had not actually been validated by anyone. The Duke was unaware of his presence and Sir Richard was of the belief he was an imposter. She had reacted, much to Gerald's disappointment, by concurring with Sir Richard. The idea of Marmaduke and Lucinda having a child seemed preposterous. Olivia knew the emptiness of a childless marriage and had once confided in Lucinda about her fear of being barren. The Duchess had empathised and had even become quite emotional; it had been a poignant moment, one that had helped Olivia come to terms with the probability of a childless life. Her eyes began to well with tears; she missed Lucinda.

Despite Olivia's stance, Gerald had returned to the castle in high spirits. "Cheerio, m'dear," he'd said, pecking her on the cheek. "I shall see you this evening, by which time I feel confident Xavier's identity will have been validated."

However, instead of bringing home validation, he'd brought home frustration. He'd been heckled (again) during the Posting Ceremony, and Sir Richard, as far as Gerald could see, had made no attempt to inform the Duke of Xavier's existence. "He is a most calculating individual, Olivia, and, sad to say, I don't trust him."

Olivia found Sir Richard charming and intelligent (two words she couldn't use to describe her husband), but Gerald was correct: he *was* calculating and untrustworthy. (Another two words she couldn't use to describe her husband.)

"What makes you so convinced that Xavier is Marmaduke and Lucinda's son?" She had tried not to sound too frustrated, but, truth to tell, her husband engendered frustration. He was so... easily led. She had known she was making a mistake when she married him six years ago, but, at that time, she hadn't cared. She had wanted to punish herself for losing the man she actually loved... but she didn't want to think about that, particularly when her 'punishment' was lying next to her in bed.

Gerald's face had lit up at the question, as if he'd been waiting for her to ask it. "That's just it, my sweet; the evidence is there for all to see. Anyone with eyes can see he is their son; even Lieutenant Swill concedes there is a resemblance."

Olivia had picked up on his use of the word 'concedes' — it didn't have the same assuredness as 'recognises' or 'believes' — but she'd kept that thought to herself.

The following day had proven to be even more disappointing for Gerald. Richard had still not arranged a definite time for Xavier to meet 'his father'.

"It's rather poor form to say the least; this young man deserves so much better…"

Olivia had never seen Gerald so intense.

"There's something about him that is *special*. He's a healer, but he's more than that. It's… it's as if he can see inside one's heart."

Olivia had arched an eyebrow at that particular comment. Gerald was apt to take flights of fancy, but they usually centred on his prowess in the political arena. Her dubious reaction brought out an even rarer, defensive response from her usually compliant husband.

"If you met him, you'd realise." He sighed, unable or unwilling to express his thoughts.

On Thursday morning, Gerald had left early for the castle to break fast with Xavier and make sure his needs were being attended to — he'd become quite obsessed about Xavier's wellbeing. However, there was no sign of what would occur a short time later. "Toodle-pip, my sweet" were his parting words… hardly prophetic.

Within the hour, Gerald returned with Xavier; not that she realised it at the time. He virtually bundled the young man down the corridor to the kitchen, ignoring Olivia's protestations. She'd *never* seen her husband like this: brown eyes gleaming, shoulders broad, back upright and determined, all wrapped up in boyish excitement. The same could not be said for his bedraggled companion; he looked uncertain and wary.

Both of them were sweating profusely — the morning was already blisteringly hot — but while Gerald's face gleamed, Xavier's looked sapped. The young man was holding a travelling case and an ornate wooden box.

"What's the meaning of this, Gerald?" Olivia demanded.

Normally, Gerald would have cowered at her tone, but, instead, he smiled. "My sweet, *this* is Xavier, the heir to the Duchy of Lower Icing."

Xavier cringed at the epithet.

Olivia was seething. What was Gerald thinking bringing him here?

"Xavier, may I present my good wife, Olivia."

*Good wife!* At that moment, she'd have gladly used his newfound bollocks as pin cushions.

"Mistress Hiepants," he acknowledged, almost apologetically, acutely aware of the tension his presence caused.

Olivia regarded the young man — sweat-matted straw hair framing a despondent expression. There was nothing immediately recognisable about him.

Gerald's proclivity for exaggeration had, once again, shown him to be all talk and no substance. Ignoring Xavier's greeting, she flicked her gaze back to her husband. He looked at her expectantly, breathing quickly behind an excited smile.

"What have you done, Gerald?" She was struggling to hold her anger in check.

"My dear," he gasped, seemingly amazed by her reaction. "Please, this is our future—"

"Right now..." She cut him off; she wasn't going to entertain this whim for a moment longer. "... I'm not sure we *have* a future."

Gerald looked shocked. She turned her attention back to Xavier. His eyes were downcast, looking very uncomfortable; it quelled her temper somewhat. "I mean no offense, Master Xavier, but my husband holds a position of trust at the castle."

"There is no need to explain, Mistress Hiepants," he said, raising his eyes, "I understand."

His eyes — full of empathy, quietly accepting... Olivia's knees had almost given way when she realised... they were Lucinda's eyes.

Gerald blurted out an explanation of his actions: that Richard couldn't be trusted because he saw Xavier as a threat to him inheriting the Duchy; that Xavier was being treated like a prisoner; that Gerald was bound by his loyalty to the Duke to take matters into his own hands; that Xavier deserved to be reunited with his father. All the while, Xavier remained silent, but Olivia had already made up her mind. She would do everything she could to reunite Marmaduke with his son. Poor Lucinda. Her quiet sadness... suddenly, it all made sense.

Gerald had then decided to make haste to return to the castle and inform Richard that Xavier was missing. "That should deflect suspicion away from the Hiepants household, what," he said, grinning confidently.

Did he really think Richard was that stupid? "Just as long as you can control your urge for the dramatic," she replied.

"Well, of course, m'dear," he said, performing a flowery bow.

Olivia spent the rest of the morning talking to Xavier. He was unable to enlighten her about his relationship with Marmaduke and Lucinda; he'd only found out their *names* eleven days before, and *that* had been a chance discovery. She realised that Gerald had already relayed these details, but she hadn't paid them much heed. He rambled on so much that her mind tended to wander.

But she *had* listened to Xavier — he had a way about him that she found compelling. She listened as he spoke fondly of his years in Missing Anchor, raised and tutored by a doctor called Horatio Manky, a man he considered a genius, and one who'd inspired him in his pursuit of medical discovery and human wellbeing. And how, sixteen months ago, their peaceful, fishing-village life had suddenly come to an end, replaced by the serene, sun-washed hilltop of Blessed Whipping. The upheaval had been necessary for their research into a particular 'potion' they were developing — one that would help heal injuries and cure disease. Xavier hadn't questioned the move, even when confronted with assimilating into a community of Sun-worshippers. And they *had* made new discoveries. Then, a week ago on Sunday, he'd accidently discovered the *true* reason for their relocation. He'd spilled *Pig Dust* — whatever *that* was — over a seemingly blank parchment. However, the dust had revealed the inscription of a previously written letter: a personal communiqué in which Horatio suggested the time had come for the Duke to be reunited with his son; that it had been *twenty* years; that it might help him recover following the death of his wife. It was written with the familiarity of a confidant; it was apparent that Horatio and the Duke had been in communication since he was two years old.

Olivia could hardly believe what she was hearing. Had Lucinda known? It seemed so incredible...

Olivia couldn't lie in bed any longer. She needed to clear her mind; thoughts of Xavier made her feel uneasy. She feared for his safety; she had ever since he'd stepped out for some air on Friday night. Olivia had wanted to accompany him, but he'd politely requested some time to himself. He needed to think about his situation. Olivia acquiesced after he'd assured her he would take care where he walked and be wary of discovery. To her dismay, he'd not returned. That night, Marmaduke had fought off an intruder. There had to be a connection, but Olivia wouldn't allow herself to believe Xavier was involved. Something must have happened to him. If only she'd insisted on walking with him.

She slipped quietly from under the sheet, careful not to disturb Gerald. Let him sleep. He'd been most distressed by the attack on Marmaduke and the disappearance of Xavier. However, he'd also assured her that everything was being done to find the young doctor. Extra patrols had been assigned to scour the streets, search suspect premises, and question persons of ill-repute.

But almost three days had passed and still no word.

Thinking on persons of ill-repute, her good-for-nothing brother had rapped on their front door the morning after the Duke had been poisoned, the morning after Xavier had disappeared — *that* was too much of a coincidence for her liking — and Gerald had welcomed him into their home as if he were a man of standing.

Olivia crept out of the bedroom, stepped softly downstairs, past the reception foyer, down the passageway to the kitchen. The back of the house was still dark — the backyard was in deep, early morning shadow and would remain so for at least another two hours. Olivia, however, didn't require light; everything had its place in *her* household.

After relieving herself on the 'outdoor seat', Olivia returned to the kitchen. Straight ahead was the door to the passageway, to her left was the door to the washroom: a place where clothes *and* bodies were cleaned. It was for the latter reason that she entered.

A burnished copper bathing tub stood against the far wall. Olivia had used it more times in the last three weeks than she had the preceding three months. The summer had been unbearably hot and her clothes — indeed, the fashion of the court — were not designed for heat. She hated feeling clammy and grimy. Still, it would take more than the weather to make her compromise her standards; her appearance was of paramount importance. And if Gerald could march through the streets of Lower Icing in his heavy red coat, she would certainly rise to *her* sartorial challenge.

The tub was empty, so she walked over to the large wooden barrel tucked into the corner of the room. It stood four feet tall and had a wooden lid two feet in diameter. Resting on the lid was a bucket. Olivia lifted the bucket and placed it on the floor. She then removed the lid and leaned into the barrel until she felt cool water on her fingertips. It was about half full: enough water for her to bathe. She'd have Beth Wringer, her washerwoman, make the necessary trips to the well to refill it. It was Monday — Beth was due in an hour or so.

Olivia emptied four buckets of water into the tub. Then she filled a fifth bucket, which she would use to rinse herself. She had taken a towel from the linen cupboard, retrieved soap from the scrubbing basin and hung her nightgown on one of the door hooks, and now she lowered herself into the dark wetness of the tub. The water was surprisingly cool considering how warm the room was. Still, it was refreshing, and that was the whole point. She slid down into the water until only her head, shoulders and knees remained exposed — the tub wasn't long enough for her to stretch out fully, but Olivia was content in her cool, dark haven.

For a while she remained motionless, listening to the sounds of the new morning: twittering robins and chirping wrens melded with the more distant sounds of a waking Lower Icing. Inevitably, her thoughts returned to Xavier.

During their time together, he had been most animated when discussing his and Doctor Manky's medicines (or potions, as he called them). He described unguents that helped reduce the effects of influenza, powders that revitalised the spirit, ointments that cured skin complaints and reduced the effects of injury, even an elixir that rendered one unconscious to pain. They had odd names that seemed just as fantastic as the contents of his marvellous wooden case: sparkling glass vials and bottles full of colourful ingredients, fastened to polished walnut trays, with matching drawers that contained an amazing collection of gadgetry, all set against a dramatic black velvet lining. It was an object to treasure.

However, it was the contents of a locked leather folder that had really brought out the passion in Xavier. He wore a silver pendant around his neck, which he'd removed to unlock the folder. Olivia had been curious about the pendant — there was something engraved upon it — but Xavier had reacted guardedly and quickly looped it back over his neck, concealing it underneath his white shirt. Inside the leather folder was page after page of notes, diagrams and strange symbols (chemical and compound formulae, according to Xavier). They looked like some sort of ancient code, something you might find carved into one of those stone circles that were dotted around the Five Duchies (not that Olivia had seen one for herself, of course, but she'd seen drawings in books). And as she'd listened to Xavier describe some of his discoveries, she'd felt there *was* something mystical about this young man. It wasn't what he said, it was the way he said it. She had been entranced by him.

Olivia was snapped out of her reverie by the sounds of movement from above. Gerald had obviously woken. She wondered how his mood would be today — he'd been oddly distant since Xavier's disappearance. Yesterday, he'd even raised his voice at her; something Olivia had been well and truly shocked by. She'd put it down to the guilt he felt for Xavier's disappearance and the duress he was under from the powers that be — Sir Richard was *not* happy with him. And then, of course, there was Marmaduke, the real victim in all this. Again her mind made the unwanted connection between his attack and Xavier's disappearance.

Dull footfalls on the wooden staircase heralded her husband's descent. They were slow and plodding. Why couldn't they be smart and self-assured? So much for her peaceful soak. She picked up the cake of soap sitting in its small dish and began washing herself; now that Gerald was up, she wouldn't stay in the tub.

She managed to scrub her legs and feet before the inevitable knock at the door, followed by Gerald's sleepy voice. "Morning, m'dear."

"I'll be out directly, Gerald," Olivia responded. "You can set a fire for me, if you'd be so kind."

She heard him sigh and take a few steps towards the kitchen's hearth. That would keep him busy for fifteen minutes, by which time she would have cleaned and dried herself. Suddenly, the washroom door opened. Candlelight spilled into the dawn gloom, followed by Gerald, dressed in his nightshirt.

Olivia sank down into the tub and crossed her arms over her breasts. What did he want? Surely he could manage to light a fire.

"Sorry to disturb you, Olivia; however, I…" he said, lowering his gaze.

He looked so downcast that Olivia decided to refrain from airing her annoyance. Instead, she reverted to an impatient sounding, "Well?"

His gaze flicked back to her. "I fear, m'dear, I have something rather important to tell you."

Olivia would have normally dismissed a remark like that; Gerald's idea of 'rather important' usually turned out to be 'rather trivial', but she'd never seen him blink away tears before.

## CHAPTER 4

# *Start talkin', Master Muggins*

OPHELIA WAS DRESSED appropriately, in her opinion, for a visit to Bert Muggins' stall: a white bodice worn over an open-neck white shirt accentuating her full breasts. She was well aware of the effect her body had on men, and she knew how to use it to her advantage. That, along with her (unfounded) promiscuous reputation, could turn even the most upstanding gentlemen into lecherous fools (although, Master Prestwich had proven to be a frustrating exception).

She didn't anticipate much resistance from Bert Muggins, but this was not a time for subtleties — she had to find her father and Bert was the last person to have seen him.

Ophelia pulled her lace shawl over her cleavage before marching purposefully through the market. There was a laconic air to the usually bustling collection of stalls; even though the sun had only been up for half an hour, it was already oppressively hot. Still, it didn't stop the ogling stares, cheeky winks and hopeful greetings. Ophelia smiled and carried on. She was Frank Offcut's only daughter; no-one would take advantage.

Underneath the tattered canopy of Crockery & Curios, Bert was placing what *he* referred to as objet d'art on a table stand when Olivia announced herself with a chirpy, "Mornin', Master Muggins."

He spun around at the sound of her voice, almost dropping a cracked earthenware jug, glazed with what looked like a one-legged frog. He squinted in her direction, baring his disgusting arrangement of teeth. To aid in the focusing process, Ophelia let the shawl slip from her grasp to hang loosely from her shoulders.

"Ah, Mistress Ophelia," he said, and then ran his tongue over his lips.

Forcing herself to smile, and attempting to sound pleasant, Ophelia spoke with a directness her father would have been proud of. "Master Muggins. I'd be much obliged for your assistance."

He looked wary as he placed the jug carefully on a stand.

"My pa is missin, an' I'm hopin' you can point me in the right d'rection, since you saw 'im last an' all."

Bert scratched his spiky grey stubble as if considering the question. "I saw Frank at your 'ouse roun' midnigh'," he eventually conceded. "Tol' 'im wha' I knew 'bout a certain matter. He wen' to The Pits. I ain't seen 'im since."

"I'm sure you ain't, Master Muggins," Ophelia responded, remaining pleasant. "'Cause if you 'ad, y'woulda tol' me already, wouldnya?"

Bert's face twitched. "'Course. Goes without sayin'."

She moved closer to the scruffy stall owner, causing him to briefly flick his eyes away from her breasts in the direction of her face. She smiled at him. "You're an honest man, ain't ya, Master Muggins?"

He looked at her as if she'd asked him a trick question. There was a big difference between purporting honesty and *confronting* it. After a momentary deliberation, he settled upon a response Ophelia considered to be more or less truthful.

"When I need t'be."

She beamed at him and leant forward slightly. His pupils bounced up and down from her cleavage to her face and his smile became lascivious (in a dental-disaster sort of way), but Ophelia stayed focused on his eyes. "Wouldn't 'spect nothin' less, Master Muggins. Thing is, *this* is one of them times when y'need t'be."

He took a deep breath while leering at Ophelia's close-proximity cleavage. "I swear I ain't seen your pa," he said, almost mesmerised.

"I ain't askin' 'bout wha' ya *seen*. I'm askin' 'bout wha' ya *know*."

His eyes dragged themselves upwards. Ophelia actually preferred them at bust level — he really was an unpleasant-looking person.

"I'd be mos' grateful," she added.

"Well, maybe I did overhears a partic'lar conversation."

"I'm all ears, Bert."

"I wouldn' say *that*," he retorted, ogling her breasts and guffawing at his lecherous little joke.

Ophelia wanted to slap his face, but she continued to smile as if he was the most charming man she'd ever met. "So wha' did ya 'ear then, Bert?"

"Wha's it worth?"

*A kick in the bollocks*, thought Ophelia. She was quickly losing patience. "I orready tol' ya, Bert. I'd be mos' grateful."

"Wha's tha' mean ezackly?" he said, running his tongue across his mangy chin.

That was enough for Ophelia. She could stand a certain amount of disgusting behaviour, but Bert Muggins had just crossed into revolting territory.

Before he had a chance to react, Ophelia grabbed the stall owner by his mad, grey hair. He cried out in alarm and his arms flailed towards her, but Ophelia had already stepped behind him, twisting the clump of hair as she moved. The noise of his protestation was swallowed up, somewhat, by the hubbub of the awakening market, and, being in a corner, Crockery & Curios was out of sight of most people. Just to make sure, Ophelia yanked him behind the stall. Bert continued to bellow out his alarm.

"Stop y' squealin', Bert. 'Less, o'course, y' *wan'* me to make ya squeal." She gave his hair another tug and he cried out in genuine pain.

"Orrigh! Orrigh!"

Ophelia stopped tugging. "Now, if you don' wan' me to rip this flee nest from ya poxy scalp, start talkin', Master Muggins."

Ophelia marched straight from Bert Muggins' stall to the castle. She was fuming, and it had nothing to do with the morning heat. Bert Muggins… that shithead! She'd wanted to smash all his Crockery over his indignant face and shove some well-chosen Curios up his cowardly arse after he'd spewed out what he knew.

Sometime during the small hours of the morning, he'd been awakened by a rhythmic jingling and clopping of hooves. "I always sleeps with one eye and *bofe* ears open," he'd remarked. Two men were leading their horses down the poky lane that ran past his first-floor bedroom. It was too dark to make out who the men were and they weren't making a sound — it was obvious they were trying to slip out of town on the quiet — but Bert wasn't stupid; he knew who the two men were. "Like I tol' y'pa, them Molseon Twins were plannin' to scarper town." As they approached, Bert noticed that one of the horses had been packed quite heavily with bags. "Then I realised it weren' no bags; it was a body." As the twins passed, Bert heard the dangling body groan, and one of the brothers whispered, "Let's jus' drop the friggin' butcher 'ere. 'E ain't gonna say nothin', an' I ain't carryin' 'im all the way to friggin' Great Naff." The other one had hissed back, "You won' 'ave to, orrigh'. I know a nice big 'ole we c'n drop 'im into. Let the wolves finish 'im off."

Ophelia had reacted to this revelation with fear and anger. "An' *when*, exactly, were y'gonna tell us 'bout this, y'bastard?" she yelled, tugging his hair.

He screamed.

She flung his head forwards, letting go of his hair — she suddenly felt dirty. "I'd be plannin' on scarperin' town as well, Master Muggins. If anythin's 'appened to Pa, you're pig food." Then she'd left him cowering behind his stall. The altercation had drawn a few looks, but no-one approached as she marched out of the market and headed towards the castle.

Walking past the leering guardsmen at the West Gate, Ophelia turned right towards the barracks compound. It was about this time yesterday she'd walked through here on her way to visit Billy and her pa in The Can. Yesterday, she'd flirted with the guardsmen; today, she ignored them. Yesterday, Billy was her main concern; today, he would have to wait. The Can was a revolting piss-hole, but at least it was safe. She would sweet-talk her way into her brother's cell *after* she'd made sure she'd organised a band of men-at-arms to find her pa. She tried not to think about what state he might be in.

Ophelia headed towards the Officers' Quarters. It was behind the blacksmith's, next to the barracks. The giant Longbotian smithy was hammering away at something that clanked loudly, long blond hair tied back in a ponytail (as was his beard), muscular arms rhythmically taut and sheened in sweat, bold forehead furrowed in concentration, focused on the red-hot object in front of him. He paid her no heed as she steamed past.

Ignoring a gathering of men-at-arms who'd just appeared out of the barracks, Ophelia fixed her gaze on the entrance to the Purple Peril's quarters and marched purposefully towards it. Upon reaching it, she felt like bursting in without knocking, but decided she might be better served by displaying a *certain* amount of decorum, particularly since she required their assistance.

She was about to rap forcefully against the reinforced wooden door, but her hand was stayed by an authoritative voice.

"Mistress Offcut!"

It came from behind her. Turning around, she saw Brandon Swill marching in her direction, his purple and gold uniform gleaming in the bright morning sunlight. She waited at the door while he closed the distance between them.

"Morning, Mistress Offcut," he said, doffing the felt peak of his feathered hat. "I'm afraid this area is restricted to—"

"Y'gotta organise a search for my pa," Ophelia interrupted.

He looked confused.

"Them Moleson Twins 'ave got 'im and they're gonna chuck 'im t'the wolves somewhere on the way to Great Naff. They could've already—"

"Ophelia!"

Suddenly, he was holding the sides of her arms, clamping them still, forcing her to stop talking and look at him.

"Calm down," he said, softening his voice.

She wanted to fling his arms away and yell at him that she *was* calm, but, instead, she took a deep breath and sighed. "Please, Lieutenan'. Pa needs 'elp."

He released her arms, a concerned look on his face. "Very well, but you need to tell me exactly what's happened."

She did exactly that. Fifteen minutes later, she found herself in a place she'd never imagined ever setting foot in.


Ophelia found it hard to believe she was actually being ushered into Sir Richard Upson's private quarters. Brandon Swill had escorted her past the door to Prestwich's office, straight up a palatial marble staircase and into a plush antechamber — a far cry from four days ago, when her and Seth had been marched out of the Upper Bailey after waiting hours to speak to Sir Richard about Billy.

Brandon left her in the antechamber while he disappeared into Sir Richard's quarters. She stood, regarding four horse statuettes carved in dark marble, rearing in her direction from each corner of the room on waist-high, ornately turned mahogany pedestals. There was a black velvet divan to her left; its silver trim and stitching gleamed in the muted candlelight. She didn't even *think* about sitting on it. A few minutes later, the lieutenant returned, saying Sir Richard did indeed want to speak to her.

Brandon Swill led her across the black-and-white-check marble floor of the antechamber. Clasping her shawl to her chest, Ophelia tried to remain calm and focused as she entered the Seneschal of Lower Icing's reception room. However, she was momentarily bedazzled by its opulence. Paintings (mostly portraits of Sir Richard) adorned walls that were covered in silver wallpaper, highlighted with thin, black diagonal lines which produced a diamond pattern. The wall to her left faced south and contained three large windows which were draped with black curtains held open by silver cords. Built into the centre of the right wall (the town-side of the room) was a large fireplace bordered by a beautifully embossed, black metal hearth and a silver-seamed, white marble mantle. On top of the mantle stood two hand-painted vases containing wonderfully colourful arrangements of flowers. Hanging between them was the largest painting in the room: a portrait of Sir Richard mounted on a large black horse.

Ophelia had barely absorbed her surroundings when she found herself approaching a large, polished mahogany table at the end of the room. Two men regarded her approach. She recognised both. Sir Richard, dressed immaculately in black and silver (as if to match the décor), sat opposite the more casually attired Tom Skinner. A collection of plates with the remnants of a hearty breakfast had been pushed to one side of the table and the smell of Offcut bacon still lingered in the warmth of the room.

Ophelia suddenly felt self-conscious as she and the lieutenant came to a halt before the table. Sir Richard regarded her impassively; his dark eyes betrayed no hint of what he may be thinking. Tom Skinner smiled nervously — she wondered if he was still embarrassed about their tryst on the banks of the Icing. She found herself hoping he wasn't, even though the entire evening was a bit of a drunken blur.

The lieutenant suddenly stood to attention and saluted.

Sir Richard kept his gaze on Ophelia; she wondered whether she was expected to curtsey. Eventually he said, "At ease, Lieutenant." He sounded bored.

Brandon obliged by relaxing his stance, moving his arm from its position across his heart to his side.

Sir Richard's gaze didn't falter. Ophelia felt distinctly uncomfortable. Most men undressed her with their eyes — she could handle that — but Sir Richard's penetrated much deeper than her clothing.

"So, what do you have to say for yourself, Miss Offcut," he said without preamble. The sound of his voice made her heart jump. She didn't like this at all.

"It's my pa, 'e's—"

"Been abducted by the Moleson Twins," Sir Richard finished, impatiently. "Lieutenant Swill has already apprised me of your father's... indisposition."

Ophelia suddenly flushed with anger. What did Sir Richard want from her then? Permission to start searching for him? She wanted to tell him to get off his high-horse and get on a real one, to start combing the bleeding countryside with all the bloody men-at-arms he could bloody well muster! However, she managed to hold her tongue. Then she glanced at Tom Skinner. He looked uncomfortable.

"Miss Offcut…"

Ophelia immediately flicked her gaze back to the man in black.

"My concern lies with this trader…" He paused and eyed Brandon, "What is his name, Lieutenant?"

(As if *she* couldn't answer that question.)

"Bert Muggins, sir."

Sir Richard grimaced. "Not a name that fills one with confidence." Then his eyes were back on Ophelia. "So, what did Bert Muggins say to you about the Moleson Twins' involvement in the disappearance of a man called Xavier?"

Was *that* why she'd been allowed admittance, to help them find this *dead* man? Ophelia couldn't hold her tongue any longer. "'E don' know nothin' 'bout wha's 'appened to this friggin' Xavier! If them Moleson Twins 'ave done 'im in, then they've ditched 'im somewhere where you ain't gonna find 'im. An' righ' now, while y'sittin' y'soft arses on velvet cushions, my pa's—"

"Enough!" Sir Richard slammed his fist on the table, sending a tremor through the crockery and utensils.

"My pa's ou' there somewhere, all 'cause of some ou'sider—"

"Ophelia, please!" It was Tom Skinner.

She felt Brandon grab her arm. She shrugged it off, without shifting her gaze from a simmering Sir Richard. "Wha' nobody's never bleedin' 'eard of or gives two shits abou'!"

Brandon grabbed her arm again, with more force this time. She turned to face him; he looked concerned and flushed. Again she dislodged her arm from his grasp. "Let go o' me!"

Then she advanced on the two men sitting at the table. Sir Richard remained seated, unflinching, like one of his black statues, while Tom stood up and tried to placate her. "Please calm down, Ophelia. There are things at stake which you don't—"

Ignoring him, she placed both her hands on the table's gleaming surface and leant towards the unflappable Seneschal. "Wha' are y'goin' t'do abou' my pa, Sir Richard?"

He regarded her for a moment; his clenched jaw relaxed and the hint of a smile grew from the corner of his mouth.

She suddenly felt very hot and somewhat light-headed.

Then he looked at his companion and asked quite casually, "Do you feel it, Tom?"

Tom appeared befuddled by the question. "Feel what, Richard?"

"A sense of already having experienced an event; the Escargotians call it déjà vu."

Tom didn't answer; he looked uncertain how to. Ophelia was also dumbfounded. She could hear blood pumping through her head.

Sir Richard's smile grew as he regarded her again. "Alas, Miss Offcut, you seem to be under the same misapprehension as your father. Allow me to enlighten you, as I did *him*. My duty is to the *Duke* and the Duchy of Lower Icing, *not* a butcher."

Ophelia was too emotionally spent to argue; her world seemed to be reeling.

"Since you are unable to aid me in my duty, there is no need to prolong this… discussion."

She felt Brandon's hands on the back of her shoulder, softly this time, and allowed him to pull her back from the table. Truth be told, she was grateful for the support — her vision was beginning to swim.

"And since, as you assert, the Moleson Twins dispose of their victims without a trace, it would be an exercise in futility to send—"

"*I* will look for your father," a voice interrupted. It sounded like Tom's, but Ophelia couldn't be sure; she was in the process of fainting.

## CHAPTER 5

# A rather delicate situation

THE MORNING BATH had done wonders for Mary; she felt refreshed, both physically and mentally. By the time she'd washed and dressed for another day of clicking with the clique, she'd decided what she was going to do about Sid and the silver button. She would say nothing to Richard — not yet, at least. Not unless Sid did something to betray her trust. And she *did* trust him, against all reason and common sense. But, more importantly, she believed he was innocent. He'd have to have the brains of sty-mucker to keep that button if he'd actually committed the attack. No, it was all too obvious. Sid was right; the person who'd beaten him had planted the button. It was just a question of who that person was.

It was nearly eight o'clock by the time Mary checked on Sid. He was asleep. She stood over him for a while. The left side of his face looked like it had been filled-to-bursting with red wine. Whoever had attacked him had done a good job. She left him in peace. Doctor Whysman had said he would visit again sometime this morning.

The Harey Rabbit didn't open to the public for another hour, and since Sid was the only guest, she went straight to the kitchen. John was helping Patricia — her authoritative senior cook — prepare food. Mary bid them both good morning, then poked her head into the laundry where Juanita was busily wringing an assortment of linen.

"Morning, Meestres," she said happily. That was a good sign; Mary never knew what sort of mood she would find Juanita in. "I use dee bathwater to doo dee washeeng."

"Well done, Juanita." Mary nodded and smiled indulgently; every time Mary had a bath, Juanita used the water for washing, and, each time, the young Icarumban seemed compelled to inform Mary of the fact.

Turning her attention back to the two figures in the kitchen, Mary asked Patricia what was on offer for today's patrons.

"Col' pork pies, col' lamb, garden salad," the cook announced, without looking up from her chopping. "Too bleedin' 'ot fer cookin'."

John glanced back at Mary, looking bemused or embarrassed — it was hard to tell with John. Mary moved towards them.

"Ain't gonna learn nothin' gazin' in *that* d'rection," Patricia said, without missing a chop. John snapped his attention back to the action on the table.

Mary smiled to herself as she walked around the other side of the table. She liked Patricia's no-nonsense manner, even if it *did* mean she occasionally forgot who, exactly, was running The Harey Rabbit. It turned out she was in the process of slicing a large bowl of cooked and peeled beetroot. Her palms were a similar colour to the left side of Sid's face. Her method was simple: cut the beetroot in half, place the flat side on the chopping board, and use a forward/downward motion to slice. Her proficiency with the knife was impressive; she could perfectly slice both halves of a beetroot into thin slices in a matter of seconds.

Patricia hardly acknowledged Mary's presence. She was a stout woman in her fifties, mostly made of muscle. Her figure was apparent beneath her tightly tied white apron and close-fitting brown dress. Her thick grey hair was arranged tightly underneath a white coif. Her complexion was ruddy and a sheen of sweat glistened on her forehead, but that was mostly due to the temperature in the kitchen — the morning sun had been baking it for over two hours. Normally the door to the courtyard and stables would be closed, but in such heat, any fresh air was better than nothing.

John was also looking hot; no doubt he'd already made a dozen or more trips to the well this morning. Fortunately it was close. There were a number of wells dotted throughout the town, but some villagers had journeys of two hundred paces to fill their bucket; she wondered how they were coping with the heat. As she emerged from her thoughts, she realised both John and Patricia were looking at her.

"You gonna leddim in or aincha?" asked Patricia, glancing to her right.

Mary followed the cook's gaze. Standing in the sunlit doorway to the courtyard was a tall man. He smiled. "I did try the more conventional entrance, but the door was locked."

"Sorry, Tom." She blinked, clearing her thoughts of water collection. "I was away with the water sprites. Come in."

Tom stepped into the kitchen and acknowledged John and Patricia with a nod and a "Good morning."

"I've been wondering what happened to you since you last graced us with your presence. Spending some time with a certain butcher's daughter perhaps?"

She liked teasing Tom — he always took the bait. However, today the Gamekeeper just looked a bit awkward.

"Would you like something to eat? Perhaps a beetroot salad?" Mary noticed Patricia raise an eyebrow.

"No, thank you; I've just come to retrieve my saddlebag."

There was something definitely amiss with Tom; he seemed distracted. "I see," she said. Then she noticed Juanita standing by the washroom doorway, gazing adoringly in Tom's direction. She clapped her hands. "Juanita!"

The girl jumped, but still managed to keep smiling at Tom — the subtleties of flirtation obviously weren't part of the Icarumban culture.

"The Gamekeeper's saddlebag is in the storeroom under the stairs. Fetch it for me, please."

"Yes, Meestress," she said, without taking her eyes of Tom, who was looking even more uncomfortable now.

"Well, Master Skinner," Mary said, folding her arms. "Are you going to tell me what's going on?"

He looked torn. "It's a rather delicate situation."

She nodded her understanding, then said, "Well, don't let the clothes fool you. I do 'delicate' quite well."

Mary took him by the arm and led him outside into the stables. Wildflower was tethered to a post, as was another chestnut mare. Wildflower snorted, as if in greeting, her blaze a bright white streak in the shade of the stables. Both horses were saddled. Rubbing her hand down the side of Wildflower's neck, she said, "I'm listening, Tom."

He sighed. "Frank Offcut's gone missing."

Of all the things Mary thought he might say, *that* wasn't one of them. She found it oddly disturbing. She turned to face him to see if he was making fun. Judging by his countenance, fun was the last thing on his mind. Mary didn't know what to think. Eventually she quipped, "I'm not sure I would call Frank Offcut a *delicate* situation."

Mary had met Frank on a number of occasions since taking over the running of The Harey Rabbit — she'd had to negotiate the price of her meat orders and had commissioned a number of varieties of gourmet sausage to assuage the demands of her clientele, most of whom regularly visited Escargotia (much to Frank's disgust).

"No," Tom agreed, without humour

Mary regarded him; this was all very strange.

"He was aiding Richard and the Purple Peril in finding…" he paused, as if he'd said too much, then finished with, "a person of interest in regards to the incident at the castle."

Mary would have burst out laughing had Tom not seemed so serious. "You sound like you've *joined* the Purple Peril."

He remained silent.

"So, where's he gone missing?"

"Somewhere between here and Great Naff."

He made it sound like it was a casual stroll across the Town Square. Mary couldn't help but react with sarcasm. "Oh well, I'm surprised you bothered dropping round for your saddlebag, Tom — you'll be back before lunch. Can you tell Frank we're running low on the pork and apple sausages?"

Before Tom's withering expression could become words, John and Juanita burst into the courtyard. They appeared to be playing tug-o-war with Tom's saddlebag.

"Meestress told *me* to get dee saddlebag," she yelled, yanking the strap in her direction.

"I 'elped y'find it," John argued, pulling back.

"I no need help from baybee gringo like you." She tugged again.

John let go of the strap and disappeared back inside the kitchen (no doubt at the behest of Patricia).

Juanita nodded in satisfaction, then marched towards Mary and Tom, her face transforming from angry frown to flirtatious grin. Normally, Mary would have reined in such behaviour, but she decided Tom could do with a serving of Juanita this morning, to get his blood flowing a bit.

Tom's face had certainly turned red, and when Juanita handed him his saddlebag, he almost dropped it. Mary had to stifle a laugh. It was funny how easily a strong, self-assured man like Tom could be turned into a clumsy fool by a pair of fluttering eyelashes.

"Thank you…?" said Tom, silently asking for her name.

"Whan*ee*ta." She said it like it was an invitation to explore her body.

"Yes, *thank* you, Juanita," said Mary, deciding Tom had suffered enough. "I'm sure you have more pressing tasks to attend to."

"Yes, Meestress." She pouted, and then flounced back towards the kitchen, turning her head one last time in Tom's direction before disappearing inside.

Tom walked over to Wildflower. "Quite a washer girl you have there."

"Yes…" Mary acknowledged, before steering the conversation back to the matter at hand. "So, what do you mean by *missing*, exactly?"

"Pardon?" he said, straddling the saddlebag across the saddle.

"Frank Offcut. You said he was missing."

"Yes."

"How?"

He didn't reply, just began fastening the saddlebag. If there was one thing Mary didn't react well to, it was being ignored. She slapped his right arm. He responded calmly and turned to face her.

"Well?"

He was conflicted, hazel eyes locked onto hers. Eventually he said, "We believe he's fallen foul of the Moleson Twins."

Again, not the answer she'd expected. "The Moleson Twins? I heard they'd been locked up."

"They were released on Friday, and they were seen leaving with Frank in the early hours of this morning."

"Why's Frank Offcut mixing himself up with *those* two?"

"As I said, he's been helping the Purple Peril."

This made no sense to Mary. "Since when has the Purple Peril needed a butcher to—"

"Mary." His tone stopped her. "Someone has attacked the Duke. We are trying to get to the bottom of it. That's all I can tell you." He regarded her earnestly for a moment. "Now, I must be on my way. Time is of the essence."

Mary nodded. Tom turned his attention back to the saddlebag. Her thoughts immediately went to the man who was recovering in her bed. Should she tell Tom about Sid and the silver button? Trouble was, he'd be treated like a criminal not a victim. Mary knew how things worked. She'd overheard enough conversations at The Harey Rabbit to know that justice only existed for those who could afford it. For someone like Sid, it meant time in The Can… or worse. Maybe she could say *she* found it in the stables this morning.

"There, that should do it," Tom said, pulling down on the last buckle strap.

"Tom…" He turned to face her. "The silver button… is it…?"

"I really don't have time to discuss this with you. I'm sorry, but there have been developments which I'm required to attend to as a matter of urgency."

She pressed him. "Are you saying the Moleson Twins are responsible for the attack on the Duke?"

"I'm saying nothing of the kind," he replied, untethering Wildflower.

"Then, what are——?"

"Mary!" His patience was at an end. "I have already divulged more than I should. Suffice to say I am in the service of the Duke."

"As opposed to the service of my brother?" Mary shot back, immediately regretting her words.

He shook his head and began untethering the other horse.

"I'm sorry. It's just that…"

He looked back at her, his gaze defiant. "What?"

The words were on her lips — I have the silver button — but they didn't come out. Instead, she whispered, "Be careful, Tom."

A curious look crossed his face, relaxing into a smile. "No need to worry about me. I'm good at finding and trapping rats; the Moleson Twins won't know what's hit them."

Mary nodded, but her mind was elsewhere. If the Moleson Twins *were* involved, they would have been hired by someone. They were thugs not schemers.

Tom mounted Wildflower. "Cheerio, Mary,"

"Good luck, Tom."

He smiled as he secured the other horse's rein to the girth ring of Wildflower's saddle. Why *did* he have an extra horse? Was it a spare for Frank? She was about to ask, but he stole the moment with, "Just remember, everything I have told you is for your ears only. I trust you'll keep my confidence."

Mary nodded.

Tom nudged Wildflower out of the stables, across the courtyard and then, with a final wave, he added, "I'll be sure to remind Frank about your sausages."

She smiled as he disappeared through the courtyard gate. She *would* keep his confidence. Whoever had attacked the Duke, it wasn't Sid, and that was all Mary was really concerned about.

## CHAPTER 6

# *A most disturbing discovery*

OLIVIA QUICKLY SCRUBBED the rest of her body, dried herself, and put on her nightgown. As she emerged from the washroom, Gerald gazed sadly at her from the kitchen table. This was not like her husband at all. She noticed a book resting near his right hand. She recognised it straightaway — it was the only book she'd ever seen with a white leather cover. It contained recipes for the potions, ointments, lotions, and unguents Xavier had talked about so passionately. She'd never felt the need to read it — *listening* to the young man enthuse about his research had been wondrous. The written word would have been a poor substitute. But she knew Gerald had a scientific mind and had spent many more hours in Xavier's company. A cold chill suddenly ran down her spine.

"What is it, Gerald?"

"Sit down, m'dear." His voice, normally so loud, was barely a whisper.

She immediately sensed the worst. "Is Xavier…?"

"I think it's best if you sit down."

She didn't want to; she feared what he was about to say. "Gerald, this better not be some kind of inane jest."

"Please, Olivia." His eyes pleaded.

Reluctantly, Olivia moved towards the table and sat down opposite her husband. He continued to stare miserably at her, prolonging the dreadful suspense.

"Well?"

He sighed. "Alas, m'dear, I have made a most disturbing discovery." He dropped his gaze. "I fear Xavier may have been involved in the attack on the Duke."

Olivia's heart sank. Even though she'd entertained a connection between Xavier's disappearance and the attack on the Duke, the reality of it seemed unbelievable. "What do you mean 'involved'?"

He was sitting there like a mourner at a funeral.

She snapped. "Gerald!"

Her voice jolted him into action; he pushed the book towards her. The white leather cover looked ethereal in the feeble candlelight, but its gold-leaf lettering shone.

### POETRY IN POTION
### Doctor Horatio Manky

Olivia opened the book. The first page contained the same information as the cover. She flicked over to the next page: the contents. It seemed the book had been printed. She was surprised by that. For some reason, she had expected it to be scribed by the author.

Aches and Pains
Breaks and Sprains
Coughs, Colds and Influenza
Cuts, Abrasions and Bruising
Fevers
Nausea and Morning Sickness
Poisoning
Poxes
Relaxants
Special Potions

"At the back, in the Special Potions section," he whispered.

Her gaze moved from the page to her husband's grave visage. This was ridiculous. Xavier wouldn't harm anyone, he was a healer. Surely this was just another monumental misreading of a situation.

Olivia went straight to the back of the book and started leafing backwards through the pages. She'd flicked back two pages, past potions called *Voracious Loquacious* and *Vigour Morphis*, when Gerald spoke.

"There." He indicated with his finger. "The warning under *Paloma Coma*."

WARNING:
Any variance in measurements will affect the efficacy of the potion. Be particularly wary of Orange Spotted Mushroom: too much will cause the imbiber to become delirious and feverish and may well prove fatal.

The name of the potion had been underlined in ink and the warning circled. Olivia immediately recognised its significance; Gerald had kept her informed about Marmaduke's degenerating condition. However, the fact that the warning married with the Duke's symptoms did not mean that Xavier had poisoned him; not in Olivia's mind, at least. Gerald, on the other hand, had seemingly accepted the obvious connection at face value. Olivia didn't trust in face value. The castle clique was a perfect example of *that* — it was a case of 'two-face value' where *they* were concerned. And because she'd moved beyond face value with Xavier, she knew in her heart that he was not someone who would, or *could*, poison a Duke, let alone a Duke who was also his *father*. No, it was too incredible. And his disappearance… well, that was a worrying coincidence.

She looked at her despondent husband. "I'd like to say I'm surprised, Gerald, but, unfortunately, you have been your predictable self."

Confusion crossed his crestfallen features. "What do you mean, m'dear?"

She shoved the book back towards her husband. "That doesn't prove a thing."

Gerald regarded the incriminating page, his sadness transformed into confusion. "Surely—"

"There's no 'surely' about it, Gerald!" She didn't want to hear his inane explanation. "For a start, how could you *possibly* think Xavier would harm Marmaduke — you of *all* people?"

"That's what makes it so upsetting. To think he—"

"Think? Hah! Hope springs eternal, Gerald!"

He looked indignant, but Olivia paid him no heed. She wanted her husband to listen and realise that he hadn't actually *thought* at all. "Why would Xavier mark this book?"

Gerald's eyebrows furrowed; clearly he was struggling with her reasoning.

"It makes no sense, Gerald. I'm sure he could recite *every* syllable in here," she said, prodding down on the book.

Gerald's eyes remained focused on her.

"And someone with *that* kind of knowledge wouldn't even need to *open* the book, let alone leave an incriminating indication of his intent."

Her husband continued to stare at her, his expression becoming more thoughtful. In response, Olivia softened her tone. "This is the action of someone *discovering* information. So, what you need to *think* about is who else had an opportunity to read *Poetry in Potion*."

Gerald's expression brightened. "Of course, m'dear. What you've said makes perfect sense. After Xavier was sent to The Keep, his possessions were retrieved from The Bloody Bell by Lieutenant Swill and taken to Sir Richard. They weren't returned to him until the next day."

"There you have it," Olivia responded, although she very much doubted that either Richard or the lieutenant would be stupid enough to make such an obvious error.

A whole new world of possibilities seemed to dawn on Gerald's face. "Oh, I say, this *is* good news. You were right, m'dear; I wasn't thinking properly. Oh, this is a relief, what."

Hardly, thought Olivia. Xavier was still missing, Marmaduke was still suffering, and his assailant was still at large.

## CHAPTER 7

## *Since you're the Gamekeeper*

THEY HAD BEEN on the North Road for two hours; the midday sun was burning and her saddle was starting to rub. However, Ophelia wasn't even going to *breathe* discomfort, not after all the reasoning, coaxing and demanding she'd gone through trying to persuade Tom to take her along…

It hadn't been easy, particularly since she'd fainted in Sir Richard's office and had to be revived with a tumbler of cold water while suffering disparaging comments about being a wilting flower. Then she'd been escorted out of the royal quarters like she *was* a fragile bloom. And, besides all that, Tom had maintained that he stood a better chance of finding her pa alone, that she would be more of a hindrance than help; his main concern being her ability to cover the distance and terrain on horseback.

"This is not some jolly jaunt across a meadow, Ophelia," he'd replied after she'd declared her intention to accompany him.

They'd been walking across the stone courtyard in the Middle Bailey, momentarily spared the heat of the morning sun by the shade of The Keep. Ophelia had felt quite revived by then and was more annoyed than anything else for having shown such 'feminine frailty', particularly in front of Tom and Sir Dick-Up-Himself. Men just didn't understand the burden of emotion that women carried, and what she definitely hadn't needed at that moment was a load of patronising bullshit from a glorified huntsman. "Yeah, an' I ain't no preenin' princess what needs her arse wiped!"

Annoyingly, he'd smiled at that, but still refused to take her, listing a dozen practical reasons why she shouldn't come along, *including* the way she would have to wipe her arse, but Ophelia had been resolute. By the time they reached the West Gate, he'd acquiesced, but it was because she'd resorted to feminine charm, suggesting that her sense of adventure would really come to the fore should they have to camp overnight (which, he'd informed her, was most likely).

"Very well, Ophelia. If you're *that* game."

"I am." Openly studying his muscular frame, she couldn't deny she was attracted to him. "Since *you're* the gamekeeper."

The last time they'd talked in the vicinity of the West Gate, they had ended up drunk at The Harey Rabbit and sleeping together on the banks of the Icing. This time, however, they went their separate ways: Ophelia back home to change into something more suitable for riding, while Tom organised a second horse from the castle stables and retrieved his saddlebag from The Harey Rabbit. Before they parted, she made him promise to collect her outside the Offcut abode on Market Street, which he did so readily enough.

Her ma had been surprisingly supportive, and Seth had eventually agreed that he could best help Pa by staying at home; looking after Ma and the family business. She packed all the things Tom had told her to bring: a blanket, a bladder of water, and some food (a leg of ham, some sausages, a loaf of bread, a wedge of cheese and some apples). She also brought along a bottle of rum and some clothes for Pa.

Tom laughed when he saw the linen cloth bulging with her supplies. "I knew I forgot something."

"Wha's tha', then?" Ophelia asked, not picking up on his bemused tone.

"A cart," he replied. However, he still managed to pack everything except the ham and bread into Ophelia's saddlebag.

Tom slowed Wildflower from a canter to a walk, and Ophelia, trailing behind by some four or five horse lengths, drew level before also reducing pace.

He regarded her with concern. "How are you faring?"

Ophelia wondered if he could see her discomfort. Just in case, she went on the offensive. "It ain't *me* what's been hauled away by a coupla thugs."

He nodded. After an extended pause, he added, "We'll rest the horses soon." Then, pointing at the brown-tinged, tree-dotted open space to their right, he informed her that the Icing River was half an hour's ride away; they would stop there.

*Another half an hour!* She groaned inwardly; she was grimy with sweat and dust and could feel the sun burning her face, but she nodded her agreement. He smiled and spurred Wildflower back into canter, then wheeled right, off the North Road, into the open land.

It was actually less of an ordeal than Ophelia anticipated. For one thing, the grassland wasn't as hard underfoot as the compacted dirt road, and there were more trees, which meant more shade. The trees became quite thick, and even Tom, who seemed to have an innate ability to navigate between low branches, had to slow to a walk.

Not long afterwards, the grass began to give way to thick underbrush. Tom reined in Wildflower. "We'll have to lead the horses from here. There's a goat run over there; that will take us to the river."

Ophelia regarded the mass of tangled bushes just ahead; she couldn't see any way through it at all. "Pretty small bleedin' goat."

Tom dismounted. Ophelia braced herself to do the same. Swivelling her torso, she swung her right leg behind her and felt it thud into the ground. She managed to free her left foot from stirrup on the third attempt. Thank goodness her horse (Hazel was her name, because of her colour) was a placid animal and remained steadfast throughout the whole procedure. It wasn't until Ophelia had both feet on the ground that the soreness between her legs reared itself. She gasped involuntarily.

"It'll get worse before it gets better," Tom informed her. "I've brought an unguent that will help a little."

Ophelia was hot and in pain, and she wasn't sure how she was going to be able to walk without grimacing; the last thing she needed was a man with a know-it-all expression, even if he *was* trying to help her. "You know where you c'n stick your friggin' unguent."

Tom burst out laughing, adding insult to her injury. He was a handsome devil, damn him; she couldn't help but smile back.

Recovering his sense of purpose, he made a clicking noise with his tongue and led Wildflower towards the wall of bushes and brambles. He pulled out his sword and began slashing at the greenery. Surprisingly, the thick undergrowth didn't impede his progress much at all, and soon only Wildflower's rump was in view. Ophelia took a painful step forward and followed the chestnut mare through the mass of leaves and branches.

She was in a world of bright green: trees had given way to thick bushes filled with buzzing insects. However, apart from a constant leafy caress, the going was remarkably easy, and they *were* actually walking on a goat run; the ground was soft and well-trodden, forming a path some two feet wide. Hazel and Wildflower certainly weren't spooked by the choice of trail. The rhythmic slash of Tom's sword ceased after only a minute, and the insects suddenly seemed less outraged. As the bush cleared, the sound of gurgling water permeated through the green.

Suddenly, they were standing just above a small cove of slate-grey sand, bordered by reeds, overlooking a wide and rather shallow-looking Icing River. It was as if the goat run had transported them to another world. They were at a bend in the river. From the opposite bank, a peninsula of grey sand and shale protruded some thirty paces. On either side of the peninsula, reed beds reasserted themselves along the bank, a gentle border to the rugged land beyond. Directly in line with the peninsula, some two hundred paces in the distance, a steep range of rocky hills rose from the woodland like the back of a giant dragon lumbering its way towards the north-east.

Tom halted just before he and Wildflower reached the sand. Ophelia drew level with him. The sun beamed down, but the air was fresh, not cloying as it had been along the North Road. It was a relief, to say the least. Ophelia couldn't wait to splash some of the cool river water over her face and slake her thirst. Her water-skin was still half full, but the last swig she'd had just after turning off the North Road had been warm.

"Hold Wildflower for a moment," Tom said, handing her the mare's reins. Something had caught his attention.

Olivia watched as he stepped carefully into the cove. Squatting down, he regarded the coarse grey sand near the river's edge. Now that Ophelia was focusing on where Tom was looking, she could see the sand had been disturbed. "Wha' y'found?"

He looked up. "What I was hoping to find." Then he stood up and walked back towards her. "Two horses and at least two men — the human footprints overlap each other, so it's hard to tell, but I'd guess two — and I'd say they were within the time frame of our friends the Moleson Twins."

Ophelia was impressed. From her vantage point, some ten paces away, the sand just looked messy — she couldn't discern *any* footprints *or* hoof-prints for that matter. "Howja know they'd come this way?"

He tapped a finger against the right side of his nose. "Trade secret," he said, taking Wildflower's reins back. "Come on, let's freshen up. We've got a hard ride ahead."

## CHAPTER 8

# *Pride successfully swallowed again*

**A**FTER TOM HAD ridden off, Mary decided to check on Sid. He was asleep on his side, the damaged part of his face exposed. It was distorted by swelling and bruising, the eye wept and the gash on his forehead was stitched into an angry ridge. She was relieved she had kept his secret; he deserved *that* much from her, because, since speaking with Tom, she'd begun entertaining thoughts that one of her regulars could well be behind what had happened at the castle and, consequently, the attack on Sid. And, if that was the case, she meant to see justice done.

Doctor Whysman didn't arrive until midday, by which time Mary was busy with a thirsty lunchtime crowd. (The cold meat with beetroot salad was also proving to be a popular choice of fare.) Mary escorted the doctor down the passageway to Sid's room and then asked him if he wouldn't mind seeing himself out, unless, of course, he had something unusual to report about Sid.

"Of course I don't mind. I'm sorry to have called at such an inconvenient time, although it couldn't be helped I'm afraid. I was delayed at Mistress Hattie Chapeaux's. Fell down the stairs, poor woman. I had to—"

"That is perfectly understandable, Doctor," Mary cut in, trying to avoid a step-by-step account of Mistress Chapeaux's injuries. "I'll leave you to Sid."

Doctor Whysman smiled. "I'm sure our friend is on the mend, but I will let you know anything to the contrary."

"Thank you; you've been most attentive. Won't you at least accept—"

He held up his hand. "I won't take a single copper coin."

"Very well, but you must allow me to treat you and Petronella to breakfast… tomorrow if it suits."

"Sounds delightful, m'dear. I will—"

The noise of breaking plates crashed over the muted hubbub of the lunchtime diners. It came from the bar room. "Your pardon, Doctor Whysman," Mary said, already moving down the passageway. "I think my presence may be required."

The doctor waved her away with a smile and disappeared into Sid's… *her* room.

As Mary entered the bar, she found what she'd expected to find: a table of guests being particularly unforgiving and unpleasant to a waitress who had had the misfortune of dropping some plates. Mary couldn't tell who the waitress was; she was crouched on the ground, picking up the broken remnants. The guests, however, were immediately recognisable. Two of them were standing, barking insults, while two remained seated, venting their indignation. Mary groaned inwardly. The Limpdickers, as Mary called them, were four 'renowned' lawyers whose opinion of themselves was higher than a dozen Lower Icing Keeps.

She quickly made her away across the room to the accompaniment of pompous outrage. Some of the other guests were already beginning to look uncomfortable at their display of displeasure. Mandy — one of her serving girls — suddenly appeared with a bucket and a wet cloth. Then Mary caught sight of the unfortunate employee — Lillian Surefoot. She was one of Mary's best serving girls and not prone to accidents.

"You're not fit to carry the slops of my pissman's piss bucket," berated the closer of the two standing lawyers — one Jeremy Dupree Esquire — as Lillian stood up with a handful of large broken pieces. She was understandably flustered and curtsied an apology.

Usually, Mary was very diplomatic in situations like this — fortunately, they rarely occurred — and she had a knack of diffusing and placating, particularly where the Limpdickers were concerned. Today she felt like doing neither. However, these men were important regulars and did, unfortunately, have a certain amount of influence amongst the castle-set. As much as she hated herself for it, she wasn't prepared to risk the consequences of speaking her mind.

She smiled reassuringly at Lillian as the waitress rushed past with a handful of broken plates. Tears ran down her cheek; she was clearly upset. Again, Mary had to quell the desire to let these pompous twats know exactly what she thought of them.

Mandy was cleaning the floor when Mary made her presence known to the self-absorbed foursome. "Gentlemen," she said, forcing the word out over their continued grumbling. They all looked at her. The seated lawyers groaned, as if turning their heads added to the inconvenience. "What seems to be the problem?"

"I would have thought that was rather obvious," bellowed Jeremy, indicating the smudges of beetroot on his white waistcoat.

He was joined in his outrage by the other standing lawyer, Marcus Ironcase Esquire, whose lilac waistcoat also displayed, to a lesser extent, evidence of a spilled beetroot salad. "One of your slap-dash wenches dropped her bundle all over Dupree and I. Rather poor show, what!"

One of the seated lawyers, Oliver Lawson Esquire, responded with a supportive "Here! Here!" while the last of the quartet, Rupert Smythe-Wheaton Esquire, just shook his head in disgust.

On the surface, it appeared Jeremy and Marcus had a legitimate grievance, but Mary certainly wouldn't make any judgements until she'd heard Lillian's account, and, in any case, it was no excuse for treating one of her staff like vermin. "Please accept my deepest apologies for any inconvenience, gentlemen, particularly to you, Jeremy and Marcus." They liked Mary addressing them by their first name. "I will, of course, make recompense for any damage, and please allow me to treat you to lunch today, should you decide to stay after this unfortunate incident."

They all grumbled their displeasure. However, they were mollified enough to accept her offer. She also assured them that she would serve them personally, and to ask her for anything they needed. They nodded their approval. *Pride successfully swallowed again,* thought Mary as she walked back to the kitchen. Still, there was no use turning a stained waistcoat into a grubby lawsuit.

Juanita and Patricia were comforting a very upset Lillian when Mary entered the kitchen. Lillian was resting her head on Patricia's shoulder. They were propped up against the large kitchen table with their backs to Mary. Juanita was standing with her arms folded, looking like she could start a fire with her dark eyes. "Don' worree, Leellian, sumting *bad* is going to happen to dat gringo. Hee's a bad man, so dee bad speereets will come to heem, an *then…*" — she punched her right fist into her left hand — "Pow! Hee pays for hees badness!"

Both Patricia and Lillian flinched, more at the 'pow' than the punch.

As much as Mary admired Juanita's passion, the last thing she wanted was a staff revolt. "Just as long as *you* don't organise any of those bad spirits, Juanita."

They all looked in Mary's direction. "Meestress, look what dee bad man do to poor Leellian," she said in explanation. Lillian *did* look particularly shaken — something Mary had never seen in her.

"Yes, I can see that she's upset," Mary replied as she walked around the table and stood next to the simmering Icarumban washerwoman. As much as she felt for Lillian, there was already enough emotion in the room to boil a pot of potatoes; Mary wasn't about to turn up the heat. Lillian extricated herself from the mothering embrace of Patricia and tried to compose herself.

"What happened, Lillian?" Mary asked in a more sympathetic tone.

Lillian inhaled a shuddery breath, and Patricia took it upon herself to answer. "It was tha' bastard, Dupree. Groped 'er, 'e did!"

"Hees a *deeablo!*" added Juanita.

Mary wasn't sure what a diablo was, but obviously it wasn't anything complimentary. Lillian's chin began to quiver. Mary reached out and squeezed her arm. "I'm sorry, Lillian," she said, earnestly. "Are you going to be alright?"

She nodded half-heartedly.

Patricia sniffed in disgust. "Bastard lawyers."

"You keek them out, Meestress! Tell them to sleeng their chook!"

Mary understood their outrage (and Juanita's attempt at 'sling their hook'). However, as much as it galled her, she couldn't afford to entertain it; she had a business to run. "You've done nothing wrong, Lillian, and you have every right to be upset, but you'll just have to accept what's happened I'm afraid. You know what they're like."

Again she nodded, then whispered, "Yes, Mistress."

Mandy suddenly appeared, holding the bucket she'd used to clean up the spilled plates. "I swear, I was *this* close t'emptyin' this lot over that limp dick's 'ead!"

"You should have *smashed* eet eento hees porreedge face!" Juanita responded, using the appropriate smashing action with her arms.

"That's enough!" Mary shouted, then quietly added. "I think we're all agreed the lawyers aren't our favourite patrons, but *patrons* they are and ones with influence. If we lose their patronage, others will surely follow, and that *would* be a problem… for *all* of us." She gazed at their sullen faces. They all nodded in agreement, except for Juanita, who looked confused.

"I no understand. Een my country, we keell dee rats, not feed dem dee cheese."

Mary was momentarily lost for words. "Thank you, Juanita," she eventually said, somewhat lamely. "However, this is not Los Nachos, and I *do* intend to feed our rats, and *personally* see to their rodent requirements."

Juanita shook her head.

Mary's gaze shifted to her cook. "Patricia, please prepare four more meals for them." Then, to her aggrieved serving girl: "Mandy, put the bucket down and get back into the bar room." Then, to her distraught serving girl: "Lillian, pull yourself together and get back to serving as soon as possible. Just stay well away from the lawyers." Then back to Mandy, who had just placed the bucket on the floor: "You and Carol serve that side of the bar, but leave the lawyers to me."

Mandy nodded and walked off. Mary turned back to Juanita. "Juanita, I take it you have washing to do."

Juanita nodded and flounced off to the laundry. Mary waited for her to leave before addressing her cook. "Patricia, I want those meals ready in five minutes."

Patricia looked defiant, but nodded nonetheless.

Mary carried the tray of freshly-prepared plates to the Limpdickers' table. Dave, her head barman, had had the good sense to provide them with a bottle of fine Escargotian red wine. They seemed content, which was a relief. However, the fact that she felt relieved made her feel guilty, and Juanita's words echoed in her head.

## CHAPTER 9

### *The height of indecency*

OLIVIA WAS WORRIED — Gerald's discovery had rocked her. Even though she was convinced Xavier had nothing to do Marmaduke's attack, she was now of the belief his disappearance *was* connected to the attack. It filled her with a dreadful foreboding.

Olivia was also agitated. She was not one for sitting around, waiting for others to act, particularly her inept husband, who, conversely, had left for the castle in high spirits shortly after the *Poetry in Potion* revelation. No, Olivia was one for taking action, making things happen, and tackling things *her* way, and that was exactly what she was doing now.

The intensity of the midday sun was blinding and the heat almost took her breath away as she stepped onto Plumduff Street. The wall-mounted brass plate that identified the Hiepants' residence flared golden-white, like the sun itself. Closing the front door, she took a moment to collect herself for the short-but-sweltering cobblestone walk ahead.

She adjusted her cream bonnet, pulling its brim down towards her forehead. The dress she'd chosen to wear was loose-fitting and simply made. In fact, Olivia had made it herself and she was very pleased with the result. She had quite a skill for dressmaking; something she'd honed over the last six years in an attempt to escape the disappointment of being Mistress Gerald Hiepants.

During that time, she had created all manner of items: gloves, hats, scarves, jackets, even undergarments. Today, however, was the first day she'd worn any of her dresses out in public. The outfit was not designed around current castle fashion — apart from a lace collar and cuffs, the only embellishment was some light-blue beading that ran down the front of the bodice to the waist. The cotton fabric had been dyed a similar colour to the beading, not the darker hues of purple, maroon and deep-green favoured by the clique.

No, this was *far* too plain to be seen at any castle gathering, but it was *perfect* for walking the baking streets of Lower Icing.

Olivia felt strangely liberated as she turned her back on the castle and headed slightly downhill towards Merchant Street. To think, just this morning, she had been determined to maintain her dress standards in the face of this unbearable heat; the ridicule of the castle-set would have been far more unbearable. However, her *mind*set had changed dramatically after seeing the incriminating *Paloma Coma* markings; she was convinced someone in the castle was responsible for them. She was even reassessing her initial dismissal of Richard being involved in some way. Still, regardless of any conjecture, the fact remained that the Duke of Lower Icing had been poisoned and Xavier was missing, perhaps lying dead somewhere. So, to concern herself with such a trivial matter as her appearance had suddenly seemed to be the height of indecency.

The markings still befuddled her, however; surely no-one planning to poison the Duke would actually be so obvious in their intent. The only explanation was that the person or persons responsible had planned to expose Xavier as the culprit. Unfortunately for them, Gerald had ruined their machinations with his out-of-character decisiveness, whisking Xavier (and the book) away from The Keep before they could spring their trap. Yes, someone in the castle was cursing their ill-luck. Olivia smiled to herself, imagining the look on the perpetrator's face when they discovered they'd been outwitted by her husband.

So, it was with comfort, rather than conformity, that Olivia strode purposefully onto Merchant Street. She was going to track Xavier's movements in Lower Icing from start to finish; she was determined to find the young healer (dead or alive) and bring those responsible for poisoning Marmaduke to justice. As she crossed Noble Street, her destination shimmered into view, its red and black sign motionless in the still heat.

Olivia had never set foot in The Bloody Bell — she'd never had reason to (and never thought she would).

The entrance to the inn was via double doors facing the corner of Merchant and Market Streets. As Olivia approached the intersection, the odour of drunkenness permeated the stifling air. The doors were wedged open, revealing a gloomily, raucous interior. It was like looking into the festering maw of some giant demon, complete with guttural sounds and foul breath. She paused, wondering if she could actually bring herself to go inside. The answer was simple: if she was going to find Xavier, she had no choice but to follow in his footsteps.

Ironically, Olivia appeared to have more effect on The Bloody Bell than *it* had on *her*. Covering her mouth and nose with a white lace handkerchief (another of her creations), she entered the dark, hot cacophony of boozing men. Her presence caused conversations to cease and eyes to appraise. By the time Olivia had taken half a dozen self-conscious steps towards the bar, the roaring din had become a grumbling murmur, as if the demon had swallowed something unpleasant.

A hundred or more men ogled her as she made her way to the bar. She wasn't at all surprised that there were only a handful of women (of the disreputable variety) in the bar. Surely no woman with a modicum of self-respect would consider frequenting The Bloody Bell for pleasure.

Olivia fixed her attention on the two people standing behind the bar. Both wore the same bemused expression as they watched her approach. Clearly, they were related — father and daughter, Olivia surmised.

"Arf'noon, ma'am," said the big, burly chap. Beads of sweat covered his face and neck, but his manner was easy-going and friendly. Olivia, however, was neither of those things, and the best she could do was to nod non-committally, still holding the handkerchief tight against her nose.

"Don' believe we've 'ad the pleasure of such a fine lookin' lady as yourself in The Bell," he continued amiably. "Leas' ways not since Bertie an' me was invited to the castle for a posh nosh-up, and tha' was back when *this* one" — he indicated the young woman standing next to him with a nod of his head — "was still makin' mud pies an' feedin' them t'the pigs."

The young woman smiled ruefully at the man; yes, they were definitely father and daughter. Olivia presumed he was the innkeeper, Bar Swill. She only knew his name because he'd been mentioned numerous times over the years in Gerald's proclamations, usually relating to an outcry over the amount of drunk and disorderly behaviour emanating from his establishment, manifesting itself in the form of thieving, mugging, raping and, most disgustingly of all, vomiting at the entrances of respectable people's homes (including the Hiepants' residence on more than one occasion). How his son had become a lieutenant in the Purple Peril was a mystery to Olivia.

"So wha's y'poison then?" continued Bar, obviously unsure how to take Olivia's hovering presence.

Olivia hid a sardonic smile behind the handkerchief and resisted the urge to say 'orange-spotted mushroom'. She scanned the room. Many of the patrons were still regarding her with either curiosity, lasciviousness, or, in the case of the odd wanton female, contempt. There were also half a dozen barmaids flitting around the stinking cauldron, replenishing tankards from their ale jugs. Turning her attention back to the hulking innkeeper, she reluctantly removed the handkerchief. "May I have a word with you in private, Master Swill? It concerns Xavier."

Her attire blended in perfectly with the décor of the Swill's private residence; she had dressed appropriately for the occasion after all. Upon entering the living room, she had been surprised by its clean, neat presentation. The blue theme was also strangely soothing, and the room pleasantly cool and quiet; it couldn't be more opposite to the room on the other side of the door.

She had introduced herself, and Bar had sent his daughter, Bethany, to fetch his wife, Bertie, to join them — obviously they had a penchant for names beginning with 'B' as she mentally added Lieutenant Brandon Swill to the list. Bertie was a rotund woman, a good foot and a half shorter than her husband, but she had a pleasant face, with an open expression and sparkling blue eyes.

"Ooo wha' a loverly dress!" were her first words to Olivia.

Olivia smiled awkwardly.

"Ber'ie Swill. Pleased t'meet you I'm sure, Mistress 'Iepants."

"Mistress Swill," Olivia acknowledged in far less effusive tones. She wasn't here to make friends, and she was beginning to wonder why *they* were making such a fuss over *her*; surely they couldn't be *that* impressed by her appearance.

All four of them were now gathered around the table. It was odd to say the least, just like the large paintings of people toiling away in fields that hung on the walls.

"So, 'ow is young Xavier gettin' along up at the castle?" asked Bertie. "Loverly young lad. Made quite the impression on us, didn' 'e Bartholomew. 'Im an' his potions or wha'ever 'e called 'em fixed Bartholomew's lip in no time, didn' it, love. What did 'e call it now? Some funny name, but it worked wonders, like nothin'—"

"Bertie," Bar finally interrupted. "Mistress 'Iepants came 'ere t'tell us somethin' 'bout Xavier, not t'listen t'you prattle on."

Even though Bartholomew had said it with good humour, Bertie looked suitably abashed. "Y'pardon, Mistress 'Iepants, it's this 'ot weather; 'eats up me blood, makes me chatter away like nobody's business, still no—"

"Ma!" This time it was an embarrassed Bethany Swill. She had barely said a word the whole time Olivia had been in The Bloody Bell. Given her parentage, Bethany was a surprisingly beautiful girl; she'd inherited her mother's eyes, but, fortunately for her, not her loquacious personality. How Bar and Bertie allowed her to work in the festering environment of The Bloody Bell was beyond Olivia. If she were *her* daughter…

"Actually," Olivia said, trying to banish any morbid thoughts of barrenness, "I have *not* come here to tell you about Xavier; quite the opposite, in fact."

Bar and Bertie looked slightly confused, but Bethany's gaze dropped when Olivia made eye-contact with her. *The girl knew something.* In fact, they *all* must. Surely they had been told Xavier had gone missing from the castle; according to Gerald, Brandon Swill was playing a significant part in the search for him.

Naturally, it was Bertie who broke the awkward silence. "We 'eard 'e was bein' treated like royalty, didn' we Bartholomew… nice room in The Keep an' all."

"Really?" said Olivia, eying the Swills on the opposite side of the table. "I would have thought you'd have heard a lot more than that, considering your son's position at the castle."

"Wha' 'e does at the castle is 'is business," Bartholomew replied. "'E don' confide in us where 'is duty's concerned."

*Plausible*, she thought — certainly understandable. She regarded the family opposite. Bar looked defensive, Bertie smiled nervously at her husband, and Bethany kept her eyes on the blue tablecloth. Something was amiss here.

"Well, allow me to enlighten you. Xavier went missing from the castle on Thursday morning. He hasn't been seen since."

"Oh dear!" Bertie exclaimed, but she didn't seem shocked.

Bethany hardly reacted at all, except for casting a sidelong glance at her mother.

Bartholomew's response was, like his expression, defensive. "What makes you think *we* know wha's 'appened to 'im?"

Olivia considered herself a good reader of people — body language, tone of voice, what they said and *didn't* say — and right now she was looking at a very guilty looking trio. They knew where Xavier was, or at least where he had gone. Olivia's heart was beating quickly and she had to fight down an urge to accuse them outright.

"I don't recall asking if you knew what happened to Xavier," she replied pointedly.

Bartholomew grimaced.

"It's *shockin'* news, Mistress 'Iepants," Bertie interjected, in an attempt to rescue the situation. "Poor lad, 'e's not the type t'be wanderin' off, too gentle, like. I 'ope nothin' terrible 'as 'appened to 'im."

"Indeed," Olivia agreed. "My thoughts exactly."

That stopped Bertie in her tracks.

"Well, if you'll 'scuse us, Mistress 'Iepants," Bartholomew said, pushing himself up from the table, "we got an inn t'run an' a bunch o' patrons tha' need attendin' to…"

His wife and daughter followed his lead. Olivia, however, remained seated.

"Bethany'll show ya out the back way."

Olivia locked gaze with the innkeeper. *No*-one dismissed her, let alone someone who served drunkards and guttersnipes. She could feel blood rush to her face; the indignation must be there for all to see. Bartholomew's gaze remained steadfast and impassive as Olivia slowly stood.

"Sorry we ain't been able to 'elp you, Mistress 'Iepants," said Bertie.

"Oh, but you've been *very* helpful." Olivia smiled. "*All* of you."

The comment had the desired effect, confirming, without a shadow of a doubt in Olivia's mind, that the Swills knew Xavier's whereabouts.

Bartholomew looked at his daughter and nodded his head vaguely towards the closed door on the other side of the room. Bethany demurred with a nod and a barely audible, "Yes, Pa."

"Good day, Mistress 'Iepants," Bartholomew said.

Bertie followed up with a sympathetic, "Bethany'll show y'out, dear."

Olivia followed closely behind Bethany as she led the way down a surprisingly bright hallway, their footsteps muffled on a blue runner that ran down its length. Halfway along, a bright sun had been woven into the runner, and Olivia absently wondered whether it contributed to the brightness of the windowless hallway. The Swills certainly had peculiar taste.

At the end of the hallway, a staircase led up and down, presumably to the guestrooms and cellar. Next to the staircase was a door. Bethany walked straight towards it and reached for the latch. Before she could lift it, Olivia said, "Wait a moment, Bethany."

The young woman stopped, but kept her back to Olivia; her braided hair, tied with a blue ribbon (of course) remained motionless. Olivia gathered her thoughts; she had to tread carefully.

In a quiet, concerned voice, she said, "I know you know what's happened to Xavier, and I understand why you feel you need to keep it a secret." Bethany remained silent and motionless, but at least she was listening. "He is a most remarkable young man, yet there are people who would like to see him discredited... or worse." Still no response. "Please believe me, I mean him no harm." A movement of her hand towards the latch. "Please, Bethany, the Duke's life is at stake." Her hand dropped back to her side, and, reluctantly, it seemed, she turned around.

"The Duke," Bethany whispered.

Olivia wasn't sure if it was a question or a statement. "Yes, the Duke. He was poisoned by someone — not Xavier — but *someone* who has read his book of potions."

Bethany's blue eyes regarded her thoughtfully, in silent appraisal. Then, out of the blue, she asked, "Do y'think it was Brandon?"

The question took Olivia by surprise; she was expecting shock or outrage, not emotionless logic. She hadn't really considered who could be responsible for the poisoning, just that it *couldn't* be Xavier. Her hesitation was obviously seen as confirmation because Bethany reached for the door latch. Olivia reacted by pushing down on her arm. Bethany tensed, but didn't try to dislodge Olivia's hold.

"I don't have any idea who the poisoner is, and all I know about your brother is that my husband speaks very highly of him. My *only* concern is for the wellbeing of Xavier and the Duke."

Bethany's expression gave nothing away.

"Bethany... Xavier is the only person who can save him."

"Y'speak like y'know Xavier."

Again, her words were calm and unexpected; her clarity of thought suggested an extremely sharp intellect. Then she grimaced, and Olivia suddenly realised she was gripping the young woman's arm quite tightly. She released her hold and apologised. However, Olivia wasn't prepared to divulge the true nature of her relationship with the young healer.

"Xavier and I are acquainted... through my husband."

Bethany nodded. Then she opened the back door. Heat and light flared in. Olivia had forgotten just how unpleasantly hot it was outside; the cool blue confines of the Swill's private quarters were like an oasis.

"The truth is all I seek, Bethany."

Bethany regarded her for a moment. "Then y'best start by tellin' it," she replied, moving out of the doorway so that Olivia could leave.

Olivia bristled. *She* should tell the truth? *That* was rich, especially coming from someone who was clearly withholding vital information on the whereabouts of the one person who could save the Duke of Lower Icing.

Mastering her indignation, Olivia said, "Like you and your family, Bethany, I have not revealed all."

Bethany dropped her gaze. Olivia suddenly felt for the young woman; she probably had little say in what she could reveal.

In a more empathetic tone, Olivia added, "Truth is not the barrier here; it's the lack of trust."

Bethany flicked her gaze back at Olivia, but her face was very hard to read. She stared emotionlessly at Olivia; it made her feel quite self-conscious.

"You can trust that I want what's best for Xavier," Olivia added.

When Bethany finally responded, it was in a voice barely above a whisper. "Wha' about the Duke?"

Seizing the moment, Olivia reached out and gently touched her arm. "Believe me, Bethany, what's best for Xavier *is* what's best for the Duke."

Bethany nodded — somewhat reluctantly it appeared. "I mus' go now; Pa'll be wonderin' where I got to."

Olivia removed her hand from Bethany's arm. She couldn't help but sigh. "Very well, Bethany, I will leave you to consider your position. However, if I haven't heard from you or one of your family members by four o'clock this afternoon, I will be forced to take a more official approach, something I'm not keen to do, but time is paramount."

Again, Bethany barely nodded, but it was enough for Olivia. "Look for the brass plate on Plumduff Street. I shall be waiting within."

In answer, Bethany began to close the door, forcing Olivia to step backwards into what turned out to be a large cobblestone courtyard. As the door shut quietly, Olivia turned and regarded her surroundings. Within the courtyard, some thirty or so paces away, were the stables. They were empty, but an equine redolence was still detectable. The stables and the courtyard were enclosed by a nine-foot-high stone wall. Apart from the door she'd just been ushered out of, the only visible entrance into this area were two massive wooden gates, extending up the height of the wall, covering a ten-foot-wide entrance. The right gate was open, revealing the Town Square beyond, almost directly in line with the well. Propped up against the wall next to the open gate was a heavy-looking crossbar which, no doubt, was used to secure the area. Immediately to Olivia's right, six large barrels were lined up against the wall of the inn. They contained water. The Swills were certainly organised — surprisingly so. Olivia left the courtyard and entered the furnace of the Town Square. They had just over three hours to knock at her door; otherwise… She really didn't want to think about otherwise.

## Chapter 10

## *Recognise it?*

THE REST AT the ford was four hours behind them, but it felt like four days. After stopping to refresh the horses and themselves, they'd begun the process of fording the Icing River. The ford had been an educated guess on Tom's part: "Once you told me they'd been seen heading north out of town, my thoughts immediately went to Dragon's Back." It was the name given to the route they had been taking since crossing the ford. The ford and the path were well known to travellers who, for whatever reason, thought riding along a treacherously steep and rugged pass was preferable to the relative safety and ease of the East Road.

The horses meandered between smooth, granite boulders and jagged seams of black rock. The sun was oppressively hot, but the view was amazing. Ahead, the hills and valleys seemed to flow towards the eastern horizon, a sea of trees captured in a giant, motionless swell. However, Ophelia no longer had the energy to raise her head. She felt totally sapped, and what little strength she had left she used to keep herself upright in the saddle. They'd barely broken walking pace during the ascent. From the crunching shale of the bank, across the spiking grasses, up the steep, narrow pathway that led to the craggy ridge, progress had been painfully slow. The heat and the climb, however, were nothing compared to the agony of the saddle.

Tom regularly pointed out obscure signs they were on the right track and making good progress, but Ophelia could take little solace from it. Behind his upbeat banter, she sensed his concern for her wellbeing. He'd secured a rope from Hazel's bridle to the back of Wildflower's saddle before they'd ascended above tree height. A mere precaution, he'd assured her, but she'd been grateful nonetheless. The heat and treacherous track appeared to have no effect on him at all. In fact, if anything, he was more content and at ease — a man in his element.

Ophelia, on the other hand, couldn't imagine being more *out* of her element. Would this torturous ride ever end? She tried to focus on her pa; she could only imagine his suffering, injured and slumped across a saddle like a carcass. Her poor pa — she *had* to stay strong for him. But what if he was already…? Bert Muggins' voice echoed in her mind, relaying the words from one of the Moleson Twins: *"I know a nice big"ole we c'n drop 'im into. Let the wolves finish 'im off."*

Hazel's bobbing mane was almost hypnotic. The only thing that kept Ophelia from being lulled into a world of dazed dreams was the pain of her rubbed-raw groin. It was as if the saddle was made from the coarse granite strewn across the Dragon's Back, rather than smooth, supple leather.

Suddenly, Hazel's mane-bobbing ceased as the mare came to an unexpected halt. Ophelia looked up to see Tom dismounting from Wildflower.

Ophelia was immediately alert. "Wha' is it?"

Tom tied Wildflower's reins to a crag of black stone; he looked concerned.

"Wha' is it?" she repeated, ready to attempt a dismount.

"There are some signs ahead. I won't be long."

"Signs of *wha*?" He hadn't dismounted for any of the *other* 'signs'.

"Stay there," he said over his shoulder, then disappeared behind a massive boulder: Dragons' Eggs, Tom called them.

Ophelia kept her eyes fixed ahead. At least the sun was behind her now. But even so, in the simmering heat, her forlorn shadow looked branded onto the Dragon's Egg.

True to his word, Tom wasn't gone long. For the first time since leaving Lower Icing, he wore a grim expression.

Ophelia's heart sank. She felt sick. "Is it Pa?"

"Not exactly," he said, holding up a torn piece of white cloth about half the size of a handkerchief. It was smudged with dirt. "Recognise it?"

Ophelia took the cloth from the Gamekeeper's hand; it was a ripped remnant of a sleeve and cuff from a man's shirt. It was her pa's shirt. A wave of dizzying nausea swept across her. The Dragon's Back heaved and she lost her balance.

## CHAPTER 11

## *Wasting time on the Limpdickers*

MARY WAS TAKING a well-earned break between the lunch and dinner crowds. To be honest, she was fed up… fed up serving ungrateful patrons, fed up sorting out arguments amongst her staff, fed up with Sid's unresponsive condition and, most of all, fed up with the unrelenting heat. It was oppressive, making everyone ill-tempered and short-fused. The only thing Mary *wasn't* fed up with was food. In fact, she hadn't eaten since breakfast and had only paused a few times to slake her thirst.

Trying to find a place to keep cool in The Harey Rabbit was virtually impossible. Her only option was to douse herself in her bathing tub, but she didn't have time for that luxury today — the unusually hot weather was bringing in thirsty, demanding patrons. Her next best option was the laundry; its east-facing window was now shaded from the mid-afternoon sun, providing a small measure of relief. So, there she sat, eating a serving of cold pork and beetroot salad while Juanita and John made their twenty-something trip to the well.

As she ate, she pondered the events of the day. The lawyers had been about as enlightening as a wet wick. All her attempts at discovering information about the Duke had been fobbed off with dismissive comments and condescending remarks. They'd made it clear that she "shouldn't worry her pretty little head about matters beyond her understanding." This was followed by a slap on her behind and an equally charming, "Best stick to filling our cups and looking ravishing, what."

The only thing they'd seemed willing to talk about was the Duke of Stymouth's visit and the feast to be held in his honour in less than two weeks' time. "It's a great opportunity for us all, Mary," said Jeremy Dupree.

"Rather," added Oliver Lawson. "I've been boning up on Stymouthian law. Fascinating, really. For instance, a woman may sue for divorce if she can prove infidelity on the part of her husband."

"Outrageous!" Marcus Ironcase guffawed.

The others shook their heads in amused disbelief.

"Not only that," continued Oliver, "if infidelity is proven, the woman can lay claim to part of her husband's worldly goods."

"Preposterous!" bellowed Jeremy.

"Good Heavens. Can you imagine?" added Rupert Smythe-Wheaton.

Mary had stopped probing after that.

After finishing her late lunch, she went to check on Sid. As frustrating as his condition was, it wasn't *his* fault he'd been beaten senseless. Mary had encountered Doctor Whysman leaving The Harey Rabbit shortly after he'd arrived, and he assured her that Sid would make a full recovery.

"When?" had been her terse response; the demanding lunchtime crowd and obnoxious lawyers were already having an effect, and the insufferable heat just added to the toxic mix.

"Well, m'dear, I'd say he'll be ready to go home tonight, tomorrow morning at the latest," he replied, taking no offense at her tone. "The brain heals itself by shutting down the body, but his heartbeat is strong and the swelling is receding."

She sighed. "Sorry, Doctor. I appreciate everything you've done on Sid's behalf. It's just this damn heat, it's—"

"Think nothing of it, m'dear," he said, patting her arm. "I have left a rejuvenating elixir on your dressing table. A couple of spoonfuls in some broth or brew and he should be a new man."

He waved away her thanks, saying he and Petronella were very much looking forward to breaking their fast tomorrow.

That had been three hours ago. Since then, she hadn't even walked past Sid's bedroom, let alone seen if he was alright. Well, she'd been too busy... too busy feeding cheese to the rats. *Bloody Juanita!*

She immediately felt guilty for her absence as soon as she saw his battered face poking out from under the sheet. He was asleep. The swollen, purple side of his face was still; the other side twitched and drooled. Again she berated herself for wasting time on the Limpdickers.

## CHAPTER 12

## *Clear his mind*

**I**T WAS ALMOST four o'clock and still no knock at the door. What would she do if Bethany Swill decided not to respond to her ultimatum? Since leaving The Bloody Bell, Olivia had been weighing up her options, and there weren't many of them. It really came down to a few equally unsatisfactory alternatives. There was Brandon Swill. He was a Purple Perillian, highly regarded according to Gerald, so he obviously had some sense of duty. But how would he react to her suspicions about Xavier and his family? He'd probably require some sort of proof, and all Olivia could offer him was her intuition. In any case, he might be involved in some way… No, she couldn't risk talking to Lieutenant Swill. She could make it *very* official and tell Richard; however, according to Gerald, the Seneschal was not well disposed towards Xavier because he posed a threat to his position as the Duke's heir. For a moment she even considered confiding in her husband, and then laughed out loud — what a disaster *that* would be! She doubted if he'd ever *heard* of the word 'confide'.

There was a fourth alternative, someone she *could* trust, whose duty to the Duchy was beyond reproach, but she doubted she had the emotional strength to approach him. She'd spent the last six years trying to forget he existed — that wonderful, passionate part of her life — denying to herself that she still loved him. The wound had cut too deeply, her heart severed by their tearful parting, courtesy of her brother's ill-gotten gains.

"Paris," she whispered to the empty house.

The house answered; it was the sound of knocking.

Bethany Swill stood at the threshold of 8 Plumduff Street.

"I was about to leave for the castle, Bethany," Olivia lied, hoping it hid her relief.

Bethany regarded her with searching eyes. There was something impenetrable about the girl's demeanour that Olivia found quite disconcerting.

"Y'said I 'ad 'til four o'clock," Bethany replied.

"So I did." *How pedantic*, Olivia thought.

Bethany's brow furrowed. Then she took Olivia completely by surprise. "Come, Mistress 'Iepants, I will take you to Xavier."

They entered The Bloody Bell the way Olivia had exited it a few hours ago. Again, Olivia was struck by the relative coolness of the Swill's residence; it was if the blue interior was impervious to heat.

Bethany led Olivia to the staircase; she assumed they would be going up to one of the guestrooms, but, instead, she followed the blue-ribbon ponytail downstairs. The stairs ended in a large, dimly lit space. On first inspection, it appeared to be empty, except for a couple of barrels set upright against a wall. Sitting on top of each barrel was a candlestick with a lit candle. At the bottom of the stairs, Bethany turned and walked back along the side of the staircase. Under it were hundreds of bottles stored horizontally on grooved racks, their tops pointing outwards, caught in the flickering candlelight. Olivia was momentarily distracted by the impressive collection as she followed the Swill girl to a door on the northern side of the space.

At the door, Bethany stopped and faced Olivia. The girl had said virtually nothing during their walk from Plumduff Street, apart from informing Olivia that Xavier had met with foul play. Persistent questions regarding Xavier's wellbeing had resulted in variations of "best see for y'self" which was hardly reassuring.

So, it was with a sense of dread rather than relief that Olivia waited for Bethany to reveal what lay within.

"If you'll wait 'ere a moment," Bethany whispered, "I'll jus' tell Xavier y'here. 'E ain't comfortable with strangers."

What was the girl on about? "But, I'm not a—"

"'E ain't 'imself, Mistress 'Iepants." Her voice was quiet but firm.

Olivia's stomach sank. What had happened to him? Bethany's gaze lingered for a moment, then she turned and opened the door. Olivia had only a glimpse of the room before the door was closed, but she saw nothing of Xavier.

Thankfully, she didn't have to wait long for Bethany to reappear, but in those few moments she imagined Xavier with all kinds of horrible injuries.

"I should warn you," she whispered, "Xavier prob'ly won' recognise you." Then she pulled the door open, allowing Olivia entry.

Olivia hesitated for a moment. Her heart was pounding and she wasn't quite sure if she could bring herself to see what injuries had befallen Xavier. Why wouldn't he recognise her? Had he been beaten completely senseless?

Slowly, Olivia moved through the doorway. The room opened up to the right; it contained a rudimentary pallet bed with a feather mattress and a side table with a single candle. Most of the light, however, was provided by two small grated windows at the top of the opposite wall. From the outside, they would appear at ground level. Half-hearted spruiking from the heat-weary market vendors wafted through them.

Olivia was momentarily confused — the bed was empty. Then her gaze moved to the far corner, and there stood Xavier, looking exactly as he had the last time she saw him, wearing the same white shirt, and white pants tucked into black boots. Olivia could hardly make sense of what she was seeing; the light must be playing tricks… or was it her mind? Perhaps he *had* been killed and this was his spectre.

"Xavier?" she said.

"So I'm told," he answered.

It took some time for Olivia to come to grips with Xavier's predicament. Put simply, he'd lost his memory, or, to be more precise, had his memory knocked out of him. Bethany had been emptying the ale slops around ten on Friday night when she'd found him slumped near the water barrels, unconscious and bleeding from a blow just above his right ear. She'd alerted her father immediately and they'd carried him up to one of the guestrooms. Bethany and Bertie had fussed over him most of the night, tending to his wound and trying to keep him cool. Xavier had woken a few times, dazed and asking for water. Eventually, the heat of the guestroom had become too much, so they moved him into the cellar just after dawn.

Olivia asked Bethany why they hadn't called for a doctor.

"Ma knows more 'bout healin' than any doctor. 'Sides which, we thought it bes' if no-one knew where Xavier was 'til we found ou' who'd done this to 'im."

"What about your brother?"

Bethany's gaze penetrated uncomfortably into her eyes. "Brandon 'as 'is duty, an' we 'ave ours."

What did *that* mean? The attacks on Marmaduke and Xavier had occurred almost three days ago, and while she could understand the Swill's desire to protect Xavier, surely they could see the greater need. "The Duke's life is at stake, Bethany," she said, disbelievingly. "Surely *that* is more important than some petty family squabble."

"We didn' know the Duke 'ad been poisoned… not 'til you said."

Olivia was outraged. How could they not know? But then she quickly realised, why *should* they know? Marmaduke's condition was not common knowledge. Gerald had even made a point of asking her not to say a word about the poisoning. (As if *that* wasn't the pot calling the kettle black!) Yes, she could well see how the Swills had remained ignorant of Marmaduke's attack, particularly if there was some rift between them and their high-flying Purple Perillian son.

"So, your brother didn't inform you," Olivia said — it was more of a thought process than a question.

"'E only told us tha' Xavier 'ad gone missin' and that they were worried for 'is safety."

Olivia recalled Bartholomew's comment, alluding to the fact that Brandon had his own agenda: *"'E don' confide in us where 'is duty's concerned."*

"I see," murmured Olivia to herself.

"An' even if we 'ad known, it woudda made no diff'rence. 'E don' remember nothin' 'bout 'is potions or bein' a healer."

Somehow, Xavier had become little more than a piece of furniture during Olivia and Bethany's exchange, content, it seemed, to listen passively and allow Bethany to speak on his behalf.

Olivia faced him. He looked lost. It seemed inconceivable that he'd forgotten his passion for healing, his *raison d'être* as the Escargotians called it.

"Xavier, do you *really* remember nothing of your potions?" she asked, looking him directly in the eyes, searching for a hint of recollection.

He shook his head. "Alas, no, Mistress Hiepants."

*Mistress Hiepants?* Her heart sank; he didn't even remember that he'd addressed her by her first name. She'd insisted he do so and had corrected him on numerous occasions until he'd finally felt comfortable enough to say it without hesitation. That had been shortly before his fateful decision to stretch his legs on Friday evening. She'd wanted to accompany him, to keep him safe, to make sure he wasn't accosted by a patrol, but he said he needed some time to himself — 'to clear his mind' was how he'd put it. Well, he'd certainly achieved *that!*

## CHAPTER 13

## *Dragon's Back*

THE SUN FELT like it was flickering; waves of heat brushed across her face. She was moving, but she couldn't feel the saddle between her legs and her feet weren't in stirrups. She was aware of the pain in her groin, but it wasn't the rawness caused by constant motion, more of an aching throb. In fact, it didn't feel like she was riding a horse at all; something solid was supporting her back and she could smell meat cooking. She opened her eyes. A crackling fire danced against the darkness. A rabbit was roasting on a makeshift spit.

"Pa!" She sat upright, heart pounding. A man was sitting on the other side of the fire. It was Tom. He wore a bemused expression.

"Welcome back to the land of the living," he said.

Ophelia felt totally disoriented. Darkness enveloped everything past the fire glow; she couldn't even see the horses. How could it be night-time? Were they still on the Dragon's Back?

"Wha' 'appened?" Her voice sounded dry.

"Exhaustion, dehydration, sun-stroke and shock would be my guess."

Ophelia's mind reeled. The ride up Dragon's Back, the pain of the saddle, the unforgiving sun, Hazel's bobbing head, the torn shirt… "'Ave y' found Pa?"

"Not yet," he replied, "but I will. He survived the Moleson Twins, despite their best efforts to finish him off."

"So 'e's alive?" Her thoughts were beginning to focus. What was Tom doing sitting around a campfire, roasting a rabbit, when her pa was still out there injured?

"He was earlier this afternoon."

He was talking as if her pa had gone for a stroll by the Icing, not been beaten and abducted by a couple of thugs. She grimaced in an effort to get her feet.

"What are you doing?"

Was he seriously going to sit there and dine on rabbit while her pa was out there, fighting for his life? "Wha' *you* should be bleedin' well doin'," she answered, defiant of the pain between her legs and despite a reeling sensation.

"You need rest, Ophelia," Tom said calmly… *too* bloody calmly.

Gingerly, she stepped around the fire. "Wha' I *need* is to find my pa."

"You won't find him tonight," he replied, getting to his feet.

"Well I c'n bloody well try," she said, trying to work out which way she should be heading. "I ain't sittin' round 'ere playin' cosy campfire when me pa's ou' there fightin' for 'is life."

He drew near her, but — just as well for him — didn't touch her; she wasn't in the mood for being manhandled in *any* way.

Suddenly he was angry. "How do you imagine I've spent the last six hours, Ophelia?"

Ophelia was taken aback by his tone; it was the first time he'd raised his voice to her. She could feel the blood rushing to her face, but she held her tongue. *Six hours?*

His eyes glowed in the firelight, searching hers. "There's nothing more that can be done tonight. The trail can't be followed, only lost. I need rest and sustenance. So do you."

She took a deep breath and the aroma of roasting rabbit flowed up her nostrils; it smelled delicious, and she realised she was hungry. Tom was right, damn him. She eventually nodded her agreement. He smiled, and it was only then she became aware that he was holding her gently by her arms. She must have tensed, because he became self-conscious and his hands fell away. He quickly squatted by the fire and attended to the rabbit. "And in any case," he said, "if Frank is close by, the fire will be a beacon for him."

*True*, she thought, *if he was conscious and able to walk*. She moved back to where she had woken up — Tom had laid down her blanket on a patch of smooth ground and made a makeshift pillow by bundling together some wild grass. He'd obviously spent time preparing the camp, and had been caring for her — it made her feel bad about the way she had spoken to him. "Thanks f'lookin' after me," she said, trying not to wince as she returned to a sitting position.

"You're welcome," he said, pulling the spitted rabbit from the fire. "I'm growing accustomed to you fainting on me."

Ophelia laughed. For all his strange, woodsman ways, he was nice to be around and she felt safe in his presence. To think, four nights ago they'd coupled on the banks of the Icing, but that was just a drunken night of lust. Now, she was beginning to see him in a different light.

As they sat together, dining on the spoils of Tom's hunting skills and Ophelia's bottle of rum (the only item of her food supplies *not* to spoil), he related the events of the afternoon…

The remnant of her pa's shirt was found at a place on Dragon's Back where the southern slope fell steeply away for some two hundred paces, without a single bush to interrupt anyone's tumbling descent. There were signs of a struggle; the parched dirt and loose rocks that made up most of slope had been disturbed at the ridge. From his vantage point, Tom could also discern other parts of the slope that had been dislodged. It was obvious the Moleson Twins had chucked Frank over the edge, yet there was no sign of a body at the bottom.

After attending to Ophelia, placing her in the shade of a large boulder and making sure she was comfortable, he'd secured the horses and clambered down the loose slope. Upon reaching the base, it had been easy for Tom to see where Frank had come to rest. Not far away, he found some cut leather bindings, which suggested Frank was relatively able-bodied and still had his wits about him. He'd also been able to find tracks leading off into the valley. He'd followed them for some three hundred paces, but, by this time, more than half an hour had elapsed and he was beginning to worry about Ophelia and the horses. (Nice to know she took precedence over the horses.) So, he'd made the decision to turn back.

Climbing up the crumbling surface turned out to be an arduous task; the rocks had been baked under a full day of sun and were burning hot, and their unstable nature had caused him to slip back down the slope at least a dozen times. Eventually, however, he'd managed to reach the Dragon's Back.

There was no way the horses could negotiate the slope; the only course of action was to backtrack and find an easier route into the valley. Tom had secured Ophelia across Hazel's saddle (much like the Moleson Twins had done to her father) and headed back down Dragon's Back, the late afternoon sun directly ahead of him, blindingly hot. (Thank goodness she'd been unconscious.)

By the time Tom had reached the valley it was around seven o'clock. The trees provided welcome relief; their shading canopy was cooling, the ground blissfully rock free. He'd thought about heading deeper into the valley in search of water — there wasn't much left in the skins — but decided it was more important to pick up the trail and make camp before nightfall. He was also increasingly concerned about Ophelia's condition. The sun had treated her harshly and she had woken a number of times to vomit. (Ophelia had no recollection of vomiting, or even being conscious.) Tom had dampened the clean shirt she'd brought for her father and wrapped it around her head and neck. He'd realised she needed to rest properly; she couldn't recover slumped across the back of a horse.

Within an hour, Tom had found the spot where Frank had been dumped; the area around that part of Dragon's Back was scrubby and desolate. He'd retraced her pa's progress south, some two hundred and fifty paces into the centre of the valley, where the trees began to reassert themselves.

It was early evening by the time Tom had found a suitable place to camp. The welcome shade had become an ominous gloom, and creatures that had shied away from the burning sun now made their presence known: insects buzzed, birds called, and all manner of life rustled in the undergrowth. Added to this was the occasional crack of branches snapping from heat-stressed trees. None of it bothered Tom, but nightfall was less than an hour away, so he'd immediately set to his tasks: making sure Ophelia was comfortable, burying the spoiled food (except for the apples, which he fed to the horses), preparing and lighting the fire, searching for water (with no luck) and hunting for food (with amazing luck: he'd scored the rabbit with his first arrow).

Now, here she was, safe and feeling remarkably better after the nourishment of the unlucky rabbit. The heat of the sun still burned in her face and the back of her neck. It was extremely sore to the touch, but it would pass, and there'd be no more exposure to the Dragon's Back. The rawness of the saddle, however, was something she would just have to grin and bear. Tom had voiced his doubts about her ability to cope with the ride, and he'd been right when he'd said that he stood a better chance of finding her pa alone, that she would be more of a hindrance than a help. She would never forgive herself if they didn't find her pa alive.

They were lying next to each other, far enough away from the fire's dying embers that it made no difference to the warmth of the night. Sleep wasn't far off — the sun, the rum and the rabbit were a potent combination. Her hand found his and their fingers interlocked.

"I'm sorry, Tom."

He gently squeezed her hand and assured her that they'd find her pa tomorrow; they would continue the search at first light. Ophelia wondered if she was already dreaming.

## CHAPTER 14

# *Blow away the dust an' it's gone*

OLIVIA ARRIVED HOME shortly after seven o'clock. Much of the three hours she'd spent at The Bloody Bell had been taken up talking to Xavier, sharing all the things he had shared with her: his time at Missing Anchor, living upstairs at the Windy Sailor; moving to Blessed Whipping with all its sun-worshiping nonsense; and, of course, his research with Horatio. She'd then rattled off the names of all the potions she could remember and thought she detected a spark of recollection when she mentioned *Paloma Coma*.

"Does that mean anything to you, Xavier?" she'd prompted.

"Am I right in thinking Paloma is Icarumban for a dove?"

Olivia had no idea what the Icarumban word for a dove was, and her frustration pushed her into a subject she knew she couldn't pursue in the presence of Bethany. She'd asked the girl if she could have a moment alone with him. Bethany responded by using Olivia's words against her.

"Your pardon, Mistress Hiepants, but it was *you* what talked of trust. It weren't easy fer me t'convince Ma and Pa to let y'see Xavier. 'Is wellbein' is jus' as importan' to us as it is to you an' the Duke."

Olivia doubted that very much, but she'd held her tongue.

"So, wha'ever y'have t'say to Xavier, y'can say in front of me an' *trust* it won' leave The Bell."

Who *was* this girl? This *family*? They ran a disreputable inn. What business did *they* have in deciding what was or wasn't important? And yet, she wasn't able to fault Bethany's reasoning. Olivia glanced at Xavier — the silent observer — hoping for some spark of recognition, something to avoid revealing the whole truth, but all she could read was confusion.

"Very well," Olivia eventually conceded. "I will trust you. However, what I'm about to say cannot leave this room." She'd said that with Bertie Swill in mind; that woman stood a better chance of holding a refined banquet than she did her tongue.

Bethany treated her to one of her soul-piercing gazes before signalling her acceptance with a silent nod. Olivia had no choice but to take the girl’s word.

She sat down on the bed and asked Xavier to do the same. He complied without question. Then she’d proceeded to tell him about the accident with the *Pig Dust*, just like *he* had told *her*, emphasising the name of the powder like it was a cursed substance, and how it had led to the revelation contained within Horatio’s letter: that he was the Duke’s son.

Xavier stared blankly, before calmly saying, “If I am the Duke’s son, why am I here?”

Olivia turned to Bethany, who was now standing behind her. She’d not uttered a word and her eyes were fixed on Xavier. Was the girl all there, Olivia wondered — she’d never met anyone so… serene.

Bethany kept her eyes on Xavier and said softly to him, “It’s jus’ a name on a parchment. Blow the dust away an’ it’s gone. It’s not who you are.”

Olivia suddenly felt like a stranger in this strangely cool room. And she felt frustrated by Bethany’s words. Didn’t the girl understand what Xavier meant to the Duchy?

After some further fruitless attempts at triggering Xavier’s memory, Olivia took her leave of the Swill’s cellar. “You c’n be assured, Mistress ’Iepants, tha’ I’ll not mention this to anyone,” Bethany said in parting.

Olivia didn’t doubt that for one second as she’d bid Bethany good evening. “I shall return tomorrow. Perhaps some of his possessions may jolt his memory.”

Gerald wasn’t home when Olivia entered 8 Plumduff Street. Just as well, she thought; she was still in a quandary as to whether to tell her husband about Xavier. He deserved to know, but how would he handle the news? The thought of Gerald waltzing into The Bloody Bell like an Icarumban bull-fighter, smiling and waving at the detritus of Lower Icing, then casually asking one of the Swills if they wouldn’t mind escorting him to the Duke’s son… She cringed at the thought. No, she wouldn’t tell him just yet. In any case, it served no purpose — not while Xavier couldn’t remember who he was.

# Chapter 15

## *Person of interest*

**M**ARY WAS STANDING behind the bar talking to Dave. It was half eight and The Harey Rabbit was virtually deserted. Most of the dinner-time crowd had eaten, drunk and gone home half an hour ago. It was an unexpected relief to say the least, and she and Dave were taking advantage of the early lull.

Despite his gruff looks and beer-barrel physique, Dave was a pleasant, even-tempered man with the strength of an ox — the perfect combination for a barman. Mary felt safe with Dave behind the bar, so did the other girls. Anything more than a playful slap attracted Dave's attention. Fortunately, Dave's muscle had only been required on a handful of occasions in the three years since Mary had taken over the running of The Harey Rabbit. Those times had left an indelible impression on the patrons. No-one wanted to mess with Dave and, therefore, no-one pushed their luck with Mary or her staff. Mind you, The Harey Rabbit wasn't the type of inn to be frequented by luckpushers (apart from the Limpdickers, of course, who were a breed of luckpushers unto themselves).

Dave asked after Lillian. Mary told him that she'd sent her home shortly after the lunch shift, still a bit shaken by the incident but otherwise in good spirits. This led to the barman suggesting he could have a quiet word with the Limpdickers.

She smiled ruefully. "Don't tempt me."

"It ain't righ' they be trea'ed different, Mary. It ain't fair on the girls, an' when y'have t'send someone like Lillian 'ome — someone who wouldn' say boo to a goose — then tha's crossin' the line in my book."

"That book is also very popular in Icarumba," she replied. Juanita's words were still echoing in her head.

Dave gave her a quizzical look.

"Never mind, Dave."

It wasn't long before the topic of conversation changed. They were now in fits of laughter, reliving a lunchtime incident. It concerned one of their regular 'castle-set' ladies, one Petunia Primrose (or Prim Pet, as they called her). She was around thirty years of age, not unattractive in a physical sense, but she'd failed to attract any suitors because she was stiff and mirthless, and had the personality of a squeezed lemon. Today, Prim Pet had been rather put out by the lack of cooked food on offer. Mary had pointed out that the cold meat was, in fact, cooked, as were the pork pies and the beetroot.

"Don't be clever with me, gel," she said in her haughtily over-the-top, old-matron voice. "Co-eld meat is fit only for servants. One doesn't partake of *that* kind of food."

"The beetroot salad is—"

"Tish, gel!" Then, as if her opinion needed to be heard by the whole inn, she announced, "Beetroot is not to my taste!"

Fraser Coin, not a man for holding back in any sense of the term, responded in an even louder voice, "I should be grateful for *any* root, Mistress Primrose."

The Harey Rabbit erupted into laughter. Prim Pet, flushed with indignation, left the inn, her face the colour of… beetroot.

Mary and Dave were still crying with laughter when John entered the bar from the hallway door. He smiled awkwardly at their mirth, not sure if he should be joining in.

Mary tried to rein in her laughter. "Yes, John?"

"It's Master Sid," he said.

*That* reined it in. "What's happened to him?"

John looked taken back by her urgency. "'E's leavin', Mistress."

Sid was out of bed, already dressed in his black trousers and in the process of fastening his boots. He smiled at her when she entered.

"Hello, Mary."

"What are you doing?"

"Something I mastered around the age of five," he replied, returning his attention to the leather straps on his boots.

"Very funny," she said, without humour. He had been recovering in her bed for the best part of two days, and now, here he was… getting dressed to leave as if he'd stopped by for a quick 'how's your father'.

He looked at her. The left side of his face was still badly bruised and swollen… Again, beetroot came to mind.

"I seem to be missing a shirt," he said, favouring the right side of his mouth; obviously it was still painful for him to talk.

"I'd say you were missing more than *that*," she said, moving into the room. "Sid, you're badly injured, you've hardly been conscious for the last two days, you can't just suddenly wake up and…"

He was strapping on his other boot.

"Sid, are you listening to me?"

He pulled the strap through the buckle and stood. "I feel fine, fully rec—"

A strange look crossed his face and he stumbled towards her. She reacted instinctively to steady him, but his knees gave way and she was suddenly shouldering his weight. She fell down with him, onto her knees, but it was controlled, and he managed to steady himself by planting his right hand on the floor. He was breathing heavily. "Sorry," he panted.

Mary blew out her bedside candle and stood by the guestroom window. She was in one of the west-wing rooms, overlooking Market Street and the East Gate of the castle. It must be midnight by now. The street was dark and deserted, except for two darker shapes by the gate. The night was still and snippets of their muted conversation carried to her window. From what she could gather, they were complaining about having to be on guard duty, and one seemed to be blaming the other for their predicament. She was about to close the shutters when she heard one of the guards say, "Leas' we ain't on some wild goose chase lookin' for tha' doctor."

"Doctor?" scoffed the other. "Lad looks like 'e's jus' left 'is wet nurse's tit. Came 'ere las' Sundee afternoon askin' t'see the Duke. Ronnie pinned 'im down an' played wiv 'im for a while." Muted chuckling sounds were followed by, "Like a frightened whelp, 'e was."

Then they began talking about Ronnie and his attempt to down three jugs of cider in three minutes.

Mary closed the shutters. Her heart had raced when she heard the word doctor, but the person they were talking about sounded nothing like the ghostly individual Sid had described.

Then she remembered what Tom had revealed to her this morning about Frank Offcut: how he had been helping Richard and the Purple Peril find the person who'd attacked the Duke. A 'person of interest' had been Tom's words. She wondered if *that* was who the guards were referring to. She doubted it though; it seemed unlikely that a doctor would commit such a crime.

Then again, how likely was it that Sid — someone who three days ago she wouldn't have known from the King of Longboatia — would be recovering in her bed after being beaten, robbed and, for all intents and purposes, linked to an attack on the Duke?

Poor Sid… At least he'd agreed to spend another night at The Harey Rabbit. She'd given him some of Doctor Whysman's elixir, which he'd reluctantly imbibed in a mug of camomile tea.

She flopped onto the bed. She was exhausted, mentally as well as physically. The unrelenting heat was beginning to have an affect; her nightdress was already clinging to her clammy skin. The situation with Sid was just as sticky. She wouldn't betray him to Richard, but she couldn't help wondering what was happening at the castle, and how important the silver button was to finding this person of interest. Tom had gone traipsing after Frank Offcut and the Moleson Twins in search of information — a wagon-load of gunpowder would be less explosive than those three. And then there was this Doctor Manky. Perhaps she *should* have mentioned him to Tom. But how, without incriminating Sid?

Mary sighed and rolled onto her side. She hoped sleep wouldn't be long in coming.

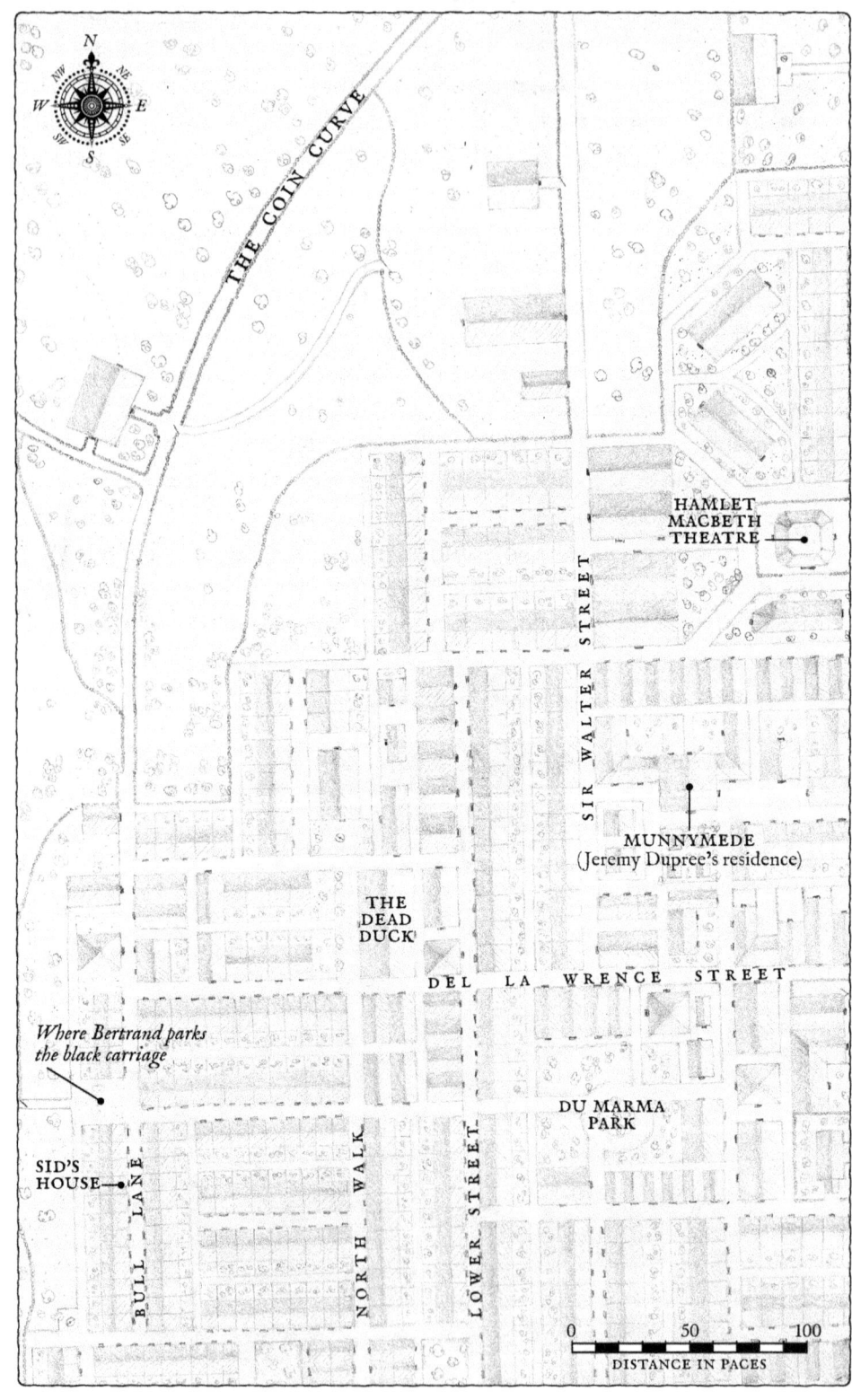

THE COIN CURVE

HAMLET
MACBETH
THEATRE

SIR WALTER STREET

MUNNYMEDE
(Jeremy Dupree's residence)

THE
DEAD
DUCK

DEL LA WRENCE STREET

*Where Bertrand parks
the black carriage*

DU MARMA
PARK

SID'S
HOUSE

BULL LANE

NORTH WALK

LOWER STREET

0          50          100

DISTANCE IN PACES

# TUESDAY, JULY 1

## CHAPTER 16

# *Like the tongue of a worn out dog*

OPHELIA WAS WOKEN by Tom's gentle shaking. She felt terribly groggy, and it was still dark. For a moment, she thought he was making advances on her.

"Time to make tracks," he said softly, his body a hovering silhouette.

*Make tracks*, she thought; funny thing for a tracker to say... tracks...

Ophelia jolted awake. Her pa! They had to track her pa! She propelled herself into a sitting position. The world took a few dizzying seconds to right itself. Squatting next to her, Tom asked how she was feeling. The dizziness transformed into a burning heat from her face and neck. Her mouth felt dry enough to catch on fire. "I'm fine," she croaked.

Standing up, her legs almost gave way in pain. Her saddle-soreness was worse, if that was possible. She inhaled sharply to prevent herself from crying out.

Tom looked concerned; his brow furrowed in the early morning grey. "I need to follow Frank's trail on foot," he said. "Can you walk, or would you prefer to ride? Perhaps you could sit side-saddle."

The thought of getting back onto Hazel made her feel ill; she'd take the walking option, painful as it was. "Jus' give me a momen' t'find me feet."

Tom nodded. "It's not light enough just yet, but it will be soon. The horses are saddled and packed; we'll be able to pick up Frank's trail very shortly."

She smiled at him as he bent down and retrieved the blanket she'd used as a mattress. "Thank you, Tom." She really was grateful for all he had done.

"You're welcome," he said. He folded the blanket and bundled it securely behind Wildflower's saddle. He returned with a water-skin and handed it to her. "This is breakfast, I'm afraid."

Ophelia was parched, the rum and rabbit a digesting memory, and she gladly took the deflated looking skin. The water was tepid and stopped flowing after four thirsty gulps — barely enough to hit the sides — but at least her tongue no longer felt like it would stick to the roof of her mouth.

Even in the shadowy light, her misery must have been plain because as Tom took the water-skin from her he said, "Don't worry, I'll find more water. In the meantime, if your mouth starts to dry up, this may help…"

He handed her an acorn. She looked at it in disbelief.

"Sucking on it makes your mouth moist."

It was amazing how quickly the light changed, almost as if someone had lit a giant candle, and suddenly they were off at quite a brisk pace. Tom knew exactly where to find the trail and he was wasting no time. That was fine by Ophelia for two reasons. One, the quicker they found her pa the better, and two, it was actually less painful to walk quickly.

To Ophelia, the trail Tom was following was invisible. The forest floor they were trudging across was covered with bracken, the more exposed plants singed by the summer sun. How Tom could say they were following her pa's trail was beyond her. He stopped occasionally to point out a snapped twig, a scuff mark on an exposed tree root, or some disturbance in the ground covering. It all looked like a natural part of the forest to Ophelia, but she was willing to put her faith in the Gamekeeper. He hadn't put a foot wrong since leaving Lower Icing, she admired his determination, and, as much as she was trying to put such thoughts out of her head, there was a stirring in her loins that had nothing to do with riding a horse.

They had been walking for about an hour. Ophelia's mind had wandered to images of Tom applying his saddle-sore unguent to her more tender areas when his voice broke through her imaginings.

"Not far now, Ophelia."

She looked up and was quite surprised to find that Tom was crouched on the ground. The last time she'd looked, he been pacing ahead with Wildflower and Hazel in tow. She wondered if she was losing touch with reality. She'd even forgotten that she'd been sucking on an acorn. Bizarrely, it *had* helped quell her thirst.

She realised Tom had found something significant and her mind snapped back into the here and now. Her heart began beating wildly. Spitting the acorn into her hand, she quickly closed in on the Gamekeeper. "Wha' y'found?"

"Take a look," he said, standing up.

Stepping past the horses, she looked down to where Tom was pointing.

Just ahead, in a hollow created by two massive tree roots, lay a pair of ruined shoes.

Ophelia's stomach lurched at the sight. She'd been expecting something natural, not something so... familiar. She stepped between the roots and picked up the shoes. They were caked in dust, the leather stitching had come away at both toes, and the soles dangled from the uppers like the tongue of a worn-out dog. She held the shoes close to her chest.

"Pa," she whispered, staring out into the sea of trees and bracken; the morning sun now dappled some of the delicate fronds.

"He can't be far away," she heard Tom say.

*No, he can't*, she thought. "Pa!" she yelled. The forest swallowed her cry, but gave nothing in return, apart from the constant sound of birdlife. Then she felt a hand on her arm.

"Let's go," Tom said. "Unless he's found water, he probably doesn't have a voice to answer."

Tom proceeded at a much slower pace; far too slow for Ophelia — her heart was beating madly, her body wanted to break into a run, all feelings of saddle-soreness had miraculously gone. She'd taken the reins of the two horses so Tom could concentrate on tracking. They'd become somewhat restless and wary, occasionally snorting and pulling at the reins.

"They're picking up on your mood," Tom informed her. "They want to run."

So did she! Again, she yelled out for her pa. Again, he didn't answer.

Some half an hour after discovering the shoes, they found the man. He was lying under a thick crop of bracken. They almost walked past him, but, ironically, it was Ophelia who spotted his grazed and dirty feet poking out from under the greenery. His left ankle looked like it had taken a bad knock — it was bruised and swollen.

"Pa!" she cried, flailing at the bracken.

Tom quickly jumped into the fray, pulling back the leafy fronds. Suddenly, she saw him, and then she couldn't move. She couldn't take it all in — the unconscious man before her *couldn't* be her sweet, beautiful pa; his raw flesh was cut, grazed and blistered, wrapped in his filthy, tattered remnants of clothing.

Her knees gave way and she slumped to the ground, then fell across her pa's chest and began to sob uncontrollably. Her pa's chest rose and she felt the word "Phelia" blow into her hair.

## CHAPTER 17

### *Quite the charmer*

MARY AROSE JUST before dawn, woken by the changing of the East Gate guards. She wondered why they sounded so clunky when they didn't wear armour. Perhaps they felt as dazed as she did. This heat; she was so tired and the nights were so uncomfortable. She'd be glad to return to her room… once Sid was better, of course.

She peeled herself off the mattress, nightdress askew and damp with sweat. She went downstairs. Sid was asleep, judging by his deep breathing; it was too dark to see him. Still half asleep herself, she made her way to the washroom where she filled the bathing tub.

Mary spent a blissful half an hour soaking and cleansing before Juanita and the dawning sun suddenly appeared. And just like the dawning sun, the Icarumban was far too bright.

"Meestress?" She seemed surprised to find Mary in the tub. "You want I should scrub your skeen, make eet all fresh an' smelleeng like dee rose petal?"

"I've already scrubbed and rose-petalled, thank you, Juanita," she said, reaching for the towel she'd placed on the floor next to the tub, "but you can leave the water for Sid. He could certainly do with a scrub and…" Mary caught the saucy look on Juanita's face. "I'm sure he'll be able to accomplish the task himself."

Juanita's expression changed to one of confusion. "What you mean… acumpleesh?"

"He can bathe himself."

By the time Mary was dressed, Sid had woken. She'd gone to check on him and found him looking out of her bedroom window, dressed only in trousers; his figure cast a long shadow across the floorboards. He seemed so strong and vital from this angle, not a victim of a cowardly attack. For a moment, she just stared at him, her thoughts conflicted by the man who'd charmed her, made her feel like… a woman. Was she doing the right thing by the Duke? He'd been attacked, and the silver button was a clue to the attacker's identity. But Richard, the Purple Peril and most Lower Icingers knew what it looked like — an image of it had been posted on the proclamation stand — so what purpose would the real thing actually serve? She had no doubt Sid was an innocent victim, but whether his attack had been opportunistic or planned, Mary wasn't sure. She didn't like the sound of this Doctor Manky character.

"Morning, Sid," she said, preventing her thoughts from spiralling into doubt and confusion.

He turned around, the image of a strong and vital Sid shattered by his battered face. He looked more gruesome, somehow, with his head framed in sunlight and his face in shadow. But there was clarity in his undamaged eye and she could see the rogue had returned.

He smiled at her. "Mary."

"How are you feeling?" she said, entering the room.

"Better. Thank you," he replied. Then, as she drew nearer, he added, "Fear not, I won't be collapsing on you this morning."

Mary smiled. "Most considerate of you, I'm sure."

Unconsciously, she reached out with her hand and gently ran it down the right side of his face; the undamaged skin was prickly with stubble. Sid's smile widened, then he grimaced in pain. Mary quickly withdrew her hand.

"Sorry," she said at the same time as he said, "Sorry."

There was a moment of awkwardness, before Mary blundered out with, "Would you care for a bath?"

Sid reacted by lifting up his right arm and smelling his pit. "Yes, I see what you mean." He grinned, ending the awkward moment.

While Sid was taking a bath, Mary sent Juanita to the market to buy some bread. Mary often did the market errands herself; she enjoyed the banter and liked most of the vendors she had dealings with. More importantly, *they* liked *her* and gave her good prices. John would usually accompany her with a small cart to carry the produce.

In the three months Juanita had been at The Harey Rabbit, Mary had never asked her washer girl to fetch anything from the market. Why would she? Why *had* she? The kitchen *was* running low on bread, but not desperately, and John could have gone.

Juanita had been just as perplexed. "Dee *bread?* Are you playeeng dee jest?"

No, she hadn't been. She been playing the fool instead, worried that the Icarumban's flirtatious disposition would somehow find its way into Sid's bath. Ridiculous!

Fortunately, Doctor Whysman and his wife arrived for breakfast shortly after Juanita went sashaying out of The Harey Rabbit, wicker basket swinging rhythmically by her side. Playing host saved her from dwelling on her insecurity.

Doctor and Petronella Whysman were the only guests in the dining room; The Harey Rabbit wasn't open for another half an hour, but Mary had told the Doctor he was welcome to arrive early if he and Petronella preferred to avoid the crowd.

Mary welcomed the unassuming couple and seated them at the table by the staircase; it was the coolest part of the room. Ironically, it was the table Sid and Gerald had been sitting at on Saturday night.

"So, how's the patient this morning, m'dear?" asked Doctor Whysman as he and Petronella took their seats.

"Much better, thank you, Doctor. He seems a lot clearer of mind and happier in spirit; your elixir worked wonders."

He smiled. "Very kind, m'dear, but the real wonder is in the recuperative powers of the body."

"And *you*, Mary," Petronella added. "Albert tells me you've taken this man in, given him your room and tended to his needs. That is most selfless of you."

Coming from any other woman who frequented The Harey Rabbit, Mary might have suspected an undertone of cattiness in the remark, but Petronella Whysman was a genuinely caring and considerate person, just like her husband. Mary had a lot of time for them both. "Thank you, but I felt it was my duty since he was attacked on my premises."

Some fifteen minutes later, Mary delivered a full breakfast to the table. Patricia was in an argumentative mood, so Mary had prepared most of it herself, but she'd been happy to do so — the Juanita incident was still playing on her mind.

"That bacon smells delicious, m'dear," enthused the doctor. "Must admit, I'm rather famished."

She was about to leave them in peace when Sid entered the room, bathed and dressed, looking rather dashing in the new white shirt she'd bought for him. Juanita had also done an excellent job cleaning his trousers and polishing his boots. The obvious flaw in this picture of rejuvenation was the left side of his face — the bruising, the swollen eye and the stitched-up gash still looked angry, even though all of them were on the mend.

"You've scrubbed up alright."

"I know. I should get bashed more often," Sid quipped.

She gave him a withering look and stepped away from the table, so she wasn't standing between him and the Whysmans. It was opportune timing — a chance for Sid to meet the man who, if not *saved* his life, had certainly brought him *back* to life.

"Sid, this is Doctor Albert Whysman and his wife, Petronella. Doctor Whysman is the person who's been treating you."

Sid bowed formally. "Delighted to meet you, Doctor," he said, affecting a noble accent. "Thank you for all your kind and timely ministrations."

Mary couldn't believe it; was he *actually* poking fun at the man who had helped him? Thank goodness Doctor Whysman had never spoken to Sid.

"Don't mention it, m'boy," he replied. "Young Mary, here, did all the work."

Mary felt the colour rising in her face as Sid shifted his stance and bowed towards Petronella. "A pleasure to make your acquaintance, madam."

*What was he doing?* She could see Petronella was slightly taken aback by his formal greeting. "Why thank you, Master…?"

"Sid will do nicely, thank you, Mistress Whysman," he responded. He really was asking for a swift kick to the shin.

"Well… Sid," Petronella said, stumbling over the familiarity of using his given name. "I am glad my husband was able to help you. You've obviously been hurt quite badly. It's dreadful to think one cannot walk the streets safely at night."

"Well, quite," Sid said. "And now, alas, I must take my leave…"

*And not a moment too soon*, thought Mary.

"Thank you again for your assistance, Doctor Whysman. I will, of course, recompense you for your time as soon as—"

"No need, m'boy," Doctor Whysman informed him.

Sid looked confused. "I insist, Doc—"

"Mary, here, has already been most generous on your behalf." He indicated the breakfast spread.

Sid looked at her and smiled, or maybe it was a grimace; she wasn't sure. "Well, it seems I am indebted to you in more ways than one, Mistress Brewer."

"Do not mention it, *Master* Evily," Mary replied, mimicking his formality. She had to get Sid out of there before the Whysmans realised he was being disingenuous. "Allow me to escort you to the door."

Sid seemed to be enjoying her discomfort. She turned her attention back to her guests. "I shall return directly, Doctor, Petronella. In the meantime, please enjoy your breakfast."

"Thank you, m'dear," the doctor replied cheerfully. "And you rest up, m'boy. Your body is still repairing itself; take care not to overdo things."

"No need to concern yourself, Doctor. I intend to take very good care of... things."

"What was *that* all about?" Mary demanded once they were outside amongst the morning stream of people going to and from the castle kitchen. The contrast in noise and heat from inside The Harey Rabbit was quite remarkable.

"What do you mean?" Sid grinned.

His attitude was beginning to annoy her. "The way you were speaking in there, all formal, like a *regular!*"

"Well y'see, me lovely," Sid said, affecting a common accent, "there ain't no 'arm done in leavin' the right impression."

Mary didn't know whether to hit him or laugh at him. Instead, she challenged him. "I didn't think you were the type to worry about what people thought of you."

He looked at her thoughtfully. "You're right, Mary," he agreed, his normal voice returning. "I'm usually quite comfortable being Sid Evily, but I don't know this doctor and I don't know the world he lives in." Then his smile returned. "It's a wise man that is wary of a Whysman."

"Oh, *very* droll," she replied, unable to hold back a smile of her own. Then the implication of what he'd just said hit her, and her smile vanished. "Surely you don't think *Doctor Whysman* is involved?"

"Who knows? I have no idea why this has happened," he said pointing at his face. "But, until I find out, you're the only one I'm willing to trust."

Mary watched Sid walk down Market Street and disappear into the tide of people that swirled in and around The Square. It was a strange feeling, watching him leave. He had burst into her life out of nowhere and wrung emotions out of her that she'd never known existed. Not even the loss of her adoptive parents, John and Kate Brewer, whom she had loved dearly and felt such sorrow at their passing, nor the death of Sir Walter Upson, her actual father, had stirred such a myriad of feelings within her. She'd been instantly attracted to him — that was a first in itself — and then to find him nearly beaten to death…

The whole situation was further complicated by the silver button and this mysterious Doctor Manky, and the fact that her brother was the Seneschal of Lower Icing. Then, of course, there was Tom and his mission to rescue Frank Offcut from the Moleson Twins. Why had the Moleson Twins taken Frank Offcut of all people? And what did *he* know about the attack on the Duke?

It was a relief to be back inside The Harey Rabbit, and not just because it was an escape from the hectic activity outside. Mary ruled the world within these brick walls; it was what she knew and where she felt at ease, where she could be herself and take care of business. There was staff to organise, books to be kept, food to prepare, patrons to look after, and a hundred other tasks to distract her thoughts from Sid Evily and that bloody silver button.

The Whysmans were still enjoying their breakfast. Albert was most effusive in his praise: "Absolutely delicious, m'dear. Certainly hitting the spot this morning."

"You're most welcome, Doctor Whysman."

"Yes, it is a delightful way to spend the morning, thank you, Mary," added Petronella. Then she smiled knowingly. "Your young man is quite the charmer, isn't he? And, I dare say, most handsome underneath all that bruising."

Mary hoped she hadn't taken offense at his patronising manner. Doctor Whysman was also smiling at her in an odd sort of way. Mary suddenly felt quite self-conscious. "Well, he's not my young man—"

"No need to be coy, m'dear," chimed in Doctor Whysman. "It is quite obvious you're smitten by Sid."

This was becoming uncomfortable. Disappearing into the simmering streets of Lower Icing suddenly seemed very appealing. "Well, I—"

"It's a *good* thing, Mary," Petronella assured her. "You could do with a man in your life."

Could she? She'd managed quite well without one. Her few romantic dalliances had proven disastrous because she refused to be dictated to by men who thought it wasn't seemly for a woman to run an inn. Yes, she'd had a few run-ins with men over the years on *that* particular point. "I'm not sure that—"

"Where does Sid hail from, Mary?" enquired Petronella, seemingly oblivious to Mary's discomfort. "Obviously he's an educated man. Which, speaking from experience, is a lovely trait." She gazed lovingly at her husband, who returned the sentiment by reaching across the table and squeezing his wife's hand.

Mary wanted to excuse herself before this became even more embarrassing.

"Did I detect the hint of a refined Naffolk accent there, Mary?"

She almost burst out laughing. "I doubt it!"

Petronella gave her a quizzical look.

Mary recovered her composure. "Your pardon, Mistress Whysman. Sid's from Lower Icing. In fact, his sister is married to the Town Crier."

Petronella's jaw dropped; a reaction Mary might have expected if she'd said Sid's sister was married to the Stymouth Slasher or the Porkshire Ripper, but there wouldn't be many people in the whole Five Duchies more harmless than Gerald Hiepants.

Petronella eventually found her voice. "Are you saying that he's *Olivia's* brother?" She sounded shocked. Mary suddenly felt a cold chill run up her spine. "So I believe," Mary replied uncertainly. Gerald had introduced him as such on Saturday night.

"Well," breathed Petronella, "I can hardly believe it."

"What is it, m'dear?" Doctor Whysman was concerned by his wife's sudden change in demeanour.

Regarding them both, she said, "Olivia has always maintained that her brother was killed in some sort of accident, that he fell from a roof a year or so before she married Gerald."

This time, it was Mary's jaw that dropped.

## CHAPTER 18

## *Like an offering*

GERALD HAD BEEN acting like a restless bear (in a red coat) all morning. He was increasingly agitated by the Duke's failing health and the uncertainty of Xavier's fate. Olivia had been tempted to confide in her husband, put his mind at rest about Xavier, but there were other, more important issues to take into account. In any case, what purpose would it serve? Xavier had lost his memory; he was no use to the Duke in his present condition. Gerald's mind would just have to do without rest, for the time being at least.

By nine o'clock, the bear had become so unbearable that Olivia suggested she accompany him on his stroll to the castle; anything to get him out of the house. He was lingering for some reason, which was very unlike him, particularly on a Tuesday — he was usually at the castle quite early, preparing for the Tuesday at Two proclamation. He'd better not come home in some last-minute fluster expecting her to add polish to his banal news; *that* would not be happening… not today. Her frustration at her husband's tardiness was compounded by her desire to speak to Xavier, to see if his possessions would unclog his memory.

After much badgering, Olivia finally ushered him outside. The sun blazed down on his red coat as she locked the door to 8 Plumduff Street. They linked arms and began strolling towards the castle.

They'd only taken half a dozen steps when some clumsy idiot knocked into Gerald. Olivia would have berated the man, but her husband favoured a more diplomatic approach.

"Mind where you're walking, there's a good fellow."

The fellow, much to Olivia's disbelief and disgust, was her good-for-nothing brother. To add injury to insult, someone had rearranged the left side of his face — he looked like some grotesque sideshow freak. *Typical*, she thought; no doubt he'd been caught carousing with another man's woman.

Gerald reacted exactly how she expected him to. "Good heavens, Sid! What's happened to you? Are you alright?"

Sid's reaction was also to type. "Oh, you know me, Gerald," he said, flippantly, "always fall for a pretty face."

Gerald actually looked concerned.

Pathetic! Sid was a selfish, immature waster, and no doubt deserved every inch of his bruising. "I'd like to say I'm surprised, Gerald," she said, gazing balefully at her brother, "but Sid looks for trouble as much as he looks for the ale jug, and both tend to leave him with a sore head."

Gerald looked pained by her response. "Come now, Olivia. Poor Sid's obviously been hurt quite badly. The least we can do—"

"The *least* we can do is let Sid go about his business," Olivia interjected, wishing to avoid a scene that would attract the curiosity of passers-by.

Sid grinned grotesquely. "Right you are, Liv…"

She hated the way he called her Liv.

"…I *do* have business to attend to. Many thanks for your concern, Gerald. I'm much better than I look. Good day to you."

He took his leave; back to the common part of Lower Icing, no doubt. Olivia had never visited his abode — if, indeed, it could be called that — and she hoped there'd never be occasion to.

"I say, m'dear, that was rather harsh, what?"

Olivia groaned inwardly. "How many times do I have to tell you, Gerald. Sid only cares about one person, and that's himself. What you've just seen is the result of *how* little he takes other people's feelings into account!"

"I've always found him quite—"

"Don't you dare say it, Gerald," Olivia said between clenched teeth. "No-one knows the true Sid Evily except me."

Gerald retreated into silence. *Just as well*, thought Olivia. If she'd heard the word 'amiable' come from his lips, she wasn't sure if her sense of propriety would have held sway over her sense of outrage.

Olivia accompanied Gerald to his office. She wanted to make sure he was well ensconced in his proclamation preparation before she went to see Xavier. Gerald's office was on the barracks' side of the Administration Section in the Lower Bailey. The thick stone wall that separated the military from the the 'quill-scratchers' provided some relief from the heat. However, he was sweating profusely by the time they reached the gloomy confines of his office.

"For goodness sake, Gerald, take that coat off."

Gerald sighed and began unfastening the gold buttons. Olivia watched in silence. *What was wrong with him?* He was usually so upbeat about the responsibility of being Town Crier. And now, with the attack on Marmaduke, there was even more reason for him to put his best foot forward and stir the populace into finding the miscreant. The Purple Peril and men-at-arms were obviously having no luck, and that's probably because they were looking for Xavier. *Idiots!* They were like a pack of dogs following the wrong scent. That had been the one good thing about finding Xavier injured: it had removed any lingering doubts about his innocence. According to Gerald, Marmaduke had been attacked just before midnight. According to Bethany, she'd found Xavier around ten, so there was no possibility he could have been responsible; his disappearance and the attack were, as she had thought, a coincidence.

A young clerk suddenly burst into the room. "Excuse me, Town Crier," he said, apologetically, acknowledging Olivia's presence with a quick nod, "but Sir Richard wants to see you immediately."

"Thank you, Master Ramekin," Gerald said, bowing his head as if resigned to some terrible fate. Then he hooked his coat to the coat stand like he was placing a noose around a condemned man's neck.

Now that Gerald was sorted for the morning, Olivia went straight back to 8 Plumduff Street and retrieved Xavier's leather folder and magnificent oak box. She placed them in his travelling case with his clothes. She decided to leave *Poetry in Potion* locked safely in the bottom drawer of the desk in the study; the room where six years' worth of proclamations were shelved. Xavier's interests would be best served with the book in her care. Should he be discovered and accused of Marmaduke's attack, there'd be no incriminating evidence to be found. And, as far as jogging Xavier's memory was concerned, she doubted the book itself would make any difference, since he'd not recognised any of the potion names. No, it would be the oak case or, more likely, the leather folder that would register with Xavier: the item so precious that he kept the key to it around his neck. She also took the opportunity to change into one of her own creations — another lightweight, free-flowing dress. It was a relief to remove the tight-fitting bodice of her castle attire.

Olivia walked through the large, open gateway that led into the back of The Bloody Bell. She could hardly wait to immerse herself in its cool, blue interior. She'd collected quite a few curious glances on her wilting walk to the inn, lugging a man's travelling case.

Unexpectedly, the back door was locked. Olivia repositioned the case in her left hand and knocked. She waited a few moments before knocking again, this time with more force. Still nothing. How inconvenient. Now she'd have to wade through the bar's steaming atmosphere of body odour, spilled ale and tobacco.

She'd taken a few steps towards the gateway when she heard the turning of a key. *Thank goodness!* Relief quickly turned to wariness when she saw the key turner wasn't Bethany, but her father.

"Mistress 'Iepants," he mumbled.

"Good morning, Master Swill."

There was a moment of silence before Bar Swill stepped back and pulled the door open. "Bes' come in then."

Olivia acknowledged the gesture with a curt smile. It was clear he regarded her presence as an intrusion. Well, that was *his* problem. Olivia had no intention of leaving Xavier's future and wellbeing in the hands of people who fuelled thuggery and lechery. The only reason she hadn't made Xavier's whereabouts official was because she believed someone at the castle wanted to frame him for the attack on Marmaduke.

"Bethany's downstairs," he said, glancing at the case. "Want some 'elp with that?"

"I can manage, thank you, Master Swill." She headed towards the stairs while he closed and locked the door behind her.

"If them things don' bring 'is mem'ry back, I'm takin' 'im back t'Blessed Whippin'."

Olivia stopped at the top of the stairs and regarded the gruff-looking innkeeper. "I don't think that will be necessary, Master Swill," she said pointedly.

Bar Swill was not cowed by her directness and continued as if Olivia had not spoken. "Tha's where 'e came from. The community will 'elp 'im, and this doctor or mentor, or wha'ever 'e is, migh' 'ave a memory brew or somethin'. In any case, 'e ain't stayin' 'ere. It ain't right to keep the lad locked away, fadin' into nothin'. 'E needs daykigh', and 'e needs t'be with people who know 'im."

"Is that right, Master Swill?" How dare he presume to know what was best for Xavier, particularly when he wasn't in possession of the full facts about his lineage. "May I remind you or, indeed, *inform* you that Xavier *fled* his mentor. Besides, I hardly think an isolated community of sun-worshipping fanatics will provide an environment conducive to recovery. No, Master Swill,

Xavier came here of his own volition, he should leave of his own volition."

He smiled knowingly as he walked towards her; not the reaction Olivia had been expecting. "The thing abou' volition, Mistress 'Iepants, is tha' we *all* got it; jus' a case of 'ow prepared we are t'*use* it."

Olivia felt the blood rush to her face; Bar Swill's manner had somehow turned threatening. Even though he was calm, his gaze was piercing (like his daughter's) and his closer proximity made her feel exposed. She took a step down towards the cellar. "I agree," she replied, hoping she sounded calm and assured.

However, judging by his patronising expression, he'd seen straight through her false bravado. "Good luck with Xavier." Then he strode down the corridor without so much as a 'good day'.

Olivia's heart was beating quickly as she hurried past the Swill's wine collection. The door to Xavier's room was shut.

"Xavier?" she called through the timber-panelled door.

The door was opened by Bethany — didn't the girl have *work* to do? She smiled serenely, regarding the travelling case. "Welcome, Mistress 'Iepants." Stepping back into the room, she allowed Olivia to enter.

It was as if time had stopped; the room and the people in it appeared exactly as they had done yesterday. Bar Swill had a point: Xavier couldn't be kept down here for much longer, but, at the same time, that didn't mean he needed to be whisked away to a community of sun-struck inbreds. She'd rather alert the authorities.

Xavier regarded her with his calm, accepting expression. He looked pale. He'd been held captive in one form or another since arriving at Lower Icing, and Olivia felt responsible for her and Gerald's part in that. "Mistress… ah, your pardon… Olivia," he said, awkwardly.

Olivia smiled at him; at least his short-term memory was intact. "Good morning, Xavier." Then she laid the case on his bed like an offering to the malady that held his memory hostage. She could only hope it'd be satisfied.

He regarded the case.

"This is yours. Inside are your clothes and items that are precious to you, particularly the folder."

Xavier bent down and ran his hands over the case's leather surface, as if the *feel* of it might trigger some recognition. His hands eventually found their way to the latches, which he unfastened slowly and deliberately. The tension was almost unbearable; Olivia wanted to push him aside and throw open the case. He was probably scared, she thought — scared of *not* recognising what lay within.

Slowly, he lifted the lid. The neatly folded clothes looked somewhat crumpled after the walk from 8 Plumduff Street. The folder lay askew, next to the box. Xavier rested his hand on the folder, saying nothing.

Had he recognised it, she wondered. "As you can see it has a lock," she murmured. "You wear the key around your neck."

His gaze flicked back up to her, his eyebrows furrowed with confusion. "I wear nothing around my neck."

Olivia looked at his neck; the leather chord that was usually visible was, indeed, missing. She immediately turned her attention to Bethany. "What have you done with his pendant?" she demanded.

Bethany's eyes narrowed, but her voice remained calm. "Nothin', Mistress 'Iepants."

Olivia snapped. "Don't take me for a fool, girl. He would never remove that pendant!"

Bethany's gaze turned introspective, as if she were listening to some inner voice. It made Olivia's skin crawl — she was a most otherworldly creature.

"I don' take no-one for a fool, an' I suggest you learn t'do the same."

Olivia was gobsmacked. The cheek!

"Xavier was beaten *an'* robbed; more'n likely it was taken then, don' y'think?"

Olivia flushed, embarrassed she *hadn't* considered that possibility. However, 'more than likely' didn't ring true. She thought it more than likely this odd family with their fetish for the colour blue and names beginning with B would have an agenda of their own.

"That is *one* possibility."

Xavier was a confused bystander, just as he'd been yesterday. He placed the box and the folder side by side on the bed. Olivia's heart sunk; there'd obviously been no recollection of what these objects were. Olivia prompted him to open the box. He nodded, like an obedient child; it wrenched Olivia's heart to see him this way. He was so... lost.

He turned his attention to the plain-looking oak box; the simple metal plate, engraved with his name, caught what little light there was in the room. The sounds of Lower Icing drifted in through the window while Olivia and Bethany waited in silence. His fingers touched the two latches, but he didn't open them.

"Open it, Xavier," Olivia said.

At the same time, Bethany asked, "Are you alright, Xavier?"

In response, Xavier stood up, stroking the front of his neck. "You are correct, Olivia," he said, looking at her. "I remember wearing a pendant. It was silver, wasn't it?"

## CHAPTER 19

# *She was Frank Offcut's daughter*

HER PA HAD been slipping in and out of consciousness for the last four hours, during which time he'd mumbled incoherently about the Moleson Twins and The Slasher and, for some strange reason, irony. They'd done their best to make him more comfortable, but they dared not move him — he barely had the energy to move his lips, let alone stand up or clamber onto a horse.

Thank goodness for Tom; he'd been a marvel. He'd treated her pa with care and concern, applying his 'saddle-soreness' unguent to the many scrapes and scratches covering his poor, beaten body. His face and back were bruised, his nose was broken, and there was a nasty-looking gash between his eyes that, fortunately, only required cleaning and bandaging. They'd found a deep cut on his left thigh; it was caked in blood and dirt and had attracted a large number of flies. It required stitches, as well as cleaning and bandaging; a task to which Tom applied himself diligently. There were also nasty raw marks around his wrists where his bindings had dug in.

Tom had then gone to find water, returning half an hour later with full skins. He'd gently dribbled some over her pa's cracked, sunburnt lips. He opened his mouth and licked his lips, looking for more. Tom gradually increased the flow, craning her pa's neck forward so he wouldn't choke. His eyes sprang open, alive and thirsty for life. Despite Tom's efforts, her pa drank greedily, and then began coughing and spluttering until he exhausted his way back into unconsciousness. Yet, it filled Ophelia's heart with joy — she could see her pa was being revived.

Tom's next task was to find food. This meant looking for edible berries, laying traps and taking any opportunity to use his bow. He'd been gone for the best part of two hours now and, in his absence, Ophelia had done her best to do what he'd asked of her: She'd made a small clearing by hacking away at the nearby undergrowth (using the fine bracken fronds as a pillow for her pa's head), dug a shallow fire-pit, collected firewood, and set the pit with dry grass and twigs. It was humid under the forest canopy and she was sweating like a pig, but it was better than being out in the burning sun.

During the preparation of the campsite, she regularly attended to her pa, dripping more water onto his lips and keeping the cloth across his forehead moist. She even took the opportunity to apply some of Tom's balm to her own tender areas. It was soothing and made her feel a lot more comfortable.

Before he'd left to go hunting, Tom had shown her where he'd found the water: it was a ten-minute trek south, where the valley ended in a steep, thickly forested slope. Sliced into the valley, like a giant sword cut, was a narrow ravine. It was completely shaded from the sun and it felt like they were entering another world. The ravine, some ten paces wide, contained all manner of exotic-looking plant life. One variety had a mesmerising purple flower and shiny black berries. Ophelia had been immediately attracted to its vivid colour and faint perfume — it appeared to be thriving in the moist, gloomy environment.

"Wha' a beautiful flower." She reached out and caressed the soft petals.

"Yes, it is," Tom agreed.

"C'n we eat them berries?"

"Of course, but I wouldn't recommend it."

"Why not?"

"Because they'd probably kill you."

Ophelia snatched her hand away. "Are you jestin'?"

"It's Deadly Nightshade," he said casually.

Deadly Nightshade — *that* didn't sound good. She stepped back from the beautiful plant.

Tom looked bemused. *Was* he jesting?

"And it's not just the berries; the whole plant is deadly. But if you're looking for certain death, I suggest munching on the roots."

Ophelia began wiping her hands on her dress.

Tom started laughing. "You'll survive, Ophelia. You have to actually ingest the Belladonna."

"The Belladonna?" she asked, bringing her wiping to a halt.

"It's what the Pastarians call Deadly Nightshade."

Pastarians? How the frig did Tom know what the Pastarians called Deadly Nightshade? Pastaria was farther away from the Five Duchies than Escargotia and Icarumba. The only thing she knew about Pastaria was the cured-meat sausage called Salami her pa made especially for the nobs.

"It means 'beautiful woman'."

Well, that made no sense. Bella and whatever the Pastarian for purple flower was would have worked better.

"I prefer it," continued Tom. "Quite apt, don't you think?"

No. She thought Bella Purple Flower was more apt, but she knew what he was getting at. And she knew he was teasing her. "'Ow 'bout y'show me where the friggin' water is."

He laughed and led her to a spring-fed pool some thirty paces into the ravine. On the way back, he used a sharp stone to scrape direction markers on the trunks of trees, making it possible for Ophelia to find her way to and from the spring on her own.

It was around midday, or maybe a bit later — it was hard to tell in the forest. She'd successfully followed the marked trees and refilled the water-skins (giving the Belladonna a wide berth). She'd kept a fast pace, because she didn't want to leave her pa for more than twenty minutes. She'd left him resting peacefully, but he was still quite feverish, and the insects buzzing around his face, seeking out the gash on the bridge of his nose, were a constant annoyance. She'd also left the horses, but Wildflower and Hazel were quite content standing in the shade of the forest, tethered to a tree twenty paces from the campsite. They even had patches of grass to munch on.

Ophelia arrived back at the campsite to find Tom had returned.

"Y'look like the cat what got the cream," she said.

"Actually, I'm the cat that got the goat." He indicated the white furred creature hanging from its hind legs on a branch of a nearby tree, blood dripping from its cut neck.

Ophelia smiled; they'd eat well today. She was already famished. It had been a hard morning, physically and emotionally. She needed sustenance and so did her pa.

"Hmm... not bad I s'pose." She placed the water-skins next to the fire-pit.

"Yes, I managed to find my way to that female's heart easily enough."

It seemed like jovial banter, but what he did he mean by that exactly? He approached her. He looked like he might want to kiss her. There was no doubt she was attracted to him, but her pa... He was just a few paces away. Imagine if he woke and found her and the Gamekeeper in a passionate embrace; the shock would be enough to kill him.

Still, he moved closer. "I have something for you."

*Well, a kiss would be alright,* she thought. Her pa *was* unconscious; the chances of him waking at this very moment were slim to say the least.

Tom stopped within arms' length. Then he reached for his belt. Surely he wasn't thinking of… The unguent had worked well, but not *that* well, and, in any case, he was making a painful mistake if he thought he could have his way with her out here in the wild like a… wild animal. She didn't care *how* well he'd treated her pa; the only part of her body his codpiece was going to connect with was her swiftly moving knee.

His hand moved away from his belt and she realised he'd pulled out his hunting knife, its handle suddenly pointing at her sun-pink cleavage. He was offering it to her. *What the…?*

"Since you're the only daughter of Lower Icing's only butcher, I thought you should do the honours." He flicked his head in the direction of the goat.

It took a moment for Ophelia to grasp the intent of Tom's words. When she did, her first thought was to tell him where he could stick his frigging hunting knife. But then, that'd be exactly what he'd expect her to do.

Instead, she smiled sweetly and accepted the handle. She'd show him. *She* was no wilting flower (as much as she felt like one). *She* was Frank Offcut's daughter!

# CHAPTER 20

## *Almost hear Juanita cheering*

FOR SOME REASON, The Harey Rabbit felt strangely empty without Sid. Mary had been looking forward to reclaiming her room, but while it was nice to be back amongst her possessions, there was a feeling of… emptiness. And then, of course, Petronella's revelation that Sid had died six years ago continued to echo into the void. Her initial reaction had been one of shock. Petronella seemed very certain of her facts, but, as Mary had explained to the Whysmans, Sid had been introduced to her by the Town Crier. Surely *he* wouldn't be party to such a fabrication. Sid's resurrection was just another piece to a puzzle she had no idea how to solve.

Mary sighed as she pulled the sheets from her bed — the only remnant of Sid's stay — and made her way to the washroom. Juanita had returned; the basket of bread sat on the kitchen table like a tribute to Mary's insecurity. It was freshly baked and filled the kitchen with a mouth-watering aroma. Mastering her embarrassment, Mary turned into the washroom. Juanita was there, tackling a pile of dishcloths.

"I get dee bread, Meestress," she said, as if Mary might have somehow missed that fact.

"Yes, Juanita, I can see *and* smell it," she replied, and then immediately changed her tone; Juanita had done nothing wrong. "I'm sorry. I shouldn't have asked you to do that."

Juanita stopped sloshing the bucket full of dishcloths. "Ees alright. I no mind. Dee market ees full of dee colour an' noise an' theengs. I like eet! An' dee baker, ees a very nice man. He geeve me extra three loaves, because he says I have…" She paused, her sultry eyes narrowed in thoughtfulness, her full lips pouting as she searched for the right words. "Nice buns?"

"Really," Mary commented, evenly; she would have a word with Paul Sourdough next time she went to fetch the bread. What *was* it with Juanita and men? There was no doubt she exuded a certain amount of sexuality;

Mary understood that. But Paul Sourdough? He was a happily married man, with four children, who'd always treated Mary with respect and had never even made the slightest of suggestive comments in *her* presence. Somehow, she felt insulted by that.

"I no understand," Juanita continued. "I have no buns or nutheeng; *he* ees dee one with dee buns. But I geeve heem dee beeg smile and say muchas gracias, but I am theenkeeng you have dee strange customs in Lower Iceeng."

"Very strange," Mary agreed.

She left the sheets with the Icarumban and began the daily task of preparing for the lunch crowd — both of them could do with something mundane to concentrate on.

Mary strolled through the streets of Lower Icing. The mid-afternoon sun beamed brightly on the fresh white dress that was dancing around her ankles; it felt so good to be out of her staid, black work attire.

She approached what she hoped was Sid's front door. He'd told her where he lived and described his terraced house as the one with a cannon-ball-sized dent in the wall to the left of the door. According to Sid, it had been caused years back by a mad bull from a visiting Icarumban Circus. Apparently, someone had thrown a tomato at it, sending the beast on a panicked run through the streets of Lower Icing, bashing and crashing and chasing a crowd of villagers who were either terrified or out for a thrill. It all sounded very farfetched to Mary, but as she studied the wall of the dwelling, she saw there *was* a round dent in the brickwork about rump-of-a-mad-bull height. Icarumba... was *everything* from that sun-baked land hot-tempered and emotionally unstable?

Mary knocked at the door. She was concerned about Sid. However, if she was being totally truthful, she also needed to be around someone who found her... desirable. *Did* Sid find her desirable?

She knocked at the door again, harder this time. He had been flirting with her on Friday night and they'd shared some tender moments during his recovery, but it could have been the drink on Friday night and then the delirium. Mary didn't know what to think.

*Where was he?* She banged on the door for a third time. Perhaps he was in the privy, or maybe he'd fallen unconscious. She banged again. "Sid!" she yelled and banged the door. What if he *was* unconscious? "Sid?!"

"Would you like an axe?"

The croaky voice came from above. Sid was leaning out of an upstairs window.

Relief flooded through her. "Well, would you believe it? I've finally made enough noise to wake the dead."

"Can't get enough of me, eh?" He yawned and stretched. "I'll be down shortly."

It was a rather dazed-looking Sid who eventually opened the door. He apologised for keeping her waiting and invited her inside. Mary's first impressions of his place were overwhelmingly underwhelming: the downstairs room was empty except for a table and a couple of chairs. It was almost as if the floorboards had felt sorry for him and arranged themselves into a few pieces of furniture.

"Welcome to the abode of Sid Evily," he said, offering Mary one of the chairs.

It was all a bit sad really, but his charm was hard to resist. She sat down. "Has a woman ever set foot in this place before?"

"Plenty of women, but never a lady."

Mary smiled, even though she suspected she wasn't the first woman to hear *that* particular line. Sid rounded the table and sat directly opposite her. On the table was a nibbled slab of waxy cheese that looked ready to crumble to dust, dried up remnants of a loaf of bread, and an empty tankard of ale. Next to where Sid had positioned himself was a quill and parchment with something written on it. Next to the parchment, shining in the feeble light, was the silver button.

"So, how are you feeling? You look a bit better, particularly for a man who died six years ago."

He looked puzzled. "Was that a jest, Mary? My head is still rather foggy."

"Not according to Petronella Whysman. She's under the impression you fell from a roof."

Sid groaned. "Let me guess… my sister?"

Mary nodded.

"And here I was thinking you'd come to cheer me up."

"I'm sorry, Sid; it's just that Petronella seemed quite shocked when I told her who you were."

He sighed. "Liv decided long ago that a dead brother was more socially acceptable than the live version."

"Well, you can hardly blame her for *that*," said Mary, not wanting the conversation to turn sombre.

He barked out a laugh, then winced in pain.

Mary shook her head — enough of this nonsense. His sister must be a very hate-filled person to perpetuate such a story. Turning her attention to the objects on the table, she reached over and grabbed the parchment. "What's this?"

She regarded the script. It was a scrawl, as if the person writing it had downed a few tankards of ale and eaten some stale bread and cheese. It contained a list of suspects — actually, more a series of ponderings about who could have attacked him.

The castle intruder? Found out his mistake after Gerald's proclamation.

Someone at The Harey Rabbit?

Yellow waist-coated tosser lawyers? No, they wouldn't have the balls!

Just the wrong place at the wrong time... probably.

No frigging idea... exactly!!!

Mary smiled at the lawyers comment. Sid had pegged the Limpdickers perfectly, but she also knew they had nothing to do with his attack; they were far too self-absorbed. She doubted they even knew Sid existed.

"Hmm... some interesting thoughts."

"Amusing ones, by the look."

He seemed so serious that Mary wanted to laugh. "In a... naïve sort of way."

"*Naïve?*" He cursed in pain as the swollen part of his face reacted to his outrage. He snatched back the parchment and began reading it, obviously trying to see what Mary found so naïve and amusing. He seemed so vulnerable and childlike that she felt an overwhelming desire to comfort him. She rose from her seat — a sense of the Icarumban stirring inside her — gently put her arms around his neck and kissed his cheek... then his mouth... then, she was in his arms… then, somehow, in his bed. She could almost hear Juanita cheering.

Mary could hardly believe what had happened. There they were, lying next to each other in the afternoon afterglow, slick with sweat — it was wonderful. But it was also deflating.

The euphoria was subsiding, being replaced by the concerns of everyday and the strangeness of her and Sid's coupling. She was confused by her feelings and amazed by her actions. "I have something to tell you," she whispered before the words had even popped into her head.

"That sounds ominous," he said, sleepily. "Should I have heard this *before* you had your way with me?"

Mary gently stroked the good side of his face. "I don't know what to make of you, Sid Evily, but I am not ashamed to admit you have made my heart fly."

"And you mine."

He was about to draw her into an embrace, but she held him at bay. "Wait. You need to know something about me."

*What was she doing?*

"If we are going to be open with each other, this must be said."

His demeanour turned from sleepy desire to focused concern. "Very well, Mary. I'm all ears."

She took a deep breath. How would he react? Why was she so worried about how he would react? "Sir Richard Upson is my half-brother."

He just looked at her… breathing, his good eye moving, taking in her features.

"Say something, Sid," Mary whispered.

When he finally spoke, his voice was strangely calm and relaxed. "Does that mean you know what happened at the castle?"

"No!" She knew he'd think that: that she had been playing him. "I know nothing about any of it. I am not my brother's confidante. We rarely see each other and, when we do, we talk of the weather or other such inane things. We live in two different worlds and have nothing in common."

He said nothing. She searched his face, looking for understanding. She reached out, took his hand, and told him about being the daughter of the late Sir Walter Upson and a serving girl, about been brought up by John and Kate Brewer who ran The Harey Rabbit, that she regarded them as her true parents, that, after they had died, she discovered Sir Walter had purchased the deed of The Harey Rabbit in her name.

She'd become quite emotional thinking about her parents and her father; John and Kate had given her love, kindness, and a belief that she was capable of doing anything she put her mind to: priceless gifts. Her father, distant but caring, had given her The Harey Rabbit.

Her vision began to blur and she blinked away the tears. She felt them run down her cheeks. Then she felt Sid's gentle touch as he wiped them away. "I swear, Sid. I know nothing of this silver button business."

"I believe you, Mary."

She drew him close and blinked away more tears. "Thank you."

Mary could have easily spent the rest of the afternoon in bed with Sid, but The Harey Rabbit required her art of diplomacy (patrons *and* staff). As they walked past the table in the downstairs living room, Sid suddenly remembered he'd discovered something about the silver button: that its engraving was not a sword and feather but rather a sword and *quill*. Hardly earth-shattering news, particularly in the context of *her* revelation.

He was perplexed by her reaction. "Don't you realise what this means?"

"The person who drew Gerald's poster has poor eyesight?" she quipped, but he didn't seem to find any amusement in it. Truth to tell, she really didn't want to think about the silver button; this last hour with Sid had been blissfully button free (apart from the ones that got her into his trousers). She smiled at the thought, then kissed him on his good cheek and whispered jokingly in his ear, "I suppose it could be a secret message."

His reaction was unexpected. He looked deadly serious as he said, "My thoughts exactly."

As Mary walked back to The Harey Rabbit, she began to feel uncomfortably hot and self-consciously sweaty. The mid-afternoon sun was baking the streets, and the silver button business was playing upon her mind. She tried to turn her thoughts to more positive things, like Sid and her together. It brought a happy smile, but there was still a fair bit of water to pass under *that* particular bridge. At least she had told him about Richard — the bridge seemed to have survived *that* raging torrent.

Richard... She felt she should speak to him, at least to find out what had happened at the castle, why this silver button was so important.

She entered The Harey Rabbit via the kitchen. The first thing she was going to do was have a bath. She couldn't remember the last time she'd had two in one day, but needs must. She couldn't serve the dainty and distinguished smelling like a copper-piece harlot.

Of course, the first person to flash into her field of vision *had* to be Juanita. "Ah, Meestress, you are back. Can you tell dee large cook woman to get her own water, por favor?"

"I assume you are referring to Patricia?" Mary was too hot and tired for petty squabbling.

"Si, Patreesha, dee water thief!"

Why did Juanita become more Icarumban when she was angry?

"Where *is* Patricia?" There was no-one in the kitchen — it was unusual, but understandable in this weather. The kitchen wasn't exactly a haven from the heat.

"She an' Leellian go to do sumteeng — she don' tell me. I send John to fetch dee water from dee well, seence Patreesha stole mine to make dee steam," she said, pointing at a couple of large fire-blackened pots simmering away atop the stove.

No wonder it was hot in here. Mary sighed; she didn't have the energy to deal with Juanita or Patricia, or anybody else. "I need a bath."

Juanita brightened. "I feex for you, Meestress."

"Thank you, Juanita," Mary said, gratefully, walking past her washer girl to retrieve a change of clothes. As she did, Juanita smiled at her, but it wasn't a 'happy to be of service' kind of smile; it was more of an 'I know what you've been up to' kind of smile. Mary blushed. *How* could she possibly know?

Mary couldn't remember enjoying a bath more. After thoroughly cleansing herself of sweat, grime and all traces of Sid — so that not even Juanita's sixth sense for the erotic would detect anything — Mary just soaked and luxuriated (to the relaxing sounds of Patricia and Juanita arguing about water: Juanita telling John to get her some more water; Patricia telling John to get *her* water first; John telling Juanita he didn't take orders from her; Juanita telling John that in Los Nachos she'd have a hundred men at her door *hoping* to be the one chosen to fill her bucket; and so on). She had told all her staff not to disturb her while she was bathing, to carry on as if she wasn't there, and, so far, they were doing just that.

Mary was about to submerge her head one last time when there was a knock at the door, followed by a quiet, "Sorry t'disturb you, Mistress."

It was Lillian.

If it had been any of the others, she would have told them to go away, but Lillian was sensible and level-headed (when she wasn't being dressed down by the Limpdickers). "What is it?"

"Um…" She seemed hesitant, as if being prompted by someone behind the door. "Sir Richard Upson is here."

"Richard?" Mary sat up in the bath.

"Says 'e'll wait for you in the private dining room."

Mary was already out of the bath.

# Chapter 21

## A much more agreeable choice

XAVIER'S MEMORY HADN'T returned — far from it — but if Olivia had been conducting experiments to retrieve it, she'd made what Xavier would call a breakthrough.

The recollection of the silver pendant had been the catalyst for other random memories; although, some of them seemed bizarre to say the least. The most puzzling of which was the description of his mentor, Horatio. According to Xavier, he had very pale skin, white hair and pink eyes. (He'd never actually described Horatio to her, but she wondered how he could've possibly omitted mentioning an oddity like that.)

He'd also mentioned something called a Sunwatcher and somebody called Butterfly (of all things). Bethany had become quite animated at this point and steered the conversation towards his time at Blessed Whipping. Olivia had no idea what the girl was on about, talking about the sun and other such nonsense.

Fortunately, she'd been able to rescue the situation by raising more pertinent issues, like the Duke. Xavier reacted by saying he thought Horatio knew the Duke, which was very encouraging. Olivia felt confident she'd set him on the path to recovering his memory.

They reached a point where Xavier had begged time to rest his mind. Bethany had been immediately solicitous, whereas Olivia thought they could make further progress. In the end, she'd agreed, albeit reluctantly, to give Xavier some time to collect his thoughts.

As it turned out, he'd been well within his rights to feel somewhat drained — when Olivia stepped upstairs, out of the cellar's candlelit gloom, she'd been surprised to find the day had progressed well into the afternoon.

The walk home was surprisingly pleasant. There was a breeze; it was warm, but at least there was some movement in the air, something to break up the stifling stillness. Olivia was in high spirits. Xavier was on the mend, which meant he'd soon be able to meet and treat his father.

Poor Marmaduke — she'd hardly spared him a thought over the last two days, except when trying to jog Xavier's memory. Gerald had said his condition seemed no different, but he *must* be deteriorating. If he was as delirious as Gerald said, he couldn't have eaten or drunk anything for almost four days now.

These thoughts carried her to the burnished brass plaque of 8 Plumduff Street, which now looked rather dim in the afternoon shadow. She wondered if her husband was home and, if so, whether his mood had improved. He'd been unusually agitated this morning and had looked most apprehensive when his clerk informed him that Richard wanted to see him.

She didn't have to wonder very long. As she stepped into the dull, stuffy entrance hall, Gerald's upbeat voice rang out from the back of the house.

"Olivia? Is that you, my sweet?"

His day had obviously ended better than it had begun; perhaps Marmaduke's condition had improved.

"Yes, Gerald," she replied, resisting the urge to respond with something sarcastic — the breakthrough with Xavier had also changed *her* mood for the better.

Her husband appeared at the other end of the hallway, smiling at her. He was still wearing his red coat, so he couldn't have been home long. "Been out for a stroll, m'dear? That's a nice dress. Is it new? I say, you won't believe what happened to Sir Richard today. Most amazing thing, really — the nobles demanded he step down as Seneschal. Oh, by the way, did you manage to get some more of that lavender-scented soap?"

Olivia was dumbfounded, but she wasn't sure what dumfounded her more — the fact that he'd announced that Richard was no longer Seneschal or that he'd followed up his ebullient revelation with a query about soap. And he was *actually* looking at her with an expectant smile. It was ridiculous, even by Gerald's standards.

"What do you mean, demanded he step down?" she said, finding her voice and marching down the hall. "Which nobles? And why?"

As she got within 'slapping-some-sense-into-him' range, he backed into the kitchen.

"I say, m'dear."

"Don't 'my dear' me, Gerald," she said, forcing him to retreat towards the kitchen table, all trace of tolerance gone. It was high time she found out what was happening at the castle. She'd been giving Gerald far too much leeway since Xavier's disappearance.

"There's no need to worry, m'... Olivia. It's actually very good news," he said, trying to calm her.

"Sit down," she ordered.

He plonked onto one of the four chairs that surrounded the kitchen table. She sat down opposite him. This time of day, the back of the house was filled with light, and Gerald's coat glowed, making his face look ruddier than it actually was. However, he still looked flushed. Perhaps he *was* flushed.

"Right, Gerald, I want you to tell me exactly what's happening at the castle: the whos, the whys, the wherefores and everything in between. And for mercy's sake, please stick to the *relevant* details."

"Very well, m'dear." He nodded, looking like he *had* taken in what she'd just said. She could only hope.

"Well," he said conspiratorially, leaning across the table towards her, "the silver button belongs to Sir Richard."

He was looking at her expectantly; she had no idea how to respond. "What silver button?"

"Come now, m'dear," he said, taken aback. "Surely you remember me telling you?"

Yes, now that she thought about it, she did vaguely remember him mentioning something about a silver button, but, for some reason, it hadn't registered as being significant. Gerald certainly hadn't made a song and dance about it, as he usually did with things he thought important. In any case, she had been consumed by Xavier's disappearance.

"I had to re-write Saturday's proclamation," he continued, attempting to prod her memory.

"Yes, I remember *that*, Gerald," she said evenly. Olivia vetted and amended all his proclamations before he submitted them to Marmaduke and Richard for their endorsement (or, as Gerald referred to it, the Okay to Oyez). She'd even *written* them on a number of occasions. On *this* occasion, however, Gerald had circumvented both her *and* Richard — obviously Marmaduke had been in no state to endorse anything — and, for the first time she could remember, delivered his *own* proclamation.

"Are you suggesting *Richard* had something to do with the attack on Marmaduke?" It was almost said in jest; the idea was so ridiculous.

"Some of the *nobles* believe so. And I must say, I wouldn't put it past him. His behaviour before *and* after the attack has been rather questionable to say the least."

This was too much. She wouldn't credit such an announcement were it made by someone with a modicum of credibility, let alone her fanciful husband — it beggared belief. "Questionable? In what way? And to which nobles are you referring? And how does this silver button—"

She stopped herself from airing all the questions that had suddenly popped into her head. She took a deep breath to clear her thoughts.

Gerald's voice quickly filled the void. "I say, Olivia, it makes me wonder if you ever listen to me at all. I have told you on many occasions this past week of my misgivings regarding Sir Richard and his attitude towards Xavier and the Duke."

*Yes, but if only you weren't such an incompetent fool,* she wanted to shout. Instead, she conceded, "Very well, I may have been less than attentive these past few days — my mind has been elsewhere — but you *have* my attention now."

Gerald's indignation transformed into a sympathetic smile. He reached out to take her hand. She quickly clasped her hands together and sat up straight.

It had the desired effect; Gerald leant back in his chair, more in acceptance than disappointment.

"Perhaps if you start at the beginning."

"Very well."

He then proceeded to tell her of the events involving Sir Richard since Xavier's disappearance. He began with the *Five at Five* meeting almost four days ago, and how animated Marmaduke had been about the Duke of Stymouth's visit.

"I assumed Sir Richard had told him about Xavier," he said, "but when I approached Sir Richard after the meeting, he seemed rather bewildered by the Duke's behaviour and scoffed at my suggestion that the Duke was upbeat because of his son. If you recall, m'dear, my *original* Saturday proclamation was full of wondrous details of the castle preparations, rallying Lower Icingers to embrace the Duke of Stymouth's visit."

Olivia nodded. In truth, she only had a vague recollection of the content — she had been far too concerned about Xavier — but her impression of it had been underwhelming to say the least; it was about as wondrous as manure. Still, she remembered giving *this* version of Saturday's proclamation her Okay to Oyez.

That night, the Duke had been attacked (and so had Xavier), his body discovered just after first light on Saturday morning by his squire, one Bradley Lamb. Of course, at the time, both she and Gerald were unaware this had occurred. In fact, Gerald had been quite chipper on Saturday morning. He'd even welcomed *Sid* into the house (knowing that she strongly objected to him having anything to do with her brother). He was recalling that particular moment right now.

"As you know, m'dear, Sid's visit delayed me by some fifteen minutes or so."

"Yes, I've been meaning to talk to you about that," she said, suddenly realising there had been quite a bit going on in Gerald's life that she hadn't involved herself in — she'd being worrying about a man who *mattered*. It was a heartless thought — even *she* recognised that — but, unfortunately, it was the truth. A despairing sigh escaped from her mouth.

Gerald mistook the sigh for annoyance. "I say, I really don't see how you can despise your brother so. He's an amiable chap, and the poor fellow has been assaulted quite badly, yet you treat him with—"

"Gerald! We've had this discussion on many occasions. How many times do I have to repeat myself? What happened between Sid and I is in the past, and I intend to *keep it there*. As far as I am concerned, my amiable brother is nothing more than a waster with his head in an ale mug!"

"Well, *he* obviously doesn't feel the same way." His tone had turned defensive. "If you must know, the reason for Sid's visit was your birthday; he asked me if I had any suggestions for a gift."

Olivia was speechless. Then she laughed at the absurdity of it all. "Gerald, that is quite possibly the most unbelievable thing I have ever heard you say and, believe me, *that* is saying something."

Gerald didn't share her amusement at all. "Be that as it may, it was what he wanted. And, since we are being completely honest, I also met him for a post-proclamation drink at The Harey Rabbit."

Her husband wore an expression of defiance, something that only reared its unattractive head when she pushed him too far. Very well, she thought, let him have his little backbone moment. Whatever his reason for drinking with her good-for-nothing brother, it had little bearing on Xavier or the Duke.

"I see... clearly *that* establishment's standards are slipping. Perhaps you should curtail your Saturday afternoon visits."

He regarded her for a moment — a pained look in his eyes, a soft shake of his head — before continuing his account. "Sid's visit here meant I was a tad late arriving at the castle on Saturday morning. Still, if I hadn't been, I would not have run into Doctor Whysman." His gaze turned inward. "Time and chance, m'dear: two things we cannot guard against."

He then proceeded to tell her how he'd met Doctor Whysman striding down, in some haste, from the Upper Bailey. He was quite flustered and appeared relieved to see Gerald. (Olivia doubted that, but kept silent.) He was on his way to retrieve some herbs from his residence — the Duke had been attacked and poisoned.

"It was quite a shock, as you could well imagine, m'dear. I asked him if the Duke's life was in danger. He said he didn't know, but that his condition seemed stable. Then he asked me if I wouldn't mind doing him a service. He handed me a silver button, saying that he'd found it clasped in the Duke's hand, and could I please give it to Sir Richard as soon as possible, that he'd tried himself, but the guards told him Sir Richard was not to be disturbed. Well, m'dear, I obliged him, of course."

"Why on Earth did he give it to *you*?" The doctor's mind must have been addled.

Gerald bristled at her incredulity. "It may have escaped your notice recently, but I *am* the Town Crier. I do hold *some* sway over the matters that affect the people of Lower Icing."

Olivia tried not to scoff. She didn't want to set him off on a tangent about his 'important responsibilities'. Then she remembered one of those important responsibilities had taken place earlier that afternoon: the 'Tuesday at Two' proclamation. She'd forgotten about it; she and Bethany had been immersed in the retrieval of Xavier's memory. For a second time, Gerald had not sought her Okay to Oyez, which was worrying. "And what matters affecting the people did you hold sway over at The Square today?"

An expression of smugness formed on her husband's face (something Olivia rarely ever saw). "If you'll allow me, m'dear, I think it best if I continue this *succinct* account of my fortuitous meeting with Doctor Whysman; wouldn't want to be accused of waffling, what."

He wouldn't want to push *that* attitude, but she managed to hold her tongue as he continued.

"I assured Doctor Whysman that I'd give the button to Sir Richard. He was most relieved and asked me to treat what he'd just divulged with the utmost discretion."

"Yet you decided to divulge it to the population of Lower Icing."

She couldn't resist the jibe. "*Most* discreet of you, Gerald."

"I had to do *something*. Sir Richard had sealed off the Duke's quarters and the guards refused to let me pass, even though I told them I was in possession of important evidence. Prestwich was nowhere to be found, nor was anyone else of worth. I wasn't about to pass the button on to some minor official. I even tried the barracks, but they were virtually empty — officers and men were already undertaking a search of the castle and Lower Icing."

"Gerald, I don't require a blow-by-blow account of your poor decision-making. Let's take it as read that all relevant parties were otherwise engaged. Am I to assume that you took matters into your own hands?"

Gerald flushed. "Well, if you must know, the inspiration behind my actions was Klob Hoofenhaus."

She was so taken aback that she thought she must have misheard him. "Did you say *Klob Hoofenhaus?*"

He nodded.

She still couldn't believe it. "Klob Hoofenhaus… the *blacksmith?*"

He nodded. "You must understand, I had—"

"Taken leave of your senses! What? Why on…?" She had no words; the situation was too ridiculous. Just when she thought her husband could not sink any lower in her expectations… Olivia shook her head; surely, this was some sort of jest.

"Obviously Klob was aware there was an intruder in the castle. I must have looked rather at a loss, searching the deserted barracks, because he stopped working and asked if I required assistance, which is very unlike our esteemed blacksmith. I told to him I had important information regarding the intruder. I revealed nothing about the button, my dear. However, he made me feel quite self-conscious; cuts a rather foreboding presence, does our blacksmith."

Hardly a difficult feat, Olivia thought; a *milkmaid* cut a foreboding presence when standing next to her husband. She wondered where he could possibly go with this.

"Then he said in his thick accent: 'In Longboatia, important news is shared amongst clan. We forge many swords with one hammer blow, not like here in Lower Icingk.'"

He looked at her as if his badly mimicked words explained everything.

"Well, of course, Gerald; no *wonder* you were inspired to scribe your proclamation after hearing such enlightening words."

He ignored her sarcasm. "I don't know how to explain it to you, m'dear.

However, by the time I'd walked back to my office, the idea of actually rewriting the proclamation had begun to take hold. Klob was right: the more people who knew… Well, it could only help in capturing the Duke's attacker. I thought *someone* might recognise the button."

Olivia sighed as she shook her head. "Oh, Gerald."

"Well, you are always telling me to use my initiative, be more assertive, don't you know. And I do believe it's all worked out rather well. Sir Richard has been asked to step down — rightly so in my opinion — *and* I did not betray Doctor Whysman's confidence. I mentioned *nothing* about the Duke being attacked or poisoned. In fact, I made a point of saying the Duke was unharmed."

So, he'd arbitrarily chosen which facts to share with the populace, and, in the process, thrown into doubt the future of the man destined to be the next Duke of Lower Icing. It didn't take the mind of a siege-engineer to work out why Richard was being asked to step down as Seneschal — nothing like an identifiable button found in the hand of the victim to arouse suspicion. However, like the markings in *Poetry In Potion*, it all seemed a bit obvious to Olivia. "Well, Gerald, let's hope the Seneschal is forgiving of your motives when he's reinstated."

"I will cross that bridge *if* I reach it, m'dear. The nobles seem quite pleased with their new Acting Seneschal. He was appointed this afternoon — a unanimous decision apparently — and I must say I already find him a *much* more agreeable choice. I think Sir Richard may find it hard to win back the support of the nobles even if he *is* found innocent of any wrong-doing."

That was interesting. She couldn't imagine Richard yielding the role of Seneschal easily, or to just anyone. "So, who did the nobles appoint?" *Probably some spineless inbred,* she thought. Someone they could manipulate.

Gerald looked fit to burst. "A man of impeccable character: Captain Paris Le Sharp."

Olivia's stomach lurched. Paris was Seneschal… *her* Paris.

"I say, m'dear, are you alright? You've gone quite pale."

She heard herself gasp out, "I'm fine." But she wasn't fine. The man she loved, the man she should be with, *would* have been with if not for Sid, had become Seneschal. She felt sick.

"Olivia?"

She stood up. She couldn't listen to Gerald's voice anymore. "Excuse me. I need some air."

She watched him stand. He looked concerned. "M'dear," he said, reaching towards her. "Are you sure you're—?"

Olivia turned away from her husband and walked out to the back garden. Fortunately, he didn't follow her.

## CHAPTER 22

# *A delicious moment of anticipation*

ANYONE STUMBLING ACROSS their campsite would be met with a relaxed scene: a party of three sitting lazily around a smouldering campfire dappled in late afternoon gold, the remains of a roasted goat skewered over a makeshift spit.

Ophelia felt like sleeping. The goat had sated her hunger and now her body craved rest. Her pa, propped up against the trunk of the nearby oak, was already asleep. His condition had continued to improve. He'd been conscious for most of the afternoon and was even able to partake in the feast of roasted goat. Unfortunately, he hadn't been able to relay much of what had happened to him at The Pits — just snippets of memory. He knew the Moleson Twins had been there; he remembered holding a knife at Mal's throat. And there was a man called The Slasher, who ran The Pits, and someone else whose name he couldn't recall, but he remembered this someone had trouble untying his bindings. However, he had no memory of whether they'd revealed any details regarding the doctor.

Ophelia could feel herself drifting into sleep. As much as she felt like succumbing, she knew she had to make another trip to the spring, and she wanted to do it before the evening gloom set in. "I'll go fetch some water," she announced, standing. She felt groggy, but she knew it would pass.

Tom regarded her with a bemused expression. "Would you like a hand?"

Yes, she bloody well would, but she didn't want Tom thinking of her as frail and needy. Still, she'd proven herself by skinning and gutting the goat; Tom had complimented her, saying that *he* couldn't have done a better job. Now that she thought about it, she bloody well deserved a hand. "Only if y'ain't got nothin' better t'do."

He smiled. "Well since your pa's sleeping off the exertion of eating, it seems I *do* have nothing better to do."

"Seems tha' way t'me too."

Tom sprang to his feet. He was so energetic — the heat and the environment appeared to have no effect on him. This was Ophelia's fourth trip to the spring and she no longer needed Tom's markers to help her find the way. She was beginning to *see* the way: 'landmark' trees and recognisable bushes, patches of disturbed ground from their previous trips, even certain smells as they approached the dank terrain of the ravine.

Leading the way, carrying Tom's two large water-skins, Ophelia was already feeling revived; even her saddle-soreness was now only a minor irritation. Walking amongst the lush undergrowth, immersed in a sea of trees, with only their footfalls breaking the green silence, it seemed as if she and Tom were the only people left in the Five Duchies. It was strangely exhilarating, even magical. Ophelia would have never imagined feeling this way about being in a forest. And she certainly never imagined she'd be feeling it because of Lower Icing's Gamekeeper. They'd shared a drunken night together, but it had been under unusual circumstances: the stress of Billy being locked up in The Can, the heat, drinking with the nobs, and the fact that he'd actually listened to what she had to say.

Now everything seemed different. Her pa was safe because of him. He'd taken care of her and treated her with respect — more than any man had ever done outside her family. Just like the forest, she was beginning to see him in a new light.

Her thoughts became words, cutting through the footfalls. "So why'ja do this, Tom?"

There was pause before the voice behind her answered. "Do what, exactly?"

"Come lookin' for me pa. I know Sir Richard didn' wan' ya to."

A longer pause followed. She was about to turn around, but he finally found his words. "Duty to the Duchy."

She waited for him to continue, but only the sound of his leather boots followed.

Duty to the bloody Duchy. "Is tha' it?" she asked, almost to herself.

"What were you expecting me to say?"

Good question — what *was* she expecting him to say.

"I didn't do it for your father, Ophelia. I'd be lying if said as much."

She felt her heart drop. She hadn't expected him to say anything noble about her father, but possibly — stupidly — she was hoping that *she* had had something to do with his decision.

"I see," she whispered.

Ophelia had barely taken another step when she felt hands clamp down on her shoulders and swing her around. The forest swirled and then disappeared behind Tom's two-day-stubble. His blue eyes glowed in the deep green of the canopy, searching her face. She stood, momentarily transfixed, mesmerised by his eyes, drawn to him by the gentle pressure on her shoulders. A tangle of sandy hair fell forward as he bowed his head towards her, his lips parting, eyes closing. Ophelia mirrored Tom's actions, and the delicious moment of anticipation ended in a passionate meeting of mouths.

## CHAPTER 23

## *Chateaux Defeat*

MARY SAT IN her room, brushing through waves of dark hair, preparing herself for the evening crowd. The afternoon shadows had crossed the courtyard to the stables, leaving only the top half of the out-building washed in coppery sun. She'd lit a candle to see herself clearly in the mirror. As she brushed, she studied her reflection. She looked presentable, as she always did, but her hair was lifeless and there was tiredness in her eyes which had nothing to do with the running of The Harey Rabbit. The events of the last few days were beginning to take their toll. The attack on Sid had shocked and worried her. However, the visit from Richard had set her nerves on edge…

Mary had entered the private dining room in a rushed state of presentation: her hair was tied into a haphazard bun, still wet from the bath. She'd quickly put on a black working dress, its bodice fastened so quickly that the shoulder sat slightly askew, but her feet remained uncovered. She hadn't seen her brother for at least three months, and he never arrived without *some* fore-warning.

The dining room was located at the other end from the kitchen, next to Mary's bedroom. It was reserved for private meetings or functions — the guild of merchants used it for their monthly get-togethers, the Limpdickers had the occasional private dinner, and she'd even hosted soirées for the castle-set. Richard, however, had never deigned to partake of his sister's hospitality.

The dining room had no windows, just a few ventilation holes near the top of the wall. Her parents had used it as a store room, but after Kate and John died, Mary had decided to rejuvenate The Harey Rabbit. She'd redecorated, reconfigured and reassessed how she wanted the inn to work, and part of the rejuvenation included creating a space where people could meet or entertain privately. The fact that the room had no windows made it ideal for the purpose, and, as it turned out, it had been a most profitable decision.

Richard was standing at the far end of the large oak table with his back to the door, his arms at his side and the fingers of his left hand flexing. He was agitated about something, or perhaps just impatient at being made to wait.

He turned smoothly to face her; his familiar patronising smile was paired with an appraising gaze. She immediately felt self-conscious, quickly positioning an errant lock of hair behind her ear.

"Hello, Richard. Sorry to keep you waiting. I was just freshening myself for the dinner crowd."

He smiled indulgently as she pushed the door shut behind her. "Not at all, Mary. No doubt the dinner crowd have high expectations of your freshness."

What did he mean by *that*? "It's more a case of setting a high standard," she said, pointedly. "In that, at least, we were born of the same yolk."

He nodded and smiled wryly. "It is good to see you, Mary."

"Thank you, Richard." She returned his smile. Reaching his side, she added, "It's a surprise to see *you*."

"Today is a day for surprises." There was little mirth in his black eyes.

So, the usual game of double meanings and half-truths was about to begin; Mary wasn't sure whether she had enough energy to play.

"Shall we be seated?" he said, pulling out a chair for her.

She flushed with embarrassment — the guest was offering the hostess a chair. Richard *excelled* at being charmingly disarming.

Mary made no move to sit; the hostess had been awakened. "I was about to ask if you required any refreshment before we settled ourselves."

"Very well, perhaps one of your fine Escargotian wines," he said almost dismissively, then his eyes focused on hers. "Whichever you deem best complements deceit and treachery."

Mary fetched a bottle of *Le Coq Rouge*, a fifteen-year-old red from the Chatonnay region of Escargotia, which, at two gold pieces, was one of her most expensive wines. If Richard was impressed by her choice, he kept it to himself, but he smiled ruefully when he saw the red cockerel seal on the neck of the bottle.

"Puts me in mind of our Town Crier; he's another puffed-up creature who thinks his red coat is a license to disturb the peace with inane noise."

It was an odd thing for Richard to say, and there was a touch of rancour in his tone. He grabbed the bottle and filled two goblets with the dark red liquid. Mary winced inwardly at the callous treatment of the *Le Coq Rouge*: the wine should have been decanted and allowed to breathe, then tasted and appreciated.

"Has Gerald done something wrong?" she enquired as he took a large swig from his goblet.

Finishing his mouthful, he replied, "The man is a buffoon."

"Surely *that* is not news to you."

This brought about another rueful smile. "News…" he mused. "Your choice of wine and words has been impeccable today."

She really wasn't in the mood for intrigue and insinuation. "Please, Richard, just tell me what has brought you here. Obviously something is amiss, otherwise you wouldn't—"

"The Duke has been attacked with a poisoned blade and I am no longer Seneschal."

He said it so matter-of-factly that Mary wondered if he was jesting, but as she searched his face, she could see he spoke the simple truth. She could only stare while he drained his goblet, unable to voice the thoughts that were racing through her head: how, when, why… Then realisation… "Is the Duke dead?"

"No." He poured himself another wine. "He lives… just."

"But… why are you no longer Seneschal?"

He shook his head and smiled, drained his second goblet of *Le Coq Rouge*, then went on to explain the events that had led to his appearance at The Harey Rabbit.

Early on Saturday morning, the Duke had been discovered lying unconscious on his bed with a knife wound to the upper arm. Doctor Whysman had been summoned, and Richard immediately sealed the Upper Bailey. The doctor arrived in good time. However, he could not begin his assessment because the squire, who'd discovered the Duke, was in a state of shock and refused to leave his side. Richard knocked him unconscious and had him carried out of the chamber. Doctor Whysman was then able to confirm what Richard already knew: the Duke had been poisoned. Judging by the dark blood stains on the bed and the coagulation of the wound, the attack had occurred some hours before — late Friday night was the doctor's guess. Richard left the doctor to administer to the Duke; no purpose was served watching the man go through his process of elimination and guesswork. His duty lay in finding the person responsible. He met with the Captain of the Guard, Paris Le Sharp, to co-ordinate a search of the grounds and increase security throughout the castle. During this time, the squire, Bradley Lamb, regained consciousness. He was questioned by Richard, who had left orders not to be disturbed save for news of change in the Duke's condition.

He sighed and poured the last drops of *Le Coq Rouge* into his goblet. "That order turned out to be my downfall. Then again, when fate conspires against you, I'm not sure any action can change an outcome."

"Shall I fetch some more wine?" Mary asked out of habit.

Richard shook his head and flicked his hand in a dismissive motion. The gesture filled Mary with chagrin. She'd interrupted him in the middle of his recounting; he must think her extremely rude  or, worse, a woman not able to grasp the gravity of the situation. "Your pardon, Richard; please continue." Then, wanting to assure him that she *was* absorbing his words, she added, "Obviously matters unfolded without you being made aware. Did the Town Crier do something foolish?"

"Ha! That takes the prize-winning cake for understatement!"

He then revealed that Doctor Whysman had found the silver button clasped in the Duke's hand. He'd tried to inform Richard, but Richard was questioning the squire and had given the order not to be disturbed.

On his way back home to retrieve some herbs, the doctor had run into the Town Crier and had entrusted *him* with giving the button to Richard. However, the Town Crier, puffed up with his own importance, had kept the button and displayed it to the populace during his proclamation, where he not only fabricated events but posted a likeness of the button in the news stand and offered a reward of one hundred gold pieces. Richard had been none the wiser until later that afternoon.

Mary, of course, had heard the news soon after Gerald's proclamation: the theories, the amount of the reward, and the man himself reiterating his version of events. However, Mary hadn't paid much heed to Gerald; her attention had been diverted by his roguish drinking companion.

Now she felt sick. The silver button had suddenly taken on a far greater significance. It was no longer the button of an intruder; it was the button of a potential murderer. She felt even more conflicted.

"Richard... I—"

"Mary," he said, cutting across her indecision. "The silver button was mine."

"Yours?" That couldn't be true; it made no sense. "Are you sure?"

"Well, of course I'm sure!" he snapped. "Do you think I would say such a thing otherwise?"

"No. It's just that…" If the button was Richard's, no *wonder* he was upset with Gerald. "How did it come to be clasped in the Duke's hand?"

"Ah… therein lies the mystery." He smiled bitterly. "The button itself is easy to explain; it was loosened the day before in an altercation with Frank Offcut. No doubt it was pulled off during the fracas with Squire Lamb, but how it found its way into Marmaduke's *hand*…" He sighed. "Perhaps I *will* have some more wine."

*It*, thought Mary. "So, you are only missing *one* button?"

He frowned at her and held out the left sleeve of his black doublet, "As you can see, I still am."

Sure enough, there was an obvious gap in the row of silver buttons that lined the sleeve. There should have been four, but the second button from the cuff was missing. Even in the dim candlelight, Mary could make out the quill and sword etching — there was no doubt these buttons were the same as the one she'd found in Sid's pouch. But how?

"Satisfied I speak the truth, Mary?" he said, resting his arm back on the table.

She nodded… But, if what he said *was* true, where had the silver button in Sid's pouch come from? And why was it planted there? Someone was obviously desperate enough to knock him senseless… but… it just didn't make sense.

Mary returned with another bottle of wine — this time, a less expensive but well-regarded vintage from a town called Crushing Defeat in the Southern Vales of Naffolk. She'd already removed the cork and, before sitting down, filled both goblets with the rich red hue of *Chateaux Defeat*.

As she poured, Richard enquired if something was amiss. "You seem distracted."

"Well, it's not every day your esteemed brother drops by to tell you he's suspected of poisoning the Duke," she said flippantly, but in truth her mind was racing. What to say about Sid? She looked up to find him staring at her, his dark eyes appraising. "I take it you didn't willingly step down as Seneschal," Mary added, trying to deflect his gaze.

It brought a sardonic smile. "Let's just say I have relinquished the epithet… for the time being." He picked up his goblet, tested the wine's nose, then swallowed a delicate mouthful. His gaze turned to the bottle. Again he seemed bemused by what he saw. "A wine from Crushing Defeat. Excellent choice, Mary."

Mary ignored the jibe. Richard then went on to explain how, for the last four days, they had been searching in vain for the assailant, and as each fruitless day passed by, the nobles had become more and more sceptical that there had actually been an intruder. In fact, they felt it was more likely the assailant was known to the Duke, perhaps even knew the Duke well. "I can appreciate their point of view, but I have reason to believe external forces are at work here."

"Have you any suspects?" Mary asked, hopefully sounding matter-of-fact. *Should* she tell him about Sid… about Doctor Manky?

"I'd rather not discuss that with you, Mary. Suffice to say there is a specific individual who is central to our enquiries."

A specific individual? According to Tom Skinner, Frank Offcut had been assisting the Purple Peril in their search for a 'specific individual'. Then she'd overheard the two guards talking about the search for a young doctor.

"So, the silver button has no significance to your search?"

Richard's left eyebrow arched. "Is there something you'd like to share with me?"

Mary sighed.

Then she told him about Sid, about the *other* silver button, about Doctor Manky, about Tom and Frank Offcut, and even about the guards. Throughout her explanation, Richard's expression barely changed: a slight furrowing of the brow, a soft pursing of the lips and a narrowing of the eyes were his only outward signs of emotion. His silent, appraising gaze and stony demeanour made her feel very self-conscious, and she found herself spilling out more and more information.

"I see," he said after she'd finished spilling.

"I'm sorry I didn't tell you sooner, it's just that—"

"You were waiting for the right moment? How fortuitous I decided to visit at such an opportune time."

"Richard, I—"

He waved a dismissive hand at her. "As it turns out, what you have told me changes very little. If anything, it reinforces my suspicions. Although, I am surprised at Tom's loose tongue."

"I'm to blame for that."

"Really? I fail to see how that's possible. As long as I have known Tom, he's chosen his words most carefully. Perhaps his tongue was loosened by the thought of gallivanting off with the irrepressible Ophelia Offcut."

"Ophelia Offcut?" Mary was incredulous. So *that's* who the other horse was for.

"Tom's always had a soft heart for wild creatures." Richard took another swig of his wine. Then, as if thinking out loud, he added, "Still, if they find Frank alive, he may prove useful."

He said it so casually, as if Lower Icing's butcher was no more important than one of his pigs. It shocked Mary. Frank Offcut was not a particularly likeable man, but, even so, his life was worth more than any information he might have about the Duke's attacker.

"Do you think the Moleson Twins might have actually killed Frank Offcut?"

"According to Ophelia, they were seen leaving The Pits with Frank's body draped over a horse — not exactly a promising sign. Mind you, *her* source is hardly what I'd call reliable."

Mary shook her head. "Poor Frank."

Richard took another swig of Chateaux Defeat. "So, this Sid character, Mary…" It sounded like an accusation. "You say he is the Town Crier's brother-in-law; I didn't realise he had one."

"He's Olivia's brother," Mary supplied.

"Really?" he said, sounded mildly curious. "I seem to have some vague recollection he'd been killed years ago, falling from a roof."

"That is something *she* has perpetuated. They're… estranged."

Richard nodded, but his expression was dubious. "Well, it matters not whether Sid is who he claims to be, but rather the company he keeps."

Mary reacted defensively. "Sid is a victim in this, Richard."

"Aren't we all," he countered. "The point is, Mary, I *will* discover the truth behind the attack on the Duke. As I said, there are things at play which I am not prepared to discuss with you."

"What about this Doctor Manky?" Mary blurted.

"I know who he is. Though why he decided upon such a covert course of action is beyond me. He could have simply…"

A few seconds of silence followed, with Mary thinking Richard was going to continue with his thoughts, while Richard said nothing.

Mary broke the silence. "So, he's not the doctor your guards were talking about?"

"Guards," he scoffed, followed by more silence.

"Well?" she pressed.

"No."

"So what doctor *were* they talking about?"

"At this stage, the fewer people who know the—"

"Does he have anything to do with Sid's beating?" Mary interrupted, becoming fed up with her brother's obfuscation.

Richard stared at her, as if considering what he should reveal. "Mary, let me make this perfectly clear: my priority is the Duke's wellbeing. If you want to talk about victims, I think you'll agree that his need is greatest."

Mary flushed at his admonishment. "You're right, Richard; it is a terrible thing that has happened."

Richard nodded, seemingly satisfied with her contrition. "As for Sid's attacker," he added, "I assure you I have no idea who is behind that, although the silver button is an interesting development."

"Development? I thought you said—"

His eyes narrowed.

She sighed. "Very well, Richard; keep your secrets."

"Which brings me nicely to the reason for my visit — not that your company hasn't been most pleasant and… enlightening."

"Delighted to be of service," she replied.

"I require the use of this room tomorrow evening."

"I see…" It was a bit of an anti-climax, truth be told. "Well, of course, Richard; what do you require?"

He leant back in his chair, taking on a more casual pose. "Just the hospitality of The Harey Rabbit and some privacy. There will be six of us in all. Is that agreeable to you?"

Mary nodded. "Will you be six *gentlemen*?"

A wry smile played across his face as he reached for the bottle of *Chateaux Defeat.* "I will share *one* thing with you, Mary." He topped up Mary's goblet, refilled his, and then raised it. Mary acknowledged the gesture by doing the same. Touching his goblet to hers, he finished with, "*This* is the closest I ever intend to come to tasting defeat."

Richard's play on words brought a brief smile to the face reflected in the mirror, and she hoped his assertion was more than just bravado.

Mary opened the top drawer of her dressing table and pulled out a sapphire-blue ribbon. It was her only concession to fashion. Her clothes were made for working: hard-wearing, comfortable, and black or dark grey to hide the stains. Still, it didn't bother her; she wasn't a fashion sort of person. She'd served enough of the preening castle-set to know their fine clothes were a thin and fragile façade — pretty eggshells containing yolks of distrust and insecurity.

She used the ribbon to tie back her hair. Then she applied a small amount of rouge to her cheeks; not something she usually did, but it put some life into her face. However, it did nothing to improve the way she was feeling. She was tired and stressed, caught in the middle of two men, both victims of violent acts: one directly, the other indirectly; one physical, the other in reputation. However, both acts revolved around the appearance of a silver button. Her mind whirled just thinking about it.

Mary reached over to her scent bottles and chose one that was redolent of roses. She dabbed it on her wrists and neck. Tomorrow, The Harey Rabbit would have to do without her front of house; Richard had been most insistent that she serve his gathering personally, that no-one else should enter the room, stressing the future of the Duchy could well depend upon what was discussed. Tonight, however, she had a crowd of expectant patrons to attend to.

## CHAPTER 24
# *A need for retribution*

**O**LIVIA WAS SITTING at the desk in their den, a single candle barely illuminating the desktop. She could feel the oppressive presence of six years' worth of proclamations looming over her right shoulder, the twice-weekly account of her husband's prowess as Town Crier stacked chronologically on shelves. To Olivia, it was a twice-weekly reminder of how little she'd settled for. The man she would have been with if not for the villainous pursuits of her selfish brother was now the Seneschal of Lower Icing. *That* revelation had been the last straw; after six years of being weighed down by Gerald's inadequacies, something inside her had snapped.

She'd left him in the kitchen and headed for the relative privacy of the summer garden situated at the end of the backyard. It consisted of a birch tree surrounded by the pink, white, blue and purple hues of blossoming hydrangeas and petunias; although, the normally vibrant blooms were looking rather frazzled. On the far side of the tree, two chairs were set around a small table. On the other side of the setting, the high corner walls created a sense of seclusion. Gerald used it more than she did; he liked to read outdoors and sometimes contemplated the content of his proclamations there. On this occasion, the summer garden had been a place of emotional release; pent up anger and frustration flowed through her silent tears. It wasn't, as she'd thought it might be, an emotional cleansing; it turned out to be more of a clarification process, one which left her *more* resentful (if that was possible).

Olivia's resentment, however, was not directed towards Gerald; as much as he annoyed and frustrated her, he was who he was. In a way, she felt sorry for him. He would have been much happier with someone else, someone more simple-minded, happy to play the goodwife. If only she hadn't caught his eye, and he hadn't caught her at her most vulnerable, they both would have lived more contented lives.

No, it was Sid — he was the one who'd caused her life to turn out this way. Even after all these years — no, *because* of all these years — the bitterness had remained and… festered.

The den was silent, as was the entire house. Gerald had finally retired for the evening. They'd barely spoken after Olivia's return from the summer garden, but she'd made an effort to reassure him that all was well, that it was just the stuffiness of the kitchen and the heated conversation that had left her short of breath. As usual, he accepted what she told him at face value, and she'd been just as willing to accept his suggestion that they resume their conversation tomorrow morning. "We're both hot and bothered, m'dear," he'd said. "And, in any case, I feel I have shared with you the most pertinent details surrounding events at the castle. Who knows what lies ahead. If only Xavier hadn't disappeared, all would be well. The Duke… alas, who could have foreseen this happening." He'd looked oddly introspective, and Olivia had experienced a rare feeling of empathy towards her husband; he had been right about time and chance. She stared at her ghostly reflection in the den's window — six and a half years ago, both had conspired against her…

Back then, Olivia and Sid had shared a house on Backflush Lane: a cramped street of twenty terraced dwellings located a block away from The Pits on the castle side. Castle-side… she smiled bitterly to herself; being thought of as a castle-sider had been quite important to her — there was a certain amount of esteem associated with the epithet (well, at least from the villagers who lived north-side). It was also safer; the men-at-arms tended not to patrol as much north of The Pits.

She'd inherited the house at just fourteen years of age; her mother had finally drunk herself to death after her father had run off four years earlier. She'd been left to raise her nine-year-old brother. It was a task she had taken to with purpose, vigour and determination, and it had proven to be both rewarding and fulfilling, because Sid had been a most willing and able student. By the time of his twenty-first birthday, he had worked his way into Castle Administration. It was the perfect foundation for a career in commerce or politics. She'd even instilled in him the necessary refinement and social graces required to interact with the noble class. She could not have been prouder. Then she'd stumbled across a massive stash of gold coins hidden under the floorboards of his bedroom, and her world had turned upside down. She'd invested over ten years of her life giving him the best opportunity to become successful and socially accepted, and he had repaid her with a cache of ill-gotten gains.

It took Olivia three days of soul searching to decide what to do. There was no question of keeping the money (as Sid wanted), nor was she going to leave Lower Icing and use the money to set up somewhere else (as Sid suggested). No, she'd decided she would 'discover' it in the alleyway that ran behind their home and report it to the authorities or, more precisely, to Captain Paris Le Sharp... Paris...

Her reflection in the window blurred as her eyes began to fill with tears; the memory of Paris was all too clear, even though she'd managed to avoid seeing him for almost six years.

Her heart had literally skipped a beat when she'd first laid eyes on the dashing man. It had been a mild, mid-February morning, and Olivia had just entered the West Gate of the castle on her way to see Sid. As she turned towards the Administration Section of the Lower Bailey, she couldn't help but notice the resplendent figure in purple and gold walking towards her — he'd gleamed against the dull grey backdrop of the castle and winter sky. Olivia hadn't been able to take her eyes of him as he approached; his upright bearing and confident gait had mesmerised her. As he passed by, he'd smiled and doffed his gold-plumed cavalier's hat. Olivia's heart had started to pound, and suddenly she'd felt quite light-headed. She'd stopped and turned back to look at the man who'd had such an effect on her, only to find that he'd also stopped and was gazing back at her. He'd then retraced his steps, introduced himself, and enquired, most charmingly, after her name.

A trickle ran down her left cheek. Damn it all! She didn't *want* to remember. Her life had been bearable a week ago, before Xavier had appeared out of nowhere, before she'd felt moved and inspired for the first time since Paris had swept her off her feet.

Paris was exactly the kind of man she'd hoped Sid would eventually become: strong-minded, impeccably mannered, commanding and considerate. He'd escorted her to dinners at the Upper Baily, taken her on jaunts in the countryside, invited her to fencing competitions, and treated her like she was the only woman in the Five Duchies he wanted to be with.

Then, three months into their courtship, she'd been forced — by the disreputable activities of her brother — to come to him with her fabricated story about a cache of gold. Upon seeing it for himself, he'd been amazed, but seemingly accepting of her version of events. He hadn't pressed her (or Sid) for details, but he *had* assured her that a discovery of such importance would be investigated thoroughly. Olivia had felt terrible about lying to him, but she had no choice — she couldn't betray Sid.

Sid! She slapped her hand down angrily on the desktop, catching the edge of a parchment and knocking it to the floor. She bent and retrieved it. The script hadn't smudged; the letter was still intact.

After the return of the money, Olivia had noticed a subtle change in her relationship with Paris; nothing she could put her finger on, he just seemed more… formal, or *regimented*, in his demeanour. On the occasions she'd asked him if anything was amiss, he'd shrugged away her concern, assuring her all was well. Olivia, however, hadn't felt reassured. In fact, she'd become so immersed in her own concerns that she'd paid little heed to Sid's increasingly wayward behaviour. Even when he resigned from his position at the castle, she hadn't reproached him, because, at that stage, she'd been devoted to making Paris happy. In any case, she'd made enough sacrifices to ensure Sid's success. If he chose to throw it away on ale and women, then that was his lookout; he was no longer her priority.

The week that had begun with Sid ending his employment at the castle, finished with Paris ending his relationship with Olivia.

"I am sorry, Olivia," he'd said through tears. "I can duel with my conscience no longer." He'd then revealed that he'd stymied the investigation for fear of what he would uncover. The implication had been clear: he knew she'd lied to protect her brother.

"What would you have me do, Paris?" she'd pleaded. "You are my life; there must be a way to remedy this?"

"Alas, my love, there *is* no way," he'd replied, and Olivia knew she'd never be able to convince him otherwise. She'd collapsed into his arms, and he'd embraced her, whispering "I'm sorry" over and over. However, it had been Olivia who had been sorry over and over ever since. When they'd finally let go of each other, she'd felt as heavy and emotionless as the castle walls that surrounded their final farewell; like all traces of warmth and love had been sucked from her. Even his promise that no harm would befall her or Sid had felt like nothing more than cold comfort.

Olivia heard the floorboards creak. She readied herself for the voice that would soon follow.

"Are you all right, m'dear?" Gerald's voice was muffled by the closed door.

"I'm fine," she replied wearily… and she *was* weary.

"It's just that I heard a rather loud bang, and I thought—"

"As I said, I am fine. I shall join you directly."

"Very well." More creaking signalled his departure.

Olivia made sure the ink on the letter to Reg Puffy was dry and then sealed it. She'd known about Sid's little scam with the Head of Kitchen for some time now, thanks to a conversation Gerald had had with Sid and then shared with her. Up until now, she couldn't have cared less; in fact, in a way, she felt it was poetic justice that Sid's life had become so trivial and pointless. But now there was a need for retribution, and the best way to hurt Sid was through his money pouch.

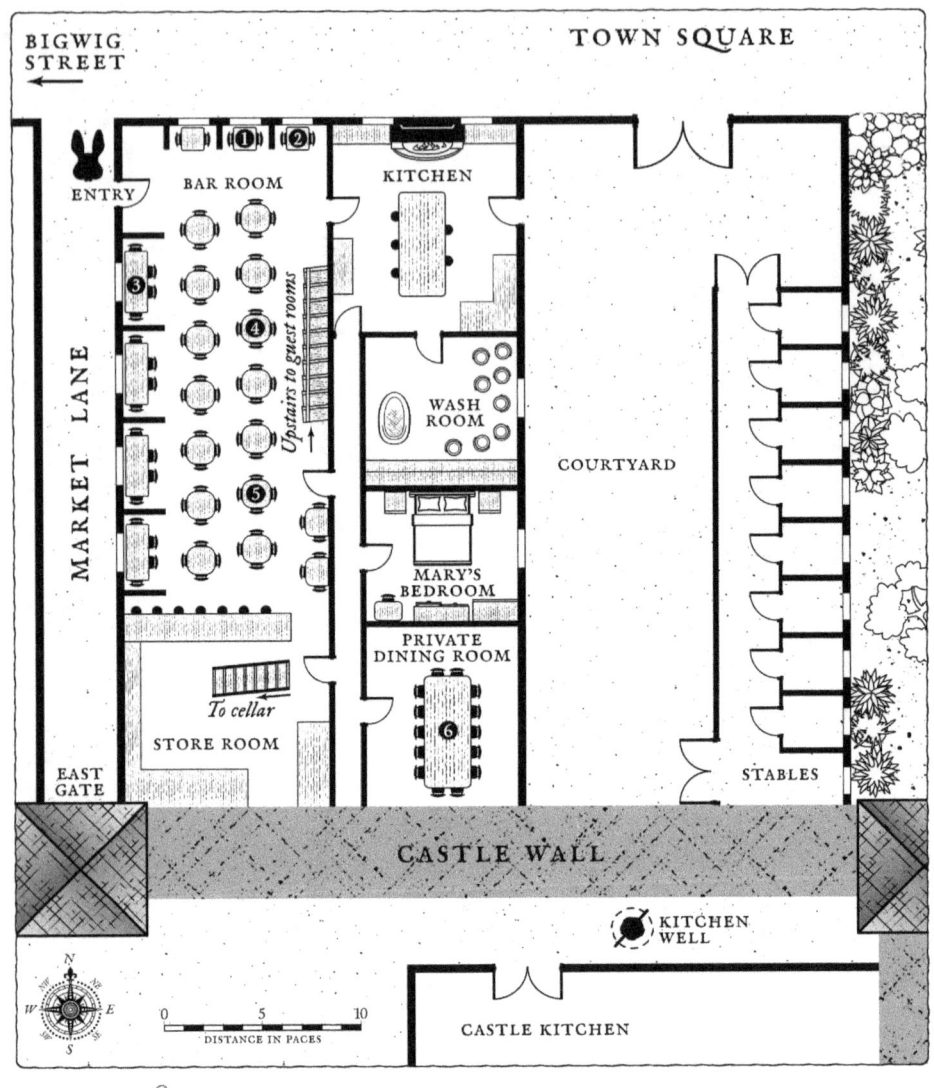

# THE HAREY RABBIT

*Ground Floor Floorplan*

1. Where Sid sat
2. Where Tom and Ophelia sat
3. The Limpdickers' Table
4. Where the Whysmans sat for breakfast
5. Prim Pet's Table
6. Scene of the Wednesday night dinner

# WEDNESDAY, JULY 2

## Chapter 25

# *Rather pleased with herself*

GERALD LAY ASLEEP, quietly snoring, as Olivia gently closed the door of 8 Plumduff Street and made her way to the East Gate. The early morning sky was clear and the air was hot, but Olivia thought she detected a hint of moisture in it. Then again, it was probably just the sheen of nervous perspiration on her forehead.

Walking along Big Wig Street, she could see a flow of people and carts ahead, coming and going from the castle kitchen. As she approached the intersection of the Town Square and Market Lane, she pulled her wide-brimmed hat over her face; it was black and non-descript, like the 'house dress' she was wearing. Olivia wanted to dissolve into the flow as much as she could.

No-one paid her much heed as she turned right up Market Lane and fell in behind a pair of young lads around twelve years of age. They were pushing a large wooden barrow filled with marrows. Olivia detested marrow — it reminded her of growing up in Backflush Lane, when her parents hardly had two copper coins to rub together. In those days, they'd virtually lived on boiled marrow.

Up ahead, the procession of kitchen supplies trickled through the East Gate. The two guards seemed to be a jovial pair, welcoming those making their regular deliveries. How would they react to her, Olivia wondered. The key was to project a sense of purpose. She smiled to herself; she shouldn't have much trouble achieving *that*.

Olivia regarded The Harey Rabbit on her left as she walked into the shadow of its façade. The inn was closed, but she could see candlelight and movement through the open windows. She hadn't set foot in The Harey Rabbit for over six years; she had very little in common with the twittering, gossipy women who frequented the place, and the chance of seeing Paris was far too high — just the thought of such an occurrence made her tremble. She pressed her right hand over her heart and took comfort in the parchment secreted against her left breast. Her letter to Reg Puffy was safe from prying eyes.

As she approached the East Gate, the guards' eyes looked far from prying; they were more bemused. After saying good morning to Garth and Gareth (the marrow boys), the guard to her left stuck his arm out sideways, blocking her progress through the gate.

"S'cuse me, Mistress," he said, smiling. "If I might be so bold as to ask, what bus'ness might *you* be havin' 'ere?"

Olivia smiled back; she knew how to play this game. "Why certainly, guardsman," she replied, eyeing his extended arm. He dutifully lowered it. "I simply wish to inform Master Puffy about a small error in one of his orders. It will take but a moment, and I'm sure he will be most grateful."

The guard grinned knowingly at his fellow guardsman. Olivia had no idea what they found so amusing, but both seemed to be enjoying some sort of private jest at her expense.

"Well, Ronnie," said the other guard, "best not keep the lady waitin'."

Ronnie chuckled. "Aye. Wouldn't want Master Puffy t'miss out on 'is chance at bein' mos' grateful."

They both burst out laughing as Olivia walked through the gate. Normally, she would have taken them to task about their rude behaviour, but she was too excited about gaining entry to the kitchen. In any case, she was more perplexed than offended by their behaviour.

The marrow boys were now well ahead of her, so she fell in behind a man lugging a sack of what she supposed was flour. She followed him across the courtyard into the main entrance of the kitchen. Olivia had never set foot in this part of the castle, and she was taken aback by the amount of activity. The noise coming from inside the kitchen was incredible — the barking of orders and crashing of pans could be heard above the general din of voices and other workplace operations. However, the noise and activity went to another level entirely as she stepped through the wide entrance. It was the most chaotic scene Olivia had ever witnessed — it made the bar room of The Bloody Bell seem like one of Petronella Whysman's fabric-viewing soirees. (That reminded her; she was yet to finish writing her reply to Petronella's drapery luncheon.)

Olivia didn't have time to think about where she was heading. She found herself being buffeted along the laneways of preparation tables, steaming pots and wood-fired ovens. The heat was intense. Eventually, she spilled out of the bustle near the waste barrels. Olivia almost gagged. There were at least twenty of them; most were filled with vegetable matter, but some contained bones and other unusable body parts. She had to get out of here.

Grabbing the nearest kitchen hand, she asked to be directed to Master Puffy.

"'Is office is just up them stairs," yelled the young man over the cacophony, while pointing to a timber mezzanine structure some twenty feet away. "But 'e ain't in yet."

Olivia nodded her thanks as the kitchen hand hurried about his business. This was perfect; she could drop off the letter anonymously. No-one would remember her amongst *this* madness.

Olivia arrived home some fifteen minutes later, task accomplished. It had been surprisingly easy — she'd arrived and departed Reg Puffy's office without anyone noticing her place the parchment on his desk. As for her exit from the castle: the guardsmen had been too busy helping a farmer with a spilled cartload of potatoes to see her leave. Oddly enough, she felt quite exhilarated by the whole affair and wondered, ironically, if this was how Sid felt after he burgled a home. Regardless, she entered 8 Plumduff Street rather pleased with herself.

The house was quiet, which was strange — she had expected to see Gerald up and preparing for the day. However, after checking the kitchen and washroom, she went upstairs and found him still asleep. That was unusual. Gerald was usually up by half six each morning (particularly this time of year) and it must be near seven by now.

She was tempted to let him sleep, but that would only delay her seeing Xavier. She felt confident of a breakthrough today. And she felt vindicated (and exhilarated) by her actions this morning. She wondered how Reg Puffy would react to her letter. Regardless, yesterday's maudlin mood was over. She couldn't change the past, but she could shape the future. She began by rousing her husband.

It took Gerald nearly an hour to wash and dress. He seemed particularly lethargic this morning, while Olivia felt exactly the opposite — it was almost as if she'd sapped the energy out of him to double up on hers. She even felt inspired enough to prepare a full breakfast of bacon, eggs, bread, honey and cheese. It was most unlike her.

However, instead of regarding the spread with effusive pleasure, Gerald grazed through his breakfast in dutiful silence, which was most unlike *him*. She wondered if yesterday's sharp words were still playing upon his mind.

She couldn't deny that she had been particularly prickly towards him lately, and now it seemed she might have finally popped his pep. For some reason, that disturbed her; inane as it was, his upbeat chatter was an inherent part of his personality.

"You're unusually quiet this morning, Gerald," she finally remarked as he finished off a honey-soaked piece of bread. "Is something amiss?"

"Well, m'dear," he said, regarding her with a considered expression, "I *could* tell you, but I dare say you would not approve, and the appointment of the new Seneschal... Well, m'dear, I have no wish to upset you."

The directness of Gerald's words went straight to the pit of her stomach. She suddenly found it hard to breath and could only watch as he excused himself from the table.

"Thank you for a delightful breakfast." He smiled at her sadly, and then walked out of the kitchen.

As he left, she finally found her breath and had to steady herself against the kitchen table. For a moment, she thought she was going to faint, but, fortunately, the world righted itself. She could hear his footsteps retreat down the passage and climb the stairs to where his signature red coat waited to be worn, despite the fact it was another hot day.

Collecting herself, she went about clearing the table and cleaning the dishes. Any distraction at this point... Her husband's words often engendered a feeling of anger or frustration, boredom on a good day, but they'd never made her feel what she was feeling now: guilt.

She was sweeping the kitchen floor when she heard the front door close. Gerald had left without saying goodbye. He'd never done *that* before. Suddenly, the pit of her stomach erupted.

## CHAPTER 26

### *Most considerate of him*

THE KITCHEN HAD been in action-stations since dawn. Not only did Mary have to cater for the normal Harey Rabbit crowd, she also had to prepare for Richard's impromptu dinner. However, the chaos was a good thing — it took her mind off Sid and the silver button. She'd barely slept last night thinking about it. Richard had lost only one button, yet *two* had been discovered. She'd asked him if he wore the same button on other clothing, but he'd answered in the negative. Therefore, there could only be *one* silver button with an etching of a quill over a broken sword. So where had Sid's come from? Strangely, the anomaly hadn't seemed to concern Richard; he'd referred to it as an 'interesting development'. *Interesting development!* It was unbelievable! How could he be so blasé?

Her hectic thoughts had been superseded by the hectic organisation of her staff. Today, Patricia had the assistance of two kitchen hands — Pearl and Vera — where, more often than not, she had none. Mary had also decided that her most experienced waitresses — Mandy, Carol and Lillian — would take charge of serving lunch and dinner. (Lillian had assured her she was fully recovered from the dressing-down she'd received from the Limpdickers.) She'd bundled John and Juanita off to the market to purchase extra food supplies, much to John's dismay and Juanita's excitement. Mary would oversee the preparations for Richard's dinner.

The morning hadn't taken long to heat up, and the kitchen hadn't taken long to reach boiling point. Patricia was in her element, ordering people about: chop this, boil that, mix faster, stir slower — the vociferous eye of the storm. Had it just been Pearl and Vera caught up in the whirlwind of instruction and abuse, everything would have blown over without much damage. Unfortunately, Juanita had been swept up in the maelstrom. After returning from the market, Mary had asked the Icarumban to clean the best crockery for Richard's table. The task involved heating water, and heating water meant vying for space over the kitchen stove. Mary should have foreseen the consequences of such a conflict, particularly after the 'water thief' incident, but, at the time, she'd needed to go through the wine, cider and ale inventory with Dave. They were in the cellar when they heard a screech followed by a loud crash. Bizarrely, Mary's first thought was that the two sounds were in the wrong order. She rushed up the cellar steps, across the empty bar room to the kitchen.

The sight that met her would have been comical if it hadn't been so serious. Patricia was standing there, completely saturated. Underneath her (now opaque) white linen coif, strands of grey hair clung to the sides of her dripping face, and her uniform was body-huggingly drenched. At her feet, a large metal pot lay on its side, still rocking slightly. It was the only sound and movement in the room. Vera and Pearl were at the table, respectively frozen in the process of chopping carrots and swedes, while Patricia just stood there like a dripping statue of disbelief.

"What the…?" Mary rushed to her cook's side. "Patricia, are you alright?"

At the sound of her voice, everyone snapped back to life. "Oh, Mistress," Patricia cried, holding out her apron, "jus' look wha' she's done t'me!"

"It was Juanita," supplied Pearl, unnecessarily. Vera nodded her affirmation.

"Are you sure you're alright, Patricia?" Mary asked again, guiding her to a nearby stool. Her waterlogged clothes felt warm; the water had obviously been quite hot.

Patricia nodded as she sat down. "Jus' such a shock, Mistress."

Yes, she could well imagine.

"Everythin' alrigh', Mary?" The voice came from behind her — it was Dave.

"Yes, thanks, Dave," she replied, keeping her attention on Patricia. "Just a case of Icarumban hot-headedness."

"Righ' y'are, then." There was mirth in his voice. She heard the bar room door shut behind him.

Vera and Pearl were still standing on the other side of the preparation table, wearing similar gormless expressions. Mary found it irksome. "Would you two mind helping Patricia out of these wet clothes? There are spare uniforms in the washroom."

They jumped to do her bidding.

Then John appeared at the courtyard doorway. He looked agitated. "Mistress! It's Juanita, she's…"

"She's what?" Mary snapped, annoyed at John's inability to express himself. She didn't have time for all this nonsense. Today of all days!

He cowered at her tone.

"Oh, never mind, John," she said, angrily. "Where is she?"

"In the stables, Mistress," he mumbled, retreating out of the doorway as she stormed towards him.

The stables — what on earth was Juanita doing out *there?* Mary glanced back towards the saturated Patricia. Vera held her left arm, Pearl her right, carefully escorting her into the washroom. She *really* didn't need this.

Juanita was huddled against the wall of the stable closest to the Town Square. Her face was buried behind her knees; black hair cascaded down her legs. She didn't look up as Mary approached.

"Well?" Mary said without preamble. She was in no mood for Icarumban histrionics.

Juanita didn't acknowledge Mary's presence in any way.

"Juanita, I won't ask you again."

Her threatening tone had the desired effect. Juanita looked up; her tear-streaked face looked rather pathetic. Mary had never seen her like this before. "I'm sorry, Meestress." She sniffed, running the back of her hand across her nose.

Sighing, Mary squatted down next to her, more out of frustration than sympathy. "Tell me what happened," she said, directly.

"She no let me feeneesh heateeng dee water for dee deesh washeeng, like you say for me to do." Juanita eyes gleamed with injustice.

Mary shook her head. "So you reacted by *emptying* it on her?"

Juanita pouted with indignation.

"It's unacceptable, Juanita. If you can't control—"

"I try Meestress!" Juanita blurted out defensively. "I know you are beesy today — your brother has hees deener — so I try to be nice, grab my tongue, but Patreesha she just yells at me over and over: I need dee water! I need dee water! I need dee water! All dee time, I need dee water! So, I *geeve* her dee water!"

Mary could well imagine the scene, but it still didn't excuse the Icarumban's behaviour. "And what would you have done if she'd been shouting for a knife?"

Juanita looked abashed. "Dat ees deefferent, Meestress."

Mary wasn't convinced. "So you say, but in the heat of the moment,

Juanita, how would you react? You realise you could have scalded her with that water!"

"You theenk I am dat stupeed?" Juanita said, defensively. "Patreesha ees dee stupeed one — stupeed old cow with dee dried-up teets."

"That's enough, Juanita!" Mary snapped. "If you wish to continue working at The Harey Rabbit, you're going to have to find a way of working *with* Patricia. Do you understand?"

Reluctantly, her washerwoman nodded.

Mary stood up, offering her hand. Juanita looked at it sullenly before taking it. It was obvious she felt hard done by, but she would just have to lump it. Mary helped her to her feet. "Now, Juanita, when Patricia is dried and clothed, I want you to apologise to her."

"*Me?*" Juanita cried. "*She's* dee one what should be doing dee apology! Dees ees no fair, Meestress."

"Listen to me, Juanita," she said, holding her hands against the Icarumban's arms and looking her straight in the eye. "I realise Patricia can be very rude and demanding — she is rude and demanding to *me* on occasions, and I'm her *employer!* So, when you apologise…" Juanita moved her mouth to interject, but Mary squeezed her arms and reinforced her position. "*When* you apologise, Juanita, you'll do it with sincerity, because you will *actually* be doing it for *me*."

Juanita nodded her compliance, if somewhat reluctantly, and then said quietly, "I *am* sorry to you, Meestress."

"After your apology, I don't want you anywhere near the kitchen. You can help clean and prepare the dining room for the dinner."

The left corner of her mouth turned up in a half-smile; the idea obviously appealed to her. However, Mary didn't want her to think she was being rewarded for her behaviour, and added, "Tomorrow, I'll work out what I am going to do with you both."

Juanita's smile vanished. Mary left it there; she didn't have the time or inclination to drag the episode out any longer.

Thankfully, the apology went off without a hitch. Juanita did an acceptable job of sounding contrite, and Patricia did an equally acceptable job of accepting her contrition. The fact that Mary had also privately warned Patricia not to play the stubborn card probably helped matters.

Juanita had then set to cleaning the dining room with vigour (or, as she called it, gusto). She was a hard worker, Mary had to credit her that.

Around midday, Mandy popped her head into the dining room. Juanita was helping Mary polish the silver candelabra for the table setting. "There's a Lieutenan' Swill 'ere t'see you, Mistress."

Mary nodded. "Thank you, Mandy. Show him in."

Brandon Swill — she hadn't seen *him* for some time, not since he'd been made lieutenant anyway. They'd used to see each other quite regularly before he'd become a guardsman, mainly because they both worked at an inn. The Brewers and the Swills used to order ale in bulk together, before Mary took over the running of The Harey Rabbit and began catering more to the tastes of the castle-set.

She hardly recognised the man who appeared in the doorway. His purple and gold doublet shone in the muted light of the passage, as did the highly polished black boots that flared at his knees. He'd removed his black cavalier's hat, holding it formally at his side, its purple feather brushing against his gold-brocaded sleeve. The only imperfection in his appearance was his slightly matted brown hair and the sheen of sweat on his forehead. It was a far cry from her memory of an easy-going lad who always looked like he'd woken up in the clothes he was wearing.

"Hello, Mary." He smiled, and suddenly the lad was back.

Mary smiled too. "Hello, Brandon… Or should I say Lieutenant Swill?"

His smile turned wry. "I save that for people I can order about. I don't think that's ever worked with you."

Mary laughed.

"May I come in?"

"Of course."

Then his eyes deflected to his left. Mary looked to find Juanita eyeing Brandon with unabashed lasciviousness. Did the girl have *no* self-control?

Rolling her eyes, Mary introduced her. "Brandon, this is Juanita, my treading-on-thin-ice washing girl."

Juanita gave her a quizzical look before performing some sort of exotic bow in which her cleavage was displayed to full advantage.

Brandon looked unsure how to react. He settled for a formal sounding, "Pleased to meet you, Juanita."

Mary felt a flush of embarrassment. "Juanita," she said. "Go and see if Dave needs a hand down in the cellar, the lieutenant and I have private matters to discuss."

Juanita pouted, but wisely decided not to gainsay her. She and her come-hither expression sauntered out of the room without a sound. Mary followed her to the doorway and watched as she disappeared into the bar room. Satisfied Juanita was out of earshot, she turned to face Brandon. "Sorry about that," Mary said. "I think it's the hot weather." Brandon dismissed her apology with a bemused shake of his head.

They sat at the dining table; the smell of polish was quite strong. "You look well," Mary said, replacing the cork seal on the earthenware jar of polish. "Congratulations on being made lieutenant — the youngest ever, I hear. The Purple Peril obviously suits you well."

He nodded, and his smile was boyish. Again Mary was reminded of simpler times. "Thank you, Mary. It is true; the last three months have been the most rewarding of my life. Well, at least until the attack on the Duke. I must admit, this past week has been most strange and frustrating, which brings me to why I am here."

He sounded so formal, so... on duty. And it was obvious why he was here: Richard had sent him to make sure everything was in order.

"Sir Richard wishes to know if you need any assistance in preparation for tonight's proceedings."

"*Most* considerate of him." She folded her hands and leaned forward on the table.

Brandon's expression conveyed a certain amount of awkwardness. He obviously didn't feel comfortable playing lieutenant with her.

"Yes..." Then he sighed. "Look, Mary, I realise you have been brought into a situation you should not have to concern yourself with, but unfortunately—"

"I'm a stupid helpless woman without the wherewithal to grasp the gravity of the Duke's attack?"

Brandon looked confused.

"How *is* the Duke, by the way?" Mary enquired.

He regarded her for a moment, either trying to work out what he'd just said to upset her or considering whether he should answer the question. When he finally spoke, it was in a guarded tone. "I have not seen the Duke. However, according to Doctor Whysman, his condition is unchanged. Occasionally he is feverish, but for the most part, he sleeps."

Mary considered this. What purpose did the attacker have? To gain access to the Duke's quarters required a lot of skill or knowledge (or both). So, why go to all that trouble just to put the Duke into some sort of delirium?

And why use a knife? It seemed too messy somehow. Unless the attack was a moment of opportunity… but who walks around with a poisoned blade? A doctor would certainly carry knives, but poison…?

"Are you alright, Mary?" Brandon now wore a more solicitous expression.

"I'm fine," she replied, distractedly. "And I don't require any assistance for tonight's dinner."

He nodded, though he didn't look convinced. "Very well. You know there will be six in total?"

"Yes. Richard deigned to tell me *that* much. Apart from the fact, of course, that he is no longer Seneschal because *he* is suspected of poisoning the Duke. *You're* obviously convinced of his innocence, Brandon."

Brandon nodded, but hesitated slightly before answering. "I truly believe Sir Richard had nothing to do with the attack on the Duke. However, that is *all* I'm prepared to say on the matter."

"Very well… So, Tom and Ophelia haven't returned with Frank?"

Brandon looked surprised, which was gratifying.

"Sorry, did I forget mention that Richard also told me about Frank Offcut's pivotal role in searching for some mysterious doctor? Forgive me, Brandon; it must be the burden of so much information taxing my feeble womanly mind."

Brandon leaned forward. For an odd moment, she thought he was going to take her hands in his. "Mary, I apologise if I sounded condescending in any way." He folded his hands in a mirror image to hers. "I have nothing but respect for you. There is no doubting your ability and intelligence. Ma, Pa and Bethany struggle to run The Bell, yet you manage The Harey Rabbit single-handedly. It is a remarkable achievement. However, the fact remains that I cannot speak to you about the investigation into the attack on the Duke."

Mary realised there was no point in trying to push Brandon further; he wouldn't compromise his position in the Purple Peril or his duty to Richard.

"What I *can* tell you are the names of the people who will be attending tonight."

Mary bit back a sarcastic response and settled for a diplomatic, "That might be helpful."

However, her words must have conveyed a hint of sarcasm because Brandon's eyes narrowed. "As you know, you will be the only person outside the group permitted to enter this room. You are being trusted to keep anything you may overhear to yourself."

"Yes, I understand."

"Very well. Sir Richard will be joined by his secretary, Prestwich, the merchant, Fraser Coin, a lawyer, Rupert Smythe-Wheaton, a comrade of mine, Lieutenant Sebastian Fitzbadly, and I will be the sixth."

"I see," Mary said, noncommittally. Truth be told, she thought it an odd mix, particularly Fraser Coin (who was loud, brash and egotistical) and Rupert Smythe-Wheaton (the least offensive Limpdicker, but a Limpdicker nonetheless). Neither man was known for his discretion.

"We will be arriving individually from seven o'clock via the stable entrance. If you wouldn't mind arranging your kitchen staff to be otherwise engaged for a period of fifteen minutes while we arrive, it would afford us a certain amount of anonymity."

Mary wasn't happy about that particular concession: at seven o'clock the kitchen would be in full swing and fifteen minutes would severely disrupt the flow of service. "They already know Richard is having a dinner."

"Be that as it may, the fewer people who know about the rest of us the better."

"People will find out, Brandon. I can't imagine Fraser Coin holding his tongue. If ever there was a man who loves the sound of his own voice..."

Brandon smiled. "Even so."

Mary sighed in resignation. "Anything else, Lieutenant?"

He regarded her appraisingly — very Richard-like — before responding in the negative. Then, eyeing the half-polished candelabra, he added, "Except there's no need to waste your time on finery. All that is required is sustenance and privacy."

With that, Brandon took his leave. Mary thanked him and suggested he visit The Harey Rabbit more often.

He smiled. "I'll see you tonight."

## CHAPTER 27

## *You patronisin' me, Ophelia?*

OPHELIA WAS WORRIED about her pa. It had been a day since they'd found him and he continued to drift in and out of consciousness. Tom was also concerned, but it was more about the *time* it was taking for her father to recover — he was keen to return to Lower Icing as soon as possible, hopefully with information about the whereabouts of this doctor.

Tom had been gone most of the morning, exercising Wildflower and Hazel, while Ophelia stood vigil over her pa (apart from two trips to the spring). His skin was beginning to peel where it had been exposed to the sun, mostly on his face, neck, arms and the top of his head (where he also had some blistering). However, the many scrapes and scratches he'd received after being dumped into the valley were looking cleaner. His blistered feet and swollen left ankle were less bloated; the nasty bruise across his ribs was vividly apparent, but not as angry; his wrists were still raw from where the bindings had bitten into the skin, but there were signs of mending; and the stitched-up knife wound to his left thigh also seemed to be healing fairly well. And it was all thanks to Tom's ministrations — he'd continued to dress and bandage her pa's wounds. The only injuries that still concerned Ophelia were the ones to his head: the broken nose and the gash between his eyes radiated bruising across his sun-cooked face. It must have been a severe blow.

Tom returned just before midday with, of all things, a brace of trout.

"Where did y'catch *them*?" Ophelia tried not to sound too impressed, even though she *was* impressed. Tom was a marvel; there was something primal about him that she found very attractive.

"There's another ravine farther along the valley, towards the Icing," he informed her. "A feeder stream runs through it."

The brown, dark-spotted fish were almost two feet long. "Jus' as long as you realise I ain't no *fishmonger's* daugh'er." She'd butchered the goat; she wasn't about to gut the fish as well.

He smiled. "How could I *not* realise — you smell *far* too sweet to be a fishmonger's daughter."

Ophelia blushed. It was something that rarely happened. However, since her and Tom's romantic interlude at the spring yesterday evening, she'd felt more exposed, more vulnerable. Their coupling had been passionate and much more meaningful than the drunken night by the Icing. When they'd eventually disentangled their bodies and made their way back to camp, she'd felt both elated and guilty. It was wonderful to be in Tom's presence, in a place that seemed magically theirs, and in which Tom was clearly in his element. But she couldn't help thinking that she had just betrayed her pa and her brother. She'd barely given Billy a thought since they'd left Lower Icing. He was stuck in the stinking Can while she was surrounded by pristine wilderness, indulging in carnal pleasures with the man who had helped put him there. Her pa would never forgive her. Still, she didn't regret it. And she desired to have him again.

They lunched on the trout. Her pa seemed relatively lucid. So much so, in fact, that he was able to relay more of what happened in The Pits…

He'd been set upon the moment he'd stepped into Crapp Alley, and then bundled off to see The Slasher — Paul Peabody was his actual name. (Tom had never heard of him, and Ophelia only vaguely remembered his name when her pa told them about the side of beef he'd supplied for Paul's fortieth birthday.) Bert Muggins had told her pa that the doctor had fallen foul of the Moleson Twins and that they were planning to leave Lower Icing in a few hours. So, if Frank was going to find them before they left, The Slasher was the man to see: he was a person who *did* know what was happening in the lower layers of Lower Icing.

"Anyway," her pa rasped; his parched throat was still sore. "All I got for me troubles was some Pits 'ospitality, a drink o' rum with a madman, an' a joy ride through the friggin' countryside with a cuppla friggin' thugs. Still, leas' I managed to prick one of 'em with me bonin' knife."

"What about Xavier?" Tom asked.

"Wha' abou' 'im?" Her pa sneered.

Tom looked and sounded frustrated. "Did you find out what happened to him?"

The animosity between them was palpable. From her pa's point of view, Tom was a meddling nob, chief ass-licker to Sir Richard, and the man who'd apprehended Billy, while Tom saw her pa as a means to an end: someone to be tolerated as long as he stuck to the task of finding this doctor.

Her pa leant forward from the trunk of the tree he was propped against and cleared his throat. For a horrible moment she thought he was about to gob at Tom, but he just grimaced and swallowed. "They beat 'im up an' stole 'is money," he said, as if he'd already answered the question a dozen times before.

"I take it you mean the Moleson Twins, Frank?"

"Well, I ain't talkin' 'bout the bleedin' needlepoint club!"

"Where and when?" pressed Tom, sounding more like a Purple Perillian than a gamekeeper.

Her pa glared at him. "Near the back o' The Bell last Friday nigh'. Musta been fairly early as they said they were lookin' for some coin for drinkin'."

Tom seemed to consider this. "Are you sure? Not trying to fill in the rum-filled blanks are you, Frank?"

"No, I *ain't* sure, nature-boy," her pa snapped, "but tha's wha' I was tol' by Mick Moleson when I 'ad 'is brother's throat at knife point, so I *s'pect* 'e was tellin' the truth."

Her pa was becoming worked up; his face was reddening around the bruise. Ophelia was worried he was about to do himself harm, and she also didn't like the way he was speaking to Tom. "Pa, please," she said, soothingly, reaching over and placing a light hand against his shoulder, hoping he would relax back against the trunk.

He shot her an angry look. "You patronisin' me, Ophelia?"

Ophelia felt the blood rush to her face.

"Don' tell me you been charmed by this woodland wimp?"

"That's enough, Frank," Tom said, evenly.

Her pa didn't acknowledge Tom's warning; his attention was fixed entirely on her as she blushed furiously under the scrutiny of his battered and bandaged face. Although she tried, Ophelia couldn't maintain eye contact.

"What the frig, Ophelia!" He grabbed her hand and pulled her towards him.

Ophelia was too shocked to react. Tom, however, sprang up from where he was sitting and rescued her from her pa's grip.

Frank slumped against the trunk, breathing heavily.

Ophelia was close to tears and her anger flared. "Tom saved your life, Pa!"

"Saved my life!" he rasped. "I wouln' need no savin' if it weren' for 'im an' 'is 'igh an' mighty bunch of schemin' nobs. All this pissin' doctor business —

tol' you wha' that's about 'as he?"

"*You* tol' me it was somethin' t'do with the Duke o' Stymouth's visit," Ophelia yelled. What was her pa saying exactly? She looked across to Tom; he still had hold of her arm. Why did men feel the need to grab her? Tom's expression was serious. She pulled her arm away from him and he suddenly looked apologetic.

Ophelia turned back to her pa, whose head rested against the trunk once more.

"Thought y'was sharper than tha', Pheel," he whispered. Then he closed his eyes and his head lolled to the left.

Ophelia's heart almost leapt out of her mouth. "Pa!" she cried.

Tom had taken over then. Her pa had passed out, so Tom laid him down, removed the bandage from his forehead and placed a water-soaked cloth over his head. The gash had started to bleed, but Tom staunched the flow.

Ophelia felt gutted. Her pa had never spoken to her that way. He always told her how proud he was of her, how smart she was. Now she'd disappointed him. No, more than that, she'd betrayed him.

Her pa regained consciousness a few minutes later. Ophelia apologised over and over, lightly kissing the damp cloth on top of his head. He smiled at her weakly, but said nothing. For the rest of the afternoon, he lapsed between sleep and grogginess. Ophelia sat with him the entire time, while Tom constructed a shelter. He said it was going to rain, even though there wasn't a cloud to be seen. Sure enough, by late afternoon, the sky had turned grey.

## CHAPTER 28

### *Slap the impertinence out*

IT WAS NEARLY midday before Olivia stepped out into the heat of Plumduff Street. She'd bathed and changed into her summer clothing, and now felt a lot better, putting her unusually emotional state down to the excitement of her morning escapade, the heat of the kitchen and the rich breakfast. She'd dismissed Gerald's mood as an aberration, probably also brought on by the continuing heat. If not, well… whatever duress he was experiencing at the castle had been brought on by his own inexplicable behaviour. Delivering a fanciful, half-baked proclamation was one thing, but being inspired to do so on the unwise words of a Longboatian blacksmith bordered on madness. Olivia shook her head at the incredulity of it all, and then turned right towards the castle. She'd decided to approach The Bloody Bell from the Town Square, thereby avoiding the group of malingerers who always seemed to loiter at the corner of Market and Merchant Streets.

After a brisk walk along Big Wig Street to The Square (retracing her steps from earlier this morning) a feeling of excited expectation filled her. Crossing The Square at a quick pace, perspiration already forming on her forehead, Olivia approached the stable entrance of The Bloody Bell. However, before she reached it, she noticed the stable gates were shut. Much to her annoyance, they were also locked. It left her no choice but to enter via the main door.

She steeled herself for the lascivious expressions and bawdy remarks her presence would no doubt evoke. Sure enough, the clientele of The Bloody Bell didn't disappoint, with boasts of sexual prowess and the size of their manhood, but Olivia kept her eyes fixed ahead and reacted to none of it. What she *did* react to, however, was the globular shape of Alistair Bean. The poet was leaning against a table just inside the entrance, holding a large mug of ale and gazing indignantly across the room at someone. Olivia had met Alistair Bean at numerous castle functions, where his stirring poetry was always a highlight of the evening's entertainment; in fact, his ability to relay the emotions of love, bravery, sacrifice and the like was such that one almost forgot the man behind the words was physically grotesque. Here, at The Bloody Bell… well, the man behind the ale mug looked more tragic than any of his poems of lost love or wasted sacrifice. Olivia wondered if some tragedy *had* befallen Alistair Bean; she couldn't imagine why someone of his intelligence and refinement would *choose* to drink at The Bloody Bell.

She halted by the swaying figure; his red, watery eyes regarded her with disdainful curiosity. "How now," he suddenly boomed, "what trick of the light is this?"

"Master Bean," Olivia responded, curtly.

"Madam." He leaned forward, then belched, forcing Olivia to recoil from the resultant ale (and pickled something) fumes. However, his eyes were now focused and alight, and his voice rang out across the bar. "Avert thine eyes and block thine ears lest the detritus which inhabits this miasma of tainted humanity gnaws away at the very marrow of your soul," he said, theatrically, while performing a sweeping gesture with his ale mug. The room of tainted humanity responded with jeers and laughter. Olivia doubted whether any of them had understood a word of what Alistair had just said, but that didn't appear to be the point — it seemed a dramatic reaction was all that was required to fill the small minds of this mob.

As if on cue, someone yelled out, "This y' latest squeeze then, Runna?"

This brought uproarious laughter from the crowd. Alistair stiffened and glared balefully at the heckling audience. Olivia flushed with embarrassment and indignation, and realised she was about to be caught up in this drunken sideshow. Suddenly, a strong hand grabbed her left arm and pulled her roughly into the crowd. It took her a few stumbling steps to realise it was Bar Swill.

It wasn't until they'd reached the peaceful confines of the Swill's blue living room that the innkeeper unhanded her. He flung her into the room and then slammed the door shut.

"What friggin' game are y' playin at 'ere?" he hissed at her, barely controlling his anger.

"How dare you!" Olivia yelled, rubbing her soon-to-be-bruised arm.

Her protest went unheeded. "It's bad enough 'im on 'is own, withou' you dippin' y' oar in."

He couldn't possibly think she'd encouraged that performance, *surely*? But this was no act; he was glaring at her — furious and intimidating.

"Let me assure you, Master Swill, if I *had* an oar, I *certainly* wouldn't dip it into *that* pond of bottom feeders!" Olivia was trembling with shock and anger now, and her voice was beginning to take on a hysterical tone. "If your stable gate hadn't been locked, I wouldn't have had to subject myself *or* you to that behaviour. It's *your* bloody inn! *You* run this cesspit! *You* choose the scum you serve! How *dare* you blame—"

Olivia's emotions got the better of her and she burst into tears. Then her vision swam and she stumbled forward into Bar Swill. He grabbed her and sat her down on one of the dining chairs. What was happening to her?

"Stay 'ere, Mistress 'Iepants," he said in much calmer tones. "I'll fetch y'some water."

Bar Swill returned within a couple of minutes, by which time Olivia had recovered her senses somewhat. However, her behaviour was a concern. She had just sworn at Bar Swill, for goodness sake! She'd always been able to keep her emotions in check, no matter how angry or frustrated she became. She could justify yesterday afternoon's outburst, when she found out about Paris — that had been an emotional release — but this morning she'd been physically ill, and now... *this*.

Bar Swill held out a large cup. He looked concerned. "Here, drink up."

Olivia obliged and drank deeply. The water was cool and refreshing. She felt a lot better. "Thank you," she whispered, placing the cup on the table.

Bar nodded and sat down across from her. "I take it you've come t'see Xavier."

"Of course," Olivia replied, ignoring the opportunity for a more sarcastic response.

"Well, he's indisposed, an'—"

"What do you mean indisposed?"

"I mean *not* disposed t'seein' *you*, Mistress 'Iepants."

Olivia wanted to slap the impertinence out of the innkeeper's defiant face, but she couldn't afford to allow emotions get the better of her again. Taking a deep breath, she said as calmly as possible, "Do you really expect me to believe that, Master Swill?"

"No... but it don' matter; it ain't goin' t'change nothin'."

"Really." She bristled. "I wouldn't be too confident about *that*, if I were you."

Bar Swill treated her to a sardonic smile. "Well you ain't me, an' it's *you* what shouldn' be too confident. There's been developments since you was last 'ere."

"Has his memory returned?" Olivia interjected, her heart suddenly pounding.

He regarded her for a second as if weighing up what to reveal. "Nothin' 'bout his healin', but... other things."

"Like what?"

"Like why 'e came t'Lower Icing."

"I see." It was inevitable they would find out. At least the Swills might finally see how important it was to keep Xavier safe *and* in Lower Icing.

"Bethany said y'knew who Xavier was, that you'd told her, that she'd promised to say nothin'." He made it sound like an accusation.

"Believe *me*, Master Swill, I would have preferred to keep your daughter ignorant of Xavier's relation to the Duke, for Xavier's sake, but she left me with no alternative."

"Bah!" He spat, distastefully. "Xavier's sake! Y'really think we're *that* stupid?"

Olivia bristled at the innkeeper's tone. Was he *actually* accusing her of being disingenuous where Xavier was concerned; the nerve of the man.

Bar Swill was shaking his head, glaring at her contemptuously. "You sit there lookin' all shocked an' offended an' such, tryin' to act like you give two shits 'bout Xavier, but all y'really tryin' t'do is cover you an' y'husband's arses."

Olivia felt her mouth drop. No-one had *ever* spoken to her this way.

"'E's also told us 'ow Gerald snuck 'im out of The Keep and kept 'im 'idden away in y'house. No wonder you was so keen t'get 'im back."

Olivia could hardly believe what she was hearing. "Yes, because he was being treated like a *prisoner!*" Olivia fumed. "Gerald was the *only* one at the castle who believed Xavier!" She had never felt so angry. "He didn't force him to leave The Keep, Master Swill — he came of his own volition. He was *grateful* to Gerald! So don't you *dare* twist his words!" She stood up and began moving around the table towards the door that led into the Swills' private quarters. "Where is he? I want to see him!" The blue room no longer felt cool and calming; all she could see was red.

Bar moved to block her path. "Tol' you, Mistress 'Iepants, you ain't seein' the lad."

Olivia continued towards the door regardless. "Move out of my way, innkeeper."

Bar Swill stood firm.

She glared at him. "If you don't stand aside, Master Swill, you'll regret the—"

"I ain't no eighteen-year-ol' lass, so keep y'empty threats to y'self, Mistress 'Iepants." He accompanied her name with a sharp prod to her left shoulder, forcing her to take a step backwards. Then she felt the pain. Her hand automatically clasped the spot. This was unbelievable. Had he really just *done* that. "An' jus' in case you was 'bout t'say how you'd go runnin' t'Sir Richard an' the like, ya too late; they already know. I tol' Brandon yest'day evenin'."

Olivia regarded the bear-like man in front of her; his breathing was more pronounced and a rivulet of sweat ran past his right ear. The look he gave her was one of defiance, and Olivia knew she stood no chance of convincing him to let her see Xavier. Suddenly, she no longer had any fight in her.

"When?" Her voice sounded feeble and croaky.

Bar Swill looked puzzled. "When wha'?"

"When did he remember?"

"I tol' you, late yesterday. Not long after y'left, matter o'fact." Then his features softened as he noticed the tears welling in her eyes. Sighing, he unfolded his arms and moved towards her. Olivia flinched and stepped backwards — she felt vulnerable. She cursed herself for her weakness, for the tears that *showed* her weakness; to think, she'd felt so *elated* walking back from castle kitchen this morning, so upbeat about what the day would bring, but now she just felt… bereft.

Bar Swill was holding up his hand. "I ain't gonna 'urt ya."

His voice and demeanour were non-threatening, but Olivia didn't want him near her. She walked back to the other side the table, trying to stem the flow of tears with her sleeve.

The innkeeper sighed and stayed where he was, shaking his head. "I couldn' let y'see Xavier even if I wanted to. 'E's under 'ouse arrest."

Her heart sunk; what must Xavier be thinking. "Well, I hope you're satisfied, Master Swill. Whatever you may think of me or my husband, Xavier has done nothing more than try to reunite himself with his father."

Bar Swill shrugged. "That's for others t'decide."

Her throat tightened and she felt more tears welling up. All she could do was shake her head at the injustice of it all.

"You should know that Xavier ain't told no-one about you an' Gerald's part in this." His voice was a calmer, almost sympathetic. "'E tol' Brandon 'e still can't remember 'ow 'e left the castle. We won't tell no-one neither, but Xavier ain't no longer your concern. You understand?"

Olivia nodded, but it was more of a response than any real understanding.

She didn't understand it at all. It was all too much — Xavier, Paris, Gerald, Sid, the Swills. Her hands began to tremble, the tears started flowing and she collapsed onto a chair, sobbing her heart out.

Somehow, somewhere along the way, Bar Swill had been replaced by Bertie Swill. Her hand rested softly on her prodded shoulder. "Come now, Mistress 'Iepants," she said, softly. "Ain't no good you bein' this way; no 'arm's gonna come to Xavier."

No harm? He was under house arrest. And if he was saying he couldn't remember how he left the castle, then what would become of him? Olivia took a deep breath and let out a ragged sigh. Then she forced herself to stand up and face the squat figure of Bertie Swill. "Tell Xavier to… remember us if he needs to."

Bertie Swill smiled at her and nodded. "Strange 'ow life throws things at you, ain't it? Things thought left in the past…"

Olivia said nothing; she could only absorb the truth in the words. Then Bertie Swill extended her arm in an ushering movement. "Come, Mistress 'Iepants," she said, kindly. "Allow me t'escort you out of The Bloody Bell; it ain't no place for a woman of your standin'."

It was the nicest compliment anyone had paid her in a very long time. She nodded her acquiescence and fell in beside the innkeeper's wife. The journey through the bar was noisy but eventless. Alistair Bean was snoring at a booth and the rest of the mob refrained from making salacious jibes and inappropriate tongue gestures. The reason for their change in behaviour was possibly due to Olivia's obviously upset appearance, but, more likely, it was because Bertie Swill commanded a great deal of respect.

The heat and light assaulted her tear-raw eyes. She found herself squinting through the rabble that spilled out onto the street. Fortunately, she still had Bertie by her side. It wasn't until they'd walked some twenty paces down Merchant Street that she left Olivia to continue alone. "Y'should be right from 'ere."

"Thank you, Mistress Swill," Olivia murmured.

"An' try not to worry 'bout Xavier," she said, gently squeezing Olivia's arm. Then she turned and marched back into the morass of unwashed.

Olivia hardly remembered the walk to 8 Plumduff Street; just a vague recollection of a female voice wishing her good afternoon and a street vendor enquiring whether she'd like to buy one of his fans. She was mentally wrung out and physically worn out; her resilience and resolve had been dissolved in the Swill of betrayal.

She glanced at the brass plaque by her front door. She was usually meticulous about its appearance, buffing it two or three times a day, but she hadn't attended to it for almost two days now and it was already wearing a light coat of dust. How poetic, she thought. Well, let it stay that way; she didn't have the energy, nor, for the first time in over six years, did she care. Instead, she opened the door and headed straight upstairs to her bedroom. There she collapsed onto the hand-stitched bed cover and cried herself to sleep.

## CHAPTER 29

# *The average Lower Icinger*

AFTER BRANDON LEFT, Mary set Juanita back to the task of polishing the silver. She wasn't prepared to risk the reputation of The Harey Rabbit by providing a basic spread to the likes of Fraser Coin and Rupert Smythe-Wheaton. And she doubted whether Richard would be content with just sustenance and privacy. She even questioned Brandon's expectations of 'no finery' now that he was in the Purple Peril — they weren't known as Cake Eaters for nothing.

The afternoon gradually settled into a rhythmic pattern. Patricia had recovered from her Icarumban dousing and was working efficiently (even happily) with Pearl and Vera. Mandy, Lillian and Carol handled their duties without incident. Dave completed the monthly drink inventory, while keeping the patrons refreshed. Juanita polished away at the silver like it was some kind of treasure trove, and John happily went about the many jobs and errands Mary gave him.

It wasn't until later in the afternoon that she remembered Sid was expecting to see her tonight. She'd meant to send John around earlier to tell him that she could no longer make it, but the dinner preparations, not to mention Patricia and Juanita's behaviour, had distracted her. She suddenly felt worried about him. What if he'd relapsed into some sort of unconscious state, or over-exerted himself and collapsed?

Grabbing her hat from her bedroom, she hurried down the passage to the kitchen, informing all within earshot that she was stepping out for half an hour.

She strode out of the courtyard, through the stables, and then headed across the Town Square to Merchant Street. The sun was still blasting out its heat, even though the afternoon shadows had grown surprisingly long. Where *had* the day gone. The air was cloying, and by the time she had walked across The Square, she could feel her clothes beginning to stick to her. Hopefully, the clinginess was a sign of rain.

The corner of Merchant and Market Streets was, as usual, a hive of activity — the place where the traffic from the market collided with the spillage of people from The Bloody Bell. This time of day, the drinkers far outnumbered the vendors. As Mary walked by the inebriated gathering, she was the focus of a few leering gazes, but she knew she was in no danger. Most of The Bloody Bell's patrons knew who she was. If any one of them decided to try their luck, there'd be a dozen who'd jump to her rescue, and if Bar Swill found out, the chancer would more than likely find himself with a jaw that no longer worked. In fact, as she walked past, she noticed some of them doffing their hats to her.

As she headed down Merchant Street, Mary's thoughts turned to the average Lower Icinger: the market vendor, the farmer, the goodwife, the tanner, the maid, the farrier, even the drinker at The Bloody Bell; those who slogged away to make ends meet. How would *they* react to what was happening at the castle? Would they care that the Duke had been attacked or that Richard had resigned as Seneschal? Would it *really* affect their lives? The Duke of Stymouth was due to arrive in less than two weeks, but she doubted many of the villagers cared. If they did, you certainly wouldn't know it from walking the streets; they looked the same as they always did. Yet, within the walls of The Harey Rabbit, the patrons were abuzz with excitement and conjecture about the Duke's visit.

By the time she reached Sid's abode, some ten minutes later, she was feeling quite sapped of energy. Annoyingly, there was no answer to her persistent door knocking. Again, images of an unconscious Sid ran through her head, so she walked around the back to see if she could gain entry that way. The door was locked, but there was a window she could peer through. However, its grime-filled panes revealed nothing. She began yelling and banging at the back door until the upstairs window of Sid's neighbour flew open.

"Will ya shut the frig up!" shouted down a large, red-faced woman in her twenties. "Can't y'tell 'e ain't friggin' well 'ome? I got a baby what I'm tryin' t'put t'sleep 'ere, an' I ain't got no chance with you bleatin' away like some friggin' los' sheep!"

Mary flushed with embarrassment. "I'm sorry, goodwife. I meant no offense."

The woman nodded, somewhat mollified by Mary's contrition.

"May I ask if you actually saw Sid leave?"

"Left a cuppla hours ago. Slammed 'is front door loud enough to wake the friggin' dead; never no mind I got youngins t'look after."

"I see. Well, I will leave you in peace."

With that, the woman slammed shut her window: another Lower Icinger who had more than enough on her plate already, with no need or desire to spare a single thought about the Dukes of Lower Icing and Stymouth. Mary's plate was also full. Well, full enough, at least, not to expend any more energy looking for Sid. He was alive; that was the main thing.

By the time Mary returned to The Harey Rabbit, she was sweating so much she felt as if Juanita had emptied a pot of hot water on *her*. The air was increasingly humid, and a dark bank of clouds had crept into view from the north. Thank goodness, Mary thought. If ever Lower Icing had needed a drenching, it was now — the smell of rubbish, rotting food and effluent in the streets was as bad as she could remember. If the Duke had arrived today, it would have been a diplomatic disaster.

Fortunately, there'd been no disasters within the confines of The Harey Rabbit: Patricia had control of the kitchen; Mandy, Lillian and Carol were preparing the bar room for the evening trade; John had swept the courtyard and was now cleaning out the stables; Juanita had finished polishing the silver and was in the process of sweeping the dining room floor, and Dave was lugging some ale barrels from the cellar to the bar. Since everything was in order, Mary decided to fix herself a bath; she couldn't very well serve Richard and his band of merry men in her current state.

Fifteen minutes later, she was alone in the washroom, relaxing in a tub of cool water. It was soothing, peaceful, and, best of all, cleansing. The soapy water was a disturbingly dark shade of grey when she finally extricated herself from the tub half an hour later. It was an indulgence, but she'd needed it, and she felt much better for it.

During her soak, Sid had re-entered her thoughts. He was still expecting her to stay with him tonight.

By the time Mary re-emerged into her innkeeper's world, John had finished mucking out the stables. Not that there was any muck. Apart from Tom's two horses, the stables hadn't been used for over a fortnight. However, John was a mess and he looked like he was ready to collapse. She ordered him into the tub. What was good for the goose was good for the gander.

Once he'd washed and dressed himself in a clean set of clothes, she sent him to Sid's with strict instructions: "If he's not home, wait for him and tell him…" She suddenly felt self-conscious. "Tell him that I'm sorry I can't see him tonight, but I have to host a private dinner."

"Righ' y'are, Mistress," he said, smiling.

As he headed out the kitchen door, Mary pulled him up. "Oh, and John, don't mention that the dinner is for Sir Richard." If Sid knew Richard was the reason she couldn't see him, she'd have a lot of explaining to do.

"Very good, Mistress." John nodded. Then he was gone.

# CHAPTER 30
## *Let's drink to saying nothing*

OLIVIA WOKE TO the sound of Gerald's excited voice. She could hear his footsteps bounding along the passageway downstairs. "Olivia, my sweet; are you home?"

Her head felt heavy, her mind fuzzy. Then she realised she was lying on her bed. Propelling herself off the cover, she moved to the window. How long had she been asleep? It was still light, but the sun no longer beamed into the room.

"Olivia?" Gerald bellowed again, from the kitchen by the sound of it.

She looked at the sky; it was clouded and dull. For a moment she thought she'd slept through summer. Groggily, she turned around and stepped towards her dressing table. There, she regarded herself in the mirror. Her neatly pinned hair looked frayed and a few wisps stuck out at unkempt angles, but that was nothing compared to her face. It looked like the population of the Five Duchies had grieved through her. Olivia had always felt she looked quite young for her almost thirty-three years, but the woman who gazed back at her, red-eyed and drawn-faced, seemed more like some grotesque vision of the future than a reflection of the here and now.

"I say, are you home, m'dear?" Gerald's voice boomed from the bottom of the stairs.

She couldn't let him see her like this. "I'll be down directly, Gerald," she called back.

Instead of cheery acquiescence, Olivia was confronted by the sound of heavy footsteps stomping up towards the bedroom. "My dear, I have great news."

"I said I will be down directly!"

The footsteps didn't miss a beat as they reached the landing.

Olivia sat down at the table and quickly began applying some powder to her face. Moments later, the red coat burst into the room. Olivia continued puffing her face with powder. She didn't need to turn around; she could see Gerald's animated features in the mirror. "Gerald, I'm busy. Surely whatever it is can wait a few minutes."

Gerald, however, was undeterred by her tone; perhaps he was immune to it after all these years. "My dear, I've been waiting all day to tell you. I came home at lunchtime, but you were out, and I haven't had a chance since… Oh, such good news, m'dear — Xavier's been found!"

Olivia stopped puffing her face. She wasn't sure how to react; did she pretend that it was all a wonderful surprise or…

"Did you hear what I just said, Olivia?" He'd moved next to her. All she could see in the mirror was his gold braided cuff and red sleeve almost touching her shoulder.

Placing the puff on the table she stared straight ahead at her bizarre reflection and said quietly, "I am well aware of that fact, Gerald."

Olivia relayed the events of the last few days while seated at her dressing table. It was as if the bizarre-looking woman in the mirror was someone else and Olivia was just a witness to a tale of good intentions and betrayal. She held nothing back. By the end of her account, Gerald's initial outrage had become hurtful disbelief. "You talk of being betrayed by the Swills, Olivia, and yet you've done the same thing to *me*."

"I didn't tell you because I wanted to *protect* you, Gerald. Xavier couldn't help the Duke, so there was no point. If you'd known, there's no doubt you would have found some inadvertent way of letting the cat out of the bag."

He huffed. "I say, m'dear, you really must think me an incapable dolt. I am your husband, and while it's a long time since I believed I had your affection or admiration, I was, however, under the impression I had your loyalty. It is a sad day."

She was ready to defend her stance, but the poignancy of his words prevented her. He was right, she thought, it *is* a sad day… the saddest since…

She looked up at her husband's face. He looked defeated; cheeks that were always puffed up with blustering good cheer were deflated and sagging, a mouth that always wore a natural smile was pursed into a thin straight line, and eyes that always shone with optimism were dull.

She felt so ashamed that she stood up and actually embraced her husband, powder-faced horror that she was. His heavy woollen coat still radiated the heat of the day. "I'm sorry, Gerald," she whispered into to it. And she truly was.

Then, looking him in the eye, she asked him to forgive her. His expression was one of surprise and confusion; her sudden show of affection had obviously befuddled him. Truth to tell, she felt rather befuddled herself.

"Well, I suppose I…" he mumbled. Then, he sighed. "I say, m'dear, you *do* test my patience, what."

She nodded her acceptance, but took it that he *had* forgiven her. Moving away from him, she noticed a white smudge of powder just below his right shoulder. Brushing at it, she said, "I'm afraid I'm a bit of a mess…"

She looked up from the powdery smudge. His expression was guarded and… uncertain, perhaps. She didn't blame him. "Just give me a moment to make myself more presentable. Then perhaps we might share some refreshment in the summer garden."

Gerald's expression turned wary, but eventually he acquiesced. "That sounds most pleasant, m'dear."

Olivia sat across the summer garden table from Gerald. Yesterday she'd come here to *escape* him. She'd done her hair and made up her face, and now she felt more at ease, not only with what had happened today, but sitting here talking openly with her husband.

Gerald was right about loyalty. After six years of being married to a man with a bell, he'd finally said something that had rung true. No-one had been loyal to her: not the Swills, not Sid, not even Paris. In fact, Gerald was probably the only person who *had* remained steadfast. And that counted.

The evening was upon them. The sky looked threatening, and the humidity was closing in, but it was, as Gerald had said, most pleasant. They'd even found a bottle of white wine from the Chutin Blancs region of Escargotia (a popular destination for castle-set honeymooners) to help lubricate the discussion.

"As I see it, Gerald, we have two choices." Olivia was responding to Gerald's comment about Xavier's recovering memory. "Either we admit our complicity in his disappearance and take the consequences, or we say nothing and trust that Xavier will be able to keep our secret."

"If we say nothing, it puts rather a lot of pressure on the lad, what?"

"Yes." Olivia agreed. "If Xavier maintains he can't remember what happened until he woke up at The Bloody Bell, then the Swills' version of events may be called into question, particularly the *time* they found Xavier."

"Oh I say, I see what you mean, m'dear," he said, thoughtfully. "Sir Richard may convince Captain Le Sharp that Xavier *does* have a case to answer."

"Exactly, Gerald."

"Then we have no choice," he said, slapping his hands overdramatically on the table. "We must admit our part."

"What good would *that* do? At best, we could only vouch for his whereabouts until just after nine-thirty on the night Marmaduke was attacked. Assuming, of course, *we* are believed."

"Yes, I dare say my word is not held in such high esteem at the castle since Saturday's proclamation."

"Well, quite," Olivia agreed, suppressing her irritation. A pained look crossed Gerald's face, but Olivia ignored it. "So, what I propose is that we say *nothing* and let events unfold as they will. After all, we have done nothing except treat a young man with kindness and respect — a young man who could well be the next Duke of Lower Icing."

Gerald nodded. "Very well, m'dear." He sounded determined. Then he raised his glass of wine. "Let's drink to saying nothing."

Olivia smiled to herself; she would never have thought to hear those words coming from her husband's mouth. As they touched cups, the first drops of rain began to fall.

## Chapter 31

# *Good Riddance!*

THE RAIN WAS steady, but thanks to Tom's intuitiveness and ingenuity, they were dry. He'd constructed a lean-to against the massive trunk of the oak tree. The oak's lush summer canopy provided good cover against the downpour, and the sturdy lean-to (constructed of hewn branches and woven underbrush) protected them from the drops that managed to filter through.

Tom was sitting to Ophelia's left, their backs supported by the trunk, while her pa was lying to her right, sleeping peacefully through the refreshing sound of rainfall. The air was still warm, and the forest had turned a dismal dark green as the afternoon approached evening.

Ophelia was conflicted. She fancied the pants off Tom and she'd never felt that way about anyone. He was something… unexpected. And he had a caring nature — he had saved her pa… and her. On the other hand, her pa was right: they'd never have been in this situation if it hadn't been for Tom and that Lieutenant Swill. She broke the silence with a question, one that had been playing on her mind since the lunchtime altercation.

"Wha's this all abou', Tom? This doctor, why's 'e so importan'?"

Tom said nothing.

"'E ain't got nothin' t'do wiv the Duke o' Symouth, 'as 'e?"

"No," Tom whispered.

Ophelia nodded. The doctor hadn't really been her concern; she'd been focused on finding her pa, looking after him, and… being with Tom.

"He claims he is *our* Duke's son."

She turned her head towards him. He kept his gaze forward, a shadowy profile framed in gloomy green. She knew she should be shocked, but all she felt was mild surprise. "And 'is 'e?"

The profile nodded. "From what Richard says, I believe so."

"Wha' does the Duke say?" Her voice was a whisper now.

He turned his head towards her. She could barely see his eyes underneath his mop of sandy hair, but she could sense their appraisal. He breathed in, and then exhaled. "On Friday night, the Duke was attacked — cut on the arm with a poisoned blade."

This did shock Ophelia. "D'ya mean the Duke is dead?"

He shook his head. "No. That is to say, he wasn't when we left Lower Icing."

Ophelia could hardly believe what she was hearing. "Bloody 'ell!"

"That's why Richard used your father to find Xavier."

"So y'reckon this *doctor* poisoned the Duke? That ain't the act of no son."

Tom agreed. "No, it seems unlikely Xavier was responsible. Particularly if your father's information is correct — seems the Moleson Twins got to him before the Duke was attacked. But Xavier could well be the only person who can save the Duke. If he's alive…"

"Bloody friggin' 'ell, Tom." She shook her head, trying to make sense of it all. "So wha' 'appens now? If them Molesoen Twins beat 'im up, someone must've found 'im, 'less o'course 'e recovered an' wandered off. Migh' 'ave been so dazed tha' 'e walked into the Icin' an' drowned."

"Exactly. That's why we can't spend time waiting for Frank to fully recover. I want to get moving at first light."

Her father had barely been awake since lunch. "Don' like y'chances, an' I ain't gonna let y'risk movin' Pa if 'e ain't well enough. Not for some missin' doctor, Duke's son or not. Pa was right: 'e wouldn't be 'ere at all if it weren' for Sir Richard usin' our Billy to get 'im t'do 'is dirty work."

It was Tom's turn to shake his head. "Your father is *here* because of his defiant inability to see reason where *your Billy* is concerned. Your brother tried to force himself upon a young girl, Ophelia. I would have thought you'd have more of an understanding of her plight."

Ophelia bristled. Tom had no right to judge her pa, her brother *or* her — *particularly* her; he didn't *know* her. "Yeah, an' I woulda thought since *you're* such a friggin' master tracker an' Sir Richard's such a friggin' smart arse, you'd've been able t'find the son of the Duke *without* havin' t'get me pa's 'elp. You must be thankin' y'lucky stars Billy 'ad a go at that girl!"

Ophelia was fuming now. Her pa stirred in his sleep.

Tom suddenly sprang out of the shelter and disappeared into the rainy gloom.

Good riddance!

A drop of water spilled on her cheek. Her immediate thought was that the shelter had sprung a leak. Then she blinked and realised it was her eyes that were leaking.

## Chapter 32

# *A remarkable woman*

THE FIRST GUESTS arrived with military precision at seven o'clock. It was the out-of-uniform lieutenants — Brandon and Sebastian Fitzbadly. As ordered, the kitchen and passageway were clear of staff; no-one would see them or the other guests enter the dining room. Mary had sent a grumbling Patricia upstairs to one of the guestrooms with Vera, Pearl and Juanita. (Fortunately, Juanita and Patricia had come to some sort of understanding and now seemed to be on quite good terms. Mary could hardly believe it.) Dave, Lillian, Mandy and Carol were on strict instructions to remain serving in the bar room, and John was yet to return from Sid's. He'd been gone for at least an hour — probably still waiting for Sid, poor lad. However, she didn't have time to think about that now; Richard's party was upon her.

The remaining guests arrived within the allotted fifteen minutes: Fraser Coin appeared a few minutes after the lieutenants. He gave Mary a conspiratorial wink and patted her on the rear as she led him down the passageway. Next was Rupert Smythe-Wheaton, who acknowledged Mary with a smarmier than usual expression. Then a fidgety whippet of a man suddenly appeared in the kitchen and introduced himself as Sir Richard's secretary, Prestwich. He walked speedily past Mary down the passageway and into the dining room. Mary had never met Prestwich before, and still felt like she hadn't. The only thing she'd had time to notice, apart from his plain grey clerk's clothes, was that he carried a ledger, ink and quill. The last to arrive was a very subdued Richard, both in manner and appearance. Instead of his striking black and silver attire, he wore a rather muted ensemble of plain black trousers, shirt and boots. His only concession to grandeur was an intricately engraved silver buckle through which a three-inch-wide polished black leather belt was fed.

"Good evening, Mary." His tone was matter-of-fact. "I take it everyone has arrived?"

Mary nodded. "Yes."

"Very good." He seemed eager to join them.

Mary was about to escort him down the passageway when he stopped her. "One moment, Mary. I would speak to you briefly before the formalities begin."

That sounded ominous, and Richard certainly looked serious.

"Without revealing the nature of what will be discussed tonight, I want you to understand why I have assembled such a group."

"I see; most thoughtful of you, Richard."

A quick, sardonic smile played across his face. "Normally a meeting like this would be conducted in my private quarters and consist only of military personnel. However, since I am no longer Seneschal, I have been forced to take a more... unorthodox approach."

Mary remained silent; she suspected her half-brother was quite adept at the unorthodox.

"For the sake of the Duchy, I have decided upon a course of action that requires the co-operation of certain influential people — Fraser Coin is one of them. I have included Smythe-Wheaton purely from a legal perspective. Every word of what is said in that room tonight will be recorded by Prestwich, and that document will be legally ratified by Smythe-Wheaton as a true and faithful account of the meeting. In fact, Mary, I am also having him draw up a Declaration of Occurrence — where and when the meeting took place et cetera — which, if you have no objection, you will witness."

Richard paused. Mary said nothing, waiting for him to continue. Then she realised he was expecting a response from her. "Oh... yes, of course."

His eyes narrowed. "Thank you. Your co-operation is appreciated." Then, flicking his gaze in the direction of the passageway, he said, "Very well, let the games begin."

He strode across the kitchen and down the passageway. Mary followed in his wake. "What about the lieutenants?" she said to his back.

"What about them?" he replied without stopping.

"If you're no longer their Seneschal, what are *they* here for?"

Richard reached the door to the dining room before he turned to face Mary. "Insurance." He smiled, and then opened the door.

Now that the party was assembled, Mary played the host, welcoming them and assuring them of complete privacy. *She* would be the only person to enter the room and would only do so after been given leave; her staff had been told not to use the passageway.

She then drew their attention to the well-provisioned table where three loaves of freshly baked bread were surrounded by a selection of cheeses, cured meats, pickled onions and chutney, as well as a selection of dried fruit and nuts. Despite Brandon's comment to the contrary, she and Juanita had also spent some time adorning the table with 'finery' like lace placemats, pewter plates and crystal goblets; they complemented the two silver candelabras beautifully. There were also two crystal decanters filled with an Escargotian red, and Dave had tapped a barrel of prized Wurstland ale from the cellar. Mary had also filled the room with fresh summer flowers, not just for appearance, but to mask the odour of urine that would eventually emanate from the piss buckets she'd placed in two corners of the room.

She smiled proudly, her gaze lingering slightly on Brandon. "As you can see, gentlemen, all your needs have been considered. I can see no reason to disturb you until main course, which should be ready within the hour. However, in the meantime, should you require anything, I suggest either Lieutenant Swill or Sir Richard inform me, since their presence has already been noted at The Harey Rabbit."

The reaction to Mary's directness was varied: Fitzbadly gawped, Brandon smiled, Smythe-Wheaton guffawed in outrage, Prestwich twitched nervously and Fraser Coin leered at her and licked his lips. Richard's expression, however, was unreadable. "Most acceptable," he said. "Thank you, Mary."

Mary nodded and left the room. She then went upstairs and retrieved her kitchen staff.

The evening progressed without incident or interruption. Mary delivered the main course of roasted quails and vegetables an hour later, refilled the wine decanters and left without hearing or seeing anything that gave her any clues as to what was being discussed.

It wasn't until after the main course that Mary started to worry about John — he'd been gone for almost three hours now and it was starting to get dark. Vera and Pearl were busy washing dishes, while Patricia and her new best friend, Juanita, were taking a well-earned break in the courtyard. The sky was now covered by cloud and the air felt heavy with moisture.

"Yes, but dee Meestress ees very worried, I theenk," Juanita was saying as Mary walked out of the kitchen to join them.

"Really, Juanita," Mary chipped in. "And what, exactly, apart from your behaviour, have I to be very worried about?"

Juanita's flush of embarrassment was caught in the weak light spilling from the doorway. "I sorry Meestress, but you say to me you are worried for Seed, and you are worried why dee gringo bash hees head in, and den your important brother has deener dat ees beeg seecret, and that make you more worried, I theenk."

It took a few moments for Mary's brain to decipher the rapid fire Icarumban-laced words. Patricia looked completely confused.

"Be that as it may, Juanita, it is not *your* place, or Patricia's, or Dave's, or anyone else who I employ to question my behaviour."

"I no question your behaviour!" Juanita blurted out defensively.

"She's jus' worried 'bout you, Mistress," Patricia added quickly.

She'd heard it *all* now: the hard-nosed cook sticking up for the 'mad Icarumban' who'd emptied a hot pot of water over her. "I'd rather she worried about controlling her tongue!" Mary realised that she was shouting. She sighed. "I'm sorry. I'm just tired."

Patricia moved towards her, holding out her arms. Mary accepted the woman's motherly embrace. "We're all feelin' the strain, Mistress," she said, patting her back. "You push y'self too 'ard you do."

Mary nodded into Patricia's solid shoulder. Juanita joined in, embracing them both. For a few moments they just hugged each other. Then Mary felt a heavy splash of water on top of her head, then another. They separated and looked at the sky. Then they all laughed and ran inside just before the downpour.

A drenched John stumbled into the kitchen some twenty minutes later, much to Mary's relief. She accosted him as he dripped his way to the washroom.

"Where have you been? Is Sid alright?"

He belched. "Sorry, mishtress. You said t'wait f'Sid, like. And 'e only got back reeshen'ly."

"Did he now," she said, fanning the ale fumes away from her face.

"'E's a good bloke," John informed her. "'E's worried 'bout you an' this dinner."

"Is he now." *Another* person who was worried about her: *just* what she needed.

He nodded, and Mary handed him a dry towel. "I'll get you some dry clothes. Can you undress yourself?"

He looked at her, his eyes swimming. "'Course, mishtress."

What had John said to Sid, she wondered.

It was close to midnight when Richard finally announced the meeting was coming to an end. He asked her to make sure their exit would be just as private as their arrival. *That wouldn't be hard*, she thought — everyone except Juanita and John had gone home. Juanita was asleep in her room upstairs (where she boarded) and John had eventually passed out at the kitchen table; he was now in one the guestrooms. Mary was beyond tired herself after all the preparation and stress of making sure everything was as it should be for Richard's dinner. It had been a long, hard day for all of them.

"You may leave at your leisure, gentlemen," she said, trying not to sound too eager. "I am the only person left to see you."

"Very good," Richard said. He looked and sounded exactly as he had at the beginning of the night, which was surprising; he wasn't one who refrained from drinking. As a party, they'd certainly not skimped on the wine or the ale, and they'd hoed through the food. Prestwich and Brandon also appeared sober. In fact, Prestwich was still scratching away at his notes, his quill flicking hurriedly across the page, but she couldn't see what he was writing. Predictably, it was Fraser Coin and Rupert Smythe-Wheaton who looked worse for wear, as did Lieutenant Fitzbadly. Still, none of them had become loose-tongued enough to reveal any part of what had been discussed. At the beginning of the evening, she'd been hoping they'd let some details slip; now she was hoping they'd leave.

They were all staring at her and she suddenly felt like an intruder. She made to leave when Brandon spoke up. "Mary," he said. It sounded like an order. All eyes were on him as he rose from his chair. "Thank you for a superb meal and excellent hospitality. You are a remarkable woman."

He was looking at her with admiration. Like Mary, the other guests weren't sure how to react; it seemed so out of place with the tight-lipped formality they'd maintained throughout the evening.

Richard was the first to react. "Well said, Lieutenant." He also stood. This set of a chain reaction of people springing, jumping and staggering to their feet.

Brandon then orchestrated three cheers.

Fifteen minutes later, everyone had left except Richard. He asked to stay in one of the guestrooms.

Mary duly obliged. "Of course, Richard. Have you been thrown out of the Upper Bailey?"

"Not as yet." He yawned, looking as tired as she felt.

Mary escorted Richard to the room she'd used while Sid had been recovering. It wasn't the best The Harey Rabbit had to offer, but it would certainly do for someone who only needed a place to sleep. In any case, she was in the process of preparing the other seven guestrooms for some of the Duke of Stymouth's entourage who were due to arrive in nine days. The rooms had been appropriated on behalf of the Duke by Sir Cecil Paisley, Lower Icing's most renowned proponent of fashion and culture.

"I do appreciate all you have done tonight, Mary." Richard stifled a yawn as she opened the guestroom door.

She yawned in response. "I hope it achieved what you wanted."

Richard smiled wearily. "So do I."

Mary bid her brother goodnight and went back downstairs. Entering the passageway, her bedroom and the dining room lay to the right, the kitchen to the left. She was sorely tempted to head straight for her bedroom and collapse into a deep sleep. However, she couldn't leave the dining room in its current state: full of dirty plates, spilled food and drink and, of course, the piss buckets.

Gathering her last reserves of energy, she began the process of tidying up and cleaning. She scraped the plates and cleaned the crystal; Juanita could wash the lace tablecloth, clean the table and sweep the floor tomorrow. She also thought about leaving the job of the emptying the piss buckets to Juanita, but the smell would be much worse by morning. Amazingly, the party's aim had been quite good; most of the piss had actually made it into the two buckets. Trying not to think about their sloshing contents, she grabbed the buckets and took them outside.

The rain had become a drizzle, but it was good to feel the gentle drops against her face. She opened the courtyard gate and headed along the southern edge of The Square, past the stable block, following the dry-stone wall that bordered The Square from open farmland. Some twenty paces along, she stopped and emptied the pungent liquid over the wall. A guard tower on the massive castle wall loomed over her — an eerie presence, barely discernible in the darkness. She felt as though it was watching her as she returned to the courtyard and locked the gate.

Just as Mary was about to head back into the kitchen, she heard hoof beats echo against cobblestones. As they grew louder, they slowed from a trot to a walk, until eventually they stopped at the other side of the gate. Then she heard the rider dismount and try the locked gate. The person — it was a man — cursed in frustration and banged against the barred gate.

"Who is it?" Mary demanded.

"Mary?" he asked, sounding surprised.

Mary was just as surprised. "Tom?"

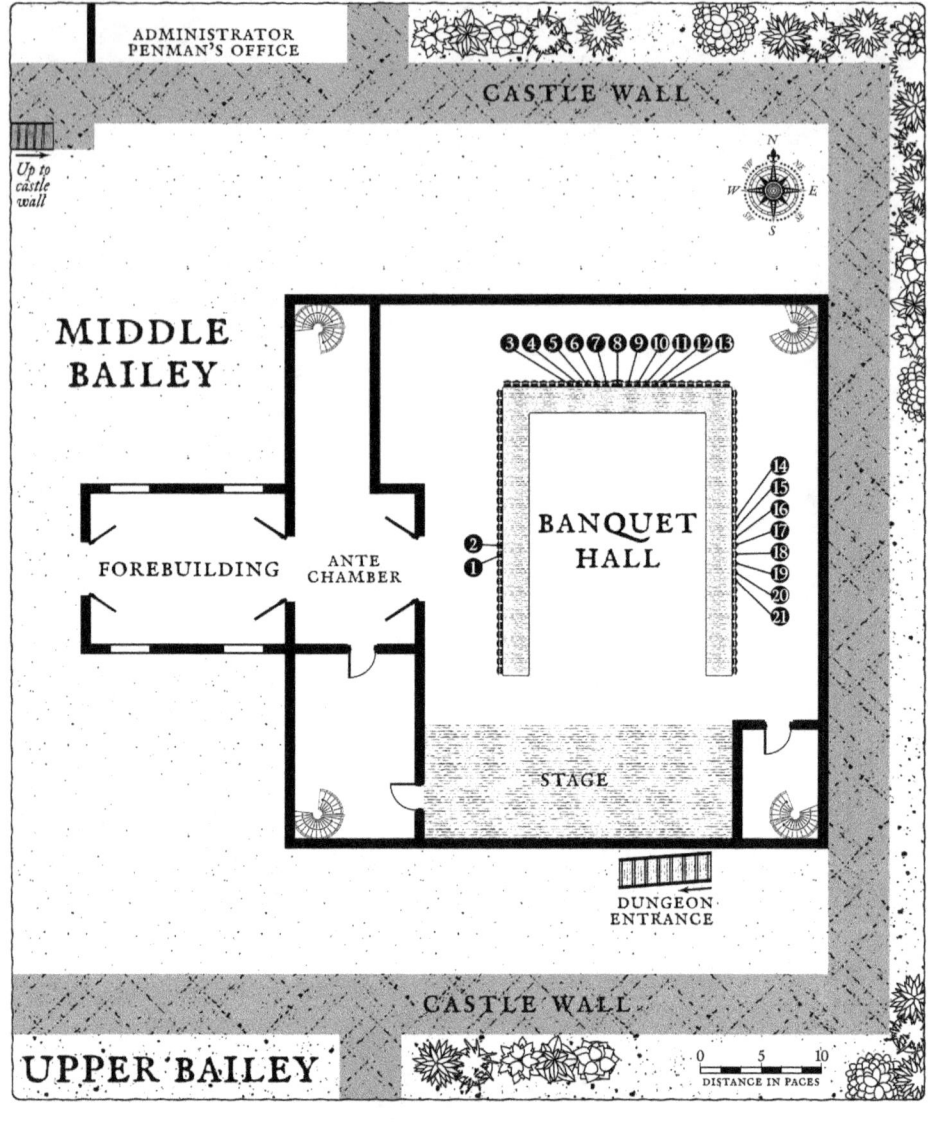

# BANQUET HALL

*Floorplan of the Castle Dinner at* The Keep

| | | | |
|---|---|---|---|
| 1, 2 | Regina and Jonathon Nitter | 13 | Ariadne Smythe-Wheaton |
| 3, 4 | Hillary and Marcus Ironcase Esq. | 14, 15, 16 | Eloise, Henry and Candice Bowler |
| 5, 6 | Esther and Jeremy Dupree Esq. | 17 | Sir Richard Upson |
| 7 | Captain Paris Le Sharp | 18 | Olivia Hiepants |
| 8 | The Duke? | 19 | Gerald Hiepants |
| 9, 10 | Fraser and Miriam Coin | 20, 21 | William and Cecily Dyer |
| 11, 12 | Beatrice and Oliver Lawson Esq | | |

# THURSDAY, JULY 3

## CHAPTER 33

### *Shitload of firewood*

OPHELIA WOKE TO the call of birds. It was her third morning in the forest and she was becoming attuned to life in the wild. For a while she just lay there listening to sounds bounce through the trees — chirps, squawks, croaks, chatters and whips, all vying to be heard in the gloom of dawn. It was quite cosy in the warm confines of the shelter, her pa's breathing was deep and…

*Tom?*

She bolted upright; he wasn't next to her. Suddenly wide awake, Ophelia leapt from the shelter into a misting rain. Hazel snickered, but there was no sign of Wildflower; Tom hadn't returned.

She'd lain awake for what seemed like half the night, waiting for him to suddenly appear out of the darkness. Every noise — scampering feet, rustling bushes, creaking branches, even drops of rain — became a hope for Tom's return.

She'd regretted her harsh words well before the thud of Wildflower's hooves had been swallowed by the clatter of rain on trees. But she'd been too stubborn to call out an apology, and now, it seemed, she'd been left high and dry.

Looking around the campsite, there was no sign that anything had been disturbed. Shock gave way to disbelief. Had Tom really left them to fend for themselves? Maybe he'd been injured travelling at night. He could have knocked himself unconscious on a low branch, bashed his head on a rock, fallen down a ravine, or drowned in the Icing… her mind raced with possibilities. Maybe she could follow his tracks, she knew *some* of the things to look for; he might be lying less than fifty paces away with two broken legs. Then again, maybe she should take Hazel; that way she could cover more ground.

Her thoughts were interrupted by a croaky, "Wha's wrong?"

Ophelia walked back to the shelter. Her pa had levered himself up against the trunk of the oak.

"It's Tom, Pa," she said. "'E lef' las' night an' 'e ain't come back."

"Good riddance," he muttered, echoing her thoughts from yesterday evening. She wished she could take them back.

"Pa…" She crouched under the shelter. "It *ain't* good riddance. It ain't *good* at all. 'E could be 'urt."

"Listen 'ere, Ophelia," he said, grabbing her wrist. His grip was stronger than it had been yesterday. He was definitely recovering. "Don' y'go worryin' 'bout that friggin' tree hugger; 'e ain't worth it. You 'n' me can do jus' fine without 'im. Understan'?"

"Yes, Pa," she agreed meekly.

He released his grip on her wrist and gently ran his hand down her left cheek. "You do me proud, Pheel."

To take her mind away from Tom's departure, Ophelia set to the task of restarting the fire. There'd been enough rain overnight to douse the flames, but, fortunately, Tom had covered the fire with two large logs and dull red embers still glowed underneath them.

Her pa wanted to help forage for dry wood, but the effort of standing up made his head spin and after a few stubborn steps he'd accepted that he'd be more of a hindrance than a help. Leaving him propped up under the shelter, Ophelia walked away from the dawning sky and headed west towards the Icing, to where Tom had said he'd caught the fish, in the direction he'd disappeared yesterday evening.

Despite what her pa said, Ophelia knew they'd struggle without Tom. And while she wasn't in fear for their lives, it might well be a day or two before her pa was strong enough to walk without assistance or clamber onto Hazel. During that time, they'd have water and fire, but unless Ophelia stumbled across a dead animal, they'd be going without food. And her pa needed food to regain his strength.

As Ophelia moved into the forest, she kept her eyes peeled for signs of Tom and Wildflower's passing. Amazingly, she spotted some — mainly broken or trampled bracken, but she also identified the occasional hoof mark and footprint. It was clear that Tom had walked Wildflower, not ridden her. He'd been cautious at least. That was a relief; chances were he was safe.

Ophelia silently admonished herself; if only her temper wasn't ignited by the tiniest spark. Then again, what could she do? She was her father's daughter. Right now, all she wanted to do was fall into Tom's arms and tell him she was sorry.

She'd moved about two hundred paces to the west and had just finished marking a third tree when she came across an outcrop of rock running north-south. It became higher as it trailed up the southern edge of the valley. So, she headed north, following the outcrop for some hundred paces until it petered out into flat ground. She could find nothing to indicate a man or a horse had been this way. She'd lost Tom's trail.

Retracing her steps, she made her way back to the campsite. Along the way, she collected an abundant amount of twigs and small branches to encourage the fire back to life.

By the time Ophelia emerged from the trees, the campsite was dappled with sunlight and the drizzling rain had stopped. Hazel whinnied out a welcome.

"Zat you, Pheel?" her pa called out. He was still propped up against the oak.

"Yes, Pa," she replied, walking towards the dying fire.

"Where y'been?" He sounded put out.

His tone irked her. Where the frig did he *think* she'd been? She dumped the armload of branches by the fire. "Well, I ain't been powderin' me nose."

Her pa emerged from the shelter. He looked angry. "Don' get lippy with *me*, Ophelia. It don' take an hour t'grab an 'andful o' firewood."

An hour? What was he on about? She couldn't have been gone *that* long? "*You're* the bleedin' 'andful! *This...*" She sent the pile of sticks flying with an angry kick of her boot. "Is a *shitload* of firewood!"

There was a moment of stunned silence as sticks and twigs crashed into the fire pit, smacking against the burnt logs and disturbing the damp ash bed.

They both laughed at the same time. Then Ophelia winced as the pain in her right foot kicked in. Her pa also grimaced as he laughed, grabbing onto his bruised ribs. What a fine pair they made.

## Chapter 34

### *Offcut meat is good*

MARY WOKE TO the sound of splashing rain on her window. She groaned. Could it really be morning already? Surely it was only minutes ago that she'd finally laid down her head. Though barely awake, her body automatically reacted to the new day by flinging off the bed sheet and springing out of bed.

She walked groggily to the window and peered out at the courtyard and barely illuminated stable. The cobblestones looked slick, and a number of puddles had formed within the uneven surface. It must have been raining all night. It was good to see; Lower Icing could do with a good wash. Come to think of it, so could she.

Mary stuck her head out the window; more to wake herself than any attempt at cleanliness. The air was still warm, but cooler than the stuffy confines of her room. For a few minutes, she stayed there, half dazed, staring into the empty courtyard and listening to clattering noises emanating from Reg Puffy's kitchen. As she stood there, her mind drifted back to Tom's unexpected arrival…

After establishing it *was* actually Tom behind the courtyard gate, Mary had welcomed him in with a bombardment of questions: What are you doing here? What's happened? Have you found Frank Offcut? Where's Ophelia? and probably half a dozen more, all in quick succession, before Tom had been able to get a word in.

"Everything is fine, Mary," he assured her. "Is Richard here?"

"Yes he is, but how—?"

"Lieutenant Swill suggested I try here. Sorry to be rude, but would you mind informing him of my arrival while I stable Wildflower?"

Mary was too bewildered to take offence; his sudden appearance was just so bizarre, and there was a sense of urgency in his voice. She complied without further question.

Predictably, Richard reacted with minimalistic efficiency. Apart from his boots and his belt, he hadn't undressed. "Tell him I will meet him in the dining room directly."

She returned downstairs to find Tom standing over the kitchen table, hoeing into the leftovers from the dinner. It was only then that she realised he was soaked to the skin. "Tom, what have—?"

"Excuse me," he said as he chewed on the remains of the roast quail. "It's been somewhat of an arduous day."

That was patently obvious: not only was he saturated, his clothes were covered in dirt and his shirt was torn in a few places. "You need to get out of those clothes straightaway. You'll catch your death."

In answer, he picked the bones of the quail.

"Tom, what's going on? *Did* you and Ophelia find Frank?"

"A most pertinent question, Mary," Richard said, entering the kitchen.

In answer, Tom revealed that he had, indeed, found Frank alive, although quite badly injured, in a valley just south of something called the Dragon's Back; apparently, he'd been chucked over its edge by the Moleson Twins. He was now in the more-than-capable hands of his daughter. Richard had raised a dubious eyebrow at that particular remark and said, "I think it best if we continue this conversation alone, Tom."

*So be it*, Mary thought. Let them have their private discussion. However, at her insistence, Tom took the time to change into some ill-fitting dry clothes. She kept quite a few spare outfits for her staff — they tended to get quite messy — but none had the Gamekeeper's tall, muscular physique. Dave's spares would have to do. (John's certainly wouldn't.) The two men then disappeared into the private dining room, Tom taking the leftover cheese and bread with him.

Twenty minutes later, they returned to the kitchen. During their absence, Mary had scrubbed Tom's clothes and hung them over the stove. He acknowledged her efforts with a tired thank you and a request to stay the night, informing her, "I have an early start tomorrow."

"Of course," Mary replied. "Take the room next to Richard."

"Thank you." Then he followed Richard out of the kitchen.

She called after them; they weren't getting away *that* lightly. She moved towards the passageway as the two men turned to face her. Folding her arms, she said, "I think I deserve *some* sort of explanation. Did you find out anything from Frank?"

Expectedly, it was Richard who answered. "We've been through this, Mary. Suffice to—"

"You know where you can stuff your suffice, Richard." She was tired and in no mood for playing his games. He treated her to one of his disdainful smirks. It infuriated her. "Don't you dare patronise me," she snapped, unfolding her arms and walking towards him. "I'm not some dullard serving wench, Richard, *nor* am I some wanton floosy," she said, flicking her gaze at Tom, who bristled at the barb. "I *can* be trusted to hold my tongue."

Again, it was Richard who responded (with whip-like speed and accuracy). "Unfortunately, Mary, your tongue was compromised the moment you stuck it into Sid Evily's mouth."

Chagrin filled every fibre of Mary's being; she felt the blood rush to her cheeks. She wanted to slap his moral-high-ground face, but somehow — *somehow* — she managed to stay her hand.

"Richard! That was uncalled for!" Tom interjected on her behalf, though he looked surprised by the revelation.

Richard regarded Tom wearily. "Perhaps we are *all* overtired." Then he cast his gaze back at her. "I am sorry, Mary." It was perfunctory at best and did nothing to quell her indignation.

Tom also looked unimpressed by Richard's effort. "I know this must seem terribly unjust, Mary, but I assure you, it *is* for the best."

Mary wanted to respond, but her throat had tightened and her eyes — damn them — had begun to fill with tears.

The two men shared a meaningful look. Richard sighed. "Very well," he murmured, reluctantly. "Since *Tom's* tongue has let slip Frank Offcut's involvement..." His black eyes glinted in the candlelight, while Tom's narrowed. "Yesterday afternoon, the person Frank was assisting us to find was discovered in Lower Icing. I am not prepared to go into details, but the fact that he was found alive is what triggered tonight's meeting."

Mary thought about interrupting Richard to ask him if this person was the mysterious doctor she'd overheard the guardsmen talking about, but it seemed obvious it was. Instead, she wiped her welling eyes before they overflowed down her cheeks.

"Then, this morning," Richard continued, "I made a discovery that shed a different light on how the Duke was attacked. Again, I am not willing to go into details; however, both these events are significant and were discussed tonight in depth. It is imperative that we keep our cards very close to our chest if we are to bring to justice the person responsible for Marmaduke's attack."

"So you know who attacked the Duke?" she whispered.

"It's more a case of we know who *didn't* attack the Duke. However, our list of suspects *has* become rather more… focused. Which is why secrecy is paramount, you understand?"

All Mary could do was nod and wipe away an errant tear. She had more questions than ever, but knew it was no use asking them.

"Then we'll bid you good night."

Tom added a more heartfelt, "Good night, Mary."

She watched as they walked down the passage; Tom's side illuminated more than Richard's, because the Gamekeeper held the chamber-stick. Just as they'd reached the stairs, she finally found her voice for the one question she *did* want answered. "What about Sid?"

They both turned around. There was a moment's silence before Richard spoke.

"I am assured that your… *dalliance* does not have the wherewithal to undertake an attack on the Duke."

He could be such an arrogant bastard. And *who* had assured him? Whoever it was didn't know Sid very well.

"However, if you wouldn't mind asking him to return the silver button, it might save the embarrassment of men-at-arms at his door."

Leaning out the window, half asleep in the drizzling dawn, Mary wondered who the suspects might be. Then her thoughts turned to the day ahead. Once Richard was out of her hair, she could get back to running The Harey Rabbit, which seemed a much easier proposition after the effort of last night's dinner. She also needed to see Sid. Apart from the fact that she desired to, she had to tell him that Richard knew about the button. He wasn't going to like that one bit — she'd betrayed his confidence — but at least she could reassure him that he wasn't a suspect.

Her dreamlike ponderings were broken by the sound of creaking footsteps from the passageway. She rushed, barefoot, to her bedroom door and opened it. Tom, still wearing the clothes she'd given him, had just come down the stairs and was walking towards the kitchen. He bid her good morning and informed her that he would be leaving directly. Mary nodded and offered to fix him some breakfast, which he readily accepted.

By the time Mary entered the kitchen, Tom had changed back into his clothes. He gave her a weary-looking smile, his mouth surrounded by a spiky growth of sandy-coloured hair. "I was just about to go and saddle up Wildflower," he informed her.

"You do that, Tom," Mary replied.

He nodded and disappeared through the back door of the kitchen. Mary lit a couple of candles to add some colour to the early morning grey. The kitchen bench was stacked with the remnants of last night's dinner, but at least she'd scraped the plates and dishes — it was now a matter of washing everything. Fortunately, she had Juanita and Lillian for that. Instead, she set to the task of cooking Tom (and herself) a breakfast of eggs and bacon.

The bacon was sizzling away by the time Tom returned. The curling pink rashers put her in mind of Frank Offcut and, now that Tom had reappeared, Ophelia.

"Smells good," he said, cheerfully.

"Yes," Mary agreed, turning the rashers over. "Offcut meat *is* good." She looked across to where Tom was standing on the other side of the table. He wore a bemused expression. "Though you'd probably know that better than me."

He took it with good humour. "I'd be wary about going down *that* track if I were you, particularly since *you* have apparently taken a shine to The Dead Duck's Pork Pie King."

Mary laughed. "Good point." Sid had mentioned that he had a lucrative pastry arrangement with Reg Puffy and Will Plucker. "Sit down," she said, indicating the places set at the table. "Breakfast won't be long."

Minutes later, Mary served up two plates of eggs and bacon. She'd also brewed some tea, which she poured into a couple of mugs. "So, do you and Ophelia have more in common than Lower Icing's butcher?" she asked casually.

He gave her a wry smile. "I think she is uncommonly her own person — reminds me of you in many ways."

Mary wasn't sure how to take that. Her expression must have spoken volumes because Tom quickly added, "It was meant as a compliment."

"I see. Then thank you, Tom." She needed to change the subject; she didn't really want to delve into the intricacies of Tom's attraction to Ophelia Offcut. And, as Tom had pointed out, she didn't want him plying *her* with questions about Sid. "So, how *is* Frank? You said last night that he was badly injured. Are you *sure* he's going to be alright?"

Tom nodded, swallowing a mouthful of egg and bacon. "He's a tough nut; he'll pull through. He just needs rest and nourishment. I'll grab some supplies from my cabin and hopefully he'll be right for travelling in the next day or two. The urgency is not so great now that Richard has—"

Mary raised a curious eyebrow. "Richard has…?"

Tom looked abashed. "I'm sorry, I'm not at—"

"Spare me, Tom," Mary interjected. "I've heard *that* cockerel crow enough in the last day to last me a lifetime."

"Fair enough," he said, sipping at his tea. "In any case, I must be off soon. It's almost light and I have a good half day's travel in front of me. I suspect my prolonged absence has not been well received."

"Well, I can understand that, Tom. *I* wouldn't be overjoyed at being left to fend for myself in the middle of… Where are they exactly? I've never heard of the Dragon's Back."

He smiled at that. "Yes, that's because you serve the well-to-do rather than the well informed."

"Or, in your case, the well-out-of-order."

Ignoring her jibe, Tom explained that the Dragon's Back was a mountain ridge that rose from the Icing River and ran in a north-easterly direction for some hundred miles before descending into the Naffolk Plains. "It's known in certain circles as a safe route to Great Naff. Frank and Ophelia are in a valley on its southern side, some fifty miles upriver from here. They have water and ate well yesterday afternoon."

"Oh well, what *more* could they want?"

Tom took her sarcasm in good humour. "Ophelia is a resourceful woman and, I might add, whole-heartedly endorsed my leaving. Speaking of which, dawn is breaking."

With that, he shoved the remaining fried egg into his mouth and washed it down with three noisy gulps of tea. Then he wiped his mouth and stood up. Mary also stood.

"Well, thank you again, Mary."

"Good luck with the Offcuts. Hopefully they haven't been eaten by wolves or strangled in their sleep by some well-informed travellers."

He smiled. "Send my regards to Sid." Then, almost as an afterthought, he added, "Richard told me what happened, by the way — how you found him."

Mary suddenly felt quite self-conscious, and even to herself, her response sounded defensive. "Yes, well, I couldn't just leave him sprawled unconscious next to the stables. If John hadn't discovered him, he might not have—"

"Mary. It wasn't an accusation. Neither Richard nor I think Sid had anything to do with the attack on the Duke. And there's no doubt the silver button was planted on him."

It suddenly occurred to Mary that Tom was speaking as if he knew Sid personally. Sid had mentioned he had a loose arrangement with someone who supplied him with furs. "So *you* were the one who assured Richard that Sid wasn't capable of attacking the Duke."

"Now *that* sounded like an accusation."

Mary shook her head, trying to focus her thoughts. "Sorry. It's just…" She sighed. "Oh, never mind."

He regarded her with a mixture of compassion and confusion.

"I'm just tired," she added.

"Yes, I know the feeling."

Looking him in the eye, she asked, "Do you know who attacked Sid?"

He stared at her, no doubt weighing up what he should reveal. *Did* he know? Her heart was suddenly racing. "Tom?" she prompted.

"Can't be sure," he replied. "But there's a good chance it was the Moleson Twins. It seems Sid was just in the wrong place at the wrong time."

She nodded thoughtfully; if the Moleson Twins had beaten up Frank Offcut and chucked him down the side of a mountain, they were certainly capable of bashing Sid and emptying his purse. But what was their connection to this mysterious silver button, the one identical to Richard's, but not his, the one he'd downplayed as an 'interesting development'. She wanted to ask Tom if *he* knew its significance, but there was no point — she knew what his answer would be.

"Well, it's time to take my leave," he said, moving towards the back door.

"Yes, of course," she said, following him.

When they reached the stable, Tom mounted Wildflower and bid Mary farewell. Then, almost as an afterthought, he asked if she would mind informing Frank's wife that her husband and daughter were safe.

"Not at all," she agreed, readily. "Good luck, Tom." There was a tangible sense of familiarity about the scene, but unlike Monday morning's farewell, he was riding into steady rain rather than the blistering sun.

"Fear not. All will be well."

Then, with a couple of clicks of his tongue, a pull on the reins and a gentle nudge of his heels, he steered Wildflower out of the stables, through the gate, across the Town Square and towards the East Road, presumably to retrieve supplies from his cabin.

An hour later, the kitchen was in full production for another Thursday at The Harey Rabbit. Juanita and Patricia — their new friendship still intact — were making quick work of the dishes, while Lillian and Mandy set about cleaning up all traces of last night's dinner in the dining room. Strangely, Richard was yet to put in an appearance.

Mary walked up to his room and knocked on his door. "Richard? It's Mary."

Footsteps followed. Then the door opened. Richard was in a state of half dress — unbuttoned shirt and black trousers were the extent of his sartorial progress. It took Mary by surprise; she'd never seen him look anything but immaculate.

"Good morning," she said as pleasantly as possible.

He nodded. "Excuse my appearance, but I wish to further prevail upon your hospitality."

"Of course," Mary said, coming to attention. Richard had that affect; she wondered if anyone had ever said no to him.

"I wish to wash and shave. Can you arrange that?"

"I'll have some water heated and brought to your room. Do you require a blade?"

He nodded. "Thank you, Mary."

He was about to close the door when Mary enquired in her best hostess voice, "Will you also be requiring breakfast in your room?"

That brought out a bemused grin. "That would most agreeable."

"I'll leave you in peace then, Richard."

He nodded and closed the door.

## CHAPTER 35

### *Never felt so proud*

**T**HE SOUND OF Gerald entering the front door barely two hours after he'd left for the castle was unexpected. And judging by the urgency in his voice as he called out to her, he brought with him unexpectedly bad news.

"Olivia!" he bellowed again; he hadn't given her time to respond to his first call.

"Yes, Gerald," she called out to the approaching footsteps. She was in the middle of washing clothes. Beth Wringer's weekly washing service usually sufficed, but, with the hot weather and the visits to The Bloody Bell, the pile of washing had built up quickly. She couldn't leave it until next Monday, and now that the rain looked like easing up, it was a good opportunity to make inroads into the accumulation.

Gerald appeared at the washroom door, his face almost as red as his coat.

"What is it, Gerald?" she said, concerned by the amount of concern on his sweating face. His expression was in complete contrast to the ebullient one he'd worn upon leaving 8 Plumduff Street.

"I say, Olivia," he gasped. "I've just heard that Sir Richard held a secret meeting at The Harey Rabbit last night."

Olivia stared at him panting in the doorway. Her usual reaction would be something sarcastic like 'It couldn't have been *that* big a secret if *you've* heard about it', but after the emotional events of yesterday and the realisation that Gerald was the only person who'd been loyal to her, she chose a more supportive response. "I see," she said, seriously. In truth, it was a potentially significant development (if, of course, it wasn't just castle rumour).

Discarding the blue blouse she'd been scrubbing, she asked how he'd heard about the meeting. "Well, m'dear, it was more a case of *overhearing*." He paused to catch his breath. "I say, would you mind if we sat down? I'm feeling a tad light-headed, what."

Olivia agreed readily enough; her back had begun to ache from leaning over the tub, scrubbing out grime and sweat.

Fifteen minutes later Gerald had filled her in on the details surrounding the discovery of the meeting. Fraser Coin had been speaking to Rupert Smythe-Wheaton outside Prestwich's office. Apparently, the lawyer was delivering a parchment to Richard's secretary, something he referred to as a Deed of Occurrence. Fraser had then quipped that the deed was aptly named and that Sir Richard certainly knew how to host a secret meeting. Then he mentioned something lurid about Mary and having to frequent The Harey Rabbit more often.

Olivia had brought Gerald to task after his retelling, querying why Fraser Coin and Smythe-Wheaton would speak so openly in front of him. He'd explained that they weren't aware of his presence, that he'd been upstairs in Sir Richard's quarters where he thought to find Captain Le Sharp. (He'd stammered over the words, eventually referring to Paris as the new Seneschal.) However, Paris had not yet taken up residence in the Upper Bailey and Gerald had been on his way back down to the reception hall when he'd overheard the conversation. He'd stopped and listened as soon as the words 'secret meeting' passed Fraser Coin's lips.

However, any further information the lawyer and the merchant might have divulged had been thwarted by the appearance of Prestwich. Smythe-Wheaton had bid Fraser Coin good-day, then entered the secretary's office. By the time Gerald had descended the stairs, Fraser Coin had also disappeared.

He then went on to tell her that he'd bumped into Lieutenant Swill on the way out of the Upper Bailey. The lieutenant had informed him that Captain Le Sharp was in The Keep. "This is where things became even more worrisome, m'dear," he said. "You see, even though Master Scaffold and his team were still in full swing preparing the Banquet Hall for the Duke of Stymouth… I must say, Olivia, it's going to look rather fantastic. They're even erecting some sort of gallery overlooking—"

"Gerald," Olivia interrupted as kindly as possible; her newly found tolerance towards her husband's quirks didn't extend to his penchant for digression. However, her tone must have been sufficiently curt, because he apologised smartly enough.

There was a moment of silence before he continued with an anti-climactic, "Now, where was I, m'dear?"

"Even though Master Scaffold and his team…?" Olivia prompted, trying to rein in her growing agitation.

"Oh yes, quite. In the midst of all this preparation, the new Seneschal was talking to Sir Cecil Paisley… Well, I say talking, but placating would be a better word, I fear. You know what Sir Cecil is like, m'dear — all those foppish dramatics, what. I really don't know how—"

"Gerald. Will you *please* concentrate on the topic at hand? What occurred in The Keep that you found so worrisome?"

"Your pardon, m'dear, I do tend to—"

"Gerald!"

"They're holding an impromptu dinner at The Keep tonight. The Seneschal told me it was for an important announcement, but would say no more, adding only that I would find out at the same time as all the other invited guests."

To Olivia it could only be one thing: Paris was going to declare the existence of Xavier. She wasn't sure she had the emotional fortitude to bear witness to that (if, indeed, she was invited).

Olivia saw Gerald to their front door, encouraging him to remain steadfast, as nothing untoward had come of Sir Richard's secret meeting, and that tonight's dinner could be exactly what they'd been hoping for. "Paris is a man of principle and honour, Gerald, not a politician and schemer like Richard. He will do right by Xavier, and, if our part is revealed, he will do right by us."

Gerald nodded half-heartedly; clearly, he was finding the machinations of politics rather overwhelming. Olivia, on the other hand, was ready and willing to face the consequences of their actions.

Reluctantly, Gerald began walking back to the castle. Olivia shut the door of 8 Plumduff Street, and was about to return to the arduous and thankless task of scrubbing when she heard a voice outside cry out her husband's name. She hurried to the front living room and peered out the window.

Gerald had been accosted by her good-for-nothing brother. She watched as he stood in Gerald's way, demanding to know what was happening at the castle, virtually accusing Gerald of knowing who'd bashed him.

*How dare he!* And in front of their home! The only thing that prevented Olivia from yelling out to Sid was the fear of attracting unwanted attention from the gossip-hunting castle-set with their parasol-shaded faces and butter-wouldn't-melt-in-their-mouth smiles.

Gerald, surprisingly, seemed to be holding his own. He even had the good taste to appear indignant at Sid's ranting. In the end, it was Gerald who held sway over Sid — he'd actually put her slacker of a sibling back in his ale-filled box. Gerald tipped his hat and left Sid fuming in the middle of the street.

"You will let me know if you *do* find out anything, won't you, Gerald?" Sid yelled after him.

Gerald didn't miss a step as he strode purposefully towards the castle, nor did he acknowledge Sid's words in any way. Olivia had never felt so proud of him.

Gerald's cool handling of Sid's aggressive behaviour had put Olivia in a rather buoyant mood. No doubt her brother was suffering the effects of another ale-filled night; he'd certainly looked rather seedy as he'd trudged up Plumduff Street and then turned left down Big Wig Street. *Hah!* she thought, perhaps he was going to visit Charles Bling 'Jeweller to The Duke' to steal her another birthday present. She was turning thirty-three tomorrow. Funny, it was the first time she'd given it any thought since Gerald had brought Xavier into their home... almost exactly a week ago. It seemed as if a lifetime had passed since then. And, in many ways, it had.

As she watched her wretched brother disappear, a momentary break in the cloud highlighted the homes on their side of the street in shimmering sunlight. A glint by the front door caught her eye. The brass plaque — it needed attending to. Today, more than any day in their six-year marriage, Olivia felt it deserved to shine.

## Chapter 36

### *Time for a fresh start*

IT WAS AT least another hour before Richard appeared downstairs. During that time, John had been to the well a dozen times to replenish their stocks of water; not just for Richard's bath, the kitchen and washroom barrels also needed refilling. The poor lad was quite soaked by the end; the early morning drizzle had become steady rain. Still, it had washed away the fogginess of last night's adventure with Sid and he was now in good spirits, as was everyone else in the inn — the rain and cooler temperature was a massive relief.

It was Mandy who, after retrieving the breakfast tray from Richard's room, brought the news that he was waiting for her in the dining room.

"'E's done a good job with that blade, Mistress," she quipped as she placed the tray on the kitchen table.

"Put them plates in the washin' bucket, missy, an' stack that tray in the cupboard where it belongs," Patricia said, without turning around from the bench where she was peeling potatoes.

"Yes, Patricia," Mandy answered. Then she poked her tongue out at the rotund cook's back.

Mary left them to it and headed down the corridor. The dining room door was open. Richard stood at the table with his back to her, resplendent in black, gazing down at a spread of parchments. He was back to his immaculate best. He turned as she entered the room, but it was a stranger's face that greeted her, one who was clean shaven.

"Richard?" It was hard not to stare — the sculptured beard was such an inherent part of who her brother was. It almost defined his personality. *And* his dark, shoulder-length hair was pulled back into a tight ponytail.

"Time for a fresh start, Mary," he said, matter-of-factly, dark eyes as appraising as ever.

"I see," she said, still mesmerised; she couldn't get over the transformation —

he'd shaved at least five years off his thirty-seven.

"I want you to read this," he said, handing her one of the parchments.

She blinked away her fascination and took the sheet. "Your pardon, Richard, it's just that you look so—"

He forestalled her, indicating with his eyes that she should focus her attention on its contents. "The document, Mary."

Obediently, Mary cast her eyes down to the parchment. Written in large, flowery lettering at the top of the page was *Deed of Occurrence*. Underneath was a summary of the dinner: where it occurred, who was present, what time it began and finished. However, it was written in pompous legal jargon with phrases like 'fit and proper', 'true and accurate', 'the said', 'the aforementioned', and a plethora of thereofs and whereofs. It was mindboggling how complicated a simple gathering could sound. At the bottom was space for three signatures. Rupert Smythe-Wheaton and Richard had already signed the document.

"When was this prepared?" She tried not to sound too incredulous, but she was amazed that the Deed of Occurrence had been written so quickly.

Richard cocked an eyebrow. "Sometime between the end of the dinner and fifteen minutes ago when Prestwich delivered it here."

"*Prestwich*?" She hadn't seen him arrive, and she hadn't been informed of the fact. "Prestwich was *here* in The Harey Rabbit?"

"You have the proof in your hands. Now if you wouldn't mind—"

"How did he get in?"

"My guess would be through a door," he said, irritation beginning to show.

"But…?"

"Prestwich is a most nimble individual, Mary. He often takes *me* unawares, suddenly appearing out of nowhere and the like. I suppose I am used to it. However, Prestwich's movements are neither here nor there. The Deed requires your signature."

Mary had to wrench her mind away from the perplexity of Prestwich's appearance. She would speak to Dave; maybe *he* had let him in. Placing the parchment on the table, she reached over to a quill sitting in its inkwell — had Prestwich brought *that* too? She signed the Deed without hesitation; the nib scratching Mary Brewer across the parchment underneath Richard Upson and Rupert Smythe-Wheaton.

"Thank you," he said perfunctorily. "Now, as you can see, I have other matters that require my attention."

Mary gave the other parchments a cursory look, and then gazed back at her half-brother. "Even though you are no longer Seneschal?" she asked, knowing that Richard would never relinquish complete control of the Duchy.

He smiled his sardonic smile. "Even though."

Mary nodded. "Well, it's time I returned to the matters that require *my* attention. If you need anything…"

"I will be fine. Thank you."

Mary went straight to the bar and asked Dave about Prestwich. Dave hadn't seen him arrive *or* leave. How could that be? Dave didn't have any answers for her.

She then marched into the kitchen. Patricia was deboning chicken. John hovered over her left shoulder observing her technique, while Mandy and Lillian sat at the table chopping carrots and turnips. However, there was *one* anomaly: Juanita was standing at the bench, peeling onions.

"What are you doing, Juanita?" Mary asked her.

Patricia piped in with, "She's jus' 'elpin' me, Mistress. Bit o' catchin' up t'do, after yesterday, like."

Mary glared at the robust cook, but she was too involved in her deboning operation to notice.

Juanita, on the other hand, was more than happy to look away from her task. "Ie yie yie." She sniffed, eyes streaming tears. "Dees oneeuns are so… how you say?"

"Oniony?" Mandy suggested.

"No. Ees… picante." Juanita sniffed, wiping her eyes with her sleeve.

Mandy giggled. "Pee wha'?"

This was a conversation Mary could do without. "When you have finished with the onions, Juanita," she said, cutting off Juanita's response, "there are a couple of bedrooms that need making up with fresh linen."

Juanita nodded while wiping her eyes.

Then Mary added, "If that's alright with *you*, Patricia."

Patricia didn't bat an eyelid or pause from the task at hand. "Don' pay me no mind, Mistress," she said, wearily. "I'm jus' goin' 'bout me bus'ness."

*If only*, Mary thought.

John gave her a wry smile.

"Eyes this way, boy," Patricia ordered.

"Actually, Patricia, I have another task for John."

His face brightened. "Yes, Mistress?"

"I want you to check on Sid for me."

John greeted the news with an enthusiastic smile. Patricia deboned without comment. Mandy giggled. Lillian nudged Mandy reproachfully. Juanita sniffed.

Mary beckoned John down the corridor; she didn't want *that* bunch listening in.

Aware that Richard was working in the dining room, Mary kept her voice low. "Right, John. Listen to me carefully."

John nodded seriously.

"I want you to make sure Sid is alright. If he doesn't answer his door, come straight back here and tell me, no hanging around waiting for him this time — straight back here."

"Yes, Mistress," he whispered, obediently.

"If he *does* answer his door, tell him I will see him this afternoon if that's convenient. Say that I am too busy this morning — there's no need to go into details."

John looked uncomfortable. "I think I migh' 'ave told 'im 'bout Sir Richard an' the dinner, like."

"Bloody hell, John!" Mary hissed.

John winced. "Sorry, Mistress."

"How did he react? Can you remember?"

He shook his head. "Don' think he was best pleased, like."

*That* was undoubtedly an understatement.

He hung his head. "Sorry, Mistress."

She sighed. "What's done is done, I suppose." She was going to have some explaining to do now. Still, it could have been worse. Sid could have decided to come back with John last night, demanding an explanation. Perhaps Richard had been enough of a deterrent.

"Right, John. Listen carefully."

John looked up.

"Tell Sid I'll be at his place at three this afternoon." If she gave him a definitive time it was more likely he'd be there. "Say that I am very sorry about last night and that I'm looking forward to seeing him." She wanted him to know she *was* sorry, and that she missed him — it seemed like ages since he left The Harey Rabbit.

"Sid's at three," John confirmed.

"Off you go, then," she said, ushering him back into the kitchen.

As John made his way to the back door, the ensemble of food preparers watched him with expressions ranging from mild disapproval (Patricia) to barely controlled mirth (Mandy). Lillian smiled pleasantly, while Juanita still battled with her onion tears.

He was just about to disappear into the courtyard, when Mary called him to stop. John halted immediately and turned around to face her, like a puppy desperate to be let off its leash. "Just make it clear to Sid that *I* will come to *him*." The last thing she wanted was some sort of confrontation at The Harey Rabbit.

"Right y'are, Mistress; I'll be sure to tell 'im." He shuffled in the doorway. Mary let the puppy go.

Ignoring the various gazes from her staff, Mary went into the washroom. Richard's request for a shave made her realise that more handtowels were probably required in each guestroom; she didn't want the guests from Stymouth to want for anything. She walked past the empty bathtub (she planned to make use of that this afternoon, just before heading off to see Sid) and opened the linen cupboard. She was taking stock of the towels when she heard John yell out, "No, wait! Please, Sid!"

*Sid??* Mary's heart hardly had the chance to leap before she heard the man himself call out for her. He was in the kitchen!

"Now listen 'ere!" Patricia responded in an indignant tone.

This was snapped off by Sid's angry, "Where's Mary, John?"

"You leave that boy alone!" countered Patricia.

This was a disaster. If Richard met Sid... Well, it didn't bear thinking about. Mary hurried across the washroom. As she did so, she heard Juanita comment about the romance of it all (of all things!) while John pleaded Mary's case. As she entered the kitchen, Sid stood near the back door, facing the courtyard and an upset-looking John who was saying, "The Mistress said to tell you that she'd—"

"Visit you this afternoon," she cut in coolly, crossing her arms. She understood Sid's frustration, but there was no need for him to take it out on John. Sid whirled around to face her. His face looked hurt in more ways than one. "At three o'clock to be precise." Damn him, why couldn't he just have listened to John?

He moved to hold her, but she stepped into the kitchen and restrained his arms. She had to get him out of here.

"You have to leave," she said meaningfully, keeping her voice low.

Understandably, Sid was upset and wanted to know what was going on, but as much as she wanted to, and *would* do, now wasn't the time. She said as much while edging him towards the doorway. They'd only taken a couple of small steps when Sid stopped and held her arms. "Please, Mary," he said intently, "I need to know what's going on."

She was about to promise him that she would tell all later when Patricia piped in with a gruff, "You 'eard the Mistress."

Mary suddenly understood Juanita's urge to douse the cook in hot water. She steamed her disapproval. However, all Patricia did was shrug her shoulders and return to her task at hand (water off a duck's back). Looking back at Sid, Mary could see his frustration. He deserved an explanation; if the shoe was on the other foot… "I *will* tell you, Sid," she said, keeping her voice low, "but not now. There are…" — What could she say? — "things I have to take care of first."

"Things?" He let go of her arms and looked at her questioningly. She wanted to scream 'Not now, Sid! Richard is just down the passageway!'

Mandy, for whatever reason, chose this moment to giggle, just to add insult to Sid's injury. Mary flushed with chagrin. "Mandy, I don't employ you to chop vegetables." She was fed up with the barmaid's childish behaviour. "You and Lillian get back to the bar."

Both women stared at her as if she'd just ranted something in Icarumban. "Now!"

That sent them jumping and heading straight for the bar room door. Mary immediately felt guilty, and Juanita's disapproving gaze wasn't helping. "Be quick about those onions, Juanita; that linen won't wash itself!"

The washer girl nodded her compliance, but it was compromised by her annoyingly knowing smile. Mary shook her head in frustration. Then she took a deep breath — now to make Sid understand it was in his best interests to leave. She didn't want to hurt him, but… It wasn't until she opened her eyes that she realised she'd *closed* them. He was looking at her with a confused expression, which, combined with his injured face, made him look quite tragic, like he'd just stepped out of a Hamlet Macbeth play. Just to add to the poignancy of the moment, a tear escaped from his swollen eye. She reached out and gently wiped it away. "I'm sorry," she whispered. "I know how this must seem, but you have to trust me."

Sid took her hand. "I could ask the same of you."

"I *do* trust you," she said, squeezing his hand to emphasise the point.

Before she could further reassure Sid, John entered her field of vision.

"Um… Mistress," he said, nervously, eyeing someone behind her.

Mary knew instantly who that someone was. Flinging Sid's hand away, she turned around. Sure enough, her brother stood there, framed in the doorway, eyeing the scene with an appraising smile. Even without the beard, he'd retained his mocking expression. *No!* She wanted to scream. Instead the words "What do you want?" blurted out from her. They sounded as guilty as she felt.

"Come now, Mary," Richard purred. "I heard an aggressive male voice and was concerned for your wellbeing. However, this gentleman — though *clearly* not gentle — seems to have your… confidence."

Richard stepped into the kitchen. "Allow me to introduce myself," he said, turning his gaze towards Sid. "I am Sir Richard Upson."

Mary looked back at Sid, but his attention was now on her brother.

"Sid Evily," Sid replied, holding Richard's gaze.

This was not good. "Sid was just leaving, Richard."

"Evily?" he said, ignoring her. "Curious name."

"You could ask my father about it, but it's been a long time since I've seen *him*." She could hear the contempt in Sid's voice.

Richard was not averse to a show of contempt, just as long as *he* was the one showing it. He smiled knowingly. "Ah… That would explain the…" He twirled a finger near his left eye. "…lack of discipline."

Mary felt a tingle run down the back of her neck. She had to get Sid out of here quickly before Richard decided to… Well, who knew what he might do, particularly if Sid was in possession of the silver button. She wished she'd never spoken of Sid to her brother — Richard might have relinquished the title of Seneschal, but she doubted very much he'd relinquished any of his power.

Mary grabbed Sid's arm. "Sid, you said you were in a hurry."

Like Richard, Sid was focused on his opponent. "More like the lack of discipline in your so-called men-at-arms," he countered. It looked as though speaking was still causing him some pain.

Richard's smile widened, as if acknowledging Sid's wit. Mary knew, of course, it meant nothing of the sort. "Speaking of which, you could save me the mundane task of ordering a couple of them to—"

"Richard! Please!" Mary implored.

She was suddenly aware that they had a captivated audience; Patricia and Juanita had ceased their tasks, and John stood wide-eyed by the door, riveted by the unfolding drama. Mary attempted to calm her voice as Richard's dark eyes bored into her. "Do you really think *this* is the appropriate place to be discussing your affairs?"

Richard flicked his gaze at Sid, silently considering his options, before his eyes returned to meet hers. "You are quite right, Mary," he acknowledged. "I should know when to… *button* my lip."

For the second time in less than twelve hours, Mary had an urge to slap the arrogance from her brother's face. Instead, she turned her back on him. Unsurprisingly, Sid looked stung, as if she'd slapped *him* on the face. He'd obviously realised what Richard's snide little jibe meant. She felt awful, but hopefully he would give her a chance to explain later. "I think you should leave, Sid."

He regarded her impassively, and for a moment Mary thought he was going to refuse, but then he nodded and said, "You're right, I *do* have important things to attend to."

She smiled, and gently squeezed his hand, hoping it would convey how sorry she was.

He smiled back, but it was hollow. Then he addressed Richard in his put-on gentleman's voice. "Alas, Sir Richard, it seems we are not to become better acquainted, for the moment at least."

Richard raised an eyebrow. "So it seems, but no doubt you'll be invited to another family gathering — perhaps when you're looking a touch more… presentable."

*Why did men have to be so combative?* She felt that Sid was one retort from being arrested. She squeezed his hand harder, silently pleading him to leave.

"I will see you later," he responded, barely containing his displeasure.

"Yes, you will," she assured him.

He smiled, gravely, and kissed her on the cheek. The awkwardness of the moment was compounded by Juanita's dreamy, "Oh! El amor es bello!" followed by Patricia's admonishing, "That's enough of that kind o' language, my girl!" followed by Juanita's, "No. You no understand. Ees—" followed by Mary's angry, "Enough!"

In the heat of the moment, she returned Sid's kiss and said she would see him at three. He nodded his acceptance, but looked far from happy with the situation. He squeezed her hand and headed for the door. On impulse, she told John to go with Sid. John looked surprised and delighted. She had no idea how Sid reacted; he didn't look back as he stepped out into the courtyard.

## CHAPTER 37

### *Some sort of ornate knife*

THE MORNING TURNED out to be quite productive for Olivia — the plaque now looked brand new, and the washing had been done and was hanging out in the backyard. The sun was beginning to reassert itself and the fresh rainy morning had become a stiflingly humid day. Still, the hard work had been worth every drop of sweat, with the added benefit of focusing her mind on the tasks at hand. Yes, a dose of routine had done her good. She decided to continue her rejuvenated productivity upstairs. The den, in particular, could do with a good tidy up.

On first inspection, someone might mistake the den for a library. Gerald's collection of proclamations, stored in leather-bound volumes, spanned the entire far wall across the top shelf and halfway along the shelf below: a six-year documentation of news and events in Lower Icing. Absently, she wondered if last Saturday's proclamation should be added to the collection. It *was* a record of the most significant event since Lucinda's death almost eighteen months ago, but it was hardly a true and accurate record. And yet, Gerald's fanciful version of events did have a certain resonance; his manipulation of the truth had, after all, resulted in Richard being asked to stand down as Seneschal. The whole thing was preposterous, of course — Richard would never hurt Marmaduke.

Poor Marmaduke; he'd been in some sort of feverish sleep for almost six days now. Just like Lucinda, he seemed to be slipping quietly away. No-one had been able to save Lucinda from *her* malady, and, now, it seemed, no-one was capable of saving Marmaduke from *his*… apart from Xavier, of course, but *he'd* lost his memory and Olivia wasn't allowed to… *No! This would not do!* She couldn't let her thoughts become maudlin.

She wrenched herself back to the domestic here and now and regarded the state of the den with a critical eye. Dull light filtered into the room through the window that overlooked the back garden and filled it with what Olivia thought of as an optimistic gloom.

As she moved into the room, she realised it was as much a case of sorting out the old clutter as having to clean. Below the volumes of proclamations, the shelves were filled with paraphernalia, including some rolls of dress material, a threadbare pin-cushion, Gerald's collection of novelty tankards, and an ugly painted ceramic statue of a Town Crier he'd received last year as acknowledgement of his service to the Duchy. (Fortunately, thanks to his Klob Hoofenhaus-inspired madness, the chance of him receiving another one was about as likely as her brother having an ale-free day.)

She bent down to take a closer look at the other items on the shelves. She pulled out things she hadn't seen in years, some of which she'd forgotten she still had, including a set of ornamental plates that Gerald had presented to her on their first wedding anniversary. She'd told him in no uncertain terms that their marriage required no such trivial acknowledgement, so they now represented the *only* keepsake of their marriage (apart from her wedding ring).

At the far end of the lowest shelf was a stack of books. She smiled to herself as she read the cover of the top one: *Do Well-To-Do Well* by Lady Violet La Fleur.

It had been her guide to improving her life well before she met Gerald, in the years when she was becoming a woman, when she'd taken on the responsibility of educating herself and teaching Sid. She picked it up and flicked through the pages — it was like being transported back fifteen years. Some of it was laughably trite and old-fashioned. (The castle-set would think it pertinent and contemporary.) As she refreshed her memory with its contents, she paused at a chapter entitled *Caviar and Sangfroid*. It basically described how to remain composed under testing social occasions. (The eating of fiddly delicacies like fish roe could prove quite frustrating.) However, the chapter also delved into more robust scenarios and the tactics one could employ to keep one's demeanour relaxed and serene. She certainly could have used some of Lady La Fleur's words of wisdom this past week.

Olivia stood up and arched her back; she'd done far too much bending this morning and it was beginning to ache. She walked over to her writing desk, situated by the window, and placed *Do Well-To-Do Well* next to the still-unfinished reply to Petronella Whysman's invitation to morning tea next Wednesday. She would definitely have to complete the acceptance before the day was out — Lady La Fleur would be most critical of her tardiness.

Walking around the desk, Olivia stood at the window and breathed in the sticky air. At least the rain had freshened things up a bit. The plants and flowers looked less sad than they had yesterday (which wouldn't be hard) and the dust and grime had been washed from the brick pathway and courtyard. Hopefully, the next downpour wasn't weeks away.

As Olivia turned back into the room, her foot collided with an object on the floor and sent it skittering across the floorboards. It came to a halt under the shelving, next to an old wooden jewellery box. At first, Olivia thought it was some sort of ornate knife, but as she bent down to retrieve it, she realised it was too small and had a polished walnut handle. It was one of the tools from Xavier's case of potions — she'd seen him use it to unfasten a tray of glass vials contained within its magnificent, velvet-lined compartment. She desperately wanted to speak to Xavier. Perhaps fate had just sent her an excuse to do so.

## CHAPTER 38

# *Between bored and grumpy*

IT WAS NEARLY midday and all Ophelia had managed to do was light the fire and fetch water. She'd also led Hazel to a new patch of grass and foraged around for berries and the like — something to sustain her and her pa until he was strong enough to leave. However, she found nothing she considered edible and, after her brush with Deadly Nightshade, wasn't about to try anything she didn't recognise.

Still, her pa seemed much better in himself today, which was a relief. He was still physically weak and sore, but at least his senses had returned, and he wasn't slipping in and out of consciousness. Instead, he was slipping between bored and grumpy. He'd tried moving about a few times, but the effort of standing for long periods was still too much for him.

The day had turned out to be clear and, for the most part, sunny. However, the humidity was still high and the forest had become steamy and uncomfortable. It seemed the more they drank, the more they sweated.

"This bleedin' 'eat, and these friggin' insects," he grumbled, waving away a nasty-looking orange and black specimen about double the size of a wasp.

She'd just about had enough of his complaining — what did he expect *her* to do about it? *She* wasn't the one keeping them here. Her thoughts turned to Tom again. What if he *had* left them to fend for themselves?

"S'pose I shouldn' be complainin'," he continued. "Not with our Billy in The Can."

Once again, Ophelia felt a pang of guilt. Of course she was worried about Billy, but she was also worried about Ma and Seth and how they'd be worrying about her and Pa. Hopefully Tom had had the decency to tell Ma and Seth they were both alright. Tom, blast him, she was also worried about *him*. What if he *hadn't* deserted them? What if he *had* come to some harm?

"Wan' me t'fetch some more water, Pa?" Anything was better than sitting around here feeling guilty and chewing over possibilities like a piece of overcooked rump. In any case, the water-skins could do with refilling.

"Aye. Might as well, Pheel." He took a swig from the skin next to him and tipped the dregs over his pink, peeling skull. Then he tossed the skin over to where she was sitting; not a huge distance, but his strength was definitely returning.

Ophelia grabbed the other water-skin and headed south along the now-well-trodden path to the ravine. The incline was slight, but she felt sapped of energy, and she was hungry, hot and uncomfortable. So, the normally effortless journey had suddenly become an effort.

To think, this time yesterday, Tom was returning with a brace of trout. The fish had been delicious. Even her pa had grudgingly expressed his appreciation, but that was before the altercation about this bloody doctor, the altercation that had ultimately led to Ophelia standing up for her family and sending Tom off into the night. The truth was she could see both sides — Tom and her pa were both men of principle.

The slope became steeper just before the entrance to the ravine, then levelled off before dipping down towards the spring. The final push left her breathless. She paused at the top, relieved that the darker, cooler confines of the ravine were just a few steps away.

A jingling flutter echoed out from its depths. It didn't sound natural to Ophelia. Suddenly she was alert. She couldn't see the spring from where she was, so she crept forward. The fluttering noise was repeated, and now she could hear someone talking. As she moved into the shadow of the ravine, the spring came into view, and she could see a man patting the neck of a horse.

It only took a second for her eyes to adjust to the gloom. "Where the bleedin' 'eck 'ave *you* been, Tom Skinner?" she yelled into the serenity.

She ran into Tom's arms. He'd shaved and changed his shirt and trousers. He even smelt different. She kissed him on the lips quite forcibly, as if she was taking back ownership of him, leaving her scent on him. Some kind of animal instinct had taken over; the forest was beginning to have a wild effect on her. Still, Tom didn't appear to mind.

When she finally let go of him, he said, "So you didn't miss me then?"

She punched him on the shoulder; he was being too knowing for her liking. "I'm jus' friggin' 'ungry." She tried to sound cross, but failed dismally.

Tom laughed at her, then he smacked her on her rear. Normally, Ophelia's response would be a swift kick to the bollocks, but with Tom it engendered quite a different reaction. However, it still involved the bollocks.

Half an hour later, Ophelia and Tom (with a fully provisioned Wildflower in tow) were walking along the trail back to the campsite. She could hardly keep her eyes off the Gamekeeper; their coupling had been the best she'd ever experienced. Whatever it was about Tom and the forest, it was working its magic on her. For the first time in her life, she imagined a life outside Slaughter & Offcut.

As they approached the campsite, the guilt returned. Her pa would know what they'd been up to — she'd been gone too long. Well, he might have to get used to it. She brushed her fingers through her tousled hair and removed a couple of errant twigs. Then she stopped.

"Hold, Tom," she whispered.

"What is it?" he said, immediately wary.

"Nothin'." But it *wasn't* nothing.

Tom wore a confused expression.

"It's jus' me pa," she said, almost apologetically.

"What about him?" He now looked slightly annoyed.

"Well…" She wanted to say that no matter what her pa thought of him, she didn't feel the same. But that felt disloyal. It wasn't her place to make excuses for him — he was her pa. Instead of airing her thoughts, she took him by surprise and kissed him tenderly on the mouth. When their lips parted, Tom looked even more confused.

"I'm with you, Tom," she whispered, gazing into his clear blue eyes.

A minute later, the campsite came into view. Her pa was still propped up against the oak tree under the shelter. He turned his head in their direction. He didn't look happy.

## CHAPTER 39

## *Heed my words or not*

RICHARD HAD LEFT The Harey Rabbit shortly after Sid, leaving Mary in no doubt as to his opinion of the scoundrel who was 'clearly taking advantage of her good nature'. While Mary escorted him across the rear courtyard, he'd remarked, "Apart from your Upson blood, you're an intelligent and successful woman, Mary. It's obvious that Sid Evily is not a match for you in either category. My advice is to leave well enough alone and be done with him."

He really was an arrogant man. Thirty-seven years old, with no wife or woman by his side — what would *he* know of matching? "Well, thank you for your concern, Richard," she replied as pleasantly as possible, "but I'm no fool and neither is Sid."

"And yet you are both acting foolishly."

She stopped and regarded her brother. "It's high time you got off your high horse, Richard. Not everyone has such lofty ideals as you. You treat people as if they are pieces in a game. You revel in outwitting and out-manoeuvring, convincing yourself it's for the greater good of the Duchy, but the people don't care about your political machinations. To them, you're just another powerful nob they have to bow to."

Richard's black eyes glinted balefully in the dull light; not even a sardonic smile played across his clean-shaven face. "It's clear that Sid Evily is already having a deleterious effect on you," he said, evenly. "Heed my words or not. It is your choice. I am simply offering some brotherly advice."

Mary felt her indignation wilt under his gaze. What had possessed her to speak to him in such a way?

"And as for the people of the Duchy, it's rather ironic, don't you think, that someone like yourself, who serves the noble class and gentry so deferentially and *profitably*, should feel empathy towards the common folk. In fact, it smacks very loudly of hypocrisy. Something, I dare say, you'd find hard to accuse *me* of."

With that, he turned and walked towards the gate. Mary felt mortified. "Richard!" she called after him. "Please! I'm sorry."

He paused at the gate, but didn't turn to face her. "When you visit your fool this afternoon, retrieve the silver button for me." He turned to face her; the sardonic smile was back. "It is, after all, stolen property."

Then he was gone.

As much as Mary busied herself in the running of The Harey Rabbit, the noisy lunchtime crowd could not drown out the angry echo of Richard's words. And every person she served was a vivid reminder of the sickening truth they contained. Not even a visit to the Offcuts', where the joyous news of Frank's discovery had coincided with the return of Billy from The Can, had been able to lift her spirits.

John arrived back during lunch. Juanita informed her that he was waiting in the courtyard for her.

"Why is he in the courtyard?" she asked, immediately thinking something was amiss. "What's happened?"

Juanita shrugged. "He just say to get you, Meestress. And because he says eet nicely to me, I say hokay to heem."

Mary shook her head and brushed past Juanita, leaving the lunchtime crowd to indulge themselves without her 'deferential' presence.

John was wet… *again*. This time it was because he'd fallen into the Icing River on the way back from Tom's cottage with Sid.

Mary was incredulous. "Why were you visiting the Gamekeeper?"

"Sid wanted t'see 'im," he explained, unhelpfully.

"Yes, I gathered that." Her altercation with Richard had put her in a bad mood and her patience had deserted her. "*Why* did Sid want to see the Gamekeeper, John?" she said, as if speaking to someone touched in the brain.

"Dunno, Mistress. 'E wasn' 'ome, like. We tried knockin' on the door an' all."

Mary wondered if John was actually as simple as he sounded. "Never mind." She really couldn't be bothered pursuing the matter, "You can stay out here until those clothes dry and, in the meantime, make yourself useful by helping Juanita hang out the washing."

"Yes, Mistress."

She'd taken two steps back towards the kitchen when John called out to her. She wheeled around. He looked uncomfortable.

"Well?"

"It's Sid," he mumbled.

"What about him?" She couldn't afford to think about Sid right now; there were too many rich diners waiting for her to fawn over them. *Bloody Richard!*

"'E said t'tell you that when y'visit 'im this afternoon…" He paused, as if trying to remember Sid's exact words.

"Just spit it out, John. I'm sure I'll get the gist."

"'E said t'tell you that y'should bring plenty of answers, 'cause 'e's got plenty of questions."

*Did he bloody now! Who the frig did he think he was?* She may well owe him an explanation, but it was hers to give, not his to demand.

"Thank you, John," she replied evenly. Three o'clock couldn't come quickly enough.

# CHAPTER 40

## *They serve no purpose now*

THE REVOLTING ENVIRONS of The Bloody Bell assaulted every one of her senses as, once again, Olivia found herself wading through a morass of moronic meatheads. It was now just after midday and the inn was even more packed than it had been during her last, upsetting visit. Bar Swill's manhandling of her was fresh in her mind, as was the bruising on her arm. However, her determination to see Xavier and put things right far outweighed the wrath of a simple innkeeper. In any case, she felt fairly sure he wouldn't dare lay hands on her again.

Olivia had put Xavier's tool into a black cloth bag she'd found amongst the odds and ends in her sewing room. She'd then placed the bag into one of her plainer leather handbags. She was now clutching the handbag close to her side as she pushed forward through the noisy rabble. Ironically, the bigger lunchtime crowd paid her far less heed than yesterday morning's uncouth bunch. She wondered how Alistair Bean had fared after his shameful performance. Imagine passing out in a drunken stupor at The Bloody Bell; the man must be distraught with remorse.

"What c'n I be doin' y'for, love?" yelled a squawky voice.

Somehow, Olivia had squeezed her way to the bar and was being addressed by one of the barmaids. After mentally rearranging the girl's words into something resembling syntax, she replied, "I'd like you to fetch Mistress Swill for me. Tell her Olivia Hiepants is here to see her."

The girl looked at her as if she was doing some mental un-jumbling of her own.

"Go and get Mistress Swill, girl!" Olivia yelled.

The barmaid jumped and disappeared through a door behind the bar. The girl was only gone for a minute or so, but it was long enough for Olivia to have to fob off lecherous advances from a couple of wishful-thinkers. Upon her reappearance, the barmaid glanced briefly in Olivia's direction before returning to her serving duties. *What was the girl playing at?* Olivia called out to her, but she'd moved down to the other side of the bar. Then she felt a hand upon her shoulder. Didn't these imbeciles realise they had no hope of entertaining their debauched fantasies with her?

She whirled around to give the latest chancer a piece of her mind. However, her words caught in her mouth at the sight of the purple and gold uniform.

"Mistress Hiepants…"

Although they'd yet to be introduced, Olivia quickly realised that she was being addressed by Brandon Swill. He sounded as formal as he looked.

"Please follow me."

Without another word, he turned and began walking towards the door that led to the blue room. Olivia trailed close behind. He opened the door, held it open for her as she walked into the empty room, then closed it behind her.

"Please be seated."

It sounded like an order. Olivia dutifully complied.

"I take it you are here to see Xavier," he said, sitting opposite her, the width of the large table between them, its sky blue tablecloth smooth and clean.

She could tell he was not best pleased by her appearance. "How is he?" she ventured.

"Yesterday you were informed of Xavier's situation and told not to concern yourself with it."

So, Bar Swill had not kept his mouth *entirely* shut. "It was your father who told me that Xavier's *situation* is none of my concern," she replied, evenly. "I'm sorry, but I do *not* take orders from an innkeeper, and I *am* concerned about him."

The lieutenant stared at her, seemingly considering her words.

"You may suspect I have some ulterior motive," she added. "However, I can assure you I don't."

"You have put me in a difficult position. The knowledge of your involvement with Xavier, at this point in time, is limited to my family. However, as an officer of the Purple Peril, I have a duty to pass on such information to my superiors. Fortunately for you, the situation is… delicate and there are many things at stake."

Yesterday, Olivia would have reacted to such officious patronising with righteous indignation. Today, however, she responded to this 'caviar' moment with Le Fleur sangfroid. "Well, Lieutenant, allow me to make things *easy* for you. There's no need to feel conflicted on *my* account — inform your superiors, and whomsoever else you deem worthy, of my involvement with Xavier. Neither my husband nor I have anything to hide or to be ashamed of. And, as far as I know, we have broken no laws. In fact, Lieutenant, I'd say *your* family, though clearly well-intentioned, are the ones who have put you in a difficult position."

There; *that* had put the upstart in his place; Brandon Swill's face had turned a rewarding shade of pink. Three cheers for Lady La Fleur! Olivia suddenly felt quite empowered. Indeed, empowered enough to play the part of a fragile woman. "Please, Lieutenant, I just want to speak to Xavier. I'd like to see how he is and explain that…" She paused, wondering what she should reveal. There seemed no danger in holding back, now that the Swill boy was aware of her and Gerald's involvement. Even so, it was probably best to keep her cards close to her chest "…that we haven't deserted him."

Apart from the colouring, the lieutenant's face remained impassive; weighing up his options, no doubt. Olivia knew her remarks had hit home — literally.

"Very well, Mistress Hiepants," he said, nodding his acceptance of the situation. "I will ask Xavier if he wishes to see you."

"He *will*, I'm sure," she said, pointedly, and smiled as the lieutenant rose from his chair.

Xavier entered the blue room. He looked wan and undernourished. This shocked Olivia; she'd expected him to look… better. He nodded to someone down the hall and then shut the door.

She stood up and approached him, suddenly feeling horribly self-conscious. "How are you, Xavier?"

He looked pensive, but, as she stepped closer, a thin smile played across his mouth. "It is good to see you, Olivia."

The use of her first name filled Olivia with hope. "It's good to see *you*, Xavier." She gently touched his arm. She could have easily hugged him, but that would be too familiar.

"Shall we sit?" he said, indicating the table.

She agreed readily.

"I'm afraid I can't spend much time with you, Olivia. I shall be returning to the castle within the hour."

He looked as if he should be returning to a sick-bed. He was very pale, like he hadn't seen the sun in days. His golden-blond hair had also lost its shine;

it was limp and drab, and hung over the collar of his light blue shirt like a wig of wet straw. But it was his eyes that shocked her the most; the brown pools that had once radiated empathy and intelligence now looked empty and lost.

"Oh, Xavier." She reached out and gently touched the side of his face. "What are they doing to you?"

He twitched a smile, like she'd hit nerve. "They are taking me to see my father."

"Your memory… has it returned? Are you able to…?" She left the sentence hanging; she could tell by his downcast gaze that his memory was still not intact.

"I remember everything, Olivia," he replied. "Everything *except* my knowledge of healing."

"But… your beautiful case of vials and the folder with all your notes?"

He shook his head. "I can remember all the powders, unguents, oils, extracts and other ingredients contained within the case, but their nature, their nuances, their properties, their essence… everything that is required to *understand* how they work… It's hard to explain. There is, or should I say there *was*, a certain innate ability to my healing: things that I didn't need to memorise, that I just knew instinctively." He sighed. "I don't even know how I know this. I just… feel it to be true." Then his eyes focused directly on Olivia's. "I may *never* be able to heal again."

"Of course you will." She reached out and squeezed his hand. "As you say, it is an *innate* ability. It *will* return."

He looked unconvinced.

"What about your folder? Your notes? Haven't they provided some clues?"

"I haven't looked at them."

Olivia was momentarily dumbstruck. "Why?"

He twitched out another smile. "It seems your memory has failed too, Olivia. I cannot open it without my silver pendant."

She hadn't forgotten; his bare neck was a glaring reminder. "But surely you could force it open?" she said, trying not to sound incredulous.

"Yes… but I won't. It was designed to be opened by the pendant. Unless the pendant is retrieved, it will remain closed."

"Xavier!" she pleaded, squeezing his hand again. "It may help you to—"

"You don't understand, Olivia!" he snapped, withdrawing his hand from hers. "It's not about notes and papers and formulas and ingredients. They are just… things that exist. I remember them all. They serve no purpose now."

Olivia didn't know what to say. She felt like weeping.

Xavier's expression softened. "Imagine you know all there is to know about riding a horse — you've read books, you've spoken to accomplished horsemen, you've even studied the anatomy of a horse. It counts for *nothing*, Olivia, when you're confronted with having to *ride* one."

Olivia nodded her acceptance, although she didn't really understand his analogy; he'd *been* a healer, he'd *ridden* his horse. "Why, then, are you being taken to see Marmaduke?"

"I haven't been given a reason. A belated recognition of my relationship, perhaps?" He smiled mirthlessly.

It was so sad. He'd come to Lower Icing after discovering he was the son of the Duke and Duchess — his mother dead just eighteen months before. And, if that wasn't enough to cope with, his appearance had been treated with suspicion and derision, particularly by Richard, when it was patently clear, even to Gerald, he was who he claimed to be. And now, it seemed, it might well be too late for him to ever speak to his father. Damn Richard and his bloody politics.

"Do they think you had anything to do with the attack?" she asked. Xavier was still under house arrest; well, she *assumed* the lieutenant's presence meant he was still under house arrest.

"Judging by this latest concession, I'd say not. However, as you know, I am not at liberty to come and go as I please."

"I'm sorry, Xavier. This is so unfair." She suddenly felt terribly guilty. If he hadn't been brought to 8 Plumduff Street, he wouldn't have gone out into the streets to stretch his legs, wouldn't have been bashed and robbed… "I will tell Richard of our part in your disappearance," she said. "I will *make* him see reason, that you couldn't possibly have had anything to do with Marmaduke's attack."

He smiled. "Thank you, Olivia, but there's no need."

"But there *is* need. There must be something or some*body* who…" It suddenly occurred to Olivia that there was, indeed, someone who could help — not only Xavier, but perhaps Marmaduke as well, "What about your mentor? He's a doctor, isn't he?"

Xavier dropped his gaze. "Yes, he is…" He looked as if he was about to say something else, but his brow furrowed and the words remained unsaid.

"Then couldn't—?"

"I've asked the lieutenant to send for Horatio," he interjected softly, as if he were talking to himself. Again his eyes met hers. "He is yet to confirm whether or not he has done so."

Olivia shook her head — this was unbelievable! What sort of men were in charge of Lower Icing? No wonder Gerald had welcomed the news of Richard being made to stand down as Seneschal.

"So you see." He shrugged. "There is nothing else to be done."

He looked forlorn, his eyes haunted and his expression... resigned.

"You must stay strong, Xavier." She took his hand again. "The truth will out. *None* of this is your fault."

"Isn't it?" He smiled, bitterly. "My presence here is my fault. *That* is what led to the Duke being attacked."

"You mustn't think that way, Xavier!"

"There is no other way *to* think!" He calmed himself. "I came to Lower Icing because of a life I'd lost, now I've lost the life I had."

Olivia was speechless.

"I'm sorry, Olivia, I must go now; Brandon was defying orders allowing me to see you. I don't wish to cause him any trouble. The Swills have been good to me."

Piss on the Swills. They'd done nothing but treat him like a glorified prisoner in their strange blue world. He was even wearing a light blue shirt!

Xavier stood up from the table.

She followed his cue.

"Thank you for coming to see me, Olivia."

She nodded — she suddenly felt quite choked for words.

"I'm sorry for any trouble I may have caused you and Gerald."

She shook her head and managed to choke out, "It is *we* who are sorry." There was so much more she wanted to say: to reassure him, to give him hope, to make him believe in himself again. But she knew, even if she *had* the time, there was nothing she *could* say to make him feel any of those things.

Xavier escorted her to the door; the soothing peacefulness was about to be replaced by a stinking, sweat-filled miasma of noise. She turned to face him. "Good luck, Xavier."

"Thank you, Olivia. I appreciate your good wishes."

Olivia entered the bar room of The Bloody Bell. The door closed behind her. Clasping her handbag, she braced herself for the march through the obnoxious crowd. Then, she remembered the tool: the whole reason she'd come here!

She turned around and knocked on the door. She would enter unbidden if no-one answered after she counted to five. The door opened on four.

Xavier regarded her with concern. "Are you alright, Olivia?" he said, flicking his gaze over the rabble behind her. "Shall I ask Brandon to escort you from the bar? The back entrance has been locked."

"Thank you, Xavier, but I will be fine on my own," she replied, raising the volume of her voice against the din. She'd rather be accosted by a dozen drooling denizens than escorted unscathed by an officious hypocrite like Brandon Swill. "I've remembered that I have something of yours."

"I see," he said, warily.

"I'm sorry; my mind was distracted by our conversation."

His gaze was penetrating. She looked away and unfastened the strap on her handbag. Reaching inside, she felt the smooth-handled tool within the cloth bag. She pulled it out and presented to him. "It's a tool from your potion case."

He nodded as he took hold of the bag. "Yes, my screw-remover. I've been using one of my spatulas instead."

"I'm sorry, Xavier; I only found it this morning."

He nodded, acceptingly. "I'm also missing my copy of Horatio's book of potions. Do you still have it?"

Olivia flushed with embarrassment. Looking into his serious face, she could invent no plausible lie. And, in any case, he deserved honesty; something of which he'd received precious little since arriving in Lower Icing. "Yes… but I have good reason." Then her words spilled out in a rush about the incriminating markings and how she feared it would be used against him. It didn't matter that her words were heartfelt and expressive, no-one except Xavier could hear them.

She felt his hand squeeze her arm, his eyes filled with compassion. She'd expected anger or, at least, annoyance. Instead, he *felt* for her. "Don't upset yourself, Olivia. You did what you thought was best. I understand."

He didn't need his potions; Xavier could heal with words. "I shall keep it safe until I am able to return it." Then, impulsively — a word she would never normally use to describe *any* of her actions — she stepped forward and kissed him on the cheek.

He recoiled slightly at the unexpected advance, and smiled awkwardly as she stepped back. "I'm afraid I must take my leave, Olivia," he said, self-consciously. "Thank you for returning the screw-remover. Hopefully, we will see each other soon."

Olivia nodded and hoped her expression looked reassuring. She watched him as he shut the door, and then turned around to confront the raucous rabble. Adjusting the brim of her hat so it covered more of her face, she kept her eyes fixed on the exit — the light at the end of a rat-infested tunnel. She'd taken two steps when, nearby, something metallic clanked loudly. Olivia's gaze didn't flinch.

The walk home was quite pleasant; the thick humidity of the streets was refreshing compared to the thick humanity of The Bloody Bell. As she reached the threshold of 8 Plumduff Street, she noticed a smudge mark on the brass plaque. How irritating; it had taken her half an hour of hard polishing to make it gleam spotlessly. She reached out and used the sleeve of her dress to rub off the smudge. As she entered their home, she found herself hoping Gerald had come home for lunch — she actually wanted to see him.

## CHAPTER 41

# Son of a friggin' woodcutter!

**T**HEY SAT IN the early afternoon shade of the oak, dining on cold pheasant (of all things), cheese, bread, apples, dried apricots and peaches, nuts and a bottle of Escargotian red. The newly prepared fire provided unwanted heat, but at least it kept the infernal insects away. Her pa's mood had improved from angry to surly.

"Wha's this crap, then?" he said, eyeing the label on the wine bottle.

*Couldn't he just be grateful?* She cast Tom an apologetic look as her pa read out loud: "Poison Gliss Ant?" He treated Tom to a distasteful glare. "Sounds friggin' delicious."

Tom smiled. "Pwahson Gleesont," he said, affecting an Escargotian accent. (He seemed quite unruffled by her pa's rudeness, which was a relief.) "It means 'Slippery Fish'."

Her pa shook his head. "Only the friggin' Escargotians would call a wine slippery friggin' fish." Then he took a large swig. This was followed by an exaggerated display of spluttering, like he'd actually drunk poison.

"Tastes like it's been *made* from friggin' slippery fish!" He gasped. "Not even our Billy in The Can would be given this slop."

Ophelia's heart sank at the mention of her brother's name; it was the spark that could ignite the blazing point of contention between Tom and her pa, and this time there'd be no middle ground. Ophelia would be forced to choose.

Fortunately, Tom seemed oblivious to her pa's provocative words. "You can rest easy on that point, Frank. Your Billy will have been released by now, back to the nurturing confines of household Offcut."

Relief flowed through Olivia. She wanted to kiss Tom, but instead she leant over and hugged her pa. "Oh Pa… our Billy is free."

Her pa managed to twitch a smile at her, but his attention was on Tom. "Did y' *see* 'im released or you jus' *supposin'*?"

"Pa!" She was finding it harder to support his antagonistic attitude. He was beginning to sound like a victim, and that was something Frank Offcut had *never* been.

"Be quiet, Ophelia. Nature boy 'ere might've cast some pixie charm over *you*, but *I* still got sense enough t'know wha's real an' wha' ain't!"

Ophelia slapped her pa's face. She'd never even *thought* of hitting her pa before. Where the frig had *that* come from? The shock on her pa's face must have mirrored her own.

"Oh, Pa," she whispered, and reached to touch his reddened cheek.

He glared at her and pushed away her hand.

Then she felt a soft touch on her shoulder. Holding back tears, she turned towards Tom. Looking her in the eye, he gently squeezed her arm. "I assure you that Billy has been released." This was met by a derisive 'bah' from her pa, but Tom paid him no heed; he didn't take his eyes off her. "I have not signed the Witness Statement. Without it, Billy cannot be kept in The Can for more than seven days. Today marks his seventh day and, although I did not actually witness his release, Administrator Penman is a stickler for procedure. Believe me, Ophelia, he's back with your mother and brother."

Ophelia fell into his arms and sobbed. She heard her pa say she was being soft, but all she felt was the soft cradling of Tom's arms.

The afternoon was uncomfortable for many reasons — the humidity was cloying (Ophelia had never sweated so much), the constant swatting of buzzing insects was driving her mad (the fire no longer seemed to deter the little shits), and her pa had retreated into a sullen silence under the shelter.

Well, if he wanted to sit there, stewing in his own juices, that was *his* lookout. He'd behaved badly; badly enough, in fact, for Ophelia to feel completely guiltless about siding with Tom — the man who could have abandoned them, but instead had brought them food and good news about Billy. The man who, at this moment, was preparing them another campsite along the river somewhere. He was determined that they begin the journey back to Lower Icing tomorrow; if Frank was well enough to complain about drinking Escargotian wine, he'd reasoned, he was well enough to get on a horse.

Ophelia wasn't convinced, but her pa, puffed up with pride, had stated that he was ready to leave whenever nature boy and his pissing pony were. And so Tom had headed off alone, leaving her with her pa who, looking far from a man ready to go horse-riding, had retired to the shelter, grumbling about the insects and how the wine had given him a gut ache. Well, *he* was giving *her* a gut ache.

She'd really wanted to go with Tom, but he'd convinced her it was better if he went alone; he could ride faster without her, and, as much as he thought Frank would be fine left alone for a few hours, he didn't want to further antagonise the situation between her and her pa. She wasn't sure it could get more antagonistic. All he'd done for the last two hours was doze and complain.

She was contemplating another trip to the spring (not that they were in desperate need of water, but the ravine was so much more pleasant) when her pa rasped out her name. She asked him what he wanted without moving from her sitting position underneath the tree Hazel was tied to. She'd been exploring the theory that the horse would draw insects away from her.

"Come 'ere, Pheel. I ain't got the voice f'yellin'."

Ophelia sighed to herself as she stood and made her way to the shelter — he'd better bloody start improving his attitude.

"Yes, Pa," she said, squatting under the roof of branches and bracken. He looked hot, and flies were buzzing around his bandaged forehead, his face bruised and peeling. She immediately felt sorry for him. "Can I get y'somethin'?"

He shook his head. "Jus' wanna talk t'ya."

She sat down. "Yes, Pa."

"Don' wan' us t'fall ou' over the Gamekeeper."

She nodded; relief flowed through her.

"I understan' y'gettin' carried away by the romance of where we are an' all — y'prince charmin' 'as rescued y' poor ol' pa an' knows 'ow to survive in the wild an' talks all posh an' all that…"

Ophelia tensed; she could feel the 'but' coming.

"…but 'e ain't Offcut material, Pheel. 'E's from diff'rent stock. You'll see that when we get back t'town."

No doubt her pa had intended his words to be conciliatory, but they had the opposite effect on Ophelia. "An' wha' if I don'?"

"Now, Pheel—"

"No, Pa! You ain't me! You don' know 'ow I'm feelin'!"

He pushed himself into more of a sitting position. Suddenly he wasn't looking quite so feeble. "No, but I know wha' I know, an' I *know* tha' bein' ou' 'ere is a friggin' *world* away from bein' at 'ome with y'ma and brothers. You're a smart girl, Ophelia; surely you c'n see there ain't no future in bein' with the friggin' Gamekeeper."

Ophelia was shocked and angry. Did he *actually* think she was going to spend her whole life at Slaughter & Offcut? Did he *expect* her *never* to leave home?

"Wha' would y'do? Spend y'life pluckin' friggin' pheasants an' collectin' firewood?"

"Ha! *That's* friggin' rich comin' from the son of a friggin' woodcutter!"

This time, her pa slapped *her* in the face.

Ophelia couldn't believe it had happened. For a moment she was stunned; her pa had never hit her.

This time *he* looked shocked — the same reaction *she'd* had — but instead of reacting with sullen silence, Ophelia ran away. She needed to put space between them. She could hear him calling after her. It made her run faster. Right now, she wanted to forget he existed.

She soon found herself on the now-familiar trail to the spring. She slowed to a walking pace and began to breathe again — her gasps becoming sobs as she made her way towards the ravine.

## CHAPTER 42

# *Did he really care what she thought?*

**I**T WAS WITH mixed emotions that Mary walked down the narrow street that Sid lived on. Bull Lane, as it was known, ran along the western-most edge of the township. Further north, just past Sid's place, it became the arcing dirt thoroughfare to the North Road via Fraser Coin's massive estate.

What was she doing? Was Richard right? *Was* she being foolish? Is *this* where she wanted to end up?

But, then again, there was something about Sid; he was his own person, even though she wasn't sure who that person was. He clearly hadn't succeeded in life, but she was still intrigued by him, and he made her feel like a woman — in *that*, he'd succeeded… where all others had failed.

She was now standing in front of his terraced house. The dent in the wall amused her. The house was a bit like Sid; it had taken an unexpected blow. She smiled to herself. At least Sid hadn't been hit by a runaway Icarumban bull.

She knocked on the door. There was no answer. She knocked again, and still there was no response. She tried the door. It was open. She called out his name. No answer. He'd better be unconscious, she thought, as she entered the sparse interior. To her dismay, he was.

An hour later, a still-unconscious Sid was in bed being tended to by Doctor Whysman. It had been a frenetic hour. She'd been expecting to work up a sweat visiting Sid, but for far more amorous reasons than trying and failing to revive him, racing back to The Harey Rabbit, sending John to fetch Doctor Whysman, racing back to Sid's, trying to keep him cool while waiting for the doctor to arrive, then, when he did arrive, helping him and John carry Sid up the stairs to his bed.

She watched, along with John, as Doctor Whysman gave Sid a more thorough examination. Apart from the comfort factor, the natural light in Sid's bedroom was better. Along with the usual poking and prodding, the doctor mixed a sample of Sid's drool into a small bottle of clear liquid, which, when shaken, turned light blue. Apparently, that was all perfectly normal. Then he mixed a grain of green powder into the bottle and shook it again. The liquid turned a murky green colour and, even from a distance of six feet, Mary could smell its pungency. He waved it under Sid's nose and Sid immediately regained consciousness.

"Welcome back, young man," said Doctor Whysman.

Sid looked vague, seemingly unaware of his surroundings. Then he tried to sit up, but Doctor Whysman settled him back. "Be at ease, Sid."

"How is he, Doctor Whysman?" Mary asked, feeling on edge.

"Mary?" Sid called out.

She moved closer so he could see her. Her presence appeared to relax him.

"He'll be fine if he rests and gives his body a chance to heal," Doctor Whysman answered, keeping his attention on his patient.

Her concern was now tinged with frustration and annoyance — why had he gone off looking for Tom? Exerting himself like that. If *he* didn't care about his health, why should *she*?

Sid was suddenly alert. "What's happened?"

Mary wanted to yell that it should be bloody obvious what had happened, but, instead, he received the far more measured tone of Doctor Whysman. "Now, Sid, listen to me. You've been overexerting your mind and body. To fully recuperate you need rest and proper nourishment."

Sid was still gazing at her and didn't appear to be paying any attention to Doctor Whysman. He was *really* testing her patience.

"And that means no more gallivanting around the countryside or drinking gallons of ale."

Sid's attention was drawn back to the man who was trying to help him recover from a savage beating. "Doctor Whysman," he said in his put-on noble voice, "I have been foolish in the extreme. I will, of course, heed your wise council."

That was enough for Mary. "You're impossible, Sid Evily!" Her raised voice exploded into the room. "Don't waste your time on him, Doctor Whysman."

She hated that he made her sound so emotional, and, right at that moment, she felt like punching the good side his face. Instead, she stormed past an embarrassed-looking John and slammed the door as she exited the room.

She needed air. Downstairs was stuffy, so she opened the back door and stepped into the yard. The air was still and thick, but she breathed it in —

deeply — trying to calm herself. The only thing she was aware of was the sound of a crying baby coming from next door. Apt, she thought; she felt like a cry baby, running away like that, but Sid… damn him!

"Are you alright, Mary?"

Mary jumped at the sound of the unexpected voice. Doctor Whysman regarded her from the back door.

"Sorry, I didn't mean to startle you."

For a moment she tried to hold back the tears, but was overwhelmed. Then the doctor's arms were around her and she sobbed into his shoulder; all this business with Sid, the Duke and Richard, as well as running The Harey Rabbit, had taken its toll.

She felt his hand pat her back, but he said nothing. Eventually, the sobs subsided and she pushed herself away, suddenly self-conscious. "Forgive me, Doctor… most unseemly behaviour."

He smiled, full of compassion. "Not at all, my dear. Release of emotion is a balm for the humours, like lancing a boil."

Mary nodded and tried to smile.

"Sid will be fine. I think he'll take better care of himself from now on."

"Hah!" She scoffed. "Don't be fooled by that act he puts on."

"Oh, I am under no illusion my words mean little to Master Sid Evily. *Your* words, however, speak volumes. Believe me, Mary, he cares very much what you think."

Really, she wondered — did he *really* care what she thought?

"And remember, Mary, the blow to his head was quite severe. It would certainly be clouding his judgement and making him act irrationally."

She nodded. No doubt he was right about that, but she wasn't sure how much more irrationality she could take.

As if reading her thoughts, Doctor Whysman said, "I have a draught — it's stronger than the one I have been using. I will give you some to administer to him if you wish; it will help with his sleeping, give his mind a chance to recuperate."

Mary sighed. It sounded more like a shudder. "Thank you." She then followed him back inside.

He walked over to the table in Sid's living room and retrieved a small brown bottle from his medical case. Taking the bottle, she noticed Sid's list of suspects was still lying on the table, covered in rim marks from the bottom of a tankard. Sid's attempt at deduction now looked rather pathetic, and she felt her heart go out to him — Doctor Whysman was right, the blow had affected more than just his appearance.

"Be careful with this, Mary," the doctor was saying to her. "Just a small spoonful mixed into a broth or brew is enough."

Mary nodded.

"I would normally see to this myself, but... well, as you are aware, the Duke's condition is a... challenge. John was lucky to find me at home; I'm having to dedicate more time towards finding a curative."

He shook his head as he shut his case.

"Is he faring badly, Doctor?" The only information Mary had on the condition of the Duke was what Richard had told her: that he had been poisoned and was suffering some sort of delirium.

He regarded her seriously; wary, perhaps, that he'd already spoken out of place. "He is able to take fluids, so he remains nourished, but the poison has a hold over his consciousness, the likes of which I have never experienced before. I am worried for him."

Mary reached out in reassurance. "He couldn't be in better hands, Doctor Whysman. You are a most—"

The moment was interrupted by the sound of enthusiastic footsteps descending stairs, shortly followed by the appearance of John.

"What is it, John?"

He jumped at her tone. "Nothin', Mistress... jus' makin' sure, like... you were... I think Sid wants to speak to you."

Mary shook her head, irritated by his meekness as much as his vagueness.

"Well, I must take my leave, Mary," said Doctor Whysman. "Just remember what I said about that draught."

"I will. Thank you." Then, addressing John, she said, "You can leave too. Tell Patricia that I may be a while and that Lillian's in charge of serving until I return."

"Yes, Mistress."

She escorted Doctor Whysman to the front door. He stepped out onto the street with John in tow.

"Well, good afternoon, Mary."

"Good luck, Doctor Whysman," Mary replied meaningfully.

He tipped his hat to her; then he and John began walking up the lane.

Mary shut the door and made her way upstairs. She placed the small bottle of sleeping draught into a pocket of her dress. What Sid didn't know, wouldn't hurt him.

## CHAPTER 43

# *No recriminations*

GERALD DIDN'T ARRIVE home until just after three o'clock. He was in a most agitated state: his face was covered in sweat and he was *still* clad in his infernal red coat. Why did he persist in wearing it in such oppressive weather?

He went straight to the kitchen — the coolest room — where Olivia poured him a mug of water while he removed his coat. Underneath, his green shirt was saturated in sweat; it looked like a bucketful of water had been thrown at him.

He hooked his coat to the wall-mounted rack, plonked himself at the kitchen table and downed the mug of water like he was boozing in The Bloody Bell. It actually felt like Gerald was heating up the kitchen — he was oozing humidity. After he'd taken his fill, he handed her a rolled-up parchment. It had a seal of gold wax stamped with five crowns below the head of a unicorn that fixed a purple ribbon in place. It was the Ducal Seal of Lower Icing — it was *Marmaduke's* seal.

Olivia eyed the parchment as if it couldn't possibly exist... unless... Marmaduke had recovered.

"What is *this*?"

Gerald still looked as if he was about to pass out. He wheezed his reply in short statements. "As I told you, m'dear... a dinner has been arranged at The Keep tonight... for the Seneschal's important announcement. This... I believe... is our invitation."

"Yes, I remember you saying," she said, trying not to be put off by his laboured breathing. In truth, she'd given little thought to the Seneschal's dinner or his announcement; Xavier's plight had filled her mind. Yet, this dinner could well prove Xavier's salvation. Why else would Paris feel it appropriate to use Marmoduke's personal seal? "What I'm referring to, however, is not the parchment but the seal."

Gerald poured himself some more water. "Ah, yes, my dear… well spotted."

*Well spotted?* Had his brain been fried? The seal stood out more than Olivia did at The Bloody Bell. Shaking her head in disbelief, she broke the seal and unrolled the parchment while he gulped down another mug of water. What *had* he been doing? The contents were, as Gerald surmised, an invitation.

### The Duke of Lower Icing
*requests the pleasure in the attendance of*
### Gerald and Olivia Hiepants
*at The Keep of Lower Icing Castle*
*Tonight at 7 o'clock*

That was it: no details of the occasion; no indication of the dress requirement; no mention of a dinner; no requirement to accept or refuse. At the bottom, the invitation was stamped with Marmaduke's insignia. This was the work of a soldier, Olivia decided. She couldn't imagine Sir Cecil Paisley allowing such an invitation to be sent out.

Gerald placed the mug back on the table and wiped his well-watered mouth. "So, m'dear, it seems we have but a few hours to prepare for the reckoning."

She regarded her husband; he looked more than just worn out, he looked resigned. "This is not the time to be dispirited, Gerald. On the contrary, I believe we are about to be vindicated, and perhaps even heralded as true and worthy subjects of the Duke."

He nodded, but it was half-hearted.

This wouldn't do; she needed him ebullient and confident. They needed to walk *proudly* into The Keep and convey to everyone they were above reproach. "I saw Xavier again this morning," she said, trying to spark some enthusiasm. "I found one of his tools while I was cleaning the study. I thought it best to return it to him."

Gerald nodded noncommittally.

Undeterred, Olivia explained what had happened at The Bloody Bell: how she had confronted Brandon Swill and defended their involvement with Xavier — that it was nothing to be ashamed of (quite the contrary, in fact).

She described how she had been taken aback by Xavier's appearance, that his memory had returned, but not his healing ability, and mentioned that he was about to see the Duke, though they hadn't told him why. She spoke of how Xavier had told Brandon Swill to send for his mentor to help Marmaduke, but nothing seemed to have been done; how she'd returned the tool and he'd asked about the book of potions, that she'd admitted to keeping because of the markings; and how he'd been most gracious and thankful for their support.

"So, you see, Gerald," she said in summary. "Unlike the Swills, we have *nothing* to worry about."

He'd listened in silence during her account and seemed somewhat revived by the end of it. "No doubt you are correct, m'dear," he said. "However, there has been no news of Xavier's arrival at the castle."

"Well, of course not, Gerald," she said, becoming frustrated with his attitude. Picking up the invitation, she waved it in front of him. "What do you think *this* is all about? The Ducal seal wouldn't be used for some run-of-the-mill occasion! Paris is obviously planning to make a grand announcement about Xavier. It's not every day the heir to a Duchy is revealed; it requires a *certain* amount of ceremony."

"Yes, it all makes sense." He yawned.

Olivia regarded him with a mix of disbelief and agitation.

"Your pardon, m'dear. I'm rather exhausted, truth to tell."

She put the parchment down, suddenly concerned for her husband; he looked quite unwell. "Are you alright, Gerald?"

He nodded. "It's just been a rather taxing day, my sweet." He sighed. "Quite the challenge, in fact."

"In what way?"

"This 'saying nothing' business, m'dear… it plays on one's mind, what."

"We no longer need concern ourselves about that, Gerald." She covered his sweaty hand with hers, pressing them to emphasise her next words. "Xavier is about to be recognised as heir to the Duchy. If Marmaduke doesn't survive, Xavier will become Duke; there will be *no* recriminations."

He smiled at her. However, it appeared forced. There was definitely something amiss. He still looked flushed and she could *still* feel the heat radiating from him.

"Right, Gerald," she said, patting his hands, "I'm going to prepare you a bath. You can't go to the castle looking like you've just been scooped out of a boiling cauldron."

This time his smile was genuine.

It wasn't the first time Olivia had prepared a bath for Gerald, although those occasions were few and far between, but it *was* the first time since the very early days of their marriage that she'd actually scrubbed him. The reason for today's scrub was twofold: she wanted to be sure that he was clean — they both needed to be immaculately presented tonight — and she needed to get to the bottom of his dispirited countenance. Looking the part was one thing, but they also had to appear happy and confident — *guiltless* in other words. As she scrubbed her husband's back, she asked him for an account of his day at the castle...

He'd returned to his office in the Administration Section and spent a couple of hours with his assistant, Master Ramekin, sifting through the pile of notes that had been left on his desk from the Office of Petitions. (Some of the more interesting squabbles were passed on to the Town Crier's Office for possible mention in a proclamation.) However, his mind hadn't really been focused on the trivialities of village life, not with Sir Richard's secret meeting and Captain Le Sharp's impromptu dinner party playing on his mind.

Around midday, he'd left his office to find the captain. It had occurred to him that Sir Richard's meeting might have had nothing to do with the attack on the Duke, and been more to do with undermining the new Seneschal and his supporters. He roamed around the castle for fifteen minutes or so, but the Seneschal was nowhere to be found, and no-one seemed to know where he was. He thought about going to Prestwich, but Gerald didn't trust him: he was Sir Richard's man.

Eventually, he'd knocked on Administrator Penman's door. The administrator was also uninformed regarding the captain's whereabouts. Gerald had then returned to his office and begun documenting (in secrecy) his version of events — in *and* out of the castle — since the arrival of Xavier. He wanted to make sure that if he (and Olivia) *were* brought to task that all the facts had been written down: the treatment of Xavier by Sir Richard and the consequences thereof, including his part in enticing Xavier to take refuge at 8 Plumduff Street.

He'd been interrupted at two o'clock by a message from Administrator Penman informing him that Captain Le Sharp was currently to be found at The Keep. Leaving his account of events locked in his desk drawer, Gerald had made his way to The Keep, where he was informed that the Seneschal was atop the massive structure. Gerald had then laboured up the six levels of spiral stairs. Emerging from the dark grey stairwell into light grey sky, the dizzying heights of The Keep had opened up before him.

Upon scanning the parapet-enclosed rooftop, there'd been no sign of Captain Le Sharp, or anyone else for that matter. Then he'd heard voices coming from the north-west lookout tower. The thought of having to wind his way up another level of stairs had almost defeated him; it had been years since he'd clambered to the top of one of The Keep's towers, and even in those younger, fitter days, the ascent had been a struggle. He'd taken a moment to catch his breath before the final push.

Having reached the summit, he'd been greeted by Captain Le Sharp and Lieutenants Fowler and Potts. They were surveying the township, planning out the route the Duke of Stymouth would take upon his arrival. The captain had been most solicitous of Gerald and insisted he recover his breath and take a swig of claret (of all things) before sharing his important news. Gerald had been reluctant to speak in the presence of the two lieutenants, but the Seneschal vouchsafed for them.

Captain Le Sharp had reacted to the news with thoughtful consideration — Potts and Fowler had appeared bemused and dismissive — and he'd assured Gerald he would raise the matter with Sir Richard. He'd then thanked Gerald for his diligence and informed him that the invitation to tonight's dinner should be delivered to his desk within the hour.

After exiting the tower, Gerald had paused before descending into The Keep itself. If his breath hadn't already been taken away by the climb, it certainly would have been by the view. Lower Icing looked like an artisan's miniature village — only the movement of the miniature villagers and their carts, animals and livestock spoiled the illusion. The overcast, still conditions made for pristine clarity, both in sight and sound. He'd wondered if this was how those intoxicated by power felt: the exhilaration of being *above* everybody. His gaze had stretched northwards, following Market Street, which eventually became the dirt trail known as the North Road, following it until it met the West Road a mile or so out of the village — the road to (or from) Stymouth.

The Duke of Stymouth and his entourage would arrive along this road in seven days' time. He'd wondered why Captain Le Sharp found it necessary to prepare a route through the village; there wasn't much choice and, in the end, all the Duke of Stymouth would care about was the kind of greeting he received. The question was, *who* would officially receive him? Gerald hoped, with all his heart, it was Duke Marmaduke Du Marma.

Descending the corkscrew stairwell had been almost as taxing as the journey up; his knees felt as if they were about to give with every downward step. He'd rested on the third level, before continuing to the bottom, where he'd rested again.

He'd thought to look in on the dinner preparations before he left. However, the chaotic noises echoing from the Banquet Hall had been enough to put him off the idea. Instead, he'd made his unsteady way across the black-and-white tiled floor of the fore-building, out into the steaming Middle Bailey and back to the Administration Section. He'd collapsed at his desk to find the invitation had already been delivered.

No wonder he'd come home in such a state, Olivia thought, as she rubbed the soap into his shoulders. He'd obviously overexerted himself running around after Paris. Still, Gerald had made a good point — Richard wasn't a man to step meekly aside, particularly at the behest of those he considered inferior to him, yet it seemed Paris had treated Gerald's revelation with polite indulgence rather than suspicion or outrage. Perhaps he'd already been informed. Nonetheless, Gerald had proven he *did* actually possess a certain amount of fortitude and initiative; his decision to document events from the arrival of Xavier showed an intelligence and foresight of which she wouldn't have thought him capable. And, she reminded herself, he'd also put her rat of a brother back in his hole.

As if reading her thoughts, Gerald murmured, somewhat sleepily, "Oh yes, I forgot to tell you, m'dear, I saw Sid again this morning. He seems to be popping up everywhere. He's under the impression..."

After an extended pause, Olivia stopped sponging his shoulder. She was about to prompt her husband, when he began snoring.

## CHAPTER 44

### *Someone I can turn to*

**M**ARY'S RESOLVE WAS diluted with frustration and embarrassment as she re-entered Sid's room. Her reaction to his behaviour had been emotional — something she'd expect from Juanita; she promised herself that she would *not* be upset by his words again. However, if he continued to play with her affections and disregard those trying to help him, she would heed her brother's words: *My advice is to leave well enough alone and be done with him.*

Trouble was, it was easier said than done. And when she saw him lying on his bed, looking abashed and so… bashed, she could feel her head already surrendering to her heart. When he apologised, all she wanted to do was comfort and restore him.

She sat on the edge of his bed, stroked his messy black hair away from his damaged eye and kissed his forehead.

"I'm sorry too," she said. "I shouldn't have yelled at you. But I'm worried about you and… other things." Then she leant towards the small bedside table and lit the candle.

Richard's appearance at The Harey Rabbit had, no doubt, complicated matters between them, especially since she'd told Sid that she and Richard led separate lives and rarely saw each other. He must feel betrayed or, at least, suspicious of her. Yet it was Mary who found herself wondering whether *she* should trust *him*. He was still too ready with flippant remarks about things he didn't understand, particularly regarding Richard. Still, it was too late to say *nothing*; if that had been her intention, she could have left with Doctor Whysman and John. Instead, compelled by her feelings for the man in front of her, she'd forgone her chance to leave well enough alone.

So, after being reassured that he would keep her trust, Mary told Sid that Richard had come to see her two days ago, on Tuesday afternoon, that he was agitated because of the Town Crier's concocted proclamation, that a silver button had been found with the Duke, but the Duke wasn't the victim of an attempted robbery, he'd been attacked and poisoned and remained in an unconscious delirium.

Sid's reaction was predictable disbelief. "I can hardly credit this, Mary."

Mary concurred. "Yes, it is hard to take in."

Mary had to move as he threw off his sheet and swung his legs over the side of his bed. Then he stopped and teetered in a sitting position, before collapsing back onto the mattress. It shocked her to see him flop back so helplessly.

"Sid!"

He looked confused, his good eye searching the room as if he didn't know where he was. She gently touched his forehead — it was warm and clammy.

"Are you alright?"

"I'm not sure," he answered. Mary was worried; his breathing had become more rapid. "The silver button — you told him!"

"Yes, but only because—"

"You talk about trust." He lifted his head, trying to force himself back up.

Instinctively, Mary held him down. His gaze locked onto hers. She breathed deeply, taking a moment to steel herself — she was about to betray her brother's confidence. "The silver button is Richard's. He told me so himself; it was found clasped in the Duke's hand and, because of it, he is no longer Seneschal."

Sid's good eye searched hers, looking for some kind of explanation that she couldn't provide. She relaxed her position, stopped holding him down. "Richard is as much in the dark as you are. That's why he held a meeting at The Harey Rabbit. I think he suspects someone at the castle, but I know nothing more than that."

She could see him trying to think through the logic of it all. "So, why doesn't he suspect *me*?" His voice was still breathy. "Surely, I'm the obvious candidate, or at least the easy mark?"

She shook her head; his logic was flawed. "That's why you're *not* a suspect. Richard isn't stupid — he realises you've been set up. The perplexing thing is the button. Richard can't understand how…"

She caught herself. It would serve no purpose telling Sid that Richard had lost only *one* button (as displayed by the Town Crier). It provided no clue to the identity of Sid's attacker and she was acutely aware that she might have revealed too much already, particularly about Richard stepping down as Seneschal. *It is clear that Sid Evily is already having a deleterious effect on you, Mary.*

"How what?" Sid asked, interrupting her scattered thoughts.

"Oh, it matters not," she said, attempting to gather them up. "If Richard knows anything, he certainly isn't sharing it with *me*." Which, in most ways, was true. There was Richard's 'person of interest', but Mary deemed it would only complicate matters. And she didn't have any answers to the questions Sid would no doubt bombard her with, just some unsubstantiated guesswork and a lot of 'not at liberty to say'.

Sid looked unconvinced. The barely open, puffy slit that was his left eye had begun to weep. She felt like weeping herself. She reached out and gently stroked the unharmed side of his face, thinking, subconsciously perhaps, he might be reassured by her touch. However, it had the opposite effect.

He levered himself into a sitting position, then questioned whether Richard might actually be the one behind the Duke's attack. He'd have had the opportunity, could have easily manipulated the proclamation, and then arranged for one of his buttons to be planted on some unsuspecting person like *him*.

He looked at her expectantly, but what could she say? Richard would have to be missing *two* buttons for *that* theory to have any credence. *And* Richard had known nothing of the proclamation; he was furious with the Town Crier.

Shaking her head, she said, "Doctor Whysman is right; the knock to your head *has* addled your senses."

He looked at her oddly (as if confirming her remark).

"If what you are suggesting were true, Richard would have arrested you by now. Yet, here you are, being confided in by his sister as well as being tended to by the Duke's doctor."

He continued to stare, saying nothing, not even moving his head. It was Richard's words, echoing inside Mary's head, that filled the silence: *When you visit your fool this afternoon, retrieve the silver button for me. It is, after all, stolen property.*

Prompted by her thoughts, she added, "In fact, Sid, he asked me to get the silver button from you. He wants it back. Hardly the act of a man trying to deflect blame in your direction."

*That* triggered a response. "I think I lost it while plucking John from the Icing."

Mary was dubious. "Richard won't be pleased."

Sid shrugged; either he hadn't grasped the significance of the loss or… he was lying. Regardless, the mention of John's drenching put Mary in mind of John and Sid's little adventure together. "Why did you go looking for Tom Skinner?"

"I know him."

It sounded like something *John* would say. "Is *that* the extent of your explanation?"

"I thought he might know what had happened at the castle."

Again, his attitude was very matter-of-fact. Then again, what did she expect him to say? Perhaps it *had* been nothing more than a fact-finding mission. "If only I'd known, I could have saved *you* the walk and *John* the drenching, *and* you'd still have Richard's button."

His eye narrowed slightly, questioningly.

"Tom also stayed at The Harey Rabbit last night," she explained. "He's helping Richard, and he's just as tight-lipped."

His breathing had settled down and he seemed quite relaxed, but his gaze felt appraising. "Yes, well, you weren't exactly in the mood for a conversation this morning, and I wasn't about to announce my intentions in front of your high-and-mighty half-brother."

And there it was again: his rigid spitefulness towards Richard.

Mary pushed herself off the bed and walked over to the window. This wasn't going to work. Richard would always be a barrier between them. She could accept Richard's distrust of Sid. That wouldn't matter; he really wasn't part of her life. However, from Sid's point of view, Richard would *always* be a thorn in his side.

She looked up at the grey sky; the humidity was breaking, there was freshness in the air. She breathed deeply, hoping it would cleanse her mind.

From behind her came, "I'm sorry, Mary."

She continued to stare out the window. Light grey sky over slate grey roofs, grey cobblestones — it was like some drab dream. "It's just that bad things are happening," she said, dreamily.

A creaking sound drew her gaze back into the room. Sid was walking groggily towards her. Again, her heart tugged at the sight of him. She *wanted* this to work — they both needed someone to save them from themselves. She felt her throat tightening, and spoke to stop herself from crying. "I need someone I can turn to, Sid, not someone who will turn on me."

Sid moved next to her, the tragic clown, wrapped an arm around her waist and drew her close. It felt right; it was tender and compassionate. Mary rested her head against his shoulder. They stood together in silence, the warmth of his skin on one cheek, the cooling air on the other. And for a while, there was no poisoned Duke, no silver button, no Tom and no Richard — just her and Sid.

"Will you stay with me tonight?"

There was an uncomfortable pause before he replied, "Are you sure it's safe for me to be surrounded by all that ale and wine? You know what Doctor Whysman said."

A remark like that would have annoyed her fifteen minutes ago — now it seemed right. He was who he was, keeping his feelings at bay behind a wall of quips. "That's just it, Sid. *I* will be in control of everything that passes your lips."

She turned to face him. Then she kissed him. It was lingering and passionate. He didn't resist, kissing her back, and holding her tightly to him. Then she pulled away and smiled. "See?"

He broke into laughter, and then gasped in pain.

## CHAPTER 45

# *Let's go and appease the wolf*

SITTING BY THE spring, Ophelia had lost track of time. She'd immersed herself in its cooler confines, not bothered by the biting insects; they paled into insignificance against the sting from her pa's slap. It wasn't a physical pain, of course, but emotional; she wondered whether it would ever fully leave her.

This last week, since Billy's arrest, had been life-changing for Ophelia in ways she never would have imagined. Most of it revolved around her relationship with Tom and, by default, her pa. Ophelia was caught in a battle between two men she loved — it was quite a concession to admit that she loved Tom, even if it *was* just to herself. She could feel her heart beginning to side with the man of her future, not the one who'd been her entire past… who'd raised her. And *that* made her feel shameful, weakening her resolve. Her mind was buzzing with emotion, or perhaps it *was* just the insects.

The lush greenery enveloped her as she stared at her dark outline reflected in the still surface of the spring. It seemed a lot gloomier all of a sudden. How long *had* she been sitting here?

More unknown time had passed when Ophelia heard her name being called. It was Tom. She stood up slowly; remnants of her day astride Hazel could still be felt. However, her movement was more out of a reluctance to leave the serenity of the ravine. Tom called her name again, but she didn't answer; she just waited for him to appear. Then he was walking towards her, past the enticing purple Belladonna. He said nothing as he approached her. She did likewise. He took her hands and gently kissed her cheek — an act of… love? His blue eyes glowed like the Belladonna, and he whispered that all would be well. She nodded. Yes, she thought, with Tom beside her, all *would* be well.

They exited the ravine hand in hand, Tom leading. As they stepped out into the forested hillside, Ophelia was surprised by the early evening murkiness. She must have been sitting in the ravine for hours, transfixed in thought, while the world progressed without her. She let go of Tom's hand, and all her thoughts suddenly found voice. She spoke about how she and her pa had fought, how she felt torn, how she felt guilty, and, ultimately, how she felt about Tom.

By the time she'd finished, they'd almost reached the camp. Tom hadn't responded in any way — she hadn't given him the opportunity — he'd just listened, like she'd asked him to.

Now they came to a halt, and Tom regarded her intently. "We've all been tested one way or another this past week. Your father blames Richard for his current predicament and me for Billy's arrest. You have been conflicted between your father's wishes and the feelings we have for each other. And I... well, to be honest, Ophelia, I have questioned the role I've taken in the hunt for the Duke's attacker. I feel like I could have been more... useful."

He diverted his gaze, looking unsure of himself. She didn't want to see him like that, at least not because of *her*. "You got nothin' t'feel guilty abou', Tom."

"I know." Then he smiled. "That's the problem — when I'm with *you*, I *don't* feel guilty."

She wasn't exactly sure what he meant by that, but she took it to be a good thing. She hugged him. He squeezed her close. It felt... right.

"Come on," he said, patting her back, signalling the end of their embrace. "Let's go and appease the wolf."

She smiled. "Pa'd like y'thinkin' of 'im as a wolf."

He nodded, his moment of introspection seemingly passed. "No doubt he would. However, he was looking decidedly sheepish when I left to find you."

# CHAPTER 46

## *An innkeeper and her battered beau*

MARY WOKE WITH a start. She was lying beside Sid on his bed. The last thing she remembered was listening to him saying something about his sister… something to do with The Bloody Bell. It was all a bit hazy and she felt quite groggy. *What time was it?*

Panic arose when she realised it must be well past six o'clock. The dinner crowd would be arriving; she needed to get back to The Harey Rabbit. Mary jumped out of the bed, but Sid remained undisturbed by her sudden movement; she had to shake him awake.

He jerked into a sitting position. "Mary?"

"We have to go."

"What's happened?" His face twisted in pain.

"We've slept through the afternoon. It's past six o'clock. I have to get back to The Harey Rabbit."

He looked unwell. Perhaps it would be better if he stayed here and rested properly. She suggested as much — Doctor Whysman's sleeping draught was still tucked into the pocket of her dress — however, Sid was adamant he was fine. He arose from the bed and gracefully kissed her hand. "Lead on, my lady," he said in his noble voice.

Mary had to hand it to him, he certainly had charm.

The narrow streets in Sid's part of Lower Icing were oddly deserted. Then again, it *was* dinner time — most families were probably sitting down for their evening meal (just as her patrons would be). She quickened her pace, virtually tugging Sid along as they walked arm in arm. He looked bemused by her sudden urgency, but increased his pace to match hers.

They walked in silence for a while, just breathing in the freshening air. As they made their way towards the castle, Mary's thoughts turned to the silver button. If, indeed, it had been lost, what would that mean to Richard?

Did he need it to prove his innocence? Was it *that* vital to him? And, if it was, what would it mean for Sid? How would Richard react?

As they approached Merchant Street, Mary noticed there were a lot of people out enjoying the more temperate conditions. As they progressed towards the corner of Plumduff Street, the traffic of people increased, all dressed in their finery. Mary recognised every one of them… well, just about. By the time they reached Noble Street, it was clear they were all heading in the same direction: towards the castle.

She and Sid drifted along with the flow, up Noble Street towards the West Gate. She was aware of the strange looks she was receiving from the castle-set, who were no doubt puzzled by her appearance *outside* The Harey Rabbit, arm in arm with a man who, in their eyes, must look like he'd been dragged out of a back-alley in The Pits. It suddenly occurred to her, between polite nods, they must also think that she and Sid were part of whatever *they* were involved in. She smiled inwardly. That would be causing them some consternation. To think, an innkeeper and her battered beau being considered in the same breath as these refined ladies and dashing gentlemen — outrageous!

As they approached the corner of Big Wig Street, a loud, exuberant voice broke through her musing. It was the Town Crier.

"Goodness gracious, Sid. We *do* seem to be running into each other rather a lot lately."

He was dressed in green trousers, white shirt and yellow waistcoat — his expression brighter than his outfit. On his arm was Sid's estranged sister, Olivia. Mary had never actually met Olivia before and her first impressions were of a woman who bore herself with pride and composure — the type who wouldn't suffer fools (even though she'd married Gerald Hiepants). Unlike her effusive husband, she was regarding Sid with barely concealed contempt. Sid appeared slightly dazed.

"So, how are you, old chap?" the Town Crier continued amiably, as if trying to conceal his wife's surliness. Again there was no reply; not that Gerald really gave Sid a chance to. "Not too bad, I'd say, having a pretty lass like Mary on your arm, what." Before she had a chance to acknowledge the compliment, Gerald asked her how she was.

Suddenly, Sid found his voice. "We're both well, Gerald. You're looking rather dashing. In fact, there seem to be a few people out in their finery tonight."

"Yes, and we must be joining them, Gerald," interjected Olivia, coolly.

*No, she wasn't a woman to be messed with,* thought Mary.

Although Mary was more than happy for Olivia and Gerald to be on their way, it behoved her to show some courtesy towards them. And, in any case, she was curious to know what was happening at the castle. The parade of people seemed odd, to say the least.

"Is there some occasion then, Mistress Hiepants?" she asked, respectfully.

Mary was treated to a condescending smile — the kind that could wilt a rose. "We have been invited, along with other distinguished guests, to dine with the Duke at the castle."

The words were spoken clearly and calmly, but Mary was still uncertain whether she'd heard them correctly. She felt her jaw drop. "Surely the Duke is not—"

Sid squeezed her arm hard enough to stifle 'yet recovered'.

Olivia's response was cutting. "I hardly think *you're* in a position to query anything to do with the Duke. You should attend to matters more appropriate to your station. *And*, if you'd take some good advice, I suggest you choose your associations more wisely." She glanced disdainfully in Sid's direction.

Mary tensed. *That* was uncalled for. Not surprising then that Sid no longer had anything to do with her. In fact, he'd do well to count his blessings that she'd disowned him. However, Mary knew how to play someone like Olivia; after all, she'd had enough practice with the Limpdickers and other stuck-up patrons. She would simply confound her with politeness. "Thank you for the advice, Mistress Hiepants. However, I know a bad apple when I see one."

Mary knew Olivia had felt the prick of the barb, but she, too, appeared adept at controlling her emotions. "Then you should see that Sid is rotten to the core."

"Really, my dear, I rather think—"

"Be quiet, Gerald!" she snapped at her husband, without deigning to look at him. Gerald winced at the biting tone. "And as for *you*," she said, glaring at Sid. "Why don't you crawl back to your world of dirty whores and pathetic drunks?"

*What a bitter, hateful woman.*

Sid just shook his head and smiled at her sadly. "I think you'd be surprised by *my* world, Liv. You see *all* types at the places I drink… particularly The Bloody Bell."

Mary detected a slight twitch in Olivia's left eye. He'd hit the mark there. What *had* happened in The Bloody Bell, she wondered, trying to recall their sleepy, afterglow conversation. He'd mentioned something about his sister…

"Come, Gerald," Olivia ordered. "It's time we were on our way."

"Right you are, m'dear." He sounded deflated.

He wished her and Sid a good evening before guiding Olivia back into the flow of fashion funnelling into the West Gate. What was Richard up to? Is this what he and his cohorts had spent half the night planning? Who was he trying to out-manoeuvre? The Duke couldn't possibly be well enough to host a dinner.

She aired her thoughts as she and Sid continued towards The Hairy Rabbit. Sid's response was, once again, laden with suspicion regarding Richard — even suggesting that he and Doctor Whysman had fabricated the Duke's poisoning. It was almost comical the variety of ways Richard was guilty in Sid's mind. At least he didn't seem serious about his latest postulation; he was more distracted than anything else. Then he revealed the reason why: he'd been presented with a rare opportunity.

She could almost hear his mind buzzing. "What rare opportunity?"

He didn't reply, just increased his pace. Now it was Mary's turn to keep up with *him*. "Sid?"

"I'll tell you when we get back to The Harey Rabbit."

# CHAPTER 47

## *Stiff upper lip and all that*

THE BATH HAD done Gerald wonders, invigorating him in body and spirit. Oddly enough, Olivia had quite enjoyed the experience of washing him. It was a bit like dusting off Lady Violet Le Fleur's *Do Well-To-Do Well* and finding there was actually some substance amongst the frippery. Thinking on that, Olivia remembered she was yet to finish her reply to Petronella Whysman's invitation to morning tea. Oh well, it would have to wait. The castle dinner was upon them; she needed to ensure both she and Gerald were looking their best and ready to confront, with sangfroid, whatever lay before them.

They left 8 Plumduff Street at quarter to seven. The temperature had dropped markedly — the evening was most pleasant, in fact. And so, it was with defiant optimism that she linked arms with her husband, and proudly joined the flow of other distinguished guests making their way towards the West Gate.

Olivia played the part of the dutiful wife as Gerald effusively greeted and hallooed any guest that came within welcoming range. Normally, she would have cringed. Tonight, she silently applauded her husband's ebullience. In fact, Gerald was so upbeat, she wondered whether he was feeling the same sense of anticipation and excitement as she, the same sort of thrill she'd felt leaving the note for Reg Puffy… What was *happening* to her?

"Goodness gracious, Sid!" Gerald's voice bellowed through her thoughts. "We *do* seem to be running into each other rather a lot lately."

Olivia felt her blood rise. She could barely stand the sight of her brother. And here he was, amidst the parade of Lower Icing's clique, looking like a drunken bar room brawler, being held upright by Mary Brewer — the *innkeeper* of The Harey Rabbit. This was not good; they were already attracting curious glances. She squeezed Gerald's arm, but he continued with the idle pleasantries, enquiring after Sid's wellbeing and flattering the

Brewer woman — of all the people to stop and chat to, for pity's sake!

"We're both well, Gerald," said Sid, eyeing him with his good eye. "You're looking rather dashing. In fact, there seem to be a few people out in their finery tonight."

Olivia could hear the condescending tittering and feel the judgemental gazes. "Yes, and we must be joining them, Gerald."

"Is there some occasion then, Mistress Hiepants?" asked the Brewer woman. She was dressed in her plain black work clothes (stained and wrinkled) and her hair was dishevelled, giving the overall appearance of someone who'd spent the day… cavorting.

Olivia informed her of the dinner, and the Brewer woman was quite taken aback by the news, even to the extent of voicing her doubt. *Who did she think she was?* "I hardly think *you're* in a position to query anything to do with the Duke. You should attend to matters more appropriate to your station. *And*, if you'd take some good advice, I suggest you choose your associations more wisely."

Sid was gazing at her with disdain, or perhaps it was pity — who could tell under all that bruising? Well, if it *was* pity, then he should look at his *own* pitiful life of drunken whoring, and the ruined chance of being something… better.

"Thank you for the advice, Mistress Hiepants," Mary Brewer was saying, "However, I know a bad apple when I see one."

Olivia smiled inwardly. Was *that* the best she could come up with? "Then you should see that Sid is rotten to the core."

"Really, my dear, I rather think—"

"Be quiet, Gerald!" When would he learn not to interfere where Sid was concerned? "And as for *you*…" She addressed her brother, not attempting to conceal her contempt. "Why don't you crawl back to your world of dirty whores and pathetic drunks?"

Sid smiled at her, shaking his head slightly, as if *she* were some sort of lost cause. "I think you'd be surprised by *my* world, Liv," he said, softly. "You see *all* types at the places I drink…" His smile lost its pity and became more… calculating. "… particularly The Bloody Bell."

Olivia felt her stomach drop. Her mind raced with possibilities. Had he seen her there? Had someone told him she was there? Or was he just playing games? He *loved* playing games, thought he was so clever… sangfroid, sangfroid…

"Come, Gerald. It's time we were on our way."

It wasn't until they'd passed though the West Gate that Olivia felt able to speak or even breathe. Her heart was still pounding at the thought Sid might have seen her with Xavier. Not that it changed anything, of course — it was just that she didn't want him ruining her (and Gerald's) chance of being in favour at the castle... again.

Gerald's mood had swung towards taciturn and he barely managed a cordial good evening to those who funnelled through gate with them. She knew she was responsible for the swing; she shouldn't have berated him like that in front of Sid and his wanton, ale-pouring wench, but, damn him, he was just so... unaware of the obvious. Surely he must have realised that talking to Sid would set her hackles up.

She sighed. "I'm sorry, Gerald."

He gently squeezed her arm, but said nothing.

"Remember, we have nothing to feel guilty about. Our actions *will* be vindicated," she said, confidently. And she *did* feel confident about that.

"Yes, of course, m'dear; stiff upper lip and all that, what."

To say the statement lacked conviction was an understatement. Surely he wasn't going to let her momentary loss of temper affect the rest of the evening. For goodness sake, he must be used to it by now.

They were about to leave the Administration Section and enter the Middle Bailey. She patted his hand fondly. "I'm proud to be walking on your arm this evening, Gerald." Oddly enough, she was, and her words had the desired effect.

"And I you, m'dear." He smiled at her.

He *did* look rather dashing, particularly in his black cavalier's hat with the green plume that perfectly matched the hue of his trousers — it was so nice to see him out of red. She found herself smiling back.

## CHAPTER 48
### *It's bloody unbelievable*

THE HAREY RABBIT was bizarrely deserted, except for a smattering of those deemed unworthy or not important enough to be invited to the castle. Mary had to hold back a smile when she saw Prim Pet was one of the indignant leftovers.

Dave, Lillian and Mandy were at the bar, sharing a private joke. They greeted her and Sid with open smiles.

"It seems we have competition from the castle tonight, Dave," said Mary.

He looked particularly chuffed with the situation. "Aye; given me a chance to work me charms on these two beauties 'ere."

Mandy hit him playfully across the arm, while Lillian shook her head and laughed, before they both wisely decided to resume serving customers.

Dave gave Sid a jovial wink. "'Ow y'feelin', Sid?"

"Much more clear-headed, thanks, Dave." He sounded almost cheerful, amused, no doubt, by Dave's playful flirtation with Mandy and Lillian.

"So, when did you find out about this dinner?" Mary asked, nipping the lads-only banter in the bud.

"Jus' after y'sent John to fetch Doctor Whysman. A few hours ago, I s'pose… Same as the guests, I reckon."

*Surely the guests were given more warning than that?* Mary leant across the bar towards Dave; she didn't want the handful of patrons overhearing their conversation. Sid hunched in closer as well.

"What do you mean?" asked Mary.

Dave spoke in conspiratorial tones, but there was mirth in his expression. "Well, two castle servants, dressed all formal like, come in 'ere an' started 'anding out sealed parchments to the more importan' folk. It caused a big to-do, I can tell ya. Just about ev'ryone went rushin' for the door; it was like somebody 'ad fired a cannon or somethin'. Turns out the parchments were invitations from the Duke to dine with 'im at the castle tonigh'." He chuckled.

"Blimey, you shoulda seen them ladies when they realised they only 'ad a few hours to get ready."

Mary, however, wasn't in the mood for seeing the lighter side of tonight's surprise dinner. Richard was up to something, and, so, for that matter, was Sid. He'd promised to tell her about his rare opportunity when they returned to the inn. Well, they were here.

Dave had cocked a curious eyebrow when Mary told him that she and Sid had some private matters to discuss. She'd grabbed a bottle of *Red Herring* (a popular red from the coastal vineyards near the southern township of Cutty Shag in Naffolk) and told him they were not to be interrupted. Out of the corner of her eye, she'd caught Dave giving Sid another knowing wink, but she'd chosen not to react. Instead, she'd headed, with Sid in tow, into the private dining room.

Sid closed the door and sat down at the table with Mary. While pouring the wine, she got straight to the point. "What do you think is going on at the castle?"

"I have no idea, but, as I said, it's given me an opportunity to delve into something else." He had a glint in his good eye.

"You mean your sister's appearance at The Bloody Bell?" Mary placed a glass of wine in front of him.

"Have I told you?" He looked surprised.

"Only vaguely," she said, taking a sip of wine; she liked the Red Herring, it was light and uncomplicated. "I don't remember anything significant. It was just before we fell asleep."

He joined her in tasting the wine, then proceeded to tell her how he came to see Olivia at The Bloody Bell. Basically, he'd needed a drink after his little sojourn with John. Then, while waiting to order, he'd spied a man and woman having a conversation by the doorway under the staircase. (Mary had been in The Bloody Bell enough times to know the spot Sid was describing. It was the entrance to the Swills' private quarters; the Blue Room, as she called it.) Sid had been intrigued by their body language and the man's expression. He couldn't see the woman's because she'd had her back to him, and, therefore, he didn't realise at first that it was Olivia he was observing. Then, she'd pulled a cloth bundle out of her bag and handed it to the man. He'd received it with a certain amount of gravitas, according to Sid. Then Olivia had kissed him on the cheek. Sid was talking like he still couldn't quite believe it.

Mary could well understand that. "Yes, it *does* seem an odd place for you to see your sister, even though I've only just met her. Are you *sure* you weren't mistaken?"

"As you say, you've just met her — would you now mistake her for anyone else?"

She shook her head by way of an answer. However, she was actually more intrigued by the *man*. Olivia had *kissed* him… She wondered if it was the kiss of a lover.

"The point is, my sister was in a public house."

The point was lost on her. *Obviously* she was in a public house, but what was the *man* doing there? Was he staying at The Bell, she wondered. "Is that… unusual?" she said, trying to focus on what Sid was saying.

"Unusual?" He winced in pain, and then said more calmly, "It's bloody unbelievable."

She must be missing something.

He placed his empty glass on the table and reached over for the *Red Herring*. "Let me put it this way: Gerald drinks here every Saturday afternoon, brown-nosing with all the nobs of Lower Icing, but I'd wager he's never been accompanied by Liv."

She acknowledged the truth of the statement as he topped up her glass and poured himself another. "I've only ever seen her *outside*, walking with Gerald. This evening was the first time I've spoken to your sister."

He put the bottle down. "That's because she believes public drinking is beneath her. And if that includes the salubrious confines of The Harey Rabbit, what the bloody hell was she doing in The Bloody Bell talking to some strange man? And what the frig was she giving him?"

Yes, indeed, Mary thought, what *was* she giving him, and what was *he* giving her in return? "She *did* flinch slightly when you mentioned The Bell."

"Ha! Yes! I wanted to see her reaction."

Mary nodded. "So, what do you have in mind? Remember what Doctor Whysman said about resting and…" She paused as he downed his second glass of wine. "…drinking."

"I remember," Sid said, dismissively, "but this is a chance to *put* my mind at rest."

Mary doubted that was the case; he looked too… eager.

"I'm serious, Mary. This dinner at the castle is the perfect opportunity for me to look around my beloved sibling's home and possibly find out what she's been up to."

"Do you think she's involved with what's happened at the castle?"

"Your guess is as good as mine, but I wouldn't put it past her. Gerald's been tied to that Town Crier's bell for over six years now and I reckon Liv's more than ready for him to have a position that has a better ring to it."

Or, thinking about the stranger in The Bell, a man who's *already* in a better position. "Yes, I can imagine that," she said to herself. Then, realising she'd actually voiced her thoughts, she added, "But going to such lengths as poisoning the Duke?"

He stared into his empty glass as if pondering the absence of wine. "I have no answers, Mary, but I may find some at 8 Plumduff Street."

Then he looked up at her as if seeking her approval.

"Just be careful, Sid," she said, meaningfully.

# CHAPTER 49

## *Your soft-arsed daughter*

**T**HEY WERE SITTING by the replenished fire as two rabbits roasted on one of Tom's makeshift spits. The day had an hour or so left, judging by the light. Ophelia's ability to read the movement of the sun (even on an overcast day) was one of the many ways she was becoming more attuned to the natural world. Of course, it had been Tom who'd explained the path of the high-arcing summer sun and how it differed to the weaker, shallower winter version.

Ophelia and her pa had said their apologies and made their peace. For the first time since they'd all been together, there was a semblance of goodwill around the camp. Her pa had even skinned and gutted the rabbits. And, just to add to the pleasantness of the evening, cool air wafted through the trees.

Ophelia sat between Tom and her pa, breathing in the mouth-watering aroma of the roasting rabbits, listening to the earthy richness of Tom's voice as he talked about his plans for tomorrow: how they would break camp at first light and make for the campsite he'd prepared on the other side of the Icing, near the ford he and Ophelia had crossed three and a half days ago.

"We'll take it easy, Frank," Tom said, "and see how you go, but even with the horses at walking pace, we should make camp sometime in the early afternoon."

Her pa grunted his assent.

"Then, on Saturday, we'll make another early start and should be back in Lower Icing by mid-morning."

"Thought y'said it'd only taken you 'alf a day t'ride 'ere," her pa said gruffly, but there was nothing aggressive about his tone.

"That's correct," Tom replied, amiably, "but I think you'll agree I have a *slight* advantage when it comes to riding ability *and* I haven't had to go through the rigours of a night in The Pits or being dumped down the side of a ridge."

"True enough, Gamekeeper. Tough ol' bastard, ain't I?"

Tom laughed.

Ophelia smiled. She could hear the sound of bridges being built.

"That you are, Frank… unlike your soft-arsed daughter."

Ophelia's smile vanished. *Soft-arsed, my arse!*

Her pa barked out a laugh, which ended up being more of a cough, while Ophelia turned on the man whose attempt at bridge-building was suddenly sounding very dodgy. He was smiling at her. She knew he was only jesting, but she'd never been one to back down when challenged; he might as well find that out sooner rather than later.

She smiled sweetly. "Is tha' right, Tom?"

He caught her tone, yet his smile grew wider. "Well, if the saddle fits…"

Then he began laughing.

Bastard! He hadn't given her a chance to respond. So she did the next best thing — she feigned a swift punch in the vicinity of his codpiece. *That* jerked the humour out of him, as his hands and legs reacted defensively. She smiled at his shock. "Ha! I wouldn't be talkin' 'bout *me* bein' soft, if I were you, Tom Skinner."

He pa nodded in approval. "Tha's me girl."

## CHAPTER 50

## *Would that I could*

THE FORE-BUILDING OF The Keep was illuminated by hundreds of candles set in large, wrought-iron candelabra stands. Everything seemed to glow, from the gold and purple pennons above to the chessboard-tiled floor below. It was… mesmerising. In fact, it was hard to take it all in.

The two massive tapestries, each running the length of the fore-building, looked vibrantly real in the bright light, particularly the one to her right, depicting the celebration of Marmaduke's succession. She had been thirteen at the time, just coming into womanhood. Her pa had run off three years earlier and her ma was less than a year from drinking herself to death; for the previous two years she'd been responsible for both Sid *and* her mother's wellbeing. It had been a struggle, but her life had been put into some perspective when the news about the sinking of the *Happy Mermaid* reached Lower Icing. The Duchy's entire royal family drowned and lost at sea… as if they'd never existed. Then, a few months later, Marmaduke and Lucinda had arrived at the castle and the town's spirit had lifted. Yes, the succession had truly been a celebration.

Wrenching herself from her reverie, Olivia observed the chatty stream of guests had also been hushed by the display of grandeur, and she wondered if the Duke of Stymouth would be equally impressed. She smiled to herself; there could be no doubt the heir to the Duchy of Lower Icing would be revealed tonight. She squeezed Gerald's hand and glanced up at him. He smiled and nodded reassuringly at her.

Through the splendid entrance, she and Gerald moved into the relatively muted antechamber where guests were lined up, waiting to be shown to their seats. Olivia peered ahead to see if she could catch a glimpse of what lay behind the open double-door entrance, but her view was obscured by the guests in front. She could hear the hum of polite conversation from within, and, as they moved closer to the archway, the strumming of a lute. The anticipation was almost overwhelming. Then, suddenly, they were being acknowledged by one of the ushers. The young man, resplendent in a purple doublet with gold trim, escorted them to their seats.

The Banquet Hall had been transformed from a dark, empty, unwelcoming grey-stone space to a place of light, warmth and vibrancy. Twelve massive candle chandeliers, in three rows of four, were suspended by chains from the ceiling, bathing the hall in an enticing glow.

Before them, guests were being seated at the large U-shaped table arrangement — the base of the U faced a newly-built stage erected against the southern wall. The stage was relatively dark, except near the centre where two lute players, highlighted under a large candelabrum, strummed out a whimsical tune. They looked rather insignificant on the impressive stage, with its mock balcony and painted backdrop of a fine-looking house. Perhaps a performance of Hamlet Macbeth's *Star-crossed Lovers* was being planned for the Duke of Stymouth.

They were led to the far side of the hall, giving Olivia ample opportunity to admire the table setting. The entire U-shape was draped in purple satin, decorated with yellow blooms of daisies and roses and laid out with burnished bronze plates and cups. It was spectacular. Olivia felt the thrill of anticipation; she could just imagine the scene as she and Gerald were acknowledged and rewarded for their loyalty to the Duke and Duchy. Even Paris would be admiring of her resolve in supporting Xavier. He might even feel a tinge of regret that he... No, she couldn't think that way... not tonight.

Their usher stopped halfway down the length of the table and pulled out a wooden chair for Olivia. She acknowledged the gesture with a gracious nod and then sat down. Gerald followed suit, his yellow waistcoat a perfect match to the floral arrangements. *What a fortuitous choice*, Olivia thought. The planets seemed to be aligning. It was her thirty-third birthday tomorrow, but she had a strong feeling she'd be celebrating it tonight.

Now that she was seated, Olivia had the opportunity to see who was sitting where. About half the guests — of what looked to be around a hundred in total — had been shown to their places. The four seats to her right were still vacant. To her left, Gerald was already saying hello to a cloth merchant named William Dyer. His wife, Cecily, was a good friend of Petronella Whysman. (No doubt, Cecily had already responded to the morning tea invitation.) Olivia bid both of them a courteous good evening, but, truth to tell, she was far too distracted for pleasantries; she could hardly wait for the evening's formalities to begin.

Gazing around the room, all the faces were familiar to her. However, only a handful would she call acquaintances, and, sad to say, none would she call a friend. That was another thing that had been lost to her since Paris.

"I say, my dear, pucker up," Gerald murmured in her left ear.

It was unexpected to say the least. What was he on about? She *was* puckered. She turned to face him.

"Is something amiss?" he asked. "You look a tad concerned."

She suddenly felt self-conscious. "Of course not. I'm merely soaking up the atmosphere."

He looked unconvinced.

"Truly." She smiled, her sense of occasion returning. "The hall is most impressive. If anything, I'm feeling quite—"

Gerald's gaze flicked to someone or something behind her; now it was *his* turn to look concerned. Turning around, she saw the object of his attention: he was dressed in black and silver and had just rounded the corner of the U. Other people were also looking at the man. He had a commanding presence, self-assured gait and wore the superior expression of someone who… *Richard?*

It *was* Richard. There could be no doubt that the man heading towards them was the former Seneschal, but he looked so… different: clean shaven, with his raven hair pulled tightly back across his head. She heard Gerald stand as he approached. Olivia had to fight the urge to join her husband. Richard's gaze fell upon her momentarily as he came to a halt, and for that moment she felt open and vulnerable.

He nodded, perfunctorily. "Town Crier."

"Sir Richard," Gerald responded.

"Good evening, Sir Richard," William Dyer added in a much more buoyant voice.

Richard's eyes flicked towards the merchant. All this was going on behind her, but she couldn't take her eyes of Richard.

"Master Dyer," he acknowledged, followed by an equally non-committal, "Mistress Dyer." Then a more genuine, "Please, do sit down."

Then his gaze was back on her. He addressed her with informal courtesy. "It seems I have the pleasure of being seated next to you, Olivia. You are looking most becoming tonight," he said, pulling back the vacant chair to her right.

It felt like a hundred pairs of eyes were on her. "Why, thank you, Richard." She hoped her sangfroid was holding up; she doubted Violet La Fleur had ever experienced someone like Richard Upson. "You also look very… polished."

He laughed as he sat down. Gerald had resumed chatting to the Dyers, relieved, no doubt, to avoid conversation with the man he'd been at odds with over Xavier, and, of course, the proclamation. Olivia, however, knew Richard on a more personal level, from the time she and Paris were courting. In any case, she was intrigued by his change in appearance.

As Richard pulled his chair in, she realised that he *was* actually seated next to her. That couldn't be right; surely he should be at the head of the table. Just because he was no longer Seneschal…

The copper-piece suddenly dropped. *This* was about Xavier, and where Richard now stood in the eyes of the castle elite. Olivia couldn't resist the opportunity to assist putting him in his place, "Passing strange you're seated next to Gerald and I, Richard."

"Well, as you know, Olivia," he replied, casually, "I am no longer Seneschal. Your husband's meddling has, unfortunately, for *everyone* concerned, put into question my character. It's obvious the seating arrangement is a further lesson in… character building."

Olivia felt her face flush. Gerald was in conversation with the Dyers; she doubted he'd have heard Richard's opening salvo. Well, if he was going to be *this* direct, then so was she. She leaned towards him and lowered her voice. "Surely, Richard, you are not admitting that you have been outplayed by my husband?"

He smiled, and, now that it wasn't framed in a manicured beard, it was even more disarming. "Touché, Olivia. However, it is more a case of underestimating the capacity for stupidity."

Olivia bristled at the insult; she'd be the first to admit that Gerald had a blithe attitude to just about everything, and that it frustrated and annoyed her to distraction, but he'd shown over the last week that he *did* have qualities that she'd failed to recognise, like integrity and conviction. "Come now, credit where credit is due. While you played politics with Xavier, Gerald treated him as a person; while you wanted him hidden, Gerald wanted him reunited; while you doubted, Gerald believed. You chose your path and Gerald chose his. I know who *I'd* rather be walking alongside."

Richard regarded her with his unfathomable black eyes. She was vaguely aware that people were being seated next to him, but his gaze held her attention. Eventually, he said, "I agree with you completely."

Olivia felt her stomach sink. He was playing with her. Looking behind him, three more guests had taken their seats: the milliner, Henry Bowler, who ran a shop called *Hats on Big Wig*, had just sat down with his wife and daughter.

Richard, following her gaze, turned his head and politely greeted the Bowlers. The daughter, whose name escaped Olivia, was almost overcome with excitement when she realised she was seated next to Sir Richard Upson.

Olivia cast an eye over the hall; most places at the table had now been filled. Then her eye fell upon Paris as he appeared at the entrance, looking the epitome of a Seneschal in his captain's uniform, and suddenly time stopped. For six years she'd managed to avoid him, removed herself from the cloistered world of the castle-set women, and, now, here he was, a mere twenty paces from her. Six years... He hadn't changed; he still looked dashing, proud, confident... perfect.

Richard had also noticed the Seneschal's appearance. "It seems the night is about to begin."

Paris looked over in their direction and his expression became more... self-conscious? However, she couldn't tell if it was she or Richard who was responsible for his change in demeanour. The look was only fleeting, and, as he made his way towards the head of the table, he acknowledged guests with an open and genuine smile. Olivia hoped that it *was* her that had made the impression, but she suspected not.

"And what, exactly, is tonight about, Richard?" she said, forcing her gaze away from Paris. She wondered where the words had come from — she hadn't intended to broach the subject with him. He regarded her, considering his response, compelling her to add, "And please don't insult my intelligence by denying you've had any part in it." She could always bring up his 'secret meeting' if he did.

"Why would I deny it? This night *is* partly due to me. In fact, I'd go as far as saying that it's *largely* due to me."

She was momentarily taken aback by his openness, but he still hadn't answered her question. "To what end?"

"Of *that*, Olivia, I cannot be certain. The intention, however, is for Lower Icing to be *fully* prepared for the Duke of Stymouth's visit."

It was a political response; Olivia knew that. Well, she wasn't in the mood for being political. She and Gerald had nothing to fear, not from Richard, not from Paris, not even from her game-playing brother. "Come now, Richard, speak plainly. I take it you are referring to Xavier."

He reacted with a sardonic smile, but any further conversation was cut off by a blast from a horn. It had come from the stage. All eyes turned towards the horn-blower. He was standing in front of the musicians, dressed in the ubiquitous purple and gold. Talking murmured into silence. She felt Gerald's hand close around hers, as if he was seeking reassurance. She squeezed his hand. In truth, she was also in need of some comfort after talking to Richard. The silence was prolonged, but no-one whispered a word.

"Ladies and Gentlemen…" Paris' voice cut through the silence.

There was a jingling of jewellery as a hundred heads turned from one side of the room to the other. He was standing in front of his chair. Olivia noticed the chair to his left was vacant: the chair that would normally be occupied by Marmaduke. Who would occupy it tonight, she wondered.

"Thank you for your attendance, particularly at such short notice. No doubt you are all curious as to the nature of tonight's proceedings. Firstly, allow me to apologise for the sparseness of the tables — we shall not be feasting tonight."

That brought about a susurrus of quizzical whispering. For her part, Olivia was grateful the night wasn't going to be drawn out with food and wine; she was not in the least bit hungry; she was too full of nervous energy.

"However, let me assure you, in nine nights' time, when Lower Icing officially plays host to the Duke of Stymouth and his entourage, the spread of food will be lavish. As to the reason for this gathering, the Duke of Lower Icing will be joining us directly and all will be revealed. In the meantime, please enjoy the music. Wine and a light supper will be served shortly."

Paris nodded in the direction of the stage, and the musicians resumed their playing, but they were quickly drowned out by the rumbling of conjecture from the guests. Still clasping hands, Olivia looked to Gerald. He appeared concerned. No doubt he was thinking the same as she: had Marmaduke made a miraculous recovery? Had he died? Perhaps Xavier's memory had returned… Would it be *he* who took the seat next to Paris?

Paris had been most ambiguous in his welcome; it could well have been Richard speaking. Then again, Olivia thought, it probably *had* been. Twitching out a feeble smile, she tried to reassure her husband; they needed to be strong. "Remember, Gerald," she said in a voice modulated for his ears only, "whoever occupies that chair, we have acted in the best interests of the Duke."

He nodded, but it lacked conviction. "Have we?" he said; more to himself, it seemed, than to her. Then he let go of her hand and smiled, but it was a sad smile. "Don't worry, m'dear. I shan't take a backwards step." He patted her hand.

She knew how he was feeling; she also felt conflicted. There were so many 'if onlys.' At least she'd been spared the frustration of dealing with the castle regime. Nor had she had to worry about being at odds with the man sitting the other side of her. She felt a sudden urge to give Richard a piece of her mind, but he was indulging the whimsical fancies of the Bowler girl. The girl caught Olivia's expression. Richard immediately picked up on her distraction and smoothly turned his attention back to Olivia.

"Something amiss, Olivia?" he enquired as if he genuinely had no idea.

"That rather depends on who sits next to Paris," she said, trying not to be overheard by the silly, pouting Bowler girl.

"I believe the Seneschal just announced it is to be the Duke. Do you have someone else in mind?"

His patronising tone barbed. "Richard. You *know* to what I am referring!"

His expression was smug. "Of course I do. However, since your husband's interference, and, to a certain extent, *your* role in harbouring a suspected outlaw, I am no longer in a position to tell you *anything* concerning the Duke. I'm afraid it's now a case of 'would that I could', Olivia."

He was lying, but what could she do? Accuse him of such? No, she wasn't prepared to do that... not without anything to substantiate such an accusation. "We both know Xavier is no outlaw, Richard. You can stop singing that tune."

His black eyes narrowed. Olivia felt a chill run down her back, but she held his gaze.

"Are you truly this naïve, Olivia?"

His tone was condescending, eyes unflinching in their appraisal. She wanted to slap his face, Lady Violet Le Fleur be damned.

"It's a remark I might expect from your dolt of a husband. Perhaps he has finally begun to wear off on you..."

*How dare he!* She was so affronted her cheeks were tingling and her eyes were welling; it was as if Richard had slapped *her* face.

"...Xavier's arrival precipitated the attack on Marmaduke; surely that is patently clear."

The only thing patently clear was that Xavier was Marmaduke's son, a man of gentle intelligence, who had *such* empathy and a unique gift for healing. But she couldn't speak the words, it was taking all her self-control not to break down or lash out.

Richard must have taken her silence as acquiescence, because he nodded his satisfaction. Then his gaze flicked to the entrance. "Ah, the wine and food," he said, as if they'd been discussing culinary delights.

Sure enough, servants were filing into the hall carrying trays of food and decanters of wine. Olivia didn't have the appetite for either.

"I say, m'dear, are you alright?"

All she could do was nod and force a smile, but it was hardly convincing. Gerald's concern was obvious. He regarded Richard and actually looked as if he might confront him. She placed a gentle, restraining hand on his arm; now was hardly the time or place. "Let it be."

He seemed not to hear her.

"Please, Gerald."

She felt the tension in his arm relax, but the tight expression on his face remained. A servant placed a decanter of wine and a platter of savoury pastries between them, and the moment was broken. Gerald reached for the wine. She waved away his offer to fill her goblet, but watched as he filled his own and gulped down its contents; she had never seen him drink like that before.

"Not partaking of this fine fare, Olivia?"

It was Richard's sarcastic voice in her right ear. She refused to look at him; instead, she cast her eye in Paris' direction. "No."

"I don't blame you. Pork pie isn't exactly food fit for a Duke..."

Paris was looking up from his chair at Brandon Swill, nodding at whatever the lieutenant was saying.

"...unless, of course, you're the Duke of *Sty*mouth..."

*Was that an attempt at humour?* She turned to face him; he wore his usual, calculating smile.

"...Still, I suppose we should be thankful Reg Puffy had an unexpected surplus, or we might have been eating a more... *humble* pie."

Olivia felt the blood rush to her face (again). Surely he didn't know about the letter. She'd been most careful. No-one could have possibly noticed her.

"I take it you dislike the Duke of Stymouth." *What was going on?* First Sid's remark about The Bloody Bell and now Richard...

His smile widened. "Let's just say that the Duke of Stymouth wears his name better than his title."

Richard's attention was then deflected by the fluffy Bowler girl. It was just as well; Olivia needed to recover her sangfroid and, in any case, she was far more interested in the conversation Paris and Lieutenant Swill were having. She could only judge by their expressions, but whatever they were discussing, it didn't look good.

## CHAPTER 51

### *Crème de Poire*

MARY HAD GIVEN Sid an hour. Even though he seemed quite focused and clear-headed, who knew what duress searching his sister's house would put him under. And the wine wouldn't have helped — she'd regretted bringing out the bottle the moment Sid had told her what his 'rare opportunity' meant. She'd intended to slip some of Doctor Whysman's elixir into the *Red Herring*, then put him to bed for a recuperative night's sleep. Instead, he'd drunk half the bottle and was eager to go *Adventuring*, as he called it. She couldn't really blame him, and, truth to tell, she was just as curious to see what he might find.

For Mary, the stranger was more intriguing than Olivia Hiepants; he must be someone very important or influential. As Sid had pointed out, his sister had never been in The Harey Rabbit, so what kind of person could have enticed her into The Bell? Did Richard know about him, she wondered. Was he connected to the 'person of interest'? Was *he* the person of interest? It seemed unlikely if he was at liberty to meet Olivia Hiepants and take possession of... what?

Perhaps this was all part of Richard's elaborate scheming. Perhaps Olivia Hiepants was just part of his plan to catch the Duke's poisoner.

Mary sighed. Her mind was overwhelmed by possibilities. Hopefully, Sid's foray into his sister's domain would provide some answers. If not, then whatever was happening at the castle probably would. Mary knew Richard wouldn't make such an extravagant play if he wasn't holding the trump card.

Mary had been back in the bar room for just over half an hour. She'd spent her time mingling with the smattering of guests — they had all voiced their surprise and outrage at not being invited to the castle, they all knew people less well-connected who were attending, and they all knew they must be victims of some clerical error.

Mary couldn't help but take secret delight in their social snubbing, particularly the plight of Petunia Primrose. She was surprised to see Prim Pet so soon after her last embarrassing departure. Either Fraser Coin's comment had been forgotten or she was a glutton for humiliation. There was, however, a price to pay: Mary had to suffer through her haughty indignation and perceived importance.

Prim Pet clicked her fingers. "Gel!"

Mandy rolled her eyes while clearing plates from one of the other tables. Lillian was at the bar, giving Dave a drink order. Mary was at another table talking to Earnest Pepper, a spice merchant. Earnest was a jovial man who couldn't understand the fuss being made about the castle invitation; a view not shared by his wife and daughter.

Mary excused herself and approached the lone diner. Smiling indulgently, she asked, "Mistress Primrose. Is there something you require?"

"I should say!" Prim Pet puffed up; she really was an old woman in a young body. "I have been waiting far too long for my... aperitif."

She'd actually paused to pronounce the word in an Escargotian accent. Mary almost burst out laughing, but managed to control herself enough to reply, "Dave is just organising that now." She'd ordered the drink less than two minutes ago. "Your Crème de Poire" — Prim Pet raised an appraising eyebrow at Mary's pronunciation — "will be with you shortly."

Prim Pet sniffed dismissively.

*What a sad person,* Mary thought as she walked to the cellar to find the bottle. Dave and Lillian could get on with keeping the relatively less-demanding patrons lubricated; she didn't want the night suddenly turning pear-shaped.

She located the bottle relatively quickly; it was covered in a sticky dust and Mary wondered how long it had been since it was last opened. She pulled the cork and sniffed the contents, and was somewhat surprised to find that it actually smelt of pear. Oh well, it was what the old maid wanted.

Mary ascended the stairs and presented the bottle to Dave.

"Well, I'll be stuffed. We 'ave still got some of that cat's piss!" He reached under the bar and produced a small glass.

Mary pulled the cork and poured. It *did* look like piss.

Placing the glass on a tray, Mary beckoned Lillian over. "Take this to Prim Pet, please, Lillian."

She nodded, bravely accepting her fate.

"Tell her it's with my compliments," Mary said as Lillian picked up the tray.

"Very good, Mistress," Lillian replied, before carefully making her way towards the upright figure sitting condescendingly by herself.

"Let's hope she chokes on it, Dave."

"*I* friggin' would," he replied, chuckling.

As Lillian reached Prim Pet, the door to Market Street opened and in walked Sid. He looked agitated, and Mary felt her stomach sink. She quickly made her way over to him.

"I'm fine, Mary," he said, but there was an urgency in his voice and he was gazing at her intently — *something* had happened. Then he leant towards her, "We need to talk in private. You won't believe what I have discovered."

## Chapter 52

### *Some friggin' point to it*

ONCE AGAIN THEY dined in fine style. Her pa found nothing to complain about and even complimented Tom on the roasting of rabbits. "Course, it's all got t'do with the way they're gutted an' prepared."

Tom produced another bottle of wine, but this one was a white from the Southern Vales of Naffolk. Her pa wasn't that impressed — he wasn't much for wine — but at least it wasn't Escargotian. However, by his second glass, he conceded that it wasn't too bad at all.

"Don' know why you drink that Escargotian crap," he said, by way of a compliment. "An' drinkin' somethin' called *Summer Breeze* sounds a damn sight better than friggin' *Slippery Fish*."

Still, that didn't stop him spitting out a whole mouthful when Tom casually remarked that Xavier had been found alive in Lower Icing.

"Thought you'd be pleased, Frank," he said, repositioning a half-burnt branch. The fire sputtered, and so did her pa.

"Bloody friggin' hell!" Then he began coughing.

Ophelia was also shocked. Why hadn't he told them before now?

"Tom?" She smacked him across the arm, interrupting the repositioning of the branch, sending sparks flying, but not as many as there were going to be if he didn't wipe that smile from his face and start explaining what had happened, and why he'd kept them in the dark. "When did *this* bleedin' well happen?" She smacked his arm again while her pa continued to cough.

For some reason, Tom seemed to be finding their reaction amusing. He held up his hands in mock capitulation. "Hold," he said, jovially, "I will tell all."

"Y'bloody well better!" her pa retorted, trying to hold back another cough.

The orange glow from the fire played across Tom's face, his mirth fading as he regarded her. "I didn't tell you before because neither of you were in the right frame of mind to receive such news."

Who the frig did he think he was? Even if there *was* some truth in his words, who *the frig* did he think he *was*?

Her pa was equally unimpressed, "Well, I ain't sure I'm in the righ' frame o'mind *now*, Gamekeeper, bu' I still wanna know whether all this *shit* Sir Richard put me an' mine through 'as some friggin' *point* to it!"

*Exactly!* Ophelia thought. How dare Tom keep the news to himself; he could have at least told *her!*

The joviality of the campfire had disappeared and Tom was now regarding both of them with what, in the dusky firelight, looked like contrition. "You have the right of it, Frank," he said. "I apologise to both of you."

Her pa grunted his acceptance.

Ophelia said nothing, just listened as Tom told them about the discovery of Xavier at The Bloody Bell and how Bar Swill had informed his Purple Perillian son yesterday afternoon that they'd found the young doctor unconscious on Friday night and had been tending to him since.

"Bloody Bar Swill!" Her pa spat out the words. "Slung '*im* in The Can, 'ave they? 'Arbourin' a wanted man's gotta be worse than liftin' the skirt of some bar girl. Wha' d'ya reckon to *that*, Gamekeeper?"

Tom bristled at the dig, but his voice remained calm. "As far as I know, nobody has been arrested. The Swills thought they were doing what was best — the lad had his memory knocked out of him."

"Ain't *that* bloody convenient! I've had the *shit* kicked out of me, while our Billy's been locked up in a shit-hole, an' frig knows wha' worry poor Maizie an' Seth 'ad to cope with. All the friggin' while, them Swills been playin' *doctor* to this friggin' *doctor!*"

Tom accepted her pa's outrage with good grace; he even nodded his understanding.

"Pa, it ain't Tom's fault," she interjected, softly. She could see why Tom had been reluctant to break the news earlier.

He snapped at her, "I ain't said it *is*, Pheel!"

Ophelia felt a hollow stab in the pit of her stomach. He began to cough again, but recovered quickly and continued in much calmer tones, "Point is, us Offcuts 'ave been made to suffer for somethin' trivial our Billy did, while them who's responsible for this so-called disappearance been protected 'cause their son's in the bleedin' Purple Peril."

Tom agreed. "Yes. In hindsight, the matter—"

"I'll tell you wha' the bleedin' *matter* is — Sir Richard friggin' Upson!"

Tom shook his head. "Frank, I can understand your anger, but Richard is not—"

"'Course, 'e bleedin' well is… For frig's sake, *you're* part of the castle-set. Thicker than thieves you lot. Don' think I don' know wha' this is about, Gamekeeper."

"Oh, do please enlighten me, Frank," Tom said, his patience wearing. "I really *would* like to know."

"Well, I woulda thought it was bleedin' obvious, even to a tree-hugger like you. Sir Richard's tryin' to cover 'is arse 'cause 'e's shit scared that this doctor is gonna be the next friggin' Duke!"

The only sound that met her pa's remark was the popping of the fire. Tom just stared into its flickering flames, while her pa nodded in a self-satisfied kind of way. Again, Ophelia's heart was torn — caught between loyalty and desire.

## CHAPTER 53

### *The moment is upon us*

AT LEAST AN hour had passed since Olivia and Gerald had been seated and there was still no sign of Marmaduke… or Xavier. The guests were becoming restless. Paris looked more agitated, and his communications with Lieutenant Swill were becoming increasingly intense. Something had happened. Not that you'd know looking at Richard; he seemed calm and relaxed, one might even say jovial, acknowledging compliments on his new appearance and indulging in inane conversation with the Bowlers, particularly the daughter, who gushed over him like an over-ripe tomato. Admittedly, Olivia herself had had a brief conversation with Henry Bowler about the latest millinery fashion and how he'd just ordered some pieces from the renowned Escargotian boutique, Chateaux de Chapeau. Gerald had also tried to busy himself in idle chatter with the Dyers. However, it hadn't prevented either of them from becoming more and more concerned about the empty chair next to Paris.

Olivia was observing Paris as the lieutenant approached him for the fourth time in the past half hour. He leant down and whispered something in his ear. Whatever was being conveyed, it was good news, because the hint of a smile (or relief) broke across Paris' face, followed by a determined nod. Then the Swill boy saluted and took his leave, striding at a quick pace back towards the entrance.

Paris stood up, but now many of the guests were consumed in conversation and the lack of food meant the wine had taken hold. He had to yell for attention a few times before the room rumbled into silence. (Where had the horn-blower gone, Olivia wondered absently.)

"Ladies and gentlemen, my apologies…"

He had *such* presence.

"The Duke has been unavoidably detained. However, I'm assured he will be joining us very shortly. Thank you for your patience."

Fraser Coin blurted out, "As long as the wine keeps flowing, I'll be as patient as you like, Seneschal." This was followed by a guffaw of laughter from certain guests. Surprisingly, Richard was one of them. Paris acknowledged the comment with good grace and sat back down.

"I would have thought such base humour beneath you, Richard," Olivia remarked.

He wore a mirthful expression. "Really? Perhaps it's more a case of clever wit being *above* you, Olivia."

He turned his back on her and continued playing with the frothy Bowler girl. Candice was her name; she'd been formally introduced during the conversation with her father. Clearly, Richard was not a good judge of wit.

Olivia's gaze was drawn, once again, towards Paris... so handsome. Someone caught his attention; he smiled and nodded. Olivia followed his gaze. Doctor Whysman was standing at the entrance. He returned Paris' nod, before disappearing back into the antechamber.

"Gerald..." she said, tugging at her husband's arm.

He was immediately attentive.

"The moment is upon us."

She felt him tense.

# CHAPTER 54

## *The best plan I've heard all week*

AFTER ASSURING DAVE all was well, Mary took Sid up to one of the guestrooms — the one Richard had stayed in on Wednesday night. However, she saw no reason to inform him about *that*.

They sat at the small dining table provided for guests who preferred to dine in their room. A single candle burned in a small brass holder, illuminating the table, but hardly making a difference to the dusky gloom of the room. The flame bent gently in the cool evening breeze. On any other occasion, the mood would be considered romantic. However, Mary could tell that romance was the last thing on Sid's mind.

"Liv has something to do with the attack on the Duke," he said as soon as they were seated. Before Mary could gather the fragments from *that* particular bombshell, he began hurling out other explosive news: Liv had a copy of a book called *Poetry in Potion* by Doctor Horiatio Manky. In it, a potion called *Paloma Coma* warned the potion maker about using too much orange-spotted mushroom. The warning had been circled, and the side-effects matched the purported condition of the Duke.

Mary could hardly believe what he was telling her.

"And, to top it all off," Sid continued, bitterly, "she also wrote the threatening letter to Reg frigging Puffy!"

"What threatening letter?" He'd never mentioned anything about a threatening letter.

He looked puzzled. "Didn't I tell you?"

She shook her head. "When did this happen?"

"Yesterday morning… I thought I told you."

"No." It was hardly surprising; they hadn't seen each other yesterday because of Richard's dinner and today… well, his ability to think clearly had been severely compromised. "Understandable, given the circumstances."

He nodded, accepting the comment, then proceeded to inform her about the mysterious letter Reg Puffy had received early yesterday morning, advising him to cease all association with Sid or suffer the unpleasant alternative.

Mary had never considered Olivia Hiepants as anything more than the reclusive wife of the Town Crier; out of sight, out of mind. Now she was front and centre: the bitter sister of her new lover; someone who was having clandestine assignations at The Bloody Bell, who knew Doctor Manky — bloody hell, she *knew* Doctor Manky — and who, unbelievably, appeared to be involved in the poisoning of the Duke. Mary couldn't conceal her incredulity. "What the frig, Sid!"

"Exactly."

"What are we going to do?"

He sighed. He looked drained. "I'm seeing Manky tomorrow… Well, supposed to be, at least. The bloodless creep might not come back if he's heard what's happened."

Mary hoped he *had* heard and *didn't* come back; Sid could well have become dispensable.

He yawned, then apologised.

Mary stood and moved over to him. Rubbing his shoulders, she said, "I'll fill you a warm bath, and then put you to bed."

"That's the best plan I've heard all week," he said, sleepily.

It probably wasn't necessary to slip Sid some of Doctor Whysman's elixir, but Mary did so anyway. While John filled the bath in Sid's room, she went to the kitchen and asked Patricia if there was any broth left. There was plenty, of course; most of the expected broth-eaters were at the castle. Mary poured some into a bowl and then added a few drops of the elixir. Stupidly, she did it in front of Juanita who was drying dishes.

The Icarumban smiled knowingly at her.

"Something the matter, Juanita?"

"No, ees all good, Meestress," she said, continuing to smile. "Ees for Meesta Seed?"

"Yes, Juanita — to help him sleep."

Juanita burst out laughing, and, surprisingly, she was joined by Patricia, who was sloshing and clanking away at the dirty dinner plates.

Mary felt her face flush.

"Sorry, Meestress," Juanita apologised through her mirth. "Eet's happy for us to see you happy."

What was the girl on about? "Juanita—"

"She thinks y'addin' a love potion to the broth, Mistress." Patricia was still chuckling.

Juanita was firing up now. "Si. Many gringos in Los Nachos try to—"

Unfortunately for Juanita, Mary wasn't in the mood for firing up. She was tired and worried. "We're not in Los Nachos, Juanita; Sid is *not* a gringo and *this…*" — She shook the small bottle — "*…* is *not* a love potion!"

Juanita's expression cooled, but she retained her annoyingly knowing smile. Without another word, Mary picked up the bowl and left them to their world of make-believe romance.

As she walked back upstairs, Mary's thoughts turned to Richard. What was he up to? Did he know about Olivia Hiepants and Doctor Manky and the stranger in The Bell? He must. He *had* to be Richard's person of interest, didn't he? And if Richard knew about him, then surely he'd be aware of Olivia Hiepants and Doctor Manky's involvement. Yet, what if he was being played? She very much doubted it, but still… what if?

Mary sighed as she reached the top of the stairs. It was just after nine o'clock, but it felt more like midnight. She was exhausted, even though she'd had the luxury of sleeping through some of the afternoon… with the man she would lie beside tonight… the man who'd somehow been entangled in an attempt on the Duke's life… the man who had just discovered his sister must be involved with Doctor Manky and *his* machinations. Mary was worried about what tomorrow would bring. Despite her exhaustion, she felt like sleep would be a reluctant bed partner tonight. Perhaps she should have some of the broth.

## CHAPTER 55

## *There is no proof!*

WATCHING XAVIER ENTER the hall, escorted by two guards, felt oddly dream-like — too unreal to be happening. And yet, here he was, wearing the gold doublet and purple sash of House DuMarma. He looked… resigned.

Olivia felt her heart drop. This was meant to be a moment of elation, vindication and triumph. Instead, she felt sad; sad for Xavier and sad for Marmaduke. Oh, Marmaduke… did he still live?

The hall hushed at his appearance. She felt the squeeze of Gerald's hand on hers as Xavier was led to the seat next to Paris. The Seneschal stood as he approached. He was quickly joined by the two couples sitting next to him: Jeremy Dupree and his wife Esther, and Marcus Ironcase and his wife Hillary. This set the rest of the guests into motion and the hall was suddenly filled with the sound of scraping chairs as everyone found their feet. Well, almost everyone… Richard remained seated.

The noise of the chairs broke the spell and the guests found their voices. Most people wore confused or questioning expressions. Olivia, however, had no words. And now that she was standing, she felt light-headed. Leaning on her left hand, she braced herself against the table. Xavier remained expressionless as he came to a halt next to Paris. The Seneschal nodded and bowed. Xavier looked uncomfortable as he returned the gesture. Voices raised in astonishment. Paris held up his hand for silence and the guests quickly obliged. Olivia could now hear her heart pounding. Her breathing was fast and shallow.

"Ladies and gentlemen, please allow me to present—"

Olivia jumped at the sound of a jingling crash.

Richard had thumped his fist against the table. "Enough!" he yelled. "Enough of this farce!" Then he shot up from his chair, buffeting Olivia towards Gerald. "You've overreached, Captain." His voice hissed like a red-hot sword in a blacksmith's slack tub.

Olivia could feel her body shaking as Gerald held her upright.

"I say, m'dear, you're trembling."

A wave of nausea flowed through her. Richard was ordering everyone to sit down… thank goodness.

Gerald guided her back to her chair. "Here. Have some wine, m'dear," he said, reaching for the decanter.

She nodded, mutely. Perhaps that was it; she hadn't eaten or drunk anything all day, not since… She couldn't remember when she'd eaten last.

She watched Gerald pour a generous fill of the dark-red liquid, and was only vaguely aware of the curious grumblings filling the hall; some voices were raised, calling out for an explanation.

Gerald handed her the goblet. It began to tremble in her grasp. He steadied her hand and guided it to her mouth. As she began imbibing the aromatic vintage, Richard demanded silence from the guests. The gathering hushed as the red wine spread through her body like a warm blanket. She gave Gerald a weak smile. He took the goblet and placed it back on the table in front of her.

Looking around the room, Paris and Xavier were still standing, as were the two guards who'd escorted Xavier into the hall.

"I suggest *you* sit down, Sir Richard," Paris said, forthrightly.

"And I suggest you *stand* down, Captain," countered the black figure standing next to her.

Olivia couldn't see Richard's expression. Truth be known, she couldn't take her eyes off Paris. He was… irresistible.

"Your position requires judgement and leadership," Richard continued. "If your intention is to present this… unknown, then clearly you have neither."

Paris shot back, "I hardly think *you* are one to talk of judgement and leadership. Not from where *I'm* standing."

Olivia wanted to cheer, but the room had fallen silent, no doubt mesmerised by the war of words between the current and former Seneschals. Or maybe it was just the way Paris filled the room with his presence.

"Very well, *Seneschal*," Richard said, mockingly. "Present this boy, and then explain, if you can, *how*, exactly, he came to be standing here in the Duke's place. May I suggest you begin with his arrival and the subsequent attack on Marmaduke."

As the hall filled with the sound of shocked voices, Richard casually returned to his seat. Paris glared at him, and then held up his hand for silence. Poor Xavier looked forlorn: head bowed, arms limp at his side. Far from a crowning glory, he looked like a man condemned to an executioner's axe.

As the guests quietened, Olivia looked to Gerald; she could do with some more wine. Gerald regarded her with an empathetic smile. It was a fleeting effort. She could see that he, too, felt the occasion had turned sour. She picked up her goblet and he duly obliged by refilling it. Then he refilled his own.

The hall reverberated with a low rumbling of discontentment and confusion. Paris' crisp voice rang above it. "Ladies and gentleman, it is true the Duke has been the victim of an attack. However—"

Again the hall erupted.

Olivia turned towards Richard. He looked smug. Such a self-serving individual, she thought, sitting there like he... like he was *satisfied* with the uproar he'd caused. He glanced in her direction and smiled; she could hardly bear the sight of him. At least the nausea had passed, and she felt calmer — no doubt the wine was having an effect.

Just to test her nerves, the sound of a horn blasted through the noisy outrage. This time it came from the entrance to the hall.

As the room fell silent, Jonathon Nitter, a wool merchant, shouted out, "What's all this about, Seneschal?"

"Yes, explain yourself!" Henry Bowler agreed.

"That's exactly what I'm attempting to do!" Paris shouted back.

Xavier looked as if he wished he could melt into the flagstone floor.

Paris took a deep breath and gazed defiantly towards Richard. "As I was saying, the Duke was attacked, poisoned, we believe, on Friday night, and has been in a feverish delirium since."

"Skip over that part of the proclamation, did you, Town Crier?" It was Fraser Coin. Richard sniggered. Gerald bristled, but remained silent. Why oh why hadn't he kept to his original proclamation and not been 'inspired' by the words of a Longboatian blacksmith?

"However..." Paris placed his hand on Xavier's shoulder, "this young man had nothing whatsoever to do with the attack, despite Sir Richard's insinuation to the contrary. Instead, he came to Lower Icing to *introduce* himself to the Duke, whom he had cause to believe was his father. Good cause, as it turns out."

This revelation created a collective gasp of shock. A few more men began shouting out questions. Olivia was feeling distinctly light-headed and her vision was beginning to swim. Xavier... he was standing there... exposed... an exhibit... expressionless... *What had they done?* She tipped down the last mouthful of wine in a most un-castle-set-like manner; Lady Violet La Fleur would not be impressed.

Paris' voice rang out against the hubbub. "Sir Richard's motive for accusing this young man lies in the fact that *he* was derelict in his duty, allowing the personal safety of the Duke and the wellbeing of the Duchy to be compromised. I believe, as do others close to the Duke, that this young man, Xavier by name, is the son of Marmaduke and Lucinda."

Fraser Coin shouted out, "Belief is one thing. What *proof* have you, Seneschal?"

"Exactly," Richard concurred under his breath.

The hall rang out with the reiteration of Fraser Coin's question.

"There is no proof!" The voice was loud and clear, but it hadn't come from Richard. The voice belonged to Xavier. Paris urged the young man to silence, but it was too late; the words had been spoken and many of the guests were now out of their seats, demanding an explanation.

Xavier stood strong against the yelling. Olivia's mind was spinning; she had an urge to rescue him, to take him away from all these doubters and accusers. If they couldn't *see* who was standing before them, if they couldn't *recognise* the proof *staring* at them, then they didn't deserve to have him as their Duke.

She looked to her husband. Gerald was shaking his head; he obviously felt the same way. She turned to face Richard; he now appeared indulgently bored, like he was listening to a poetry recital by Alistair Bean. Emboldened by the red wine, she shouted over the din, "Is *this* what you wanted, Richard?"

He glanced at her. "Not quite."

Smoothly, Richard rose from his seat, rearing like the snake he was. He had a mesmerising effect on the gathering — the yelling quickly became silence.

Paris, confronted by the man in black, took the initiative. "You have made your position quite clear, Sir Richard. If you find the presence of Xavier so unpalatable, I suggest you leave the hall."

"Thank you for your kind offer, Captain Le Sharp. However, the only thing I have found mildly unpalatable tonight is the selection of food."

This brought a titter of amusement from some of the guests.

"Perhaps if you'd said unconvinced or *unimpressed*, or even *underwhelmed* by his presence, then you and I would be in full agreement. And may I say, since we're on the topic, I feel much the same way about *your* presence."

Paris remained steely-eyed, but Olivia could see the twitch in his jaw as he clenched back a retort.

"The crux of the matter, Captain, is not *who* this man claims to be, but *why* he is standing here at all. Has the Duke died? Is this man complicit in an assault or a *murder?*"

The gathering rumbled. Paris clutched at the pommel of his sword, hands flexing as if he was fighting the urge to draw it. Xavier stared at Richard, but his expression was unreadable; he seemed… blank… empty. Olivia's heart filled with sorrow. Tears flowed. Looking up at the man standing to her right, his back angled towards her as he addressed Paris, "Please, Richard," she whispered, "stop this."

Suddenly, Gerald stood up. "Enough of this taunting, Sir Richard. Xavier has been through enough."

Richard turned on him, the snake ready to strike. "And what of the Duke, Town Crier?"

"I know who is responsible."

Why did he say such outrageous things without thinking? Still, at least he'd drawn Richard's attention away from Xavier. Olivia looked at her husband. He looked defiant and, for the first time in a long time, perhaps *ever*, he looked handsome. Then again, it might be the wine…

His gaze shifted to her. "I'm sorry, m'dear."

Sorry? What had he to be *sorry* for?

Then his eyes flicked to Richard and he nodded as if some silent agreement had just been reached. Olivia swung around to face the former Seneschal. He was smiling.

"*Now* I have what I wanted, Olivia."

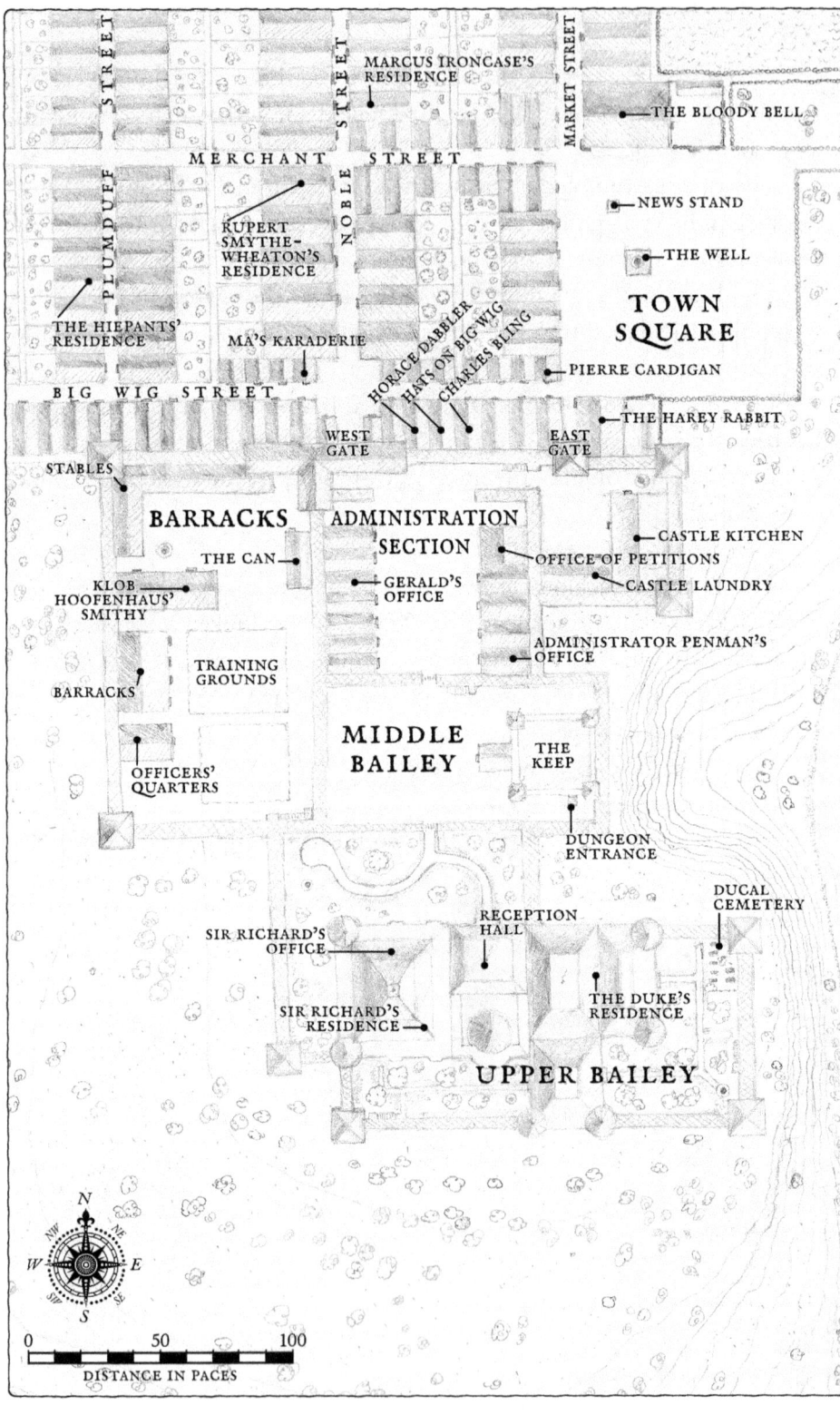

PLUMDUFF STREET

NOBLE STREET

MARKET STREET

MARCUS IRONCASE'S RESIDENCE

MERCHANT STREET

THE BLOODY BELL

RUPERT SMYTHE-WHEATON'S RESIDENCE

NEWS STAND

THE WELL

TOWN SQUARE

THE HIEPANTS' RESIDENCE

MA'S KARADERIE

HORACE DABBLER

HATS ON BIG WIG

CHARLES BLING

PIERRE CARDIGAN

BIG WIG STREET

WEST GATE

EAST GATE

THE HAREY RABBIT

STABLES

BARRACKS

ADMINISTRATION SECTION

CASTLE KITCHEN

OFFICE OF PETITIONS

THE CAN

GERALD'S OFFICE

CASTLE LAUNDRY

KLOB HOOFENHAUS' SMITHY

ADMINISTRATOR PENMAN'S OFFICE

BARRACKS

TRAINING GROUNDS

MIDDLE BAILEY

THE KEEP

OFFICERS' QUARTERS

DUNGEON ENTRANCE

DUCAL CEMETERY

SIR RICHARD'S OFFICE

RECEPTION HALL

SIR RICHARD'S RESIDENCE

THE DUKE'S RESIDENCE

UPPER BAILEY

N
NW NE
W E
SW SE
S

0        50        100
DISTANCE IN PACES

# FRIDAY, JULY 4

## CHAPTER 56

# *Smiling seemed perfectly in order*

**T**HEY'D BEEN TRAVELLING for couple of hours, after waking with the birds and packing up the campsite. For the first time since the beginning of her adventure with Tom, the morning felt crisp and clear, without a hint of humidity or sapping heat. It was actually pleasant to be astride Hazel, moving at a leisurely walking pace through the dappled undergrowth.

Ophelia had been dreading getting back on the mare, but the expected soreness was yet to manifest itself. In fact, she felt quite relaxed. The same, however, couldn't be said of her pa; his mood remained steamy, no doubt compounded by the fact that he was sharing a saddle with Tom. He looked distinctly uncomfortable sitting behind the Gamekeeper, holding on to his waist. It was something Ophelia could well relate to, but she suspected that her pa's disposition was as much to do with his pride as being on horseback.

He'd been reluctant, to say the least, stating, "I ain't ridin' if I gotta hug onto a bleedin' tree-hugger." However, he'd bowed to the inevitable… eventually. He wasn't strong enough to ride by himself and Ophelia wasn't a competent enough rider to support him. In any case, Hazel wasn't big enough to carry them both. It was a relief, truth be told.

Still, she *had* been concerned about the gash on his thigh. Even though it was healing, she thought the movement of the horse could well unsettle the stitches. He'd fobbed off her concern. "No need t'fuss 'bout that, Pheel; 'ad worse nicks cuttin' me toenails."

After two hours in the saddle, the wound didn't appear to be aggravating him and there was no sign of blood seeping through his bandage and trousers. Luckily, the Number Four Boning knife had stabbed him towards the outside of his thigh — it wasn't rubbing against Wildflower's flank — and at the pace they were moving, there was hardly any jolting.

They were due for another rest soon, more for the horses' benefit (particularly Wildflower's) than that of the riders'. They'd already stopped once, after the first hour. Tom's delayed revelation of the doctor's discovery was still a bone of contention with her pa. She understood and even agreed with his point of view — how the castle-set made decisions that were important to *them*, and bugger the consequences to the lives of the common folk — but Tom didn't deserve to be the focus of his anger.

Still, the odd conversation they'd engaged in during the morning had been begrudgingly civil; her pa had wanted to know whether Tom thought Sir Richard would be held accountable for his actions and what recompense would be made to him and his family, while Tom had wanted to know whether her pa felt any responsibility for Billy's behaviour and if he really thought making a stand against Sir Richard was a wise course of action.

Ophelia had decided *her* wisest course of action was to remain silent. She found, oddly enough, she got more of an insight into both arguments by listening, rather than putting in her two-coppers' worth.

"'Ow much further, Gamekeeper?" her pa grumbled.

"At this pace, another couple of hours or so to the river, but there's a stream up ahead; we'll stop there and refresh the horses."

"Thank frig f'that!"

Ophelia welcomed the stop and was glad to feel solid ground under her feet, even though the ride wasn't causing her any duress. She had to stifle a laugh watching her pa trying to dismount without assistance. He could hardly lift his leg over without overbalancing and having to slump back onto the saddle. Wildflower snickered (or perhaps sniggered) and had to take sideways steps to counteract the shifting load. Eventually, her pa conceded defeat and allowed Tom to assist him. It was an awkward dismount, more of a controlled fall really, with Tom catching her pa's flailing boot in his hands while pulling him down towards him. Both men ended up on the ground. Wildflower shook her head and walked to the nearby stream for a drink.

"Nice t'see you two becomin' so close."

They both gave her a withering look as they righted themselves. Ophelia smiled as she led Hazel to the stream. Her pa was much better; she could see it in his eyes — the sharpness was back. The gash in his head was still swollen and, no doubt, his ribs were still sore, but they would heal, as would all the other cuts, bruises and abrasions he'd suffered at the hands of The Slasher and the Moleson Twins. Last night's argument with Tom seemed so unimportant now. What difference did it make if he'd kept the news of the doctor to himself for a few hours? And he was right: neither she nor her pa had been in the right frame of mind. She'd still been emotional over the argument with her pa, and he'd have been feeling bad about slapping her.

Ophelia breathed in the morning freshness. It was time to think ahead, not wallow in the past. Her pa had been right when he'd said this was a world away from her life at Slaughter & Offcut, but he was mistaken if he thought it was a passing fancy or a romantic interlude. She'd never felt so alive… out here in the wild… with her Gamekeeper.

She reached the stream and let Hazel nuzzle next to Wildflower — Tom's horse was already sloshing up her fill with gusto. She removed the water-skin from Hazel's saddlebag and started gulping down what was left of the spring water she'd collected from the ravine early this morning. It seemed sweeter than usual, and she wondered if she'd ever taste its sweetness again.

By the time she'd finished, Tom and her pa were approaching the stream: Tom with a smile and an easy gait; her pa following behind awkwardly, grimacing with every step. Again, she tried not to smile; it really wasn't funny, but she was in an upbeat mood. They were on the way back to Lower Icing and tomorrow she'd be reunited with her ma, Seth and Billy. *And* she was with Tom. The world seemed right today, and smiling seemed perfectly in order.

Tom returned her smile as he stepped past her to tend the horses.

"'Ow y'feelin', Pa?" Olivia asked, trying to sound concerned, but failing dismally.

"Shut up, Ophelia," he snapped.

Ophelia burst out laughing.

## Chapter 57

## *Gel!*

THE HAREY RABBIT was bright and welcoming. The Friday morning sun streaked diagonally through the northern windows that overlooked the Town Square. Everyone, including Patricia, was in a good mood; the heat and humidity were gone, the air was fresh and reviving.

Mary, however, was struggling to involve herself in the upbeat mood of the kitchen and bar. She'd woken alone in her bed after deciding to let Sid sleep by himself. He'd virtually passed out in the bath, then collapsed into bed like he'd drunk a keg of ale. Whatever was in Doctor Whysman's elixir certainly packed a punch.

Sleep hadn't come quite so easily for Mary. She'd spent most of the night thinking about Richard and the silver button, about Sid and his sister, about Doctor Manky and this other doctor, about the Duke and the mysterious dinner at the castle, about everything that had happened since she'd found Sid lying unconscious near the stables in the early hours of last Sunday morning. She'd thought about taking some of Doctor Whysman's elixir, but if it had the same effect on her as it had on Sid, she might well have slept through breakfast (and lunch for that matter). Ironically, she'd woken up feeling like she'd downed the whole bottle.

Stumbling to the washroom, she'd splashed some cold water on her face from one of the freshly filled barrels; John was obviously up and about early this morning. Then she'd gone upstairs to check on Sid. He was sound asleep, like a child — a battered and bruised child.

She'd been sorely tempted to slide under the covers next to him, hold him and feel his warmth as he breathed. Instead, she'd left him in peace and prepared herself for another day at The Harey Rabbit. Although, of course, it wasn't just another day — it was the day they would supposedly find out what happened at the castle... if Richard's plan had, indeed, borne fruit. It was also the day Sid was due to meet Doctor Manky. That worried Mary, particularly in light of what he'd discovered at the Hiepants' residence. No, this was *not* just another day. The question was, what would it reveal?

Well, to start with, it was Lillian's day off, Carol was unwell (according to her husband who'd dropped by earlier) and Mandy was at the castle kitchen, negotiating an emergency order of bacon. (Mandy had a knack for negotiation, particularly with men.) So, she'd decided John would help with the serving this morning. He'd proven quite good at it on previous occasions; he engaged confidently and politely with the patrons (which was completely at odds with his actual personality). Still, she only used John on an 'as needed' basis; no matter how competent he was, he didn't have the essential attributes most of the influential clients were looking for, namely fulsome breasts and a ripe arse. Juanita had offered her assistance, and while her attributes were ideal for serving, her attitude certainly left a lot to be desired. Mary could only imagine how the Icarumban would react to an unexpected pinch, slap or pat. She'd pouted her disappointment when Mary told her that her assistance would not be required. (Point proven.)

The first patron to enter was, to everyone's disappointment and consternation, Prim Pet. From Mary's point of view, not only was she torturously fussy, but she'd also have no idea what had occurred at the castle dinner (unless she'd spoken to someone who'd been invited, which seemed unlikely). Mary was tempted to send John out to serve her, but his abilities didn't extend *that* far. So, as was often the case, it was Mary who attended Mistress Petunia Primrose.

She welcomed Prim Pet with a cheerful smile. It was met by a cheerless, upward curve of her lips. (No-one would call it a smile.) As Mary took her order, it became apparent that Prim Pet was on a fishing expedition of her own.

"I take it I am your first patron this morning?" she enquired.

Mary smiled as she casually indicated the empty room. "As you can see, Mistress Primrose."

Prim Pet stiffened at the flippant retort. Mary took silent delight in her indignation.

"Yes I *can* see, gel. I'm not a fool. I was merely engaging in social intercourse."

Mary had to bite her tongue; if only Fraser Coin were here.

"You've not heard any news?" Prim Pet said. Obviously, she was as much in the dark as Mary. Well, at least Mary could gain some enjoyment from being unable to enlighten the young old maid.

"News, Mistress Primrose?"

"Yes, gel, news! Are you so dim-witted to have forgotten what occurred yesterday evening?"

"Oh, of course," Mary said, feigning absent-mindedness. "Dave will be ordering some more Crème de Poire for you."

Prim Pet's expression turned from sour indulgence to bitter impatience. "I am *not* referring to your inadequate selection of aperitifs, gel! I am enquiring…" She shook her head in frustration and waved her hand dismissively. "Oh, never mind; clearly you have no idea what is occurring outside your very door. Just bring me some breakfast."

"Yes, Mistress Primrose."

Mary smiled to herself as she headed towards the kitchen, but was stopped just as she reached the door. "Oh and gel…? Instead of Jeedarling, I'll have a pot of the Earl Beige."

Not long after Mary had left Prim Pet, another couple, Henry and Henrietta Taylor (known amongst the staff as the 'two hens') entered the bar room. Henry Taylor was only a tinker, but his shop, Tinker Taylor (just opposite the market), did very well. They often breakfasted on a Friday because the market was closed. However, they were not part of the castle clique and would not have been on last night's guest list — a fact confirmed by John after he'd taken their order. The Pennyworths (father, mother and daughter) were the next to arrive. They, too, were part of the great uninvited. Bloody hell, where were her castle-set regulars?

Mary had escaped Prim Pet's haughty gaze and was half-heartedly overseeing the food preparation. Not that she needed to; Patricia had everything in order (apart from the short supply of bacon). It was more to distract her thoughts.

"Maybe dey all have dee hanging-over," Juanita said from the kitchen table, where she was peeling potatoes.

"Yes, perhaps," Mary replied.

"Or maybe dey all geeven dee magic potion like Meesta Seed."

Patricia, who was standing at the bench beating eggs, stifled a laugh. Mary shook her head.

"When I go to change dee sheets…" There was a more suggestive tone in her voice. "Meesta Seed still in bed, sleepeeng like dee baby dat got dee cream."

"Juanita!" Mary snapped. "It's hard enough trying to understand you when you're *attempting* to make sense! So, whatever *nonsense* is spinning around inside that Icarumban head of yours, I'd very much appreciate it if you kept it there."

Juanita gave her a quizzical look. "Sorry, Meestress, I no understand what you sayeeng."

Patricia burst out laughing.

John burst through the door from the bar room. He wore an animated expression, fit to burst.

"What is it, John?" Mary asked.

"The Limpdickers jus' arrived!"

There was a sense of nervous anticipation as Mary approached the table where the four lawyers had been seated. For the first time in many years, she was genuinely pleased to see them.

"Good morning, gentlemen."

Jeremy Dupree eyed her cleavage. "Ah… Mary. Radiant as usual."

Marcus Ironcase chimed in with, "Really, Dupree. I know you've had a shock, but try to keep your tongue in your mouth until breakfast arrives."

This drew a guffaw from Oliver Lawson.

Rupert Smythe-Wheaton smiled indulgently. "Forgive him, Mary, the poor chap's had to come to terms with…" He grinned knowingly at Dupree, "… drawing the short straw."

They all chuckled, except Jeremy, who shook his head ruefully. However, there was mirth in his expression. It was obviously some private joke they were sharing.

Mary smiled indulgently. "Actually, gentlemen, I was rather hoping that your tongues might be somewhat *loose* this morning."

The comment had the desired effect. "Is that so, Mary," said Smythe-Wheaton. "Pray tell, what do you have in mind for our tongues?"

Their laughter sent a shiver down her spine, but she managed, somehow, to laugh along with them.

"Well, Rupert, the four of you are very important men in Lower Icing and were, no doubt, high-ranking guests at last night's dinner."

They were nodding at her, smiling indulgently. Oliver Lawson's eyes appeared to lose focus; no doubt thinking about what his tongue could be doing.

"I was wondering, since it was quite an impromptu affair…"

She had to be careful. As far as she knew, Smythe-Wheaton was the only Limpdicker involved in Richard's plan. She couldn't single him out, nor sound as if she knew about what was going on at the castle.

"… Was it a… significant occasion?"

Their indulgent expressions remained, but their eyes turned from her to each other, as if in some silent communication. It was Jeremy Dupree who broke the silence; his expression had become somewhat curious. "It appears you have a resident guest to attend to."

Mary looked to her left, following the lawyer's gaze. She knew, before clapping eyes on him, that Sid had entered the bar room.

"Seems to have woken on the wrong side of the bed," said Oliver Lawson.

"By the looks of him," added Jeremy, "he *went* to bed on the wrong side."

"Oh, very good, Jeremy," Marcus Ironcase complimented.

Mary felt her face flush. The Limpdickers and Sid were not a good mix. She quickly turned her attention back to the lawyers. She smiled, trying to join in on the humour. "Yes, bit of a charity case there. He arrived last night, a bit worse for wear as you can see."

"Really?" Smythe-Wheaton mused. "Perhaps it might have been more charitable if you'd sent him to The Bell; no doubt he would have felt more at home there."

Mary tried to keep smiling, but her heart was pounding and Smythe-Wheaton was regarding her with a disarmingly direct expression — no wonder he never lost a case.

"If you'll excuse me, gentleman," she said, feeling quite flustered, "I will quickly attend to… my guest. Your breakfast will be with you shortly."

Smythe-Wheaton smiled… knowingly?

Jeremy Dupree looked slightly put out, while Oliver Lawson and Marcus Ironcase kept their eyes firmly on her breasts.

Sid smiled at her mischievously as she walked towards him. From the corner of her eye, Prim Pet was daintily waving her arm in an attempt to gain her attention. Mary ignored her — Prim Pet could wait, *Sid* couldn't.

"Good morning, Master Evily," she said formally, as if she was actually speaking to a resident guest. She had her back to the Limpdickers, but she could feel Rupert Smythe-Wheaton's watery grey eyes gazing at her. "I trust your stay at The Harey Rabbit was to your satisfaction?"

Sid's brows furrowed in confusion, no doubt wondering who this woman greeting him was. Hopefully he'd pick up on her tone and play along. However, his smile just grew wider and, to her chagrin, he replied in a far too suggestive tone, "I'm not sure, Mistress Brewer. I seem to have fallen asleep prematurely."

*No, no, no, Sid!* Mary wanted to scream; surely he was smarter than this. She looked at him, imploringly, and then he realised — thank goodness — what she wanted from him.

"Please excuse my foolish jest, Mistress. Your hospitality is unsurpassed. Thank you for a most satisfactory stay."

He even performed a courteous bow. She wanted to kiss him. "Why, thank you."

As tempting as it was for Mary to get Sid out of there, she had to be seen to provide Master Evily the same hospitality as any other guest; anything else would appear unusual and certainly raise a questioning eyebrow from Rupert.

"No doubt you are hungry. May I suggest you take a seat at one of the booths overlooking the Town Square?" She indicated the seating away from the lawyers. "I'll have a hearty breakfast sent to you shortly."

"Sounds delightful." Sid was using his castle-set voice. "I'm sure it will be most… fulfilling."

*Hopefully,* she thought. It depended if the Limpdickers deigned to impart something of what had occurred at the dinner. "We aim to please. Depends how—" Her 'hungry you are' was cut off by Prim Pet's snapping fingers.

"Gel!"

Mary had had just about enough of the preening old cow. Petunia Primrose was one patron Mary *could* afford to lose. She rolled her eyes and sighed. "If you wouldn't mind seeing yourself to your table, Master Evily, I'll be with you soon."

Sid cast a distasteful gaze towards Prim Pet. "Not at all, Mistress Brewer."

The rigid-postured woman was still snapping her fingers as Mary turned around to face her table. Before Mary had a chance to ask her what was wrong, Prim Pet let loose with a disagreeably loud, "This tea is too weak and co-eld."

"I apologise, Mistress Primrose. I will attend to it straightaway."

"And I do believe this is Jeedarling, when I *distinctly* asked for Earl Beige."

Bloody hell, so she had. However, Mary was finding it hard to be hospitable to Prim Pet this morning. The best she could manage was a frustrated, "Of course."

Prim Pet picked up on her tone and treated Mary to a disapproving glare.

"Your pardon, Mistress Primrose," she added, picking up the pot and cup, and then she hurried past the jovial Taylors and the silent Pennyworths to the kitchen door.

Before entering, she noticed the booths were empty. Where was Sid? She felt her stomach lurch as she realised he was standing next to the Limpdickers' table talking to Jeremy. Though their voices were muted, neither looked like they were sharing pleasantries. Bloody friggin' hell!

She pushed the kitchen door open and virtually dropped the pot and cup on the kitchen bench.

"Ees somedeeng wrong, Meestress?" Juanita was now peeling turnips. "You look like dee cheekin dats seen dee fox."

"What?" Mary replied distractedly, and then realised she was about to begin a conversation she didn't want to have. "Never mind," she added quickly, then turned to Patricia who was busy frying sausages, scrambling eggs, roasting tomatoes, sautéing mushrooms and grilling the remaining bacon. What the frig was keeping Mandy? Bloody hell.

"Where's John?" Mary asked her cook.

"'Elpin' Dave with somethin'. S'pose t'be 'elpin' me with this lot. It's jus' 'bout ready t'be served."

"You want for me to get heem?" asked Juanita, joining in on the urgency of the moment.

"No, thank you, Juanita. However, if someone could make Mistress Primrose another pot of tea — Earl Beige this time — that would be helpful."

As Mary headed out of the kitchen and down the hallway, she heard Juanita say, "I do eet, Meestress." Prim Pet was in for a treat.

Mary almost collided with John as he burst through the door that opened behind the bar and led to the storeroom and cellar. He apologised, of course, but Mary brushed it off with an annoyed-sounding, "Go and help Patricia, and *stay* helping her until Mandy returns."

"Yes, Mistress," he replied, meekly. "Sorry, Mistress."

"It's alright, John. Just… go and help her."

He nodded and scampered down the hallway. Mary tried to collect her thoughts before entering the bar. Taking a deep breath, she opened door.

The bar itself was directly ahead. Behind it, steps led down to the cellar. She could see candlelight emanating from the opening. That was a good sign — there can't have been any conflict if Dave was going about his business. And come to think of it, John would have come running if anything was amiss. She was being stupid. It was those bloody lawyers, particularly

Jeremy Dupree, who had put her nerves on edge.

Moving towards the bar, she scanned the dining room. Everything appeared normal. The Limpdickers were sitting at their Market Lane table, chuckling amongst themselves, and Sid was half slumped in one of the Town Square booths, head turned away from her, staring out the window. The Taylors were at ease, the Pennyworths looked like they were listening to a poetry recital, and, a few paces away, at her small table for two, Prim Pet was eyeing her with undisguised impatience.

She didn't feel like dealing with any of them at the moment; she needed time to focus her thoughts. "Your tea will be with you shortly, Mistress Primrose," she said politely, before taking the stairs down to the cellar.

As she descended the steep stone stairs, she could hear the scraping of oak barrels.

"Dave?" she enquired into the candlelit gloom.

"Aye." He sounded as if he was exerting himself. This was followed by a dull thud and a heavy exhale. "There, that's got the bugger back in place."

"Everything alright?"

He was wiping his hands on his smock as he came into view. "Aye. Couple of them brackets are a bit dodgy; the barrels ain't sittin' on 'em prop'ly. Prob'ly need t'get 'em replaced soon, I reckon."

Mary was staring at the barman, listening to his words, but not really taking them in until he said, "Somethin' amiss, Mary?"

"Did anything just happen between Sid and the Limpdickers?"

His confused gaze looked quite menacing in the gloomy light, but his voice was jovial. "Frig knows; I been down 'ere all bleedin' mornin'."

Mary nodded. Of course he had.

"Ain't *heard* nothin' though. Why? Watcha think 'appened?"

"Nothing... hopefully."

He looked perplexed.

She shook her head and smiled. "Oh, don't mind me, Dave. I think I must be overtired. Please look into replacing the brackets."

He nodded.

"Right," she said, trying to sound upbeat, "back into the fray. Let's see if I can get the Limpdickers to talk about what happened at the castle last night."

Dave smiled. "Just be sure they don' charge y'for it."

They exited the cellar together. Even before she clapped eyes on the patrons, she could smell the cooked breakfasts and hear the sounds of utensils on plates. Stepping up behind the bar, she was in time to see John disappear back into the kitchen. Her gaze flicked to the lawyers, who were hoeing into their platter, then to the booth where Sid… no longer sat.

Mary entered the bar room. Where the frig had Sid gone? Had he left? Without saying goodbye? Something must have…

She'd hardly taken two steps before she was bailed up by Prim Pet, who wanted to know why her food hadn't arrived before the lawyers since *she* had arrived before them *and* why her tea was taking so long. Once again, Mary had to placate the pedantic woman with reassurances that both her breakfast and tea would be out shortly.

Then the lawyers held her up about the meagre amount of bacon on their platter. She apologised and explained that they had run short after an impromptu dinner on Wednesday night. Smythe-Wheaton hardly batted an eyelid, just nodded at Oliver Lawson's "Rather poor show, what!"

By the time she reached the booth, minutes had passed. She peered out the window, hoping to catch a glimpse of Sid ambling across The Square, but the space was filled with barrows, stalls and peddlers trying to capture the attention of passersby. It was a ramshackle version of the actual market, which was closed on Fridays for some reason lost in time.

She was more than annoyed by the fact that Sid had just up and left. What had gotten into him? Was he *that* upset by her play-acting or was it, as she suspected, more to do with the Limpdickers.

As if confirming her thoughts, Jeremy Dupree's voice rang out across the bar room. "Your guest has left; looked to be rather put out. I do hope he's paid for his board." Then, as an aside, he added, "*One* way or another." This was followed by muted chuckling.

Mary felt the blood rush to her face and a cold anger fill her. She slowly turned around to face the Limpdickers. They were scoffing down their breakfast. Jeremy Dupree was biting into a sausage; he'd just yelled out in between mouthfuls because he thought he was entitled to.

Of all the things they'd said and done — their boorish behaviour, their superior attitude, their lecherous looks and wayward hands — Mary had never felt as angry as she did right now. The words were bad enough, but what really had her swallowing bile was the way they were delivered; as if they *believed* she was capable of whoring herself! Bastards! Pigs! They'd pushed her too far this time.

Smythe-Wheaton and Marcus Ironcase were in her line of sight as she approached the table, the former looking at her curiously (perhaps even warily), the latter slurping up eggs with a piece of crusty bread. Mary felt removed from the situation, as if she were in a dream, and each step closer seemed to take minutes. She could see the nuance of movement: the jelly-like jowls of Ironcase working away at the bread and eggs, the narrowing eyes of Rupert Smythe-Wheaton. Mary inhaled deeply, in preparation for unleashing five years' worth of pent-up anger.

However, one perfectly timed word stopped her; saved, as it were, by the "Gel!"

Mary's anger deflected towards the sound of the pompous summons. She marched over to Prim Pet, who looked taken aback even before the words were out of Mary's mouth, but out they came anyway.

"Listen, you preening piece of puffery. I am *not* your gel! You know very well what my name is, *who* I am, so I suggest you start treating me *and* my staff accordingly. And if you can't bring yourself to show *some* semblance of civility, then I suggest you take your sour disposition elsewhere!"

The woman looked gobsmacked. Mary couldn't fault her for that, but nor did she regret saying the words, particularly when they'd felt so right.

"Well, I never!" Prim Pet huffed, indignantly.

"Yes, we all *know* that, Petunia!" Mary wasn't going to be cowed by the old cow this time. "*That's* your problem!"

Somewhere in the back of her mind, Mary was aware her venting was being conducted in a public arena. She knew the Limpdickers would be nothing more than amused, but she wasn't sure about the Tinkers, and very much doubted the Pennyworths were appreciating the diatribe.

Prim Pet stood up, as if someone had jabbed a fork in her sour disposition, treated Mary to a disdainful glare, and walked stiffly towards the exit, her angry steps the only sound in the room. Mary's heart was thumping as Prim Pet slammed the door behind her. All eyes turned back upon her. Even John and Juanita had stuck their heads around the kitchen door.

"My apologies, ladies and gentlemen," she said, barely aware she'd spoken. The lawyers wore, as predicted, amused expressions. The rest just looked stunned. She needed to get out of here before she completely lost her reason. Holding back tears, she retreated through the hallway door to the sound of Henry Taylor's, "Good on you, Mary. She's 'ad that comin' for a while now."

She saw Dave move towards her from behind the bar. He wore a concerned expression, but she waved him away; she didn't want anyone's sympathy.

She was too bloody angry.

As soon as she reached the other side of the door, Mary began gasping for air, trying to keep the tears at bay. If she gave in to them, she'd sob uncontrollably. She headed towards her bedroom; she needed time to regain her composure. Then the kitchen door burst open behind her.

"Oh, Meestress!" Juanita cried down the hallway.

Mary turned to face the approaching Icarumban. What was wrong now?

"You geeve that stupeed cow a peece of your mouth, jus' like in Icarumba. I'm so happy to you!"

*Happy to her?*

Then John's sheepish countenance appeared at the kitchen door. Mary wanted to yell out to be left alone, but her throat felt too constricted. Fortunately, Patricia came to her rescue, barking through the open door, "You two, get back t'work now! What sort o' kitchen y'think this is?"

John immediately ducked back into the kitchen. Juanita stopped advancing down the hallway, but Mary could tell she wanted to hug her or something. Then the Icarumban's expression changed — no doubt Mary's face had betrayed her.

"Oh, Meestress, is somedeeng wrong?"

"Juanita! You listenin' t'me?"

Mary found her voice, but it was barely more than a whisper, "I'm fine. Do as Patricia says."

Mary could tell Juanita was conflicted, but Patricia yelled out her name again and she reluctantly returned to the kitchen.

## CHAPTER 58

## *Wine-soaked haze of disbelief*

OLIVIA WOKE UP surrounded by grey stone walls. Golden light filtered through a narrow window. She leapt up from the bed. It was morning. The blackness was gone, but the emptiness remained. She stumbled dizzily to the heavy, iron-bound door. Her mind was foggy, her head hurt and she felt groggy, but her heart was thumping at the realisation: the nightmare was real.

She tried the latch, but it was locked. She vaguely remembered being escorted to this 'guestroom' sometime last night. She'd been in a daze, a wine-soaked haze of disbelief, after Gerald had…

She had to get out of here. She banged on the door and yelled to be let out, but there was no answer, apart from the throbbing in her head. A wave of nausea crashed through her. She hurled herself over to the copper bathtub in the corner of the room and heaved out the contents of her stomach, beginning with gushes of purple and ending with spits of bitter saliva. After a few minutes of retching, she lifted her head from the edge of the tub and gazed, teary-eyed, at her surroundings.

In other circumstances, she would have been quite pleased with the room's presentation: the bed was sizeable and quilted in purple with gold stitching, there was a dressing table with a mirror, an ornately carved wardrobe, a dining setting and writing desk. All the furniture had been polished recently and clean rugs had been placed at the base of the bed and underneath the dining table. A brazier stood beside a neat pile of cut timber and tinder, ready to be lit, ready to provide warmth and light… ready for the guests from the Duchy of Stymouth.

She remembered Lieutenant Swill saying this was the room in which Xavier had been kept. Yes, she thought, but only after Gerald had insisted he be removed from the cell-like room Richard had chosen for him. Oh, Gerald; he'd taken the path of common decency from the beginning, and all *she'd* done was scoff, telling him to stop meddling.

Olivia tried to stand, using the rim of the tub to push herself up, but the room began to sway and the smell of sandalwood polish and acrid vomit was too much. She collapsed back over the tub and heaved until she thought her insides were about to spew through her mouth.

Olivia woke with a start. It took a moment for her to realise she'd fallen asleep with her head lolling over the side of the tub. She felt worse than she had when she'd first woken, if that was possible. Below her, a murky purple splatter of...

She pushed herself away from the tub, then used the wall to clamber into a standing position. The room reeled again, but this time she managed to stagger over to the window. She needed fresh air. Closing her eyes to the bright morning light, she leant against the sill and took slow, deep breaths.

She kept her eyes closed and concentrated on breathing. The world became smell, feel, sound and taste — the redolence of baking from Reg Puffy's kitchen, the warmth of the morning sun on the side of her face and the caress of a wispy breeze, the hubbub and clamour of people going about another day, all wrapped up in her mouth's bitter reminder of last night's disaster.

"I know who is responsible," Gerald had announced in front of the entire banquet. Initially, the gravity of the statement had been lost on Olivia and she was befuddled by his whispered apology to her.

"Now I have what I want, Olivia." It wasn't Richard's words so much, more the expression on his face that made her realise Gerald had been referring to *himself*, that *he* was responsible for poisoning Marmaduke. She remembered the chill that had run through her wine-warmed bones.

Olivia kept her eyes closed. Her lids were heavy and so was her head. She turned it to the side and rested it on her arms — the sill was quite comfortable in this position. Below, the world went by; it was mainly sounds and smells now. Olivia had never realised how much activity occurred in Lower Icing. Just the noise from the castle kitchen: the crashing, calling, yelling, cart loads of comings and goings, laughter... laughter... It was strange to hear so much of it. Olivia couldn't remember the last time she'd laughed.

From that point on, the night had become a blur of faces and voices.

The other guests had sounded confused, unaware of what had just occurred. She remembered Henry Bowler asking Richard what was happening and Richard replying that the show was almost over. It'd seemed a strange thing to say, but Olivia's head was spinning with repercussions, and she hadn't fully appreciated what *had* just taken place.

Curious, bewildered, confused, knowing, judgmental expressions swam across her vision as she and Gerald walked side by side behind Richard, with two guardsmen bringing up the rear. Only two faces had resonated with her: Xavier's expression was forlorn and, standing next to him, Paris looked — of all things — sympathetic. Thank goodness for the dulling effects of the wine, otherwise she would have been overcome with emotion. She couldn't bear to look at Gerald; she'd been too angry with him. Richard's words echoed inside her head: *"A case of underestimating the capacity for stupidity."*

What *had* Gerald been thinking?

Her head felt clearer and her stomach more settled; the fresh air was working wonders. Even the headache and grogginess were dissipating. She slowly opened her eyes. Her eyelids fluttered and blinked at the brightness, but she persevered and eventually the world came into view. It was a sideways view — Olivia's head still rested on her arm — but that didn't matter. In any case, she was reluctant to move; she didn't want the head-spinning or nausea to return. Straight ahead, the mid-morning sky was blue and cloudless. Below, the rooftops of the Administration buildings were coated in sunshine. They flowed almost seamlessly into the rooftops of buildings outside the castle wall. Everywhere, people went about their business, minding their own business, as if last night's business hadn't happened.

It wasn't long after the doors to the Banquet Hall had been closed behind them that Olivia realised the dinner had been nothing more than an elaborate ruse. The Swill boy had come up to Richard and saluted. "Sir Richard, Captain Le Sharp sends his compliments and will meet you in your quarters directly."

Richard nodded, his dark eyes aglow, reflecting the bright candlelight — the hundreds of candles that had looked so impressive and magical on arrival now seemed harsh and glaring. "Very good, Lieutenant. Tell the captain I look forward to congratulating him in person. It has been a most successful outcome," he'd said, casting a self-satisfied glance in the direction of her husband.

A successful outcome? For whom? Marmaduke? He was either dead or on his deathbed. Xavier? His hopes had been dashed by Richard's meddling, his gift bashed out of him, his self-worth and belief in tatters. Gerald? What *would* become of Gerald?

She'd turned to face her husband — to finally look him in the eyes — but his gaze was unfocused and far away… or was it deep inside? Her simmering anger subsided; the bombastic, ebullient man she'd spent the last six years with looked deflated, empty, broken…

Olivia, half asleep, listened as raised voices broke through the lulling clamour of Lower Icing, echoing off the stone walls that surrounded the Middle Bailey. They were accompanied by the sound of heavy boots marching across cobblestones. She kept her head rested on her arm and continued to breathe deeply. She wasn't interested in seeing who they were. It all sounded rather mundane anyway.

"Yes, but do you really think it was wise to send Martin with Lamb?" questioned male voice one. "Martin's a cadet, greener than fresh cow shit, and Lamb… Well, Lamb's become obsessed with *redeeming* himself."

The tone sounded vaguely familiar, but not familiar enough for Olivia to raise her head.

"True, Lamb is a leg short on a spit, but it wasn't my idea," replied male voice two. "It was Le Sharp's decision. Martin was keen to go, and I didn't have anyone else to spare, so he got the job. Nice ride in the countryside — do him good."

"I don't like it, Jethro," stated male voice one. "If it comes to a confrontation, I can't see Martin being of much use."

"Yeah, but who'd want to get on the wrong side of Bradley Lamb for frig's sake!"

"I suppose we'll find out when they return. They should be back by late evening."

The words, almost dream-like in her foggy state, suddenly resonated as real. Olivia sprang out of her stupor. Craning forward, she scanned what she could see of the Middle Bailey. It was empty. She could only hear the receding sound of boots on cobblestone, marching towards the Upper Bailey.

Predictably, the dizzy queasiness returned. She slumped back onto the sill, but she couldn't get comfortable, and her head was aching. To think her waster of a brother did this *every* night. How could he possibly function?

It was no good; she couldn't prop herself against the sill any longer. She needed to lie down again. Her mouth was dry and tasted like vinegar; she needed water.

Her head spun as she staggered back to the bed. She should have stuck to water last night, but Richard's damn mind games had unnerved her.

"This way," Richard had ordered, and started walking towards the black-and-white tiled floor of the fore-building. Gerald moved straight away, without question, as if he were under some sort of spell. The two guards who'd escorted them from the Banquet Hall also reacted, falling in line either side of Gerald, ushering him along at a smart pace to keep up with their commander. They seemed oblivious to Olivia as she moved to follow them. However, she'd barely taken two steps when the Swill boy called out her name. She ignored him. Regardless of her husband's stupidity, her place was with him. And, in any case, she didn't take orders from Swills, no matter *what* uniform they were wearing.

"Mistress Hiepants!" The voice had been more authoritative the second time. However, it made no difference to her; she'd been full of inebriated defiance and indignation. To humiliate her in this way was just… bad manners.

Then she'd felt a strong hand grab her arm and swing her around. She'd almost fallen in the process, but somehow managed to keep her feet. The Swill boy's face came into focus — it was concerned and determined. She lashed out with her free hand, but he easily caught her arm well before it contacted his face.

"Unhand me!" Her voice was a hiss. "I will accompany my husband!"

He'd kept a firm hold on her arms as she struggled to free herself. "That won't be possible, Mistress Hiepants. I have orders to take you upstairs. You will be spending tonight in one of the guestrooms."

She'd been so shocked that she'd stopped struggling. The Swill boy kept hold of her regardless. "You can't do anything for your husband."

She'd felt like crying out to Gerald, but what could *he* do?

"Please, Mistress Hiepants." His voice and expression softened. "Save yourself further indignation."

Then she realised there were still other people in the antechamber. Standing in the corner, among the muted rumblings of the departing throng, were Rupert Smythe-Wheaton and the Whysmans. The lawyer looked condescendingly bemused, Albert concerned and Petronella shocked. Everything seemed like a bizarre dream and she suddenly found the whole scenario quite amusing. She started giggling. Then she started laughing. The castle-set's expressions were hilarious, so beautifully affronted.

She'd almost collapsed in a fit of laughter. The Swill boy grabbed her by the waist to support her. It made her laugh even more.

She heard Petronella gasp, "My dear!"

Priceless! But she couldn't laugh any harder; the sides of her corsetry would have split.

"Lieutenant," said Albert, "I think you'd better take Mistress Hiepants to her room. The poor woman… this is not right."

The room had begun to spin; faces became blurs and she'd found it hard to breathe.

"Here, sit her down." Albert sounded concerned.

"That's not possible, Doctor Whysman," replied the Swill boy. "As you know, there are pressing matters to attend to."

"Why not dump her in the corner?" It was the drawling voice of Smythe-Wheaton.

"Really, Rupert!" Petronella was outraged.

Albert agreed. "Poor form, sir."

The Swill boy's arms shifted position. "I'll carry her up."

Olivia realised she was no longer laughing, and reality suddenly reared its sobering head. She pushed herself from the Swill boy's grasp and, staggering backwards, announced, "I am quite capable of walking, Lieutenant!"

Her vision was still swimming and the faces watching her still looked concerned (with the exception of Smythe-Wheaton).

"Then, *please*, Mistress Hiepants, allow me to escort you to your room." The Swill boy held out his arm and indicated the spiral staircase.

"Very well, Lieutenant; since I have no choice."

"Oh, Olivia." Petronella moved towards her, eyes full of pity.

It was mortifying — she'd rather Smythe-Wheaton's contempt. Olivia held out her hand, halting her friend. "Thank you, Petronella; I shall be fine. I'm afraid I've indulged in a little too much wine this evening. My apologies."

The pity increased.

"Oh, and I have been most tardy in responding to your invitation to morning tea. My reply remains unfinished on my desk, I'm afraid. I do apologise; I shall send it to you as soon as I am…" Her gaze swam over to the Swill boy. "…at liberty."

Petronella smiled, warmly. "Of course, my dear."

Olivia moved towards the stairwell without further ado. She gazed disdainfully at Smythe-Wheaton as she passed him. Stepping into the stairwell, Albert's voice rang out behind her, "Take care, Lieutenant."

The Swill boy didn't reply. Whether or not he'd acknowledged the remark with a gesture or not, Olivia didn't notice; she'd been too busy concentrating on putting one foot in front of the other.

Lying on the bed, remembering what had occurred, she wanted to squirm under the covers. Sinking her head deep into the soft pillow, Olivia closed her eyes. She now also felt sick with embarrassment.

# CHAPTER 59

## *Made him a doctor*

MARY HEARD A soft knock at her door. She wasn't sure how long she'd been lying on her bed; it seemed like a few minutes, but it was probably more like fifteen.

She'd been mulling things over in her head — Jeremy Dupree's words had cut deep. However, rather than dwelling on the castle dinner, Sid, Richard or the Duke, her thoughts had turned introspective.

What sort of person had she become? Was she nothing more than a panderer to the whims of the rich and pompous, who, no matter how much she tried to make them feel special, would never see her as anything more than a servant... or a whore?

Sid saw them for who they were: the snobbery, the privileged attitude, and the disdain for anything below their standards. He didn't trust them, nor did he want to know or associate with them. She could only imagine what the lawyers had said; she didn't blame him for leaving. At least he was honest and open about how he felt, while Mary smiled and made excuses. Even Juanita's fiery disposition contained a perceptive understanding: *"We keell dee rats, not feed dem dee cheese."*

Perhaps Jeremy Dupree was right; maybe she *was* a whore after all.

The person knocked a second time, but this time she identified herself. "It's Mandy, Mistress."

Mary eased off the bed and stepped towards the door. At least she hadn't cried; the wave of anger hadn't crashed into a flood of tears, it had ebbed, gradually. She quickly fluffed her hair and opened the door. Mandy regarded her with a concerned expression — Mary could only imagine what she'd heard from John and Juanita. Bloody hell... Juanita!

"I'm fine, Mandy," she said, anticipating the question. "How did you go at the castle?"

"They could only spare five pounds of rashers, Mistress," she replied, "but I managed t'wheedle some pork pies ou' of Reg; they was left over from las' night's dinner."

"I see." It was an odd sort of fare to be served at a castle dinner. "Did he say anything else?"

"Well…" She sounded like she had something juicy to reveal. She even glanced towards the kitchen to make sure no-one was within earshot.

"Here, come in," Mary said, ushering Mandy into the room and closing the door behind her.

"The dinner finished quite early, like; roun' 'alf-nine, 'cordin' t'Reg. *And none of the servants was allowed anywhere near the hall, only t'bring an' collect the food an' drink — no actual servin', like…*"

That *was* unusual; obviously Richard didn't want anyone other than invited guests to witness what he had planned.

"Only," Mandy continued with more excitement in her voice, "some of the servants 'eard from the guardsmen tha' there was a lotta shoutin', 'cause 'parrently the Duke 'as a bleedin' *heir!*"

Of all the things Mary was expecting to hear!

"An heir! Who?" How? When?

"Dunno. Jus' some young lad what rolled into town outta bleedin' nowhere."

Mary shook her head in disbelief; this sounded like gossip gone wild, unreliable sources passing on unreliable information. Lucinda had never been with child!

"It's not possible, Mandy."

"S'pose not, Mistress," she said. "Still, y'know wha' they say: ain't no smoke withou' fire."

"It's been *all* bloody smoke recently. I wouldn't mind seeing some fire."

Mandy gave her a quizzical look. "Well, bes' get back to servin', like. But there ain't 'ardly any of the regulars in this mornin', no-one tha' was at the castle dinner least ways."

"So the Limpdickers have left?"

"'Bout 'alf hour ago."

"Half an hour?" How long *had* she spent in her bedroom? "What time is it?"

"Near 'leven."

Mary swore; an hour had passed. "I see," she said, collecting her thoughts. "I take it everything else is alright?"

"Yes, Mistress. Jus' thought y'needed checkin' up on, like."

"Thank you, Mandy."

"An' I 'eard 'bout Prim Pet an' all. Wish I'd been 'ere t'see *that!*"

Mary smiled. "Can't deny it felt good."

Mary followed Mandy into the hallway and shut the bedroom door behind her.

Mandy waited for her. "Passin' strange what y'said 'bout bein' too much smoke, like."

"Oh?" said Mary, half lost in her own thoughts. "In what way?"

They began walking towards the kitchen. "Well, this lad what claims t'be the Duke's son…"

"Yes, I think we can agree that is nonsense."

"'Course, Mistress, but… if the story *is* all smoke, odd tha' they made 'im a doctor, like."

Mary came to a halt just before the kitchen door. "What do you mean, made him a doctor?"

"Well, word 'as it 'e's a doctor."

Mary's heart was suddenly pounding, her mind racing.

*A doctor!*

The one the guards had been whispering about, the one every patrolmen (and butcher) had been sent to find, Richard's 'specific individual', his 'person of interest', the secret meeting, the documents and deeds, the dinner at the castle… For frig's sake, he wasn't searching for the Duke's *attacker*; that was just a ruse. But *how* could there be an heir, unless… Marmaduke and Lucinda had had a son *before* they came to Lower Icing!

"Mistress? You alright?"

She was sick of people asking her that. "Never been better," she replied, trying to hold her shock in check. She needed to calm down and think straight. She needed to speak to Sid.

Mary despatched John to retrieve Sid. As keen as she was to see him, John would be a quicker option; he could run to Sid's place in five minutes, and if he wasn't there, better John stood waiting for him than *her*. She'd impressed upon him the importance of getting Sid to return *with* him. "If he puts up a fight, say that I know who the doctor is."

He nodded, then asked, "What doctor?"

"You don't need to worry about that. Sid will understand." Then she grabbed him firmly by the shoulders and looked him straight in the eye. "John, it's important. Can I trust you to do this?"

He held her gaze. "'Course, Mistress."

Mary nodded. He rushed out of the kitchen, sprinted across the courtyard and disappeared through the gate.

## CHAPTER 60

# *Tail of the Dragon's Back*

JUST BEFORE MIDDAY, the forest came to an abrupt end. Half an hour before, Tom had deviated from their westerly path to a more north-westerly route. It hadn't been long before the ground began to slope upwards and become rockier. Then they'd turned west again, and suddenly the trees opened onto a spread of grey shale that spilled into a glistening river: the tail of the Dragon's Back.

Ophelia recognised the spot immediately; the ford where, four days ago, she and Tom had crossed the Icing in pursuit of the Moleson Twins.

"We'll walk the horses from here," Tom said. He'd switched positions so that he now sat behind her pa. (Her pa had started to complain of saddle-soreness, and his grumbling had gradually worn down Tom's resilience. "Now who's soft-arsed?" Ophelia had quipped, to which her pa had responded, "Well, if the friggin' thing didn't sway so bleedin' much!" Again, Ophelia had only seen the funny side.)

Tom sprang easily from Wildflower's back, landing lightly on his feet. Ophelia followed suit. She was beginning to enjoy riding. Well, riding at a walking pace at least. Her pa also managed a half-respectable dismount; sitting on the saddle obviously made a difference.

Walking out of the forest, along the craggy foothills of the Dragon's Back, was like stepping back in time... Not just four days; there was something more *primal* about the ford and the river, like a dragon's tail *had* thumped down and smashed all the rocks and boulders into grey shards. The horses seemed to sense it too as they stepped tentatively across the loose shale towards the Icing. However, unlike four days ago, everything seemed wonderfully refreshing — even the flies and insects were absent.

They gathered at the edge of the ford. The horses stepped into the crystal clear water and sloshed up their fill. Tom doused the water-skins, while her pa grumbled about having to be led across the ford on horseback like a child.

"It doesn't look it, Frank, but the current is strong," Tom explained. "And the water reaches over waist height in the middle."

Her pa wasn't impressed. "Well, I ain't ezackly a feather-weight, Gamekeeper. Think I c'n 'andle a pissin' bit o'water runnin' 'cross m'legs."

Tom shook his head. "Can you swim, Frank?"

"No, but I can friggin' *wade!*"

Tom reacted, angrily. "Well, when you *do* lose your footing and find yourself being forced downstream because the current *is* too bloody strong, and you discover that you *don't* actually have the strength to cope with it, because you're *not* fully recovered from your ordeal, then please don't start yelling for *me* to save you!"

Her pa looked defiant. *Bloody pride*, thought Ophelia. Why couldn't he just accept Tom's advice; surely he must realise by now that Tom was acting in his best interests. Bloody pride!

"Pa! You're gettin' back on the bleedin' 'orse and tha's a friggin' end to it!"

He pa glared at her as he approached Wildflower, "Y'coulda bloody well tol' me before I got *off* the friggin' thing!"

## CHAPTER 61

### *Like a cornered dog*

**T**HE BAR ROOM of The Harey Rabbit was virtually deserted. Perhaps the supposed heir to the Duchy had commanded everyone to stay home today. Mandy was chatting to a young couple: Dudley and Eleanor Hotspur. They rarely ventured into town because Dudley's family bred horses on a stud farm just south of Lower Icing. It was a hands-on business, and time away from it was limited… something Mary could well relate to. Still, the rewards were there: Hotspur Stud was widely regarded as one of the best thoroughbred studs in the Five Duchies.

Once Mandy had cleared their table, Mary went and said hello to Dudley and Eleanor. They were delightful, warm-hearted people, full of praise for The Harey Rabbit and complimentary of her staff.

Mary found herself sitting down at the table with them; not something she'd normally do, but it was such a pleasure to converse with relaxed, genuine people like the Hotspurs. In any case, they had the bar room to themselves. For fifteen wonderful minutes, Mary felt like a real person, one who could interact as herself, not as a hostess or an employer or a… whore. Then Mandy interrupted her make-believe world, saying she was needed in the kitchen. Reluctantly, she excused herself from Dudley and Eleanor's enjoyable company.

John was wet *again*, but this time it was because he was covered in sweat.

"Where's Sid? Did you speak to him?"

He was still panting. "Yes, Mistress."

"Then why isn't he with you?"

John was standing by the table where Patricia sat having a cup of tea while Juanita was in the process of washing dishes at the sink. Luckily for them, neither said anything. John also remained pathetically silent. Mary felt like slapping him.

"Well?" Mary said, folding her arms (possibly to stop herself from slapping him). "What did he say? Did you tell him about the doctor?"

"Yes... that is... no... 'e said tha' 'e was fine, like..."

"John!" she snapped, exasperated by his fidgety mumblings. "I thought I made it perfectly clear. Doesn't the word *important* mean anything to you?"

"Wheech doctor?"

"Be quiet, Juanita!" Mary snapped again. Then she grabbed John by the arm and marched him out of the kitchen. She didn't stop until they'd reached the stables, out of earshot of Patricia and Juanita.

"Well?" she said, trying to keep her temper in check. John was clearly upset. However, Mary had little sympathy for him.

"'E didn' wan' t'listen, Mistress." His voice was little more than a whisper, his gaze cast down to the cobblestones. "I tried, like... but 'e said tha' 'e was tryin t'keep y'safe."

*Keep her safe?*

"Safe from what?"

John looked up. He looked close to tears. "Dunno. 'E jus' said he'd see you at The 'Arey Rabbit when 'e got things sorted, like."

Mary shook her head in frustration. There was no use berating John any further; she could imagine the exchange between him and Sid. The lad just wasn't strong enough to stand up to anyone. She should have known.

Once again, Mary found herself hurrying through the streets of Lower Icing towards Sid Evily's abode. Again she took the route past The Bell and down Merchant, over Noble, Plumduff and Blancmange, right on Meringue before meandering north and west, down the smaller streets and lanes that led to his house.

She turned into Bull Lane some hundred paces to the south of Sid's terraced home. Much to her surprise, he was standing in his doorway talking to a small, scrawny figure dressed in an ice-blue robe. It took a moment for Mary to process the scene, then she quickened her pace towards them. Judging by Sid's defensive posture, he wasn't finding the conversation to his liking. As she drew nearer, he barked out a derisive laugh, but the robed individual who, Mary surmised, was Doctor Manky's messenger, appeared calm.

Bloody hell, what was going on? Mary wasn't sure whether to be relieved or annoyed by the scene; it hardly looked like something she needed to be kept safe from. Well, there was only one way to find out. She called out to Sid.

He glanced in her direction, but didn't respond. It was like he hadn't recognised her, or didn't *want* to recognise her.

Mary waved her hand and called out to him again. She was close enough now to see the expression on Sid's face. He looked like a cornered dog, eyes darting in hope of spying an escape route. He muttered something to the man, who seemed quite unflustered by Mary's appearance. In fact, he'd not even turned in her direction. From side on, she couldn't help but notice his large beaked nose and protruding Adam's apple. Together with his bald scalp and tufts of grey hair, the man put her in mind of a turkey.

Suddenly he took flight, with Sid sprinting after him.

*What was he doing?* "Sid!"

She started running after them, but they both continued to sprint away from her. Amazingly the small man was out-running Sid.

"Wait!" she yelled. "Sid! The Doctor!"

Mary slowed to a halt as the robed whippet sprung atop a black carriage parked in a clearing between houses. Sid paused as he opened the carriage door and looked back towards her. He looked conflicted and remorseful, and for a moment, it seemed, he was about to run back to her.

Mary stood there, panting, watching, hoping…

Then the man in ice-blue leant over and said something to Sid. Sid jumped inside the cab. The carriage took off immediately and the single horse was in full trot before Mary could even begin to wonder what had just happened.

She stared at the back of the carriage as it hurtled north up Bull Lane and along The Coin Curve, until it arced out of sight. Its disappearance brought her back to herself and her surroundings. She was standing in front of Sid's house, or, more precisely, the dent in the wall left by the bull. The street was deserted… exactly how Mary felt.

"You righ', love?" a voice called out from above.

She looked up to her left. The goodwife who'd berated Mary about waking her baby was looking down from her first-floor window, cradling a baby-shaped bundle of cloth. She looked concerned.

"My apologies, goodwife, if I have disturbed your child." Then, almost to herself, she added, "I assure you; it won't happen again."

She nodded, knowingly. "You're orrigh'. Y'best off wivout Sid Evily anyways. 'E ain't nuffin' more than a drunken layabou' wha' pretends 'e's somethin' 'e ain't."

Right at that moment — given how she was feeling about Sid — Mary couldn't have put it better.

CHAPTER 62

## *High expectations*

OLIVIA WOKE UP on the bed for a second time. She sat up. Her head throbbed — if anything, she felt worse. Fighting an urge to lie straight back down, she forced herself into a standing position and stumbled over to the window. She didn't dare look in the bathtub, and held her breath until she was gazing out over the rooftops of Lower Icing.

The day had progressed without her; it must be near midday judging by the lack of shadows. Again, the fresh air worked it wonders, clearing her head and reviving her senses. Lower Icing was abuzz — clatters, crashes, cries, cackles, clops and clanks sounded from all directions. It was an amazing spectacle, but not as amazing as the spectacle Richard had master-minded last night…

The stairwell had seemed to wind upwards endlessly. Even if her head hadn't been spinning from the wine, it would have been spinning from the climb. And the dim, flickering light from the Swill boy's candle wasn't helping matters.

Every time she stopped to gather her balance (or her breath) he'd been right behind her, gently prodding her forward with a "Not far now."

After the third or fourth such occurrence, she snapped at him. "Stop pushing me, Lieutenant!"

"Then walk faster!"

She stood her ground. "Why am I being locked away in The Keep? And what is to become of my husband?"

His sigh echoed up the stairwell like a wisp of breeze. "I'm just following orders, Mistress Hiepants."

She turned around to face him; his candle-lit face looked tired and impatient.

"You have colluded with your husband in harbouring a person—"

"Quite correct, Lieutenant; *harbouring* is *exactly* what Gerald and I did.

We *harboured* the Duke's son from the *maltreatment* provided by the Duke's *Seneschal*."

"It is not for me to comment. However, the fact remains that your husband has admitted to poisoning the Duke — hardly an *altruistic* act — and until such time as he has given a satisfactory account of his actions, you are to be held in The Keep."

A few dizzying moments passed while she absorbed his words.

"Now, *please,*" he said, taking a step upwards, "keep moving."

Olivia continued up the stairs. What if Gerald *couldn't* give a satisfactory account? And in all probability, he wouldn't. Was she to spend her days locked in The Keep?

Olivia gazed out over the township and wondered if *this* was the view she would have for the rest of her life. Her chin rested on her hands. The sun felt warm on her face. On the northern edge of Lower Icing, something was catching the sunlight. It was moving. From this distance it seemed slow, but Olivia realised it was actually travelling at a pace. It arced around to the right, no longer catching the sun, revealing itself: a black, horse-drawn carriage. *Someone* was in a hurry to leave town.

It made her feel even more trapped. Her thoughts became maudlin. She wasn't sure she could stand being confined, tormented by the life below her. Still, the window was big enough for her to squeeze through, should she become *that* desperate.

Adding to her misery, she'd just remembered that today was her thirty-third birthday. Last night, walking to that sham of a dinner, she'd had such high expectations of what it would bring. High expectations. She laughed to herself as she gazed out over rooftops.

The carriage caught her eye again, shimmering its way towards the North Road. Well, one thing was for sure; *she* wouldn't be leaving town, not today at least, and there *certainly* wouldn't be any happy returns…

Once they'd exited the stairwell, the Swill boy had taken her by the arm and led her to the door. She hadn't objected; the passageway was dark, and her head was spinning, so she needed his steadying hand.

Then he opened a door and ushered her into a room. "Here you are, Mistress Hiepants. You should be comfortable; Xavier seemed content enough… until your husband unwisely deemed otherwise."

Olivia remained silent. She suddenly felt drained, and no longer had the will to argue.

He walked over to the bedside table and lit a candle, using the one he was holding. Then he moved back to the door. "I bid you goodnight, Mistress Hiepants. Someone will attend to you tomorrow."

The door was shut, the key was turned. She was now locked in… a prisoner. She desperately needed to relieve herself, but there was no sit-upon to sit upon. All she could find was a piss bucket. Thankfully, it had been emptied.

Olivia suddenly felt the need to empty her bladder. However, she felt too comfortable, propped against the window. And she was afraid any movement might have disastrous effects.

So much for being attended upon. Why had nobody come to see her? What had happened to Gerald? And poor Xavier? The Duke? Did he still live?

Eventually, the need to relieve herself outweighed her need to remain motionless. Taking a deep breath of fresh air, she stumbled over to the piss bucket. Holding her breath, not daring to smell the contents, she gathered her skirts and answered nature's call. She completed the process without inhaling, then flung herself back on the bed, gasping in air. When she closed her eyes, the room began to spin, and her head throbbed. She groaned, but somehow controlled the urge to vomit. Once again, she fell unconscious.

The dreamless void of sleep lasted moments or hours — Olivia couldn't tell. The pounding was still there, but this time it was coming from *outside* her head. Through the grim after-effects of overindulgence, she realised someone was knocking loudly at the door.

## Chapter 63

# *Her life in clothes*

B Y THE TIME Mary had made it back to The Harey Rabbit, she'd resolved to take matters into her own hands. Sid had deserted her; she didn't care what chivalrous intentions he may have had; he'd *deserted* her! She deserved better than that. *Far* better!

Mary was steaming as she marched across the courtyard to the kitchen, and it had very little to do with the fact she'd rushed back through the over-heated streets of Lower Icing. All the men who thought she wasn't strong enough to handle herself or express an opinion could go piss in their codpieces; she would not be playing the cheerful hostess or the pride-swallowing peace-keeper this afternoon. After Prim Pet and the Limpdickers, Sid had been the last straw; she'd had enough of waiting, of pandering meekly to the whims of those who considered themselves her betters (or thought they knew better). She was her own woman, and it was time she showed herself to the world outside The Harey Rabbit. And woe-betide anyone who tried to stop her.

Mary burst into the relatively sedate kitchen. "Fill me a bath, Juanita!"

Juanita jumped up from her vegetable chopping. "Has somedeeng happeneeng to you, Meestress?"

Yes! Something *had* bloody well *happened* to her, but she wasn't prepared to discuss it with Juanita or Patricia (with her raised eyebrow) or any other staff member for that matter. She ignored Juanita's question and left the kitchen through the hallway door.

"Meestress?" Juanita called after her.

"Bath!" Mary yelled as she continued down the hallway.

Mary shut her bedroom door. The room was (and had always been) a haven from the chaos of The Harey Rabbit, a place she could shed her innkeeper's clothes and be Mary Brewer. The room was welcoming, light and airy and… feminine; another part of her that was consigned to this room, because there was certainly nothing feminine about been groped and ogled by old, lascivious men.

The scent of lavender permeated the air; sprigs of it were placed within arrangements of daisies, cornflowers, marigolds and other wildflowers in a vase on her bedside table and two on top of the polished oak mantelpiece. Between the vases on the mantelpiece, her prized possessions glimmered against the pale blue wall. Three exquisitely crafted, glass figurines — an owl, otter and squirrel — sat in ornate reclusiveness, softly patterning the walls with refracted light. They were a gift from her father to her mother, to show her how deeply he felt about her.

Sir Walter had given them to Mary on her eighteenth birthday, explaining that her mother (after whom Mary was named) had been a free spirit, enchanted by woodland creatures and the world outside the walls of the servants' quarters. He'd taken her on a few outings into the woods, and they had been the happiest times of her life (and his fondest memories of her). He'd given the figurines to Mary's mother on *her* eighteenth birthday — they were handcrafted in the Pastarian capital of La Sagne by the renowned glass sculptor, Enzo Glitterati — and she'd treasured them until the day she'd died, shortly after her twentieth birthday, while giving birth to Mary.

Mary had often wondered what Lady Mildred (Richard's mother) had thought about Sir Walter's relationship with a lowly maid. She'd never asked her father, and she certainly had never broached the subject with Richard. Maybe Lady Mildred hadn't known about the affair, but Mary doubted it. More likely she'd turned a blind eye for the sake of appearances. It certainly came to light not long after Sir Walter's death, when Lady Mildred moved to Great Naff to live with her sister. Mary didn't blame her — Richard was hardly a doting son.

She gently stroked the squirrel with her index finger. It was her favourite of the three. To think a maid had been given *Glitterati*, to think an innkeeper had inherited *Glitterati*. Only the wealthiest homes and royalty could afford such pieces.

Moving past the mantelpiece, she stepped towards the window and opened the white cotton curtains, fastening them in place by wrapping a matching sash around each curtain and hooping it to a hook on the wall. Mary wanted more light, because she was about to air out her wardrobe and choose an outfit *not* made for the rigours of running The Harey Rabbit.

The wardrobe was set in the corner of the room by the window. It had two doors that opened outwards from the centre. In each door was a key. She unlocked both and opened up the wardrobe. The left side was packed full of her drab work clothes, the right side was sparse and colourful by comparison. Three lonely dresses lay folded between drawers of undergarments and shoes. She smiled ruefully at the pitiful collection — it was her life in clothes.

It felt good to slide into the tepid warmth of the bathwater. She had to hand it to Juanita, she prepared a good bath. She'd infused it with lavender and rosehip; there was also a redolence of ginger root.

She'd sent the Icarumban to choose an outfit for her. Mary had spread out the measly collection on her bed and tried matching them with her limited collection of shoes and hats, but couldn't decide what worked. She wanted to appear feminine, but not dainty; commanding, but not overbearing; refined, but not snobby; herself, but not... herself.

Juanita had jumped at the opportunity to be her fashion consultant, and left the washroom saying excitedly, "Don' worry, Meestress, *I* know what you are wanteeng."

Mary wasn't sure if she should be nervous or excited. In truth, she was both. Juanita returned fifteen minutes later, as Mary was in the process of drying herself. In her hand, she carried a dress, shoes and undergarments. She looked very pleased with herself. "Oh, Meestress, you be turning dee heads in dees."

She'd chosen Mary's pale blue, silver-tissue court dress and her white ankle-high shoes. Not that the shoes would be on show; the voluminous skirt, flowing out from the tight bodice, reached almost to the ground. The thought of squeezing into corsetry, pulling on underskirts, fiddling with stockings, and then been wrapped up in a heavy dress suddenly filled her with dread.

"I'm not sure I can—"

"Oh no no no, Meestress; you *have* to wear dees dress. Ees perfect for you. It weell glow to your brown skeen and make your eyes shineeng like dee sapphires."

Mary couldn't help but smile at Juanita's enthusiasm. No-one had ever spoken about her skin and eyes that way; she felt... flattered.

"Really?"

"Si si, Meestress. Trust me, you weell be... *hermosa.*"

"Pardon?"

"Beauteeful," she said, translating the Icarumban.

The sound of a dropped plate broke through the closed washroom door, shortly followed by the sound of Patricia berating John. The breaking plate was far less jarring.

"Please, Meestress," Juanita pleaded, waving the clothes in front of her.

The commotion had distracted Mary; she almost felt compelled to sort it out. However, she reminded herself that was exactly why she *shouldn't* — she'd marched home determined *not* to be Mary Brewer, Innkeeper.

She nodded. "Go on then, Juanita."

The Icarumban squealed in delight.

The dressing process took over half an hour. The garments felt tight and heavy, but Juanita's continuous encouragement and flattery had overcome Mary's doubts and frustration. She also received nods of approval and compliments from Patricia and Mandy as she stepped from the washroom into the kitchen. (John just smiled and looked uncomfortable.) Mary couldn't judge for herself because there was no mirror in the washroom. So, with Juanita following in her wake, she walked back to her bedroom.

The first thing she noticed was her bare bed. Juanita had obviously re-folded the remaining clothes and placed them back in her wardrobe. Mary thanked her and then stood in front of the dressing table mirror. The cumbersome dress looked as strange as it felt, but it was having the desired affect: Mary felt more… empowered.

"What about a hat?" she thought out loud. "I can't be bothered with braiding."

"No hat, Meestress. Your hair ees beauteeful just like eet ees. I no understand all dee hair over here. Dee ladees look stupeed with dee seelly reenglets and preesy braideeng. You have dee raven hair. Eet should fly wild and free."

Mary nodded. Juanita was right; she preferred her hair down, and she quite liked the way it waved across her shoulders. Mary couldn't remember the last time she'd regarded herself so critically. "What about makeup?"

"Just a leetle, Meestress. You have dee oleeve skeen, like Icarumban. I'm theenking your madre was Icarumban."

She doubted it; she and Richard's dark hair came from their father. Lady Mildred was brown-haired and pale-skinned, which was probably why Richard's features were so severe. Mary's looks had obviously been tempered by her mother: a blue-eyed beauty, according to her father, with hair the colour of freshly harvested wheat. Mary always thought she sounded more Longboatian than anything else. Mary sat down at the dressing table and let Juanita go to work on her face.

## CHAPTER 64

# *The perfect campsite*

THEY REACHED CAMP just after one o'clock, about an hour after crossing the ford (without incident). Basically, they'd followed the reed-lined edge of the Icing as it meandered its way south towards Lower Icing, occasionally having to veer inland because of an outcrop of dense vegetation.

The spot Tom had chosen was, of course, the perfect campsite, only ten paces from a calm, shallow part of the river, protected and shaded by trees. True to his word, the campsite had been prepared; a campfire pit had been dug and firewood collected.

She and Tom took care of the horses while her pa slumped against the trunk of a large willow. He looked tired, and she wondered whether they'd overdone things. He'd complained about his ribs being sore just after fording the Icing, but he'd not said anything since.

"I'm worried 'bout Pa, Tom," she whispered as she helped unbuckle Wildflower's bridle.

Tom gazed in his direction. Her pa looked as if he was sleeping, his chest slowly moving in and out. "He'll be alright after a rest," he said, thoughtfully. "That's why I broke the journey here. It's his ribs; they're still tender." Then his demeanour became more playful. "Might take his mind off the saddle-rump."

Ophelia smiled at Tom. He made her feel at ease, like nothing could hurt her (or her pa) while he was with them. They finished unsaddling the horses in silence. All the while, Ophelia was thinking how much more perfect this campsite would be if it was just the two of them.

# CHAPTER 65

## *Rather fragile armour*

MARY COULD HARDLY wipe the smile from her face as she strolled up Big Wig Street. Juanita had been right — she was turning heads. While some of the castle-set ladies showed disdain — no braids and hatless — many of the men smiled, and some even doffed their hats. Mary recognised them all, but she doubted any of them recognised her.

Juanita had transformed her; the dress was understated elegance and the makeup accentuated her features, rather than painting over them. She'd even transformed her hair by placing a single Cornflower behind her left ear, the dazzling blue bloom pinning her hair back on that side. Such a simple touch, but it had worked wonders, complementing the dress, her eyes, her skin… Mary had hardly believed the person staring out from the mirror was her; she'd become quite emotional, which was unexpected to say the least.

"Oh, Meestress," Juanita had breathed, a tear in her eye (which hadn't helped). A heartfelt collection of Icarumban words followed, of which *hermosa* was repeated several times. Mary stood up and embraced the young Icarumban washerwoman. She'd performed a feat Mary wouldn't have thought possible an hour before: washing away Mary's dark mood.

Mary smiled to herself as she strode confidently towards the West Gate. Yes, she definitely felt *hermosa*. If only it was Sid she was striding towards, rather than her brother.

The guardsmen regarded her with what she might possibly describe as admiration (in a leering-guardsmen sort of way). Oddly enough, it made her feel even better about herself. She continued into the Lower Bailey, through to the Administration Section. A smattering of townsfolk were assembled outside the Office of Petitions, but Mary only received cursory glances from them; petitioners were, by nature, an aggrieved bunch.

Heading up the cobblestone courtyard towards the Middle Bailey, Mary spied more guardsmen. Half a dozen stood casually at the arched entrance cut into the massive internal wall. The portcullis seemed to be positioned quite low, barely a foot above head height. It looked quite foreboding. Still, not foreboding enough; she was determined to confront Richard, and she was looking forward to seeing the expression on his face when he saw her in all her finery. She smiled at the thought; he might not even recognise her.

The guardsmen eyed her as she approached the entrance, their blue and gold doublets shimmering in the early afternoon sun.

"Sorry, miss," said one of them, casually. "Can't let y' pass, 'less you gotta pass."

Some of the other guardsmen sniggered at the remark. Mary knew their sort — dim-witted and juvenile, and easily manipulated.

"Oh." Mary feigned consternation. "Silly me, you have the right of it Captain, Sir Richard did, indeed, tell me to bring my pass. Oh dear, he won't be happy. He was *most* insistent that I be punctual and I'm afraid I…"

Mary put on a show of helplessness. She knew the guard was only a corporal, but could see her 'mistake' had already had an effect; he was looking self-conscious and the sniggering of his fellow guardsmen was adding to his embarrassment.

Pressing her advantage, Mary took a few tentative steps towards him, her lightly rouged lips forming into a hopeful smile. "Captain, I don't suppose you could see your way to letting me pass with*out* a pass?"

He was looking distinctly sheepish. "Well…"

One of the other guardsmen chimed in with, "C'mon, *Captain* — ain't goin' t' follow the orders of a lowly sergeant, are ya?"

The rest burst out laughing.

Mary pretended to be flustered by their behaviour. "I'm sorry," she said, "I didn't mean to cause any trouble. It's just that Sir Richard is expecting me."

"Go on, Grippy," said a peculiarly thin guardsman, "let the lady go. Las' thing we need is Sir Richard on our bleedin' case again."

Grippy nodded in agreement. "Right, Miss… be about y' business then."

She beamed at him. "Why thank you, Captain. I'll be sure to tell Sir Richard about your helpfulness."

"Thank you, Miss." Grippy nodded, touching the tip of his cavalier's hat.

Mary walked under the portcullis and through the eight-foot-thick wall accompanied by sounds of laughter and puerile comments. It was the same kind of banter she heard every day at The Harey Rabbit, just a less toffy version.

The Middle Bailey was really just a large cobblestone courtyard, a seemingly useless open space that was completely overshadowed by the massive, looming Keep. The fore-building presented a welcoming ground-level introduction to the giant stone tower — it was sculptured and ornate, with smooth stone sides punctuated by clear leadlight windows and a buttressed roof covered in shimmering slate tiles. Impressive as it was, it was dwarfed by The Keep. Mary craned her head towards the parapet summit. From where she was looking, she could see three of the four corner towers — their dizzying heights made her head spin.

She hadn't set foot in this part of the castle for over a year — last year's May Day Festival to be exact. The empty greyness that surrounded her was a stark contrast to that vibrant, busy, music-filled day. It was the one day a year Lower Icingers were admitted en masse into the Middle Bailey; no doubt, the only day of the year when the area was fully utilised. Mary hadn't attended this year's festival because she'd been hosting a private party of winemakers from the Southern Vales.

As empty as the area was, it wasn't devoid of sound. Arrhythmic hammering pounded from inside The Keep through the fore-building's open, arched doors. Peering to her left, Mary spied more guardsmen milling inside like aimless blue and gold chess pieces on its chessboard floor.

Mary continued the gentle ascent towards the Upper Bailey without further thought to the workings inside The Keep; she was far more interested in the workings inside her brother's head.

The wall that separated the Middle Bailey from the Upper Bailey was about two-thirds the height of the wall that separated it from the Lower Bailey. The entranceway was also smaller. There was no portcullis and there were only two guardsmen. Mary smiled at them as she approached. Their expressions barely changed; they both looked bored. One of them mumbled "Afternoon" as she breezed past. Mary was surprised by their apathy, even though it had worked to her advantage.

The grounds of the Upper Bailey were beautifully manicured; it was as if all the life and colour had been sucked out of the Middle Bailey to enhance the lush greenery and blooming colour of the noble section of the castle. The spectacular grounds surrounded what could be best described as a fortified manor house — it was both graceful and imposing, fine architectural touches mixed with the practicalities of defence. This East Wing was the private living quarters of the Duke. The West Wing was given over to the running of the Duchy, overseen by the Seneschal of Lower Icing. It was here that many of her influential patrons came to discuss matters of trade, taxes and security with Richard (and possibly the Duke). From what she could ascertain, it was like some high-brow, exclusive men's club, where egos were fed with palatial aplomb.

Mary had no such pretentions, but she wouldn't be leaving the Upper Bailey until Richard had explained exactly what had occurred at The Keep last night. Could there *actually* be an heir to the Duchy?

She walked down the central pathway, taking the left fork some twenty paces in. Her progress was observed by two elderly gardeners, one digging out weeds, the other clipping away at a highly manicured box hedge. On her left, the outer wall rose high above the garden, separating the grounds from the steep drop on the other side. (The castle sat on a hill, above a rocky outcrop, where the Icing River changed direction from south-west to south. It had been built there to take advantage of the imposing topography and was virtually impregnable from the east and south.)

Ahead, stone steps led up to an ornate marble portico supported by two marble columns. On the portico's façade was a relief depicting knights on horseback, charging towards each other from either end. In the centre, where the knights would clash, was Lower Icing's coat of arms (five crowns beneath a unicorn's head) entwined in a blossoming vine. The portico was the grand entrance to the West Wing.

Standing under the portico, openly appraising her, were a couple of men-at-arms. However, their open smiles suggested they were being good-natured. Still, hardly what Mary called professional.

Mary took the initiative as soon as she stepped underneath the portico. "Good afternoon, gentlemen."

"'T'be sure, 't'is now," said the taller, thinner of the two. Obviously, he was from Clover Isle.

The stumpy one, who had an amazing mop of red hair and a wild beard to match, punched his fellow soldier playfully in the arm, although with enough force to make him stumble half a step sideways. "Och, Paddy! Tha's noo how to speak to a bonnie lass," he said, in a thick Sporrendale accent.

"An' how would you know, y'feckin eejit?" retorted Paddy, pushing red-beard's shoulder.

"I knoo enough to knoo yoo shouldnee be swearin' in front o' one." Red-beard jabbed a stubby finger into his comrade's chest. (He'd made a good point, thought Mary.)

"Ha! Y'call tha' swearin'? T'be sure, Jock, tha's what I call *fec-kin' fore-play!*" Paddy jabbed his finger into Jock's chest in time to the last four syllables.

This was becoming entertaining.

"Ha! A truer word ne'er been said!" Jock growled, facing up to Paddy, spit coming out of his mouth as he spoke. "Cloover Isle, where men are men and the nanny-goots are nervous!"

"Well, if tha' ain't the gruel callin' the porridge sloppy!" Paddy scoffed, leaning into Jock with his forehead. "T'be sure, you'd be strugglin' to tell the diff'rence between a Highland beauty and a nanny-goat's arse!"

Mary was starting to wonder whether she should intercede, but, truth be told, she was finding the experience refreshingly humorous. And, in a way, quite flattering; after all, it was her 'beauty' that had started this argument.

Jock reacted by stamping his boot down on Paddy's foot. Paddy yelled out and began jumping around in pain.

"Och, Paddy," said Jock, "'tis only a wee bit o' Highland foreplay."

Pain was replaced by anger; the Clover Islander's pale, white face had become a flushed-looking pink. (It was hard to tell the colour of Jock's face underneath all that red hair.)

Paddy launched himself at the Highlander, toppling him backwards, as both of them tumbled onto the marble floor in a clattering thud of sword hilts and uniforms.

Mary watched them struggle for a moment, rolling on the floor, punching at each other, grunting and groaning as each tried for ascendency. If this was the calibre of the men charged with protecting the populace, the streets of Lower Icing were far more perilous than she'd imagined. "I think I'll leave you to it, gentlemen. I'll see myself in."

Paddy grunted; he almost had Jock in a headlock. "Y'pardon, miss, but I'm not sure y'lowed insi—" His words were left unsaid by a punch to the stomach.

"Noo sure, Paddy?" Jock said, free from Paddy's hold. "How cannee be? T'be sure t'be sure; yoo're always friggin' sure!"

Paddy lashed out with his left leg and managed to collect Jock in the kneecap with the heel of his boot. Jock hooted in pain.

It had been just under two years since Mary had stepped inside the manor house — the occasion was her father's funeral. Unlike the polished emptiness that greeted her today, the reception hall had been filled with refined ladies and gentlemen, dignitaries (including the Duke and Duchess), visiting nobles and other esteemed individuals, all spilling up the staircase leading to Richard's private quarters, all there to pay their respects to her father and to pass on their condolences to Richard and his mother, all unaware that Mary was his daughter.

While Richard had supported her attendance, he'd made it known that she could not divulge her identity; even in death, Sir Walter's reputation was at stake as, of course, was that of the very-much-alive Lady Mildred.

So, at her father's funeral, she was Mary Brewer, one of the three 'worthy citizens' representing the villagers of Lower Icing. Mary had been running The Harey Rabbit for just over three years when her father died. She'd already established an acceptable reputation with the castle-set, and many of her patrons were at the function. Some expressed their surprise and curiosity at her attendance. Obviously they didn't regard the 'girl from the inn' as being worthy enough.

In the following weeks, rumour and conjecture about Sir Walter's fidelity had spread throughout the castle-set, particularly regarding Mary. Shortly after the departure of Lady Mildred to Great Naff (some three months after the funeral), the rumours were finally put to rest and Mary's relationship to Sir Walter (and Richard) was acknowledged. Not in any formal way, of course, and it certainly hadn't changed Mary's life, but it *had* boosted her credibility. She suddenly became more… acceptable. And her patrons were suddenly able to remember her name.

Her shoes echoed on the polished marble floor as she crossed the hall to the staircase, drowning out the grunts and groans from the still-wrestling men-at-arms. *What was going on?* Everything looked the same, but it certainly didn't *feel* the same; the whole castle felt like a hollowed-out version of a place that was usually full of life. And the behaviour of the men-at-arms was odd. Not just the two idiots outside; they all seemed to be—

"Can I help you?" The voice came out of nowhere.

Mary jumped and swore.

A grey-robed figure was standing next to an open door to her right. It was Prestwich.

"Sorry," she said, heart racing, "you took me by surprise."

His expression remained bland, but his eyes darted appraisingly. "I could say the same of you, Mistress Mary," he remarked just as blandly. "The Upper Bailey is closed until further notice. The guards should have explained—"

"Clearly they didn't, Prestwich," Mary interrupted, the rush of blood refocusing her thoughts and refuelling her determination; she wasn't about to be fobbed off by a parchment-scratcher. "They had more pressing matters to attend to."

As if on cue, the Highlander let out another hoot of pain. Prestwich's gaze flicked towards the entrance. Mary also turned her head in the direction of the open door. Another guffaw broke the air.

"Perhaps you should…"

Richard's secretary had disappeared; her gaze had only been diverted for a couple of seconds, yet he was nowhere to be seen. She covered the distance to his office in a few hurried strides and knocked on the heavy, wooden door. She hadn't heard it shut. There was no response, nor could she hear any movement behind it. How had he closed it so quickly and… *quietly?*

She waited a few moments before knocking again. The door sprang open, but it wasn't Prestwich who appeared — it was Brandon. He looked taken aback, but whether it was to do with her elegant appearance or her presence, she couldn't tell.

"Mary?" he said, eyeing her. "Why are…?" Then the clatter of metal on stone echoed through the hall. "What the frig are those numbskulls…? I'm sorry, Mary, Sir Richard is busy. You'll have to… Look, just wait here a moment while I sort those two out."

With that, he rushed across the marble floor. Mary, however, had no intention of waiting — she was done with that. Brandon had left the door ajar. Mary didn't hesitate; she pushed it open and entered.

Prestwich's office was surprisingly empty. She'd been in here once before to sign the *Deed of Ownership* for The Harey Rabbit. Her memory was of rows of shelving filled with documentation. Now, there were only a few piles of ledgers and parchments placed haphazardly along the walls. The door opposite led to Richard's office. To the right of the door was Prestwich's desk. Here, the ledgers and parchment theme continued, accompanied by an impressive arrangement of quills and seals. To the right of Prestwich's desk, a stairway led downwards. *That* hadn't been there last time… or had it? No matter; the organisation of the secretary's work space was hardly her concern right now.

Mary reached the door to Richard's office, and she had no doubt that it *was* still his office, regardless of his supposed loss of status. She suspected it had all been part of the ruse. Well, she would find out soon enough.

Her instinct was to knock, but then she wondered whether she should just open it and add a touch of drama to her entrance (if not surprise). Disappointingly, her instinct prevailed.

The door was opened almost instantaneously. "I have already informed you the Upper Bailey is closed," said Prestwich, eyes darting back and forth from a parchment. "If you would please see yourself out and arrange a time more—"

Just like Prim Pet, Prestwich had chosen the wrong moment to test her patience. She would not be fobbed off! She pushed the door with some force, hitting the secretary in his expansive forehead. He gasped in pain, dropped the parchment and stumbled a few steps backwards. She stepped past him into the opulent centre of her brother's world.

As much as Prestwich's office was a tribute to documentation, Richard's was a tribute to himself. He was sitting at his beautifully crafted mahogany desk underneath a larger-than-life portrait of himself. In the far corner of the room near a window that overlooked the gardens, his highly polished suit of armour caught the afternoon sun. Moving into the bright room, three pairs of eyes regarded her: Sitting opposite Richard at his desk were Rupert Smythe-Wheaton and Paris Le Sharp.

Richard wore a mildly curious expression, Smythe-Wheaton regarded her with a leering hunger, while Le Sharp, officer and gentleman, stood. "Madam, enchanting as your presence may be, you must be under some misunderstanding. There is no function here today. The Upper Bailey is, as Prestwich here so rudely informed you, closed. However, if you'd care to brighten our day a while longer, I shall organise some men to escort you back to your residence."

Prestwich was still groaning behind her.

"That is most gracious of you, Captain. However, there is *no* misunderstanding, and I am quite capable of finding my *own* way back to my residence. In *fact*, Captain, I have no doubt I could accomplish the task far better *unescorted*. From what I have just witnessed, your *men* are totally inept."

Smythe-Wheaton's jowly features wobbled as he chuckled silently.

As usual, Richard's sardonic expression gave nothing away.

However, Le Sharp's chivalrous demeanour had taken a blow; he made no effort to conceal his affront. "I say, madam, this is most unbecom—"

"Sit down, Paris," Richard interjected; it was still odd seeing him without his sculptured beard. "Surely you recognise my sister, even in... costume."

Le Sharp looked indignant, then slightly abashed, as he sat down.

Rupert Smythe-Wheaton took the opportunity to ingratiate himself into the moment. "I must say, Mary, I have never seen you look so ravishing."

Mary had come to a halt some six feet from the desk. She eyed the lawyer — his leering made her skin crawl. She wanted to respond with 'And I have never found you more repulsive'. Instead, she treated him to a disdainful glare, which, judging by his reaction, must have eloquently conveyed the sentiment.

Prestwich suddenly appeared in the vacant seat at the end of the desk, between Mary and Richard. He glared at her from underneath a red mark swelling in the middle of his forehead.

"So, Mary," Richard said; he sounded tired. "I assume this… performance has some point to it. Have you retrieved the silver button from your… confidante?"

Despite herself, she felt the blood rush to her face. Richard's words, weary as they might be, had, invariably, made her feel self-conscious. The last time she'd spoken to Richard was after he'd tussled insinuations with Sid — he'd advised her to put an end to the association, and she'd accused him of being too high and mighty. His response still stung: *"It's rather ironic, don't you think, that someone like yourself, who serves the noble class and gentry so deferentially and so profitably, should feel empathy towards the common folk. In fact, it smacks very loudly of hypocrisy."*

It had made her feel ashamed, and was one of the emotional prods that had spurred her towards where she now stood. She suddenly felt like an actress on stage, trying to remember her next line. She glanced at her audience — they regarded her with varying degrees of expectation.

The plot had changed. *She* was meant to be the one asking the questions and demanding answers. She'd forgotten about the bloody silver button. *"When you visit your fool this afternoon, retrieve the silver button for me. It is, after all, stolen property."*

Well, she *hadn't* retrieved it. Sid had lost it pulling John out of the Icing, or so he claimed. From that point, events had overtaken her, beginning with the castle dinner, then Sid's discovery of his sister's meddling, and then all the emotional confrontations this morning.

Reeling in her thoughts, she eventually managed to speak her line. "No. It's lost."

This brought a guffaw from Smythe-Wheaton.

"How convenient," murmured Le Sharp.

Richard remained silent, dark eyes assessing. All Mary's determination and confidence withered under it. Her dress and makeup had turned out to be rather fragile armour.

Her meek voice edged into the silence. "I don't understand, Richard; why is the button so important?"

"Because it's not a button," Richard replied, casually. So casually, in fact, that Mary wondered if she'd misheard.

"Pardon?"

"Sir Richard," Smythe-Wheaton interjected, "Dupree agreed to take the case sub judice; he is yet to advise us on how his client wishes to plead."

Case? Defendant? Client? Smythe-Wheaton had ribbed Dupree about drawing the short straw at breakfast this morning. "You've caught the Duke's attacker?"

She saw Richard's jaw muscles clench.

"We have apprehended a suspect," Smythe-Wheaton confirmed.

"Suspect!" Le Sharp blurted out in disgust. "The man's admitted his crime!"

"Which man?" Mary asked.

"The case is, indeed, *prima facie*, Captain, but due process must be adhered to," Smythe-Wheaton explained, somewhat patronisingly.

"Don't you lawyers already have enough gold lining your pockets?" was Le Sharp's riposte.

Smythe-Wheaton treated the man in uniform to one of his condescending glares. "Surely, Captain, you can do better than that." Then he looked in Mary's direction and smiled mirthlessly. "Although, judging by the obvious lack of discipline within your ranks, perhaps such a *basic* observation is to be expected."

Le Sharp looked like he was ready to challenge the lawyer to a duel.

"Enough!" Richard barked. Then, in calmer tones, "Gentlemen, we have discussed all that needs to be discussed. Now I suggest we go about the tasks at hand. Rupert, see to it that you and Prestwich have all the relevant paperwork finished by midday tomorrow. Paris, I can see no reason why the accused's wife shouldn't see him now — if she is in a fit state, of course. *That* should ease Lieutenant Swill's conscience somewhat. I take it you have no objection, Rupert?"

The lawyer shook his head as he levered himself into a standing position. "Dupree should be finished with him soon; the facts are quite clear cut."

"And, Paris…" Richard remained seated while the officer also rose from his seat. "Is it too much to expect that the men guarding the castle *can actually guard the castle?*"

Smythe-Wheaton treated Le Sharp to a self-satisfied smirk. The captain bristled, but acknowledged the truth of the comment. "Rest assured, Sir Richard, Lieutenant Swill will have those buffoons cleaning The Can until they forget what fresh air smells like."

Obviously Brandon had already set about doing just that, because he hadn't returned. (It was now *very* obvious to Mary why he'd been promoted to lieutenant at such a young age.)

Richard nodded. "Very well, gentlemen, you are excused. You, too, Prestwich; I wish to speak to Mary privately."

The wiry figure sprang out of his seat. "Of course, Sir Richard."

"Remember, Sir Richard," purred Smythe-Wheaton, casting his smarmy gaze in Mary's direction, "sub judice."

"You forget yourself, Rupert," Richard said, evenly. "What *you* need to remember is to whom you are speaking." He shot out of his chair, his head the same height as his portrait's knees. Smythe-Wheaton jerked backwards, his smile shocked away by Richard's sudden movement. Leaning forward on his desk, fingertips pressed against the surface, Richard regarded the flustered lawyer for a moment. Even Le Sharp looked slightly taken aback. "I suggest you put your mind to your own business and afford me the same courtesy."

Smythe-Wheaton's jowly face wobbled its assent. "Of course, Sir Richard, I meant no disrespect."

Then all three of them bowed and exited the room. As they left, Mary was treated to three suspicious gazes. Prestwich's also contained a good amount of resentment — the bang on his head had turned into a swollen lump. However, none of their posturing affected her. After five years of running The Harey Rabbit it was like water off a duck's back.

Richard waited for Prestwich to close the door before asking Mary to sit down. She had to gather her dress to fit between the ornately carved armrests. She suddenly felt quite silly outfitted in her finery. Still, it had served a purpose; she was sitting opposite the man she had come to see.

## CHAPTER 66

# *Light and airwy*

THE KNOCKING PERSISTED, accompanied by the calling of her name.

"Just a moment," Olivia croaked, as she stumbled out of bed and banged into the chair by the side table.

"Are you alright, Mistress Hiepants?" the voice outside the door enquired.

"Yes." However, that was far from the truth; she still felt incredibly groggy.

She caught a glimpse of herself in the mirror next to the table; from her dishevelled hair to her crumpled clothing, she was a grotesque parody of grace and elegance.

"Mistress Hiepants?" the voice insisted.

"One moment!" she shot back at the door, and her head responded with a dizzying shot of pain. She tried to fix her ruined appearance, but the damage was too severe.

Reluctantly, Olivia turned towards the door; at least the person on the other side had had the good grace not to barge into the room.

The person turned out to be Lieutenant Swill. "I have come to escort you to the dungeon," he said without preamble, although he couldn't hide the concern (or distaste) in his expression. "That is, if you feel up to seeing your husband?"

They exited The Keep through the fore-building, amidst workers and guards. The blinding sun had dipped towards mid-afternoon as they walked around the massive structure to its south-eastern corner. Here, steps led down to a small cobblestone courtyard, mercifully in shadow, where an impressive iron-bound door was built into the stone foundation.

The Swill boy had escorted her, arm in arm, like they were courting, because, to put it simply, she couldn't have managed the journey without him. The staircase had been particularly challenging; the spiralling descent made her feel giddy and nauseous, the tapering steps twisting endlessly downwards, the clack of shoes stabbing her brain, as if Lady Violet Le Fleur was taunting her with loud, echoing tut-tuts of disapproval.

It took some time to gain entry into the dungeon. The Swill boy banged away at the door for what seemed like five minutes (it was like pounding nails into her throbbing head) before a metal panel in the door slid open, revealing a wary set of grey eyes below a bushy pair of grey eyebrows. The panel slid shut abruptly, and was followed by clanging, clunking and banging before the door finally scraped open. Olivia had yet to step inside the dungeon, but the torture had already begun.

The Swill boy acknowledged the man as they entered an antechamber, which was dimly lit by two torches sitting in sconces. "Afternoon, Riley."

The man's face and hands were coated in grime, his hair stringy and grey. He nodded absently as he banged the door shut, slid a bar into place and turned a large key. He appeared to be as dim as the antechamber.

Although it was a relief to be out of the blinding sun, the air in the antechamber was thick and smelt of smoke and, when he was within six feet, Riley. It was all Olivia could do not to retch.

"Is Master Key in his office, Riley?"

"Nah-down-in-cells," Riley mumbled, as if opening his mouth was a skill he was yet to master.

"I see." The Swill boy appeared to be annoyed. "Please go and fetch him. And *remind* him that I'm here with Mistress Hiepants."

Riley nodded and made some sort of guttural sound as he shambled across the room.

The Swill boy turned to face Olivia, torchlight dancing lightly across his face. He looked concerned or, perhaps, burdened. "Hold a moment, Riley," he said over his shoulder. "We'll follow you down to his office and meet him there." Once again, he offered Olivia his arm. "Come, Mistress Hiepants."

"Thank you," she whispered, accepting it.

Riley led them along a short passageway and then down half a dozen steps. At the base of the steps was another corridor, again sparsely lit with ensconced torches. The stone was beginning to feel oppressive, closing in on her like the reality of Gerald's situation. Some five or so paces later, the passageway opened into a large room which, surprisingly, was filled with a generous amount of natural light.

It was a corner room — obviously they'd traversed the base of The Keep and were now roughly positioned some floors below the room Olivia had just left. The light was provided by three barred openings set high in the northern wall (ground level to those outside The Keep). There was another one at eye-level on the eastern wall — an iron-striped painting of blue sky and distant green hills, framed in six-foot-thick stone. In front of this window was a solid-looking desk, on top of which a large ledger lay open over a haphazard collection of documents. To the left of the desk, a collection of keys hung limply on individual hooks that were fixed into the wall. Apart from a few chairs arranged in front of the desk, the room was devoid of any other embellishment.

Olivia shivered, and allowed the Swill boy to lead her to one of the chairs. "Thank you, Lieutenant," she said as she sat down.

"The dungeon is a confronting place, Mistress Hiepants. Riley will be back shortly with Master Key."

Olivia nodded absently. Poor Gerald — had he been here all night?

She heard Riley disappear down more steps. She wasn't sure if she could handle going down further, the thought of being confined under so much stone filled her with dread.

Clearly, the Swill boy sensed her anguish. "Your husband is being looked after, Mistress Hiepants."

*Looked after?* How could anyone be looked after in a place like this? What was to become of Gerald? What was to become of *her*?

"Jeremy Dupree has been with him all morning. He will have proper representation."

Jeremy Dupree, Olivia thought to herself. Not even the legendary prowess of Jeremy Dupree could save Gerald; her husband had admitted to poisoning the Duke. He was beyond help.

They waited in silence as the minutes passed. Then the sound of footsteps came echoing up the staircase from below.

"I should warn you, Mistress Hiepants, Master Key is a rather… unusual person. His manner is somewhat unorthodox."

Olivia nodded; she had no idea what to expect. She wasn't sure what unorthodox meant in a gaoler, but whatever kind of man Master Key was, he couldn't possibly make Olivia feel worse than she did at that moment.

The Swill boy stood and faced the direction of the sound. Olivia remained seated, and, for the first time, she noticed the opening in the wall opposite the Gaol Keeper's desk. A flickering light emanated from it. The torch, or torches, however, could not be seen — it must be a steep descent. Olivia's stomach turned at the thought of it.

A shadowy outline appeared in the opening. As the footsteps grew closer, the outline became smaller and more defined until it resolved itself into a short, round-faced man of about forty years. He had a shiny bald head with an incongruously thick hedge of reddish hair spiking out just above his ears. It was almost as if he'd shaved the top of his head, like the monk people who inhabited the colder climes of Sporrendale and Clover Isle. However, the oddest thing about the man was his expression: he wore a large smile, and his eyes glistened with merriment, as if he'd just heard a particularly humorous jest.

"Ah, my apologies, Lieutenant Swill," he said merrily, walking towards them. "Had a little discipline pwoblem with one of our guests. Still, more of a misunderstanding than anything else; he's now become *much* more accommodating, which, of course, has a *lot* to do with his new accommodation."

He shook his head ruefully, but his expression remained cheerful. In stark contrast, the Swill boy's demeanour was regimented as he formally introduced Olivia.

"Oh!" the gaoler exclaimed, as if her presence was an unexpected surprise. "The Town Cwier's wife."

As she stood to meet him, he performed a snappy bow.

"Pleased to meet you, Mistwess! Gewald is a most amenable fellow. Bit down in the dumps at the moment, o'course, but I'm sure *your* pwesence will waise his spiwits wemarkably."

Olivia was speechless. Unorthodox didn't even come close; the man was clearly mad. He had a speech impediment, which Olivia always associated with some sort of mental deficiency.

He was looking up at her expectantly, but Olivia was unsure how to respond. Not many men looked *up* at her, and the few who did managed to do so without a gormless expression.

The Swill boy began speaking on her behalf. "Master Key, I'm sure you appreciate that this has been a traumatic experience for—"

However, Olivia had always spoken for herself. "Please lead me to my husband, Master Key," she said with authority.

"Wighty-o, then," he replied, as if they were about to embark upon a jolly jaunt. Olivia glanced over at the Swill boy.

"After you," he said, "or do you require assistance?"

Olivia responded by walking unaided behind the bizarre gaoler. It was time to overcome the ill-effects of her drinking and confinement; Gerald needed her to be strong, and she'd be damned if she'd show any more frailty in front of the Swill boy (no matter how sympathetic he'd been).

"I think you'll be pleasantly surpwised by Gewald's woom," the gaoler chirped as they descended the stairs. "It's wather light and airwy."

The only response he received was the sound of shoes on stone steps. After about twenty of them, the steps turned ninety degrees to the left. Olivia surmised they were now under the spiral staircase — how *far* under she didn't want to think about.

"Visitors to the dungeon tend to be vehwy impwessed by the facilities," Master Key enthused as they rounded the corner. "It's not just manacles, chains and dirty stwaw. Oh no, the pwisoners here are quite comfortable, welatively speaking o'course."

They continued downwards, hugging the west side of The Keep's foundations. After a brief pause, Master Key continued his upbeat dungeon sales banter. "Not to say we don't have manacles, chains and dirty stwaw, but they are used sparewingly, more as a detewent than standard pwocedure. Captivity is usually punishment enough, especially when you're under *this* much stone. Does tend to cwush the spiwit. Still, I'm sure—"

"That's enough, Master Key," said the lieutenant from behind her. "Neither I nor Mistress Hiepants require any further assurances from you. We are well aware that the dungeon is not a place people *choose* to stay."

*Well said,* thought Olivia, but she remained silent. Then it occurred to her — the Swill boy's voice; *he* had been one of the men she'd overheard in the courtyard below her room talking about a mad lamb and a green cadet. It was all a bit hazy.

She felt strangely detached from her immediate surroundings, and the bobbing of Master Key's shining bald head, ringed with its mop of dark-red hair, was almost hypnotic. Olivia was aware, however, the dungeon had become stuffier; there was obviously little to no ventilation, and smoke from the torches hung in the air as they descended the steps.

Then, suddenly, they were walking along a flat passageway. Shortly afterwards, they stopped in front of a door. Master Key produced a large key. It was attached to a chain, which appeared to be attached to his belt.

He used the key to unlock the door. It revealed an open space. Master Key had not been exaggerating; it *was* surprisingly light and airy, particularly after the gloomy, torch-lit passageway. He held the door open as she and the lieutenant entered the dungeon. Then he shut and locked it behind them. The open space turned out to be another reception area of some kind.

There was a desk (with more keys hanging from metal hooks) set against the opposite wall. Riley was slouched on a chair behind it. To Olivia's left was a row of cells, divided by stone walls, which prevented the prisoners from seeing each other. However, from a gaoler's point of view, each cell was fully visible between the floor-to-ceiling bars.

Natural light filtered in from a number of openings at the back of each cell, which were clearly roughly hewn rock. The openings looked more like holes and cracks than anything man-made. They ranged in shape and size, but none were big enough to crawl out of. Of the four cells in view, none contained Gerald. In fact, only two contained prisoners: motionless outlines, slumped upon their respective pallets.

"I thought you'd be impwessed." Master Key's voice jangled, enthusiastically. "Eighty fwee feet undergwound and we warely have to light all the torches."

Olivia looked at the gaoler. His smile was beginning to irritate her.

"A lot of wain wuns down the east wall of The Keep. It's ewoded the wock face and caused these splendid cwacks."

"Where's my husband?"

Master Key shook his head, mirthfully. "Apologies, Mistwess, I do tend to get wather cawwied away when entertaining visitors." He turned towards the lounging assistant (or whatever he was). "Wiley, you slovenly lump! Is the Town Cwier's woom open?"

Riley shrugged, indicating that he didn't know and obviously didn't care.

"Well, get off your lazy arse and make sure it is!" There was no humour in Master Key's voice now.

Riley, however, remained disinterested as he slowly moved his lazy arse into a standing position. Eying the keys on the wall, he mumbled, "Which-one-he-in-again?"

"The same one he's been in the entire time!"

Riley reached uncertainly towards the keys.

"The Icing Suite, you dullard!" shouted Master Key.

The Icing Suite was situated at the southern end of the row of cells. Once again, the lieutenant offered his arm, which she accepted, before following Master Key past a dozen or more cells. About half were empty, but the occupied ones *were* almost like… rooms. Master Key obviously allowed prisoners to have a certain number of personal possessions to help ease their confinement. Still, it must be cold comfort.

With the exception of one man, who bowed formally as they passed, the prisoners largely ignored her. The only voice that could be heard was that of Master Key.

"These pwisoners have been our guests for a wather long time, so we afford them some comforts," he explained. "Our short-term guests, or the ones who don't appweciate a spacious, airwy woom, are kept in the cells below… along with the chains, manacles and dirty stwaw."

Olivia wondered where Gerald would be kept. That is, of course, if he didn't wind up at the end of the hangman's noose. She felt a sense of dread as Master Key stopped and indicated they had reached the Icing Suite. "Gewald, your wife is here to see you," he said happily, and then beckoned Olivia to step forward.

For some reason, she was reluctant to do so; she'd never imagined she would ever see Gerald in a prison cell. She could feel her hands shaking as the Swill boy edged her forwards.

His appearance shocked her. He looked… normal. In fact, he probably looked better than *she* did. Apart from a smudge of stubble and slightly messy hair, he appeared as he had last night, ready to attend an official dinner at the castle. He was still dressed in the same clothes. His white shirt, yellow waistcoat and green trousers looked as clean as they had when he'd put them on. For some reason, she'd expected him to be covered in grime and wearing prison rags.

He smiled wanly as Master Key ushered her through the cell door. "I would wish you a happy birthday, m'dear, but I'm afraid I've rather spoiled things for you, what."

Tears sprung from her eyes and she felt her legs giving way as she fell into his arms.

"I think we can afford them some privacy, Master Key," she heard the lieutenant say as Gerald held her close and whispered sorry over and over in her ear.

## CHAPTER 67

## *Dressed so well for the occasion*

AFTER THE DISGRUNTLED trio had left, Richard apologised for his outburst. "It's been a rather taxing few days," he added by way of explanation.

He looked tired. No, more than that, he looked shattered: his sharp features were blunted and his dark, piercing eyes were dull and sleepy. Mary suspected he'd been up all night.

"So…" He yawned and rubbed his eyes. "If you don't have the button, why the theatrics?"

"I thought you said it wasn't a button," Mary replied.

"True."

"Then what is it?"

"A key."

"A key to what?"

Richard considered his response. "Knowledge."

"What kind of knowledge?" He was being remarkably forthcoming — perhaps his sleep deprivation could work in her favour.

After another considered pause, he answered, "The kind that might save the Duke."

What kind of knowledge could possibly…? Then she realised. "The missing doctor."

Richard nodded.

The missing doctor who, according to Mandy, was the subject of gossip in the castle kitchen and rumoured to be heir to the Duchy. "Is he Marmaduke and Lucinda's son?" The words just jumped out.

Richard's brow furrowed, but he seemed otherwise unperturbed by Mary's question. "So, the word is out."

Mary felt her heart leap. Was that an admission? He seemed so… ambivalent. "Is this some sort of jest?"

He let out a mirthless bark of laughter. He must be delirious. She was suddenly concerned for him, "Richard, are you alright, you seem—"

"Amused by your wit?"

What did *that* mean? "More like at your wit's end."

He responded with one of his condescending smiles, as if she couldn't possibly understand what he was thinking.

"Please, Richard," she said, leaning forward on the chair. "I didn't come here to play word games or compete in some challenge of the mind. Can't you just tell me, without rhetoric and nuance, what all this has been about — the doctor, the dinner, the button, the attack on the Duke. *Does* he have an heir? What the frig has been happening in Lower Icing? Clearly you have been reinstated as Seneschal, that is, of course, if you were ever made to stand down, which I doubt — just another one of your manoeuvres, more like. So please just—"

She suddenly realised she was ranting; there were so many things she wanted answers to that she didn't know where to start… or stop. Richard was regarding her impassively now; his smile had disappeared. She felt scrutinised. She sighed. "Your pardon, Richard. As you say, it's been a taxing few days."

He nodded. "Would you care for some wine?"

The question was unexpected, but not unwelcome — as it happened, she could do with a drink. "Thank you."

He stood and walked over to a cabinet near the suit of armour. Mary watched in silence as he retrieved a crystal decanter of red wine and two goblets. She needed a breather to collect her thoughts, and sensed Richard did too. She had to hand it to him; no matter the pressure, he still presented himself immaculately: hair tucked back neatly into a ponytail, his beardless face showing just a hint of stubble, and his black and silver garb looking like it had just been personally fitted by Pierre Cardigan (Lower Icing's foremost tailor).

As he placed the two goblets on the desk and began filling them, three silver buttons on his left sleeve caught the light. Pierre Cardigan would be outraged by the missing button. "Well, it seems Paris and Lieutenant Swill have relieved us of our guards," he said, handing her a goblet and placing the decanter on the desk. "We should now be able to discuss things without fear of intrusion."

It might have been an attempt at humour — there was a smile on his face — but, then again, it could well have been a statement of fact.

He sat down and raised his goblet towards her before imbibing. Mary followed his lead, taking a large gulp of the pepper and blackberry-nuanced wine; she was actually quite thirsty.

"You have to hand it to the Escargotians," said Richard, "they certainly make an excellent red."

Mary had to concur; the wine was deliciously smooth and lingered pleasantly on the palate. "Indeed, Richard — like you, they excel at complexity."

He smiled. "Very well, sister, since you have dressed so well for the occasion, it would be churlish of me not to come to the party."

This time it was Mary who raised her goblet to Richard. He responded. They both downed more of the wine. Then, after Mary assured him that she would listen without interruption, Richard refilled the goblets and began his account of events...

It started seventeen months ago with the sudden appearance of two individuals at Blessed Whipping. They were accepted into the sun-worshipping village at the request of the Duke. They were both doctors of some sort and assimilated quickly into the community — the elder of the two was particularly welcomed because he was an albino (and white was a revered colour).

Richard was obviously talking about Doctor Manky, and Mary assumed the 'young doctor' was Richard's 'person of interest' and possible heir to the throne. So the two doctors *were* connected. Why hadn't the Duke brought them to Lower Icing, and how had Richard found out? Mary found herself biting back all kinds of questions.

On February 2nd this year, almost a year into the doctors' stay at Blessed Whipping (and the day before the first anniversary of the Duchess' death), information was relayed to Richard about the contents of a letter written by Doctor Manky to the Duke. It was one of many, apparently, penned over the previous twelve months. The content was remarkable, to put it mildly. In it, Doctor Manky suggested the time had come for Marmaduke to be reunited with his son, whom he referred to as X.

Bloody hell! Marmaduke and Lucinda *did* have a son. Either that or the doctors were trying to cause trouble. Richard had known since early February there could be an heir.

X, as it had turned out, stood for Xavier. He'd arrived, without warning, at The Bloody Bell in the early hours of Sunday morning, almost two weeks ago. He mistakenly went to the Office of Petitions that Sunday afternoon, seeking an audience with the Duke. Administrator Penman told Xavier that he was not in a position to grant him such a meeting. The young doctor then declared he was the Duke's son, and he had a document to prove it. However, he didn't have the document on him, so Penman arranged a meeting for the following day. Penman then informed Richard. It had caught him unprepared — there had been no indication such an event was impending. Richard swore Penman to secrecy and set about taking control of the situation.

Mary was confused. Why would the young doctor suddenly demand to see the Duke after all these years? Unless… *he'd* only just discovered he was the Duke's son!

Richard conducted the meeting himself. He'd confided in only one other person — Brandon. There were two reasons for this. Firstly, he was, in Richard's judgement, about the only trustworthy and capable officer in the entire castle, and secondly (and possibly more crucially) he was a Swill — his parents, coincidently (or not), were once Blessed Whippingers.

*Were they?* Mary had no idea Bar and Bertie were from Blessed Whipping. For as long as she could remember, they'd been running The Bloody Bell. She had childhood memories of Brandon as a baby and clearly remembered Bethany being born — Mary and her parents had been part of the naming day celebrations. The Swills had never even mentioned Blessed Whipping as far as she could recall.

The moment Xavier was escorted into Administrator Penman's office, Richard realised his claim could well be valid. He could see Lucinda in him, particularly in his eyes.

It seemed odd to Mary that Richard referenced Lucinda rather than Marmaduke; a man bearing *her* features did not prove he was the *Duke's* son.

Xavier produced his document: a letter, or, more accurately, a *copy* of a letter written by Doctor Manky to the Duke. Even so, the message had been partly lost because Xavier had sweated through the parchment. In it, Doctor Manky espoused the positives of a reunion with a person he referred to as X — that it had been twenty years. To Xavier, the words constituted proof of his claim. To Richard, the contents of the letter were neither here nor there. As Seneschal, he was duty bound to act in the Duke's interests, and he wasn't convinced that presenting Xavier to Marmaduke would serve that purpose. After all, for whatever reason, the Duke had clearly resisted such a reunion. Richard found himself in an awkward position. The letter did not constitute evidence; he couldn't present Xavier on the strength of it. Even the original would not be enough; literally anyone could pen such a letter. Much to Xavier's dismay and confusion, Richard told him as much. Then he dismissed Xavier, ordering Brandon to escort him back to The Bell; he needed more time to assess his options. However, as he was being led out of Penman's office, Xavier mentioned the name of Richard's observer at Blessed Whipping — a town elder called Bertrand. It set alarm bells ringing.

Mary interrupted him to ask what an observer was, and he had no qualms about explaining Bertrand's role. Richard was being amazingly forthcoming; perhaps it was fatigue, or maybe the decanter of wine they were steadily emptying into their goblets. A combination of both, no doubt.

Apparently, Richard no longer trusted Bertrand. He'd become aggressive on an unrelated matter, a matter Richard wasn't prepared to discuss in any detail. Suffice to say, the mention of Bertrand automatically made Richard question Xavier and his motives, and reconsider his position about allowing him to stay with the Swills — their connection to Blessed Whipping, tenuous as it might be, was still a connection. He needed to accommodate Xavier somewhere more in keeping with his position. So, he ordered Brandon to escort him to one of the older guestrooms in The Keep. Admittedly, it was hardly what anyone would call luxury, but it would do for now. In any case, Richard *wanted* Xavier to feel uncomfortable and uncertain about his predicament; if he truly was Marmaduke and Lucinda's son, he'd remain steadfast regardless of any perceived hardship or injustice.

Mary couldn't help but admire Richard's ability to take decisive action. As much as she was curious about this 'unrelated matter', it was intriguing enough just listening to Richard air his thoughts and the reasoning behind his actions.

Brandon was sent to retrieve Xavier's belongings from The Bloody Bell. What he returned with was most intriguing. Apart from a travelling case full of clothing (and a bag of charcoal pencils), Xavier was in possession of a beautifully crafted box. Its interior was superbly made and its contents quite wonderful: vials and small bottles of colourful powders and liquids placed in purpose-made shelves. The box also contained drawers of tools and other odd-looking pieces of apparatus. Xavier was obviously a practitioner of some sort of medicine or... chicanery — a matter Richard decided he would pursue the following morning.

After dismissing Brandon, Richard had a closer look at the travelling case. He felt there was something odd about it. Emptying out the neatly folded contents, he examined its interior. It looked empty, but there was something about the dimensions, and it was weighted strangely. It didn't take long for Richard to find what he was looking for: a secret compartment.

Mary could hardly believe what she was hearing. It was like some troubadour's tale, full of entertaining exaggeration, except... *this* was real.

The compartment contained a leather folder. It was held shut by a thick silver clasp, some three inches in width, which ran from the edge of the back cover to the centre of the front cover. Richard realised a key of some sort was needed to open it. There was a coin-sized indentation in the centre of the clasp with a smaller, deeper indentation at its centre. The key could possibly look like a button.

*The silver button!* Had Sid *really* dropped it in the Icing?

What struck Richard, however, was the engraving on the clasp: a motif of a quill above a broken sword. Richard could hardly believe it. The same insignia *he* used, the one his father had bestowed upon him on his eighteenth birthday, when he became Marmaduke's squire.

Mary had been six at the time and knew absolutely nothing about Richard's life back then. Her world had revolved around living with her parents at

The Harey Rabbit. Up until the death of Sir Walter, she and Richard had shared little more than a few passing conversations, and certainly nothing about his life as a squire.

It had been a challenging time for all concerned. The Duke and Duchess had only been in Lower Icing for six months, plucked from obscurity following the demise of the royal family on the *Happy Mermaid*. Marmaduke was only twenty-three and Lucinda twenty-two, and suddenly they were expected to rule the Duchy. Of course, it was Sir Walter who actually held the reins, making sure diplomatic ties within the Five Duchies remained intact, while Richard was able to navigate them through their daily duties. Still, they were reluctant to rise to the challenge of the royal mantle. Lucinda, in particular, seemed lost. Richard did his best to buoy her spirits, and they had many jovial conversations together. Sadly, moments of happiness were always fleeting with Lucinda. Yet, Richard stuck to his task of helping her adapt to life in the Upper Bailey. Over time, his feelings for her began to change from a formal kind of friendship to something more unattainable.

This was incredible. Mary wondered if Lucinda was part of the reason why Richard had never married. She'd always assumed her brother was too involved with the running of the Duchy to have time for a wife.

However, most of his time was spent in the company of Marmaduke. They became good friends and, because they were roughly of an age, shared many of the same views about the Duchy. Together they began reforming the archaic laws that had been perpetuated throughout the generations. For example, the Office of Petitions was established — Lower Icingers could now have their disputes arbitrated fairly and legally. There were a number of other social reforms, which basically gave people more freedom; the old feudal system was at an end. It took nine years to achieve, fighting the lords and nobles (his father included) and their prophecies of economic doom.

Mary remembered when the Office of Petitions came into being. She'd been a sixteen-year-old serving girl, and the mood in The Harey Rabbit had been one of outrage. Adding to the atmosphere of indignation had been the loud celebrations flowing across The Square from The Bloody Bell. The memory brought a smile, even though it hadn't been funny at the time. Mary had no idea until this moment that Richard had been involved in any of these laws. It was eye-opening to say the least. She wondered what else her brother was going to reveal this afternoon.

Richard apologised for digressing. The point he was trying to make was that the discovery of the insignia on Xavier's folder — the one he'd thought of as *his* for the last twenty years — added another layer of complexity to an already complex situation. And *this* layer was much more personal, and possibly best left uncovered. The sifting process, however, *would* begin when he next met Xavier.

Richard paused to refill their goblets. Mary was beginning to feel the effects of the wine and wondered how long it would be before she wasn't able to keep her thoughts to herself.

The meeting, however, did not go to plan. The Town Crier found Richard in Penman's office shortly before Xavier was due to arrive. He proceeded to inform Richard that he'd just come from Xavier's room in The Keep, that he'd spotted Xavier earlier that morning, had gone up to investigate and found out that he was there at Richard's behest, that he was waiting for an audience with the Duke, and that he claimed to be the Duke's son. Of all the people who could have stumbled across Xavier! Richard immediately refuted Xavier's claim, telling the Town Crier there was absolutely no factual basis behind it. Of course, the Town Crier, being the Town Crier, had taken everything Xavier said at face value. He asked Richard about the letter. Richard replied that it could have been written by anyone. He challenged him with the fact that he resembled Marmaduke. Richard countered that any *perceived* resemblance was coincidental and used to proliferate a fanciful claim. The Town Crier became quite indignant at Richard's attitude and took him to task about Xavier's accommodation, saying it wasn't fit for *any* guest, let alone one who might well be the Duke's son *and*, what's more, he'd already had a hearty breakfast sent up to his room.

Richard lost his temper — something he rarely did. But the Town Crier was in danger of single-handedly bringing the Duchy into political turmoil. The fool had no idea what was at stake; he was full of ideological romance. Richard had no such illusions. He very much doubted Xavier's appearance would end in a happy reunion between father and son — if, indeed, Xavier was who he claimed to be. Richard insisted, in the strongest terms, that the Town Crier tell no-one about what he'd seen. He referred to Xavier as a likely imposter and attempted to explain the ramifications of such information reaching the Duke's ears, but the obstinate idiot maintained that the Duke should be the one to decide.

In the end, Richard agreed to treat Xavier like a visiting noble and even allowed the Town Crier to personally attend to his needs. However, it was on the condition that he maintained his silence until Richard deemed it appropriate to approach the Duke with this highly delicate matter. This seemed to mollify the Town Crier, which, for the moment, was all Richard was trying to achieve. And, in a way, there was a chance it might work to his advantage — let Xavier have an idiot as an advocate. However, he realised that all he'd really done was buy some time, a few days at the most.

There were several rooms being set up in The Keep for the Duke of Stymouth's entourage. He instructed the Town Crier to choose one of them. And, since the kitchen had been alerted to Xavier's presence, it was better that he appeared to be a noble.

Mary was trying to take it all in. *Was Xavier the Duke's son or not?* Even when Richard was being forthcoming with the facts, they were obscured by his reasoning. She took another mouthful of wine.

Shortly after Richard's tete-a-tete with the Town Crier, Xavier was delivered to Penman's office by Lieutenant Swill. Richard then sent the Town Crier (with Brandon as an escort) to find suitable accommodation in The Keep. And by suitable, Richard had made it clear he meant secure. Then he began the sifting process with Xavier. He came straight to the point, stating that he'd retrieved his belongings from The Bell and had discovered the secret compartment in his travelling case and the leather folder within.

Xavier looked weary and somewhat bedraggled. His expression, though, was one of surprise mingled with a muted kind of acceptance. There was no outrage or accusation of foul play. Richard was silently impressed by that. Xavier informed him that the folder contained research notes; that he was working on a rejuvenation potion with Horatio, his mentor — the 'imaginary man' who'd penned the letter to the Duke, and that he'd be happy to show Richard its contents once it was returned. Richard had never met anyone as serenely naïve as Xavier. If he *was* an imposter, he'd chosen a very unusual role.

Richard, however, said that he was not so much interested in the folder's contents as its design, particularly the motif on the clasp. Xavier told him it was the insignia Horatio used. It signified the pursuit of knowledge being worthier and more beneficial than the pursuit of power. The folder was a gift, as was the wooden box. Richard knew what it signified: it was a tenet he believed in. As far as Richard was concerned, knowledge *was* power.

Richard asked Xavier if he knew how Doctor Manky had come to choose that particular insignia, but Xavier had never asked him; as long as he could remember, Horatio had used it. Xavier, himself, wasn't particularly interested in insignias. He had no reason to have one; it wouldn't change the person he was.

Although he didn't show it, Richard was warming to the young man; he was refreshingly simplistic and there appeared to be no pretence about him. Yet, Richard still had his doubts. He also didn't know what to make of the insignia. Was it a coincidence, or was it more evidence of a connection to the Duke? Or *was* it part of an elaborate charade? Xavier's connection to Blessed Whipping and Bertrand worried Richard.

Mary wondered if it was Bertrand she'd seen with Sid. Was Sid really being protective of her, or was he involved after all?

Richard asked Xavier why he'd mentioned Bertrand and what type of relationship they had. Xavier replied that he was a community elder who had been assigned to them as a type of aide when they first arrived at Blessed Whipping. Xavier had very little to do with Bertrand and found him unpleasant to be around. He'd mentioned his name because he was known to the Swills — they too disliked him — and so had thought it would make his story more credible.

So, it probably *was* Bertrand Sid had run off with. He'd never really been brought up in conversation, just once or twice that Mary could remember, and Sid had only referred to him as Doctor Manky's servant. Did he also know he was Richard's un-trusted observer? And what connection did Bertrand have to the Swills… or the Swills have to *him*?

Xavier's story was compelling, but, at the same time, Richard was dubious. Richard aired his misgivings, challenging Xavier with the obvious: why, if the letter was genuine, had the Duke kept his relationship to Xavier from him all these years? Why, despite the urging of Doctor Manky, hadn't the Duke sent for him? Xavier had answered — Richard quoted his exact words: "The very questions I had in mind to ask, Seneschal."

And, so, Xavier agreed to remain in The Keep, as a guest of the Duke, while Richard organised an audience. Richard, in turn, agreed to return all his belongings. Xavier had appeared satisfied with the arrangement. Richard, however, wasn't satisfied with *any* of it. Still, he was determined that Marmaduke would, indeed, be the next to hear of Xavier's arrival.

The wine seemed to be affecting Richard as well (which was unusual). He looked as if he was about to drift off. No doubt, lack of sleep was playing a part. Wearily, he continued.

Before the Town Crier and Brandon returned to collect Xavier from Penman's office, Richard revisited the topic of the insignia. He asked Xavier where he'd lived before Blessed Whipping. He replied that he had spent all his life with Horatio at Missing Anchor. That had sparked Richard's curiosity, because, according to Sir Walter, Marmaduke and Lucinda had been living in a hamlet in the northwest of the Duchy called Prickly Thicket. Richard asked Xavier if he had any memories of growing up there. He replied that he'd never heard of such a place as Prickly Thicket.

Mary had never heard of it either. It didn't sound particularly inviting, and certainly not a place you'd expect to find the next in line to the Duchy. Despite Richard's insistence that she not interrupt, Mary was beginning to lose the thread of the tale her brother was weaving. Wasn't it meant to be about the silver button being the key to saving the Duke?

"Sorry, Richard," she said. "Is Xavier the heir to the Duchy or not?"

He looked at her sleepily and smiled, frustratingly non-committal.

"Is he the *poisoner*?" Mary persisted. "The box, with all its potions…?" It made sense. A naïve lad with a sheltered upbringing is suddenly confronted with the fact that his father is not only alive, but the Duke of Lower Icing. His appearance is met with suspicion, he's seemingly spurned by his father, he'll never know his mother, he feels lost and confused, and a sense of betrayal begins to overwhelm him. It was like a Hamlet Macbeth tragedy.

Then realisation struck. "The cure's in his folder. You need the silver button to open it!"

She could feel her heart beating, but her brother just stared at her.

"I'm right, aren't I?"

"No," Richard replied quietly, "you're not." Then he added, "At least, for the most part."

Her boldness melted under his gaze, and she quaffed some more wine. Its peppery finish lingered at the back of her tongue. "So, who is the—"

"I'm feeling rather weary, Mary. Perhaps we should call it an afternoon."

"No, Richard." Not now, not after all he'd revealed. "Please continue; I won't interrupt again."

He rubbed his eyes. "Very well." Then he looked towards the window, out into the mid-afternoon colour where sunlight played upon the leaves and blooms.

Mary had almost forgotten about the world outside. Normally she'd be involved with the preparations for dinner, but that seemed rather insignificant compared to what was being served in Richard's office.

# CHAPTER 68

## *The Icing Suite*

FOR A CELL in a dungeon, the Icing Suite was, in fact, quite spacious and surprisingly well appointed; it had a pallet with a feather mattress, a desk, a couple of chairs, shelving (with a few battered old books) and a piss bucket. It was like a Sporrendalish version of *her* room in The Keep. However, the most luxurious feature of the Icing Suite was the three-foot vertical crack on the back wall. It illuminated and ventilated the cell and was wide enough to provide a restricted view of the Duke's Forest and the eastern hills beyond. It was a relief to be able to see the outside world; it helped lift the oppressive weight of stone.

They were seated at the desk; their tears had been shed and their composure restored. Now Olivia was waiting for Gerald to explain how and why he had come to poison the Duke. Gerald's hands were folded on the desk in front of him. He looked lost, or introspective, as if still searching for his *own* explanation. Olivia reached out and clasped his hands. His eyes focused on hers. She smiled encouragingly. How differently she felt towards him now he'd been stripped of all the pompous puffery that had made him Gerald Hiepants, Town Crier… the pompous puffery *she* had created. Now that he'd been reduced (or reinstated, more like) to Gerald Hiepants *the man*, she felt nothing but respect for him.

"I don't know where to start." His eyes fell from hers.

She squeezed his hands. "It's alright, Gerald," she said, softly and his eyes returned to hers. "I haven't come here to judge you, just to… listen. And I *mean* listen."

He smiled, ruefully. "It's a damnable business, what. You must believe me, m'dear, what has transpired… It never entered my mind to… Oh, if only Xavier…"

Again his eyes dropped.

"Gerald, please," she whispered. "I *know* who you are, the kind of man you are — the *kind* and *gentle* man you are. I have no doubt you meant well."

"Thank you, m'dear. I don't deserve such kindness, not after what I have put you through. The embarrassment must be hard to bear, and I suspect the castle-set have…" He shook his head. "Forgive me; I'm waffling already. One of my many traits you find annoying, what."

She squeezed his hand again, as much for herself as for him; his words were so raw, tearing at her heart. She felt a tear run down her right cheek, but she wasn't about to let go of her husband's hand to wipe it away.

"Well, you see," he began. "I felt I had to do something about Xavier and Marmaduke. It was clear by Wednesday afternoon that Sir Richard was in no hurry to introduce Xavier to his father, refusing to concede his claim was legitimate, referring to him as the imposter and confidence-trickster. That's why I brought him to our home, m'dear, rather than let him be treated like a criminal." He sighed. "What am I saying? You know this already."

"It's alright," she said, "I *want* to hear what you have to say."

Again, he twitched out a smile. "I thought I was doing the right thing."

"Of course."

"Who knows what would have become of Xavier if I hadn't…" His whispery words fell silent and his gaze became introspective. "Then again, he wouldn't have been attacked, wouldn't have gone missing, wouldn't have lost his memory or his ability to heal, then the Duke would have been treated and you wouldn't… be here. You have been right all along, Olivia — I *am* a fool!"

"Gerald, of all the things you have done since we have been together, believing in Xavier has been the *least* foolish and *most* honourable. I am proud of you."

He nodded through his watery eyes, then freed his hands to wipe them. "If only that was *all* I had done. Instead, I… overreached, became puffed up with self-righteousness, and I wanted to…" He suddenly looked self-conscious. "I wanted to show you I was capable of more than just yelling out proclamations."

"Oh, Gerald," she whispered, taking back his hands. More tears welled in her eyes; surely there could be no tears left. What had she done to her husband? Her damnable pride.

He shook his head. "Vanity, my sweet, is a curse."

He was referring to himself, but the words should have been directed at her. It was too much — a shuddering breath was followed by a fit of sobbing.

"Please don't upset yourself, Olivia," he said, softly, "the fault is mine."

She tried to speak, but all she could do was shake her head. Now it was Gerald's turn to squeeze *her* hand.

"After all, it was I, and I alone, who acted against the Duke; you need not reproach yourself for anything, m'dear."

Olivia wanted cry out that it *was* her fault, that *she* had driven him to act, but no matter how she tried to control her emotions, they would not allow her to speak.

"I shall attempt to explain; hopefully you can find it in your heart to forgive me."

Olivia nodded; she already had.

"To think, almost exactly a week ago, I was sitting in the Duke's quarters for the Friday *Five at Five* meeting. Marmaduke was rather chipper — unusually so, in fact. He was upbeat about the arrival of the Duke of Stymouth, but it was more than that. There was an air of excitement about him, and that's when it occurred to me that he must know about Xavier. Perhaps I had misjudged Sir Richard after all.

"I approached the Seneschal after the meeting. He looked rather concerned, but, then again, he *always* looks that way. In any case, I remarked, casually of course, about the Duke's high spirits and how nice it was to see him so happy. I was hoping, indeed, *angling*, for confirmation that Sir Richard had, in fact, told the Duke about Xavier. Instead, he asked me if I wasn't *alarmed* by the Duke's behaviour. Well, I was momentarily taken aback, but then I realised Sir Richard might be worried about being overheard. So I made some off-hand comment about the next proclamation being somewhat more momentous, meaning, of course, the *following* Saturday's."

He paused and regarded her fondly. "It matters not what I meant. It has no bearing on what has occurred... what *actually* happened."

Last night, Olivia would have been frustrated and annoyed by the meanderings of his mind. This afternoon, she was savouring every turn.

"You see, my dear, I went back to see the Duke; he'd been so effusive about the Duke of Stymouth's visit, I needed to clarify what was to be conveyed to the townsfolk. I mean, it would have been a rather long proclamation otherwise. Not sure my voice would have gone the journey, what.

"Marmaduke was still very upbeat; so much so that I felt the need to offer my congratulations regarding Xavier. I saw no harm in it — we were alone in his study."

Gerald sighed. Olivia followed suit. Poor Gerald, he really was the victim of his own misguided enthusiasm.

"He looked at me as if I had thrown a bucket of cold water on him. Then he became angry. He said he didn't have a son and that this cruel rumour was tantamount to treason. Then he asked me if Sir Richard had put me up to coming to see him, and wanted to know how many other people were under the foolish impression he had a son. It was most shocking to see the Duke in such a temper. I really didn't know what to say. I apologised for offending him and told him that, as far as I knew, the only other people who knew about Xavier were Lieutenant Swill, Administrator Penman and you, m'dear. He looked at me — composed now, but still angry. 'It stops here, Town Crier,' he said. 'Whoever this Xavier is, he's not my son.'

"I could hardly believe what I was hearing. Foolishly, I challenged him with 'He has a letter, Your Grace' to which he snapped, 'It's nonsense! Whatever it contains, it's nonsense, fabrication, forgery. Call it what you will — I have no son!' Well, m'dear, of course I had to demur to the Duke even though I believed otherwise: that if he met Xavier, he couldn't help but admit…"

His words trailed off as if he was silently reliving the moment. Olivia was astounded by what her husband was telling her. If Xavier *was* indeed a confidence trickster, he was remarkable at it. But, no… the resemblance was too strong; she could see and *feel* Lucinda and Marmaduke in him.

"Sorry, m'dear, I realise you are well acquainted with all this."

"No, Gerald, this is the first I've heard of your altercation with Marmaduke."

"I say! Really?" He seemed quite surprised; then realisation dawned. "Ah yes, of course. You and Xavier were in deep conversation when I returned from the *Five at Five*. Thought it best to leave you to it, what. And, in any case, I had to write the proclamation and return it to the Duke's chambers by nine o'clock. He was rather keen on checking the details personally — a task usually given to Sir Richard, but, as I said, the Duke of Stymouth's visit rather consumed him."

Yes, Olivia thought, she *had* been engrossed in Xavier's world, listening to him speak about treatments and cures for illness and disease, for the ease of suffering, that it was all attainable. His view of life was remarkable in its simplicity; he was devoted to his research, yet he exuded a sense of worldliness and wisdom beyond his years. Gerald's comings and goings that Friday evening had hardly registered with her, apart from a brief read of his proclamation… the one he *didn't* cry, of course. (To think Gerald had been inspired to cry an entirely different proclamation by a blacksmith. It still made no sense to her.)

Gerald sighed and bowed his head. She could feel his hands squirming to be released, but she held them tight, encouraging him to continue.

"Go on, Gerald."

He inhaled deeply, then looked up. "My mind wasn't really focused on the proclamation. I couldn't stop thinking about father and son — the calamity of it all, don't y'know. If the Duke would only *meet* Xavier, he would *see* he'd sired a young man of which to be proud. But I knew he'd never agree. He was so… adamant.

"I began thinking of ways I could bring them together, perhaps presenting him under another name." He shook his head. "Alas, no; Xavier would not be party to such subterfuge and, in any case, Sir Richard would have certainly resisted such an idea.

"Regardless of such distractions, it didn't take long to complete the proclamation. It was rather straightforward actually: rallying the townsfolk to prepare a favourable welcome for the Duke of Stymouth, how it could mean greater trade and more prosperity for Lower Icing et cetera. I'd written similar proclamations many times before. It certainly wasn't as rousing as I would have liked, but I couldn't muster much enthusiasm for the task, truth be told." A rueful smile appeared momentarily. "I remember you reading it with a distinct lack of enthusiasm."

It wasn't an accusation, just an observation. Olivia returned his smile. "Yes, I believe I *was* somewhat distracted by Xavier that night."

"It mattered not. You see, by that stage I'd already decided to… take a different course of action."

Olivia nodded. She could feel him tense.

"As I was rummaging through the desk drawers, looking for some blotting paper, I happened across Xavier's book of potions. Or, to be more accurate, *Horatio's* book of potions. That's when it occurred to me the answer to reuniting father and son might well lie within the pages of *Poetry In Potion*.

"While he was in The Keep, I spent quite some time with Xavier and, as you know, m'dear, he is most enthusiastic about sharing his knowledge. He talked about many of the potions, what they are used for, their ingredients, how they are formulated; all of them quite fantastic, don't y'know. And he was more than happy for me to leaf through the pages of *Poetry In Potion*.

"One that caught my eye was *Paloma Coma* — the name has a rather nice ring to it and the potion itself is fascinating. I mean, imagine being able to put a person into such a deep sleep that they feel no pain, even being able to amputate a limb. Incredible, really, but Xavier assured me he and Horatio had performed many painless procedures using *Paloma Coma*.

"The only danger is in the *creation* of the potion: making sure exact amounts are added, particularly of orange-spotted mushroom. Xavier referred to it as the active ingredient. Too much would send the imbiber into a feverish delirium. So, when I saw the book of potions in our desk drawer…"

He shook his head and pulled his hands away from her grasp, then buried his head in them.

"Gerald," she said soothingly, rubbing his arm.

Taking in a deep shuddering breath, Gerald clutched her hands in his — she could see he was fighting to retain his composure. "So…" He exhaled. "When I saw the book, I thought…"

Gerald's eyes began to well with tears. "If the Duke were to become ill with a mysterious fever — a fever only Xavier knew how to treat — then…" He shook his head again, blinking remorseful tears from his eyes.

"I opened the book to make sure my memory served me correctly and, sure enough, the details of *Paloma Coma were* as I remembered them. I knew Xavier had a bottle already made up in his box. He also had a small vial of orange-spotted mushroom. It's actually a powder."

A tear rolled down Gerald's face. "In any case, it was simply a matter of pouring some of the *Paloma Coma* into an empty vial and adding a small amount of the orange spotted mushroom."

Suddenly, Gerald's focus was back on Olivia. "I assure you it was only a smidgeon. I knew too much could be fatal — the warning, don't y'know. It was I who marked it."

*Yes, the warning*, Olivia thought. Why *had* he incriminated himself by circling it?

"A stupid thing to do, I know. A case of absent mindedness, I'm afraid. I'm sorry, m'dear, I've made rather a botch of—"

"Please stop apologising, Gerald," Olivia said, a hint of her traditional impatience returning.

"Yes, quite. What's done is done and all that." Gerald belatedly wiped his teary eyes. Then, without warning, he stood up and stepped over to the opening in the wall.

She stood up after him. "Are you all right, Gerald?"

"Just need some air, m'dear."

She moved towards him.

"Truly, I shall be fine in a moment. Rather stuffy in here, what?"

He faced the opening, then began to breathe deeply. A cool breeze wafted through. It was refreshing and soothing, even to Olivia; the sight of the tree tops and blue sky provided a calming reassurance that there was a world outside.

Olivia placed a comforting hand on his shoulder, but he didn't acknowledge the gesture, just continued to inhale the fresh air. She could only imagine what he was going through: the guilt, the uncertainty and the fear. *And*, no doubt, a certain amount of frustration at the vagaries of fate. It *could* have ended so differently, just the way Gerald had imagined.

His moment took a few minutes. She smoothed his back until he turned to face her.

"That's done the trick." He smiled. "Thank you, m'dear."

Olivia, however, wasn't convinced; he didn't look well. "Gerald, are you sure you're—"

"Truly, I feel quite recovered," he said, somewhat dismissively, as they sat back down at the table. He looked at her or, to be more accurate, *through* her. "It's the memory, you see," he said quietly, almost to himself.

The silence that followed was prolonged. Olivia was about to break it with a question, but Gerald spoke first.

"He *knew*, m'dear," he said, simply.

"I'm sorry, Gerald, I don't understand."

"Marmaduke… I'm sure he knew I'd put something in his wine… When I returned with the proclamation… He didn't say anything, but the way he looked at me… He seemed… *grateful*. 'To your health, Town Crier,' he said before downing the goblet. It all happened so quickly. It was shocking. I felt ill — it *still* makes me feel ill. I wanted to tell him what I'd done, I began to, but he stopped me. He handed me the proclamation and said, 'Well done, Gerald. Thank you. That will be all.' He'd never called me Gerald before… at least not when I was acting in my official capacity. And I don't believe he was thanking me for what I'd *written*. He was talking about…"

Again, her husband rushed up from the table. This time it was far more explosive and instead of heading for the opening, he dived into the corner of the room and began retching into the piss bucket.

## CHAPTER 69

### *Entangled on the bank*

**T**HE AFTERNOON MEANDERED by, flowing slowly like the Icing River. It was idyllic really — the warm sun sparkling down on the water. Ophelia was lazing on a blanket by the edge of its calm shallows. There was nothing else to do. Tom had already prepared the campsite and her pa seemed content to sleep and recuperate. And, truth be told, Ophelia was content to let him; she was beginning to lose patience with his grumblings. While her pa seemed to have formed a begrudging respect for Tom, he still needled him with comments about being a tree-hugger and the like. It annoyed her. Tom had gone way beyond what was expected of him. Her pa had become dispensable as soon as the doctor had been found, yet, instead of abandoning him, Tom had taken it upon himself to bring him back to Lower Icing in some sort of fit state. Of course, the fact that Tom had feelings for Ophelia obviously contributed to his endeavour. Even so, her pa could start showing a little gratitude.

She propped herself up on her elbows. It had to be around five o'clock. She was starting to feel peckish and the sun was beginning to lose its warmth. She gazed around her. Her dress, blouse and bodice still lay stretched out on top of the reeds with Tom's shirt and trousers. The drying clothes brought a smile to Ophelia's face. The afternoon hadn't been *all* lazing around…

Shortly after settling into the camp, she'd decided she could do with a wash (and so could her clothes). She made her intentions known to Tom, with a rather obvious undercurrent in her tone.

He reacted with practical ambivalence. "Be careful not to wade out too far; the riverbed is uneven, the current is deceptive from the surface, and there are sink-holes."

It certainly wasn't the response she'd been angling for. Her pa was asleep, the river was hidden from the campsite by trees, bushes and reeds, and she…

*wanted* him. The circumstances presented an opportunity to *have* him.

"Oh," she said, feigning concern. "Praps y' better come with me then."

He gave her a quizzical look.

*For frig's sake!* She pulled open the laces at the top of her bodice. The bodice began to stretch open, revealing a luscious portion of her fulsome cleavage. "I c'n think of one sink-hole I'd like you t'plunge into."

Her coquetry finally hit the mark. He blushed profusely, eyes darting from her to her pa. "What about…?" He nodded towards the slumped figure, sleeping peacefully against the tree.

"Like y'said, Tom," she said, delighting in his discomfort as she continued to unlace her bodice, "'is body needs rest. Pa ain't goin' nowhere soon."

"Be that as it may…" He was whispering, his expression looking more panicked as the bodice became more undone.

"But *my* body don' require no rest; the opposite, in fact." She freed herself of the stiff garment.

"Ophelia!"

She could tell her pa was sleeping heavily; she recognised the sound of his breathing. A stampede of squealing pigs wouldn't wake him. Not that Tom knew that, of course. She then began undoing the buttons of her blouse, allowing the fabric to fall where her body allowed.

It was too much for him; he closed the gap between them in two quick strides, gathered her up in his arms and carried her to the edge of the river.

They thrashed about in the shallows like a couple of adolescent otters. It was passionate and intense, the cold water and coarse sand adding to the vitality of their coupling.

Some minutes later, they lay side by side, panting at the blue sky. Ophelia had never felt so alive. She rolled over and rested her head on his heaving chest; his skin was cool and wet and smudged with brown sand. She ran her fingers through his chest hair. "I love you, Tom."

There was a rise and fall of his chest before he replied, "I love you, Ophelia."

The memory sent a warm flow through her body. She'd never even thought about saying she loved someone before, apart from family members, of course. But this was different … *very* different. This was… *desire.*

They lay entangled on the bank, clothes half torn off, soaking in each other. It didn't last long; even their body heat and the warmth from the sun failed to lift the chill the afternoon breeze sent through their wet clothes. They wrestled out of their garments, doused them in the river, and then hung them over a thick bed of reeds. Naked, they waded into the Icing. After four or five steps, the knee-deep water suddenly became waist-deep. Ophelia gasped, but Tom seemed immune to the icy water.

"This is far enough." He smiled, taking her hand. "Don't want you getting carried away downstream."

Yes, she thought, there were much better ways to get carried away. However, they didn't linger long; the water was too cold, despite the unusually hot spell. Back on shore, they clung to each other, Ophelia shivering in Tom's embrace. Reluctantly, Tom decided to retrieve a blanket from the campsite (even though he didn't relish the idea of sneaking past her pa with no clothes on).

"You'll be righ', Tom. Pa's seen 'is fair share of danglin' sausages."

He looked self-consciously at his groin. She laughed and pushed him into motion. "Go on! I'm bleedin' freezin'!"

He returned without incident; her pa still slept, oblivious to the carry-on just twenty or so paces away. Tom wrapped the blanket around them. Soon they were warm and dry, but the same could not be said of their clothes. Ophelia didn't mind being naked, particularly here by the river where they seemed a world away from anyone. Tom, however, was preoccupied by the proximity of her pa and said he'd feel better if he was at least partially dressed. Eventually, he gave in to his need to be clothed and reclaimed his sopping woollen breeches from the reeds.

Ophelia laughed as he struggled to put on the undergarment. "Lucky for me y'don' 'ave this much trouble takin' 'em *off*."

Tom treated her to a withering look. Eventually, he mastered the mechanics of legs through openings, and the breeches were in place, in a sagging sort of way.

"An' tha's *better* is it?" Ophelia enquired, genuinely amused.

He smiled; he actually looked relieved. "Put it this way, it's *safer*."

"Won' get no arguments there," she said, alluding to the lack of appeal they presented.

He laughed at her playful dig. "There's plenty of other fish in this river. Think I'll go catch one."

"Won' catch one like me, Gamekeeper."

"True." He leant towards her as if he was about to kiss her. Instead, he said, "*They'll* put up a fight."

She punched him hard in the shoulder.

Ophelia stood up and shook the sand and dirt from the blanket. Then she folded it and carried it over to the reeds where their clothes still hung. She hadn't seen Tom since he went fishing, well over two hours past. She wondered if he'd had any luck. What was she thinking — of *course* he'd had some.

The clothes, for the most part, were dry. There were still tinges of dampness in her bodice and in Tom's trousers. Still, they were a lot cleaner and far less odorous than they had been a few hours ago. She dressed. It felt odd to be encumbered again, constrained somehow, but at least it kept the chill at bay. Laden with the blanket and Tom's clothes, she made her way back to the campsite. However, before leaving the little cove, she cast her eyes over the spot where she and Tom had lain. Would there ever be a moment like that again? Would they ever come back here? Yes, she'd make *sure* they did.

She'd spent the rest of the time lying on the blanket in a contemplative doze. What were they going to do about Billy? He'd been running amuck for a while now. Tom was right: he needed more discipline, otherwise he could well end up like the Moleson Twins. For some reason, her pa looked the other way where Billy was concerned. None of this recent trouble would have happened if her pa had been stronger with Billy. And it wasn't fair on her ma, or Seth for that matter. Maybe they should send him to stay with the family in Great Naff, set him to work in the Naff Office. Baby brother or not, Len, Bert and Tad wouldn't put up with any of his nonsense. Yes, the more she thought about it, the more she thought it was a good idea. Her ma wouldn't like it, but it was better than Billy winding up in The Can again… or worse. The little brat. She couldn't wait to see him… and her ma… and Seth. Poor Seth, always a last thought.

Ophelia pushed her way through the undergrowth towards the campsite. The leafy battle lasted less than ten seconds. Emerging from the greenery, she was surprised and concerned to see her pa still propped up against the tree, eyes closed. Tom was nowhere to be seen. She walked hurriedly towards him, and his eyes popped open.

"Well," he said, croakily, "if it ain't the fish tha' *didn'* get away."

Ophelia halted, taken back by his accusatory tone. "Whatcha mean, Pa?"

"Don' play games with me, Ophelia. Ain't in the mood for it."

"Dunno wha' ya on abou'."

He shook his head and jerked himself into a sitting position. He grimaced in pain. Dropping Tom's clothes, she moved to help him.

"Leave me be," he growled. "I c'n manage."

"Pa?" She was worried now. Something had happened.

He regarded her; he looked tired.

"Pa?" she repeated. "Wha's wrong? Is it your ribs? Are y'thirsty? Do you wan' some—"

"Wha' I *want* is a daughter what shows some respect an' don' go trollopin' off with a friggin' tree-hugger within earshot of her pa who's recuperatin' from a bleedin' beatin' from a couple thugs 'e was forced to friggin' well hunt down '*cause* of 'im.'"

Ophelia flushed with a mixture of embarrassment and anger.

"Wha' the *frig*, Ophelia! 'E put our Billy in The Can, an 'ere y'are puttin' out like 'e's some sortta friggin' knight in pissin' armour!"

Anger overpowered embarrassment. They'd been through this; she thought it was behind them.

"It weren' Tom's fault, Pa!" she yelled back. "It was Billy's! And *yours!* You let 'im run 'round doin' wha' 'e wan's with no friggin' consequences. Billy was *lucky* it was Tom what arrested 'im. Least 'e c'n see wha's what!"

"Ha! Wanna know wha's what, girl? I'll *tell* ya wha's what. Will Plucker was bleedin' right: I've sired Lower Icing's sauciest tart!"

Ophelia couldn't believe those words had just come out of her pa's mouth. Not because it was news to her — her reputation was based on wishful thinking more than substance — but because her pa seemed to give it some credibility. He'd always *defended* her.

She was dumbstruck and could only watch as her pa edged himself into a standing position, using the tree trunk for support. He looked momentarily disoriented. She moved to help him, but he waved her away. He closed his eyes and rubbed his right temple, his face pinched in pain. Then he teetered.

"Pa!" Ophelia sprang towards him and managed to soften the fall as he collapsed back onto the ground. She shook him by the shoulders. He showed no sign of consciousness. His injured face suddenly looked more battered; his broken nose was still swollen, the gash between his eyes looked raw, and the skin on his head was still peeling and pink in patches. A wave of panic flooded through her. "Tom!" she screamed.

# CHAPTER 70

## *She didn't have the key*

OLIVIA SHIELDED HER eyes as Riley opened the door to the outside world.

"Come, Mistress Hiepants," said the Swill boy, "I shall escort you back to your residence."

She allowed him to take her arm as they emerged from the gloom. The air was sweet, and Olivia breathed it in greedily. It didn't take long for her eyes to adjust to the late-afternoon light. Olivia looked up at The Keep — the looming behemoth had swallowed her and then spat her out. She *felt* spat out; everything was awry and she must look a sight.

As they entered the Administration Section, she could feel eyes upon her: scornful, amused, contemptuous, bemused and wary. However, in the grand scheme of things, it scarcely mattered. To think, this time yesterday, she was preparing (at scandalously short notice) for the dinner that was to be her and Gerald's vindication… which, now, was their humiliation.

Gerald… She hadn't wanted to leave him, but he'd insisted. He'd said his piece, explained the madness in his method, and said there was nothing she could do. Jeremy Dupree had matters in hand and was in possession of Gerald's notes: his documentation of the events surrounding Xavier's arrival. It wouldn't excuse what he had done, but it would certainly *explain* it. Hopefully that would be enough to save him from the gallows.

They were approaching the West Gate. The relative peacefulness of the Administration Section had been replaced by the clamour of the barracks. A couple of men-at-arms strode up to the Swill boy and half-heartedly punched their fists to their chests in a rather slap-dash attempt at a salute.

"Lieutenant," said one of them. "McHaggis an' O'Limerick 'ave finished cleanin' out The Can."

The Swill boy didn't look impressed.

"But the inmates are complaining about the smell, y'see," said the other one in the sing-song tone of someone born and raised in the Duchy of Stymouth.

"Well, Ap Bleddyn, you can tell them to refill their buckets and start again. I dread to think what those two consider clean."

"'Tisn't the smell of sh—" Ap Bleddyn stopped himself, realising Olivia was within earshot. "Ah, that is... 'tisn't the usual smell, y'see."

"Wen' overboard with the aromatics," said the other one.

"What are you talking about, Greyson?" The Swill boy looked fed up.

It was Ap Bleddyn who answered. "See they've only gone an' stuffed a whole bunch of peppermint in the buckets, then mixed in lavender and the like; eye-waterin' stuff, sir."

The Swill boy winced, but it was clearly in frustration. "So, just to clarify, lads, you're telling me the prisoners are complaining because their cells smell too *pepperminty?*"

The two men-at-arms looked at each other, before Greyson spoke up. "Aye, that's the gist of it, Lieutenant."

Olivia could see the muscles in the Swill boy's jaw twitch. He unhooked his arm from hers. "Excuse me a moment, Mistress Hiepants."

Olivia nodded — what choice did she have — and watched as he marched the two men out of earshot. However, it wasn't hard to ascertain that he was less than pleased with them. He jabbed a finger at both of them, then pointed to his temple, indicating he wanted them to use their brains (or, perhaps, questioning whether they had any). Then he pointed in the general direction of The Can. Olivia heard the question 'Is that clear?' Both men, now looking quite chastised, nodded, saluted, then did an about-face and began walking back in the direction of the barracks.

The Swill boy then returned his attention to Olivia, closing the distance smartly. "My apologies," he said, offering her his arm again. "A small discipline matter that needed attending to."

Olivia smirked, linking her arm in his. "No doubt you handled the situation with aplomb. I imagine you must have to discipline your men quite often."

He regarded her curiously, wondering, no doubt, whether she was questioning his ability to command. Well, let him think she was, because it was clear to Olivia those in authority had acted very questionably where Xavier and Marmaduke were concerned — particularly Richard. If he'd just let Xavier meet his father. She sighed. There was no point thinking about 'ifs'; the damage had been done.

"Something amiss, Mistress Hiepants?" They were walking through the West Gate, his voice was amplified by the tunnel of stone. The question seemed ridiculous; where would he like her to start?

"Nothing *you* will concern yourself with."

They walked in silence. Turning left down Big Wig Street, they passed Ma's Keraderie on the corner. A shop window of garishly painted masks stared out at Olivia, their hollow eyes following her with mocking expressions. *Just* what she needed!

"Passing strange that we use peppermint to clean out The Can."

The Swill boy's words came out of the blue. (Or, to be more accurate, the late-afternoon shade.) Olivia didn't respond; she wasn't the least bit interested in the goings-on within the world of common reprobates.

"It's purely for the smell, of course," he continued, as if she *was* interested.

They approached the corner of Big Wig and Plumduff. It would be a relief, to say the least, to shed her tattered finery and wash away the grimy remnants of her drunken disgrace. However, there'd be no sanctuary at 8 Plumduff Street: waiting, wondering when she'd be called upon to… What? She had no idea of what to expect next. She assumed Jeremy Dupree would ask her to corroborate Gerald's version of events, but…

"Xavier uses it to help with stomach maladies. He used it to help me, in fact."

Xavier: the memory of him being paraded into the Banquet Hall, standing numbly while Richard and Paris performed for the crowd. She understood now. The whole Seneschal/ex-Seneschal by-play had been a well-rehearsed drama, and the presentation of Xavier in the Duke's clothing all choreographed for the benefit of her husband. And, right on cue, he'd dutifully played his part. Not that she blamed him; she could only imagine his sense of guilt, especially upon seeing Xavier looking so forlorn and resigned. Olivia stopped walking and removed herself from the Swill boy's arm. He looked puzzled.

"I have to see, Xavier," she said before he could ask her what was wrong.

"I'm afraid that's not poss—"

"Of course it's possible!" In a more reasonable tone, she added, "I can help, Lieutenant. He… trusts me."

The Swill boy looked sympathetic, but he was shaking his head. "I'm not sure how you *could* help, Mistress Hiepants. His memory has returned, as you know. It's his inability to—"

"I'm not referring to his memory, Lieutenant. You saw him last night at the dinner. He blames himself for what has happened to the Duke. He's lost belief in himself, and is surrounded by people who only think of him as an heir, not a person. People who are only prepared to use him for their own ends."

The Swill boy's eyes narrowed at the remark. She'd probably overstepped some boundary, but she didn't care. "He needs compassion, not politics."

He looked at her thoughtfully. "I agree with you, Mis—"

"Then you'll allow me see him?"

He paused, his eyes darting, considering. "I'm sorry; I don't have the authority and—"

"But you could ask on my behalf?" Olivia persisted.

"*And*," he said more forthrightly, "my sister is already… attending to Xavier."

"Bethany? She's barely a woman, what would *she* know about the ways of…"

Her voice trailed off under the Swill boy's indignant gaze.

"I'll think you'd find my sister *quite* capable. She has a nurturing spirit and… *empathy*. Xavier is in good hands, I assure you."

In good hands? How could he *possibly* be in good hands? Bethany knew nothing of the world outside that pig-pen of an inn. "Where is Xavier? He's not still being kept—"

"His whereabouts are not your concern."

"Lieutenant Swill, I must insist that you ask—"

"I'm afraid you are not in a position to insist upon *anything*, Mistress Hiepants. My instructions were to escort you to the dungeon, *then* escort you home. I intend to do *just* that. I suggest you put your mind towards your husband's predicament, rather than involving yourself in Xavier's fate."

Olivia could feel herself bristle. "Too late, I'm afraid, Lieutenant," she said, and began walking down Plumduff Street. The Swill boy marched next to her. Neither of them said a word until they reached the door of number 8. It was then she realised that she didn't have the key.

She turned around. The Swill boy was rummaging inside the pocket of his trousers. Eventually, he extricated a key. Olivia held out her hand. Instead of giving it to her, he moved towards the door.

"Please, allow me, Mistress Hiepants," he said, formally.

"That won't be necessary," she responded, moving in front of the keyhole. "May I have my key?"

"No."

"No?" She was incredulous. "What is the meaning of this?"

"Please step aside."

"I shall not! This is my home!"

The Swill boy regarded her, wearily; he looked fed up. The purple of his doublet merged into the shade of the entranceway. The gold braiding glowed bronze, or perhaps it was just the reflection from the Hiepants' plaque. He was standing near enough to it, insinuating himself.

"Mistress Hiepants, I am to escort you home and see you safely inside."

"I am quite capable—"

"Stand aside!" he ordered. Then, more quietly, "This is not something in which you have a choice."

## Chapter 71

## *Couldn't come soon enough*

IT HAD BEEN a shock to see her pa collapse. He was so strong, nothing floored him — a rogue bull would come off worse if it butted heads with her pa, so to see him just drop like that…

Fortunately, Tom hadn't been far away. He'd heard her scream and had come rushing. If the circumstances hadn't been so serious, he would have looked comical bounding into the campsite in his breeches.

He'd taken one look at her pa, lying face up, eyes closed, barely breathing and raced over to Wildflower. He came back with a small pouch. It contained a white powder.

"Wha's tha?" she asked.

"Harts-horn," he replied, pinching a small amount out of the pouch.

"Wha' the frig is Harts-horn?" She could hear the panic in her voice — she *was* bloody well panicking.

"Powdered deer's horn," he said, calmly.

But Ophelia wasn't calm. How the frig was powdered deer horn going to help her pa? She grabbed his hand. "Tom. What—?"

"It's smelling salts, Ophelia," he informed her. "It'll revive him."

She let go of his hand and he sprinkled a small amount of the powder under her pa's nose. The effect was immediate. Her pa's eyes shot open and he began coughing and spluttering, rubbing away the powder. Then he began swearing. That's when Ophelia relaxed.

"It's alrigh', Pa," she said, placing a gentle hand on the side of his beaten face.

His eyes darted from where Tom was squatting to where she knelt. He looked confused. Tom reached over and grabbed the water-skin.

"You'll be alrigh'," she reassured him, but it was just as much to convince herself as it was her pa.

"Here, Frank," said Tom, offering him the water-skin. "You need water."

Her pa looked as if he might spit at Tom, eyeing his lack of attire. Instead, he nodded begrudgingly. Ophelia tried to help him as he attempted to lever himself into a sitting position. "Leave be!" he snapped, croakily.

"Jus' tryin' t' 'elp you, Pa!"

"Yeah, well… it's time I got used to not needin' your 'elp." His gaze flicked back to Tom as he grimaced his way into sitting position.

She felt her heart drop; so he was *still* mad at her. Well, maybe he *should* get used to not having her around… beginning now. She stood up. "Fine; 'ave it your way then, Pa."

She turned her back on them both and headed for the river, in the direction from which Tom had appeared. Tom called out to her, but she didn't reply; she was too angry and upset to speak.

Ophelia sat by the side of the river on a small rise. The reed bank below, coated gold by the waning sun, rustled in the breeze. Overhead, a lone bird crowed, breaking through a chorus of contented frogs. It was a wonder they had time to croak, Ophelia mused, what with the amount of insects buzzing around. The river itself was silent: a giant molten serpent snaking its way south.

Still, it was good to be alone… good to breathe the cool air; it'd give her time to calm down and clear her head, stop her from saying something she'd later regret… again.

Regardless of Tom, this adventure had opened her eyes. There was more to life than Slaughter & Offcut and she wanted to experience as much of it as she could. Maybe she could visit Great Naff; she'd never been there. See her brothers, her nieces and nephews, take Billy with her. She'd like to think Tom would be by her side… she didn't like the thought of him *not* being there. What had he *done* to her? The way he said her name, like it… *meant* something to him — it made her feel special.

Then she realised he *had* said her name. She withdrew her gaze from the hypnotic river as he sat down next to her. He put an arm around her shoulder and held her close. That felt good too.

"I'm fine, Tom. Jus' needed t'get away before I gave 'im a good bollockin'."

"He heard us," Tom said, sounding way too embarrassed for her liking.

"So bleedin' what. I've 'eard 'im an' ma too. Don' hear *me* goin' on about it."

"It's not the same, Ophelia."

"Wha' y'sayin', Tom?" she said, pushing away from him. "Regret it, do ya? Wish ya hadn' been with me?"

"Of course not!" He looked shocked.

"Well, it don' *sound* like it!"

"Ophelia," he said, reaching out and touching the side of her cheek. "You have captured my heart. And like all things captured, the predicament is unexpected."

*Predicament?* What the frig did *that* mean? "You sayin' y'feel trapped?" she said, slapping away his hand.

"No… not at all…" Shaking his head, he sighed. "What I'm trying… bloody hell, I'm not good at this… don't know how to say what I feel… I just think you are… beautiful in every way. I never expected to feel this way about anyone. I love you."

He looked like a boy in this light; his ruffled sandy hair was burnished bronze, his bright blue eyes aglow, searching hers… hopeful.

Yes, Ophelia thought, he *does* love me. She wrapped her arms around his shoulders, kissed him on the cheek and hugged him as tightly as she could.

On the way back to the campsite, Tom stopped to retrieve the brace of salmon he'd caught and gutted earlier. Then they attended to the horses together. Her pa was in his usual position, propped up against a tree, wearing a surly expression. Ophelia realised, apart from being in pain, her pa was probably bored shitless. It was something she hadn't really considered; he was an active person, hands on, up to his elbows in blood and guts, always doing something, so sitting around twiddling his thumbs… Still, being bored only excused his mood, *not* his words.

They dined well, as they had every night, thanks to Tom. He'd stuffed the salmon with the remaining dried apricot and peach he'd brought from his cabin and they washed it down with the last bottle of wine (another bottle of *Summer Breeze*) which Tom had chilled in the Icing.

The mood around the fire was muted to say the least. The conversation, if you could call it that, revolved around what time they were breaking camp. Her pa made it perfectly clear the moment couldn't come soon enough.

## CHAPTER 72

# *Your part in his actions*

IT WAS THE silence Olivia found disturbing. Her husband had filled 8 Plumduff Street with colour and sound — traits she had found distracting and annoying. Now, in his absence, the house was cold and silent, like a tomb. The emptiness was playing upon her mind, prodding her with memories of prideful indifference where Gerald was concerned, and taunting her with the injustice of her predicament.

To distract herself from the maudlin, Olivia had prepared a bath. It took over an hour. The stack of wood in the inglenook needed replenishing and the fire itself had to be set and lit. Then she had to twice-fill the large metal pot with water from their rainwater pond and heat it over the fire. Still, it was worth the effort, and the distraction had worked.

She hung a towel to warm next to the fire, lit some candles and then, finally, rid herself of the noble gown she'd made: her hand-sewn work of art, her crowning glory for a crowning glory. Now it was little more than a tragic rag, soiled and crumpled, much like her hopes for recognition amongst the castle-set. Amazingly, the only odour still trapped within the fine cotton and silk embroidery — even after a morning of retching and an afternoon spent in the dungeon — was that of Reg Puffy's pork pies. Fortunately, Olivia wasn't a superstitious person, otherwise she might have thought it was fate's retribution for ruining her brother's pathetic little venture. Still, she'd never go near a pork pie again.

She edged into the warm bathwater scented with lavender and rose-petal. The sky's burning sunset had become dying embers of purple. Purple… She submerged herself up to her neck, tendrils of water-vapour gently caressing her face, and thought of the Swill boy. His insistence that he see her 'safely inside' her home had bridled, as had his clinical dispatching of her 'conditions of freedom' — as if *she* were some kind of criminal. His aggressive manner — she still couldn't believe he'd actually slapped her — had been a shock, but what had really stung her, what had left her sobbing at the kitchen table, were his parting words...

"Well, Lieutenant," Olivia said, after she'd stepped across the threshold of 8 Plumduff Street, "you have seen me safely home. I believe I can manage from here."

Instead of bowing and bidding her a good evening, the man in purple followed her inside. Then she realised he still had the front door key. Olivia huffed in frustration, and marched down the hallway to the kitchen; she would not allow a puffed-up son of a bar-keep in her lounge room. She heard the front door shut and his booted steps echoing behind her.

The sun was just high enough to streak the kitchen in gold. She usually enjoyed this time of day; she almost expected to see Gerald sitting in the summer garden, reading.

"Mistress Hiepants," the Swill boy's voice cut through her musings like a blade scraping on stone, "before I take my leave, I am required to inform you of your conditions of freedom."

She spun around to face him; his uniform, brightly illuminated by the sun, momentarily dazzled her. "My *what*?" she said, evenly. How dare he!

"Your husband removed Xavier from The Keep against the express wishes of Sir Richard, *then* he kept the fact secret while we wasted valuable time and resources searching for him. In *this*, Mistress Hiepants, *you* are also culpable."

Olivia was almost too offended to respond, but she managed to breathe out, "May I inform you—"

"No, you may not. It is *I* who shall be informing *you*. I suggest you sit down and listen to what is required of you."

Olivia was stunned. Stiffly and silently, she pulled a chair out from under the kitchen table. The man in purple sat down opposite and proceeded to tell her that she was at liberty to come and go as she pleased between the hours of seven in the morning and seven in the evening. Outside those hours she was to confine herself indoors. She was also prohibited from setting foot in The Bloody Bell (no hardship there) and anywhere within the castle walls (outrageous) until further notice.

Before Olivia could interject, he added, "If this is not agreeable to you, my orders are to escort you back to The Keep where you will be lodged indefinitely."

Her sangfroid was quickly reaching melting point. "And what of my husband?"

"The preliminary hearing is tomorrow morning. You will be notified of the outcome, and a time will be arranged for you to see him."

"And *where* might this occur, since I am not permitted to set foot within the castle." She knew she was being pedantic, and possibly even provocative, but she wasn't about to be compliant in the face of such injustice.

"Wherever it pleases Sir Richard," he replied, his manner matter-of-fact.

Olivia remained silent; there was no use arguing with a mere barrel-boy, regardless of the clothes he now wore. No, she would save her reasoning for someone who could understand a woman of her standing. Someone like… Paris. Her heart sank. How could she possibly bring herself to face him ever again?

"Mistress Hiepants," the Swill boy was saying, trying (and failing) to sound reasonable, "I'm not sure you're grasping the severity of the situation. Your husband has poisoned the Duke, and you have both knowingly harboured a man whose—"

"I am *well* aware of the severity, thank you, Lieutenant; more than you could possibly realise."

He stared at her for a moment. *Go on,* Olivia thought, *just ask me what I mean by that.*

Unfortunately, his reaction was resigned. "Very well. I will take my leave. Suffice to say you are not to discuss what has occurred with anyone save me or Sir Richard. This is also a condition of your freedom."

"Of course," Olivia acknowledged, bitterly. "In fact, Lieutenant, you may inform Richard that I would be *most* keen to have a private audience with him." Pleasingly, her familiarity with Richard was not lost on the man in purple.

He stood. "I believe I have said all that needs to be said."

Olivia remained seated. "Before you see yourself out, Lieutenant, may I have my key?"

He pulled the key from his pocket and placed it in her outstretched hand. Then he wished her a good evening. As he turned to leave, a thought occurred to her.

"Lieutenant?" she called as he disappeared down the hallway.

His footsteps stopped. "Yes?" he enquired, somewhat impatiently.

In truth, no matter how officious the Swill boy was being, she didn't like the thought of being left alone. The sound of footsteps began again, heading back towards her. When he appeared at the kitchen door, he halted. "I'm rather pressed for time; Sir Richard is expecting me to return directly to his office."

Of course he was — no doubt he was busy fanning the flames of treachery in Gerald's direction. "I am curious. The dinner… a rather elaborate charade for conjecture. You must have *known* it was Gerald who poisoned the Duke."

He looked conflicted. "Mistress Hiepants, I'm afraid I—"

"Please, Lieutenant," she pressed, "I had no idea until last night that Gerald… I still find it incredible that he had the wherewithal to carry out such a… *Please*, it would help me come to terms with what has happened."

The Swill boy regarded her for a moment, as if measuring her sincerity. Surprisingly, she'd never *been* so sincere.

He sighed. "Very well. Your husband's undoing came about through the discovery of blood on the Duke's suit of armour, more precisely, his sword." Olivia was about to interject, but the Swill boy forestalled her with a raised hand. "Originally, it was thought the Duke was attacked in his bedroom with a poisoned dagger. He had a cut on his upper arm, from which Doctor Whysman was able to determine the time of the attack: an hour either side of midnight."

"Gerald returned home at nine-thirty!" It suddenly occurred to Olivia that Gerald could be taking the blame for someone else.

"If you'll allow me to finish. *When* it was discovered the Duke had *actually* cut his arm on the sword, the focus of the investigation changed; we were no longer looking for someone who'd broken into the Duke's chambers around midnight. In fact, it made more sense to assume the poison had been administered earlier in the evening, particularly since none of the Ducal staff had seen or heard anything out of the ordinary before *or* after the Duke retired to his chamber. The poison could well have been slow acting; its delirious manifestation supports such reasoning. Therefore, it is reasonable to assume that it probably caused the Duke to become unsteady on his feet, enough, at least, to stumble against his armour."

It sounded far-fetched to Olivia. "Who discovered the blood on the blade?"

"Sir Richard made—"

"How convenient." And it *was* convenient; Richard had been embarrassed and bettered by Gerald, something he wouldn't take kindly to.

"On the contrary, the upheaval in the castle has been anything *but* convenient."

"When did Richard make this *incredible* discovery?"

The Purple Perillian's expression became guarded. "The time is irrelevant. However—"

Olivia jumped out her chair. "Of course it's relevant!" She stepped towards him. "*When* was it discovered?"

He remained silent. His reluctance only spurred Olivia on. She came to a halt less than a pace away from him. "Well?"

"Wednesday morning."

Wednesday morning! Almost *five days* after the attack! It could be *any*body's blood, put there *any* time!

"There you have it. If the crime has no evidence, then *invent* some, and be sure it incriminates the right person." Then, more contemptuously, she added, "Is *this* what it takes to become an officer of the Purple Peril? You're still just a barrel boy, except now it's *Richard* who has you over a barrel!"

She felt a sharp pain on her left cheek. He'd slapped her. She could hardly believe it. Tears welled in her eyes as the smarting blow fizzed across her face. Fortunately, he'd been somewhat restrained, because Olivia was able to hold her ground.

With tear-filled eyes, she rushed into the washroom to escape the sight of him, but she couldn't escape his caustic words: "I can well understand why your husband poisoned the Duke, Mistress Hiepants. I, too, would rather spend my life in the dungeon than be holed up with you. Even the hangman's noose would be a welcome relief from your spitefulness. Let me assure you, if we were to fabricate evidence against anyone, your husband would be well down the list. We have not schemed or manipulated — your husband poisoned the Duke, as you are *well* aware. *And* you know *full* well his reason for doing so. Do you *really* think we would contrive such a ridiculous plot. He has readily admitted his guilt. It's time you looked to *your* part in his actions."

His footsteps disappeared down the hallway. The front door opened, then slammed shut. Then there was silence. She leant against the water barrel and sobbed.

# Chapter 73
## *Behind the façade of life*

MARY WAS LYING on her bed, the noise of a Friday night crowd permeating through the walls of the bar room. She'd barely had the energy to remove her clothing before collapsing onto the mattress. She was only vaguely aware of the time. It had gone past five o'clock when Brandon escorted her from the Upper Bailey (Was he *never* off duty?) and that felt like a while ago now. The light in her room looked dusky… it must be around eight o'clock.

Occasionally, she heard noises from the kitchen — the usual crashing, smashing and yelling. But Mary had made it clear to all and sundry that she was off duty; she wasn't to be disturbed for anything short of a disaster. She'd expected a barrage of questions and complaints, but everyone seemed very understanding (which was odd, now that she thought about it). Patricia assured her the kitchen was running smoothly, Mandy told her she was enjoying playing up to the nobs (she could just imagine), Lillian said she was happy because none of the Limpdickers had shown up, nor had Prim Pet. John just kept washing dishes (wasn't that Juanita's job?) and Juanita, who appeared to be doing nothing in particular, just smiled.

Mary's head was spinning. She'd drunk far too much wine with Richard, but she couldn't fall asleep; her mind was also spinning from all the things she had and *hadn't* been told…

When Richard stood to refill the decanter, Mary joined him. She could feel the effects of the alcohol drawing her into a sleepy haze; she could only imagine how fatigued it was making Richard.

"Is that your armour?" she asked him, staring at the polished silver suit standing proudly in the corner.

"Yes," he replied, carefully pouring a bottle of red into the decanter.

It was impressive; even in shadow it seemed to gleam golden, as if the late-afternoon sun had bent its rays around the window. In fact, now that Mary was looking at it more closely, it looked alive, and she was sure it was about to move... She stumbled forwards. Then the world righted itself. *Bloody hell, how much wine had she drunk?*

If Richard noticed her unsteadiness, he didn't show it. "Not that I have worn it in the last ten years. My tournament days are over and, fortunately, we seem to be living in a time when battles are won over a banquet table."

He paused while he tipped the last drops into the decanter — it was a bottle of *Chien Extraordinaire*. The label depicted a dog balancing a goblet on its nose. Mary used to serve it at The Harey Rabbit, but her wine merchant, Vincent Quaffer, hadn't been able to obtain any in the last year. Apparently, the eponymous canine had died and the winemaker decided he could no longer make the wine (even under another name). Fraser Coin had been most disappointed — even with *his* vast network of contacts, he was unable to source any bottles. So, the fact that Richard had one...

He'd just said something to her, but her wine-filled musings had momentarily taken her away from the plush surrounds of her brother's office. All she'd managed to catch was 'expert at banquets'.

Mary flushed. "Sorry Richard; the wine... it's just... Never mind." Her words sounded confused.

He cocked a curious eyebrow.

"I'm fine. You were saying..."

"Merely that the Duke of Stymouth, being the pig that he is, is somewhat of an expert at banquets."

"I see."

Richard's expression turned dubious. "I doubt it, Mary. Then again, I doubt *anyone* in Lower Icing really appreciates the ramifications of Stymouth's visit. Even Marmaduke, with his feast full of goodwill and generous intent, doesn't truly understand what Stymouth is capable of devouring. Still, that's not something you need concern yourself with."

Richard led her back to his desk and topped up her goblet. Mary was feeling even more mentally disoriented.

"So, are you saying that Xavier's appearance has something to do with the Duke of Stymouth's visit?" Then another thought occurred to her, one that shocked her. "Richard... do you think he was *sent* by the Duke of Stymouth to spy or... worse?"

Richard shook his head. "I believe that he is, for the most part, all he claims to be. And I even believe he believes he is Marmaduke's son. Who knows, he may *well* be. However, no matter how genuine his claim, the fact remains his presence is a… complication. If Stymouth gets wind there is a blood heir to the Duchy, this banquet could well become a feeding frenzy of bad trades, increased levies, more taxes… not to mention pushing his farcical claim over Spitting Dipthong — he'd not stop until he'd picked Lower Icing's bones clean."

Mary hadn't realised the Duke's visit was anything more than just a chance for the castle-set to throw a big party. That's the way her patrons talked about it, at least; she hadn't heard any of them mention economics. (And the townsfolk didn't give a toss about what happened at the castle as long as nobody stopped them drinking.)

"Surely, Richard, you can—"

"Do absolutely nothing! Do you *really* think my position hasn't been compromised by this silver button nonsense? Stymouth will refuse to have anything to do with me."

"I thought you had caught the attacker?" Mary countered, voice rising against her brother's heated words.

Richard shook his head and smiled his sardonic smile. She hated that smile. "It makes no difference, Mary. The fact that the Duke was poisoned — on my watch — is enough to condemn me." His eyes turned inward, then he let out a sigh. "If Marmaduke doesn't survive, my position as Seneschal will be untenable." His voice was little above a whisper now. "It's taken twenty years for the Duchy to recover from the *Happy Mermaid* tragedy… to right the ship, so to speak." He smiled weakly at his poor joke. "And now, just as stability and prosperity have returned…" He gestured airily with his goblet, as if his next words were patently obvious.

Mary felt overwhelmed by the magnitude of Richard's predicament. She couldn't imagine what Lower Icing would be like without the Duke, let alone her brother.

"So you see, despite appearances to the contrary, my first and foremost concern has been for the wellbeing of Marmaduke… not *only* for the benefit of the Duchy, but because, more than *anything* else, he is my friend."

Richard slowly, almost dreamily, brought his goblet of *Chien Extraordinaire* to his lips.

Mary wasn't sure how to react; the conversation had drifted in a different direction, caught in the eddies of Richard's wine-filled exhaustion. Politics was not Mary's cup of tea; she was vaguely aware of events happening in and around the castle simply because of what she overheard at The Harey Rabbit. And patrons like Fraser Coin and the Limpdickers were always blowing their own horns. However, she had no idea about the internal workings of politics — that was one job men *could* keep for themselves.

Her brother was teetering on the edge of sleep. However, she couldn't let him fall; he still hadn't finished telling her about Xavier: how he came to be missing, the secret meeting at The Harey Rabbit and the dinner last night.

"Richard," she whispered. His drooping eyelids shot upwards and his gaze refocused. "What happened to Xavier? Tom said it was probably the Moleson Twins who—"

"Oh, spare me, Mary," he said, placing his goblet on his desk.

"—Attacked Sid and planted the silver button or key, or whatever it is, on him."

He sighed. "The Moleson Twins are just opportunist thugs."

"Opportunist thugs who almost did away with Frank Offcut in a most *calculated* manner," she countered. "I take it they also attacked Xavier. And yet—"

"Forget about the Moleson Twins," he said, wearily. "They have no real part in what's happened. Let them run off to Great Naff — good riddance, I say."

Mary was shocked. Her brother couldn't be *that* unfeeling; it must be the exhaustion talking. "Richard. Surely you don't—"

"Mary, *all* the attacks occurred because of the misguided judgement of one man. A man who thought that poisoning the Duke would *benefit* the Duchy, because his intentions were *right* and *just*. He acted without any thought to consequence and *certainly* didn't expect the vagaries of fate, misfortune, call it what you will, that brought the Moleson Twins to the back of The Bloody Bell last Friday night, where, if you can *possibly* credit it, Xavier was taking in some night air after been holed up at the bloody T—"

Richard dropped his gaze to his goblet. He'd almost let something slip. "Richard?"

He shook his head and looked towards the window. Mary followed his gaze. Most of the garden was in shade now, enveloped in the shadow of the Upper Bailey wall.

"It matters not," he said, almost to himself. "Suffice to say one action set into motion many other actions and now…" Mary looked back at her brother. He was regarding her through sleep-filled eyes. "Here we are."

Shortly after her brother's dreamy musings, they'd been interrupted by Prestwich. He'd appeared and disappeared, and then, suddenly, Brandon was in the office, apologising to Richard and her for the behaviour of his guardsmen and assuring them that they were being disciplined. He also reported that he'd just escorted the accused's wife back to her home and that she was aware of her rights. He seemed a little awkward delivering this piece of news in front of Mary. The announcement further flamed her curiosity; however, she was resigned to the fact that the identity of the accused would remain undisclosed... until tomorrow at least.

Brandon's entrance marked the end of her audience with Richard. There were so many questions left unanswered, but it was clear Richard was unwilling, and possibly unable, to continue. Brandon, of course, offered to take her home. She'd accepted, not only because she was feeling light-headed, but because it was an opportunity to delve for more information.

She apologised to Prestwich on the way out; she felt guilty when she saw the size of the bump on his forehead. He nodded a twitchy acceptance and went about his bookwork; he was an odd man.

Exiting the reception hall, Mary felt like an age had passed. The early-afternoon sun had been replaced by the shadow-splashed world of late afternoon. The air was mild, with refreshing wisps of a cool breeze carrying the sound of bees buzzing in the garden — a far cry from the comical abuse and clash of bodies that welcomed her *into* the manor house. That *did* seem like an age ago.

Brandon took her arm and led her through the Upper Bailey. They walked in silence, Mary breathing deeply, taking in the fresh air, trying to clear her head from the wine-filled stuffiness of Richard's office.

The guards at the gate were back on duty. They'd obviously escaped the *complete* wrath of Captain Le Sharp. Still, their lackadaisical attitude had disappeared. They saluted Brandon smartly, fist to heart.

"Ev'nin' sir," one of them said, and then nodded respectfully in Mary's direction, "Mistress."

Without unlinking his arm from hers, Brandon saluted back. "That's more like it, Hawkins."

As they emerged from the Upper Bailey, Mary felt a further reconnection to the 'real world'. From her elevated position, she could see rooftops beyond the northern wall of the castle, half-coated in waning sunlight. For some reason, it made her feel more relaxed. Her gaze drifted towards The Harey

Rabbit, but that view was interrupted by the towering Keep, its western face, illuminated in gold, like a giant monument to the sun, soaring spectacularly out of the greyness of the Middle Bailey.

Her thoughts shot out just as spectacularly. "I never knew Bar and Bertie were from Blessed Whipping."

She felt Brandon's arm tense against hers. "That was a long time ago," he said, defensively, "*before* I was born."

She'd obviously touched a nerve. "Excuse me, Brandon, I meant no disrespect. It's just that Richard has told me about Xavier's claim and how he was brought to The Bell from Blessed Whipping by this Bertrand character, who, from what Richard said—"

Brandon stopped walking and turned to face her. "What, exactly, *did* Sir Richard say about Bertrand?"

His tone was aggressive. It was something she'd never heard in Brandon before.

The shock must have shown on her face, because his features relaxed and his expression became one of embarrassment. "Forgive me, Mary," he said, bowing his head.

"What is it, Brandon? Who *is* this Bertrand?" She was concerned now. Who had Sid got himself mixed up with?

He looked back up at her. Then cast his eyes around the eerily quiet courtyard. "Come," he said, keeping his voice down, "let's keep moving; I shall tell you about Bertrand once we leave the castle."

As he escorted her through the Middle and Lower Baileys, Mary's mind turned again to Sid. All along, she'd believed him an innocent victim; at worst, someone who had been played for a fool (and ten gold pieces). Now, she couldn't help but wonder if he'd been playing *her* for a fool. Why else had he run off with Doctor Manky's servant if, indeed, that's who Bertrand was? She had a feeling Brandon was going to tell her something quite different.

As soon as Brandon saluted his way through the West Gate, he began talking. It was almost as if he *needed* to talk and, in Mary, he'd found someone he could confide in.

He began by revealing that Bar and Bertie had left Blessed Whipping because they'd fallen pregnant with Brandon before they'd been 'Sunblessed'. That meant, before he was even born, Brandon was marked as a 'Shade' and would not be able to hold any position of responsibility within the community, regardless of his ability.

Mary shook her head. This was bizarre. Blessed Whipping was only half a day's ride north, but it seemed like another world. How could people so close be so different? And how could she be so ignorant of their beliefs? Quite easily, it seemed, particularly since she'd only just found out about the Swills' Blessed Whippingness.

"That's unbelievable," she commented, as much to herself as the Purple Perillian on her arm.

"Yes, but the Blessed Whippingers believe in it. And none more so than Bertrand."

Instead of leading her right, into Big Wig Street, Brandon continued down Noble Street. Mary didn't question him; he obviously had quite a bit to say.

"Ma and Pa wanted to give me a life without... restrictions." Brandon was becoming quite emotional, and Mary gently squeezed his arm. He acknowledged the gesture with a twitchy half-smile. "They took passage on a passing coach and ended up at Lower Icing. A few days later, Bertrand found them at The Bell, where they'd been offered food and board in return for cleaning rooms and other odd jobs."

*Really?* Mary had thought Bar and Bertie had always *run* The Bell. Her childhood memories were of a jovial couple busy with this and that, but perhaps there *had* been an innkeeper behind the scenes.

"Bertrand was not pleased they'd left Blessed Whipping, particularly without telling anyone. He tried to convince them to come back, but they held firm. However, after spending their whole lives in Blessed Whipping, Ma and Pa weren't ready to break all ties with the community. Lower Icing was a strange place to them — chaotic and noisy — and they were unsure whether they'd made the right decision. Bertrand played on their uncertainty by telling them they would only be welcome back to Blessed Whipping if..." Brandon sighed and shook his head. He now looked angry. "If they signed a *Deed of Promise* stating that any future children born on the summer solstice would be presented to the community by their eighteenth birthday."

"What do you mean by presented?" Mary asked — it was all so odd.

They'd reached Merchant Street. She thought he might be heading for The Bell, but Brandon continued to lead her north. Noble Street narrowed once it crossed Merchant and the terraced homes became slightly less grand.

"The summer solstice, the twenty-first day of June, when the sun shines the longest, is the most important day on the Blessed Whipping calendar," Brandon explained. "The community call it Forging Day. It is a day of celebration and also marks the annual regeneration of the Sunwatcher."

"Sunwatcher?" Mary said, almost bemused by Brandon's explanation. It sounded like some sort of made-up world you'd find in children's fairy-tales.

"It is the most honoured position in the community, even more so than the Elders. Between the ages of eighteen and twenty-five, worthy Blessed Whippingers are presented to the Elders in the days leading up to Forging Day. And then one is chosen to become the next Sunwatcher."

"*Worthy* Blessed Whippingers?"

"A person must be of good character, but more important than that is the time of their birth. The closer to midday — or Sunhigh in Blessed Whipping — on Forging Day, the more likely they are to be chosen."

Mary shook her head and suddenly felt light-headed. She missed her footing and stumbled into Brandon. He held firm, saving her the embarrassment of falling over.

"Are you alright?"

She assured him that she was.

"I'm sorry, Mary," he apologised. "I have been most self-absorbed. Come, I'll take you straight back to The Harey Rabbit."

"Don't be ridiculous, Brandon," she said, freeing herself from his support. "I've just been stuck inside Richard's stuffy office all afternoon, drinking too much wine, and these shoes are... Oh, never mind. I *want* to know about Bertrand and the Blessed Whipping customs. It's fascinating. You talk as if you grew up there."

"Ma and Pa still hold true to some of their old customs," he said by way of explanation. Then, eyeing the deserted street, he whispered, "I think we should keep our voices down."

Mary fought back an urge to laugh; they were hardly discussing Duchy secrets, but it was obviously a very sensitive subject to Brandon and she didn't want to upset him. And there *were* quite a few open windows and, now that she was paying more attention, sights and sounds of life behind the façades of red-brick and timber. They'd just passed Marcus Ironcase's residence and Oliver Lawson's was just ahead. They were two of the last people she'd want overhearing her voice.

"Sorry, Brandon," she whispered, holding out her arm. "Please continue. I take it Bethany was born on Forging Day?"

"Yes," he said, linking his arm to hers, "and what made it worse, she was born within minutes of Sunhigh. That meant she would be highly favoured to become Sunwatcher and, despite not being born in Blessed Whipping, the promise was expected to be honoured."

They continued their progress down Noble Street towards Book Street, where they would have to turn right or left, because the continuation of Noble was the entrance to Lower Icing College. (The Limpdickers were LIC scholars, as were most of the young men of the castle-set, and anyone else who needed to be educated in the fine art of LIC-arse.)

Four years must have passed between the Swills signing the *Deed of Promise* and Bethany being born. "How did Bertrand find out? Couldn't your parents have lied about the day she was born?"

"Ha!" He shook his head, a look of distaste on his face. "Bertrand is an adherent: a man turned bitter by the fact that he was born premature and could never become a Sunwatcher. He visited Ma and Pa every three months, and when he found out Ma was pregnant, he stayed at The Bell for the last month of her pregnancy."

"I can't imagine Bar and Bertie putting up with that kind of scrutiny," she said, making an effort to keep her voice down, "and, in any case, I remember Bethany being born; I don't recall seeing anyone like Bertrand."

"No, you wouldn't; he kept very much to himself and left for Blessed Whipping as soon as the time of birth was confirmed by the midwife. As for my parents allowing him to stay, they were still unsure of their future — they had yet to take over the running of The Bell and fully establish themselves in Lower Icing. The Bar and Bertie of eighteen years ago were far different from the people they are today."

They were approaching Book Street. The entrance to the college was more of a gap in the ground floor of the terraced homes (although, they weren't actually homes but student accommodation for those who hailed from further afield than the town of Lower Icing). Mary wondered if a Blessed Whippinger had ever boarded at LIC. From what Brandon had told her, she very much doubted it.

The building that spanned the entrance was constructed of wattle and daub, the tar-coated wattle supporting the lime-washed daub. It was a remnant of an older Lower Icing, although there were still quite a few such dwellings in Book Street and Reader Street (which bordered the college to the west). Of note was The Burning Candle on Reader Street, the inn frequented by The Masters and scholars. Mary quite liked the character of these 'Milk and Stout' buildings, but they weren't as sturdy or weather-proof as those made from brick.

The lintel — a massive wattle beam — displayed the college's coat of arms: two open books separated by a large candle that burned at both ends. The scroll at the base of the coat of arms read 'Studium Duro', which was ancient Pastarian for 'Study Without Fail'. It sounded tedious.

Mary was about to ask Brandon when his parents had taken over the running of The Bloody Bell when three young lads suddenly appeared from Book Street. They looked surprised by her and Brandon's presence, and though they were obviously wary of her Purple Perillian escort, they weren't cowed — not enough, at least, to prevent them from looking at her appraisingly. She knew she was safe with Brandon, but she felt oddly exposed, particularly in her finery; it accentuated her femininity.

The lads, who looked between fourteen and sixteen, smiled and doffed their caps as they made their way west down Book Street. However, as they passed, they looked at each other as if weighing up their chances against Brandon. He obviously sensed it too, because his grip on her arm loosened and his free hand moved to the pommel of his sword.

That was all it took — the lads sniggered and moved on. One of them looked back and yelled out, "Cake Eater." Then they broke into a run and disappeared down Reader Street.

"Do you know them?" Mary asked.

"No, but I have a feeling I will before too long." Then he looked back at her. "Come, it's time I returned you to The Harey Rabbit."

The pace was closer to a march than a stroll as they headed down Book Street towards Market Street. Mary also wanted to keep the conversation marching along. "You were saying how Bar and Bertie aren't the people they were eighteen years ago…"

"No," he agreed. Four or five steps clacked by without further comment. Mary was about to prompt him again, but, thankfully, she didn't need to. "Shortly after Bethany was born, Ma and Pa took over the lease of The Bell. Will Scotcher, the freeholder, wanted to move to Crushing Defeat to grow grapes and make wine. I vaguely remember Will. We used to call him Hop. He was a softly spoken man, not really someone you'd expect to run an inn, and he was very generous to Ma and Pa."

Mary wondered what world she had been living in as a child; she couldn't remember anyone called Will *or* Hop. The only connection she could make was that one of the white wines served at The Harey Rabbit was called

*On The Hop* and *that* was from Crushing Defeat. Perhaps it was one of Will/ Hop Scotcher's.

"Hop didn't ask for much rent, and this allowed Ma and Pa to make a good living from The Bell. In fact, they bought the freehold from him five years later. By this time, they were feeling more at home in Lower Icing and knew it was unlikely they'd ever return to Blessed Whipping.

"However, Bertrand was an increasingly unwelcome reminder of their previous life. While his visits became somewhat irregular, there was never more than six months between them. I remember he used to just appear without warning; it put Ma and Pa on edge. He'd only stay for a night, but the *stain* of his presence seemed to last for weeks, and Bethany… she used to get *very* upset.

"Eventually, it reached the stage where Ma and Pa had had enough and they told Bertrand he was no longer welcome at The Bell. He wasn't happy about it, and I think he threatened Pa in some way, because Pa… Well, it's the only time I've ever seen him lose his temper… and I mean *really* lose his temper. Not the bluster he uses for unruly pissheads, but…"

Brandon paused, seemingly lost in thought.

Mary said nothing; she was still absorbing what he'd told her: the life behind the façade of life. It was true of everybody, though, including herself. This Bertrand character sounded like an evil man, and Sid had jumped into a carriage with him.

"…That was about five years ago. We didn't see him again for four years, not until this time last year, just after Bethany turned seventeen."

They were approaching Market Street. Straight ahead, the wall of shops and buildings was broken by the empty marketplace. Most of it was bathed in deepening gold sunlight, but the creeping shadows were on their way to claiming the cobbled ground. Tomorrow, however, the deserted space would be reborn, filled to the last cobblestone with stalls, carts, barrows and the hubbub of supply and demand.

"In fact, it was the day after Forging Day; he just appeared out of the blue, so to speak, while Ma and Bethany were hanging out the washing. He told them he was in Lower Icing to lodge the *Deed of Promise* with the Office of Legalities and looked forward to seeing Bethany at Blessed Whipping in time for next year's Forging Day. Then he was gone."

They reached Market Street and turned right. Some one hundred paces ahead, The Bloody Bell was in full swing — the spillage of people outside, the raucous voices within — as it always was on a Friday when the market was closed. It shattered the illusion of a peaceful town settled down for the evening.

"They told Pa, and he bolted after Bertrand, hoping to intercept him before he reached the Office of Legalities, but the Elder was nowhere to be found. And, as far as he was told, no-one of Bertrand's description had been seen at the Office of Legalities. He'd just gone."

*Yes,* Mary thought — she'd seen how fast he could move; he'd outsprinted Sid.

"Mind you, those who work in the Office of Legalities are hardly forthcoming with information, so Pa came to see me. I'd been living at the barracks for over a year by then. He wanted me to find out if the Deed had been lodged, to use my position of authority, as he called it. Trouble was, my position as patrolman afforded me very little in the way of authority, particularly with the Office of Legalities. So, I sought out a more... informed source."

Mary's thoughts went immediately to her brother. She voiced as much.

Her words, however, were met with a non-committal grunt and she wondered if Richard had exacerbated the situation somehow.

"It was Humphrey Tumbridge-Wills who assured me that, as far as he was aware, there was no such legal document as a *Deed of Promise.*"

Mary knew Humphrey — he was an irregular regular, occasionally coming in for afternoon tea and scones. Very well spoken, *when* he actually spoke. Most of the time he read a book or observed the comings and goings across the Town Square from his favoured window booth. Occasionally, he would share some historical fact with Mary, and it was usually quite interesting.

"And since no-one has a greater knowledge of Lower Icing's legal history, I was able, to some extent, to allay everyone's fears about Bertrand claiming Bethany as Sunwatcher.

"However, as Bethany's eighteenth birthday drew nearer, the fear of confronting Bertrand and his bloody Deed increased. On the eve of Forging Day, the tension was so great that Bethany locked herself in her room and refused to open it for anyone."

"Poor Bethany," Mary thought out loud. "To think this happened only two weeks ago."

Brandon confirmed this with a nod.

"But Bertrand didn't arrive until—"

"The early hours of Sunday morning," Brandon finished for her, "when he deposited Xavier at the doorstep of The Bell. He must have left Blessed Whipping shortly after Sunfall on Forging Day."

"Yes," Mary agreed, "Richard told me about Xavier's arrival and his claim. What do you make of it, Brandon? Do you think he's the Duke son, or is it an elaborate plot?"

By now they were approaching The Bell and their voices had grown louder to compete with the revelry spewing out of the establishment. They had also drawn the attention of the drunken mob loitering around the corner entry.

"In truth, I'm not sure. He is a most impressive young man and certainly a very learned individual. I think he genuinely believes—"

"Wey-hey, Lieutenan'!" cried one of the mob. "Hooked y'self a pretty lookin' fish there."

The rest of them followed with a drunken cheer. Mary smiled; she'd never had *that* kind of reaction from The Bloody Bell boys before. Whether it was because of the way she was dressed or the fact she was on Brandon's arm made little difference; she felt quite chuffed by the attention. Mind you, she was still feeling light-headed.

Brandon also appeared to take the banter in good humour.

Then someone added, "'As 'e asked ya t'blow 'is 'orn yet, love?"

This was followed by uproarious laughter.

Mary also let out a giggle. However, she could feel Brandon's arm tense.

"Yeah," someone else joined in, "three quick blows an' you'll 'ave the whole *squad* t'deal wiv."

This brought about even more hilarity, and Mary couldn't help but join in. Brandon seemed less amused, but managed to eke out an indulgent smile as they passed through the mob.

Then one of them blurted out, "Bleedin 'eck! Tha's Harey Mary."

"Shurrup, Donger," said another inebriated voice. It was quickly followed by a smacking sound and an "Ow" (presumably from Donger).

Mary wasn't offended in the slightest, but she looked for her defender amongst the faces that floated around her.

Most of the men now looked a bit sheepish, realising it *was* Mary. She'd never heard anyone call her Harey Mary before, but one man had removed his cap and was looking particularly contrite. And he was standing next to a man who was rubbing his ear. "Your pardon, Mishtress Mary," he said, unsteadily. "'E meant no offence, like."

Mary halted, but was carried forward by Brandon's momentum. She almost stumbled again, but the Purple Perillian's reactions were much better than hers, particularly in her current state.

"None taken," Mary assured the considerate reveller. "What's your name?"

She could feel Brandon gently pulling at her arm.

"Rufus 'Ardbolt, Mishtress," he replied.

"Well, thank you for your consideration, Master Hardbolt. Should you ever feel inclined to visit The Harey Rabbit, I would gladly buy you a drink."

Rufus looked a bit embarrassed. "Shank you, Mishtress," he mumbled.

Mary smiled. She was feeling quite delighted with her suggestion; Rufus would make a nice change from all the stuck-up castle-set.

"Come along, Mary," Brandon said, tugging harder at her arm, "before Sir Richard's wine gives you an even *bigger* headache."

"Oh, very good, Brandon." She laughed and allowed him to pull her away. "Enjoy your evening, gentlemen."

As they departed the mob, the revelry resumed and she heard one of them say, "You tosser, Soft Nut."

"Let's hope he doesn't take you up on your offer, Mary," Brandon said once they'd moved a few paces away. Mary just smiled.

They were heading towards the well, when Brandon veered to his left and moved towards the News Stand. "Excuse me, Mary. I wish to check something."

He walked up to wooden structure and peered through the glass cover that protected the proclamations within. He paused only briefly, but seemed satisfied with what he saw. "Just wanted to see if the panel had been replaced," he said by way of explanation as they continued across the square.

Mary nodded, somewhat bemused that Brandon would be concerned by such a trivial thing. Then she tried to focus her thoughts; the mob had distracted her and the wine was affecting her concentration. "What were we talking about, Brandon?" she asked.

He gave her a wry smile. "I believe I was banging on about Bertrand and his bloody *Deed of Promise*."

That's right: all those strange Blessed Whipping customs. "Richard certainly doesn't trust him. I think he wishes he never made him one of his observers."

Brandon let go of Mary's arm and halted. "One of *his* observers; he *called* him that?"

Mary was taken aback by his reaction. It even drew the attention of a couple of women refilling their buckets at the well. He grabbed her arm and pulled her towards The Harey Rabbit.

"Brandon?"

He didn't answer until they were at least ten paces from the well; out of earshot, she assumed.

"The Gamekeeper referred to Bertrand as a Blessed Whipping observer, but I thought…" he said, almost to himself. Then he refocused on her. "So, what *did* Sir Richard tell you about *his* observer?" His voice was calm, but there was an urgent undertone. "Did he mention a letter he'd received from him? Did he say whether he—"

"Brandon!" Mary's head was spinning; the sun sitting just above the roof tops shimmered in her eyes. She shaded them with her right hand. His gaze was intensely expectant. "I don't know anything about a letter. Richard didn't mention anything about a letter to me, save for the one Xavier had shown him."

He suddenly looked preoccupied, mulling things around inside his head.

"Brandon?" she prompted.

Again his gaze refocused. "I'm sorry, Mary; most unbecoming of me — your pardon."

Mary was more confused than upset. "Clearly something's amiss. What is it?"

"Come, I shall see you to your door." He reached for her arm, but Mary moved away from him.

"I think I can make it across The Square without your assistance, Brandon," she said, annoyed by his dismissive tone.

"My apologies," he intoned.

His sudden formality irked her. "I don't want your apologies." Then her voice rose another level. "I want an explanation!"

Bizarrely, this was followed by clapping. Mary's gaze shot towards the source. The women at the well were regarding them with stern expressions.

"You tell 'im love!" one of them yelled out.

"They're all the bleedin' same," added the second.

Brandon responded by walking away, towards The Harey Rabbit. Mary stepped after him.

"In this letter," he said, "Bertrand threatened Sir Richard with 'drastic action' if he didn't ratify the *Deed of Promise*, which, he stated, he'd lodged three months ago."

"What?" Mary suddenly felt ill. The realisation that Bertrand and possibly Sid had… Richard must have arrested the wrong man, assuming, of course, it *was* Bertrand she'd seen with Sid. "So, are you saying that Bertrand is responsible for poisoning the Duke?"

"No," he said, "as much as I would like it to be the case."

"But, surely…?"

"As you are aware, Mary," he said, coming to a halt outside the courtyard gate, "we have arrested the culprit."

Mary was more confused than ever. Then what *was* Bertrand threatening to do, and what part did Sid play in his drastic actions?

"Now, I must leave you. There's a pressing matter I must attend to."

He began to walk off at pace.

"Brandon!" she called after him. He stopped and turned around, his expression impatient. "What does Bertrand look like?" She was feeling queasy.

He began walking back towards her. "Mary. Are you—?"

"Small, about fifty years of age, bald on top, feathery hair along the sides, looks like a bird?"

Brandon nodded. So, there was no doubt then: it *was* Bertrand she'd seen with Sid.

"Mary?" he said, moving closer.

"I saw him leave Lower Icing today with… Sid Evily."

"What?" His gaze was intent as he drew next to her. "When?"

Was the time significant, she wondered. "Midday."

"Does Sir Richard know?"

*Had* she told him? No, she'd just listened. She shook her head.

He nodded, but the muscles in his jaw were twitching. "Well, even *more* reason to disturb Sir Richard."

"Brandon, are you confident Richard has arrested the right man?"

"Yes," he replied without hesitation. "However, in this case, I believe the right man is actually the wrong man." He regarded her for a moment, as if he was about to reveal more, then said, "I must go."

She nodded, even though she was still none the wiser about the secret dinner on Wednesday night, and how that transpired into the castle dinner and the subsequent arrest of the Duke's attacker.

Mary watched in silence as he disappeared around the corner of The Harey Rabbit. Truth be told, like Brandon, she was more concerned about Bertrand… and what influence he had over Sid.

The last vestiges of light were playing meekly upon her Gliteratti figurines.

The shapes were obvious, but, in the creeping molasses, the intricate detail was only hinted at. Similarly, Richard and Brandon's words had given Mary an impression of a story that was undoubtedly much more complex.

## CHAPTER 74

## *Caught the flame*

OLIVIA LAY IN the bath until the water became cool and the night had well and truly settled in. She soaked away the grime and odour of the previous twenty-four hours, while her mind wandered through a myriad of 'if onlys'.

The wretched silence. She wanted to cry out, vent her frustration and fill the void with some sort of emotion. As she clambered out of the bathtub, the sloshing water seemed to echo from every empty corner of the house.

She wrapped herself in a towel, grabbed the nearly spent chamberstick, and walked upstairs. This was the first time since her marriage that she'd emerged from the washroom without a modicum of modesty. Right now, she couldn't care less; the only reason for the towel was warmth.

Olivia went straight to her dressing room, opened the chest that contained her undergarments, and removed a cotton nightdress. Under the faceless scrutiny of her dressmaker's dummy, she freed herself of the towel and put on a plain, knee-length shift. Picking up the chamberstick from the floor, she turned to exit the room. As she faced the door, she caught sight of herself in the dressing table mirror. She looked like a spectre in the dim candlelight. The white shift seemed ethereal, and her washed-out visage looked haunted — she couldn't bear to look at herself. She needed sleep. She needed the silent night to be over.

Olivia moved back into the passageway and noticed something out of place: there was a key in the door to the den. It shouldn't be there. Olivia had left it, as she always did when they left the house, hidden amongst her sewing bits 'n' bobs. Yes… she'd *definitely* left it there last night while she and Gerald had been readying themselves for the dinner.

She didn't try the key. There was no need: the door opened as she turned the knob. The flickering candlelight revealed nothing out of the ordinary; everything in the den seemed to be as it should be, as neat and ordered as she had left it.

Olivia walked over to the desk. Her shadowy, candlelit image reflected in the window as she approached. Casting her gaze across the desktop, *Do Well-To-Do Well* lay beside her unfinished letter to Petronella Whysman.

*Dear Petronella,*

*It is with great pleasure that I accept your kind invitation to morning tea next Wednesday at 10 o'clock. I am looking forward to seeing the new drapery that you*

It seemed ages since she'd written those words. It certainly felt like another life, where such things as drapery seemed quite important. She picked up the letter and held it over the candle, watched it catch alight, and then let it go. It danced towards the floorboards as it smoked and burned. It was poetic in a way: an allegory of a life no longer accessible to her.

"Happy Birthday, Olivia," she whispered to the blackening remnant of parchment. Thirty-three, and her future had never felt so bleak. Not even as a child with a drunken mother and… Sid! After everything she'd done for him! It was *his* fault she was here in *this* place… alone on *this* day… when she should have been in a *different* place living a *different* life with… a *different* man.

Olivia's attention turned back to *Do Well-To-Do Well*. Placing the chamberstick on the desk, she leant over and opened the window. The air was fresh, but she no longer felt cold. Sitting down at the desk, facing the evening outside, she flicked through the book until she found 'Caviar and Sangfroid'. She grasped the chapter's title page and tore it from the stitched binding. It came away surprisingly neatly — Lady Le Fleur *would* be impressed. She crumpled the page in her hand and held it over the candle until it caught the flame. She waited until the heat became too much to bear before throwing the flaming ball of parchment out the window. She repeated the process for the next eighteen pages of 'Caviar and Sangfroid'.

By the time the last page flared from view, the room reeked of smoke and her right hand was hurting. Olivia was feeling quite hot now; enough to feel perspiration on her forehead. She regarded the neatly mutilated book — a quarter of an inch of exposed binding the only sign of the missing pages. The next chapter's heading was entitled 'Dainties and Daintiness'.

Olivia began to laugh, and then cough as she inhaled some smoke. It was quite surprising, really, considering the open window. Suddenly there was a loud whoosh and the room exploded into light… and heat.

She jumped off the chair and turned to see six years' worth of proclamations engulfed in flames. She tried to reach the door, but the heat and smoke were too much. She had to back away into the corner of the room, using her arm to block the smoke from her nose and mouth. Her eyes were beginning to water as she wedged herself between the desk and the wall. Olivia watched — almost mesmerised — as the fire consumed her pin cushion and Gerald's novelty tankards. Then there was a loud crack as the Town Crier statue succumbed to the heat.

The noise snapped her out of her reverie; she could feel the heat singeing her eyebrows, and the smoke… a lot of it was escaping out the window. If she wanted to survive, she would have to do the same.

There was a foot gap between the edge of the desk and the window, easily wide enough for Olivia to sidle along. She turned her back on the fire and edged her way to the window. It felt like a hot wind was blowing against her back; the whooshing sound of parchment erupting into flame was terrifying and the smoke… She could barely breathe; it felt like all the air was being sucked out of the room.

It was only a few sidesteps to the window, but each seemed to be in slow motion. She could smell burning hair. She reached the window: a three-foot-wide opening, the sill at waist height. Manoeuvring into the opening was awkward, especially with the smoke billowing around her. Instead of trying to stretch her leg over the sill, she clambered onto the desk. Fortunately, her nightdress was light, her movement unencumbered, and she managed to position herself on her hands and knees after pushing *Do Well-To-Do Well* out of the way. Then she edged backwards, legs straddling the gap between the desk and the sill. She kept her head down and felt the heat licking the back of her neck. More cracking of porcelain accompanied her escape out the window.

Olivia held her breath and squeezed her eyes shut. Her shift began to ride up as her thighs scraped over the sill, but she continued; she simply had no choice. Her legs were stretched out horizontally into the night air, but, as her hips edged over the sill, her legs swung down and made contact with the outside wall. However, there was nothing for her feet to rest upon. She was dangling precariously.

Olivia felt the panic rising as she scrambled for purchase; with her eyes shut tight, everything around her was noise and heat. And then, of course, there was the smoke. She didn't dare take a breath, even though her lungs were crying out for her to do so.

Another whoosh was followed by a loud crash and a flare of heat. Fear propelled Olivia backwards, her hands finding purchase on the sill while the rest of her body dangled against the outside wall. She gasped in relief and, in doing so, inhaled a mouthful of smoke, her lungs catching on fire. She lost her grip on the sill and fell. The world tumbled into darkness, and suddenly, everything seemed quite peaceful. Then something on her right side went *crack*.

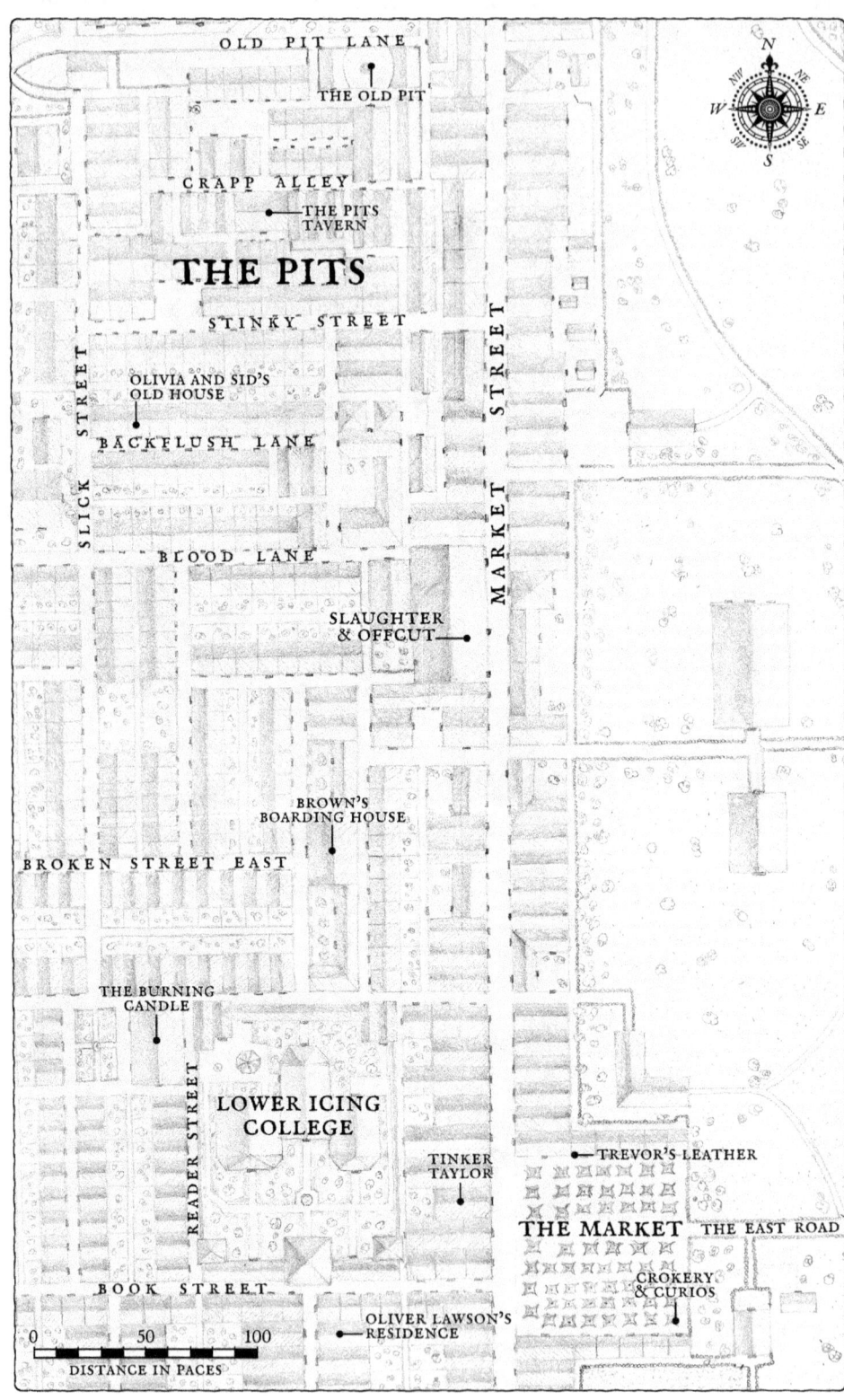

OLD PIT LANE

THE OLD PIT

CRAPP ALLEY

THE PITS
TAVERN

# THE PITS

STINKY STREET

OLIVIA AND SID'S
OLD HOUSE

SLICK STREET

BACKFLUSH LANE

MARKET STREET

BLOOD LANE

SLAUGHTER
& OFFCUT

BROWN'S
BOARDING HOUSE

BROKEN STREET EAST

THE BURNING
CANDLE

READER STREET

LOWER ICING
COLLEGE

TINKER
TAYLOR

TREVOR'S LEATHER

THE MARKET    THE EAST ROAD

BOOK STREET

CROKERY
& CURIOS

OLIVER LAWSON'S
RESIDENCE

0        50        100

DISTANCE IN PACES

# SATURDAY, JULY 5

## CHAPTER 75

## *Not out here picking bluebells*

THE MOMENT OF departure came sooner than any of them expected. Ophelia woke to the sound of her pa's laboured breathing. Tom, a shadow in the darkness, was hovering over him, in the process of placing a cloth on his forehead.

"Pa?" She shot up, realisation exploding through her grogginess. "Tom?" she cried, scrambling towards the supine silhouette. She reached her pa's side and felt the heat coming from him.

"He's come down with a fever," Tom said.

Her stomach fell. "Fever? Wha' sorta fever?"

"Don't know," Tom sounded concerned. "One of his wounds may have become infected… hard to tell."

Infected! People died from infections! "Is he gonna be alrigh'?" Her heart was pounding. Her hands were shaking. She placed one of them over the cloth (Tom had soaked it in cold water). Then she touched her pa's face. It was burning; the embers of the fire cast a dark-red glow across his features. Tom hadn't answered her.

"Tom?"

"We'll just have to wait and see. We need to keep him cool."

Gradually, her pa's breathing had become more relaxed and his temperature returned to somewhere near normal. He even managed a few gulps of water, but he was not well. She sat beside him, occasionally dabbing his neck and chest.

"I think we should break camp," Tom said.

She'd completely lost track of time, had no idea how long they'd been up. She'd been vaguely aware of Tom moving around the campsite doing… things, but she'd been attending to her pa… It must be near daybreak if Tom was readying to… Then it registered. "Break camp? Wha' you on abou', Tom —

we can't move 'im in *this* state."

"He needs a doctor, Ophelia."

"He'll need a bleedin' undertaker if we try an' move 'im."

"He'll recover from his injuries, but if there's an infection… the longer it remains untreated, the more chance…"

"Ain't you got nothin' y'can use?"

"I've done all I can; he needs a doctor."

Ophelia didn't trust doctors; they used words she didn't understand, banged on about humours and the like, and more often than not resorted to some wild concoction of foul-tasting medicine. Either that or the bloody leeches came out. But, if Tom thought her pa needed one, then she wasn't about to argue. Gazing back at her pa's battered face, his left cheek twitching as he slept, Ophelia nodded in muted agreement. Then she felt a gentle hand on her shoulder.

"Like he said, he's a tough old bastard; he'll be right once he's had a few days in a nice soft bed, with you and your ma fussing over him."

Her throat tightened; she hoped Tom was right. Right now, he looked about as tough as a new-born lamb. A tear ran down her cheek. She reached up and squeezed Tom's hand; he *was* a good man.

"See if you can rouse him, while I finish packing the horses."

It took a bit of urging and shaking, but eventually she managed to wake him. Once he was back in the land of the living, Ophelia was quite surprised by his alertness.

"Bloody 'ell, Pheel… it's the middle of the bleedin' nigh'." He struggled to prop himself up against the tree; the effort was obvious and his breathing was ragged. "An' I ain't feelin' too bright neither."

"You wanted t'get an' early start, Pa." She spoke softly. "This way we'll be 'ome in time for one of Ma's big breakfasts."

"S'pose." He puffed.

Half an hour later, they were on their way… just. They'd had to hoist her pa onto the saddle; he'd barely had enough strength to lift his leg over. But after a lot of grunting and swearing, her pa finally sat atop Wildflower. Neither rider nor horse looked at ease.

It wasn't safe to ride in the dark, at least until they cleared the trees, so Tom led Wildflower on foot and Ophelia followed with Hazel. She kept a close eye on her pa. He was slumped on the saddle, swaying like a closing-time drunk.

He looked like he might topple off, but he assured them he was able to stay upright. Still, Tom had taken the precaution of strapping her pa's boots to the stirrups, so if he *did* topple, at least he wouldn't hit the ground.

It was dark, but it was fairly easy going. There was enough moonlight to make out shapes. Low branches, fallen limbs, rabbit holes and other obstacles were avoided without mishap. They stopped regularly to check on her pa. There was no doubt he was struggling; he was sweating and grumbling about being tied to an oversized nag that was jolting every bone in his body.

"C'n we get this bleedin' show on the road, Gamekeeper," he complained after they'd stopped for the fourth time. But there was no venom in it — his voice sounded weak.

Ophelia was worried, and wondered if her pa would be better off resting for a while. She was going to suggest it, but Tom thought differently. "The road is not far off," he said. "Best keep going at walking pace until then."

"Rather take me chances gettin' hit by a branch than tip-toe around every blade o' grass."

"Yes, but it's not just *you*, Frank. There is Ophelia and the horses to consider."

Lucky for him he'd mentioned *her* before the horses; she doubted he would have a few days ago.

"In any case, first light is only an hour away."

Her pa groaned.

It was nearly daybreak by the time they reached the road. Her pa had barely muttered a word in the last half an hour. It wasn't a good sign.

Tom was in the process of unfastening his boots from the stirrups. "All being well," he said, "we should be back in Lower Icing in an hour."

"Bloody 'ell," her pa grumbled, but it was like he was talking in his sleep.

Ophelia was holding Hazel's reins, contemplating being on horseback again. She looked up at her pa slumped on the saddle, head lolling, eyes closed, a sheen of sweat around his face and neck. "Pa?"

"Wha?" he muttered, groggily.

So he *was* awake. "Jus' checkin' you're alrigh'"

"'Course I ain't alrigh'!" His head snapped up, eyes open and focused. "Been sittin' on this friggin' nag too friggin' long! My arse feels like it's 'ad ten types of shit kicked out of it!"

Ophelia was taken aback by his sudden energy and lucidness, but she took it as a good sign; perhaps his body was starting to win the fight if his main grievance was being astride Wildflower. Still, she could certainly relate to how he was feeling — saddle soreness was painful. And *that*, coupled with his injuries and fever… she marvelled at his resilience. However, resilient or not, the sooner they got him back home the better.

"Are you ready, Ophelia?" Tom asked.

She nodded. "Yes, Tom."

"What about you, Frank?"

He sighed. "Jus' bleedin' get on wiv it."

Tom helped Ophelia mount Hazel. Not that she needed helping, of course, but it was nice to be treated like a lady. Then he leapt on top of Wildflower, positioning himself at the rear of the saddle, her grimacing pa squeezed in front of him. With a couple of clicks of his tongue and a nudge of his heels, Wildflower jumped into a canter. Ophelia did neither action, but Hazel followed anyway.

They'd been on the North Road for at least half an hour. The purple gloom of a breaking dawn surrounded them; to her left, the waking pink sky flashed between passing trees. Ophelia was beginning to feel uncomfortable again — cantering on a hard dirt road was entirely different to walking across a soft forest floor.

She had fallen into a sort of reverie. The road had barely changed, just seemed to go on, heading south. She thought Lower Icing might have magically appeared with the dawning day, but all she could see in front of them was the road and the trees that surrounded the road. And then, out of nowhere, a man appeared, standing in their path.

The man yelled out for them to hold. Wildflower took the surprise in her stride. Hazel, however, reared, and *that* took *Ophelia* by surprise. She pulled on the reins, more for balance than any controlled manoeuvre. By the time Hazel had settled, Tom had drawn his sword.

The man was dressed scruffily in black: a smudge in the dawning gloom. "Peace be with you, travellers," he said, holding up his hands to show he was unarmed.

Ophelia wasn't convinced, however; he looked like some sort of confidence trickster. Probably had a dozen men secreted away in the bushes, waiting for the right moment to—

"Is that you, Sid Evily?" Tom's incredulous tone rang through her wariness.

The man looked equally disbelieving — obviously he *was* Sid Evily.

His posture relaxed. "Tom? What the…?"

"My sentiments exactly," Tom replied, sheathing his sword.

The scruff in black cast an appraising eye in Ophelia's direction while moving towards Tom and her pa. "What are you doing out here?"

"It's a long story."

Why was Tom wasting time with this vagabond? They needed to keep moving. The man smiled knowingly, and then he took a closer look at her pa. "Bloody hell! Is that Frank Offcut? What hap—?"

"Yeah, it bloody well is!" Ophelia cut in. She didn't like his tone, *and* he was regarding her pa like he was some prize catch on a hunt. "An' we ain't got time for no more pleasantries."

"Sid, this is Frank's daughter."

"Ophelia," Sid said, his smile returning.

Bloody Nora, was she *that* well known around town. She'd never met or heard of Sid Evily, yet he'd obviously heard of her. Were men *really* that friggin' basic? Judging by Tom's reddening face, he was in no doubt as to why Sid was smiling. He sounded pleasingly defensive when he announced, "We are on a matter of some urgency and importance, Sid."

"Well, I'm not out here picking bluebells, Tom."

He said it in a light-hearted-yet-serious kind of way. So, what *was* he doing out here? Tom glanced in her direction; he looked like he had the same question in mind.

"Tom," she said, making sure he registered her eagerness to be moving on.

Sid regarded them with a mixture of bemusement and curiosity.

"Your pardon, Sid," said Tom. "Apart from Frank, there are other vital matters to attend to."

The man in black arched an eyebrow, looking like a scruffy version of Sir Richard. "Really. Wouldn't have anything to do with the Duke being poisoned or a young doctor claiming to be his son?"

Tom remained silent, but his expression said it all.

*Bloody hell,* Ophelia thought, *the shit was about to fly in all directions.*

Her pa groaned.

If Ophelia felt uncomfortable riding Hazel by herself, she felt *doubly* so with Sid Evily pressed against her back, squeezing her into the pommel. The jolting canter wasn't helping either. Still, at least at this pace, they'd be back in Lower Icing quicker, and that was all she really cared about.

Before they'd ridden off, Tom had offered (on her behalf) a share of her saddle (something for which he'd pay later). Sid had wheedled a ride after explaining his bizarre appearance on the North Road…

"I've just parted company with one Doctor Horatio Manky," Sid explained. "He approached me at The Dead Duck just over a week ago and offered me ten gold coins to provide him with information."

Ophelia thought he spoke particularly well for someone who was clearly not noble. Perhaps he was a disgraced noble. His fine boots and ornate belt, like his voice, also seemed to be at odds with his overall appearance.

He was standing between Wildflower and Hazel, but his gaze and attention were solely on Tom, and Tom appeared… interested. *That* was not a good sign, particularly when her pa was clearly ailing, his head lolling forward, barely conscious.

"Tom," she said, butting in before the conversation could take hold. He glanced over, and she flicked her head in the direction of Lower Icing. However, he continued to converse with the posh scruff.

"What kind of information?"

"He didn't say; just suggested I speak to Gerald Hiepants, to see if there was anything unusual happening in the castle."

Their casual banter had turned serious. "Was this *before* the Duke was…?" Tom stopped himself, looking somewhat self-conscious.

Sid looked in her direction, then back at Tom. "We can talk in private, if you'd prefer, Tom."

"No y'bleedin' well can't! Pa needs a doctor!" She glared at Tom. "Or 'ave y'forgotten tha'?"

Tom regarded her pa. "Ophelia has the right of it, Sid."

She felt a moment of relief, before Tom continued with, "Hop up on Hazel; you can ride with Ophelia."

"What the frig? 'E ain't—"

"Sounds good to me," Sid agreed.

Piss off. Was he joking? "Yeah, well it don' sound good t'*me*."

Both men were looking at her. Sid wore a mischievous smile, Tom a concerned frown.

"Lower Icing is not far, Ophelia," said Tom. "Half an hour if we keep a good pace."

"For frig's sake, Tom!"

He paid no heed to her protestation, directing his next comment to the man between the horses. "We can discuss Doctor Manky and the Town Crier when we arrive back at Lower Icing."

Sid nodded, then regarded her pa. "So, what happened to Frank?"

"Got on the wrong side of Sir Richard bloody Upson is wha'."

Tom countered with, "It was the Moleson Twins."

"The Moleson Twins? What was *their* beef with Frank?" He flicked a quick smile at Ophelia. "If you'll excuse the expression."

Ophelia glowered at him.

"The same beef they had with *you*, Sid," said Tom.

Sid whirled around to face him. "What? It was the *Moleson Twins* who bashed me?"

Tom nodded. "A case of being in the wrong place at the wrong time. Just like Frank here."

Yeah, only because her pa was *forced* to be in the wrong place at the wrong time.

"Are you saying it was the Moleson Twins who attacked the Duke? Why didn't anyone—"

"It wasn't the Moleson Twins." Tom cast a wary look in Ophelia's direction. And he was right to look wary; they still hadn't friggin' moved!

"Who, then? If those bastards planted that bloody silver button on me, *they* must know who attacked the Duke."

"The button is unrelated to the attack on the Duke. In any case, they've scarpered off to Naffolk."

"Naffolk! What the frig is going on, Tom? Who is—?"

Ophelia had had enough. "I'll tell you what the frig is goin' on. Pa's ailin' in front of y'friggin' eyes and both ovya are bleetin' on about a bloody silver button!"

They both stared at her; Sid looked amused, Tom chastised.

"Either o' you say 'another word an' this 'orse is headin' t'Lower Icing withou' Sid friggin' Evily; don' care *wha'* 'e knows. Don' care 'bout them Moleson Twins nor no friggin' doctor neither, 'less 'e's fixin' up my pa."

Her pa chose that moment to cough and moan. He looked terrible, bound to the strapping of his saddle, cradled between Tom's arms — his poor damaged face and blistered head. Even in the cool gloom, he looked as if he was burning up.

Suddenly, Sid was grabbing the back of Hazel's saddle and swinging himself up on the mare. He positioned himself in front of the cantle and slipped forwards, forcing Ophelia to squash up against the pommel. This was going to be a very long half an hour.

Surprisingly, he asked after her comfort. Her response was to nudge Hazel into motion. She winced at the mare's staggering start, but eventually Hazel found her rhythm and the pommel pummelling receded into rhythmic discomfort.

Tom drew Wildflower close to Hazel to see how Ophelia was faring, raising his voice to be heard over the thudding hooves. Ophelia kept her gaze focused on the jolting road ahead, raised her left hand and extended her middle finger.

Sid barked out a laugh, while Tom steered Wildflower back to the centre of the road.

"An y'can frig off an' all," she yelled at the man pressing against her back.

He leaned forward and spoke into her right ear. "You should take Frank to see Manky. He's deranged, but he has some bloody good curatives."

Ophelia kept her eyes on the road ahead; she wasn't interested in anything except getting her pa home in one piece.

"He fixed me up, and my face was in a sight worse shape than your pa's."

How would *he* friggin' know how bad her pa's injuries were. She was tempted to fling her head back and smack him one. "Yeah, well it will be again if y'don' stop yellin' in my ear!"

That did the trick; her unwanted passenger leant back and kept his head behind hers. Ophelia focused on the road ahead and tried to ignore the rubbing saddle.

## CHAPTER 76

### *Just a sip*

**T**HE NEXT LIFE was light grey and softly billowing. It was like she was drifting along a corridor of wispy curtains. Now that she was concentrating, she could make out the fine lacework of the material. A feeble light shone behind them and they smelled of roses. She inhaled the sweet perfume... so much sweeter than the smoke. Thank goodness that was all behind her.

However, her mouth still felt dry. That seemed... strange. She'd have thought she *wouldn't* have dry mouth. She swallowed and felt an intense, prickly pain down her throat. Her body jerked, and the world erupted into spots of searing white light as a spasm of agony pulsed through her head and side. At first, all she could do was gasp — every muscle tensed, and she felt constricted. Then, as the pain subsided and the white spots began to fade, the lace curtains came back into view and the smell of roses returned, but now they were tainted with the scent of burnt hair.

Olivia wanted to cry out, but she could manage little more than a whisper and even *that* hurt. Her throat was parched. She needed water, but dreaded the thought of swallowing again. In fact, she didn't want to move a single muscle.

She closed her eyes. It couldn't have been more than a few seconds, but when she opened them again, Petronella Whysman was staring at her. Her expression could only be described as grave.

"Petro..." She couldn't manage the last two syllables; the room may have smelled of rose petals, but it felt like a *stem* was stuck in her throat.

"Hush, my dear," Petronella whispered kindly, though clearly she was concerned. "Albert says you mustn't speak; just to drink water if you are able."

Her friend hovered over her as if waiting for a response.

Olivia nodded; as sore as her throat was, she had never felt so thirsty.

Petronella seemed pleased by her response, and moved towards the side table. As Olivia turned her head to watch her, she felt a hot rawness on the back of her neck, the smell of burnt hair wafting with the movement. How badly was she burnt?

Petronella poured some water from an earthenware jug into a cup that was sitting on the bedside table. Next to the cup was an inkwell, quill and parchment. Perhaps they intended her to write out her will. That is, if there was anything left to leave. Everything in the study had gone. What of her clothes? Her home?

"Here, my dear," Petronella said, holding out the cup. Olivia's head was tilted up, supported by a number of pillows, but it was still an awkward position from which to drink. She attempted to push herself upright, but as soon as she moved, a stabbing pain shot through her right side; so much so that it took her breath away. She gasped in pain. Now it felt like a handful of dressmaking pins had lodged in her throat.

"Olivia!" Petronella gasped in shock.

Tears welled in her eyes and even *they* hurt. The pain receded quickly, but it left Olivia in fear of moving any part of her body.

"Oh my poor dear; what pain you are in I cannot begin to imagine." Petronella sat on the edge of the bed, gazing down at her sympathetically. "But take comfort; Albert assures me you will recover." She extended the cup towards Olivia's lips. "Here, my dear, water will help your throat."

Despite her thirst, she wasn't sure she could bring herself to drink it.

"It is cold and will help soothe the burn," she added, holding the cup near Olivia's closed mouth.

It made sense, but the thought of swallowing…

"Just a sip," her friend encouraged.

Somehow, her lips parted and the rim of the cup found its way between them. Then she felt a wet trickle run across her tongue. Petronella was right: the water *was* cold. Deliciously cold, in fact, refreshing her mouth like the rain on her sun-scorched garden. The water was beginning to pool in her mouth; pleasure was about to turn into pain. Steeling herself, she allowed the water to fall down her throat. For a moment, the sensation was of cool relief. Then came the involuntary action of swallowing, and relief was replaced by raw, prickling pain. Still, it was… manageable; the cold water dulled the intensity.

Petronella winced sympathetically and withdrew the cup.

Olivia shook her head. "More," she rasped.

As she took some more tentative sips, the irony of the situation occurred to her: the fire had started from her careless discarding of the unfinished acceptance to Petronella's morning tea and drapery viewing. She looked towards the drawn curtains hanging lightly in the early morning light — fine white chambray bordered by exquisite lacework wafted in the breeze.

She handed the cup back to her friend, who placed it on the bedside table. "Pet—?"

"Please, my dear," Petronella hushed her, "rest your voice."

"House?"

Her downcast response revealed all, but Petronella's words confirmed Olivia's fears. "I'm sorry, Olivia, but I believe your home is lost."

Lost… well, that was fitting. Gerald was lost, *she* was lost, their life, as they had known it, was lost. And now, everything they owned…

Petronella squeezed her hand. "I'm so sorry, my dear."

## CHAPTER 77

# *Men and their bloody posturing*

THE FOUR OF them had been riding together for fifteen minutes when the first glimpse of Lower Icing appeared through the trees. Well, it was more The Keep than the town itself. Tom let out a cheer, then announced, "The Duke lives!"

Ophelia looked at the massive stone structure, tinged with dawning sunlight, poking out in the distance like a giant version of the finger she'd given Tom. They were close enough to see the flags flying from the corner towers — they were at full mast. However, Ophelia couldn't muster much enthusiasm for the Duke's wellbeing, and judging by his derisive scoff, nor could the man pressed against her back. She looked over at Tom and he gave her an encouraging smile; damn him, he was handsome.

Five thudding minutes later, the trees began to give way to farmland, and now the entire castle was visible, set above the dwellings of the township like a grey stone crown set awkwardly upon a squashed, red-brick face. In one of those dwellings, her ma, Seth and Billy waited for their return. She suddenly felt energised, her heart pounding at the thought of being reunited with her family. It seemed like ages since she'd left with Tom.

However, as much as she wanted her pa safe and well, she was sad the adventure was coming to an end. And it *had* been an adventure; she'd felt a sense of place out there in the wild, with her wild man. Who would have thought it? Ophelia was surprised to feel tears run down her cheeks… so many emotions.

Sid's voice rang in her ear. "That doesn't look good."

Ophelia's first thought was that he'd noticed her tears. She was about to tell him to mind his own friggin' business when he extended his arm and pointed ahead. Ophelia looked up, expecting to see some sort of trouble on the road, like an overturned cart or a patrol of men-at-arms, but all she could spy was farmland, workers in the field tilling soil or reaping crops, and groups of grazing black-and-white cows.

"Near the castle," he said, raising his arm.

Now she could see what he was on about — plumes of opaque grey smoke blossomed lazily upwards from amongst the red buildings. From this distance it was hard to tell where, exactly, it was coming from, but the man behind her was right: it looked to be near the castle. Still, it hardly seemed worthy of note; the smoke looked little more than you'd expect from a large chimney, and probably less than what the Slaughter & Offcut smokehouse produced. There was no real vigour to it and it was certainly not *that* remarkable. Her silence, however, didn't deter him from yelling "Smoke" across to Tom.

"Aye," Tom acknowledged. He looked concerned.

*Really?* Ophelia looked back towards Lower Icing; her gaze following the smoke from gold-tinged Lower Icing to the clear early morning sky. It *was* quite a large plume, she supposed, but even so.

The north road veered slightly left as the Icing River came into view, farmland extending to its reed-lined banks. The road led them to within four hundred paces of the river before turning due south again, straight towards Lower Icing, straight towards Market Street, to Slaughter & Offcut and her family.

The vista ahead was no longer obscured by trees. Everything was bathed in rich gold: a sea of brown and green fields, some cultivated, others used for grazing, while some appeared fallow. Dotted here and there were lime-washed barns and storehouses. Rising out of the farmland was the township of Lower Icing and its looming castle. Ophelia had never seen it from this viewpoint, even though they had to be less than a mile away. It seemed strangely imposing — much grander and more impressive than she would have imagined. It just went to show how sheltered and confined her life had been before Tom came into it… before they'd spent a drunken night together.

She gazed towards the river; the water, hidden behind a curtain of reeds, was barely visible from where they were, but its sparkling reflection could be seen further in the distance towards the East Road bridge, near where she'd woken up with her Gamekeeper eight mornings ago, his semi-naked form sprawled out asleep next to her. All she'd been thinking about *that* morning was getting home before she was missed by her pa. Fortunately, he'd left early for the butchery and hadn't known she wasn't asleep in her bedroom. Her ma, on the other hand…

She glanced over at the man who'd captured her heart; she wouldn't leave him lying on riverbank now. He was saying something to her pa. Her pa's lolling head lifted and he looked ahead. The sight of Lower Icing seemed to perk him up, because he straightened in the saddle and held his gaze straight ahead. It was a good sign.

"Here's trouble," said Sid Evily.

*What the frig was he on about now?* And then she saw the group of riders galloping towards them. There looked to be around a dozen of them. They were in uniform.

She glanced over at Tom. He was gazing ahead intently. Then he drew Wildflower closer to Hazel. "We may have to stop," he shouted.

"Why?" she shouted back.

"That's a patrol of men-at-arms."

Well, thank you, Captain Obvious — was that meant to be an explanation?

"As I said," the voice by her ear grumbled, "trouble."

"Oh for frig's sake!" Ophelia sighed. *Men and their bloody posturing!*

As Tom had unhelpfully predicted, they were stopped by the men-at-arms. While he engaged the purple-and-gold-clad officer — it was that tosser, Jethro Fowler — and offered him a brief explanation as to why her pa was semi-conscious on his horse and what they were doing on the North Road at such an hour, Ophelia had to endure the leering gaze of twelve blue-and-gold-clad men. Bloody hell, she even recognised a couple of them from The Can, particularly that skinny Giblets one. He winked at her. She felt herself squirm.

"Friends of yours?" Sid Evily enquired. She could hear the smile in his voice.

"Howja like an elbow in the ribs?" she replied.

Ophelia was only vaguely aware of the conversation Tom was having with the Purple Perillian, but that changed when Tom explained how Sid Evily came to join their party.

"Is tha' right?" Fowler said; his voice held a hint of menace. She heard Sid swear under his breath as the lieutenant turned his attention towards him; well, *almost* towards him — it seemed Ophelia's cleavage was obscuring Fowler's view. "You travelled with that freak show from Blessed Whipping?"

"Well, not *all* the way, Lieutenant," Sid replied in an oddly cheerful voice. "As you can see, my taste in travelling companion has improved dramatically."

Some of the men sniggered at the remark, particularly the guardsmen from The Can. Fowler shot them an angry glare, and reluctantly the men controlled their mirth.

"Wanker," Sid breathed in her ear.

Ophelia had to stifle a smile as the officer looked back in their direction, taking the scenic route via her breasts.

"An' how, may I ask, did you happen to be his companion in the first place? What were y'doin' in Blessed Whipping? Didn' think Sid Evily could stumble further north than The Dead Duck."

Ophelia could feel Sid tense; Fowler obviously knew him.

Tom interjected, "I'm sorry, Lieutenant, but we don't have time for an interrogation. I will vouchsafe for Master Evily."

The lieutenant flicked an irritated glance in Tom's direction. "Very kind of you, I'm sure, Gamekeeper," he said, with mock graciousness, "but as I explained, Squire Lamb an' Cadet Martin haven't been seen since yesterday mornin' when they left for Blessed Whipping to fetch this... doctor. And since you've informed me that Sid here — who, fair to say, isn't the most upstandin' of citizens — appeared out of nowhere on the North Road an' tells you he's come from—"

"Oh shut the frig up, Fowler!" It was her pa's raspy voice. "Bleatin' on like a bleedin' sheep, an' a wool-for-brains one at tha'."

Ophelia did laugh this time.

Sid whispered in her ear, "Your father's got balls."

*Yes, he bloody well has,* thought Ophelia. Even the men-at-arms looked to be holding back smiles. Giblets and the other one she recognised, Grippy, smiled openly at the comment.

Unsurprisingly, Lieutenant Fowler failed to see the funny side. Nor, apparently, did Tom. "Your pardon, Lieutenant," he said, formally. "As you can see, Frank is in need of a doctor; he's taken quite a beating from the Moleson Twins."

"Friggin' cowards," murmured her pa. He appeared spent after his outburst.

"An' you're holdin' us up," Ophelia put in; all this pussy-footing formality was doing her head in.

Fowler glared at her. Ophelia glared back.

"Beardsley, Preston, Faulkner," he yelled over his shoulder. "Take Evily to The Can. He's under arrest!"

"Piss off, Fowler," Sid said.

"On what charge, Lieutenant?" demanded Tom, as the named men-at-arms began to manoeuvre their horses towards Hazel.

"On being a friggin' good for nothin' turd that I suspect the Squire an' Martin had the misfortune to step in."

"I'm afraid I can't allow you to do that, Lieutenant; I'm escorting Master Evily to the castle. He—"

"Can't allow, Gamekeeper?" Fowler barked, incredulously. "I don' care if you're escortin' him to wipe the Duke's arse; he's gonna eat shit in The Can until I return from my jaunt in the countryside."

The situation was no longer just an irritating delay; there was a palpable menace in the air. Ophelia watched Tom's hand move to the pommel of his sword and she felt Sid reaching down towards his right boot. Bloody hell, something bad was about to happen.

Ophelia reacted on instinct rather than any rational thought. "Hold on," she hissed at the man behind her. Fortunately, he had the sense to react immediately and wrapped his arms around her waist. Then she dug her heels into Hazel's sides and yelled for the mare to go.

As Hazel leapt into a gallop, Tom called out her name and Fowler yelled for her to stop. *What the frig was she doing?* Too bleedin' late now; they were already racing past the men-at-arms.

There was more shouting and the sound of swords being drawn, but the noise soon disappeared under the sound of Hazel's hooves thudding on the baked dirt road.

Sid let out cheer, followed by a triumphant yell. "Tom's just knocked that cocksucker from his horse!"

Bloody hell! But she didn't dare turn around for fear of losing control of the mare. "What abou' Pa?" she yelled back.

"Still on the saddle with Tom."

That was relief. Up ahead, through a frenetic haze of hazel-coloured mane, Lower Icing was looming quickly.

"Think he's knocked Fowler out cold; he's not getting up," Sid continued.

That didn't sound good. "What about the men-at-arms? Are we being chased?"

This was met by silence.

"Well?"

"I don't... I'd say not."

Ophelia didn't know what to do; she didn't even know why she'd taken off, except she could see both her and her pa getting tangled up in a situation that had nothing to do with them, and she didn't trust any of those lecherous bastards, especially that smarmy git, Fowler. He was the one who'd taken great delight in informing them that Billy had been arrested.

"Slow down!"

"What?"

"Slow down! Tom's coming. And he's not being followed."

Ophelia pulled on Hazel's reins and slowed the mare to a canter, then to a walk. It didn't take long for Tom to draw up next to them. Ophelia was glad to see her pa was still lucid. In fact, if anything, he looked more enlivened.

"What the frig was that all about, Ophelia?" Tom yelled at her, clearly unhappy about her flight.

She couldn't answer him. She didn't know the answer, and her heart was pounding, and her mind was racing, and she… well… she didn't *know!*

"Come on, Tom," Sid replied, filling the silence. "Everyone knows Fowler's a shithead. And, depending on where he hit the ground, you might have made him *more* of a shithead."

Wildflower was now walking abreast with Hazel, and if Tom hadn't looked so angry, Ophelia might have laughed at that.

"This is not something to jest about, Sid." His face looked as red as her pa's, and he was sweating quite heavily. "Fowler is a Purple Perillian!"

"*You're* the one wha' smacked 'im in the gob," piped in her pa. "Not a bad smack neither. Might 'ave even impressed me there, Gamekeeper."

"That's because he ordered his bowmen to shoot at your daughter, Frank!"

"Ha!" Sid guffawed. "Those dolts couldn't hit The Keep at ten paces."

Tom shook his head in disgust.

*Bloody hell,* Ophelia thought. All she'd done was ride towards the village; it wasn't as if she'd escaped from the dungeon or poisoned the bloody Duke. And, in any case, she'd had enough of people being put in The Can on the whims of those with authority. Still, Tom *had* acted to protect her; she couldn't deny she was also impressed by her Gamekeeper.

Poor Tom, he looked confounded by the company he was keeping. If they'd been alone, she would have shown her appreciation of his valour. Then she noticed her pa was watching her, and suddenly she felt self-conscious.

She turned her gaze back to the men-at-arms. They were still grouped around their fallen officer. "So, wha's 'appenin' with *that* lot then?"

"I'd be more worried about what's going to happen to *you*, Ophelia. *And* you, Sid. And *me* for that matter. Once Fowler recovers—"

"Oh, get off y'bleedin' 'igh 'orse, Gamekeeper," her pa grumbled, then added, "I know *I* can't friggin' wait to."

Sid began to laugh, and so did Ophelia. Then her pa joined in. Despite himself, Tom also saw the funny side. Ophelia wasn't sure why they thought it was so funny, but their laughter doused the tension.

By now the horses had walked them to within a hundred paces of where the North Road became Market Street. Ophelia gazed at the cobblestoned thoroughfare as it rose steadily towards the castle. It was already busy with vendors carting their wares to the market. She smiled and took a deep breath — she could *smell* the town from here. Looking upwards, she noticed the smoke. It looked slightly more impressive now they were closer, but she sensed the fire had been brought under control. From this angle it looked as if it might be coming from the barracks. Wherever it was, thankfully it was nowhere near Slaughter & Offcut.

Glancing across to the men astride Wildflower, squashed together on the saddle, she felt an urge to tell them that she loved them, but that would just be awkward for everyone. Tom was also looking skywards until he sensed her eyes upon him. Meeting her gaze, he wore a concerned expression, but whether it was because of the smoke or what had just occurred with Fowler, she couldn't tell... probably both. He deserved better; he'd looked after them and brought them home safely.

"Thank you, Tom," she said.

"I suppose he had it coming." Tom smiled ruefully, thinking her gratitude was aimed at his actions against the lieutenant. She didn't gainsay him; he looked pleased that she'd voiced her thanks.

"Most of Fowler's men will be bloody delighted you knocked him flat on his face," added Sid.

"Possibly," Tom replied.

"And I *also* owe you a debt of gratitude," Sid continued, jovially. "More than likely it would've been *me* who'd have copped an unlucky arrow."

Tom acknowledged Sid's remark with a nod and a half-smile. He looked preoccupied. Ophelia was about to ask him if something was amiss when her thoughts were distracted by the clopping of horseshoe on cobblestone — they had reached the beginning of Market Street. Her attention was drawn immediately to the bustling vista ahead. As the near-mile-long street sloped up towards the castle, the buildings that fronted it became more congested. From this distance, it was impossible to pick out the barn-like shape of Slaughter & Offcut, even though it was the biggest single structure on

Market Street. Ophelia's efforts were interrupted by her pa's voice, "'Ope y' ain't spectin' no thanks from *me*, Gamekeeper."

# CHAPTER 78

## *Draped over the sill*

MARY WOKE TO the first rays of sun streaming through her bedroom window. This was unheard of; she was always up before dawn. She should be preparing for the day ahead; people were depending on her. However, despite the realisation, Mary couldn't find the will to move from her bed. Her mouth was parched and her head pounded like a blacksmith's hammer, or was it just the kitchen coming to life? *How much had she drunk with Richard?*

Eventually, she forced herself into a sitting position; it felt like the red wine was still sloshing around in her stomach. Suddenly, nausea hit. Hurling herself towards the open window, she managed to lean over the sill before a cascade of vomit ensued, followed by dry retching, spitting saliva and a burning, bitter aftertaste.

Eventually, the spasms subsided and Mary was able to breathe in the cool morning air. The kitchen was bustling with activity; she should be helping. Why hadn't someone come to fetch her? Then Juanita's voice pierced through the preparations, and *that* was enough to banish any thoughts of leaving her bedroom. In any case, they'd all proven themselves to be more than capable in her absence over the last few days.

She was still draped over the sill, mesmerised by the spattered cobblestones, shimmering gold, when she heard a rattle at the courtyard gate. She didn't bother lifting her head; it was probably John going to fetch some water from the well. Mary wondered if he'd notice her dangling out the window, half awake, feeling wretched. She hoped he would give her a few more minutes of recovery time. Then the gate burst open.

## CHAPTER 79

# *Going to have to get used to it*

THE REUNION OUTSIDE Slaughter & Offcut was an explosion of emotion: an eruption of joyous cries and tears followed by a plume of relief and concern. Ophelia was smothered in hugs and kisses from her ma, and Billy clung to her like he was never going to see her again. Even Seth broke out of his normally reserved shell and hugged her warmly, telling her he loved her. Of course, her pa put on his 'no need to fuss' exterior, but after he'd been helped off Wildflower by Tom, Seth and Billy, he almost collapsed into her ma's embrace. They held onto each other for a long time, while Seth asked her questions and Billy held her hand. It was strange behaviour from her younger sibling, but Ophelia was too happy to see them all to give it a second thought.

Her pa was clearly in a lot of discomfort, as much from the public display of affection as his injuries. "So y'gonna let me inside me own front door, Maizie?" he grumbled, but it was good natured. "Spen' the bes' part o' six bleedin' days outdoors, love; wouldn' mind feelin' a roof over me 'ead."

Her ma laughed at that, and they all began walking towards the open red door. Billy lingered when Ophelia didn't follow. She shooed him. "I'll be there d'rectly, Billy, jus' 'ave t'speak to the Gamekeeper."

He acquiesced reluctantly, and she wondered whether it was guilt he was feeling or just the effects of a week in The Can. Now that the excitement was over, Ophelia was *certainly* feeling the effects of the last half an hour in the saddle; the inside of her thighs felt like they'd been beaten with a meat tenderiser.

Tom and Sid were standing next to each other, holding the reins of Wildflower and Hazel respectively. They'd been spectators during the reunion, but through the smothering attention, she'd caught glimpses of them in discussion.

"I'm heading back to the patrol; they may need my help," said Tom, without preamble. "Sid is going to the Upper Bailey to report what has occurred."

She felt her heart sink; he seemed so matter-of-fact. This wasn't how she imagined their parting. Actually, she hadn't imagined their parting at all.

"I'm sorry, Tom," she said, reaching out to touch his arm. "Didn' mean t'cause y'trouble."

He gave her a rueful smile. "I've a feeling I'm going to have to get used to it."

Ophelia wasn't sure he could have said anything more perfect. She jumped up onto him, wrapping her legs around his waist, and kissed him passionately — the sheer joy of the moment competed with the raw pain from her inner thighs. Both brought tears to her eyes. Eventually she let go of him.

Sid was smiling at them. "In with the Offcuts, Tom; you *are* a game keeper."

She laughed at that. She couldn't help herself. Sid was obviously some sort of rogue, but he had a likeable manner, and Tom appeared to trust him. To hide his embarrassment, the not-so-game keeper mounted Wildflower. Once atop the saddle, he addressed Sid. "Just remember what I said, Sid. And speak only to Sir Richard or Lieutenant Swill."

Sid was still finding mirth in Tom's embarrassment. "Of course, Tom; I'm looking forward to it."

Tom regarded the man in black quizzically, but then he turned his attention back to Ophelia. "Hopefully this won't take too long, even *with* a dozen men-at-arms slowing me down."

It was obvious he wasn't looking forward to the prospect of another search. Ophelia didn't blame him, but she admired his sense of responsibility.

"Take care, Tom," she said, placing her hand on his leg.

He gently squeezed it. "Try and stay out of trouble, Ophelia. I will call on you upon my return. No doubt we will have to account for our actions."

Ophelia nodded; when the time came, she'd be more than happy to account for her actions. A uniform was nothing more than a shiny thin wrapping that covered all manner of dirty deeds, the proof of which was waiting for her inside Slaughter & Offcut.

Tom released her hand and she let it fall from his leg.

"I'll take Hazel with me, Sid," he said, holding out his hand for the reins. "Just in case we need an extra saddle. No-one could double up with Bradley Lamb, that's for certes."

Sid obliged, walking the mare a few steps until her rein was within reach. "Good luck, Tom. I'll buy you a drink when you get back, if I'm not in

The Can, of course."

Tom nodded noncommittally as he looped Hazel's rein around Wildflower's head-collar. Edging the horses back into the middle of Market Street, he gave Ophelia one last wave before heading back out of town at a gentle trot. She would have lingered until he'd disappeared had Sid not been standing next to her.

"Better him than us," he said.

She turned to face him.

His expression was mischievous. "Not that it hasn't been a pleasure riding with *you*, Mistress Offcut."

"Yeah, well, y'owe Tom another drink for tha'. Now, if you'll 'scuse me, I got fam'ly wha' needs lookin' after."

He acknowledged the remark with a good-natured nod. "Of course; I too must be about my business. Hope Frank makes a quick recovery. If I see Manky, I'll send him around. As I said, he's a bizarre character, but his potions actually work. Half my face looked like a prize turnip a week ago."

She was tempted to tell him not to bother now that her pa was safe at home. But the turn he'd had last night was still fresh in her mind, and half an hour ago he'd been slumped, half unconscious, in a saddle. If this Manky was as good as Sid claimed, perhaps it might be for the best.

Ophelia shut the door on Market Street and gingerly made her way upstairs, grimacing at the soreness between her legs. More than anything, she was looking forward to soaking in a tub of hot water.

# CHAPTER 80

# *Don't Mary me*

MARY RAISED HER head at the loud banging of the gate, and, as she watched the black-clad figure enter the courtyard, she thought her mind must be playing tricks. Either that or she was still lying on her bed dreaming — nausea had plagued her sleep with dreams of throwing up, perhaps this was just a variation on a theme. Still, she watched as the figure headed towards the kitchen.

She cried out, but her voice was little more than a croaky whisper, not loud enough to distract the man from his purpose.

The effort of yelling had sent Mary's head spinning, and she coughed up more bitter red-wine spit. If this *was* a dream, it was a bloody painful one. Lifting her head again, the man was now walking towards her. He must have heard her coughing. He looked depressingly real, and he was smiling at her, frig him.

"Mary?"

There was no mistaking that playful expression; his slightly crooked smile creased his face with laughter lines and his brown eyes danced merrily under his dark, unkempt hair. He looked revived and his face appeared mended. And here *she* was slumped over the sill like a discarded copper-piece harlot. All Mary could do was groan.

"Bloody hell, Mary," he said, squatting down outside the window, "drowning your sorrows after just one night away from me? Understandable, I suppose."

He moved closer and kissed her softly on her cheek. "I'm sorry I ran from you."

She could barely muster a nod.

Reaching through the window, he helped her into an unsteady standing position. Then he clambered over the sill into her bedroom. All Mary wanted to do was lie back down on her bed. Images of a dog balancing a goblet on its nose swam across her mind… bottles of red wine being poured into a decanter… and now Sid suddenly standing next to her… it was too much. She needed a bucket!

Mary bolted out of the bedroom and ran down the corridor. The noise of the kitchen grew louder and then erupted as she burst into the room. She barely had time to register their surprised looks before turning into the washroom. Juanita was in there, sloshing away at the wash tub. Mary ignored her unnecessarily loud "Meestress!" and dived towards one of the buckets set against the wall.

She was vaguely aware of a chorus of concerned voices as she retched, coughed and spat up nothing. Nothing, at least, deserving of such heaving. She'd never drink on an empty stomach again. Then she felt a hand on her back. "You orrigh', Mistress?" Mandy asked, softly.

*Bloody hell, of course she wasn't!* "I'll be fine, Mandy," she gasped. "All of you go about your work, I'll be—"

Another spasm of retching ensued, during which time she heard Patricia raise her voice in alarm. "'Ere! What *you* doin' 'ere?"

"Think of me as a knight in dirty clothing," she heard Sid quip, while Mandy smoothed her back.

"Oh, Meestress!" exclaimed Juanita. "Meesta Seed ees here to sweep up your feet!"

All Mary could do was groan.

"She needs to drink some water." It was Sid's voice.

Patricia responded with a bellowing, "Who the bleedin 'eck y'think you are, comin' in 'ere, tellin' us wha's what?"

"Oh, Meestress; your poor dress, it needs dee soakeeng in da—"

"Enough!" Mary rasped, staring at the claret spittle at the bottom of the bucket. "Everyone get back to work. Juanita — fill me a bath."

She was relieved to hear a chorus of "Yes, Mistress."

"I'll get y'some drinkin' water," said Mandy.

Through her pounding head, she eked out a thank you.

Then Sid was squatting next to her. "Mary, I have to go to the Upper Bailey. Doctor Manky arrived earlier this morning and Tom Skinner has asked me—"

"You're going nowhere, Sid Evily, until you've told me what the frig you've been up to." Fighting another wave of nausea, she lifted her head and glared.

He regarded her seriously for a moment, and then a smile broke through. "Fair enough, Mary. No doubt your clever brother has things well in hand.

I'm sure—"

"Sid!" She really couldn't stomach Sid's caustic sarcasm right now. "Just go into the kitchen and leave me to my bath."

He kissed the side of her head. "Sorry."

As he stood up to leave, she added, "Have Patricia fix you some breakfast if you need some."

Getting undressed was an effort, but it was worth it once she was in the tub. She slid gingerly into the hot water until only her head and the tops of her knees broke the surface. Her head still thumped, but her stomach felt better almost immediately. It was a relief to say the least.

Just as pleasant was the fact that Juanita — who had insisted on giving her a 'Los Nachos Rub' for her *dolor de cabeza* — kept her promise not to talk. And she had to hand it to the Icarumban: she knew how to use her hands. As soon as she began to massage her fingers through Mary's wet hair, the *dolor* in her *cabeza* receded and Mary felt herself drifting towards sleep. However, the noise of food preparation permeating through the closed washroom door — scraping of pans, chinking of plates, and Patricia barking orders (mainly to John) — kept sleep at bay. There was also an unusual amount of laughter. Mary put that down to Sid; no doubt he was playing up to all the women (including Patricia).

When Mary eventually emerged from the washroom dressed in a fresh set of work clothes (retrieved by Juanita), she felt clean and refreshed. She was greeted by a collection of smiles and ow-ya-feelins from her staff, which now included Lillian. The remnants of the headache and nausea lingered, but she could cope with both now.

"Sid's been tellin' us 'ow 'e's jus' escaped the clutches of a doctor wiv no blood and pink eyes," Mandy said.

"Yeah, jumped ou' of 'is carriage an' all, Mistress," added a surprisingly animated John.

Sid looked rather pleased with himself, sitting at the kitchen table, arms resting either side of a plate which had recently contained a full breakfast.

"Did he, now," Mary responded, evenly. "I wonder if he jumped out of it as fast as he jumped *into* it."

Sid's smile disappeared, and, judging by the silence, the rest of them realised Mary was neither amused nor impressed by Sid's tale. "If only you'd stayed for breakfast *yesterday*, you could have saved yourself such an ordeal."

"Mind you," piped in Patricia from the stove, stirring a pot of something, oblivious to the change in mood. "'E looks a sight better than 'e did las' time 'e barged in 'ere. Them potions that doctor gave 'im done wonders for 'is face."

Patricia was right; his face looked to be healed. "Yes," Mary concurred. "Makes you wonder if you can credit *anything* Sid says."

"Mary," Sid said, standing up. "Let me—"

Mary held up her hand, forestalling more words from the man in black; she wasn't interested in explanations right at this moment. "Lillian, please brew a pot of tea for me."

"Yes, Mistress," she said, and immediately set about the task.

"I'll have it in the private dining room."

"Yes, Mistress. Jeedarling or Earl Beige?"

"I don't care as long as it's strong."

Mary was about to address Sid when Juanita's voice blared out next to her. "You better to have dee hair of dee cat, Meestress — eet does dee treek."

"Yes, thank you, Juanita," she said, dismissively. Mary really didn't want to get into a conversation with the Icarumban; there was something about her voice she couldn't handle this morning.

"It's dog, Juanita," supplied Mandy.

"What ees dog?"

The three words were like hammer blows to Mary's head.

"The 'air," Mandy explained.

"Air?" Juanita enquired with exaggerated confusion.

Mary grimaced.

"Yeah, 'air. It's 'air of the—"

"Right!" Mary jumped in; *this* conversation would do her head in with*out* a pickled brain. "*Fascinating* as this topic is, I'm afraid you'll have to excuse me." Then she cast her gaze in Sid's direction — he was standing, looking contrite (which was a good sign). "Feel free to join me."

"Of course," he agreed, readily.

"That is if you've finished recounting your wondrous escapades; I wouldn't want your audience left on tenterhooks."

He gave her a withering smile. "I believe my near-death experience has been conveyed satisfactorily."

"Oh no!" gasped Juanita, over-dramatically. "Meesta Sid, you almost keek dee bucket?"

Where the frig was Juanita picking up these bloody idioms? At least she'd got this one *right*.

"Oh, Meestress, ees so—"

"It's not bloody romantic, Juanita!" Mary snapped. Everyone stared at her, like *she* was the one talking about cats and dogs and kicking buckets. She felt like groaning; her head was throbbing again. "Just bring me the tea, Lillian." Then she left the kitchen.

Sid joined her in the dining room. Lillian brought the tea and some fresh bread with butter and honey. While she began to sip the tea — she wasn't ready to attempt the bread and honey at this point — Sid began relaying what Mary supposed was a less colourful version of events. Still, it was quite a story nonetheless. Blessed Whipping sounded like an odd place, and she was shocked and amazed by Doctor Manky's actions. To be able to put someone in a deathly state and then make them speak all they knew... it seemed incredible to her. Still, he'd completely healed Sid's face with a concoction of thistle and cow's urine, which was just as incredible.

However, it was Bertrand she'd wanted to know more about, particularly after everything Brandon had told her. Sid's response, however, was somewhat flippant. "Put it this way, you'd never invite him to dinner — a dried-up dog turd has more personality than Bertrand."

Then she told Sid about the Swills and the *Deed of Promise*. "I think Bertrand's even pleaded his case to Richard," Mary added. She knew she was probably speaking out of turn, but she really didn't care — there'd been too much left unsaid this past week. However, Sid could not enlighten her on the character of Bertrand, except to say there was something odd and slightly unnerving about the man. Then he added, unhelpfully, "Mind you, he can run bloody fast."

The tea was beginning to help, her body gratefully accepting the fluid, so she broke off a small portion of the bread and slowly added it to her delicate stomach.

"So, was it worth it, Sid?" Mary asked. "Did you find out anything from Doctor Manky?"

Then Sid dropped what he thought was going to be bombshell: the man he saw Olivia talking to at The Bell was Doctor Manky's protégé, who, the doctor claimed, was also the long lost son of the Duke.

Of course, it was hardly explosive news to Mary. "Yes, Richard confirmed that yesterday afternoon when I went to see him."

The way Sid reacted to *that* piece of news, you'd think it was *she* who'd dropped the bombshell. He seemed most put out, as if she'd gone behind his back.

Mary was not in the mood for his indignation. "Well, Sid, if you hadn't run off with Bertrand, you—"

"Mary—"

"Don't Mary me!" she snapped. "*That's* why I was calling after you, why I wanted to *stop* you getting on that carriage. Even before I went to see Richard..." She took a deep breath to try and calm down; her head was beginning to throb again. "After you *snuck* out of The Harey Rabbit, Mandy returned from Reg Puffy's laden with more than just a few rashers of bacon. She'd heard gossip about the castle dinner, that the Duke had an heir. I thought it ridiculous, just exaggerated rumour, but when she told me he was a doctor, well... it rang true — all the castle politics and secrecy and those bloody not-at-liberties, the person of interest, the missing young doctor, the man you saw with Olivia... it all suddenly made sense. And my first thought, Sid — my *first* thought — was to let *you* know. *That's* why I sent John."

She could hear her voice rising again, but she couldn't help it; words and emotion were spewing out of her far better than any Escargotian red.

"But *you* were too puffed up with your own importance, and John... Well, John couldn't stand up to a friggin' light breeze! So, of *course*, he didn't relay the news. Bloody hell, Sid! This is not even *about* you. You were just in the wrong place at the wrong time."

Mary grabbed the teapot. She wasn't sure whether she wanted to pour herself another cup or tip it over Sid's head. But the man opposite was no longer puffed up; in fact, he looked deflated.

"Yes... Tom said as much... the Moleson Twins."

She splashed some tea into the cup. "That's right, Sid, the Moleson Twins! They were getting rid of evidence: the silver button. But it isn't even a button! It's a *key!*"

She slammed the teapot down on the table, took a deep breath, and then a sip of tea. Fortunately, Sid was smart enough not to say a word, allowing her a moment to regain her composure.

She continued in a more measured tone. "It's a key to a book or folder or something that this young doctor uses to keep his notes. The Moleson Twins kicked the shit out of *him* on Friday night, stole his money *and* the silver key. Gerald's proclamation must have put the wind up them, so when you presented yourself, pissed and pissing in a dark stable…"

Sid was listening intently now.

Again she took a deep breath, trying to keep her emotions at bay. "The silver key was assumed to be Richard's, because it bore his insignia. As you know, he stood down as Seneschal *because* of it… because he knew it *wasn't* his."

Sid shook his head. "I don't understand, Mary… and I'm not sure I want to anymore."

Too bad; he was going to hear it regardless. "Richard is worried about the ramifications of an heir, particularly where the Duke of Stymouth is concerned, *and* he's suspicious about the timing of Xavier's sudden appearance. But to me, it's just a tragic story of a mother and father who gave up their little boy because of… I can't even *imagine* why, Sid, but no doubt Richard would probably call it their duty to the Duchy."

Sid nodded. "Doctor Manky revealed as much. Except, from what I remember, they were given no choice in the matter and feared the boy would be killed if they refused… it's all a bit hazy."

The loss of the royal family on the *Happy Mermaid* had rocked the Duchy, but Mary had been a little girl at the time, so the real significance was lost on her. And when Marmaduke and Lucinda arrived, there were great celebrations and the acceptance of a new era. Now she knew the cost, she felt like weeping, not just in sorrow, but in anger. How could anyone be so heartless as to force a mother and father from their child?

Mary regarded the man sitting opposite her. What did *he* care about, she wondered… other than where his next drink was coming from. *Was he really all show and no substance?* Suddenly, it was important to her; she didn't want to invest in a man whose heart was selfish and shallow.

"Do you believe Doctor Manky, Sid?"

His dark eyes narrowed, as if he suspected it was a loaded question. "I believe *he* believes what he says is true. It just seems so improbable, but then again…" He shook his head and sighed. "I honestly don't know, Mary — nobles, duchies and heirs; it's a different world from the one I'm familiar with."

Mary wasn't sure how she felt about his response, but it sounded sincere, and that would suffice for now. His eyes searched hers, waiting for her to speak. When words finally came, they weren't the ones Sid, *or* she, was expecting. "They've arrested the person who attacked the Duke."

His surprise was obvious, but he was oddly calm about it. "Who?"

"Richard couldn't tell me. It's a legal matter. I interrupted him in a meeting with Captain Le Sharp and Rupert Smythe-Wheaton, one of the Limp… lawyers you introduced yourself to yesterday morning."

A look of distaste crossed his face.

"That's what Wednesday night here and Thursday night at the castle was all about: to catch the culprit. The hearing is this morning."

Sid shook his head as he tried to take it all in. "Bloody hell, Mary."

"Richard also told me about Bertrand, as has Brandon Swill; it seems he's been involved in an underhanded scheme of his own, so when you ran off with him, I must admit I entertained the thought that *you* were involved in whatever he—"

"How could you think such a thing, Mary? Who do you think I am?" He seemed genuinely outraged.

She took another gulp of tea. "That's the point, Sid — I don't know."

He nodded; her words had cut him.

Bloody hell, what was she doing? This was not the right time to make an emotional stand.

"Very well. I shall take my leave while I'm still at liberty to do so."

What did he mean by *that*?

Then he stood up. "In any case, I promised Tom that—"

"Please, Sid," she said, standing as well — she already regretted her words. "I'm sorry. I'm feeling somewhat wretched this morning… so… what do you mean 'still at liberty to do so'"?

He then told her about their altercation with Lieutenant Fowler. She should have been shocked or concerned, particularly about the missing squire and cadet, but her overriding emotion was curiosity and, if she was being totally honest with herself, excitement. She found it hard to imagine Tom knocking a Purple Perillian from his horse; his feelings for Ophelia Offcut must be quite strong. Who would have thought? Still, the same could be said of her and Sid.

During the retelling of events, she managed to polish off most of the bread and honey.

## CHAPTER 81

## *In such poor presentation*

THE MORNING PROGRESSED agonisingly slowly for Olivia as she lay motionless on the bed. However, she learned from Petronella what had happened after she'd fallen from the study window…

She'd been found unconscious in the garden by a neighbour, Simon Shearer. By this stage, the back half of the first floor was ablaze. Simon had moved her to safety, then ran for Albert while other frantic neighbours rushed to the barracks for help. This was around ten o'clock.

Albert and Petronella were preparing to retire for the night when the knock at their door came. The news had been a terrible shock, of course. Petronella wanted to accompany her husband to the scene, but Albert insisted she remain in the house, for if Olivia had been burnt badly, he needed her to prepare a cool bath. Seeing sense in his logic, Petronella did as her husband bid.

Sometime later — it didn't seem that long to Petronella — Albert returned with Simon Shearer and one of his servants. They carried Olivia into the washroom on a stretcher (which had been brought from the barracks by one of the many patrolmen who were now swarming into the back of 8 Plumduff Street via the night-soil lane, trying to co-ordinate the fire-fighting effort).

Having acted most chivalrously, Simon and his servant took their leave to assist in dousing the blaze, while Albert and Petronella attended to Olivia. Petronella had lit several candles, and, in the brighter light, her husband was able to give Olivia (who was barely conscious) a more thorough examination: Her face and neck were pink and raw, and smeared black with smoke; her hair was singed, and the remains of her nightdress were covered in dirt and grime. Despite appearances, however, Olivia's burns were largely superficial. Even so, Albert decided she should be bathed *on* the stretcher, because the slightest movement appeared to cause her distress. Once they'd cut away her tattered attire, the reason became obvious — she had a large bruise on the right side of her torso, further evidence that she'd fallen from the study window. Albert ascertained that she'd broken some ribs.

Edging Olivia carefully onto her side (to half-conscious cries of pain) they could see the point of impact on the right side of her back, where the bruising was most severe. Her hair was singed more at the back and the skin at the top of the neck was bright pink. They spent some time cleaning her with cool, damp towels, wiping away the smoke-blackened grime that covered most of her body.

Albert directed Petronella to apply a wet compress to the back of her neck and head. He then began to bandage her ribs. It was a tricky process, because he had to wrap the bandage tightly around her torso, and the slightest movement resulted in cries of pain. After the bandage was secure, Olivia had a coughing fit which lasted for two or three agonising minutes until she passed out.

Petronella admitted that she had been worried for her life at that point. However, Albert reassured her that while her injuries were serious, and quite obviously painful, it was likely Olivia would recover given time to convalesce properly. They'd carried her to their guestroom, to the bed in which she now rested.

Olivia remembered nothing of her ordeal, but she was moved to tears by the generosity of her friend, particularly after the way she had disgraced herself at the castle dinner. And she was grateful that Petronella was married to such a caring person as Albert Whysman. Of course, she would have to personally thank Simon Shearer for his kindness and bravery. What must've he thought, finding her like that, in such poor presentation.

During the recounting (which occurred over a few sittings because Olivia kept falling in and out of sleep), she began to feel slightly better, which was probably due to Petronella's insistence she persevere with drinking water. Still, it was only a small improvement and it caused another problem: the need to relieve herself. Even though Petronella and Albert had witnessed her humiliating inebriation (and washed and bandaged her naked body), the thought of either of them emptying her chamber-pot was one indignity Olivia could not face; she would put off *that* moment as long as humanly possible.

Petronella left Olivia to rest while she went about some household tasks, providing her with a small hand-bell — like a miniature version of the Town Crier's bell — to use should she require assistance. Olivia wondered how Gerald was coping. Had news reached him in the dungeon? Was he aware that his wife had ruined their home?

## CHAPTER 82

# *A piece of her aching mind*

THE LATE MORNING sun was glaringly bright, but it was good to be out in it. Walking side by side, Mary and Sid headed down Big Wig Street for the short walk to the West Gate.

"Never thought I'd be walking the streets of Lower Icing with a wanted man," Mary teased.

Sid barked out a laugh. "Tom may *just* have deflected Fowler's attention from me… that's if the tosser can remember what hit him."

"Yes." Mary smiled. "Most unlike Tom to resort to fisticuffs. Ophelia must have brought something out in him."

Sid smiled. "No doubt — quite regularly I'd imagine."

She laughed out loud, then hit him playfully on the arm. He smiled and offered his arm. Mary took it gladly; she'd forgiven him, and it was nice just to do something simple together like walking arm in arm.

As they passed by Charles Bling: Jeweller to the Duke, Sid cast his gaze into the shop window, where gold and silver necklaces, gem-encrusted brooches, rings and hat pins were presented on plush beds of black velvet.

"Fear not, Sid," Mary said, "you don't have to impress me *that* much."

He smiled, but seemed lost in thought. "There was a time when I *could* have impressed you that much," he murmured. "Sadly, my Adventuring days are over."

His *Adventuring* days… what were *they?* He seemed deep inside his head, but before Mary could probe any further, he snapped out of his reverie.

"In any case, I haven't shared with you the news of my newfound wealth."

"I see." It sounded… unlawful.

He patted his belt. It made a chinking sound. "Fifty gold pieces — Doctor Manky's recompense for my troubles."

"That *is* generous, Sid."

Mary was about to follow up with something flippant about the amount of ale he could buy with it, when he added, "And, no doubt, for the safe return of the silver button… or key."

She felt her heart sink. She unlinked her arm from his and turned to face him. "So you *did* have it? Why did you lie to me?" She was annoyed, but she kept her voice down, well aware of the street she was in and the people who were strolling by.

He actually seemed taken aback by her reaction. "Well, I wasn't certain that I—"

"No, not certain, just pretty bloody sure, I'd wager!"

"It's not that I wanted to keep the bloody thing, it was just—"

"Just *what*, Sid?" She could feel her frustration rising again, and her headache was also making a reappearance. "Just too *dangerous* for me to know? Just that I'm Richard's *sister*, or is it *just* the fact that I'm *just* a simple woman?" Sid's face reddened as she continued to give him a piece of her aching mind. "Your bloody friggin' pride or whatever it is… Shit, Sid, the button may well be the key to saving—" She stopped herself; people were looking. One didn't act in an unseemly manner in Big Wig Street, and one certainly didn't swear. To calm herself, she began walking quickly towards the West Gate.

Sid trailed after her. "Well, you should be *thanking* me then, Mary," he countered, clearly upset by her reaction. "The best person to save the Duke is now in *possession* of the key."

*Hah! Pure dumb luck,* Mary thought. Ignoring the man in black, she kept her gaze fixed ahead. It was then she noticed a large plume of smoke smudging the blue sky somewhere behind the terraced homes of Noble Street.

"*And*, in any event, the Duke's standard still flies," Sid's voice was muted, but it now had a defensive tone. "He still *lives*."

She stopped and turned on him. They were now outside Hats on Big Wig and a couple of couples were browsing through the window. Once again she had to temper her anger. "And *that* makes your actions defensible, does it?"

Sid was dumbfounded, and that annoyed her more. How *could* he be dumbfounded? Clearly he'd acted selfishly, and if he wasn't able to recognise that then what future did they have together. "What if the Duke *had* died and Xavier could have saved him? After all, the key had been in *his* possession!"

"That's not fair, Mary," he said, simply. "I'm not responsible for what happened to the Duke. And I have already apologised for running from you. It seemed the right thing to do at the time, but if you cannot accept my apology, then I'll bid you goodbye here and now and not trouble you again."

Mary wasn't expecting him to say *that*. She felt his words churn in the pit of her stomach. Why did he have this effect on her? Maybe she *was* being unfair where the Duke was concerned, but surely she was being reasonable about everything else… wasn't she?

Before she could put her thoughts into words, Sid turned and continued towards the West Gate; he'd obviously interpreted her silence as confirmation of her unwillingness to forgive him.

"Wait," she called after him.

He kept walking, so she hurried to catch up. It only took a few quick, unseemly steps to reach his side. However, Sid kept his gaze fixed ahead — he looked angry and upset, and his pace matched his mood.

"I *do* accept your apology," she said, half running to keep up with him. The morning had been pleasantly warm a few minutes ago, now it felt uncomfortably hot, and it certainly wasn't doing anything for her head.

"That's all well and good, Mary," he said, without looking at her. "But as you said, you don't know who I am. You seem to think…" Suddenly he stopped. He was staring at her, like he was lost or something.

"What's wrong?" she asked.

He shook his head and sighed. "All I know, Mary, is what I feel for you I have never felt before and, truth be told, it scares me."

She nodded; she knew how he felt. She wrapped her arms around him and held him close, decorum be damned.

After a few moments (and some audible tutting from a passerby), Sid gently pushed her away. "Very well, Mistress Mary, if you wouldn't mind leaving any further interrogating to your esteemed brother, we should be on our way."

She smiled — the playful rogue was back.

As they approached the West Gate, Mary remarked about the smoke.

"Yes," Sid said casually, "we saw it from the North Road; looks like it's almost out."

They weren't the only ones casting their gaze skywards — there were quite a few people gathered on the other side of Noble Street, where Big Wig Street continued west towards Plumduff, Blancmange and Meringue Streets. As they drew closer, Mary could see that two men-at-arms were preventing the gathering from advancing any further down Big Wig Street.

"Aren't you curious, Sid?"

The air was now tainted with a faint smell of burnt wood.

"Normally I would be. However, as you say, I'm a wanted man, so the sooner I explain to your brother what happened on the North Road, the better."

"Even so, it appears to be coming from—"

"*And*, no doubt, Manky has informed Sir Richard of our little arrangement. Shit, how's *that* going to look!"

"I'd be more worried about Bertrand than Doctor Manky," Mary said, staring at the smoke as it wisped above the rooftops. It looked like it was coming from Plumduff Street, near the Hiepants' house. Bloody hell!

"Sid," she said, coming to halt, eyes still fixed on the smoke. They'd reached the West Gate.

"What is it, Mary?"

"I think we should—"

The sound of clattering hooves and heavy, rumbling wheels broke through her thoughts. Mary turned her attention towards the West Gate. The guardsmen were moving to the sides of the massive opening as she and Sid waited to see what was coming. It didn't take long.

Two draft horses pulling a large dray stacked with oak barrels appeared from the barracks. They were walking at slow pace; their heavy load rattled and shuddered on the cobblestones. Both horses snorted their uncertainty at passing under the thick wall of stone, spooked by its echoing closeness. However, the two drivers managed to guide them through without mishap and, as they rolled by, Mary estimated there to be thirty barrels, filled with sloshing water. So, she surmised, the fire wasn't completely quelled.

Sid called out to the drivers, "What's happened, lads?"

"Bloody 'ell, squire, where you been?" the nearest one retorted.

"'Ouse in Plumduff burn' down las' night," supplied his companion. "Jus' coolin' the cinders now."

"Which house?" Mary asked.

"Town Crier's," said the companion.

"Town *Fryer's* more like," added the other.

Sid hurried over to the dray. Mary followed him.

"What do you mean?" he said, keeping pace with the horses. "Is he dead? What of his wife?"

The nearest one shrugged his shoulders. "Dunno, squire. I 'ear they found 'is wife, like. Jumped outta the back winda 'parrently."

"Is she alive?" Sid persisted. Unsurprisingly, there was urgency in his voice.

The companion jumped in with, "Reckon so. 'Eard one of the men-at-arms sayin' she'd been taken to a doctor's 'ouse."

"Which doctor?" Shock made Sid sound angry.

"Steady on, squire. You know 'er or somethin'?"

"Dunno 'is name," the more helpful companion added, "but 'e's the Duke's doctor."

Sid stopped and turned to Mary, his face alight with concern. "Mary, do you know where Doctor Whysman lives?"

She nodded.

## CHAPTER 83

# *Never felt so parched*

**M**ORE TEARS CAME unbidden. But, no, this wouldn't do — she needed to be strong. She'd always been able to steel herself against adversity — the years spent taking care of her drunken mother, then raising and educating her good-for-nothing brother, and playing the goodwife to a man she neither loved nor respected… well, not until the last few days… and now it was too late.

Olivia's morose thoughts were interrupted by a loud rapping — someone was at the Whysmans' front door. The Whysmans had two servants: a cook and a maid. Olivia had often entertained the thought of hiring a maid, but, when it came down to it, she didn't like the thought of a servant being privy to her life, laughing behind her back at her ways, gossiping to all and sundry about the ineptness of her husband. In any case, she was quite capable of keeping her own house. Olivia's only concession to outside help was her washerwoman, Beth Wringer.

She could now hear snippets of a muffled conversation; one of the voices sounded quite insistent, but it was too distant to pick up any context. Then there was silence — momentarily, at least. The sound of an approaching set of footsteps soon followed. Wiping the tears from her eyes, she waited to see who opened the guestroom door.

It was only her dear friend, which was somewhat of a disappointment; she'd half entertained the hope that Paris might have been told of her plight and come to…

Petronella's flustered demeanour forestalled further musings.

"Something amiss?" Olivia rasped, disregarding her throat.

"Well, my dear," she said, "Mary Brewer has arrived with a man who calls himself Sid."

Olivia felt sick. Of all people… No doubt he wanted to gloat, him and his floosy with her insincere politeness.

"Albert treated him at The Harey Rabbit a week ago. He's quite well spoken, yet most informal in his manner. And, well…" She looked confused. "He reintroduced himself as your brother."

Damn him; this was not a topic she was prepared to engage in.

"But you've always led me to believe…" Poor Petronella seemed quite flustered. "*Do* you have a brother, Olivia?" she eventually asked.

How Olivia wished she could shake her head, but what was the point in denying it? She no longer had a reputation to protect. Reluctantly, she nodded.

"I see," Petronella said, as if she didn't see at all. "So, he didn't die falling off a roof?"

Olivia shook her head.

"Well… shall I… show him in? He seems most concerned, my dear."

*Concerned?* She doubted that very much, and even if he *was*, he was six years too late. She shook her head, then reached over for the cup of water; she had never felt so parched.

## CHAPTER 84
# *We're paid to be bored*

OPHELIA HAD NEVER been the type to sit around and wait. So, sitting around waiting for her pa to recover didn't sit well with her. And she certainly wasn't prepared to sit around and wait for Tom to return — who knew how long *he'd* be gone. So, as good as it was to be home, she was already beginning to feel restless. It was barely midday, yet their arrival home felt like days ago.

After helping to put her grumbling pa to bed and sharing *some* of the details of the past five days with her ma and brothers, she'd headed to the washroom to take a much needed bath.

As she slowly undressed, her ma prepared the bath, infusing the water with sprigs of lavender and rosemary. Her clothes, despite being washed yesterday afternoon, smelt of campfire and sweat. Her lower undergarments proved to be the most challenging to remove, being virtually wedged into her most tender areas.

Now that it was just her and her ma, Ophelia spent the next hour soaking and chatting, the conversation centring on Tom. Her ma seemed just as enthusiastic about her romance as she was. In the end, Ophelia even admitted it was Tom with whom she'd spent the night on the riverbank. That turned out to be a mistake. The look her ma had given her — suddenly the water had felt very cold. However, her ma's disapproval was tempered by the relief of Olivia and her pa's safe return, and the fact that her feelings for Tom were genuine.

Ophelia still felt slightly put out by her ma's reaction; she wasn't a child anymore, and didn't need her parents' permission to... She sighed; all this sitting and waiting was doing her head in.

Ma had taken to the bedroom, lying next to Pa while he slept. Ophelia was worried; so much sleeping couldn't be good — her pa wasn't the sleeping type.

Seth was downstairs in his office, working the books, tallying the incomings and outgoings, writing orders, collating receipts and whatever else he did to make sure Slaughter & Offcut ran smoothly.

However, her main concern, and another reason she was feeling restless, was Billy. Apart from the hour she'd spent soaking in the bath, he'd been by her side, clinging to her, but hardly saying a word. It was disturbing to say the least; she much preferred the annoying little brat of a brother she'd had before he was sent to The Can... and *that* was saying something.

When he *did* speak, it was to tell her that he loved her and that she mustn't see the 'friggin' Gamekeepa' again, because he was the one who'd put him in The Can. Ophelia didn't know how to react. On the one occasion she'd defended Tom, and explained that he had saved Pa's life, Billy had become quite agitated, eyes darting, as if Tom was hunting him. Then he began rocking and chanting, almost to himself, "'E's bad Pheel, 'e's bad Pheel, 'e's bad Pheel."

She'd had to shake him quite roughly. He'd looked momentarily stunned, then hugged her tightly. She hugged him back, but it was more out of concern than affection. She could feel him shaking within her embrace. What had the friggin' Can done to him?

The midday sun shone brightly on the grey cobblestones. It was nice to be outside, even if it *had* meant sneaking out of the family home via the coolroom. She just couldn't handle being cooped up in the dark stuffiness, not after the last five days of wild freedom. Besides, her pa needed a doctor, and she wasn't about to while away the afternoon hoping for the best, like her ma.

Her inner thighs still felt sore as she made her way towards the castle, but at least they weren't squashed against a jolting pommel, and the bath had soothed most of her other aches and pains.

Ophelia had become accustomed to taking the back route (past Brown's Boarding House) while visiting Billy in The Can. It was much quieter and more private than going up Market Street and Merchant Street, and probably safer too — she didn't have to deal with the spillage from The Bloody Bell. Then again, the students from Lower Icing College weren't exactly the gentlemen they were supposed to be.

She'd just turned right onto Book Street, and was approaching the main entrance of the college (the mouth of the house as Ophelia thought of it) from which Noble Street extended north to the West Gate like a long cobblestone tongue. As she began walking uphill towards the castle, she noticed the plume of smoke they'd seen from the North Road was still drifting lazily into the sky. If she was any judge — and she *was* — she'd say it was coming from Plumduff Street. Clearly, someone's house had come to grief, but she had no intention of finding out whose; she needed to find this Doctor Manky Sid had told her about.

The sound of someone whistling pierced the air. It was the kind of whistle that left her in no doubt who it was directed at. It came from above and behind her. Looking up at the Milk & Stout student accommodation, she saw a young man leaning out of a window. He wore a presumptuous smile. "I say, I'm having trouble with my anatomy class. Care to help me study?"

Ophelia smiled back, feigning interest. "You a doctor then?"

The man's smile widened. "Well, I'm certainly qualified to give *you* an examination."

Ophelia laughed. Then she turned her back on the wishful thinker and continued on her way. However, her dismissal didn't dissuade the student.

"Perhaps you'll feel more disposed to aid my acquisition of knowledge upon your return, Mistress."

Without breaking stride, Ophelia raised her right hand and extended her middle finger.

She heard him laugh. "I'm rather sure I can do better than *that*. Room seventeen — Wilbur Dickins at your service."

Ophelia couldn't help but smile.


The area surrounding the West Gate was unusually crowded; people were gathered around a blockade on Big Wig Street. She'd been right about the smoke on Plumduff Street. She'd found out from a passerby that the Town Crier's house had burnt down, and rumour had it that it was his wife who'd set it ablaze. Well, Ophelia mused, all that bloody bell ringing would be enough to send *any*one mad.

At least the owner of Ma's Keraderie had been able to take advantage of the disgruntled crowd. A freshly painted sign had been placed in the shop window amidst the eclectic range of colourful masks. It read: FIRE SALE.

Ophelia walked through the West Gate, followed by the usual sets of roving eyes, and veered left to the Administration Section of the Lower Bailey. As she made her way between the two wings of double-storey buildings, she could see the entrance to the Middle Bailey was guarded. That was a first;

she'd never seen it guarded before. Still, guards tended not to be a barrier for Ophelia. As she approached the four uniformed men, she put on her most engaging smile. They reacted as expected: smiling back at her, imagining her without the white cotton summer dress that flowed across her figure.

As she drew within a few paces, one of them said, "Sorry, Mistress, rest of the castle's closed."

She didn't recognise any of them, but that didn't matter. She stopped and directed her gaze at the one who'd spoken. He looked slightly uncomfortable, which was a good sign, yet… there was something unusually disciplined about *all* of them.

"Yeah, well it would be, wouldn' it." She was rewarded with a mildly surprised expression from the guardsman — apart from a charcoal black moustache, he was clean shaven. In fact, all of them were rather well groomed. Again, that was odd. Still, it didn't deter Ophelia. "After everythin' what's 'appened." They shared uncertain glances. "Shockin' o'course. It's jus'…" She shook her head as if lost for words. She didn't want to tell them *exactly* what she knew; Tom would never again trust her to keep her mouth shut. The guards were looking at her as if she'd been touched by the sun, and she probably *did* look sun-touched, particularly after five days in the wilderness. "I got some information what needs passin' on."

Two of them sniggered, including the one with the moustache; the other two just smiled and leered.

"It'll have to wait until the castle opens again," said moustache.

"Or you can tell *us* your information," said the clean-shaven one next to him.

These guards weren't behaving very guard-like — at least, not like the guards Ophelia had encountered recently. They were waiting for her reply. "Yeah, well tha' *would* be a lot easier," she agreed, "but the Gamekeeper tol' me not t'tell no-one 'cept Sir Richard."

She was treated to four bemused expressions.

"Did he now," said moustache, dubiously.

It sounded ridiculous, even to Ophelia, but ridiculous had always worked before.

"An' how did you come to be the Gamekeeper's messenger, Mistress?" said clean-shaven.

Good question. "Tha's a bit ovva tale. Don' wanna bore ya with the… ins an' outs."

"We're Ducal Guardsmen, Mistress," said clean-shaven, "We're *paid* to be bored."

Ophelia had no idea what being a Ducal Guardsman meant, except it obviously took more intelligence than being a non-Ducal Guardsman. Bloody hell — just her friggin' luck.

Then another Ducal Guardsman entered the mix, "So, what's your story then, Mistress?"

Ophelia was wondering whether to disclose her identity (she'd never really had to before), when another voice yelled it out for her.

## CHAPTER 85

### *Jus' blackness an' ruin*

SID LOOKED AGITATED. He *was* agitated. He hadn't wanted to accept Petronella Whysman's refusal to allow him to see his sister. Poor woman; she was clearly upset by what had happened to her friend and remained adamant that she not be disturbed.

"I'm afraid she doesn't want to see you, Master… Sid," she'd stated, beginning to lose patience with Sid's insistent manner. "As I told you, she can barely speak and needs rest."

Mary had to cajole him from the Whysmans' threshold by reminding him that he'd promised Tom he'd see Richard.

"Yes, you have the right of it, Mary," he'd conceded. "In any case, Manky's at the castle; he'll have a potion to alleviate her discomfort."

They were walking at a casual pace down Merchant Street, heading towards Noble Street, the sun beaming down from almost directly overhead. They'd been at the Whysmans' door for about ten minutes, during which time Petronella (under interrogation from Sid) had told them as much as she knew about the fire and the extent of Olivia's injuries. Gerald hadn't been in the house; he'd been at the castle at the behest of Sir Richard. Petronella had been most reluctant to talk about Gerald, and when Sid questioned the absence of the Town Crier at his wife's bedside, she'd become quite flustered. Still, Mary couldn't blame her for that — she'd had a traumatic night, and Sid wasn't exactly being sympathetic. Petronella couldn't tell them how the fire had started, save that it appeared to have emanated from the upstairs study — the fire was hottest there. Olivia had been found unconscious on the ground beneath the study window, and had said nothing to enlighten anyone.

Passing strange that Sid seemed to be so concerned about his sister; Olivia had disowned him and, from Mary's point of view, she seemed to be a particularly spiteful woman. Yet the man walking beside her was silent and focused, as if she'd been a most beloved sibling. Mary wanted to ask him why he'd reacted so... unexpectedly, but she didn't want to appear heartless.

As they crossed Plumduff Street, they both gazed to their right. Behind the guarded barricade, some five or so front doors away, was the blackened façade of number 8. From this angle, it was hard to tell the extent of the damage — the terraced frontage seemed to be intact and the soot-smudging appeared to be localised around the Hiepants' home.

The dray, still laden with its barrels of water, was parked outside; the horses looked relaxed and seemingly oblivious to the activity around them. There were a lot of men — some uniformed, some not — coming and going with buckets of water, but, like the horses, they appeared at ease. Obviously, the fire had been doused; 'cooling the cinders' is what the driver had said. It sounded like some sort of ritual, laying the house to rest. A tingling feeling ran down the back of Mary's neck, causing her to shiver; she dreaded to think what would happen if The Harey Rabbit ever burned down.

Unexpectedly, Sid walked up to the barricade and approached one of the guards. He was tall, in his mid-thirties, with short dark hair, but his most outstanding feature was a mole — it looked like a large pomegranate seed had wedged itself in the crevice where his nose and left cheek met.

"Good day, guardsman," Sid greeted him.

The guard nodded perfunctorily, clearly disinterested in what Sid was about to say.

"I was just wondering whether anything was salvaged from the fire."

"Waz ya now," he said, eyeing Sid, then flicked an appraising gaze in Mary's direction. A sour-looking grin appeared on his face, before he turned his attention back to Sid. "Well, wonder away; I ain't stopping ya."

Mary noticed Sid tense. However, to his credit, he remained calm. "It was a simple enough question, guardsman."

"Yeah." The guard nodded in an exaggerated manner, as if Sid was an idiot. "An' I gave ya a simple enough answer. Or are ya more simple than ya look?"

Suddenly, Mary was worried — this could get out of hand. Sid was already in a dark mood *and*, she reminded herself, a 'wanted man'. "Sid, perhaps we should be on our way. Remember..." she lowered her voice to barely more than a whisper, "... Lieutenant Fowler."

Sid looked at her, as if about to concede her point, when the guardsmen cast another barb, "Ah, so *she's* the one wiv the brains."

Sid closed his eyes, as if trying to retain his composure.

"Sid, come on," Mary urged. "Leave it be."

Sid huffed out a breath. Then he snapped back towards the sneering guardsman as if he might hit him. The guard flinched. "Ha!" Sid barked, contemptuously. "I thought as much! Best keep yourself safe behind your baric—"

"Tha' you, Sid Evily?" yelled out a gruff voice.

They all looked in the direction of the voice. Mary had to lean around the guardsman before she saw another guardsman approaching. This one was older, with thick grey hair and a generous coating of white stubble. He was quite a bit shorter than his counterpart, but he looked tougher: more solid and more seasoned.

Sid acknowledged the man in uniform. "Sergeant Barker."

It was then Mary noticed the three silver crowns on his blue collar, and, now that he was closer, she did recognise him. Usually, Sergeant Barker was clean shaven. (Must be the week for changing facial hair, Mary thought, absently.)

His gaze flicked between Sid and the guardsman, then he addressed the latter. "Wha's goin' on 'ere then, Jack?" He sounded a bit fed up.

Jack saluted. "Nuffin', sergeant," he replied. "Jus' keepin' the peace."

"Taking the peace more like," said Sid.

Jack treated Sid to a withering snarl.

"Really," said Sergeant Barker, clearly unimpressed. Then, as if just noticing Mary, he nodded. "Mistress Brewer."

"Sergeant," Mary responded.

His eyes narrowed, as if wondering what Mary might be doing in the company of a man like Sid.

"Look, Sergeant," Sid interjected, "all I did was ask jumping Jack here if anything had been salvaged from the Hiepants' residence."

The sergeant smiled, stepping in front of Guardsman Jack (who was not smiling). "An' what bus'ness migh' that be of yours then, Sid?"

"Olivia Hiepants is my sister and—"

Sid's words were halted by a loud burst of laughter from the sergeant. It was an unexpected reaction to say the least. Jack smiled, as if the sergeant's mirth vindicated his own attitude towards Sid.

"Bleedin' 'eck, Sid," said Sergeant Barker. "The bullshit you come up with... Tha' was a good'n — I needed that."

Mary wondered just how many times Sid and the sergeant's paths had crossed and what *other* bullshit he'd come up with. As if hearing her thoughts, Sid cast a sheepish glance in her direction. Mary felt like taking him to task;

however, now was not the time or place. And, as outrageous as it obviously sounded to Sergeant Barker, Mary felt she should support the man standing at her side.

"This is no jest, Sergeant. Sid and Olivia Hiepants are indeed siblings. We've just come from Doctor Whysman's residence where she is recuperating."

A grateful expression crossed Sid's face, while a disbelieving one remained on the sergeant's. Then his expression and stance stiffened. "And wha's *your* int'rest in this, Mistress Brewer, if you don' mind me askin'?"

Mary bristled at his tone; it sounded like he was accusing her of something. "As it happens, sergeant, I *do* mind," she replied. Putting up with arrogant patrons was one thing, but she certainly didn't have to accept this kind of attitude *outside* The Harey Rabbit.

The sergeant frowned. No-one said anything for a few moments; only the clatter from 8 Plumduff Street permeated the air.

"Well then, ain't no more to say is there? Time you was on y'way."

"That suits me, Sergeant," Mary replied.

"I'd go wivvout shit for brains if I waz you, love," said Jack.

"Shut it, Private!" Barker barked, keeping his eyes on Mary. Then his gaze softened. "Sorry for 'im, Mistress Brewer. 'E's jus' come from Naffolk and don't know who's what yet."

Mary nodded; it wasn't worth making anything out of it. Sid, on the other hand…

"Why don't you Naffolk back there, Jumpy Jack, or don't they have barricades to *hide* behind?"

Jack sprang forward and looked ready to launch himself at Sid, but the sergeant was in his way. "Stand down, Private!"

Sid hadn't moved an inch and looked ready to take Jack on.

"Private!" Barker yelled again. "I said stand down!"

Reluctantly, Jack complied, all the while glaring at Sid.

"Right…" said Sergeant Baker, composure regained. "You two best be movin' on."

"We're going, Sergeant," Sid said, still regarding the incensed Naffolker. Then he sighed. "But can't you just tell me if all was lost in the fire? Does my sister have a home to return to?"

"Yeah," sneered Jack, "a home full of—"

"Private," Sergeant Barker growled, "one more word oudda you an' you're on Can duty for a month."

Jack stiffened at the threat, and his face turned a similar shade to the pomegranate mole.

"You really 'er brother then, Sid?" Sergeant Barker sounded as if he was coming to terms with the possibility.

"We're estranged, but yes."

Mary stifled an urge to add her endorsement; she'd rather avoid being scrutinised by the sergeant again.

The sergeant nodded his acceptance, then said, "The buildin's in one piece, but tha's abou' all. Inside's pretty much gutted, specially roun' the back. Front 'as some furniture an' a few clothes what could be used. Ain't fit for livin' in though, 'specially for people of *them* standin'."

Sid nodded.

Standing... it was such an odd term, thought Mary. Well, regardless of their standing, they had to get back on their feet first, and that would be no easy task.

"Might 'ave to put 'em up at yours, Sid," said the sergeant. "Then again," he added with a grin, "they'd more'n likely prefer the burn' out ruin option."

Jack smiled openly at the jibe, but wisely made no comment.

Sid, too, seemed to treat it in good humour. "No doubt, Sergeant."

She thought he was about to bid the sergeant good day. Instead, he asked, "Would you mind if I saw for myself?"

Barker, understandably, regarded Sid's request with suspicion. "Ain't nothin' t'see for y'self, jus' blackness and ruin."

"Even so," Sid persisted.

Sergeant Barker rubbed his chin. "Orrigh' then, but only to the doorway; y'can see well enough from there. You don' go inside, righ'?"

"Fair enough."

The 'barricade' was little more than a portable wooden fence about four feet high and ten feet long. There were three of them spaced out across the width of Plumduff Street. Between each piece, a gap wide enough for a barrow to pass through had been left. It certainly wouldn't be of any use in a battle, but, then again, neither would any of the men-at-arms Mary had encountered recently.

Sid walked through a gap. Mary went to follow.

"Not you, Mistress Brewer," said the sergeant. "Ain't somethin' a lady like yourself wants t'see; an' ya more'n likely mess up y'dress."

His condescending words didn't register with Mary immediately; her brain still felt a bit dull.

"Sid, on the other 'and... bleedin' 'eck, 'e looks like somethin' what's already been dragged out from the ruin."

By this point his words *had* registered and her response was sharp. "Listen here, Sergeant, I *run* The Harey Rabbit. It has a kitchen, which I *also* run, and *that* has an oven, which burns with *fire* every day and has to be *cleaned* and *refilled* every day. Believe me, Sergeant, I am *no* stranger to ash and charcoal, *nor* am I afraid of getting my clothes *or* hands dirty. I do it *every* day!"

Somehow, Mary's hands had found their way to her hips. All three men regarded her with varying degrees of surprise.

"Think you're going to need a stronger barricade, Sergeant," said Sid, smiling his approval.

## CHAPTER 86

# *Would the pain never end?*

IT WAS A relief to hear the front door shut. Petronella had, at last, rid herself of her brother and his bargirl; she'd heard the muffled insistence in Sid's voice, but her friend had remained steadfast on her behalf.

The bedroom door opened shortly after the front door shut. "They've gone, my dear," Petronella whispered, as if they might be lingering at the front door.

Olivia nodded her thanks, keeping her movements to a minimum. She just wanted to close her eyes and wake up in a day or two, completely healed.

Her friend entered the room, shutting the door behind her. Then she sat on the side of her bed. "Why did you tell me your brother was dead? He seemed genuinely concerned for your wellbeing."

This was a conversation Olivia didn't want to have. Fortunately, she didn't have to. She pointed to her throat. *Every cloud,* she thought.

"Oh, of course, my dear; I don't expect you to answer, unless…" She reached over to the bedside table and retrieved the quill and parchment. "Would you like to write it down?"

Olivia shook her head.

Petronella smiled, but it was tinged with disappointment. As she replaced the items, Olivia reached out and squeezed her arm. "Later," she rasped.

This time her friend's smile contained nothing but warmth. "I'll leave you to rest. Don't forget the bell, should you require anything."

Again, she nodded her thanks.

Olivia's rest lasted about two minutes — if you could call trying to get comfortable when the slightest movement caused agonising pain 'rest' — before she heard more knocking at the front door, shortly followed by the tentative appearance of Petronella.

"Oh, good, you're awake. My dear, you have another visitor." This time she seemed quite excited about the prospect. "It's Captain Le Sharp," she said, her voice barely above a whisper, "do you wish to see him?"

Olivia's heart began to thump; she could feel it in her ribs, but the pain was numbed by the thought that Paris had come to see her. Trying to mask her excitement, she nodded.

Petronella seemed pleased by her response. "I'll show him in, my dear — he's looking rather dashing in his uniform."

Olivia couldn't quite believe it was Paris who was sitting beside her bed. After Petronella had excused herself, somewhat reluctantly, he'd kissed her formally on the hand, expressed his shock about the fire and his relief that she'd survived. Pulling out the chair tucked underneath the dressing table, he'd placed it next to her bed and sat down within touching distance.

Petronella was right: he *did* look dashing, but, then again, when didn't he.

Suddenly, she felt self-conscious, knowing she must look like something the cat had dragged in.

"Forgive the intrusion, Olivia, I…"

Olivia's heart raced at the hesitation. It was hard to read his expression; he looked… conflicted? Was he about to declare he still loved her or… Gerald — had something happened to Gerald?

"I have news."

Olivia's heart sank. *That* didn't sound good.

Her expression must have conveyed her thoughts, because he was quick to reassure her, "It is excellent news, Olivia."

He was hardly acting like someone who was the bearer of excellent news. This would not do. Too much had been left unsaid for too long; now was not the time for restraint. She reached for the parchment and quill, causing a stab of pain in her side.

Paris was quick to jump to her aid. "Here, allow me," he said, taking a sheet of parchment from the bedside table and handing it to her, while moving the inkwell closer. She smiled her thanks, dipped the quill in the ink, and began to write. He was looking at her expectantly as she scratched the nib across the surface.

*Please be honest with me, Paris. There is no need to protect my feelings.*

She turned the parchment in his direction and his eyes darted quickly across the page.

"Of course," he responded, and Olivia noticed his body relax somewhat. "If I'm being honest, I suppose I feel somewhat awkward… after seeing you at the dinner and… knowing that Gerald was responsible…"

Olivia's heart dipped further — the mortification of that night would never be erased from her memory. She could feel the blood rush to her face as she wrote her response.

*I am so sorry. I had no idea that Gerald had poisoned the Duke.*

"Yes… However, *I* knew, and it made me feel uneasy putting you in such an exposed position. Even after so many years of… avoiding each other… when I saw you… looking so radiant and proud… and knowing what was about to occur… It is *I* who should be apologising to *you*."

Olivia could feel tears welling in her eyes. This was the man she was meant to be with, who she *would* have been with if her brother hadn't… She couldn't bear it… Paris was here; the man of her dreams, within touching distance, yet as unreal and unreachable as her dreams. She shook her head. The tears fell. She swallowed painfully. Then she began to sob, and it seemed every part of her body was rebelling against her, as if the emotional anguish of being without Paris had suddenly manifested itself as physical pain. He moved to her side. She felt his gentle hands pull her to him. Would the pain never end?

It seemed like time had melted. Olivia had no idea how long she was in his arms, how long it took for her tears to run dry — all she felt was the sense of loss. Somewhere during the embrace, Petronella had knocked on the door, asking after her. Paris had answered on her behalf, and her friend had accepted his response without further enquiry.

When he finally released her, she felt exhausted, as if he'd squeezed the last drops of life out of her. He, too, looked drained, his eyes tear-stained. "I'm sorry, Olivia. I wish I… That is, I wish we—"

She shook her head and placed her hand against his mouth. She didn't want to hear his regret; it would be too much for her heart and mind to cope with.

He nodded acceptingly, and Olivia reluctantly withdrew her hand.

She doubted she'd have the willpower to stop him should he continue.

Then she noticed the crumpled parchment and ink smudges all over the white bedding. What would Petronella think? How much more of an inconvenience could she possibly be? She felt wretched.

Olivia retrieved the quill and began to write on the crinkled surface, but the nib left no mark; it, too, was drained. Again, her eyes were drawn to the black smudges. Paris gently removed the quill from her grasp and rested it on the inkwell. Then he took her hand in his. "The Duke has recovered," he said.

Olivia heard the words, but they didn't seem real.

"Xavier's guardian, Horatio Manky, arrived early this morning," Paris continued. His brown eyes took her breath away, his voice sending shivers down the back of her raw neck, but the touch of his hand kept her calm, kept her from believing this was a dream or… madness. "He and Xavier created the remedy for the poison, with help from your… the Town Crier. Fortunately, he was able to remember how he concocted it."

Olivia reached for the water with her free hand; her parched throat had just become… more parched. She drank, rather than sipped, the cool liquid; grimacing with every swallow.

"Are you alright, Olivia? I thought you'd be pleased."

*Pleased?* She was far too emotionally wrung out to be pleased. In fact, she couldn't ever imagine being pleased again.

"The Duke is quite himself again."

Still Olivia drank, the water reviving her senses, bringing her back to the here and now.

"And I believe he intends to pardon Gerald; his hearing was postponed this morning." He sounded disappointed.

Olivia emptied the cup and placed it on the side table, next to the inkwell. The man in front of her *was* just a dream. *Gerald* was her husband. She removed her hand from his and reached for the quill. He looked somewhat perplexed. She dipped the quill in the inkwell and wrote:

*It is excellent news. Thank you for bringing it to me.*

"Think nothing of it. I…" He paused; he, too, seemed emotionally conflicted. "I wanted to see you." His gaze was hopeful.

She smiled and shook her head; she had nothing left to offer him and, she realised, *he* had nothing to offer *her*… except regret. It was time to lay the past to rest.

*It was nice to see you, Paris. When will my husband be released?*

There was a subtle change in his expression as he scanned the parchment. She didn't want to make him feel uncomfortable, but she needed to snuff out any thought of a… different life. They were six years too late for that. Passing strange that it had taken the moment she'd been dreaming of to end the dream.

"I'm afraid I cannot say," he said. "I imagine it will be soon." He smiled, but it was for Olivia's benefit, she could see that — she'd upset him, but there was nothing else for it. "It is time I took my leave, Olivia."

Olivia nodded.

Again, he kissed her hand. Then he left; as simple as that… as *hard* as that.

Olivia's thoughts turned to Gerald. It was *he* who she truly needed: someone who would stick by her no matter what. She also thought about Xavier — he'd helped cure the Duke; perhaps his knowledge had returned. She hoped so. And she hoped he would stay true to himself and not allow the likes of Richard Upson to manipulate and craft him.

# CHAPTER 87

## *The correct documentation*

STANDING NEXT TO Sid at the doorway of number 8, the house seemed surprisingly intact: smoke stained, of course, but structurally in place. Men were moving around the home; she could hear water buckets being emptied, and banging and scraping sounds coming from the back. Now that her eyes were adjusting to the gloom inside, Mary realised the virtually unscathed entrance and staircase belied the extent of the damage beyond. Down the hallway, the blackness was dappled with sunlight: some of the roof had collapsed. Through the haze of smoke, a man flashed across her view holding a shovel. This was terrible — the destruction was clearly terminal. They'd surely have to knock it down and rebuild.

Mary had seen enough, and the smell of damp smoke was making her feel sick. She stepped back into the street, cupping a hand over her nose and mouth. Sid paid her no heed, but she a caught a knowing glance from Sergeant Barker.

Mary moved around the other side of the dray into cleaner air. She breathed deeply, trying to overcome an urge to vomit. She didn't want Barker thinking she had a week stomach. As she gazed up the street, her attention was drawn to another man in uniform. He was striding at pace along Big Wig Street; his buttons and lapel caught the sun as he sparkled by in the direction of the West Gate. Mary recognised him — it was Captain Le Sharp, and he didn't look happy.

Mary remained on the other side of the dray until she was joined by Sid a few minutes later.

"Something amiss, Mary?" he asked, though he seemed distracted.

Mary shook her head. "Just a little sensitive to smells today."

He nodded knowingly.

As they were about to be escorted back down Plumduff Street by Sergeant Barker, the brass plaque of number 8 caught her eye, gleaming amongst the smoke-blackened bricks:

## ABODE OF GERALD HIEPANTS
## TOWN CRIER OF LOWER ICING

Sid must have wiped it clean while Mary was collecting herself; it certainly hadn't been like that when they arrived. She glanced at the cuffs of his black shirt — they looked dirty, but they hadn't exactly looked clean before. Mary thought about asking him, but his mood now matched his clothes.

Back on Merchant Street, the man walking beside her remained silent. By the time they reached Noble Street, Mary could no longer hold her tongue.

"Sid, Olivia survived and is in good hands."

He glanced at her, but said nothing.

"Petronella seems to think she will make a full recovery…"

"Petronella is not a doctor."

His response irritated her; he knew what she meant. "No, but her husband is, and he's the one who aided *your* recovery." He didn't speak. Why was he suddenly so off-hand with her? "Have I done something wrong?"

He sighed. "No, of course not."

Then he stopped, catching Mary unawares. He turned to face her. He looked forlorn. "It's me. I'm sorry. I didn't think I'd… feel this way about Liv… She's the only family I have." Then he took her hand in his.

Mary wasn't sure how to react; it felt oddly intimate, and she was a little awkward with intimate, particularly on the corner of Noble and Merchant Streets, where a number of her patrons were likely to pass by.

"I know she's a stuck-up cow, but I am partly to blame for that."

He let go of her hands. He was wiping away tears. "Sorry," he said. "I don't know where that came from. I didn't mean to burden you, it's… For most of my life, she was a mother as well as a sister to me and… I'm sorry."

He was trying to collect himself, but Mary could see it was a struggle. It made her awkwardness feel… superficial.

"Oh, Sid," she whispered, kissing him softly on the cheek.

He tried to smile through glistening eyes.

Taking him by the hand, she said, "Right, Sid Evily, we have a task at hand."

He nodded. "Indeed we do, Mary Brewer."

As they turned up Noble Street, Mary's gaze was drawn to a lone figure in a white dress. She was walking through the West Gate into the castle. She walked as if trying to draw attention to herself, and the guardsmen seemed to be obliging. Her straw-coloured hair hung loosely over her shoulders; she certainly wasn't part of the castle-set. Then she turned left towards the Administration Section, and, even from fifty paces, there was no mistaking the voluptuous figure of Ophelia Offcut.

Sid voiced her observations. "Ophelia Offcut just walked into the castle."

"Really," Mary said casually. "Nice to know a glimpse of Ophelia Offcut can wrench you from your melancholy."

Sid bit at the barb. "I find it odd, that's all."

Mary had to hold back a smile.

"She struck me as quite determined to look after her pa…"

It sounded as if he was going to say more, but he held his tongue. Whatever he was thinking, he was keeping it to himself. The silence continued until they reached the intersection of Big Wig Street, where their attention was drawn to the gathering of people around the barricade.

"…Petronella Whysman seemed most elusive about Gerald, don't you think?"

The question took Mary by surprise. Petronella was clearly upset, and no doubt slightly put out by Sid's insistent attitude… but elusive? "She was shaken by what had happened, and *you* wouldn't take no for an answer."

Sid acknowledged the truth of the remark with a nod. "Still… something's amiss. Tom was most interested to find out why Manky believed Gerald could help me… what he might have revealed."

"*Did* he reveal anything?"

Sid shook his head. "Nothing significant — not that I can remember, at least. He just blathered on about a silver button thief who, it turns out, never existed."

Mary smiled; the memory of Gerald and Sid drinking away the afternoon and evening after the Saturday Proclamation was still very fresh. To think it was almost exactly a week ago — a lifetime, more like. "*Most* enlightening."

"I know. It sounds ridiculous, but I feel like I've missed something."

"I'd say you missed quite a lot, considering how roaringly drunk you two became."

"Was I *roaringly* drunk, Mary?"

He sounded so serious that Mary laughed out loud. "Actually, it was Gerald who was doing the roaring; *you* were doing the charming."

He smiled. "I believe that was *you*. Bloody hell, seems like an age ago, doesn't it?"

Mary nodded. "Yes, and here we are, still together after all this time."
She was rewarded with a genuine show of mirth. *Thank goodness.*

As they passed through the West Gate, the one guardsman who made eye-contact with Mary offered her a fleeting smile and a nod. Mary felt slightly annoyed by the attention, or *lack* of it. The entire bunch had turned their heads towards bloody Ophelia Offcut *and*, no doubt, offered to escort her into the castle. It shouldn't irk her — surely she was above all that. However... it *irked* her.

"What could've possibly kept Gerald at the castle?" Sid wondered out loud as they veered towards the Administration Section. (Clearly, his thoughts had run a little deeper than hers.) "I can't imagine *anything* stopping him from being at Liv's side — you know what he's like with her. Unless, for some strange reason, he doesn't know what's happened."

Sid was right; it did seem strange that the Town Crier wasn't at his wife's side, if not out of love, then certainly out of duty.

Then a thought struck her. It seemed preposterous, but... what if it was Gerald who had poisoned the Duke? Richard had said "*All the attacks occurred because of the misguided judgement of one man.*" If anyone had misguided judgement it was the Town Crier; Sid's sister was proof enough of that. Then there was his 'silver button thief' story and the fabricated facts in his proclamation. As much as she suspected Bertrand of playing a part in the attack, Brandon had been steadfast in his assurances to the contrary; he'd even sounded strangely disappointed about the identity of culprit: "*In this case, I believe the right man is actually the wrong man.*" And from what Sid had just told her, it seemed Tom was also very interested in the fact that Doctor Manky had directed Sid towards his brother-in-law. Bloody hell... was Gerald Hiepants actually capable of such an act? Is that why he wasn't at his wife's side, because he was in a cell?

"Sid, do you think it's pos—"

"Ophelia!" he called out.

The woman in white was standing next to four guardsmen at the entrance to the Middle Bailey. She turned around to see who'd called her name. Mary could tell there was something amiss even from opposite ends of the Administration Section. Sid's eyes were fixed ahead. He looked concerned, and Mary felt an uncomfortable pang of jealousy.

Ophelia watched them approach, hands going to her curvaceous hips, luscious lips pouting while, beneath her flowing white dress, her fulsome cleavage was… *over*flowing. No wonder Sid's gaze was transfixed; Mary was *also* mesmerised by Ophelia's… Ophelia-ness.

Yesterday, Mary had felt wonderful walking into the castle in her blue dress: both feminine and desirable. Today, in her grey work clothes, head dulled by too much wine, she felt neither.

Still, the four guardsmen seemed quite at ease, even bemused by Ophelia's posturing, which was *something* at least. Actually, it was bloody amazing given the ineptness of their display yesterday.

"What are you doing here, Ophelia?" Sid asked her. It sounded a bit like an accusation. "Has something happened? Have you heard from Tom?"

"No," she responded. "Jus' ain't gonna sit 'round doin' nothin' while Pa's sick. Thought I'd see wha's wha' wiv tha' doctor y'tol me about, and I reckon Sir Richard should know wha's 'appened t'Tom."

"He asked *me* to do that," Sid said.

"Why ain't y'done it then?" she said, smartly. "'Ad better things t'do p'raps?" She cast her eyes in Mary's direction and smiled. "Mistress Brewer."

Bloody hell. It really *was* a case of 'no holes barred' with Ophelia Offcut. "Mistress Offcut," Mary responded, hoping her smile appeared genuine rather than self-conscious.

The guards looked particularly amused by the exchange, which made Mary feel even more inadequate.

"Actually," Sid said, "we've just come from Doctor Whysman's home, where my sister is recovering from the fire that burnt down her house."

Ophelia's expression and body language changed immediately, from saucy posturing to open confusion. "Really? I 'eard someone say…" Then her expression became more thoughtful; something had obviously dawned on her. "So, y' sister's married to the Town Crier then?"

"Yes," Sid answered. "What did you—?"

"Bleedin' 'eck," she said, moving towards him, now sounding concerned. "She gonna be orrigh'?"

Sid appeared somewhat wrong-footed by Ophelia's changed demeanour. "I think so… but I want Doctor Manky to look at her. That's if—"

"Will 'e look at my pa too?"

"Yes, I would say so. Manky strikes me as the kind of person who would take any opportunity to display his self-proclaimed genius."

Ophelia nodded, seemingly satisfied with Sid's level of certainty.

*Well,* Mary thought, how cosy *this* was becoming. If only *she* had a sick or injured relative for Doctor Manky to see. She considered deflecting the conversation towards the Town Crier, but then thought better of it. This was not the moment to discuss the possibility of Gerald Hiepants having poisoned the Duke.

"Right then," Olivia announced to all and sundry. "Now all we gotta do is get past *this* lot."

The guardsmen smiled. One of them raised an eyebrow: he was clean shaven except for a moustache, which was unusual in Lower Icing; it was considered more of an Escargotian affectation. Then he spoke, "Before any of you waste your breath on wha'ever story y'about to tell, none of you are gettin' one step further into the castle without proper authorisation."

"And by authorisation, we mean *documentation*, signed by Sir Richard Upson," added a second guardsman.

Where had these men come from, Mary wondered; the contrast between *them* and the undisciplined, comical misfits on guard yesterday was remarkable. She could see Ophelia about to play her flirtatious card — the *only* card in her deck, of course. Well, Mary's deck wasn't quite so limited. Directing her gaze at the second guardsmen, she said, "Sir Richard is my brother — he'll want to see us."

This was met by a guffaw of disbelief, not from the guardsmen but Ophelia.

"Mary speaks the truth, Ophelia," Sid said, coming, unnecessarily, to her defence. Then he blemished his good work by adding, "The Seneschal is her *half*-brother."

Still, the clarification didn't suppress Ophelia's disbelief. "What the frig! Really?"

Mary ignored the display of amazement and concentrated on the reaction of the guardsmen. They looked a bit taken aback by the revelation. Ironically, Ophelia's performance might have added some credence to her claim. "Well?" Mary challenged them. "May we pass?"

They shared looks between themselves, before Monsieur Moustache answered on their behalf. "Certainly." He smiled.

Mary felt victorious; her card had come up trumps.

"If you're in possession of the correct documentation."

CHAPTER 88

## *At the mercy of Sid Evily*

THEY HAD BEEN arguing with the guards for about five minutes. The guardsmen were a stubborn lot, fobbing off Mary Brewer's relationship to Sir Richard. Bloody hell, who would have guessed a woman who worked in an inn would be related to a bloody nob? You'd think she'd be doing better for herself. Still, if Sid Evily had caught her eye, then her sights couldn't be set *that* high. Even so, she had a way about her and she wasn't stupid, and, if truth be told, Ophelia could see why Mary was attracted to Sid: there was more to him than just a ready wit. Although, looking at him now, he seemed more like someone who was at his wit's end. And he was still wearing the same clothes he'd had on when they picked him up on the North Road — clearly, he hadn't bathed, and he also smelled of smoke.

"Look," said Mary, frustrated, "why doesn't one of you go and inform my brother that we're here; I'm sure he'd happily provide the correct documentation."

This was met with more patronising smiles. "We are Ducal Guardsmen," the clean-shaven one intoned, "not messengers."

Mary sighed. "This is ridiculous."

Ophelia was also fed up with the guards, and she was disappointed in Sid. He'd contributed nothing to their cause. "Bleedin' 'eck, Sid," she said, "you jus' goin' t'stand there scatchin' y'balls?"

Ophelia had made the comment with the intention of firing Sid up. However, what happened was frighteningly explosive: Sid suddenly cried out in pain and grabbed at the back of his calf. Ophelia almost expected to see an arrow protruding from it. She heard Mary ask him what was wrong, and two of the guardsmen moved closer to see what had happened. Too close, as it turned out.

Sid sprang forward, elbowing one in the stomach, then kicking the other one in his codpiece. The codpiece one doubled over and Sid leapt behind him.

Suddenly, the gasping codpiece guard was standing up with one arm pinned behind him and a dagger at his throat.

It all happened so quickly; too quickly for the other two guards to react in time. Too quickly for Ophelia to take it all in… Sid was holding a frigging *dagger* to a guardsman's neck. *What the frig!*

"Sid!" Mary screamed somewhere in the middle of it all, but now she was just standing there looking shocked.

The other guards were also looking shocked, their supercilious smiles well and truly wiped. The one who'd copped the elbow gasped as he tried to straighten up. Tears ran down the face of the moustachioed one — the one who was now at the mercy of Sid Evily. Still, that was probably due to the kick in the nads. The only one who appeared to be calm was the man holding the dagger.

Mary breathed, heavily. "Sid, what are you doing?"

"Providing the correct documentation," he said.

The guards were eyeing each other, obviously weighing up their chances of overpowering him.

"Sid, please; this is not the way," she urged, clearly worried.

"I agree with you, Mary," he said, keeping his eyes fixed on the guardsmen, "but it is *a* way. And I think you'll agree, it's probably the quickest way."

His words were conversational, but that just made them all the scarier. Ophelia's heart was pounding; she felt like she was about to chuck it up.

"Sid," Mary said, trying to stay calm, "put the dagger down."

Ophelia had seen plenty of livestock slaughtered with a cut to the neck, but she'd never witnessed a human suffer the same fate. This was different, *very* different. Just the thought of it… She could feel herself shaking now.

"Listen to her, Sid," said one of the guardsmen. "Nobody needs to get hurt here. Let's all stay calm, shall we."

Obviously he was talking to everyone apart from Sid, because Sid *was* bloody calm — the blade hovered very steadily over the guard's pulsing neck.

"Actually, guardsman," Sid replied, "it's time for *you* to listen to *me*."

"Sid, it doesn't matter," Mary said, reaching out and gently touching the arm that held the dagger. "Richard will understand."

His eyes darted from Mary to the guards. "This is not just about seeing your oh-so-understanding brother. I've had it up to my neck — if you'll pardon the expression, guardsman — with being manipulated, misdirected and… misjudged. And, truth be told, I've been itching to use one of these beauties again."

*Again!* Shit!

Sid pressed the blade of the dagger lightly against the guardsman's skin and the man let out a pitiful sob.

Mary removed her hand from Sid's arm in case, Ophelia guessed, it provoked him further.

"We've talked about trust before, Mary. Nothing's changed for me."

"Nor me, Sid," Mary responded, and she sounded as if she meant it.

"Good." He smiled. "Now, why don't you escort Ophelia to the Upper Bailey while I keep these lads entertained with stories of my Adventuring days working for a madman called The Slasher."

*Was he jesting?*

The Ducal Guardsmen appeared to be transfixed, none of them willing, at this point, to put the man in black to the test. *That* was a relief.

"Go on, Mary," prompted Sid. "Everything will be fine here. After all, I'm only asking these *Ducal* Guardsmen to look like they're still on guard." Then, addressing the three guardsmen who weren't at his mercy, he asked, "You don't have a problem with that, do you, lads?"

The guardsmen looked at each other, shaking their heads warily. One of them said, "Whatever y'want, Sid. Just be careful with that blade."

"I *am* being careful with it," replied Sid. "Careful to keep it at your friend's throat until these ladies have returned from seeing Sir Richard and retrieving Doctor Manky."

Then he looked back at Mary. "Don't be too long, Mary; don't want to bore the lads."

Suddenly, Ophelia found her voice, and even to her, it sounded… wrong. "Don' worry 'bout tha' Sid; these lads are *paid* t'be bored."

All eyes turned to her. She felt like laughing.

"Come, Ophelia," Mary said. "Let's do as Sid says." Then the innkeeper looked back at the scruff-in-black-turned-smiling-assassin. "Are you sure about this?"

"Of course, Mary," he assured her.

"We won't be long."

He smiled and winked.

As they walked through the gates towards the Upper Bailey, it suddenly occurred to Ophelia that other people might have noticed the… altercation. She looked back towards the Administration Section. It was virtually deserted; just a couple of grey-clad clerks walking across the courtyard, seemingly focused on their destination. In the distance, a smattering of people and men-at-arms walked to and fro, going about their business or duty, ambling towards the barracks or kitchen, caught in their own worlds, oblivious to the unfolding stand-off. It was cold comfort.

Ophelia's heart was racing as she and Mary Brewer rushed across the sun-filled Middle Bailey; everything became a merging of grey — Mary's swishing dress hurrying over blurred cobblestones.

The Slasher, Sid had said. That's the man her pa had met in The Pits, wasn't it? The madman who'd allowed the Moleson Twins to beat him and dump him. The Slasher was the reason she was here, looking for a doctor.

"Are you alright, Ophelia?"

Mary was holding her arm, pulling her along. *When did that happen?* Her voice brought Ophelia back to the here and now; they'd almost reached the gate to the Upper Bailey. Ophelia nodded, but in truth she was wondering what and *who* she'd got herself involved with.

"There doesn't appear to be any Ducal Guardsmen on duty here," Mary said, as if it might make Ophelia feel better. "I recognise these two. They'll let us pass."

Ophelia looked ahead at the two guards. They were about ten paces away and appeared much the same as the other guards, but Mary seemed convinced otherwise.

"Just wish them a good day and keep walking," she whispered, letting go of Ophelia, and then added, "No extra charm is required."

The remark sounded slightly catty to Ophelia. She cast her gaze back towards the Lower Bailey, half expecting to see the other guards running after them, but obviously Sid and his dagger were still having the desired effect.

As Mary predicted, the guards allowed them to pass without much more than a cursory tip of their hat and a half-hearted "Afternoon, ladies". They progressed along the pathway, through the immaculately presented garden, to the imposing residence of the Duke of Lower Icing. Stepping under the grand portico, they were surprised to find an unguarded open door. Behind it, the extravagant, marble-floored reception hall spread out before them.

It had been over a week since Ophelia had been here with Seth, when they'd been fobbed off and kept waiting for hours. She'd been insulted by revolting old men smoking disgusting cigars *and* manhandled out of the castle by stuck-up servants for causing a scene. Well, she'd cause another bloody one if she was treated the same way. Hopefully, being with the sister of Sir Nob-head Upson would prevent that from happening.

Taking a deep breath, she left the tranquil garden behind and followed Mary into the white, echoing interior. They were met by silence. The room was deserted.

"Come on, Prestwich is probably in his office," Mary said, walking towards the door that had remained closed to her and Seth while others came and went as they pleased, including Tom.

Tom, she mused; her first impressions of him hadn't been good — just another bloody high 'n' mighty tosser who assumed *his* need was more important than theirs. Never in a million years would she have thought that he'd be the one she'd give her heart to. She wondered how he was getting on with his search — over five hours had passed since he'd ridden off with the troop of patrolmen.

Her wonderings ended as Mary knocked at the office door. It echoed loudly across the empty reception hall. It was quite eerie. They waited for a few seconds, but nothing happened. Mary tried opening the door, but it was locked.

"This is strange," she said, looking around the room. "Where *is* everyone?"

Strange was right. Ophelia didn't like it at all; she felt out of place here. She'd rather be with Tom, even it meant getting back on Hazel. She'd almost become used to sitting astride the saddle (without Sid Evily squashed in behind her) and she'd started to form a kind of relationship with the placid mare. Bloody hell, who *was* this Ophelia Offcut? What had happened to the butcher's daughter who regarded most animals as meat?

"Let's try upstairs," Mary said, hurrying towards the grand staircase that led to Sir Richard's private quarters.

This made Ophelia feel even more uncomfortable; the memory of the audience with the Seneschal was still fresh in her mind. She'd been escorted to his quarters by Lieutenant Swill after she'd told him what Bert Muggins had revealed about her pa and the Moleson Twins. She'd gone there for help, for Sir Richard to send out a search party, since it was *him* who'd made her pa go looking for the bleeding doctor. But he wasn't interested in her pa, just the frigging doctor; she'd lashed out at him and her head had begun to spin, and then she'd… fainted. For the first time in her life, she'd *actually* fainted.

Her head was spinning at the thought of it and they'd only climbed four or five steps. She stopped.

Mary turned to face her. "What's wrong?"

"Think I'll wait down 'ere," she replied. "Don' much fancy revisitin' y'brother's place. Didn' end well las' time."

"Last time?" Mary seemed surprised.

"Yeah, Lieutenan' Swill brang me 'ere… t'tell Sir Richard 'bout me pa an' how the Moleson Twins were gonna dump 'is body."

"Oh… I take it he wasn't particularly receptive."

Ophelia shrugged; she didn't want to regurgitate the conversation of five days ago. What good would it do? And, in any case, she really needed to sit down.

"Very well," Mary said. "I won't be long. We need to get back to Sid."

With that, she rushed up the stairs, the sound of her footsteps filling the void. Ophelia turned and walked over to the lounge area, where she and Seth had waited in vain to see Sir Richard. She sat down on one of the seats — plush and comfortable for the fat-arsed nobs — and waited for Mary.

# Chapter 89

## *Blacker than the darkness*

**M**ARY WAS GLAD Ophelia had decided to wait downstairs; time was of the essence and her absence was one less explanation, one less obstacle. Still, at the moment, the main obstacle was actually finding someone to run into. The marble staircase turned back on itself before arriving at the spacious first level landing. Again, the area was deserted. How long could Sid hold out, Mary wondered.

She raced over to the entrance of Richard's quarters. The black door was deceptively plain, the only embellishment a silver door knocker with an ornately decorated base plate with a quill and sword motif etched into it… just like the silver button.

She used the knocker. There was no answer. "Richard! It's Mary!"

She tried again. "Richard!"

Again, only silence. *What the frig was going on?*

She tried the door knob. Unexpectedly, it twisted and the door clicked opened. *Shit!* Something was amiss. She knew Richard well enough to know he would never leave his residence unsecured.

Mary called out his name again as she walked into the antechamber with its polished checker-board floor, pristine black velvet divan and imposing horse statues prancing on pedestals. Her voice sounded lost as it resonated in the imposing room. She halted and listened for some sign of life, but there was none, save for her rapid breathing. She thought about leaving, but she felt responsible for Sid; he was relying on her.

The door from the antechamber to Richard's private quarters was open. Again, it felt *wrong*. Mary tensed as she entered her brother's lavish reception room; although, in truth, it was more like a tribute room. Portraits of Richard adorned most of the walls and the black-and-silver colour scheme (if you could call black and silver a colour scheme) was overpowering. It made her think how much her brother would benefit from a woman's touch. She'd even mentioned it to him on one occasion. He'd responded off-handedly, "I have a maid who arranges the flowers; I'm *fairly* certain she is a woman." And *that* had been the end of that.

The expansive room was bathed in sunlight from a row of south-facing windows. They afforded the viewer a magnificent panorama of gently undulating, tree-covered hills and shimmering glimpses of the Icing River as it wended its way down to Spitting Dipthong. Mary's gaze, however, was on the opposite side of the room, past the impressive fireplace (above which hung a large portrait of Richard astride Black Beasty) towards a polished mahogany dining table that filled its far end. Next to it was the door that led to Richard's bedchamber and private living quarters.

As she approached the door, she could see it was slightly ajar — *more* wrongness! She called out her brother's name. The silence continued and a sickening dread began to form in the pit of her stomach.

As she moved closer to the door, a strip of sunlight highlighted a corridor that ran parallel to the reception room. Mary had only been in this part of Richard's residence to use the garderobe. It was located at the end of the corridor to her left and emptied onto a mulch pit that was used to fertilise the garden. There was a slight odour wafting from that direction and she wondered if Richard was having a bog... a moment's peace. A flush of embarrassment passed through her, but then, she realised, he must have heard her calling out to him... surely.

Mary pulled open the door and took a couple of tentative steps into the corridor. Ignoring the garderobe, she turned right towards Richard's bedchamber, the corridor extending into gloom and silence. Blood pounded through her ears as she crept along the wooden floorboards. She could feel a tingling on the back of her neck. Bloody hell; the sense of foreboding was almost more than she could bear

"Richard?" she called out, just to break the silence. No answer, but she could *feel* someone was there... waiting.

Mary stopped. She tried to control her breathing... to listen... but her pounding heart wouldn't let her. "I know someone is there," she said, attempting to keep the fear from her voice.

No answer.

Somehow, she continued walking down the darkening corridor. The door to Richard's bedchamber appeared on her left... blacker than the darkness. It, too, was slightly ajar. She stopped outside it. The three-inch gap revealed little more than a strip of silver wallpaper with the same diamond pattern as the reception room, highlighted in a dull sheen of muted light. Mary held her breath and listened, waiting for some tell-tale noise. There was nothing except her thudding heartbeat, the distant clamour of the barracks and Klob Hoofenhaus' clockwork hammering. Her mind was screaming out for her to flee, that if she went into the room, she'd meet a terrible fate.

Somehow she persisted. Taking a deep breath, she flung the door inwards, heavy iron hinges groaning as the splendour of Richard's bedchamber burst into view. However, Mary's eyes were quickly drawn to the body lying face down at the foot of the unmade, four-poster bed. She gasped — the body was clothed in a purple and gold uniform. Mary knew, even before she could see his face, that it was Brandon. He was sprawled across a large deer skin, his head turned to the side, as if he was asleep.

"Brandon!" she yelled, rushing over to him.

There was no immediate sign of injury: no protruding dagger, blood or mark. She knelt down beside him and reached out to touch his face. Her hand was trembling. She touched his cheek. His skin was warm. Daring to think he might only be unconscious, she put her ear to his heart. She heard it beating as, in her other ear, a voice whispered, "I'm afraid it wath nethethary."

Then blackness.

## CHAPTER 90

# *Shit! Shit! Shit!*

IT FELT LIKE Mary had been gone for ages. Ophelia had heard her knock on a door and call out to her brother, then… the silence had returned. As the minutes passed, her concern for Mary (and Sid Evily and the Ducal Guards) grew. What the frig could Mary be doing? Where *was* everyone? She was sitting on one of the plush lounges, trying to calm herself, but it wasn't working. The deserted silence… something was wrong.

Ophelia was on the verge of going up the staircase when she heard footsteps coming down it. She sprang up from the lounge. However, there was something odd about them — they didn't sound like Mary's, the footfalls were too light. But they were in a hurry. Perhaps it was one of Sir Richard's servants come to fetch her. For frig's sake… what was happening here?

A figure appeared on the staircase. He was definitely not a servant, more like some sort of malnourished peasant. He was short and wiry, wearing a pale blue robe that fell to his knees, tied at his waist by a cord of the same hue. On his feet, he wore simple, soft leather shoes. His skinny legs skittered down the steps with nimble ease. It wasn't until he reached the bottom of the staircase that he lifted his bald head and noticed Ophelia standing there.

His expression was one of muted surprise, like a turkey that had just spotted the axe. He acknowledged her with a wary smile. "Good afternoon, Mithtress," he lisped, and then continued walking towards the entrance.

*What the frig?*

"Oi," she called out to the quickly departing man; the white tufts of hair above his ears billowed as he picked up speed.

Ophelia started after him, but the man broke into a run and disappeared through the entrance. She dashed to the entrance in time to see him running towards the Upper Bailey gate.

"Wait!" she yelled, but clearly the man had no intention of stopping. Then she yelled at the two guards at the gatehouse to stop him.

The guardsmen turned in time to see the little man running towards them. One of them folded his arms, while the other made a half-hearted attempt at signalling him to stop. At least they were blocking his path.

Their presence, however, had no effect on the blue-robed man. In fact, if anything, he *increased* his pace, moving at a speed that Ophelia wouldn't have thought possible in a person of his age. He had to be at least fifty.

The guardsmen were totally caught off guard as he jumped into the air and let fly with a kick to the signalling one's throat, sending him sprawling to ground. Before the other one could unfold his arms, the spindly legged man landed on the ground and chopped him on the back of his neck with his right hand. The guardsman collapsed next to his companion, who was now making strange choking noises.

Ophelia stood under the ornate portico entrance, stunned at what she had just witnessed, and watched as the man ran through the gate into the Middle Bailey.

She ran over to the prone guardsmen. The one who had been chopped lay motionless and quiet — unconscious, she assumed. Her attention was drawn to the gurgling, gagging guardsman; arms flailing at his throat as he tried to breathe. His neck was swollen, and had turned a deep red colour. His bulging eyes pleaded for her to do something, but what the frig could she do?

"Help!" she screamed.

Then she went running into the Middle Bailey, screaming for anyone to come to her aid. At first her screams went unanswered, then Sid appeared from the Lower Bailey, running towards her. He still had the dagger in his hand. In hot pursuit was a Ducal Guardsmen. It was then she noticed the blade of his dagger was glistening red. Bloody frigging hell!

Time slowed as Sid closed the distance between them. In the background, the sound of choking gurgled to silence, as did the thrashing sound of boots. Ophelia felt sick. Then she felt Sid shaking her, calling her name, but she was watching the Ducal Guardsman approach. He didn't have a moustache; he wasn't the one Sid had been holding at dagger-point. The guardsman slowed down and drew his sword. What had Sid done? Then she felt a sharp stinging sensation on her left cheek.

"Ophelia!" Suddenly Sid's face was in front of her. "Where's Mary?" he panted.

"What?"

"Mary! Is she alright?"

Ophelia's head was spinning, she'd almost forgotten about Mary. "I dunno, she…"

"Put the dagger down, Sid," said the Ducal Guardsman, also out of breath, his sword hovering in Sid's direction.

But Sid wasn't paying him any heed. "Where is she?" His face was covered in sweat, his expression intense.

The Ducal Guardsman closed in, warily. "The dagger, Sid."

"She wen' upstairs to Sir Richard's. The man in the blue robe, 'e came runnin' down from there, then 'e attacked the guards. I think 'e's *killed* one of 'em."

*Oh shit! Had he killed Mary too?*

"I won't tell you again, Sid. Put the dagger down."

They must have seen him run past. "'E ran into the—"

Sid lunged to his right, then whirled around and kicked the sword from the Ducal Guardsman's grip. The man cried out in pain, shaking his hands, and Sid followed through with a punch to the face, using the pommel of his dagger. Ophelia heard something crack, and the man dropped to the ground, with blood spraying from his flattened nose.

*Shit! Shit! Shit!*

Then Sid was running past her into the Upper Bailey.

"Sid!" she yelled after him. This was a nightmare.

The Ducal Guardsman was groaning and spitting out blood. "He'll swing for this," he spluttered at her.

Where the frig *was* everybody? What had happened to the other Ducal Guardsmen? Had he *actually*…?

Then, as if answering her thoughts, three quick blows from a bugle rang out from the Lower Bailey. Well, at least *one* of them was alive.

Her common sense was telling her to stay put, but Ophelia needed to keep moving… to keep from collapsing. She ran back into the Upper Bailey, daring a glimpse at the prone guardsmen as she rushed past. She wished she hadn't. The grotesquely bloated face of the one who had been kicked in the neck stared agonisingly up at her… dead. Shit! The other one still looked like he was sleeping, but… shit!

Another three blasts rang out. Sid was nowhere in sight, but there was noise coming from inside the portico entrance. Suddenly, it erupted with a dozen or more Ducal Guardsmen spewing out into the garden. Ophelia's knees felt like they might give as she moved out of their way. "Y' too friggin' late," she yelled as they rushed past, barely acknowledging her presence.

Ophelia's vision swirled — mottled grass, colourful blooms and bright blue sky spun around her. Then all she could see was purple and gold. Someone had grabbed her arm and was walking her towards the entrance. Suddenly, there seemed to be people everywhere, the air urgent with sounds of orders and outrage, concern and confusion. She was led under the portico. Faces she didn't know regarded her with suspicion.

"Stand aside," the man leading her barked.

The faces made space and she was pulled through the entrance. Inside, the reception hall was cooler and somewhat calmer. It gave Ophelia a chance to collect her thoughts and focus on what was happening to her. She was now aware that the hand gripping her upper arm was strong, aggressively tugging her across the marble floor. And the man who was doing the tugging was dressed in the uniform of a Purple Perillian. Ophelia could only see the back of his head; the purple feather on his cavalier's hat looked damaged.

"Mind slowin' down a bit," she said. "An' y'can let go of my arm; I ain't goin' nowhere."

He was leading her towards the staircase… towards Mary and… frig knows what.

"Shut the frig up!" he growled, tightening his grip on her arm.

She cried out in pain and tried to shake herself free.

The officer whirled on her. His jaw was swollen, his bottom lip stitched and matted with congealed blood, but it was his eyes: they were baleful, full of hatred. Ophelia felt her stomach turn. Lieutenant Fowler!

"Go on," he hissed, sticking his horrible face in hers. "*Please* give me an excuse t'break your friggin' arm."

Ophelia let the lieutenant pull her up the stairs, not saying a word, and doing her best to keep pace so as not to provoke him into violence. Tom should have hit him harder, done a proper job on the shithead.

They approached the top of the staircase, where two guardsmen stood on duty. They saluted Fowler as he pulled Ophelia onto the first-floor landing. He continued to manhandle her into Sir Richard's private chambers, through the antechamber with its four black marble statues of rearing horses.

Ophelia was virtually shoved into the massive reception room; the silver-and-black wallpaper shimmered in the bright sunlight. There were a number of people in the room. Most were in uniform, but two were well-dressed civilians. One of them was the smarmy git who'd ogled her while she and Seth waited to see Sir Richard… *just* what she needed!

They'd walked into a heated discussion: the smarmy git was pointing his fat finger at a man in uniform — judging by his adornments, he was a high-ranking officer. The appearance of her and Fowler halted the discussion.

"Here's the Offcut slut, Captain," he said, pushing her roughly in the direction of the group.

"Piss off," Ophelia spat back, shaking herself free of his grip; he couldn't do anything to her here.

"Thank you, Lieutenant," said the officer.

"Don't tell me *she's* involved in this, Le Sharp," cried the smarmy git in outrage. "What sort of show are you running here?"

"You're not helping, Fraser," said another man, dressed in dark grey.

"Stay out of this, Rupert," snapped Fraser. "This is not a legal matter."

"True," Rupert retorted, "but neither is it a trade matter… unless, of course, you're intending to trade insults with the captain all afternoon."

"Haven't you got a *pardon* to attend to?" Fraser sneered.

What the frig had she been dragged into? Had they found Mary? And what had happened to Sid?

Even Fowler seemed frustrated by the aimless bickering. "So, what do you want me to do with her, Captain," he interjected.

"Seat her over there for time being, Lieutenant," Captain Le Sharp replied, indicating the large table at the far end of the room: the one she'd fainted next to.

Fowler didn't seem pleased. "Sir, are you sure—"

"Are you out of your mind, Le Sharp?" spurted Fraser.

Then another voice entered the conversation.

"Enough!"

All heads turned to face the voice — it had come from behind the group. Even though the person was obscured by the men, Ophelia had no doubt who it was.

"What's going on, Paris? I thought I'd made myself clear."

The captain responded defensively. "Yes, Sir Richard, we were just discussing—"

"I don't believe I asked you to *discuss* anything. Action is what I require! What *action* have you undertaken?"

"The men-at-arms have been despatched and Lieutenant Fowler has apprehended Ophelia Offcut." He nodded to Fowler, who then reacquainted his hand with her upper arm. It frigging hurt; he'd already bruised it pulling her up the staircase.

"Take y'hands of me, y'bastard!"

The group of men parted as Fowler pushed her towards an appraising Sir Richard standing in the doorway of a dimly lit passage. She could smell stale tobacco smoke as she brushed past the merchant; it almost made her gag.

The man before her was clean shaven and his hair was pulled back tightly in what she assumed was a ponytail. If it wasn't for his black clothing and his condescending gaze…

"Well, Miss Offcut…"

…*and* his condescending tone,

"…here we are again…"

*and* his condescending smile…

"…although, you seem to have broken quite a few Duchy Laws since last we met."

…*and* his condescending demeanour, Ophelia may not have recognised him.

He flicked his gaze at Fowler. "That will be all, Lieutenant."

Fowler saluted smartly. "Sir Richard, shall I take Evily to The Can?"

Sid was here?

The Seneschal regarded Fowler in much the same way he might regard a turd on his boot. "I believe I said that will be all, Lieutenant."

Fowler saluted again, then treated Ophelia to a sneer as he turned around and began walking back across the room. "As for the rest of you: Paris — your charge is to secure the Upper Bailey and protect the Duke."

"It's being done as we speak, Sir Richard."

"That's my point, Paris," he said evenly, "there is too much *speaking*. Go and find out what is *happening* and report back to me personally. And, as for you, Fraser and Rupert, since you both seem to have an appetite for bickering, why don't you go home to your wives."

"Sir Richard, I must insist—"

"*Must* you, Fraser?" The man in black smiled dangerously. Then he moved into the room. "Do you wish to gainsay my authority… *again*?" he said, walking past Ophelia. Hopefully, he was about to give the smarmy git a good bollocking — she'd like to see the fat slug squirm.

"Of course not, Sir Richard," he said, indignantly. "I'm just mindful of how this could affect the Duke of Stymouth's visit."

Sir Richard was now within kicking distance of the fat lump's bollocks. "Are you suggesting, Fraser, that *I* am *not?*"

The room had gone very quiet. The men in uniform, including the captain, had become very still, as if they'd been told to stand to attention; even Fowler had stopped. In fact, the only person who seemed to be anywhere near at ease was Rupert.

Fraser shook his head. "I'm suggesting nothing of the kind," he said, breathily. "However, it is clear you have more..." — the jowly-faced merchant glanced at her — "... pressing matters to attend to."

*What the frig did he mean by that?*

"Really." Sir Richard grinned with menace.

Ophelia could no longer see the Seneschal's face, but judging by the expressions of those who *could*, something unpleasant was about to follow.

The merchant sighed and dropped his gaze. "Very well, Sir Richard, I shall take my leave. Please let me know when you've..." Again, his gaze drifted in Ophelia's direction. "...cleaned up this mess."

Arrogant prick! She'd bloody had enough of this shit. She moved towards the ugly merchant; he was eyeing her with lascivious disdain. *Who the frig did he think he was?* She'd just seen a man get killed! He was frigging *nothing!*

No-one moved, but she could feel their eyes upon her. Even after she'd wiped the over-confident smirk from his fat face with a forceful slap, no-one moved. Well, apart from Fraser that is. He stumbled sideways into the other tosser, Rupert; surprise and momentum knocking *him* off-balance, sending both of them sprawling to the floor.

Ophelia was shocked and pleased with the result.

So, apparently, was Sir Richard. "My thoughts exactly, Miss Offcut."

Then there was a mad scramble from the men-at-arms to retrieve the two fat pigs who were now snorting and grunting on the floor.

Somewhere amidst the tangle of bodies and cries of outrage, Fowler appeared before her, his face cold and full of hatred. Suddenly, his fist was heading for her face. She flinched and felt... nothing. There was just a slapping sound.

Looking back, she saw Sir Richard had grabbed Fowler by the wrist. Yet, the lieutenant seemed oblivious to the fact. He was still straining to follow through with the punch, his mad gaze fixed on her; he must have flipped his frigging lid. He'd even broken the stitches in his lip and blood was running down his chin.

"Lieutenant," Sir Richard said, his voice sounded strained. "I suggest—"
Ophelia's kick to Fowler's bollocks made finishing the sentence unnecessary.

It took some time for the chaos to subside. Firstly, there'd been the aftermath of Ophelia's slap and kick. Fraser wanted her clapped in irons and put in the stocks for a week, Fowler just wanted to beat her to a pulp, while Rupert offered to act on behalf of the Duchy in prosecuting any person or persons against whom charges were laid. However, Sir Richard was having none of it; he told them all to clear off in his nob-ish sort of way. Except for Fowler. He ordered two of the guardsmen to take him to The Can where he was to 'consider the difference between the conduct of a Purple Perillian and that of a common thug'. Ophelia had felt like cheering, but managed to contain her pleasure to a satisfied smile.

Captain Le Sharp left to take personal command of whatever his men-at-arms were supposed to be doing. Thank frig the Five Duchies were at peace — Lower Icing wouldn't last five minutes against an organised threat. In fact, the pissheads at The Bell could probably out-manoeuvre Lower Icing's regiment of leerers, tossers and big heads.

Regardless of Ophelia's opinion, four Ducal Guardsmen — two outside the entrance to Sir Richard's quarters and two within the antechamber — were left with the responsibility of allowing the right people in and keeping the wrong people out. All the while, Ophelia was wondering what had happened to Sid and Mary. Once Sir Richard had finished ordering everyone about, she'd asked him as much. His response was predictably unhelpful.

"Given the circumstances, Miss Offcut, I rather think it is *I* who should be asking the questions. Now, if—"

Whether it was the tone of his voice, his offhand, condescending politeness, the way he dismissed anything that didn't concern him, or just the way he frigging looked, something inside Ophelia's head went… *ping*. Suddenly, she was way beyond caring where she was or who she was talking to and her pent-up emotion came spewing forth.

"Oh, for frig's sake, Sir Richard! Where do y'wan' me t'start? How 'bout wha' y'put my fam'ly through lookin' for tha' friggin' doctor? Billy ain't right in the head now an' Pa *needs* a friggin' doctor! *That's* why I'm 'ere, an' tha's wha' brought Sid 'ere too, 'cause 'is sister got burnt *an'* 'cause Tom asked 'im t'tell you wha' 'appened on the North Road. Don' know wha' tha' feckless shit Fowler told ya, but it was *'im* who made trouble for 'imself — posturin' an' accusin' an' arrestin' for no good reason an' then orderin' 'is men to shoot arrows at us when we was jus' tryin' to… An' then we couldn' get in t'the castle, even when Mary said she was your friggin' sister. So Sid… 'e pulled this dagger ou' of 'is boot… Oh frig, tha' poor…"

Ophelia felt strong arms supporting her before she realised she was sobbing uncontrollably. The vision of the guardsman's face as he gargled his last breath… and everything else that had happened… it was too much. The world blurred behind a stream of tears, and she shuddered and gasped for air like… someone choking to death.

Then she was weightless and the room turned sideways, the silver walls began to move and it became dark. Then she heard voices, muffled then clearer as the world brightened again. Then she was aware of other figures. A man in purple and gold was propped against the base of a bed. He looked like Lieutenant Swill. A ghost-like figure was bending over a woman lying on the ground. She was wearing a grey dress. Mary? She couldn't see her face; a man was kneeling in front of her, his right hand stained with blood. And there was another person, a man in black, who loomed towards her, blocking out the light, approaching her like death. Then she heard Sir Richard say, "I have another patient for you, Doctor."

## CHAPTER 91

### *She had an inn to run*

FOR THE SECOND time in less than twenty-four hours, Mary found herself being escorted from the Upper Bailey. This time she had *two* men by her side — Richard and Sid — and *this* time she wasn't drunk; although, Doctor Manky's *Vigour Morphis* had left her feeling a little light-headed. Not that she was complaining; the potion had completely revived her and virtually erased the splitting headache she'd had after regaining consciousness.

Walking through the beautiful, serene grounds of the royal manor, the lawns dappled in the mid-afternoon shade of elm trees, it seemed unbelievable that the events of two hours ago had actually occurred. It was unreal. Bertrand… Bloody hell, he'd actually *killed* someone! How close had *she* come to being killed, she wondered. Then again, she *really* didn't want to think about that. At least no-one else had suffered any grievous injury. Well, apart from the guardsman Sid had smacked in the face.

They'd just left Richard's office, where Richard had spent the last hour and a half questioning Sid and Mary. Prestwich had also been present, scribing all that was said. The knock to his forehead had turned into a bulging black bruise. Mary apologised (again) and Sid had looked at her with a curious expression. She explained how she'd opened the door onto his face. Sid made light of it, of course, and then suggested Prestwich obtain some of Manky's *Bruise Mousse*. Prestwich, however, didn't share in Sid's sense of amusement, and Richard well and truly had his Seneschal hat on. Mary was still trying to adjust to his new appearance; he just didn't look right cleanly shaven (although it was clear he hadn't shaved today) and his tightly pulled-back hair made him look even more severe… which was quite an achievement.

He wanted to know about Sid's involvement with Doctor Manky and, more pertinently, Bertrand. His movements subsequent to discovering he was in possession of the silver button were also scrutinised. Mary's behaviour was also called into question, particularly for colluding with Sid, a man she barely knew. Mary had never experienced Richard under these circumstances and she found it confronting to say the least, particularly after everything else that had happened… no doubt it was why he'd chosen to question them at that time. Still, Richard hadn't acted unreasonably; he listened more than he questioned and sought clarification rather than information. He appeared to accept Sid's answers at face value, questioning his judgment more than the veracity of his actions. Of course, Mary was able to corroborate some of what he said.

Sid had been surprisingly accepting of the position he found himself in — there was no trace of sarcasm or guardedness towards Richard — and he was particularly forthcoming about his sister's meeting with Xavier at The Bloody Bell; although, he was quick to add that he hadn't known it *was* Xavier until yesterday evening, when he saw a portrait of the young doctor in Manky's house at Blessed Whipping. He also admitted that he'd broken into the Hiepants' abode on the night of the castle dinner and found the doctor's book of potions and the incriminating markings within. Richard responded with an admission of his own: that they already had their man by then and the dinner was nothing more than an elaborate confessional.

It was then Mary asked Richard if *Gerald* was his 'man', the one with 'misguided judgement'. Surprisingly, and without hesitation, he confirmed that he was. Even though she'd asked the question, she hadn't expected such a definitive response. Sid was gobsmacked. He'd convinced himself that it was Olivia's doing. Richard assured him that the Town Crier had acted alone in the Duke's poisoning. However, Olivia *had* been complicit in harbouring Xavier prior to the poisoning; a self-righteous act which had led to Xavier's assault at the hands of the Moleson Twins and, ultimately, the assault on Sid himself. Both of them had found it hard to absorb. As Richard revealed more details about the days leading up to the poisoning, the more it seemed like a plot from a Hamlet Macbeth tragedy (though even *he* wouldn't be clever enough to imagine such an incredible set of circumstances).

And then, of course, there was the false proclamation and silver button fiasco complicating an already bizarre situation. For all intents and purposes, the button (or key) was nothing more than an annoying distraction; one, however, that could have proven disastrous for Richard and the Duchy. He could almost forgive the Town Crier for his stupidity in poisoning the Duke in an effort to reunite father and son, but he couldn't forgive him for his duplicity in fabricating such a misleading and incriminating proclamation.

Sid had asked what was to become of Gerald and his sister. Richard replied that while the Duke had pardoned the Town Crier for the poisoning, they would both answer for their disloyalty and scheming; he would make sure of that. The hearing that was supposed to have been held this morning would happen at a later date, where *both* of them would be facing charges. Sid wanted to know what Richard had in mind; he was understandably worried for them, particularly since Olivia had been injured in the blaze that burnt their house down. Sid suggested that perhaps *that* could be viewed as punishment enough. Richard disagreed, but, other than stating that Gerald and Olivia would not be punished physically, he was non-committal about their future.

The Seneschal had then re-visited the subject of *Sid's* behaviour, saying that he excused his actions where Lieutenant Fowler was concerned, but he couldn't ignore his aggressive, unprovoked attack on the Ducal Guardsman. This time, Sid offered no defence for his actions (and Mary kept her thoughts to herself), saying only that it was done in the heat of the moment and he was sorry for causing undue injury. Richard pondered Sid's response for some time before ending the meeting without further comment. Prestwich stopped scribing and took his leave without saying a word; it was almost as if the Seneschal and his secretary shared some silent form of communication. She and Sid had shared curious glances at the abruptness of it all. They'd shared even more curious ones when Richard offered to escort them both back to The Harey Rabbit.

Four Ducal Guardsmen snapped to attention as they left the lush confines of the Upper Bailey for the stark greyness of the Middle Bailey. Richard acknowledged them with a nod. Mary didn't recognise any of them, which was a relief, but she sensed they knew who she and Sid were; it was an uncomfortable moment.

As soon as they set foot in the Middle Bailey, Richard began to speak, and the topic was as unexpected as the conversational tone in his voice, "Tell me, Sid, how would you describe your relationship with your sister?"

It was clear Sid was just as taken aback by the question as Mary. "I'm not sure what you mean."

"Very well; allow me to elucidate... I find it passing strange that in all the time I've known Olivia — since her courting days with Captain Le Sharp — she's never mentioned having a brother."

Sid looked decidedly uncomfortable. "We had a parting of ways... of sorts."

"So I understand."

*What was going on here?* Mary had already told Richard that Sid and Olivia were estranged.

"And I believe it was not long before she married the Town Crier," Richard continued, casually, "or, perhaps, it is more accurate to say, not long *after* her dalliance with Captain Le Sharp ended."

Sid remained silent, but his face turned red.

"Which, coincidently, appears to have occurred shortly after a large sum of coin was discovered by your sister in the alleyway behind your then abode in Backflush Lane."

Mary didn't like the sound of this. "Richard, what are—?"

"Please don't interrupt, Mary," her brother said smoothly, and without a hint of annoyance.

She felt the blood rush to *her* face. Richard was adept at putting people in their place. And right now, her place was walking silently to Sid's left, while, to his right, Richard continued to peel away the skin of Sid's past.

"Of course, when the… *discovery* was brought to Captain Le Sharp's attention, he acted with the kind of alacrity and efficiency that is patently lacking in most officers today."

Where was this heading, Mary wondered, and why wasn't Sid *saying* anything? He looked… guilty. Mary's heart began to beat faster. What the frig had he done?

"So much so, in fact, that no further investigation was deemed necessary."

Still Sid remained silent, but his words outside Charles Bling, Jeweller to the Duke, echoed in her mind: "*There was a time when I could have impressed you that much.*"

"And I believe, Sid — please do enlighten me if I am wrong — that shortly after the coin was claimed by the Duchy, your association with one Paul Peabody came to a rather abrupt end."

"*Sadly, my Adventuring days are over.*"

He'd also referred to his Adventuring days when he overpowered the guardsmen with his dagger. Was he some sort of highwayman?

"I'm sorry, Mary," he said, quietly.

*Oh no! What had he done?*

They were approaching the gate to the Lower Bailey and she had the distinct feeling Sid was about to bolt. Instead, he stopped. Mary and Richard turned to face him. Her heart was pounding now.

"What do you want from me?" he said, addressing Richard. Blood still stained his right hand *and* the arm of his crumpled black shirt. His playful hair looked messy and his usually smiling eyes looked hunted. Suddenly, he looked capable of something… desperate. She cast her gaze down at his beautifully crafted boots and the tasselled affectation that disguised their deadly contents.

A sardonic smile played upon Richard's face. "I'd rather think of it in terms of what I can *give* you, Sid."

Sid regarded Richard with derision. "Really… and what would *that* be — twenty years in the dungeon?"

*What the frig?* Mary couldn't hold her tongue any longer. "Sid, what did you do?"

Sid's eyes flicked momentarily in her direction.

Her brother's smile widened. "I was thinking something a little more productive than that. Something more… *community* minded."

Sid looked wary, waiting for a hook in the bait.

"Essentially," Richard continued, "I'm prepared to give you a chance to… redeem yourself."

"Redeem himself? For what?" Mary blurted out.

"How?" Sid asked, keeping his eyes fixed on Richard.

"Who's Paul Peabody?" Mary persisted, looking from her brother to her lover and not caring which one answered.

Richard continued to smile at Sid in a challenging way.

It was Sid who relented and cast his gaze towards Mary, but he was still lost for words.

"Well? Who is he?" she demanded.

He let out a deep breath. Mary waited, not sure if she really wanted to hear what he was about to say. He took a step towards her. She had to fight the urge to take a step backwards. Instead, she crossed her arms. That — and, no doubt, the look on her face — was enough to forestall any further advance.

"He's someone I used to… work with."

Mary could feel her body tense.

"He'd do the research and planning and I'd carry out the deed."

"The *deed?*" Mary could feel herself shaking, remembering Sid's words as he held the dagger to the guard's throat. *"I've been itching to use one of these beauties again."*

He looked confused, then added quickly, "The *thievery*. I've never *harmed* anyone."

"Don't lie to me, Sid!" She could feel the tears welling, her throat tightening. She lashed out with a kick to his left boot. "What sort of *harmless* thief has daggers in his friggin' boots? Ones he's been *itching* to use again?"

He looked shocked and confused. "What? I swear to you… they are… or *used* to be for self-defence… mainly in The Pits. Paul had them made for me. I've never attacked anyone, not until… The guardsman was the first time I…" He was looking pleadingly at her now. "Mary, please believe me, I have never been anything more than a common thief."

Mary didn't know how to respond. Her emotions were all over the place; she wanted to hit him, to cry in his arms, to believe in him, to kiss him, and to walk away and forget him.

Richard, however, had no such conflict. "Come now, Sid. You do yourself a disservice; you were a most *un*common thief, one might even say a *master* thief. The homes you gained access to, the people you stole from, and the objects you pilfered… all without leaving a trace. *Most* remarkable."

Sid ignored Richard's mocking praise and regarded Mary with pleading intensity, looking for understanding. "I was a different person then… and *Paul* was the master. I was just a… means to an end."

Mary shook her head; this couldn't be happening. "And what are you *now*, Sid Evily?"

He studied her, then nodded his head in acceptance. "A drinker and a womaniser; a petty criminal and a petty person to go with it." He sighed and dropped his gaze. Then he looked up again, his dark eyes glistening. "And then a week ago, almost to the hour, I met you. And since that moment, I've wanted to be… a better man."

Mary felt a tear run down her left cheek; her throat felt raw and tightened even more. She couldn't speak, and Doctor Manky's potion wasn't helping either; her head was spinning.

"Mary, I—"

"Most eloquent, Sid," Richard interjected, "but actions speak louder than words."

The words sounded oddly distant. Mary closed her eyes and squeezed out the tears.

"I'm offering you the opportunity to *be* a better man, to use your skills and give yourself some self-worth, to work for me on the *right* side of the law."

"Is this a jest?" she heard Sid reply.

"As Mary will attest, I rarely jest. I tend to leave that for jesters, lawyers and other tricksters."

Mary took a deep breath and opened her eyes. As she breathed out, her head cleared and the dizziness passed. Not that either Sid or Richard seemed to have noticed — the former was regarding the latter with curiosity. "How did you find out about the coin? Did my sister confess?"

"No, and nor did Captain Le Sharp."

Mary suddenly felt like a bystander.

"You'd be surprised what has been documented. Prestwich is a marvel. His mind is one big ledger of names, places and dates. He records and remembers... *everything*."

Sid was grimacing now.

"After our impromptu introduction at The Harey Rabbit, I asked him to find out what records we had on one Sid Evily. A name like that was bound to stick in the mind of a man like Prestwich and, no doubt, be lodged in some incriminating documentation... and sure enough..."

Sid looked incredulous. "What documentation?"

He'd snatched the words out of Mary's mouth.

"Well, for a start, the addition of two thousand two hundred and forty-four gold coins to the Duchy's treasury was documented. Your sister and, by extension, *you* were named as contributors. I'm sure you appreciate the irony, Sid. I certainly did after Prestwich delved deeper and discovered your name was also mentioned in an official investigation entitled *People of Interest in The Pits*. Your association with Paul Peabody — also known, as you are aware, by the epithet, The Slasher — was noted."

*The Slasher!* Sid had been given a pair of *dagger* boots by a man called The Slasher? The one he'd referred to as a madman? Mary thought he'd been jesting, trying to put the wind up the guardsmen, but clearly...

Sid was shaking his head. "Then why wasn't I arrested?"

"For the same reason Paul Peabody is still at liberty after all these years: lack of evidence. Which, if I'm honest, is a result of both general ineptness and a preference by certain individuals to... how shall I put it... keep the shits in The Pits."

It wasn't hard for Mary to guess who those individuals were; she'd served enough of them over the years. However, she had no idea who *this* dishevelled man standing before her was, the one she'd been caring about and having feelings for over the past week.

"So, you want *me* to become your shit-kicker?" Sid said as if the suggestion was outrageous.

Richard smiled indulgently. "I was thinking of a more subtle role… something that requires nerve and certain amount of… guile. Something more up your alley or, should I say, for the sake of the thematic, up your *Crapp* Alley."

Sid scowled. "And if I refuse?"

A thoughtful expression crossed her brother's face. "Well… I suppose there's always your *original* suggestion, but… well, what a waste of twenty years. Hardly what I'd call a worthwhile existence, with very little opportunity for redemption."

Mary had had enough; obviously *this* was the reason why Richard had decided to 'escort' them to The Harey Rabbit. Though why he'd felt the need to include her when he could have just taken Sid aside and… Then it struck her — he was proving his point, following up on his 'advice' to *"leave well enough alone and be done with him."*

"Oh, *very* good, Richard," she said, acerbically.

Her brother regarded her with mild puzzlement.

*"Heed my words or not."* (Clearly, 'or not' hadn't been his preferred option.)

She shook her head. "Stop playing me for a fool."

"Mary?" asked Sid, openly perplexed.

She looked at them both, emotions bubbling under the surface… too many emotions to put into words. She'd heard enough though… from *both* of them. "I can see myself to The Harey Rabbit."

She turned and began to walk towards the gate.

"Mary! Wait!" Sid cried.

She kept walking, and then he ran in front of her. She moved to walk past him and he fell in beside her. She stopped and faced him. "I can't do this, Sid. Not at the moment—"

"But Mary—" He reached out for her.

"Please, Sid!" This time she *did* back away.

He looked hurt.

"I need some time to think without feeling… manoeuvred." She cast her gaze in Richard's direction; he hadn't moved. "Or manipulated."

Richard's expression remained impassive.

Sid looked crestfallen, but she had nothing to give him; not right now, at least. "I need time, Sid."

He nodded, resigned.

To her frustration, she found there *was* a sliver of sympathy still lurking within her. She sighed at the fallibility of her emotions. "Perhaps I will feel differently tomorrow."

He took her hand and gently kissed it.

That was enough; they could sort themselves out without her help, and Richard had played his hand well enough to let her go. In any case, she had an inn to run.

With one last simmering gaze at her brother, she turned and walked towards The Harey Rabbit… unescorted.

It wasn't until she rounded the corner of Big Wig Street and saw the red brick façade of The Harey Rabbit that Mary remembered it was post-proclamation time. Sid had mentioned the significance of the hour just ten minutes ago, but he'd been talking about when he *met* her and… well… she hadn't been thinking in terms of… Oh, bloody hell; Saturday afternoon was The Harey Rabbit's busiest time for frig's sake!

She hurried around the outside of the building, underneath the wooden sign that hung over the corner door. On it, a brightly painted, big-eared rabbit holding a tankard of ale regarded her with a cheeky two-toothed smile, as if it found her forgetfulness amusing. (Kate Brewer had named the inn after a pet rabbit she'd had when she was a young girl — it used to love drinking ale and *her* pa used to say it was having 'hair of the rabbit', so it became known as the Hairy Rabbit. When John Brewer had commissioned the sign writer, he'd neglected to specify the context, so it had come back as *Harey* Rabbit, as in 'hare' rather than 'hair' — hence the big ears. John offered to have it redone, but Kate loved it… and so did Mary. It was due for another touch up soon.)

Looking towards the Town Square, there was no proclamation or posting ceremony in progress. Hardly surprising. She wondered if any official announcement had been made to the townsfolk. Judging by the smattering of people in The Square and the usual crowd lingering around The Bloody Bell, she doubted it.

As Mary approached the courtyard gate, she could hear the sounds of a busy kitchen: scraping pots and plates, sloshing water, chopping knives, Patricia yelling out instructions. She opened the gate and there was Juanita, sitting on the back steps to the kitchen, madly scrubbing away at plates and cutlery in a large wooden bucket.

Mary experienced a sudden feeling of kinship towards the washer girl; she *could* be her younger sister... Juanita had remarked about Mary's Icarumban features... there *were* some similarities in their appearance.

Perhaps it was just the after-effects of Doctor Manky's potion, but Mary could *see* something in Juanita as she scrubbed away, dazzling from within. There was no doubt the girl had spirit, but she also seemed... content. True, she was opinionated and quick tempered, but she was also passionate and quick to laugh... and she was a hard worker, always offering to help, *and* she thought Mary was *hermosa*.

Juanita looked up as Mary shut the gate. "Oh, Meestress!" she exclaimed, jumping to her feet.

Immediately, Mary thought something bad had happened in her absence. "What's wrong, Juanita?" she said, closing quickly on the girl.

"Oh no no no... notheeng ees wrong," she said, flailing her arms dramatically, sending a shower of water from the scrubbing brush she still held. "We just worried for you."

Mandy poked her head through the doorway. "Mistress!"

Before Mary could respond, her staff rushed out of the kitchen as words rushed out of Juanita's mouth. "One of dee rat leempdeekers say you were heet on dee head and you were muchas lucky you weren't keelled like dee guardsman."

"I'm fine, Juantia," she assured the girl, who was now hugging her (with a wet scrubbing brush).

And then she had to say it again and again as Mandy, Lillian, Patricia and even John joined the embrace.

## CHAPTER 92

# *Just what the doctor ordered*

OPHELIA WAS LYING down, staring at a white ceiling adorned with ornate plasterwork featuring horses prancing and rearing through garlands of flowers. She knew she'd collapsed... *again*... and Sir Richard had carried her to... where other people were gathered. And then she'd been examined by the man with pink eyes, who looked like a ghost... and... had she heard someone mention Mary? It had sounded like Sid. That seemed... unlikely... but... hadn't she seen him? His hand covered in... and Lieutenant Swill? Then the man with pink eyes had asked her to drink something.

Ophelia's gaze drifted downwards, past an open window of bright blue sky to the midnight black of the velvet divan she was lying on. She became aware of two people conversing in hushed voices. As she turned her head in their direction, she realised she was in a bedchamber — a bloody *huge* bedchamber. The four-poster bed on the opposite side of the room was massive — at least ten feet across — yet there was still plenty of space for an expansive wardrobe and furniture... and the walls were covered in portraits of—

Ophelia sat up with a start; she was in Sir friggin' Richard's bedchamber! "Wha' 'appened?" she said through a wave of dizziness.

Two men began moving towards her, one dressed in black, the other dressed in white: the ghost with pink eyes. Even his hair was the colour of snow.

The dizziness cleared and was replaced by wariness. "Who are ya? Wha' y'done t'me?" she said, edging up on the divan, ready to spring away and make a run for the door should she need to.

"Please be at ease, Miss Offcut," said the one in black. "We've done you no harm and you are in no danger."

Ophelia regarded them as they loomed before her. The man in black was older (by at least ten years) and shorter (by some six inches) than the man in white, who added, "I gave you a few drops of *Oil of You Lay* — a calming potion containing passionflower and lavender."

A few drops of *what*? What the frig!

The man in black held out a placating hand. "You were traumatised; understandably so, after what you witnessed."

Ophelia stood up. "Who are you? Where's Sir Richard?"

"My name is Albert Whysman," answered the man in black. "I'm the Duke's doctor. And this is Doctor Horatio Manky, the—"

"Manky?" Ophelia blurted. "*You're* the quack Sid tol' me about?"

Strangely, it was Albert Whysman who took offense. "Miss Offcut, Horatio has—"

"It's quite alright, Albert," interjected Doctor Manky. "I have been called far worse in my time. How are you feeling, Miss Offcut?"

His soft manner took her by surprise. She hadn't really thought about how she was feeling, because she was feeling… normal… perhaps even better than normal. That took her by surprise as well. "Well enough to wan' t'know wha' the frig is goin' on."

"To answer your other question, Miss Offcut," said Albert, "I believe Sir Richard has escorted his sister and Master Evily back to The Harey Rabbit."

What? Really? "So Mary's alrigh'?"

"She was knocked unconscious by a blow to the back of the neck," Doctor Manky informed her. "However, she suffered no other injuries apart from a severe headache, for which I gave her some *Pain-o-dull*. She will make a full recovery."

*Was he making these names up?* No wonder Sid thought he was a nutter.

"An' Sid; 'e ain't been arrested?"

"Not that I'm aware of," said Doctor Manky.

Albert was no more enlightening. "I believe Sir Richard was satisfied by Sid's explanation of events."

Ophelia could hardly believe what she was hearing. "*Satisfied?* You 'avin' me on? Wha' abou' the friggin' Ducal Guardsmen? For frig's sake, Sid 'eld a dagger to the throat of one of 'em! An' the blood… I *saw* the blood on the blade!"

"That was—" Manky began.

"An' he was bein' chased by another one, an' Sid smacked '*im* in the gob!" She knew she sounded slightly hysterical, but she found it incredible that Sid was not only free but in the company of Mary and the Seneschal of Lower Icing.

Doctor Manky appeared unperturbed by Ophelia's reaction, his demeanour as odd as his appearance. "The blood on Sid's dagger was Bertrand's," he said.

Who the frig was…? Then she remembered. "Wha', the man in the blue robe?"

Doctor Manky nodded; he looked disappointed or… ashamed.

"So is 'e dead then?" Ophelia asked.

"Perhaps we should sit down, Miss Offcut," said Albert, "and take our ease for a while; we've all been through a rather harrowing day."

"Good idea, Albert," agreed Doctor Manky.

Oh shit… this didn't sound good.

"If you please…" Albert said, indicating a table positioned next to a large double-sash bay window, from which she could see an elm tree glistening in the sunshine. (It was the middle one of three such windows in Sir Richard's expansive bedchamber.) "We will explain, to the best of our abilities, all that has unfolded since your arrival at the castle."

Both men regarded her with a sense of benign expectation. She agreed readily enough, acutely aware they were yet to respond to her query regarding the man in the blue robe.

As they sat down, Ophelia glanced out the window. The garden below was a tranquil scene of manicured colour. Her eyes reluctantly sought the place where at least one guardsman had been killed. Fortunately, there was no trace of the calamity that had occurred only… When? It was then that Ophelia noticed the shadows from the trees had advanced markedly. It had to be mid-afternoon.

"'Ow long 'ave I been 'ere?" she wondered aloud, pulling back the chair and tucking her white dress under her legs.

"Three hours," Albert answered.

Ophelia nodded. She was thinking about the other guardsman — had he survived? Then Albert's words permeated. "Three hours?"

"Approximately," Doctor Manky agreed.

"Bloody Nora! Wha's in tha' bloody potion of yours?"

"You were in shock," said Doctor Manky, "and your body required rest."

Albert nodded. "Before we start, perhaps a glass of wine would also be beneficial in relaxing the mind and lifting the spirits; Sir Richard said we may avail ourselves of his stores."

"An excellent suggestion, Albert."

"Yeah," Ophelia said. "I could use a drink… or three."

Albert stood and walked back in the direction of the black divan to where a large cabinet was set against the wall. Bleeding heck; this bedchamber was unbelievable. What did Sir Richard *do* in here?

While Albert was organising the wine, Ophelia asked Doctor Manky if he'd come and see her pa. "'E's been beaten up and chucked down the side of a friggin' mountain, all 'cause o' your... or the Duke's... or wha'ever this doctor is who's so bleedin' importan'."

Doctor Manky nodded, sympathetically; at least as sympathetically as you *could* with bacon eyes and a bloodless complexion. "Sid told me of your father's condition and I am sorry for any part Xavier and I may have inadvertently played. Of course I will tend to his needs. It is the least I can do, Miss Offcut."

Ophelia nodded in satisfaction. At least the man was being agreeable.

There was a tinkling of crystal as Albert returned with a decanter of red wine and three glasses. Ophelia had only ever drunk out of a glass once in her life — at her brother Fred's wedding — and that certainly hadn't been crystal.

"Here we are," announced Albert as he placed the three glasses on the table. "Just what the doctor ordered."

Albert was the only one who chuckled at his little jest. Ophelia didn't notice Doctor Manky's reaction; she was mesmerised by the cut crystal decanter, facets twinkling in the afternoon sunlight as the three glasses were filled. It was all quite surreal.

"While you're up, Albert, would you mind drawing the curtains?"

"Oh dear!" He looked embarrassed. "Of course, Horatio; most remiss of me... my apologies."

"Not at all," Doctor Manky said as Albert hurried to close the curtains.

Doctor Manky's pink gaze turned to Ophelia. "It's my pigmentation, Miss Offcut."

Pigmentation? It sounded like some foreign way of making bacon... or perhaps he was referring to his eyes.

"Sunlight does not agree with me, and I find the sun in Lower Icing particularly harsh. I hope you don't mind if we sit in more muted light."

She shook her head. Why should she mind; it made no difference to her, just as long as she could drink Sir Richard's fancy wine from his fancy glass.

The area around the table darkened as Albert covered the window with black velvet curtains. Sir Richard really needed more imagination when it came to decor. All this black and silver — no wonder the Seneschal was so bleeding uptight. Leaving the other two windows uncovered, Albert sat down. The man in white now looked like he was glowing, and it occurred to Ophelia that if he was such a genius, why hadn't he found a cure for his pigmentation problem? "So, you can't fix y'self then?"

Again, it was Albert who seemed to take offense. "Miss Offcut, Doctor Manky's condition is congenital."

He said it as if it explained everything, but Ophelia had no idea what he was talking about. "What?" she asked, genuinely curious. "Ain't 'e got no balls?"

Albert looked like she'd slapped him in the face.

"It means it is a condition I was born with," said Doctor Manky. "There is no cure."

An awkward silence followed, and Ophelia found herself feeling sorry for the white man in white clothing. To end the moment, she reached over and grabbed one of the glasses of wine. "So… these for lookin' at or drinkin' out of?"

Both men gave her a wry smile and picked up a glass. The wine was deliciously crisp and untainted; so much nicer drinking out of a crystal glass than a wooden cup. It left her mouth zinging and wanting more. As she swallowed her last mouthful, she looked up to see both doctors regarding her: the one in black looking aghast, the one in white looking bemused. Both their glasses had hardly been touched.

"Well," she said, self-consciously, "tha' 'it the spot."


Ophelia wasn't sure exactly how long she sat with the two doctors, but her glass was refilled twice (though she could have done with quite a few more). The contents of the subsequent pours, however, were drunk at a far more leisurely pace. During this time, Doctor Manky (for the most part) gradually revealed what had unfolded at the Upper Bailey. It was like getting blood out of a… person with a pigmentation problem. Doctor Manky had begun by begging Ophelia's indulgence.

"Wha'ever… long as y'don' take me for no fool. I'm good at spottin' the offal in a meat pie."

He smiled, while Albert assured her of Doctor Manky's impeccable integrity. How would *he* bleeding know — the man in white was a stranger to everyone in Lower Icing (with an emphasis on 'strange').

Doctor Manky began by saying how he'd rolled up in his carriage at the West Gate just before dawn (around the same time Tom and Ophelia had come across Sid on the North Road). He revealed he'd been concerned about being admitted into the Upper Bailey, so much so that on the journey from

Blessed Whipping he'd asked Sid if he'd organise a diversion.

"Poor Sid," said Doctor Manky. "I now see why he felt the need to go his own way. I was rather… focused at the time."

Focused? Bloody Nora — extreme more like. Still, a diversion seemed rather insignificant to what Sid had *actually* done.

As it turned out, a diversion or any other subterfuge proved unnecessary. Doctor Manky was escorted directly to Sir Richard as soon as he announced himself to the guards at the West Gate — the Seneschal had anticipated his arrival. From there, Doctor Manky was reunited with Xavier and brought to the ailing Duke.

*How very cosy,* Ophelia thought. Never mind everyone else who had been sucked in and then spat out because of this bleeding Xavier. Emboldened by the effect of the red wine, Ophelia let her thoughts air. "Bully for you, Doctor. Still, can't see 'ow tha's got anythin' t'do with me or mine, or why I saw a man get killed."

"Miss Offcut!" Albert gasped.

"Wha'?" she snapped back. "Y'reckon tha' guard's fam'ly gives a toss the Duke's been saved?"

Albert dropped his gaze, and Doctor Manky looked… guilty.

"So, *did* Sid kill this Bertrand bloke?" They *still* hadn't told her. "Who 'is 'e anyway? Looked like some sorta crazy wizard in tha' blue robe."

Eventually Doctor Manky admitted that Bertrand was a Blessed Whipping elder and his servant of sorts. He went on to explain that, unbeknown to him, Bertrand had been conducting a private vendetta against the Swill family — in particular, the daughter, Bethany. Ophelia could hardly believe what she was hearing.

Then he began talking about Sunwatchers and Forging Day and other Sun things that made no sense at all to Ophelia. (Even Albert looked befuddled.) By the time he'd explained who Bertrand was, Ophelia had sipped her way through her second wine.

Albert hesitantly refilled her glass as Doctor Manky explained how he and Xavier (with the aid of Albert) had treated the Duke, working out how much 'extract of thistle sap' and 'cherry seed oil' would be needed to counteract the effects of too much 'orange-spotted mushroom'. This time Albert seemed fascinated, while Ophelia was beginning to wonder whether the *Oil of You Lay* had some kind of hallucinatory affect when mixed with wine. Surely she wasn't *actually* sitting here, listening to this bizarre story.

"Of course, the Town Crier was also instrumental in the Duke's recovery," said Doctor Manky.

Even under the effects of alcohol-potioning, that piece of information was way too weird to ignore. "'Ang on," she said, "did you jus' say the Town Crier?"

"I'm not sure we were meant to mention anything about that, Horatio," Albert whispered loudly.

This was spiralling out of control, and Ophelia was beginning to lose focus. "Can you both please shut the frig up," she said, trying to sound reasonable. "Sorry, but I don' give a flyin' fart 'bout wha' bleedin' oils or essences ya used t'fix the Duke *or* who did the fixin' — the Town Crier's turd collector could 'ave 'elped for all I care." She could hear her voice rising and sounding more frustrated. "An' I *really* ain' int'rested *whose* arse the friggin' sun shine's ou' of in Blessed Whippin' *or* what Bertran's done or ain't done to Bethany Swill… an' you *still* ain't told me whether Sid killed 'im or not, but I'm guessin' not 'cause Sir Richard would 'ave chucked 'im in the friggin' Can!"

The black and silver wallpaper shimmered behind the doctors' bewildered expressions.

"Please calm yourself, Miss Offcut," said Doctor Manky. "I was merely trying to provide context to your involvement."

For frig's sake; what did she have to say to make them understand? "I ain't int'rested in context; *forget* the friggin' context. *Wha' 'appened 'ere this afternoon?*"

"Perhaps I should take over from here, gentlemen." The voice came from the chamber door. It belonged to Lieutenant Swill. As he walked towards them, he added, "If Mistress Offcut is well enough, I am to escort her home, and, Doctors, I believe you have another patient to attend to."

He sounded very official (as usual).

"You should be resting, Brandon," said Doctor Manky as the lieutenant reached the table.

"This *is* resting." Then his expression softened. "However, I am appreciative of your ministrations and concern. In truth, I feel quite invigorated." Then his gaze flicked to Ophelia. "How are *you* feeling, Ophelia?"

Well; she was feeling a bit drunk and a lot frustrated, but she settled for a non-committal, "Fine."

He looked dubious, but there was also amusement in his expression. "Very well, then. Are you ready?"

So that was it then; her time with the doctors was over. She regarded the three faces staring at her. Then her gaze fell to her almost-finished glass of wine. It might be the last time in her life she drank such a fine vintage from a crystal glass. She picked up the glass and, as elegantly as possible, downed the aromatic liquid. "Now I am."

As she said her thank yous and goodbyes to the doctors, she reminded Doctor Manky about her pa. He assured her that he would attend to him later that afternoon, after they'd completed their next appointment.

She nodded, then added, "Slaughter & Offcut — jus' down from the market; the place with the red door."

He nodded and smiled reassuringly. "All will be well, Miss Offcut."

## CHAPTER 93

# *Think nothing of it*

OLIVIA WOKE WITH a start. The light had changed, but the pain in her ribs remained, so too the rawness of her parched throat. However, something worse had finally occurred: the desperate need to relieve herself. Reluctantly, she reached over to the side table and rang the bell.

Petronella appeared within moments. Olivia made no bones about her situation; there was simply no delicate way of putting it and she was in real danger of wetting the bed. Ever prepared, her friend reached under the bed and retrieved a chamber-pot.

Petronella insisted on helping her out of bed. Olivia acquiesced readily enough; she didn't have the urinary fortitude to protest. Her embarrassment soon evaporated in the sheer agony of moving her body into a squatting position. And the pissing, rather than being relieving, added to the pain. Olivia almost collapsed into Petronella's supportive arms.

The effort left her drained and sweating. She barely had the strength to get back onto the bed… and the pain… If wasn't for the fact that she was in her friend's guestroom, she would've collapsed onto the floor.

Once she was lying down again, Petronella removed the chamber-pot and returned with a cool, damp cloth. Sitting on the edge of the bed, she proceeded to mop Olivia's face and neck. It was surprisingly relieving, and the pain in her torso had ebbed into bearable discomfort.

"I'm so sorry, Petronella." Her voice was little more than a croaky whisper.

"Hush now, think nothing of it," she said, kindly.

*Think nothing of it?* If only. Paris' visit had undone the last six years of thinking nothing of it. So handsome, so… everything Gerald wasn't. She tried to banish her unfaithful thoughts, but she couldn't help but wonder if she'd been too… dismissive. No, it was for the best… wasn't it?

"There you are, my dear," said Petronella, patting the cloth around the base of Olivia's neck.

She managed a weak smile. "That's much better, thank you."

Petronella gazed at her, searchingly, and Olivia sensed she was going to ask her about Sid again. Just in case, Olivia added, "But I'm afraid I feel rather exhausted."

Her friend nodded her understanding. "I shall leave you to rest in peace, my dear." She gently squeezed Olivia's hand — it was damp and cool from the cloth — then daintily arose from the bed. At the door, she stopped and said, "I'm sorry this has happened to you, Olivia."

Olivia had no words.

"Remember the bell… if you need anything." With that, she left the room, quietly closing the door behind her.

Olivia sighed; her throat was raw and dry, but she dare not drink anymore. The thought of relieving herself again today…

Her mind wandered back to her predicament; what was to become of her and Gerald? She'd been led to believe by Petronella that their home might be salvageable, but what of their lives? A pardon was one thing, but Olivia very much doubted the Duke's generosity would extend to reinstating Gerald as Town Crier. Richard would certainly voice his objection to such a suggestion. Imagine if they were banished from Lower Icing. Where would they go? They had nothing. Olivia didn't even have the clothes on her back.

Her thoughts continued to torment her as she lay motionless on the bed. She thought about ringing the bell, just to break the monotony, but even the will to do *that* had deserted her. In any case, Petronella would only want to know more about Sid, and Olivia would rather piss a river than talk about *him*.

She wondered how Xavier was. He'd finally met his father after helping to save his life. What must he be feeling? And Marmaduke, of course. Olivia couldn't begin to imagine the emotion of such a reunion, particularly under such circumstances. It was her last thought before drifting off to sleep.

## CHAPTER 94

# *I am bleedin' concerned*

**B**RANDON SWILL WALKED at Ophelia's side as they left Sir Richard's guarded quarters and headed down the marble staircase. The reception hall was deserted except for two more guardsmen at the base of the stairs. If only they'd been there before, they might have been able to stop Bertrand and prevent the death of their comrade. But, then again, she'd more than likely have witnessed another killing.

The lieutenant had asked for her forbearance until they'd left the Upper Bailey; that he would explain all that had befallen Mary, Sid and Bertrand. Ophelia was happy enough to oblige; he'd already revealed that Bertrand was, as she'd rightly surmised, alive.

Four more guardsmen were posted at the entrance to the palatial dwelling. Like all the other guardsmen, they saluted Brandon as he walked by. And, as he had done before, Brandon returned their salute, fist to heart. Ophelia noticed they did it with conviction. Amazing what effect the death of comrade could have.

They walked along the garden path: the path to the gatehouse, where the guardsman had died gasping for air. The spot was now marked by the shade of a tree top — a shadowy pointer. Ophelia diverted her eyes. Hours had passed, the grounds were peaceful and serene… beautiful, in fact. Perhaps too beautiful. Not a sign that anything had happened; the violence had been buried in beauty. Even the soft breeze carried the scent of roses. It seemed… wrong.

"Are you alright, Ophelia?" enquired Brandon.

She nodded. "Did the other guard survive?"

"Yes."

The four guardsmen at the gatehouse saluted as they passed through into the Middle Bailey. Suddenly, Ophelia was fighting back tears. "The one what died… did 'e 'ave a wife an' children?"

Brandon nodded. "Guardsman Hopwood was husband to Polly and father to two girls, Jenny and Lucy."

"What will 'appen to 'em?"

"They'll be looked after," he replied. "The Duke has already made a point of it."

Ophelia sniffed and wiped tears away from her eyes.

"I know this past week hasn't been easy for you and your family, Ophelia. It certainly hasn't been easy for me and mine. I don't think anyone imagined such an incredible set of events. To think the Duke has a son… Two weeks ago, no-one even suspected such a person existed. Although, Bertrand seems to have known, and Doctor Manky, of course. And now…" He exhaled loudly. "And now here we are."

For a few moments, all she could hear were their footsteps echoing across the courtyard. She was walking beside the man who had arrested Billy — the person who'd put him in The Can. Yet she felt no animosity towards him. In fact, she felt as if they'd shared something… different but the same.

Ophelia inhaled a shuddery breath. "Doctor Manky mentioned somethin' 'bout Bertran' tryin' to get at y'sister."

"Yes," he acknowledged. "Still, that's something we need no longer fear."

"Where is 'e?"

"Down there about sixty feet," he said, pointing to the ground at the foot of The Keep. "I doubt he will be seeing his precious sun for a while."

Ophelia nodded. Good, she thought; he deserved to spend the rest of his life in the dungeon — the family of Guardsman Hopwood had lost a husband and father for life.

"That wha' they mean by poetic justice?"

Brandon let out a bitter laugh. "That's for certes, Ophelia."

As they marched out of the castle, through the various gates and out into the streets of Lower Icing, Brandon Swill shared his version of events with Ophelia…

After Doctor Manky had been escorted to the Duke, Sir Richard brought Bertrand to his office. There he was questioned on several things regarding the security of the Duchy. Prestwich was in attendance, recording the whole interview. Brandon wasn't at liberty to go into specifics, suffice to say that not only had Bertrand been holding the Swills to ransom, but he'd also played a significant part in manipulating the events that had led up to the arrival of Xavier.

The questioning was almost into its third hour when they were interrupted by news of the Duke's revival. Relief and joy filled the room, and further questioning was put aside. Sir Richard went straight to the Duke's chamber, while Brandon and Bertrand waited in the Duke's lavish upstairs reception room.

Word must have spread, because they were soon joined by a flood of castle clique (including Rupert and Fraser). Brandon had to repeat on a number of occasions that he knew nothing of the Duke's state, save that he had recovered and that Sir Richard and the doctors were currently attending to him. Eventually things settled down and the well-to-dos begrudgingly accepted they had no choice but to wait. Brandon had been concerned that Bertrand might use the unrest to cause trouble — he'd certainly garnered curiosity and suspicion from the ensemble. However, the Elder had been relatively engaging for the most part and appeared just as pleased for the Duke as everyone else.

(Ophelia thought about mentioning the Town Crier; she was still intrigued by what Doctor Manky had said about him being *instrumental in the Duke's recovery*, but she decided to let the lieutenant continue without interruption.)

After what seemed like a prolonged wait, punctuated by irritated grumblings, Sir Richard emerged from the Duke's chamber to assure everyone that the Duke was well, but would require a day or so to fully recuperate. The Duke also wished to have some private time with Xavier and Doctor Manky.

This caused a minor uproar of indignation, but Sir Richard was able to satiate their egos by suggesting they all gather in his private quarters, where he would brief them on what had been discussed during his audience.

Brandon was sent ahead to make sure the quarters were secure and to organise for guards to be positioned at the bottom of the staircase. Sir Richard also instructed Brandon to take Bertrand with him; he wanted to make sure the Elder was watched at all times. There were too many distractions in the Duke's residence for the Seneschal to be that attentive.

Brandon was happy to keep the scheming adherent close by. He didn't trust him any more than Sir Richard did, and Brandon knew, better than anyone outside his family, what Bertrand was capable of. Even the hours of interrogation hadn't seemed to bother him; it was as if his beliefs justified *any* course of action. However, as they walked across the first floor landing from the Duke's residence to the Seneschal's quarters, the diminutive man regarded Brandon with suspicion, wanting to know why he was the only guest accompanying him, and what Sir Richard had said to him. Brandon told him that it was none of his business. This was Lower Icing, not Blessed Whipping; he had no status here and he certainly shouldn't think of himself as a guest. Bertrand didn't respond, but Brandon had more to say to the man who'd been the bane of his family's existence for the last eighteen years; namely, that he held no sway over Sir Richard, the *Deed of Promise* would not be recognised, and he would not be taking Bethany back to Blessed Whipping. Bertrand remained silent as they entered Sir Richard's residence.

Brandon had been entrusted with the Seneschal's keys. His task was to make sure that all the windows were sealed and the internal doors locked. Sir Richard wanted everyone contained within his reception room; there'd be no using the privy, no wine or any other such distractions — he'd say what there was to be said, then they could all go about their business.

As he conducted his inspection, Brandon admitted he felt unsettled by the Elder's presence and calculating scrutiny: a malevolent ice-blue shadow following him around Sir Richard's quarters. However, he never considered Bertrand a physical threat. He'd almost completed his inspection and was walking towards an open window in the Seneschal's bedchamber when the blow to the neck came.

The next thing he knew, he was surrounded by chaos, with a head that felt like Klob Hoofenhaus' anvil: Sir Richard was ordering guardsmen to fetch Doctor Manky, Sid Evily was gently slapping Mary Brewer's unconscious face with a bloodied hand, calling out her name, before being pulled off her by two guardsmen. Sid resisted, saying the blood was Bertrand's — that he'd stabbed him in the leg.

As Sid was taken away, Brandon could also hear Fraser Coin questioning Sir Richard's ability to command. Then Sir Richard was looking down at Brandon, asking him what had happened. He remembered trying to answer, but his mouth wouldn't work. He'd panicked then. Sir Richard had sworn and told everyone to wait in his reception room.

Doctor Manky arrived with Doctor Whysman. Brandon was lifted into a sitting position, his back resting against the edge of Sir Richard's bed. Then Doctor Manky used his fingers to pry open his mouth and pour a vial of bright orange liquid down his throat, telling him it was a muscle stimulant, something called *Vigour Morphis*. It had an acrid taste and his body began to spasm. For a few moments he thought he'd been poisoned, but Doctor Manky assured him the unpleasant sensation would pass.

While he was recovering, Doctor Manky treated Mary the same way, but first he wiped away the blood Sid had slapped on her face. Brandon watched as Mary shuddered and then regained consciousness. Sir Richard was hovering over her, looking concerned. Then he was distracted by the sound of raised voices coming from the reception room, and left the bedchamber.

Sid reappeared and knelt down beside Mary. Brandon's head was beginning to clear. The *Vigour Morphis* was working remarkably well (just like the *Bruise Mousse* and *Natron Bomb* Xavier had given him); even the pounding in his head had subsided.

(*All these strange-sounding medicines*, Ophelia thought. She wondered what Doctor Manky would give her pa. She hoped it wasn't a *Natron Bomb*; he was already explosive enough.)

Brandon soon became aware of sounds outside: disturbed voices, boots running across cobblestone, someone barking out a command to secure the grounds. It sounded like Seb Fitzbadly. He wanted to find out what was happening. He tried to stand, but his body still felt clumsy. Doctor Manky told him to stay still; the potion needed more time to properly take effect.

Brandon turned his attention back to Sid and Mary. Mary was asking Sid what had happened. Then she called out Brandon's name, asking Sid if Brandon was alright. Brandon spoke up and said he was fine. Sid moved out of the way so she could see him. She asked if it was Bertrand who had attacked them. Brandon confirmed it was. Then Sir Richard reappeared in the room, carrying a clearly distraught Ophelia. Brandon had assumed Ophelia was another of Bertrand's victims.

(She was beginning to realise how bloody lucky she was that she hadn't been.)

Brandon began wondering how many other people had been injured and how long he'd been unconscious.

While Doctor Manky was concocting a potion for Ophelia, Brandon managed to edge himself onto the end of Sir Richard's bed. Sir Richard helped him to his feet, asking how he was feeling. He replied that he was well. In truth, he had a slight headache and a feeling like he'd just woken from a deep sleep, but otherwise his body now seemed recovered.

Sir Richard informed him that Bertrand had not escaped, but two guards had suffered injuries — one of them a fatal kick to the neck, the other a blow similar to the one he and Mary had received, and that Ophelia had witnessed the attack and been overcome emotionally.

Ophelia had felt the need to interject at this point and told Brandon that it wasn't just the attack, but also the fact that she'd been manhandled, threatened and nearly assaulted by Lieutenant Fowler, and basically treated like a dog turd on the doorstep by all the nobs. Brandon conceded her point and apologised, informing her that Fowler would face a disciplinary hearing, but that it was complicated because Ophelia had technically prevented a man from being arrested, and Tom had assaulted an officer of The Purple Peril. Ophelia reacted with outrage and quite a few expletives. Brandon calmed her down by saying that no charges were being brought against her or Tom, and that Sid's arrest had been overturned by Sir Richard. Ophelia then asked if Brandon had heard anything from Tom. He replied that he hadn't, and she could tell by the way he answered that he was concerned — not for Tom, so much, but the squire and the cadet who'd clearly not reached Blessed Whipping.

Brandon returned to his retelling by saying that while Ophelia was being attended to by the doctors, Sid described their attempt to gain entry into the Upper Bailey: how he'd resorted to holding the guardsman at knife point while Ophelia and Mary went to find Sir Richard; how he'd waited, playing a game of stand-off, wondering how long he could actually keep it up. Mary had defended his actions by adding that the guards had provoked the situation through their inability to see reason. Sir Richard had countered with, "So, Mary, are you saying that if you refused to serve an unruly looking stranger a mug of ale and he reacted by holding a knife to your throat, you would consider his actions defensible?"

After that comment, Sid seemed wary of incriminating himself and had proceeded in a more measured manner, explaining he'd withdrawn the dagger and set the guardsman free as soon he heard Ophelia scream for help, adding that the guardsman was unscathed. However, before he'd had a chance to run to Ophelia's aid, Bertrand suddenly appeared, launching himself towards Sid with some sort of flying kick. Sid ducked and lashed out with his knife, feeling it slice into flesh and hearing the Elder's cry of pain.

While the guardsmen were in a state of disarray, Sid bolted into the Middle Bailey. It was then he noticed his right hand and forearm were sprayed with blood, and so was the dagger he still held. He saw Ophelia across the courtyard; it was obvious she was in a state of distress. Upon reaching her, one of the Ducal Guardsmen, who had chased after him, demanded his surrender. Whereupon Sid dispatched him with a pommel-punch to the face.

Ophelia was able to confirm this was true, but also found herself speaking up for Sid, saying that he wasn't thinking clearly at the time — neither of them were — and he was worried about Mary.

(Ophelia had been too, but a man had been killed and everything had just... exploded!)

Brandon nodded his understanding. However, he believed Sid might still be facing some sort of punishment for the unprovoked knife-point incident, though Sir Richard seemed non-committal on that particular point. And clearly, since he had escorted both Sid and Mary back to The Harey Rabbit, it seemed questionable whether Sid *would* answer for his actions.

Brandon then went back to relaying Sid's version of events. He had left Ophelia with the stunned guardsman and, spurred on by the sound of three bugle blasts, sprinted through the garden, across the reception hall to the stairs. Just as he reached the stairs, the large door to the Duke's chambers burst open and Ducal Guardsmen poured into the reception hall and headed outside towards the sound of more bugle blasts.

At the top of the stairs, Sid had turned towards the open door to what he assumed was Sir Richard's residence. Just at that moment, the Seneschal, along with a number of other people, had appeared from the other side of the large landing. Sid heard a command to 'hold', but had ignored it, reiterating that his concern had been for Mary.

Sid had concluded his version of events with a wary look at Sir Richard. "The rest you know — you arrived moments after I found Mary and Brandon sprawled on the floor."

Sir Richard's expression remained impassive, but said he would be looking into 'the rest' once everyone was back on their feet.

They'd just turned past the entrance to Lower Icing College. Ophelia wondered if the medical student was still waiting for her in his room... seventeen. Bloody Nora! She'd actually remembered the number of his room and, now that she came to think of it, his name: Wilbur Dickins.

"...filled in the holes, Ophelia?"

The lieutenant was regarding her expectantly.

"Wha'?" Then, realising what he'd just asked her, she replied, "Oh righ'... sorry... I s'pose so... leas' wise, for the mos' part." In truth, she had more questions, but she didn't know where to start; it seemed this Bertrand had caused a lot of trouble, even before his murderous attempt at escape, but she wasn't sure what he'd actually done apart from being a pain in the Swills' arse.

And if this young doctor was *truly* the Duke's son… Well, she had no idea what it meant for Lower Icing. But these were questions for another person and another time. She felt the need to let the sawdust settle.

However, as they neared Market Street, she remembered one hole that *did* need filling. "There *is* one other thing, Lieutenan'."

"Yes?"

"Wha's the Town Crier got t'do with fixin' up the Duke?"

He looked uncomfortable with the question and was clearly considering his response. "It's not something you need concern yourself with," he replied eventually.

How could he say that after what she and her family had been through? "But I *am* bleedin' concerned, ain't I, Lieutenan'? My faml'y was 'eld t'ransom t'find this doctor so 'e could fix up the Duke an' all, an' now this *other* doctor what *no-one* was lookin' for says the friggin' *Town Crier* is instru-bloody-men'al in fixin' 'im up! It don' make no sense. I mean, wha's it all abou'?"

His face reddened, but he remained silent.

Ophelia was suddenly aware that she might have spoken too loudly, though the hubbub from nearby Market Street would have drowned out most of the detail. Still, it made her stop in her tracks. Brandon followed suit, regarding her with a mixture of impatience and sympathy.

"Listen, Lieutenan'," she said, looking him in the eye. "Wha'ever people think abou' me, I *ain't* loose, an' I *ain't* stupid. I know wha's wha', an' I *know* when t'keep me mouth shut."

He regarded her for a moment, clearly weighing up whether he should say anything. Then he sighed and told her it was the Town Crier who'd poisoned the Duke.

## CHAPTER 95

## *The black behind the white*

OLIVIA JERKED AWAKE to the sound of a scream. At least, she thought it was a scream. Perhaps it was *her*, crying out in her sleep. Now she could hear voices — Petronella's was the most dominant, and, as they drew nearer, it sounded like she was apologising for something. She also recognised Albert's understated tones. However, the owner of the other voice, refuting Petronella's need to apologise, was unknown to her. Olivia felt a sense of relief; hopefully Albert had brought some concoction to alleviate her discomfort.

"Truly, Mistress Whysman," the unknown voice said, "I assure you I have taken no offence."

"But to react in such an unseemly—"

"Hush now, Petronella," Albert admonished, softly.

There was a pause, then Petronella's whispered response, "Of course. Please excuse me. A pleasure to meet you, Doctor."

Doctor?

The sound of Petronella's retreating footsteps was shortly followed by the appearance of Albert at the door.

"How are you feeling, Olivia," he asked kindly, walking into the room.

Olivia grimaced, the back of her neck afire as it rubbed against the cotton pillow.

"I understand." He nodded, his expression full of sympathy. "I have brought someone to see you. I hope you don't mind, but his knowledge of medicine is most remarkable." Albert looked towards the door, motioning for the person outside to enter. "Please, Horatio," he said, "come in."

The figure who appeared in the doorway looked like an apparition; for a moment Olivia wondered if she was still asleep and this was just some sort of bizarre dream.

"Olivia," Albert said, "may I present Doctor Horatio Manky. Horatio is Xavier's guardian and mentor, and the man responsible for bringing the Duke back to full recovery."

"Mistress Hiepants," Doctor Manky said, the white skin around his pink eyes creasing into a smile. It was unsettling to say the least.

Olivia found it hard to believe that *this* was Xavier's guardian — the man of whom he'd spoken so fondly, the genius who'd raised and nurtured him and made him the person he was today. No wonder he'd never described him; the man was a freak.

Albert stepped back and allowed Doctor Manky to move closer to the bed. "May I?" he asked Olivia, indicating the chair placed by the bed.

Olivia's gaze flicked to Albert's kind face. He nodded reassuringly. Olivia looked back at the ghoulish visage looming over her, his snow-white hair dangling limply over his collar. She nodded warily.

He sat down, placing a white, rectangular case (which Olivia had only just noticed) flat on the bed by her right knee. Her gaze flicked back to Albert — again he nodded his reassurance.

"I'd like to begin by looking at your ribs, Mistress Hiepants," he said, without preamble. "Are you able to pull up your shift, or will you allow me to do it?"

Olivia had never been subjected to such... directness. However, for the sake of the little modesty she had left, she was prepared to be examined if it meant providing some relief to her discomfort. She indicated to the white man that he should proceed.

The doctor smiled and nodded; he looked a little too pleased with himself for Olivia's liking. It *was* like some sort of bizarre dream. "It will be best if I move you onto your left side first," he said. "I'll be as gentle as I can."

He placed one hand on her right hip and the other on her right shoulder. Olivia gritted her teeth in expectation of the gasping pain, but the moving process proved to be relatively bearable... surprisingly so. She was now facing the white wall of the bedroom, glad she could no longer see his white face as he began pulling up her cotton shift. Again, the discomfort was unexpectedly minor and he managed to keep most of her modesty intact.

"I think it will be easier if I cut through the bandaging, Albert, rather than unbind it. Do you mind?"

*Cut through the bandaging?* Olivia didn't like the sound of that.

"Of course not, Horatio," Albert replied; he sounded as if he'd moved closer to the bed. "Can I assist you in any way?"

"Thank you, but I can see you have already done excellent work in treating Mistress Hiepants."

Olivia wasn't quite sure what to make of that. If Albert had done excellent work, did that mean this doctor could do no better? Then she felt movement by her knees and the sound of the case being unlatched.

"I apologise for the delay in seeing you, Mistress Hiepants," Doctor Manky said, retrieving something from the case. "It's been a rather busy afternoon, I'm afraid."

"That's an understatement if ever I've heard one, Horatio."

"Yes, quite…" It sounded introspective, and tinged with sadness. Then he added matter-of-factly, "I also had to wait for the sun's intensity to wane. My pigmentation doesn't react well to prolonged exposure to sunlight, and it seems more severe in Lower Icing, possibly due the reflected light and radiant heat from the abundance of stone surfaces."

Olivia felt a slight scratching sensation through the bandaging on her exposed right side.

"As you may know, Xavier and I have spent the last sixteen months at Blessed Whipping: a community whose life revolves around the movement of the sun. Hardly the place for one such as I, you might think."

The scratching continued, and she could feel the pressure of the bandaging lessening.

"And yet, oddly enough, there the sun seems to have less effect on my condition. I am even able to partake in the outdoor midday meal without suffering any ill effects. Most remarkable really. There's no scientific explanation for it. Makes you wonder whether something more primal is at play."

*Why was he sharing this with her?* She had no interest in his condition, save that it was a most disturbing one. Xavier *had* talked about the Blessed Whipping community, but even with *his* ability to communicate and inspire, Olivia thought the place sounded as if it was inhabited by a collection of inbred fools.

"Just about done, Mistress Hiepants — you've been most patient."

Olivia felt the tension of the bandaging fall away; much quicker and far less painful than she'd expected. She had to give Doctor Manky his dues: he had a gentle hand.

The newly exposed skin itched. Olivia let it itch; she knew any attempt at scratching would turn the itch into torture. She felt his hand upon her skin. She jerked involuntarily, sending a stab of pain through her torso.

"Your pardon," Doctor Manky apologised. Then his tone became more professional. "Your diagnosis is correct, Albert; she has at least two cracked ribs. If you wouldn't mind handing me one of the green jars from my case…"

"Of course," Albert replied. This was followed by a delicate metal-sounding clink.

"Thank you," said Doctor Manky.

Olivia was tempted to turn her head to see what Albert had retrieved, but again… the consequences.

"With your permission, Mistress Hiepants, I'd like to apply an unguent to your bruising. While it won't heal your ribs — only time will do that — it *will* aid in the healing process and alleviate the pain to a certain extent."

Olivia nodded her consent.

"Very good. *Bruise Mousse* has a rather unpleasant odour, I'm afraid. However, once it's absorbed into the skin, the odour fades."

*Bruise Mousse.* She remembered Xavier talking about *Bruise Mousse* amongst other odd-named concoctions. And now, here she was, about to be on the receiving end of some. The sound of a stopper being removed was shortly followed by one of the most offensive odours Olivia had ever had the displeasure of breathing in — redolent of their 'outdoor seat' at the height of summer. It was all she could do not to gag.

"The last time I applied *Bruise Mousse* was to your brother's swollen face."

Olivia could hardly believe the words had been spoken. How in the name of normality had Doctor Manky encountered Sid? And how had he come to know that Sid was her brother? She couldn't see *that* piece of information being part of a doctor-patient conversation.

"I must say, I felt rather responsible for his condition, since he was acting on my behalf, gathering information."

*Gathering information?* Olivia felt sick, and it had absolutely nothing to do with the disgusting stench. Then she felt a cool, tingling sensation upon her skin. What was he doing to her? Was he even a real doctor? She doubted it very much if he'd had dealings with her scoundrel of a brother.

"I employed your brother eight days ago; although, I kept the reason for employing him to myself."

Eight days ago… the Friday Xavier went missing, the Friday Gerald poisoned the Duke, the Friday her world had turned upside down.

"You see, Mistress Hiepants, I thought Sid's relationship to you might stand him in good stead, that, through your husband, he might be able to find out what had happened to Xavier. It seemed the best course of action, since my appearance at the castle would have caused quite a stir."

So *that's* why Sid had arrived on their doorstep last Saturday morning, why he'd talked Gerald into having a drink with him at that floosy's establishment. Again, it begged the question, how did he find out that Sid was her brother in the first place? She'd spent the best part of six years denying he existed.

She gasped in surprise as his cool hand began smoothing the unguent into her skin, sending a shot of pain through her side.

"If you can bear with me a moment more, the *Bruise Mousse* will begin to have an effect."

She could feel herself beginning to perspire. The pain and the vile smell... and then... relief: a cool, fizzing relief. She could feel her muscles relaxing, the tension ebbing. Olivia exhaled — she hadn't realised she was holding her breath — and then curled into a ball and began to cry... in relief.

She heard Albert ask Doctor Manky if she was alright. He sounded concerned on her behalf, but Doctor Manky explained that it was her body releasing the pain, emotionally as well as physically. And he was right... unbelievably right. And, to add to her relief, the smell had already begun to fade.

"When you're ready, Mistress Hiepants," said the doctor, softly, "try stretching out your legs and rolling onto your back."

She followed his instructions; anyone who could do what he had just done...

"Take your time," he added as she began to move her legs.

There was virtually no pain (relatively speaking) as she slowly straightened her body, just a slight niggle in her side. Wiping away a tickling tear from her cheek, she couldn't help but smile. Even her throat seemed more relaxed, though the rawness remained.

Gingerly, she began to turn her body. Again, Doctor Manky's hands went to her hip and shoulder. "Allow me to support you," he said. "The pain may have eased, but the injury remains."

The pain had definitely eased — it was there, but it was dull. Her internal, dagger-wielding bandit had been banished to the edge of consciousness, lurking, but ineffectual.

Olivia lay on her back, looking up at the smiling apparition and began to laugh. It hurt her throat immediately, and the back of her neck burned against the pillow. Nonetheless, she found it hard to stop, because her side no longer felt as if it would split.

Then Albert appeared behind the doctor — the black behind the white, the expression of concern behind the one of satisfaction.

"The ribs will need to be re-bandaged," Doctor Manky continued, more to Albert than her, "and *Bruise Mousse* applied upon waking in the morning and before going to sleep. A week should be sufficient, but no heavy lifting or strenuous activity for at least a month."

Albert nodded, looking very serious. Olivia's fit of laughter subsided as she realised he was probably thinking that he and Petronella would be burdened with the responsibility of her recuperation. Well, she just wouldn't allow that to happen. She might be regarded by some in the castle-set as aloof and icy, but none of them could accuse her of being someone who imposed herself.

"I will leave a jar here," said Doctor Manky, his focus back on Olivia. "Please use it sparingly." He held up his right index finger. "Just enough to cover the tip of your finger; a little goes a long way."

Olivia nodded, pulling her shift back down over her midriff without any major discomfort. Doctor Manky smiled, encouragingly. How could such a simple, well-intentioned gesture look so wrong? Yes, she could *well* imagine the stir he would have caused arriving at the castle unannounced.

"Now, Mistress Hiepants, let's see what damage you've done to your throat. If you wouldn't mind opening your mouth as wide as you can."

Olivia complied, readily. If he could do for her throat what he'd done for her ribs, she'd give him… Another realisation struck her — how was she going to pay for this treatment? Did she and Gerald have any coin left?

Doctor Manky's face loomed towards her, glowing like a full moon, his pink eyes intense as they focused on her gaping mouth. His hair dangled just above her face, whiter than Petronella's new drapes.

"Hmm… you're right, Albert… ulceration associated with smoke inhalation and extreme heat."

He withdrew back to a sitting position.

"And there are superficial burns on the back of her neck," added Albert.

Doctor Manky nodded. "Both will mend of their own accord. Your throat looks quite raw, Mistress Hiepants."

Olivia nodded.

"Just as well you don't have your husband's profession."

Was that an attempt at humour? Judging by Albert's chortle, she assumed so. Still, it hardly seemed appropriate under the circumstances.

The doctor's pink-lipped smile drooped self-consciously as he turned around to look inside his case. "I have a potion that should lessen the discomfort somewhat."

After fiddling around with some turning device, he presented her with a vial containing a murky, yellow, powdery-looking substance — hardly what she'd describe as a *potion*.

"This is *Pain-o-dull*," Doctor Manky informed her.

Well, the name sounded promising at least. Not that it mattered — Olivia was prepared to take any potion, powder or preparation Doctor Manky prescribed.

"The active ingredients are powdered white willow bark and ground birch leaf, but I have infused it with essence of peppermint to make it slightly more palatable."

It could be powdered sheep droppings for all she cared, as long as it worked.

Doctor Manky pulled out the vial's stopper and placed it on the bedside table. Holding the vial above her drinking cup, he tapped a small amount of the *Pain-o-dull* into the water. Then he replaced the stopper and gently set the vial down on the table. Albert hovered over his shoulder, observing the procedure.

"Does the powder dissolve in cold water? It was rather tepid at the Upper Bailey," Albert enquired.

"Yes, it's particularly fine and, therefore, quite soluble," Doctor Manky responded. "However it does require a little mixing. Would you mind handing me a spatula?"

"Not at all," Albert replied, moving quickly to retrieve the required item from the case.

Moments later, Doctor Manky, spatula in hand, gave the mixture a quick stir. "That's all that is required," he said, addressing Albert. Then, turning his attention to Olivia, he picked up the cup. "Now, Mistress Hiepants," he said kindly, "are you able to sit up of your own accord?"

Good question. She felt like the answer would be yes; she certainly felt confident in trying. Placing her arms at her side, she pushed up on her elbow. The movement that would have caused her unbearable pain before the application of *Bruise Mousse* now only caused her mild discomfort.

Doctor Manky smiled. "Good."

"Remarkable, Horatio." Albert was shaking his head in wonder. "Simply remarkable."

And he was right — it *was* remarkable.

"Here, Mistress Hiepants," he said, proffering the cup. Olivia took it, using both hands to hold it. "It is not a pleasant-tasting potion, so I suggest you drink it as quickly as possible, as painful as that may be."

Olivia nodded as she brought the cup to her mouth; it looked much like a murky brew of Earl Beige. She sniffed the potion. It didn't *smell* unpleasant — quite woody with a hint of mint. She looked up and regarded the two faces peering down at her: Doctor Manky's calm and knowing, Albert's animated and enthusiastic. She suddenly felt self-conscious, as if she were part of some medical experiment.

"Try to drink the whole amount, Mistress Hiepants; it will be more efficacious."

Taking a deep breath, she opened her mouth and tipped the *Pain-o-dull* down her throat. It wasn't until the second mouthful that the pain of the first registered. The bark powder felt more like sharp splinters… and then the bitter taste came. It was all Olivia could do not to spit it out; her tongue felt as if it was shrivelling, taste-buds recoiling from the bitterness. Yet, she persisted and, one gulp later, she'd drained the cup.

"Well done, Mistress Hiepants," Doctor Manky said, taking the cup from her.

Olivia was too busy sucking on her tongue, trying to extract the acrid taste from her mouth to acknowledge the doctor.

"Do you have anything sweet here, Albert?"

"I'd say we'd have some honey. I'll fetch some."

"Thank you." As Albert left the room, Doctor Manky refilled the cup with water. "I'm sorry the taste is so unpleasant. Xavier and I have tried to neutralise the acidity and bitterness without affecting the potion's potency, but, alas, we have been unsuccessful. However, that is not to say we have resigned ourselves to accepting *Pain-o-dull* in its current form."

If it had been Xavier speaking to her now, and not his ghoulish guardian, Olivia *might* have been intrigued by the commentary. However, she had no interest in Doctor Manky's quest for *Pain-o-dull* perfection and wished he would stop talking about the vile taste of the yet-to-be-perfected version in her mouth. And, unlike the *Bruise Mousse,* it didn't seem to be working; her throat still felt raw and prickly.

"Here; take some more water," he said, holding the cup out for her.

Olivia grimaced and pointed to her neck.

"Ah yes…" He nodded. "*Pain-o-dull* takes a little longer to work. The pain should recede in a few minutes."

Olivia waved away the cup; she'd rather put up with the taste than the pain.

"Very well," he said, placing the cup back on the bedside table. Then he regarded her thoughtfully. "It might not be my place to say, Mistress Hiepants, but I think you should know that Sid has been quite concerned about your wellbeing."

Olivia shook her head; her brother's concern was *no* concern of hers. "I don't care," she rasped.

"Like you, he's been through quite an ordeal this past week, and I'm afraid his ordeal is—"

"Enough!" She couldn't bear it.

Doctor Manky dropped his gaze and sighed. "My apologies; I'll say no more about your brother."

That suited her perfectly. She didn't even want to know how he'd discovered they were brother and sister. *Pain-o-dull* was nothing compared to the bad taste *Sid* had left in her mouth.

After a minute or so, she could feel the prickling rawness subside. Doctor Manky watched in silence as she took the cup of water and drank deeply. It was… wondrous. And Olivia couldn't help but wonder about the man himself. How could he have spent twenty years in anonymity? He and Xavier should be acclaimed across the Five Duchies… But then, of course, Xavier should have grown up the son of Marmaduke and Lucinda, the heir to Lower Icing.

Olivia's thoughts were interrupted by the reappearance of Albert and Petronella, the latter holding a small, earthenware bowl. Doctor Manky stood as Petronella entered.

"Oh, please remain seated, Doctor," she said. "I've brought the honey for Olivia." Then her friend's animated gaze fell upon her. "Oh, my dear, you look so much better. I can see it in your eyes." She looked back to Doctor Manky. "Albert said you had worked wonders. Once again, please accept my—"

"Petronella," Albert chided.

"Yes, of course," she acknowledged, and then handed the bowl to Doctor Manky. "I just wanted to say… well… we are grateful."

"Not at all, Mistress Whysman," said Doctor Manky, taking the bowl.

She looked back at Olivia. "Oh, my dear…" Emotion was obviously getting the better of her.

It made Olivia feel emotional too. She could feel her throat constricting, but it did so without the excruciating consequences. "Thank you for all you have done for me, Petronella."

And then they both burst into tears.

## CHAPTER 96

## *Sail on*

OPHELIA WAS SUDDENLY alert; woken from her fitful dozing by someone knocking at the door, snapping away images of choking guardsmen, bloody daggers and poisoning Town Criers, and half-dreams of lying on the bank with Tom, and receiving strange potions from a man with pink eyes: the man she hoped was responsible for the knocking.

Billy jerked awake as well. He'd been sleeping on the couch next to her.

"Tha' the doctor y'reckon?" he asked.

"It better be." Ophelia stifled a yawn and headed out of the lounge towards the passageway. Billy leapt up to follow her. She turned around to face him; she couldn't be doing with his lost puppy routine at the moment. "Stay 'ere, Billy. I'm only goin' downstairs t'answer the door."

He looked sulkily at her.

"Don' worry. I ain't goin' nowhere."

She turned back towards the passageway and was relieved not to hear footsteps following her.

There was another rap at the front door. This was followed by her ma crying out, "You gettin' tha', love?" It came from behind the slightly ajar door to her ma and pa's bedroom.

Then Seth appeared at the doorway of his bedroom, wondering, no doubt, whether *he* should answer the door.

"I got it!" she yelled to all and sundry.

It was both doctors — the black and the white. They'd just come from the black one's home, where Sid's sister was recovering from injuries she'd sustained in the fire. *Nice,* Ophelia thought, sarcastically. The wife of the man responsible for poisoning the Duke receives treatment *before* the man who'd tried to find the doctor who'd helped *cure* him. *And,* if the rumour she'd been told was true — that Sid's sister had set the blaze herself — then she *deserved* any injury she got. However, Ophelia kept her thoughts to herself; she was grateful Doctor Manky had kept his promise.

She escorted the doctors upstairs, and even though she had prepared her family for Doctor Manky's pigmentation problem, they all reacted exactly how she'd told them not to: in varying degrees of shock and horror. Predictably, Billy's reaction was the most overt and Seth's the most circumspect. Her ma tried to be gracious, but her quivering lips spoiled what she no doubt considered to be a welcoming smile. Her pa… well… calling him all sorts; you would have thought Doctor Manky was there to perform medical experiments on him. And she felt completely mortified when he said he could see what she meant by 'pig-man-tation.' Once again, the outrage belonged to Albert, while Doctor Manky portrayed calm acceptance. Then her pa followed up by telling Albert that he was looking more and more like a frigging undertaker.

That was enough for Ophelia. She'd kept most of what had occurred at the Upper Bailey to herself, because she didn't want to add to her pa's worry, but buggered if she'd remain silent in the face of his ungrateful rudeness, *particularly* after what she had gone through to bring Doctor Manky to him. So, she let fly with a few well-chosen words at the man lying prostrate on his bed, whose head and body were blistered, peeling, cut and bruised.

"For frig's sake, Pa, y'should bleedin' well look at y'*self* fore y'start mouthin' off at wha' other people look like, 'specially when they come 'ere t'fix you an' all. I *seen* wha' Doctor Manky can do an' *tha's* wha' matters, so 'ow 'bout shuttin' the frig up an' start bein' a bit more grateful, 'cause things could be a *frig* sight worse, lemmie tell ya!"

The room was silent and everyone (apart from Doctor Manky) stared at her, dumbfounded. Then she became aware she was breathing heavily.

"Thank you, Miss Offcut," Doctor Manky said, opening his white case. "Your bedside manner is most effective."

Was he being serious? Ophelia couldn't tell, but the man in white had certainly broken the ice. And suddenly everyone (apart from Doctor Manky) was laughing.

They all stayed in the bedroom while Doctor Manky (assisted by Albert) tended to his patient. Her pa wasn't happy about it; he didn't want people gawping at him while he was being prodded and poked and made to look weak and foolish by "quack doctors who knew as much about healing as our Billy." But her ma was having none of it, telling him he couldn't *be* weaker and more foolish than he was being right at this moment; they were his family and they loved and cared about him, and that he would just have to put up with them being by his side in his time of need. Her pa eyed each of them before conceding the point with a sigh and a begrudging "'Ave it your way then."

Doctor Manky applied a bright-green ointment called *Infectus Rejectus* to all his wounds and his sun-blistered skin, paying particular attention to the gash between his eyes from the iron tankard, the stab wound to his thigh and the lacerations on his wrist. He was most complimentary of Tom's work, saying that his ministrations had saved her pa from a far more severe outcome. (Ophelia wondered how Tom was faring; she was missing him and could hardly wait to fall into his arms. She needed to feel... protected.)

Her pa grumbled at every touch, but made no more disparaging comments (apart from scoffing when Doctor Manky praised Tom). However, he *did* swear (understandably) when Albert opened a jar containing an unguent called *Bruise Mousse* and handed it to the man in white. It smelt disgusting, even to a family of butchers. Still, as Doctor Manky dabbed it on his bruised ribs, the smell faded. More importantly, the relief it gave her pa was miraculous; the grimacing tension on his face faded and his breathing became more relaxed and measured. He even managed to compliment the doctors. It filled the room with smiles, and tears of relief ran down her ma's face. She and her brothers were quick to follow.

The doctors' visit lasted over an hour, with the time spent treating her pa, explaining how the potions worked, and how he needed to relax for a few more days at least. They bound his ribs and applied new bandages to his forehead and thigh. The stitches Tom had sewn into the knife wound were still intact and it was mending nicely. Again, both doctors praised the Gamekeeper's skill. Doctor Manky said his broken nose might eventually need straightening, but he would use a special potion — something *Coma* — to perform the procedure painlessly.

By the end of it all (and regardless of all the scrapes, bruises and bandaging), her pa looked so much better; she could see it in his eyes. Frank Offcut was back. *All* of them could see it, and the mood in the Offcut household lifted as relief turned into joy. Even Billy seemed to gain strength from their pa's recovery.

The doctors left in a fanfare of gratefulness, and, as Ophelia escorted them to the front door, she broached the subject of Billy's behaviour. She explained how clingy he'd been since she'd been back from her jaunt in the wilderness; that her ma said he'd been like it ever since being released from The Can, explaining to them that he'd spent a week in there for making unwanted advances towards Will and Joan Plucker's niece.

They both listened with interest, and, as she opened the front door, she asked Doctor Manky if he had any potions that could make him… less clingy.

"Alas, Miss Offcut, the emotional brain is something Xavier and I have yet to master. Xavier, himself, is currently suffering from, for want of a better term, a blockage of the mind."

It wasn't what Ophelia was expecting to hear, and her face must have betrayed her disappointment.

"However," Doctor Manky continued, touching her arm reassuringly, his eyes mirroring the hue of the dusky sky, "I am certain he will make a full recovery, and I believe Billy will do the same. Our minds are like ships upon an ocean, Miss Offcut, drifting on a sea of vast uncertainty. Sometimes we are gifted gentle waters, sometimes we're tormented by unfavourable winds, and, every now and then, we find ourselves challenged by violent tempests. But, like ships, our minds are designed to float — to weather the most unsettling of storms and eventually right themselves. From there they are able to… sail on."

What could she say to *that*? No-one had ever spoken to her that way: so poetically and meaningfully.

Her response was neither. "Righ' then."

Albert, however, was able to convey the sentiment better. "Most eloquent, Horatio."

Doctor Manky smiled at the man in black. "Xavier and I spent almost twenty years living in Missing Anchor, residing in an inn called the Windy Sailor. My metaphors tend to be on the nautical side."

"And, of course," Albert added, "the whole reason we are standing here is because of the *Happy Mer*—"

He stopped himself, aware of the faux pas he was about to make. The sinking of the *Happy Mermaid*: the reason why the Duke had *become* the Duke, and the reason why, it turned out, he and the Duchess had been separated from Xavier. For the first time, Ophelia realised what a wrench it must have been for them… *and* for Xavier, for that matter. Billy had only been separated from his loved ones for a *week,* and he was a mess; she could only imagine the depth of loss after twenty years.

The silence was short-lived. "Well, we'll bid you good evening, Miss Offcut,"

Albert finished, tipping his finger to his black hat.

Doctor Manky smiled wryly at his associate, then directed his dusky eyes back to Ophelia. "We will visit your father again in a couple of days, but should anything unforeseen occur in the interim, please call upon us. I believe arrangements have been made with…?" He looked to the man in black for assistance.

"The Office of Petitions," said Albert, still looking rather embarrassed. "If you leave your name with the clerk, he will see to it that your request reaches us in good time."

Ophelia thanked them again, and watched for a while as they walked up Market Street. She heard the man in black apologise, and the man in white telling him to think nothing of it. Then she went inside and shut the red door.

## CHAPTER 97

## *Honey to orange marmalade*

ONCE AGAIN OLIVIA found herself alone in the confines of her temporary bedroom. She had resolved not to impose herself on Albert and Petronella a minute longer than was necessary. Of course, they'd both said that she was welcome to stay, but it had only been out of politeness, and she was determined not to take advantage of their generous nature. Still, she did wonder where she and Gerald would go. And she wondered what had become of him. Neither Albert nor Doctor Manky had been able to enlighten her on that point — just that they had last seen him in the Duke's residence shortly before midday.

The day — it felt like the longest of her life — was finally waning; the sky was now the colour of the honey Petronella had brought to mask the taste of *Pain-o-dull*. The foul concoction was now just a bitter memory, but she would happily drink it again — the benefits far outweighed the unpleasantness. In fact, Doctor Manky's ministrations had worked so well, Olivia found herself suffering from another malady: boredom. She felt like getting up, being useful in some way. She'd even offered to help Petronella prepare supper, but her friend had tutted her into submission with reminders that Doctor Manky had said she required rest.

It couldn't be more than an hour since the two doctors had departed to 'attend to another patient', but, for Olivia, time had flowed slower than… honey. Oh dear… this would not do. She couldn't just lie here with nothing but her thoughts to keep her company.

She thought about ringing the bell, just for something to do, but that was not fair on her friend. Petronella had already dedicated enough of her time to conversation. Perhaps, if Olivia offered to reveal some of the truth about Sid — nothing about his thieving or the involvement of Paris, of course. She might even suggest moving to the reception room; she felt confident she could sit in a chair without too much discomfort, and the change of scenery would be most welcome. Then she realised she didn't have the appropriate attire for such a room.

Olivia resigned herself to her situation. Her thoughts progressed through the 'if onlys' while the sky turned from honey to orange marmalade.

It was almost dark when she heard another knock at the front door. This time it was the man she had been waiting for.

## CHAPTER 98

# In the sound of people

THE WELCOME AT The Harey Rabbit had been heartfelt, but short-lived; the inn was full and they all had jobs to do. After a quick retelling of events (with predictable responses from all her staff), Mary spent the rest of the afternoon, and well into the evening, serving and playing host to her patrons. She felt a renewed sense of purpose in running The Harey Rabbit, and she was very proud of her staff; oddities aside, they always seemed to pull together.

She felt invigorated talking to her regulars, serving them drinks and hearty meals. (She'd have to get some more of that *Vigour Morphis* potion from Doctor Manky.) Even the Limpdickers were unusually subdued and less boorish; particularly Rupert, who, like Mary, had been embroiled in the Upper Bailey machinations. And now, it seemed, everything was out in the open.

Gerald Hiepants and Xavier were the two main topics of conversation. Many of her patrons had been at the castle dinner on Thursday night, and The Harey Rabbit was abuzz with opinion and conjecture. If only Gerald could see the stir he'd caused by *not* delivering a proclamation. He'd always wanted to make an impression on these people, to be seen as… relevant. Passing strange that he'd had to *be* the story to achieve it. While disbelief and outrage were the main sentiments expressed within the inn, there also seemed to be some sympathy reserved for Olivia, particularly among the women. It just went to show how appearances affected people's judgement. And, of course, gossip played its part. Every rumour was eagerly swallowed, and then consumed as fact until the truth was just a morsel lodged in the corner of a lip, inevitably wiped away without a thought. Still, it was with some reluctance that Mary bid her last patrons goodnight; she felt at ease in the sound of people enjoying themselves. Truth be told, she didn't want to be alone.

## CHAPTER 99

# Feel each other's pain

GERALD WAS STILL wearing the same clothes. However, his yellow waistcoat was now smudged in grime, the white shirt underneath was crumpled and sweat-stained, and his green trousers were torn just above the right knee. *Had no-one had the decency to allow him to change?* The fire must have destroyed his wardrobe, but, even so, she thought *someone* would have offered to re-clothe him.

"You took your time," Olivia remarked, eyeing off his presentation. She knew it sounded cold (and she really didn't want to sound cold) but she had… expectations. And somehow, without saying a word, Gerald had already fallen short.

He nodded at her glumly, as if her welcome had met *his* expectations.

She felt her stomach sink. What was she doing? "I'm sorry, Gerald."

She edged herself into a sitting position, half expecting a stabbing pain to catch her by surprise, but the *Bruise Mousse* was still working its wonders.

"How are you, m'dear?" he asked as he sat down on the chair beside the bed. There was no feeling in his words; it sounded like something he'd been trained to say — that *she'd* trained him to say. He looked… empty.

She *felt* empty. Then she was sobbing in her husband's arms, but she couldn't say whether the embrace or the tears had happened first.

During the moments or minutes she spent in Gerald's arms, nothing was said — it was just an outpouring of emotion. The only thing she was aware of was the security of his embrace and the softness of his clothes. Even the smell of his sweat seemed comforting. Then it was over.

Olivia sat on the edge of the bed, opposite her husband, but still connected to him by clasped hands. There, feeling closer to him than at any time during their marriage, they talked of their time apart.

Gerald explained his role in the recovery of the Duke: he'd demonstrated how he'd concocted the poisonous version of *Paloma Coma*. From that,

Doctor Manky was able to create an antidote using a selection of powders and oils. The doctor had been very understanding and kind. Even Sir Richard had comprehended the necessity of Gerald's involvement. And, of course, he'd been reunited with Xavier.

"How was he?" Olivia asked, imagining the toll Thursday night's performance must have taken on him.

Gerald's response was considered. "He seemed well." Then, with more conviction, he added, "He *is* well; the presence of Horatio has been a great boon to him. I would say he is himself once again."

"And his ability to heal?"

"Of that I am not sure. However, he *did* assist Horatio in formulating the antidote. It was under Horatio's guidance, but... I truly believe all will be well with Xavier."

Olivia nodded and squeezed her husband's hand. His news sounded positive — better than she'd hoped.

"And now that Marmaduke has recovered..." He released a shuddering breath. "Oh, my dear, I cannot tell you what a relief it is that he's recovered. And he has been most..." This time it was Gerald's hands doing the squeezing. "Forgiving... too forgiving, in fact. He pardoned me, Olivia... after what I did to him."

"Oh, Gerald... you deserve to be pardoned. Marmaduke knew what he was doing; you said he looked grateful when you—"

"It was just a feeling," he whispered. "I can't be *sure*. I will never be sure."

Olivia nodded. Their hands remained locked together, like they needed to feel each other's pain.

"How did Marmaduke receive Xavier?"

"I don't know, m'dear." He sighed. "I haven't been privy to any news regarding Xavier or the Duke since they've been reunited."

Olivia nodded. Despite the injustice of it all — *Richard* should be the one being held accountable for his actions — she realised that Gerald could no longer hold a position of trust within the Upper Bailey.

"And there's been some trouble at the castle this afternoon."

"What kind of trouble?" Olivia's voice was beginning to sound hoarse.

"I'm not sure exactly; it had something to do with Doctor Manky's servant... A guardsman was killed."

What madness was *this*? "*Killed?*" she rasped. "Are you *sure?* This is not just one of your fanciful interpretations, is it?"

A half-smile broke through his downcast expression. "No. There was quite an upheaval at the Upper Bailey — men-at-arms everywhere. Another guard was injured, as were Lieutenant Swill and Mary Brewer. They were treated by Albert and Doctor Manky and are now quite alright. In fact, Lieu—"

"Why was *she* attacked?" This was incredible. What was going on?

"I'm sorry, Olivia, but I don't know the details. These are just snippets I overheard during the afternoon. No-one has *told* me anything."

Olivia shook her head in disbelief. Doctor Manky's servant? It made no sense at all. How could a *healer* have a *killer* for a servant? And what did that say about Doctor Manky? He'd seemed quite at ease whilst treating her; not what she'd expect from someone whose servant had just killed a guardsman. And Albert... he'd have been more on edge, surely. No, Gerald *must* have got his facts mixed up. "Do you know if they apprehended this... servant?"

His expression turned sheepish. "I believe so."

He was hiding something. "What is it, Gerald?" Her voice was now little more than a whisper.

"Well... the person who prevented him from escaping..." It was obvious he was reluctant to share *this* snippet.

"Yes?" she prompted.

"Well... I heard it was Sid."

It took a moment for the sound of her brother's name to sink in. Had the world turned upside down while she'd been consigned to this bedroom? A killer servant of a doctor with an incurable skin condition had been caught by her waster, womanising, drunkard of a brother? What were he and his floosy doing in the Upper Bailey in the first place?

Olivia freed her hands from Gerald's and covered her face. She couldn't bear it. Their life was in ruin, literally gone up in smoke.

"Are you alright, m'dear?" Gerald's voice was soft and laden with remorse.

She wanted to lash out at him, to say that of *course* she wasn't alright: he'd ruined them with his idealism. And, because of that, *she'd* ruined their home.

Olivia shook her head; not in answer to his question, but in defiance of her emotions. In her heart, she knew she was at fault; she was the one who'd driven him to... Suddenly, the Swill boy's acerbic words echoed in her mind: *"I can well understand why your husband poisoned the Duke, Mistress Hiepants. I, too, would rather spend my life in the dungeon than be holed up with you."*

Her hands fell from her face into her lap. "I'm so sorry, Gerald," she whispered, keeping her eyes downcast, focusing on her hands. "I have been an unloving wife and made our marriage miserable." Oddly, she felt little emotion as the words spilled out. "And the blame lies with me for what has happened to us this past week."

"No, Olivia. I—" he whispered, his hands reaching for hers.

"*Please*, Gerald." She spoke over him — she was adept at doing that, but this needed to be said while she had a mind to say it. "I know why you poisoned Marmaduke, and I realise that most of it was *my* doing." She forced her gaze upwards, to look him in the eyes. "I *drove* you to desperation, Gerald." He looked stunned, but she could feel his hands close back around hers. "And I have destroyed our home — not on purpose, but in a prideful fit of pique. Xavier's book and… all your proclamations turned to ash. How will you ever forgive me?"

His eyes were welling with tears, but a hint of a smile began to form on his face. "Fear not, my sweet, I've had some practice over the years."

His compassion was too much. "Oh, Gerald," she said, her voice barely audible now, "what is to become of us?"

He brought her hand to his cheek. "I'm not sure."

The moment was interrupted by a soft knock at the door. Olivia immediately withdrew her hands from Gerald's grasp. There was a moment of silence, before the door was opened hesitantly by Petronella.

"Excuse me, Olivia. I'm sorry to interrupt…"

Her friend was addressing her as if Gerald wasn't there.

"However, the Town Crier's escort is waiting for him."

Escort? What was she talking about? And why was she being so odd and formal around Gerald?

"Thank you, Mistress Whysman," Gerald responded. "I will be out directly."

"Very well," Petronella acknowledged, momentarily flicking her eyes in Gerald's direction, before closing the door again.

"Gerald?" Olivia rasped; she needed some water or honey or something — she could feel the prickle in her throat returning.

"I am confined to The Keep at the Duke's pleasure. I have been granted this time to see you as a concession to your condition and my co-operation."

*What nonsense was this?* "But… your pardon. Surely…"

He shook his head. "It does not apply to my falsification of the proclamation or my liberation of Xavier. Sir Richard is quite determined to have me tried for those actions."

*Of course he was,* she thought, bitterly — Richard had been made to look a fool by Gerald, and now he sought retribution. She shook her head at the injustice of it all. "When?"

"Directly after the Duke of Stymouth's visit. Until then, I am to remain in The Keep… in Xavier's room." A wry smile broke upon his face. "Ironic, what?"

"Oh, Gerald," she said, brushing her hand against the side of his face.

He reached up and held it against his cheek, then kissed it. His silver, bell-shaped cufflink caught the candlelight and glinted against his dungeon-stained cuff. Her husband still had his pride, and that was enough for Olivia. They would be together come what may.

"I'd best take my leave, my sweet," he said, releasing her hand.

As Gerald stood, Olivia stood with him — the first time she'd attempted the feat since waking up in Petronella's guest room. She could feel her ribs complaining, but nothing like the teeth-clenching pain she'd experienced before Doctor Manky's ministrations.

"Goodbye for now, m'dear," he said. "I dare say Sir Richard will allow me more visits."

All Olivia could do was nod. Even if she'd had a voice left, emotion was clogging her words. It was all so unfair. As Gerald opened the door, he paused and looked back at her. "If it's any comfort, Xavier's book was removed from the house before the fire. Lieutenant Swill conducted a search while we were detained in the castle."

There *was* comfort in Gerald's news, but it was cold. However, for his benefit, she attempted a smile, but her tears betrayed her — tears that became sobs when he shut the door.

She collapsed back on the bed, sending a jab of pain through her ribs, but her greatest pain was caused by the sound of fading footsteps down a floorboard passageway.

# CHAPTER 100

## *Inhibido*

IT WAS JUST past ten o'clock when Mary locked the front door. She sent Dave, Mandy, Lillian and Patricia home, then helped John and Juanita tidy up the kitchen in readiness for the breakfast service. As she added the last dried plate to the stack, her mind turned back to the day's unimaginable events. They seemed so distant and unreal… and the way she'd left Sid… Oh, for frig's sake, surely she could go—

"You feeleeng dee sadness for sometheeng, Meestress?"

It was the unusual softness of the Icarumban's voice more than the question that took Mary by surprise. "What?" she said, pretending to adjust the stack of plates.

"You sigheeng with dee sadness."

Really? *Could* you sigh with sadness? Mary turned to face Juanita. As she did so, she saw John yawning. It triggered an excuse to avoid a conversation she really didn't want to have. "Time to get some rest, I think," she said, looking mainly at John. "You've both had a long day. Thank you again for being so professional in my absence."

"Good night, Mistress." John yawned again and began walking towards the hallway door.

Juanita, however, looked quite defiant, crossing her arms and furrowing her brow. "I know you are geeveeng me dee bum's rash."

If she was going to use these idiotic idioms, Mary wished she would at least use them correctly. "It's bum's *rush*, Juanita," she informed the washer girl. Behind her, John ducked out of the kitchen, eager, no doubt, to remove himself from a conversation with bum in it. "And, yes, I suppose I *am* giving you the bum's rush, but—"

"You no want to share your heart," Juanita finished for her. Then she shook her head. "I no understand you Duchee people, you so… *inhibido*."

It was probably the first word of Icarumban to come out of Juanita's mouth that Mary understood, and she didn't like it at all. "Well, Juanita," she responded, crossing her arms like a petulant adolescent, "at least we *Duchy people* don't pour hot water on defenceless old women." She knew it sounded pathetic.

"Ees better to let off dee steam than boil eenside. That make you crazy!" Juanita's hands were flailing now.

This was ridiculous. Mary shook her head and sighed. "And before you say anything, Juanita, *that* was a *frustrated* sigh!"

"Si." Juanita nodded, knowingly. "*Inhibido.*"

# CHAPTER 101

## *Sleep wouldn't come*

THE EVENING HAD faded into night. Ophelia lay on her bed, staring out of her window at a black sky sprinkled with stars. She was exhausted, but sleep wouldn't come. Again, her thoughts turned to Tom. Perhaps he was staring at the stars too. She hoped so… and that he was safe.

At least her pa had finally received the medical attention he needed. Sid was right about Doctor Manky: he *did* have some 'bloody good curatives'. But Sid had also said he was 'deranged', which seemed harsh to Ophelia — Doctor Manky was calm and rational. Still, Sid hadn't really seen him as a doctor, more of a bizarre benefactor. And his appearance obviously worked against him.

Ophelia knew what it was like to be judged by appearance. Not that it was the same, of course; she could *play* upon hers… to a certain extent at least. Doctor Manky, however, had no choice; his appearance was an affliction, one that evoked fear and mistrust. It certainly wasn't fair or right that a man of his ability should be judged so superficially, but Ophelia knew it was the nature of things. Well, she, for one, would sing his praises — as much for his courage as his bloody good curatives.

Ophelia closed her eyes on the night and concentrated on breathing, feeling the rise and fall of her chest. Her thoughts turned to the sea. Great Naff was on the sea — another reason to visit Len, Bert and Tad. She'd never seen the sea, and tried to imagine what it was like — the Icing River without an opposite bank — but… the reeds kept getting in the way… and the memory of guardsman Hopwood… the sound of…

She sat up in her bed. Her body ached almost as much as her mind. And she felt suffocated by the four walls of her room, closed in by the darkness. She could do with some more *Oil of You Lay*.

Ophelia swivelled to the side of the bed, leant out the window and breathed in the cool night air. Hers was the only bedroom that faced the back of Slaughter & Offcut. Below her window, the expansive roof of the coolroom extended to an alleyway. From there, other rooftops spread out to meet the night sky. She gazed up at the glittering stars. Tom had explained how travellers navigated by them… and some of them had names like *Big Bear* and *Big Dog*, which seemed strange to her. They deserved more… *sparkling* names. She wondered how far away they were. Tom would probably know. She'd give anything to be with him right now.

# SUNDAY, JULY 6

*Five minutes past midnight, to be exact.*

# CHAPTER 102

## *It's tomorrow*

MARY LAY ON her bed. She felt absolutely shattered — Doctor Manky's potion had well and truly worn off. She should be asleep, but her mind wouldn't let her rest. Images and conversations swirled inside her head, like ale being poured into a tankard: Sid holding a knife to the guardsman's neck, then looking sad, a teary-eyed, "*Sorry, Mary, I don't know where that came from*"; the whisper in her ear as she walked into Richard's silver-and-black chamber, "*I'm afraid it wath nethethary*"; Richard's full-size portrait leaning away from the wall to speak to her, "*It is clear that Sid Evily is already having a deleterious effect on you, Mary*"; Ophelia posing, pouting and playing up to Sid, but when she spoke, it was with Olivia's voice, saying, "*You should attend to matters more appropriate to your station*"; Sid groping Ophelia's breasts, "*I've been itching to use one of these beauties again*"; the look of hurt on Sid's face when she stepped back from him, and Juanita's voice taunting her with "*Inhibido, inhibido, inhibido*". Then the chant became "*Mary, Mary, Mary*" and the tone of the voice changed — the Icarumban accent melting away to the gentler, more soothing tones of a Lower Icinger. Then she felt something brush across her cheek.

Mary sat up with a start. A fly was buzzing around her face. She swiped it away. She could hear herself breathing. Her heart was racing from her twisted dreams. Sitting there, breathing heavily, she regretted walking away from Sid… leaving him with Richard. Then she heard her name being whispered. It sounded like…

"Sid?"

"Mary," he answered from the window, his silhouette framed in the square opening.

What the…? Was she awake? She clambered off her bed and moved to the window. Sid retreated slightly as she approached, stepping back into the gloom so she could push the window open.

"Sid, what are you—"

He stopped her words with a kiss, tenderly bringing his hand to her cheek. The kiss lingered. She felt her body tingle.

When their lips parted, he whispered, "It's tomorrow."

# PART 2

# MARMADUKE

## AND

# OWEN

# The Dukes are up

**M**ARMADUKE DU MARMA, Duke of Lower Icing, and Owen Llandrover, Duke of Stymouth, were two completely different people. About the only thing they had in common was their title.

Marmaduke had been plucked from obscurity after the demise of the 'true' royal family, whereas the Llandrovers had been ruling Stymouth for almost two hundred and fifty years. Marmaduke had taken the mantle of Duke reluctantly, whereas Owen revelled in his right to rule. Marmaduke courted advice and guidance, whereas Owen took his own counsel. Marmaduke was a reformer and humanist, enacting laws for the betterment of Lower Icingers, whereas Owen was a traditionalist, maintaining the laws that kept his family in power. Marmaduke and Lucinda had suffered the 'loss' of their only son, whereas Owen and his wife, Gwen, had delighted in the raising of three sons and four daughters. Marmaduke was circumspect and removed — even more so after the death of Lucinda — whereas Owen was brash and bold, quick to temper, but also jovial and good humoured. Marmaduke would meet Owen in three days' time because he sought to build stronger ties with Stymouth, whereas Owen would meet Marmaduke in three days' time to see what *advantage* he could gain from stronger ties with Lower Icing.

It had been twenty years since the two Dukes last met… twenty years since Marmaduke and Lucinda had become Duke and Duchess of Lower Icing… Owen had been the Duke of Stymouth for five years by then, and Gwen had already borne him three children, including his eldest son and heir, Cedrych. Twenty years — their passing had been as different for the two Dukes as the men themselves. Marmaduke's were haunted with the memory of a two-year-old son, with only his heartbroken wife with whom to share his pain, whereas Owen's time had flashed by in a triumphant blaze of procreation and prosperity. And, so, their reunion would be a meeting of unlike minds.

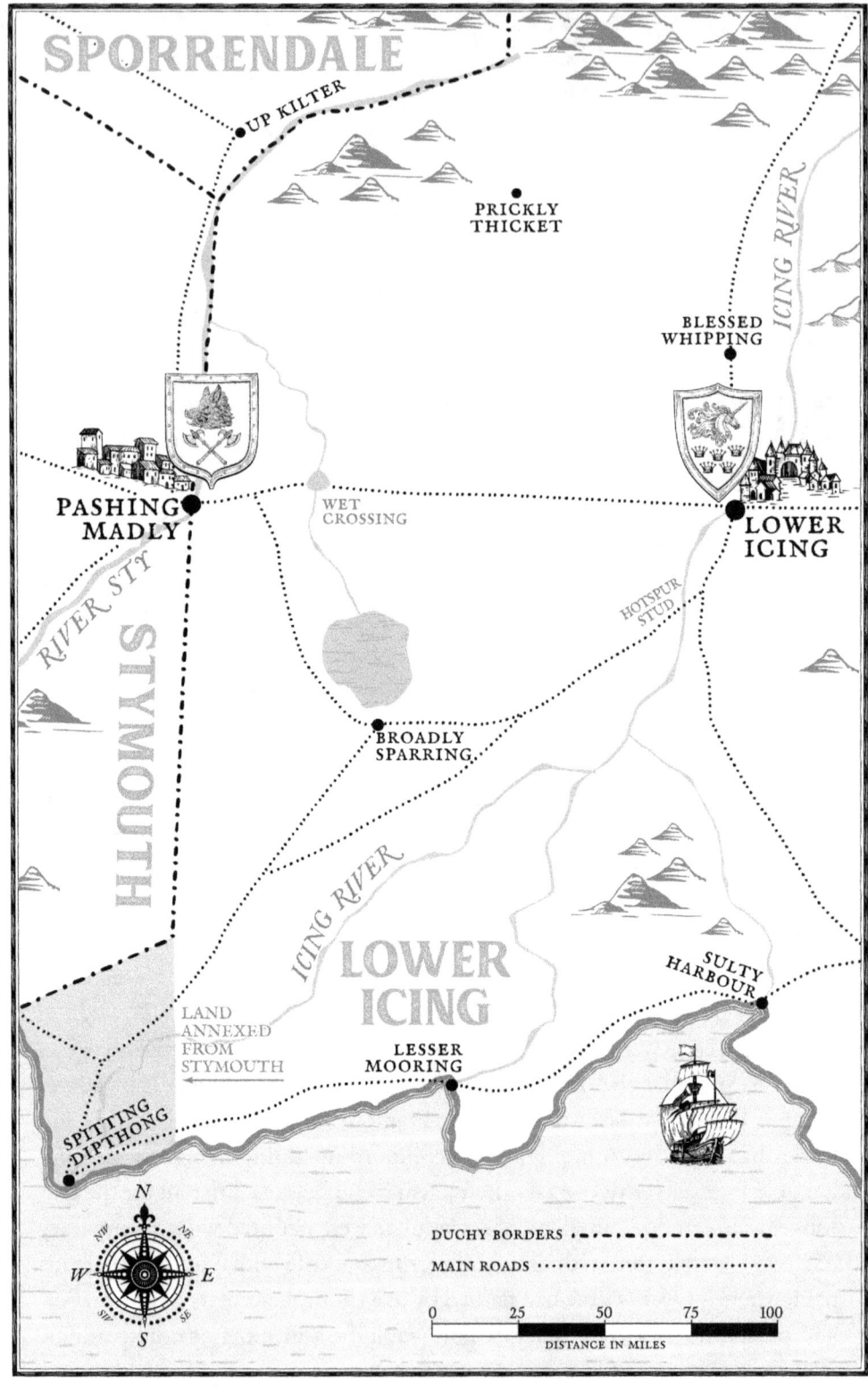

SPORRENDALE

UP KILTER

PRICKLY
THICKET

ICING RIVER

BLESSED
WHIPPING

PASHING
MADLY

WET
CROSSING

LOWER
ICING

RIVER STY

STYMOUTH

HOTSPUR
STUD

BROADLY
SPARRING

ICING RIVER

LOWER
ICING

SULTY
HARBOUR

LAND
ANNEXED
FROM
STYMOUTH

LESSER
MOORING

SPITTING
DIPTHONG

N
NW          NE
W                    E
SW          SE
S

DUCHY BORDERS ·—·—·—·—·—·

MAIN ROADS ····················

0          25          50          75          100

DISTANCE IN MILES

# TUESDAY, JULY 8

*Three days after the antidote was administered to Marmaduke by Doctor Manky and Xavier.*

# CHAPTER 1

## *An unnatural course of action*

MARMADUKE SAT WITH his back to his desk, staring out the window at a grey sky. The rain had stopped, but the trees were still dripping wet, and the beautifully presented garden looked eager for every drop; its blooms joyfully facing upwards, radiant in the overcast dullness. It was a far cry from the glaring sunshine and sweltering heat... *before* he drank the poison.

He'd known the Town Crier had tainted his wine — he'd seen it in his eyes, in his trembling hands as he handed him the goblet. Of all people, Marmaduke would never have expected Gerald Hiepants capable of such an act, and yet, there he'd been, providing him with a course of action he'd mulled over many times since the death of Lucinda; it was almost as if fate had finally made the decision for him.

And now, it seemed, fate had changed its mind.

Marmaduke sighed. He still hadn't come to terms with being reunited with Xavier. In many ways, it gladdened him beyond measure — he was a son of whom to be proud. But he was also a stranger, one who'd inherited Lucinda's thoughtful eyes and uncertain smile. Marmaduke couldn't look at him without thinking of his wife. All those years together, parted from their son, wondering if he lived, but thinking he was dead, tormented by the way they had left him, believing they'd had no choice, having been swept away by forces too hard to resist.

They *had* had a choice though. However, by the time they'd realised it, Xavier had disappeared. Or so they'd been told by Sir Walter Upson, and, as the years drifted on, a dark acceptance replaced the light of hope.

Marmaduke had the running of the Duchy to keep his mind occupied, but Lucinda had no such distraction. She was left with too many hours to reflect and, eventually, be seduced by remorse. No matter how he'd tried, Marmaduke could not lift his wife's spirits. Another child might have helped, but there was no desire in their coupling. It was as if Lucinda believed they didn't deserve more children if they could relinquish their first so easily. But they'd thought they were saving his life. Horatio had promised to keep him safe until they came for him. Sir Walter had said the separation would be temporary — a few months or so, just until he and Lucinda had established themselves. And now, the aching guilt he felt for abandoning his son had been compounded by the realisation that his son *was* actually alive.

Marmaduke stood up and leant out the window — he had to clear his head. Taking a deep breath, he let the rain-cleaned air fill his lungs. Over the wall, the horizon stretched east towards Naffolk.

Inevitably, his gaze fell downwards to the garden, to the statue of an old man delighting in the scent of a freshly cut rose. It was a statue of his second cousin, Hugo De La Wrence; a man he'd never met, the father of Olivier De La Wrence... a Duke lost to the Biting Sea. It had been Lucinda's favourite place: an oasis of contentment where she would read or, on the odd occasion, take her hand to needlepoint. It was the only place Marmaduke could recall her laughing — often with Richard — and it was the place where her ashes were scattered.

A knock at the door snapped Marmaduke's thoughts back to the land of the living. He'd finally set aside time for a private meeting with Richard. There were many things to discuss, including the funeral of Bradley Lamb — *another* death Marmaduke felt responsible for. His squire had been found by Tom Skinner dumped under a bramble patch just off the North Road, his neck broken. Bradley had left Lower Icing on Friday with the task of retrieving Horatio from Blessed Whipping. He'd been in the company of a recruit... of whom there was no trace. The horses had also gone. The patrol had returned with Bradley's body on Sunday morning. Tom had returned yesterday morning; he'd continued alone, tracking the horses until he lost the trail on the West Road.

However, the true reason for the meeting was to *confide* in Richard. It was time his friend knew the truth about Xavier, and the role Sir Walter Upson had played in keeping his whereabouts secret.

The man sitting across the desk from him looked concerned... or perhaps it was just his new appearance. It was strange to see Richard clean shaven, with his hair tied back tightly into a small ponytail. It made Marmaduke feel as if he'd been in a delirious state for months or years, rather than a week.

Richard had asked after his wellbeing… again. Marmaduke was becoming slightly irritated by all the concern. He knew people's intentions were kind, but no matter how much he assured them that he'd made a full recovery, they remained unconvinced. In truth, he felt perfectly well; it was as if nothing had happened to him. Once Horatio had administered the antidote, the effects of the poison had dissipated rapidly. All that was required was rest and sustenance: something he'd excelled at in the last few days.

However, *that* time had passed. The Duke and Duchess of Stymouth would be arriving with their entourage in three days. Things needed to be done, and said, before then.

The late morning light filtered through the overcast sky, highlighting the silver brocading and stitching on Richard's black doublet. Marmaduke had always been impressed by Richard's immaculate sense of style. No-one could ignore the Seneschal of Lower Icing when he entered a room; he commanded attention — if anyone had been born to be Duke, it was Sir Richard Upson.

"Is something amiss, Marmaduke?" he said, eyes narrowing. "You seem preoccupied. Are you sure—?"

"I'm quite myself, Richard," he interjected, fobbing off another enquiry about his health.

Richard nodded, though it was clear he wasn't convinced.

Marmaduke sighed in frustration. It was followed by silence. Now the moment had come, Marmaduke wasn't sure how to broach the subject of Sir Walter; he was concerned it would affect his friendship with Richard.

The silence was broken by the man sitting opposite, taking the lead as usual. "A messenger arrived from Stymouth this morning, confirming numbers and expected time of arrival. They should be—"

"Richard, do you remember what I said when you confronted me about Xavier?" The words were out of his mouth before he realised he'd said them.

Richard's eyes narrowed slightly. It was barely noticeable, but Marmaduke knew he had thrown his friend with the question, but continued regardless, "The night we shared wine together, the night before I shared wine with the Town Crier?"

Richard's expression remained impassive; no doubt he was weighing up the intent of the question. Eventually he replied, "You said, 'Our son died twenty years ago.'"

Marmaduke nodded and smiled bitterly; he'd wanted it to be true. "But, of course, you knew better."

Richard remained silent, dark eyes searching. "So, you *did* know he was alive?"

Marmaduke nodded. *Oh yes; he knew.*

Richard shook his head. "I don't understand. Then why deny—?"

"It was too late!" The words were a like bandage that needed to be ripped off quickly, even though the wound would never heal.

"Too late for what?" Richard asked.

Marmaduke wanted to answer, but *those* words stuck fast.

Richard was openly confused. "When did you find out?"

He thought he was ready for this, but now his mind was spinning with the consequences of what he was about to reveal. "Nineteen months ago."

Richard nodded, as if he'd suspected as much.

Marmaduke felt hollow just hearing the words; nineteen months of torment, eating away at his conscience. If only he'd acted sooner, Lucinda would have lived to see their son... and their reunion would have been joyful.

Richard's eyes bored into his, scouring his mind. "Did Lucinda know?"

It sounded like an accusation... and he was right to accuse. "No... she died before..."

The air suddenly felt thick.

"Before I could..."

What he was about to say wasn't true. He *could* have told Lucinda before she'd died, but he'd chosen not to until he was *sure*. He'd *needed* to be sure before he...

"Marmaduke?" Richard stood up. "Are you alright?"

And then his friend was by his side.

"I just need some air, Richard."

They stood together at the large bay window overlooking the garden; Hugo ever delighting in his bloom... if only life was that simple. He breathed deeply and suddenly the words flowed effortlessly.

"Nineteen months ago, in late December, I received a letter informing me that Xavier was alive, living with Horatio in Missing Anchor above a tavern called the Windy Sailor. The letter explained that he and Horatio had been residing there for over eighteen years."

"Who was the letter from?" Richard asked; his voice was soft, but there was a bite to it.

"Let me first tell you what else the letter revealed," he responded, staring out to the eastern horizon. If he told Richard who the letter was from, the context would be lost. And *this* was very much about context.

"It stated that Horatio had been, and still was, of the belief that Lucinda and I thought it best that he and Xavier remain in Missing Anchor, that we were happy for him to raise and educate our son, that we believed Xavier would live a better life away from the castle."

Out of the corner of his eye, Marmaduke could see Richard shaking his head. "Doctor Manky strikes me as a compassionate man. It seems incredible that he could accept such an unnatural course of action."

Richard was right, of course, but he and Lucinda had been just as guilty in that respect. "Don't forget, Richard, the laws were different twenty years ago, and the circumstances unprecedented. We were all, Horatio included, swept along by what was expected of us, forced into a situation we never could have imagined… the duty, the… sacrifice. Our past was drowned as surely as if *we'd* been on the Happy Mermaid."

A cool breeze caressed Marmaduke's face; it felt gentle, like the world was trying to comfort him, but it need not try — no matter how close he and Xavier became, the ghost of Lucinda would always torment him. Then he felt a supportive hand on his shoulder. He kept his gaze outwards; he couldn't face the sympathy… not from Richard.

"We have achieved much, you and I," said his friend. "We've made Lower Icing a better place, I think. The De La Wrence rule was self-serving. We changed that, you and I *and* Lucinda. Lower Icing is now the most liberal and just of the Five Duchies. It is an achievement of which to be proud."

Again, cold comfort. Lucinda was dead, and the icy guilt permeated through every fibre of his being.

"… for so long?" Richard's gaze was searching, waiting for Marmaduke to respond. His hand was no longer on his shoulder.

"Pardon?"

Richard's eyes narrowed. "I was wondering how the illusion could have been perpetuated for so long."

Marmaduke had wondered the same thing, but Horatio had explained that the correspondence had been very regular, particularly in the beginning, reiterating the need for secrecy about Xavier's identity, that not even Xavier should know. And each missive was accompanied by a promissory note, for which Horatio exchanged coin with a local money-lender. It was more than enough to support them both *and* pay for Horatio's research.

"Once a pattern is set in place, it becomes routine, expected… *accepted*," Marmaduke explained, relaying what Horatio had told him. "Horatio believed he was doing what Lucinda and I wanted… and he was being supported financially, which he saw as confirmation of our resolve. As the years passed, he stopped questioning the reasoning and began accepting it, raising and teaching our son in the ways of healing. He also admitted that, during that time, he began to look upon Xavier as his own son, that he was happy with the arrangement."

"I see," Richard said, though clearly he had doubts. "So, who was the mastermind behind—"

"Horatio is an honourable man, Richard," Marmaduke interjected, delaying the moment a little longer. "Lucinda and I trusted him with our son. He… we… *all* of us, including *you*, Richard, are victims of political manipulation."

His friend regarded him suspiciously. "What do you mean?"

"It was Sir Walter."

Richard looked at him blankly, as if the name meant nothing to him. But Marmaduke knew what it was like to hear the incredible.

"Your father was responsible for Lucinda and I being parted from our son, and he was responsible for *keeping* us apart."

Richard's jaw muscles clenched and unclenched as he chewed over the words.

"It matters not, my friend — not now. The damage has—"

"Of *course* it matters!" he hissed. "Who accuses my father? The author of the letter, I suppose. So, who are *they* to make such an accusation? And what *evidence* do they offer?"

Richard's anger didn't shock Marmaduke; it was expected. Richard had admired his father, and so had Marmaduke. Sir Walter Upson had been given a Ducal funeral in the Upper Bailey, his ashes spread in the western garden, a majestic marble tombstone carved and erected in his honour.

It was four and half months after his death that the letter arrived — the letter that still haunted Marmaduke. "Believe me, Richard, the information in the letter has proven to be true. If only *I* had believed it sooner…"

Marmaduke regarded his friend; his dark eyes afire, glaring in expectation, ready to refute the validity of any person Marmaduke cared to name.

"The letter was from your mother, Lady Mildred."

Richard remained still, unblinking, as if the mention of his mother's name had frozen his blood.

"Richard, I assure you—"

"Show me the letter," he demanded.

"I can't," Marmaduke replied, unruffled by Richard's tone.

"Why not?" He stepped away from the window and back towards the desk in the hope, perhaps, that Marmaduke might have it secreted in one the drawers.

"I destroyed it." The words sounded dreamlike.

However, to his friend they were all too real. Richard stopped, a look of incredulity on his face.

"I burnt it after Lucinda died." Marmaduke felt like he was listening to his words, not saying them. "It was the reminder of my inaction. Instead of sharing the news with Lucinda, I wanted to make sure its contents were true. After eighteen and a half years... it seemed incredible. I didn't want to give Lucinda false hope. I sent a missive to Great Naff, asking your mother to confirm she'd penned the letter. I received a reply two weeks later verifying the letter's authenticity — bad weather had prevented the messenger from reaching me earlier — but even then, I needed to be sure, to see Horatio and Xavier for myself. I sent a message to Horatio, asking him to bring Xavier to Blessed Whipping, but not to mention the reason why. I didn't want Xavier to know I was his father before he'd met Lucinda; that would've been unfair. At Blessed Whipping, I could be certain all was as the letter had stated."

"However, once again, the winter weather played havoc with travellers and messengers alike. The northern part of the Duchy was particularly affected; Missing Anchor was virtually snowbound. By the time I received Horatio's reply it was mid-February... Lucinda had gone... less than two weeks before Horatio's commitment to meet me at Blessed Whipping, but I... couldn't bring myself... not after Lucinda's passing... it wouldn't have been... right..."

Marmaduke could feel his throat constricting. Richard was regarding him intently, but his expression had softened.

"I sent a missive to the Elders of Blessed Whipping, asking them to accept Horatio and Xavier into their community. I thought, perhaps, I might feel differently about seeing Xavier as time passed. However... the guilt... I felt Lucinda's loss too greatly."

Richard nodded, seemingly accepting, but his words sounded resentful. "I know about the missive you sent; its contents were relayed to me by the Blessed Whipping Elder who now resides in the dungeon. Five months ago, he happened upon one of Doctor Manky's letters to you: *'And I hope there is now room in your heart for Xavier. He is your son, and, I believe, your salvation'*..."

Marmaduke's stomach dropped at the sound of the quote, as if he were falling in a dream... into an empty void... into the emptiness of his heart.

"...I didn't know how to react, so... Why didn't you tell me, Marmaduke? It would have—"

"I have already told you why!" *How much more of his heart was he expected to lay bare?*

Richard regarded him from the desk, his features smooth, his expression discerning. "Very well," he said, clearly annoyed. "At least Xavier can finally be your son, be who he was meant to be."

Marmaduke shook his head; poor Richard had no understanding of his despair. No-one did. "Xavier *is* who he was meant to be, Richard. And I intend that he and Horatio go *on* being who *they're* meant to be."

Richard's eyes narrowed.

"Horatio and Xavier will establish a new medical school at Lower Icing College. They will share their discoveries and teach their skills to students across the Five Duchies and I... will have a son of whom I can be proud."

"And what of *my* legacy, Marmaduke? If the accusation levelled at my father is true, how can I hope to repay *that* debt?"

Marmaduke smiled at his friend. This was an easy question to answer, one that benefitted them both. "By being what he could not."

Marmaduke leaned back on the window ledge, inhaling the fresh air, the sustenance he needed to get through this meeting. Richard rejoined him. "Would you care to explain that remark?"

"Have you ever considered why your father didn't claim the Dukedom for himself? He was, after all, the person best suited to the position."

Again, Richard regarded him appraisingly, looking for the underlying meaning behind his words, before answering: "He was not of the royal bloodline; his taking of the Dukedom would have been seen as inappropriate at best, and, at worst, it could have led to civil war."

Marmaduke smiled at his friend. *Did he actually believe that?* There was no doubt it had been the political sentiment at the time: that a claim based on land lines would have caused unrest, whereas none could argue about bloodlines. However, none would have gainsaid Sir Walter. He was clearly the most powerful noble in Lower Icing. Only one thing had prevented him from taking the title of Duke.

"It was Mary, Richard."

Richard's eyes remained fixed on his.

"Like Xavier, she'd been born out of wedlock. Worse, she was the child of a mistress. And even though most of the nobility were ignorant of that fact, there were a few influential people who knew the truth about John and Kate Brewer's daughter. She couldn't be secreted away like Xavier…"

Richard shook his head, either in denial or disbelief.

"…The laws that applied to Lucinda and I also applied to your father. That's why Mary wasn't officially recognised as your sister until after Sir Walter's death, when Lady Mildred had moved to Great Naff. Even though we'd changed those laws ten years before he died, reputation was of paramount importance to your father… which is why he couldn't allow Xavier to return to Lucinda and I."

Richard was shaking his head more vigorously. "This is just my mother's scorn, Marmaduke, trying to sully my father's character. I can understand how she must have felt after Mary was recognised, but to suggest that my father was capable of keeping you and Lucinda parted from your son… it was her bitterness speaking in that letter."

He *was* in denial.

"Richard, your mother knew the whereabouts of Xavier; the only person she could have learnt that from was your father. I daresay she only discovered the truth after his death. Perhaps she found a letter from Horatio while going through his belongings following his passing, or during the process of relocating to Great Naff."

Richard was still shaking his head.

"Your father was dead. It served your mother no purpose to besmirch the name of a dead man… it would have been beneath her dignity."

"You're expecting me to believe that my father managed, for eighteen and a half years, to intercept *every* letter Doctor Manky sent to you? How is that possible?"

"Have you *seen* any of Horatio's letters?"

"Not an *actual* letter, no."

"The seal is most distinctive: an easily recognisable insignia of a—"

"Quill above a broken sword," Richard whispered.

Marmaduke nodded. "The insignia your father bestowed on you on your eighteenth birthday, six months after Lucinda and I arrived in Lower Icing."

For a change, Richard's searching gaze turned inward… reflective… accepting. "The day I became your squire."

"From which you have become my friend, my confidante, my Seneschal and my heir."

Richard looked pained — it was unavoidable. However, Marmaduke had great faith in his friend's unerring sense of duty.

"As you say, we should be proud of what we have achieved together, and I truly believe, together, we will achieve even more."

Richard was looking down at the sleeve of his doublet where four silver buttons shone against the black fabric — the missing one had been sewn back on. A small drop of water splashed against it, the quill and sword distorted by the liquid. Marmaduke looked to the overcast sky, but he could see it wasn't raining.

## CHAPTER 2

# *A taste for Escargotian pastry*

OWEN LLANDROVER AND his party had taken over The Frisky Porker — the more salubrious of two inns at Pashing Madly. The innkeeper had been given two days' notice to clear the inn of other guests and prepare for the arrival of the Duke and his wife, Gwen, as well as his eldest sons, Cedrych and Ewan, and their wives, Lynne and Ceridwyn. Also travelling with Owen were two of his closest friends and advisors: Bryn Ap Gwyn and Dafyd Y-Coed and their wives, Bloodwyn and Marie (who was Escargotian). Bryn's sons, Angwyn and Alwyn, and Dafyd's son, Bleddyn, and nephew, Gruffydd, were also part of the party heading to Lower Icing and Great Naff. They were escorted by twenty men-at-arms, led by Captain Madog Maelgwyn. The men-at-arms were staying at the less salubrious of the two inns in Pashing Madly: The Horny Hog.

Pashing Madly straddled both sides of the river Sty, the river that led to Stymouth, the Duchy's seaport capital, from whence they had begun their journey four days ago.

The party had arrived on schedule at four o'clock (an hour ago) still damp from the morning rain and spattered with flecks of mud kicked up by the horses. Owen and Gwen, along with the rest of the honoured guests, had retired to their respective rooms to wash and freshen up for the evening meal that was being prepared downstairs in The Frisky Porker. The dinner had been arranged by the Mayor of Pashing Madly, Ifor Rhydwyn, to celebrate their 'most wonderful' visit. The town, like the Mayor, was parochially Stymouthian, even though half of it was, geographically speaking, in the Duchy of Lower Icing — in this part of the Duchy, the river Sty marked the border between Stymouth and Lower Icing. However, there was *no* doubt on which side of the Sty the Pashing Madliers' hearts resided.

*If only the people of Spitting Dipthong were as loyal,* Owen thought as he towelled his freshly shaven face. Those bloody Spitters well and truly considered themselves Lower Icingers now. The southern fishing village had once been part of Stymouth, until the De La Wrences' annexed it seventy-three years ago as 'compensation' after a failed Stymouthian uprising. How the frig his great-grandfather, Pywll Llandrover, had allowed such a concession was beyond Owen. Uprising! Bloody hell! It was just a few border skirmishes poorly orchestrated by a bunch of undisciplined rebels, not something organised and sanctioned by the Duchy. His clean-faced reflection shook its head in disgust. Pywll meant prudent and wise in the Old Tongue. In Owen's eyes his great-grandfather had been neither.

Spitting Dipthong was something he intended to raise with Marmaduke… or whoever was running the Duchy. In fact, it was one of the main reasons for travelling through Lower Icing — a place he'd managed to avoid for the last twenty years. Since the farcical coronation of Marmaduke Du Marma, he'd had no need *or* desire to visit the Duchy. Stymouth's main trade was with Escargotia and, to a lesser extent, Naffolk: places that were much easier to reach by ship.

However, the time had come for Owen to act. He would turn fifty in a month's time… he'd started thinking about his legacy: the kind of Stymouth he wanted leave his sons, and the songs they would sing in his honour. Yes, *now* was the time to act, particularly if (and it was a *big* if) the message he'd received a week ago held any truth to it. He would know soon enough. Barring unforeseen circumstances, they should clap eyes on Lower Icing's pretentiously large castle in three days' time.

He placed the hand towel next to the wash bowl. The clear, scented water was now a dirty milk colour. He reached for his clean dress shirt — the Madliers would expect some concession to occasion. In truth, Owen could do without the pomp and ceremony tonight. It had been a tiring four days on the road, and all he really wanted to do was down a few quiet ales with Bryn and Dafyd, and then have a decent night's sleep.

As he buttoned up his shirt, he regarded his reflection. He was still in good shape for his age. He had muscle definition in his chest, and, unlike most men of nearly fifty, his ale belly was negligible. (Bryn, in contrast, looked like he was about to give birth to triplets.) His shoulders were straight and his thick neck was still taut and strong. He studied his features; wide, flat nose; generous mouth; and a square jaw under a thick, wiry thatch of greying hair that covered his head like a bristly skull cap. It was a strong, solid face.

However, at this particular moment, he felt neither strong nor solid, just tired and slightly... uneasy; he could see it in his grey eyes.

Truth be known, he *was* uneasy and had been for five days, since receiving that message... the message from a man he'd virtually forgotten about. It claimed that Marmaduke Du Marma was in a feverish delirium after apparently being poisoned, and that Richard Upson had stood down as Seneschal. According to the report, that stuck-up Upson twat was up to his manicured beard in shite (although it wasn't phrased that way).

While it was good news, Owen couldn't afford to put much stock in it; he was disturbed, as much as heartened, by the report. It didn't go into much detail and cast no light on who'd poisoned Marmaduke or why, apart from suggesting a vague connection to a doctor from Blessed Whipping. However, what disturbed Owen more than the report was the man who'd written it; he was a most unsettling individual, and Owen was rarely unsettled.

The man had introduced himself three months ago, offering his services. How the hell he'd managed to approach Owen was *still* beyond his recall, as was the man's appearance, which was disturbing in itself. All Owen could remember was his name: The Fixer. *What sort of bloody name was that?*

Owen had laughed at him, and joked that if he could fix it so Sir Richard Upson was disgraced and the Duchy of Lower Icing was in disarray, he would pay him his weight in gold. The Fixer's parting words had also lodged in his memory: "I accept your offer, Lord Llandrover. I will inform you when the task is met."

Owen couldn't believe he had no recollection of the man's appearance — he never forgot a face.

Well, one thing was for certes: it would take more than a few words scribbled on a parchment to convince Owen the task had been met. None of the official correspondence mentioned such an occurrence. Still, he couldn't afford to put much stock in *that* either.

Owen finished his buttoning, except for the cuffs — Gwen would attend to those when she returned from preening herself with the other ladies. He reached over for his trousers and slipped his freshly scrubbed legs into the woollen lining. He sighed out loud. Yes, he really could do without the celebrations tonight. Gwen was of the same mind, but she, too, realised the importance of maintaining the revered name of Llandrover in such a remote town as Pashing Madly. Loyalty should be rewarded.

Owen's thoughts were interrupted by the sound of the guestroom door squeaking open — Gwen returning from her preening — but his focus remained on pulling his trousers over his waist. Perhaps he wasn't in such good shape after all. Bloody formalities; they gave Owen the shits.

"Oh friggin' heck," he said, wrestling with his trousers. "Mind lendin' me a hand with these?"

"I didn't come here for that, Lord Llandrover," replied a smooth, dusty-sounding voice. The voice of the man he'd… virtually forgotten.

Owen almost coughed up his heart, his gaze shooting towards the figure standing at the door. The man whose face he couldn't recall looked shockingly familiar. "What the frig!"

The man regarded him impassively.

"How the hell did *you* get in here?"

He shrugged his shoulders, as if it was of no consequence. "I simply walked up the stairs. No-one stopped me. All your men-at-arms are at The Horny Hog. It seemed an opportune time."

Owen's gaze flicked towards his sword lying on top of the bed in its scabbard. It would only take him a few seconds to reach over and draw it.

"Well, you can friggin' well walk back *down* them," Owen snarled, standing upright, trying to adjust his trousers — friggin' bloody things!

"Of course." The Fixer smiled. "After you have paid your debt to me."

"Frig off!" he said, moving across the room towards his sword; an action that didn't appear to bother The Fixer.

"I must say, I am disappointed," he remarked, "though not entirely surprised by your attitude, Lord Llandrover."

Owen was not a man to be intimidated, but…

"We had an agreement."

"Like frig we did," Owen said, reaching for his sword. The Fixer watched him with what appeared to be nothing more than mild curiosity… *unsettlingly* mild curiosity. Picking it up, Owen put his hand on the pommel and flexed his fingers.

"I distinctly recall our arrangement," The Fixer said smoothly, like he'd picked up a sword of his own. "Disharmony within the Duchy of Lower Icing and the disgrace of Sir Richard Upson in return for my weight in gold. I have fulfilled my part, now you must fulfil yours."

*Must?* Owen was astounded by the man's effrontery — too astounded even to draw his sword. "Are you friggin' *mad*, man? Do you expect me to take *you* on your word?"

He'd moved within two paces of The Fixer now, but the man hardly batted an eyelid.

"Yes, I do," he said, pointedly. "As I have already taken you at *your* word."

Owen had had enough; he drew his sword and waved it at the man's inconsequential torso. "Well, you can just take your friggin' expectations and shove them up your friggin' arse." Owen didn't want bloodshed, especially not here and now. It wouldn't look good. But he'd be buggered if he allowed some unhinged nobody to sneak into his room and make demands of him. "Unless, of course, you'd rather feel the bite of my sword."

"To be honest, neither really appeals."

The man was clearly mad; either that or he had no concept of who he was dealing with.

The Fixer's expression became thoughtful, "Perhaps, Lord Llandrover, after I have apprised you of my efforts over the last three months, you'll better comprehend my dedication to our agreement and be more disposed to fulfilling your part of it."

"Like frig I will!" Owen wasn't sure why the man was still standing. *Why he hadn't run the rogue through?* The Fixer's expression remained deadpan, seemingly oblivious to the sword now aimed at his heart.

"I beg to differ," he said. "The continuance of the Llandrover name depends on your ability to stand by your word."

Owen was gobsmacked. The only thing that stayed his arm from thrusting the sword through The Fixer's heart was the man's gaze — it was… disarming.

"Should any harm befall me, you and your family will not reach Lower Icing."

Amid the flood of contempt flowing through his veins, Owen felt a trickle of fear.

"And your other sons and daughters will also meet untimely ends. It will be the end of Llandrover rule in the Duchy of Stymouth."

Owen shook his head and smiled. The madman had overreached himself; what he was threatening wasn't possible… and yet…

"So, if you'd kindly put away your weapon, I shall be more disposed to *fully* apprise you of the actions I have taken on your behalf to *further* the Llandrover name."

Owen could feel his heart beating… no, *thumping*. The point of his sword was moving up and down slightly, almost hypnotically, and then he realised it was in time to his breathing.

A heartbeat — that's all the time it would take to end this man's life. Only a few inches separated the point of his sword from flesh and bone... but... almost in disbelief, he watched the point dip towards the floor, weighted down with doubt and fear, as if it were in the hands of someone other than Owen Llandrover — someone who was *easily* unsettled.

The Fixer nodded, the curve of his mouth moving upwards in time to the lowering of the sword. "Very good, Lord Llandrover. Shall we sit down?" he suggested amicably, casting his gaze at the small table on the opposite side of the room, near the window.

Owen was tired, his head was aching, and this man was... doing his head in. Sitting down was, however, a concession he was willing to entertain this madman's ramblings; a concession the *real* Owen Llandrover wouldn't even consider. But right at this moment everything felt quite... unreal. He considered shouting for help, but images of Gwen, Cedrych and Ewan with knives at their throats... "Very well." His voice sounded husky and... distant.

They sat opposite each other, no more than a pace apart. Owen had sheathed his sword and it now leant against the wall to his left. The Fixer sat with his hands clasped together on top of the table, looking completely at ease.

"Let me begin at the beginning," he said without preamble. "Shortly after arriving in Lower Icing, I enlisted as a cadet in the local militia using a pseudonym, George Martin. You can check my service record during your visit if you like."

Owen didn't respond, but it was something he *would* look into.

"I was assigned to a patrol of men-at-arms under the command of a Lieutenant Jethro Fowler. I performed all kinds of menial tasks, including cleaning the cells of excrement and vomit. Still, I was fulfilling my part of our agreement, and I have learned through experience that, more often than not, the end justifies the means."

Owen continued to gaze at The Fixer, hopefully with an expression of unimpressed contempt.

"I worked diligently, volunteering for tasks that most of my fellow men-at-arms avoided if they could. I must say, I found the average Lower Icing soldier lazy and of an imbecilic disposition. There were a few exceptions. My commanding officer, for example, was brash and uncouth, but certainly not stupid. And Lieutenant Brandon Swill seemed to be a cut above the rest — the youngest ever Purple Perillian, so I was informed. Still, generally speaking, they're a rather undisciplined bunch, bordering on what I would define as *disarray* — something you could certainly work to your advantage, Lord Llandrover."

It was nothing Owen didn't already know or suspect, and definitely not what he'd define as a *Duchy* in disarray. Still, Owen was becoming more intrigued by what The Fixer had to say. Perhaps he *had* uncovered something useful.

"I was rewarded for my work ethic with better assignments, like preparing the officers' quarters and being responsible for their uniforms — something at which I excelled, since I am a stickler for presentation. I have to be, of course…"

The Fixer clearly didn't mind sharing his high opinion of himself.

"But I digress; your pardon, Lord Llandrover. Having such assignments, I was able to insinuate myself more closely into the higher-ranking world, where I could overhear conversations and snippets of gossip. Unfortunately, nothing untoward seemed to be happening. I needed to gain access to the Upper Bailey, where I could better ascertain the… opportunity for disruption… *and*, of course, find means of disgracing Sir Richard."

The man had a compelling manner, no doubt about it, but some small recess in the back of Owen's mind was yelling at him to snap out of it.

"Sir Richard is a most commanding individual — you were right to be concerned about him — and I was beginning to doubt whether it would be possible to exploit such a man… at least, not in time for your arrival. And, truth be told, if it hadn't been for a most extraordinary set of incidents…" The Fixer smiled to himself and shook his head as if in disbelief. "Well, I wouldn't be sitting here now."

Curiosity had now replaced Owen's outrage. The man opposite was a compelling storyteller; an ability Owen had always appreciated.

"Firstly, my assiduousness earned me a posting inside the Duke's residence. Not that *that* was extraordinary, but the *timing* was, since it was the morning before the Duke was poisoned, almost a fortnight ago."

*What sort of hired thug uses a word like assiduousness*, Owen wondered, absently.

"Sir Richard had ordered a doubling of the guards in the Upper Bailey, and later that day I found out why. From what I could glean from muffled conversations behind closed doors, a certain person of interest — the doctor from Blessed Whipping I mentioned in my report — had disappeared from The Keep, where he was, for all intents and purposes, being detained. Sir Richard was most upset by that. The following night, the Duke was poisoned, but it wasn't until the next morning that his squire discovered him in bed, unconscious with a fever. Fate smiled upon us here, Lord Llandrover."

*Us?*

"My fellow guard I were given the task of escorting the Duke's doctor, Albert Whysman, to the Duke's bedchamber. Upon entering the room, we saw his squire, Bradley Lamb, kneeling by the prostrate Duke, holding a handkerchief to his arm. There was dried blood on the sheet, but the wound certainly wasn't mortal — nothing that some stitches wouldn't mend — and it was clear the Duke was no longer bleeding. However, Squire Lamb was delusional, convinced the Duke would bleed to death if he released the pressure on the handkerchief, and he refused to leave the Duke's side or allow anyone else to intercede, including Doctor Whysman. Even Sir Richard's presence made no difference to Bradley Lamb. Sir Richard's secretary, Prestwich, was particularly flustered by the scene."

*Understandable,* Owen thought. Finding your Duke poisoned in a blood-stained bed *would* be confronting.

"We were ordered back outside the chamber and told not to let anyone enter the room. We heard raised voices, and eventually Prestwich appeared at the door, telling us our assistance was required to forcibly remove the squire. We took to the task with gusto, but Bradley Lamb would not relent. He was young, tall and strong, and his delusion had given him great strength. Even with the aid of Sir Richard and the doctor, we could not better the Duke's squire. Eventually, Sir Richard rapped him over the head with the pommel of his dagger. And *this* is the moment I was presented with a fantastic opportunity."

The Fixer's report stated that Sir Richard had stood down as Seneschal, but he hadn't gone into much detail as to why, save that he'd been implicated in poisoning the Duke. Owen was most interested to hear how the man opposite him had arranged *that* particular feat.

"During the scuffle, one of Sir Richard's silver buttons was ripped from its sleeve. I only noticed it because it hit me on the hand, then landed between my feet. So, as Sir Richard pulled out his dagger and subdued Bradley Lamb, I picked up the button and placed it in the Duke's hand. It was so… *perfect.*"

The Fixer shook his head as if he could hardly believe the unlikelihood of it all. And if what he was saying was indeed true, then it *was* a miraculous occurrence.

"His hand lay open right next to me, so still amongst the chaos. It was as if time had stopped for a moment. I closed his hand over the button and the deed was done."

The Fixer clenched his hand into a fist, re-enacting the moment.

"We dragged the unconscious squire to a divan in the opposite corner of the room. Then we were dismissed, but not before I overheard the doctor say he suspected a poison blade — an even *better* outcome, wouldn't you agree, Lord Llandrover?"

Owen was beginning to warm to The Fixer. This was good news indeed, but he wasn't about to concede anything at this point. "Go on," he said, evenly.

"I spent the rest of the morning on guard while Doctor Whysman attended to the Duke and Sir Richard questioned Bradley Lamb. I gleaned nothing more until later that afternoon, when the Town Crier, a man of dubious intellect, proclaimed to the populace that the Duke had been attacked, though was unharmed. He told the crowd the attacker had left a clue to his identity — the silver button — which he *actually* produced in front of the villagers, telling them there was a reward of one hundred gold pieces for information leading to an arrest. Then he posted a sketch of the button on the news stand."

"Unharmed? I thought—"

"Yes, it was a curious distortion of the facts, one I put down to maintaining the peace." The Fixer smiled mischievously. "How wrong I was…"

The Fixer was becoming more animated; his eyes glinted in the grey afternoon light.

"To say Sir Richard was unhappy about the proclamation would be very much understating his reaction. He ordered Captain Le Sharp, the Purple Perillians and, consequently, *me* to find the Blessed Whipping doctor. It was apparent that his disappearance and the attack on the Duke were more than coincidental. Again, that assumption proved erroneous."

Owen was beginning to feel a little frustrated by The Fixer's caginess.

"For the next few days we searched for him, but to no avail. The Duke remained confined to his chamber; I heard nothing about how he was faring. There was no talk about poison amongst the men or anyone else, so the Duke's condition was obviously being kept secret. Only Doctor Whysman, Sir Richard, Prestwich and, I believe, Brandon Swill were apprised of the true facts. Even my fellow guardsman, a dullard called Beardsley, seemed oblivious to what he'd actually witnessed in the Duke's chamber. Which was fortunate, because it allowed *me* to feign ignorance and go about my… duty."

*Duty* — Not a word Owen considered appropriate; The Fixer was a man for hire, not a man of principle.

"As the days passed, rumblings of discontent and suspicion within the

senior ranks were aimed towards Sir Richard. It was the button, you see…
and the inability for anyone to find this doctor. It was beginning to look like
an elaborate ruse on Sir Richard's part, and prominent citizens were beginning
to ask uncomfortable questions."

Yes, Owen could *well* imagine. He had *his* hands full trying to keep
puffed-up-good-for-nothings and full-of-themselves-want-to-bes from
demanding this and that and everything in between.

"By Tuesday morning, Sir Richard had stepped down as Seneschal, his
mantle assumed by Captain Le Sharp. That's when I penned my report to
you. I apologise for the sketchiness of the detail; I was rather pressed for
opportunity and time. But, I assure you, my diligence and opportunism have
wrought a major upheaval."

"So you say," said Owen, even though he believed The Fixer's story to be
true. It was too incredible *not* to be.

"Yes, I do," The Fixer agreed.

"However, you said you were wrong… on *two* accounts."

He smiled. "So I did, and so I was."

"Care to share?"

"Of course. Firstly, the Town Crier's misleading proclamation had nothing
to do with keeping the peace. Secondly, the disappearance of the doctor and
the attack on the Duke *were*, to a large extent, coincidental. I only found out
these facts *after* I sent the report… last Thursday night, in fact. That's when
I discovered that the missing doctor had been found and…"

Owen waited for The Fixer to continue, but the man seemed lost in
thought.

"And what?"

"You're going to love this, Lord Llandrover."

"Am I just."

The Fixer nodded. "The missing doctor claims he is the Duke's long lost
son. He calls himself—"

"Bullshit!" The Fixer had gone too far; whatever spell he'd been weaving to
keep Owen listening to his fanciful story had just been broken. "It is common
knowledge the Duchess was barren. Almost *twenty* years without a child, man!
Whoever this doctor is, he's a charlatan." He regarded the smooth-talking
man sitting across the table. "Unless, of course, *you* are the charlatan."

"This is not my *opinion*, Lord Llandrover. I am merely stating the facts
as they occurred. If it's any consolation, Sir Richard shares your disbelief."

"Ha! I'm sure he *does!*"

"But others are convinced the doctor — Xavier is his name — *is* who he claims... Captain Le Sharp for one."

"Bah! Self-serving bullshit!" If Lower Icing was anything like Stymouth, there was always *someone* trying to gain political advantage.

"It may well be. I'm not in a position to give a definitive opinion," said The Fixer. "I left Lower Icing mid-morning on Friday. However, on Thursday night a dinner was held in The Keep... very impromptu. All the important citizens were there; it appeared to be some sort of dry run, so to speak, for the banquet to be held in your honour. It was most odd, and the guests were quite befuddled by the occasion. As it turned out, it was a trap to catch the Duke's poisoner."

For frig's sake, how much more bizarre could this tale become?

"Again, my ability to place myself in front of the right people gained me a posting at the banquet. *That* and the fact idleness runs rife amongst the Lower Icing militia — something to keep in mind when discussing... whatever it is you intend to discuss."

"Get on with it," said Owen; he didn't like what the Fixer was insinuating — as if he knew about Spitting Dipthong.

The Fixer smiled. "My apologies. The other thing I learned from the charade of a banquet is the identity of the Duke's poisoner — it was the Town Crier."

*Frig off!* "Is this some sort of jest?"

"No, I don't believe so. He admitted to the deed and was escorted from the banquet. As it transpired, his intention was not to kill the Duke, but rather to make him ill enough for the doctor to then 'treat and meet' his father. The Town Crier is also convinced Xavier is the Duke's son. The proclamation was simply written on a whim, without knowing the silver button belonged to the Seneschal. Xavier was discovered at an inn, being cared for by the family who ran it — the family of Lieutenant Swill, as it happens... read into *that* what you will. Xavier had been assaulted outside the inn by a couple of opportunist thugs the night the Town Crier poisoned the Duke. So, his disappearance *was* merely coincidence. However, I also believe the Town Crier harboured Xavier for two days before the assault occurred."

Owen shook his head — this was too much to take in.

"So you see, Lord Llandrover, disarray abounds in Lower Icing, and while I believe Sir Richard Upson has been reinstated as Seneschal, his reputation and honour have taken a battering. Undone, you might say, by a silver button."

Clearly, The Fixer thought he'd made a successful case for payment, but Owen certainly wasn't convinced. "Even if what you say is true, it seems to me that all this… disarray would have happened without your involvement. I fail to see how you can claim responsibility for causing it. As for Sir Richard Upson — if he is still Seneschal, then he is *not* disgraced and you have failed to fulfil your side of the agreement."

The Fixer began drumming the table with his right hand. "In everything, Lord Llandrover, there is a certain amount of luck, and, I agree, I have had more than my fair share where this assignment is concerned. However, I do believe that we make our own luck, and in that I have been most diligent on your behalf. I have just relayed to you information of which very few people in Lower Icing are aware — information you can use to your advantage."

Owen wasn't about to concede anything to The Fixer. "What of the Duke? You say you left Lower Icing last Friday morning. That's four days ago. Had he recovered?"

Again, a wry smile played across The Fixer's face. "Four days ago I volunteered, once more on your behalf, to accompany Squire Bradley Lamb to the small communal village of Blessed Whipping — the place where Xavier had been living for the past seventeen months and where his mentor, one Doctor Horatio Manky, still resided."

*Manky?* What sort of name was *that?*

"I learned from Bradley Lamb that the Duke was still ailing; Doctor Whysman had made no headway and Xavier's memory had been affected by a blow to his head, so he was unable to concoct an antidote. Therefore, the only remaining course of action was to bring Doctor Manky — a man of great learning, supposedly — to the Duke. The squire regarded it as an opportunity for redemption; he blamed himself for the Duke's poisoning, even though he could not have done anything to prevent the Town Crier's actions.

"As we headed along the North Road, Squire Lamb began talking about the Duke and how important he was to the Duchy — that he had to survive, that if he died it would mean ruination for Lower Icing. Squire Lamb was not enamoured by the thought of Sir Richard becoming Duke; he didn't trust his motives, saying he was too thirsty for power. He was most passionate about his feelings, which is why…" The Fixer chuckled and shook his head. "…I broke his neck."

It took a moment for Owen to absorb the words, yet he still couldn't fathom what he'd just heard. "You *killed* the Duke's squire?"

The Fixer grimaced in a comical sort of way. "I haven't known anyone to *survive* a broken neck."

The man was unhinged, and Owen suddenly felt a queasiness in the pit of his stomach.

"I thought it the most efficient way of delaying aid to the Duke. Squire Lamb had convinced me that a dead Duke would be a disaster for the Duchy and, therefore, to *your* advantage. You see, Lord Llandrover, I am the consummate professional. I leave no stone unturned and no neck unbroken. I'm sure you'll now agree that such professionalism deserves to be rewarded."

Owen looked into The Fixer's eyes. They were deadly still — the gaze of a killer. Owen could feel his head nodding.

The Fixer smiled. "Very good. I have already calculated my weight in gold. You'll be pleased to know I've lost a few pounds since beginning this assignment. I put it down to stress."

Owen put it down to insanity.

"In any case, the amount is fifteen hundred and seventy five gold pieces. A snip, don't you think?"

Owen snapped out of his reverie. "I don't carry that much gold."

"Of course not. However, I will accept a promissory note, one that is recognised in Naffolk and possibly even Escargotia. I think, perhaps, I'm due a change of scenery, and I seem to have acquired a taste for Escargotian pastry: an unforeseen hazard of being dogsbody to a bunch of Purple Perillians."

Owen waited a moment for the ink to set on the parchment before pouring a pool of red wax at its base. Then he applied the Ducal seal — a boar's head over crossed axes — to the wax. Back in Pwyll Llandrover's day, the seal had been a leek over crossed spoons. For frig's sake — what sort of message had *that* sent. Not that Owen was living up to *his* insignia right at this moment, meekly penning a promissory note to The Fixer — enough coin to fund the useless rabble of men at The Horny Hog for a year.

Still, he supposed, the price was worth the peace of mind, and even if a quarter of what the maniac standing over his shoulder had said was true, then it *would* turn out to be a profitable exchange. Placing the seal back in its box, Owen proffered the promissory note to The Fixer.

"I believe it requires your signature, Lord Llandrover," said The Fixer, before laying a hand on it.

*Worth a try,* Owen thought. "So it does."

He dipped the quill back in the ink and scratched his name underneath the seal. "Do you know if the Duke lives?"

"No."

And *that*, it seemed, was all The Fixer had to say on the matter.

Then another, more disturbing thought crossed Owen's mind. It was very odd that they hadn't been disturbed. Gwen usually fussed over his clothes on such occasions. Perhaps she was fussing over Cedrych and Ewan's. And what were Bryn and Dafyd doing? One or both of them usually barged in with a bottle of wine or ale. Perhaps *their* wives were fussing over them. It was the first time in years the wives had travelled.

Owen picked up the promissory note for a second time and blew gently across the parchment's surface. Then he turned around and faced The Fixer. "Before I give you this," he said, directly, "I want your assurance that no harm *has* or *will* befall my family."

"You have it, Lord Llandrover," he said. "I *am*, as you will soon see, a man of my word."

Owen nodded. He had no reason to believe this madman, but he sensed *this* particular madman was madly obsessive about his 'word'. And, in any case, he had no choice.

With a smile, The Fixer accepted the promissory note. "Good luck in your endeavours, Lord Llandrover. It has been a most interesting assignment. Now I shall bid you farewell. Or perhaps I should say *au revoir*. I *do* have a penchant for chocolate éclairs."

Owen watched him as he moved across the room and shut the door behind him. Seconds later, the door opened again and Gwen appeared. Relief flowed through him.

"Who was that man, Owen?" she asked, looking mildly concerned.

"No-one," Owen replied; he'd already forgotten what The Fixer looked like.

# BETHANY

## AND

# JUANITA

THE TUESDAY EVENING crowd at The Bloody Bell was in full voice. Bethany, however, was sitting in relative silence with her parents at their dining room table, each of them pondering the contents of the letter that lay upon the blue tablecloth. It was addressed to her: Bethany Swill, The Bloody Bell, Lower Icing. However, what had them all concerned was the seal. Pressed within the hard, sky-blue wax was a beaming sun.

It had been delivered thirty minutes ago and her pa had immediately sent for Brandon. Bethany wanted to open it, but her pa insisted that anything from Blessed Whipping had to be made official, regardless of Bertrand's arrest and the *Deed of Promise* being put to bed. And so they waited for Brandon to arrive.

"Remember, Bethany," he told her, "wha' affecks one of us affecks *all* of us."

She nodded and smiled indulgently at her pa's gruffness. They'd been through an emotional two weeks, since the arrival of Xavier. To think he *was* actually the Duke's son. It seemed incredible… and she wondered what would become of him. She couldn't imagine him becoming Duke. From what Brandon had told her, it seemed likely he and his guardian would continue being doctors. She hoped so… and she hoped he was feeling more at ease, more at one with himself. She felt his memory loss was due more to his state of mind than the actual blow to his head.

The door opened, crashing her thoughts with a cacophony of ale-swilling conversation.

"What's happened?" asked Brandon, shutting the door on the revelry. "Are you alright, Bethany? What's this about a letter from Blessed Whipping?"

"We don't know Brandon, love," said her ma. "We ain't opened it yet. It's 'dressed to Bethany, like, but we thought you should be 'ere, jus' in case."

Her ma looked at her pa with a worried expression. Brandon looked at her with a look of incredulity. "Just in case what?" He sounded annoyed.

"No need for that tone, lad," said her pa.

He sighed. "Look," he said, moving to the seat next to her, "Bethany is safe here at The Bell. I've already told you the Blessed Whipping Elders have been informed of Bertrand's skulduggery and murderous actions. We will hear no more about Bethany becoming Sunwatcher."

Bethany knew her brother found their Blessed Whipping heritage embarrassing and Ma and Pa's lingering remnants of their 'Sun ways' ridiculous. She could feel an argument brewing. She reached for the letter. "Let's see, shall we?"

As she'd hoped, the words focused their attention. She picked up the letter, feeling their intense gazes... like the rays of the blue wax sun.

She felt calm as she snapped the seal. Meeting Xavier had had a profound effect on her. He could see into the heart of a person... to see good in all. She felt... drawn to him, wanted to be like him. He had lived amongst the Blessed Whippingers, had spoken of his life there as she tended him... as he began to remember who he was...

She unfolded the parchment and read aloud its contents.

Greetings Bethany,

My name is Beatrice, former Sunwatcher of Blessed Whipping. It was I who arranged for Bertrand to take Xavier to Lower Icing. As such, I feel deeply responsible for what has occurred to you and your family. I hope you can forgive my actions, and the community for its ignorance – we were unaware of Bertrand's obsession with bringing you to Blessed Whipping. I assure you, you and your family need no longer fear any such intentions. However, should you ever care to visit us, you would be most welcome guests. It would please the community to make amends in some small way, and I would be most grateful for the opportunity to apologise to you all in person. I would also like to express my heartfelt appreciation of your goodwill and care towards Xavier. He and Horatio have brightened our Sun, and we hope that they will now brighten yours.

Beatrice

Bethany looked up to the tear-stained faces of her ma and pa as eighteen years of fear and anxiety trickled away. Then she felt Brandon's hand clasp hers. He was smiling at her. Bethany smiled back. Beatrice had done more than allay their fears, she had welcomed them back into the community. For her parents, that was an even bigger gift.

IT HAD BEEN an unusually busy Tuesday at The Harey Rabbit. Everyone had come out to see the new Town Crier. The people seemed happy with the choice. Juanita wasn't so sure, however. He seemed far too fat for the job, and she found it hard to understand what he was saying, but everyone else seemed to find him amusing. The only thing Juanita had found amusing was his name: Alistair Bean.

Patricia had made of a pot of baked beans in his honour, which Juanita also found funny… until they'd run out during the dinner service and Patricia had started yelling at Mandy and Lillian (even the Mistress) to stop taking orders for the beans. But the orders kept coming.

That's when Juanita had used her initiative, like the Mistress had told them all to do. She'd walked into the dining room with a pot and a spoon and banged the spoon loudly against the pot. The room went silent immediately, which was pleasing. Then, putting on her no-nonsense voice, she said, "Dee beans, dey are over, dee end… *terminado!*"

# AUTHOR'S NOTE

I guess if you've read this far, you've enjoyed *The Silver Button Saga*, so thank you for giving it go. The fact that it's ended up being two books is certainly unplanned – the story basically followed its own path from the first meeting between Sid and Doctor Manky. However, by the time I'd finished writing Frank's part at the end of *When Doctor Manky Strolled In* it occurred to me that everything had been written through the eyes of men… *very* in keeping with the medieval times. (Although, the era is not accurately represented in this story – I hardly think an establishment like The Harey Rabbit would have existed in the Middle Ages… But then again, who knows? Perhaps Crème de Poire *was* served to ladies like Petunia Primrose.)

Regardless, *When Frank Offcut Went Missing* was the time to change things up and see things through the 'clearer' eyes of Ophelia, Olivia and Mary. They added direction to the story and were responsible for it progressing down a path – Sid, Tom, Brandon, Gerald, Frank and even Sir Richard would have spent the whole book chasing their tails.

However, it created, through Mary, the challenge of rewriting scenes that had already occurred between her and Sid. It wasn't so much repeating conversations – although that complicated the writing process – it was maintaining continuity: time, place, weather, and other little details that I had to be a little OC about. For example, I discovered Mary was held up in the kitchen in *When Frank Offcut Goes Missing* at the same time she was knocking on Sid's door in *When Doctor Manky Strolled In*. The pay off, however, was being able to create two points of view for the same interaction (which was a bit of a revelation) and it triggered a whole lot of other interactions within the story.

Most of the characters are conflicted or at odds with someone, which, again, was something that occurred organically. I found Frank v. Tom (with Ophelia being 'piggy in middle'), Sir Richard v. Olivia, and The Swills v. Olivia interesting to write… there's always two sides to an argument. (And Juanita v. anybody was just fun… although she made a lot of sense to me.)

As I mentioned in my Book One notes, the medical advice, cures and potions in the story are obviously concocted, and would only work in the Five Duchies. However, Albert Whysmans' reference to the 'four humours' while treating Sid is based on knowledge at the time, and first posed by Hippocrates around 400 BC. (That's not progress for you!)

The poisonous nature of Belladonna/Deadly Nightshade is also true (so please take Tom's warning seriously if you have some in your garden).

## THE MAPS

The other thing I'd like to mention are the maps. The map of Lower Icing was my COVID lockdown project in 2020. It started off as just the castle, then I thought I'd include the surrounding streets, Town Square and the two inns (The Harey Rabbit and The Bloody Bell). Then I thought I'd include The Market, Lower Icing College and Slaughter & Offcut, then… you get the idea. In the end, the castle (drawn on two A4 sheets of paper) had become the entire town of Lower Icing (on dozens of A4 sheets, measuring roughly 1.8m by 1.5m) and six months had gone by (well past lockdown). Still, I was pretty pleased with the end result, everything was hand drawn (no ruler was used – which is fairly obvious, I guess) and it gave me a much clearer idea of the geography of the town. Of course, this caused a few rewrites; adjusting distances and times it would take to walk from one place to another… it's not all beer and skittles being a Creator.

The Five Duchies map was conceived as I was reviewing the edits of the manuscript. I had a rough idea of where everything sat in relation to each other, so it came together fairly quickly (within an afternoon). However, I did spend a couple of weeks thinking up some of the more obscure place names. Still, it was little more than a scratchy mud map before being totally transformed in the design process. Seeing it finished made me feel like the Five Duchies really exists (which it kind of does… in my head).

I also decided to add some floor plans in Book Two; as much for my benefit as the reader's. It took a few goes, rearranging the furniture, but we got there.

## REVIEW

Since you've enjoyed *The Silver Button Saga*, feel free to leave a review of Book One and Book Two on Amazon (if you purchased them on Amazon) or at Goodreads. Your review will help *The Silver Button Saga* become a number one bestseller… in The Five Duchies. (Lady Violet La Fleur would be most impressed.)

Cheers,
Tim

# ACKNOWLEDGEMENTS

Firstly, I'd like to thank the people who helped me write this book, all the guys and gals working in cafés supplying me with flat whites and toast. I reckon at least 90% of the story was written in cafés, mainly in Adelaide, but also Carlton, Bondi, Port Douglas.

Rosey's (sadly no longer Rosey's) was where most of it was written, and the last words typed… which was, literally, a champagne moment. Rosey Hume ran the eponymic Rosey's and pretty much lived every chapter of *When Frank Offcut Went Missing* with me. Even though Mary Brewer was an established character by then, I couldn't help seeing parallels. So, thanks Rosey for being so enthusiastic, entertaining and a good mate during those fab Rosey's days.

The next stage saw the story take printed manuscript form, in eight ring-bound volumes. After sifting through it and finding an amazing number of typos and grammatical errors, I shared it with any willing readers, which, as it turned out, amounted to three people. (That makes this next bit a whole lot simpler.) So, thanks, Dave Horbelt — a great friend of mine who couldn't wait to read it, and he did so with sincere enthusiasm and enjoyment. Dave, you propelled me forward; Peter Nelson — another friend, one who doesn't usually read fiction. Peter, I'm grateful for your support and your forensic ability to find twice as many typos as me; and, finally, to Michelle Dottoré (my hairdresser) who provided me with the funniest feedback: "You know what I *love* about this book?" she said. And I'm thinking *wow*, she sounds super impressed. Then she followed up with, "The ring-binding! It's brilliant – the pages stay flat, so you can just rest it on your lap." Of all the comments, this is the one that will stay with me.

After a few years of faffing around with the manuscript, I decided 2020 was the year to begin the process of turning it into a book. (COVID-19 didn't have much of an upside, but I have it to thank for getting my literary arse into gear.)

First cab off the rank was obtaining a professional overview. This fell to Nicki Markus (who also edited the story). Nicki gave the story a general thumbs up and a list of suggestions to turn it into a high five. I agreed with most of them — creativity is a subjective thing. One of her many excellent suggestions was to create a timeline. This proved to be a very worthwhile (if time-consuming) exercise, and completely changed the structure of

*When Frank Offcut Went Missing* for the better. Originally, I had Mary, Ophelia and Olivia rotating in order, but from a *chronology* point of view it was a little confusing. So, I rearranged, sliced and diced all the chapters, until they made more chronological sense. The editing process was also extremely helpful, and I now know the difference between 'further' and 'farther'. So, thanks Nicki for your diligence and availability – you helped me write a better version of the story.

And, finally, Rachel Rolfe, who transformed my word documents into what you've just read. Rachel was a 'random' discovery on my Find a Book Cover Designer journey. She was recommended by another designer, Christine Sharp (who was kind enough to respond to my query) and I'm so glad I took her recommendation. Rachel – who told me she wasn't an illustrator – not only designed the cover, but also constructed the chapter illustrations (except the Belladonna), turned my mud map of The Five Duchies into a real map and added all the information to the Lower Icing map. She did the typography and typesetting, managed to interpret my ramblings, and brought the Middle Ages to the pages. It was so enjoyable and relaxing having Rachel on the other end of the line; she is open and engaging, a pleasure to work with. So, now it's my turn to recommend Rachel and her business, Lead Based Ink, for… Anything. You can contact her at rachel@leadbasedink.com.au

# ABOUT THE AUTHOR

Tim Thompson has been writing for over 30 years, mainly as an Advertising Copywriter and Freelance Content Writer (separated by a three-year teaching stint in London). The Silver Button Saga is Tim's first long-format story, but he's had a number of short stories published. His first foray into short story writing was titled *Bradman's Thongs*, and was one of ten stories to win publication in *The Advertiser* Summer Short Story competition. Tim lives in Adelaide, South Australia. He can be contacted at timet@internode.on.net

www.ingramcontent.com/pod-product-compliance
Lightning Source LLC
Chambersburg PA
CBHW061504020726
47502CB00006B/1933